"Liar, Thief! Thief!"

Brilliana screamed, hammering at Ted's face. "Your father loves you, you are his only son, but you took his money. You used me! My background! When things were going well, I was the hostess you needed. When they were going badly, I was your servant. You didn't hesitate to lie, cheat and rob me. And for what? A crazy dream."

"Okay," Ted answered, "But what you lose sight of is that I did it for something."

"For me?" asked Brilliana.

"Of course for you." Ted replied with conviction. "And for me. For this family, the dynasty we're founding."

Ted Angstrom pushes relentlessly on for the power, the wealth, the dynasty he wants, but he comes to learn the truth of the Arab proverb, "a man's enemies are his children and his possessions."

"Reading Nancy Freedman's robust and compelling novel is to share her exuberant belief in the future of humanity, a belief all the more attractive for being so rare."—*Los Angeles Times*

ABOUT THE AUTHOR

Nancy Freedman lives in California and is the author of *Mrs. Mike* and *Joshua Son of None.*

The Immortals

NANCY FREEDMAN

WARNER BOOKS

A Warner Communications Company

WARNER BOOKS EDITION

Copyright © 1976 by Nancy Freedman
All rights reserved

Library of Congress Catalog Card Number: 75-40787

ISBN 0-446-82271-X

This Warner Books Edition is published by
arrangement with St. Martin's Press, Inc.

Cover art by Dave Blossom

Warner Books, Inc., 75 Rockefeller Plaza, New York, N.Y. 10019

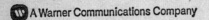 A Warner Communications Company

Printed in the United States of America

Not associated with Warner Press, Inc. of Anderson, Indiana

First Printing: October, 1977

10 9 8 7 6 5 4 3 2 1

This book is dedicated to Benedict
and to the future: Benedict Charles
Shauna Lin
???

I wish to express my appreciation for the thoughtful help and expert advice I received from

Joseph H. Birman, Ph.D.
Norbert M. Werk, M.D.
Kenneth J. Atchity, Ph.D.

The sun: an orgastic litany of heat, momentary mountains thrust from turbulent oceans of gas flows. Radioactive cataclysms hurl spirals, vortices and funnels, to create and cannibalize energy. Swirls of plasma in restless beds produce suction spots like cavernous, pursed mouths dissolving into polarized light spheres. Subsonic pulses, troughs of cresting flamelike emanations torn by shock waves, erupt in clouds of nucleons, in filamentary streams of bright penumbra. Great flares of scarlet vapor swell, sheerest bubbles, to burst a hundred thousand miles in space. An ionized zone thinner than gas wraps an electrical field on which a dazzling corona shimmers, crowning the boiling mass.

This cauldron, the size of 333,400 earths, holds moons and planets in place. A cycle established itself, solar heat shafted the third most distant mass and lifted water to the air. It returned as storm, as rain. Oceans sank and rose in shuddering upheavals, washing marine deposits, gravel and sand into anticlines of stratified rock. Faulting land masses spilled mountain ranges upward, lagoons tilted, drained and were buried. Dead shores were washed by salt seas. Time settled the world.

Microorganisms floated, trilobites clung, vase-like sponges drifted. The bodies of preglacial creatures were entombed in sediment and silt, compacted into strata, waiting to release their chemical energy. Life in the sea was pressed into what would become oil.

The skin of the earth wrinkled, its convolutions not yet done. Algae, lichen and mosses invaded the land. The amphibians, goggle-eyed, spiny-shelled, jointed legs, bony heads, thrived in a new environment. Salamanders and flying lizards migrated to laze in the heat that was day. Giant insects buzzed through reeds. Soft trees in steamy forests laid down thick mulch. The great experiment was underway.

It began with the sun.

Oil marked him. When he was eight his mother died. Irv Angstrom's solution was to take the boy into the fields with him. Ted came to know a dozen sites from Pennsylvania to California. Each field was alive with the same smells, sounds and dreams. A kind of vibration got into you, whether it was from the star bit driving into rock, or whether it was expectation, he didn't know.

When he was small, Ted ventured from the doghouse, a shed invariably erected near the first pumping well on which his father nailed a board with the word OFFICE daubed in white paint. Ted wandered seemingly with no direction, but he always ended up hanging around the crew. The driller was the boss, his dad made that clear. Even the leaseholder did not tell the driller what to do. The derrickman was next in line, but he didn't get extra for a night tower the way the driller did.

Ted would sit a little way off so as not to be told to clear out. He watched endless games of poker and craps and understood that each player had his eye on some piece of land, for which the winnings were a "down." Sometimes one of the men, drunk on cheap whiskey, took Ted to view the spot where his fortune lay. It could be anything, a peculiar depression in the earth, a small hummock, a sulfur outcropping, traces of tar in a farmer's well. Ted nodded his blond head sagely, but peer around as he might, could discover no overt sign of the oil he was earnestly assured was beneath his feet.

He imagined the oil to be like his own blood, only black and lying in lakes. He was quickly disabused of this idea. "Naw, there ain't any holes in the earth, kid. It's solid. But the oil sort of seeps, pushed along by gas pockets, and it collects in the rocks like water in a

11

sponge. We wring it out, that's all. Wring out enough and you got it made."

Ted was disappointed it wasn't a lake or an ocean that he could one day syphon dry. But if the black rock was down there for these men and his dad, it was down there for him too.

After a while the crew got used to having him around, especially as he was cheerful about running errands. "Get off your butt, boy, and tell the boilerman he's dying on us again." Away Ted would shoot. The boiler, for reasons of safety, was situated several hundred feet from the rig. Tending it was a lonely occupation, and the boilerman taught Ted seven card stud, or else sent him to bum chewing tobacco, cigarettes being strictly forbidden.

School authorities caught up with him each fall, but summers were his. When he was fifteen he was as tall and husky as the next man, and was taken on as a temporary hand. He was part of the crew, no favors asked. As the leaseholder's son he was kidded a lot, but there was no deference. These men were an independent bunch—each a dreamer, each a gambler. And the stakes were under their feet.

Andy McNulty was his dad's new driller. He seemed to take a special pleasure in making life tough for Ted. It made no difference if Ted was off a twelve-hour tower, McNulty could be counted on to have a task lined up for him. Ted didn't mind much, his enormous energy was elastic, it stretched like a rubber band. He could always sleep later. But, strenuous and physically demanding as the job was, a great deal of time was spent standing around, loafing and passing the flask. This new driller could really yarn. Sometimes he'd rescind an order, "That can wait. There's no tearing hurry about that." Then he would put his feet up on the wooden bench, settle back, and Ted knew one of his stories was coming up. "The word *derrick*, that was from a hangman, John Derrick, who plied his trade at Tyburn in London, in the seventeenth century. He built these goddamn high towers, you see, so the audience would have a good view. People streamed in from hell and gone to see them jerk, watch their eyes and tongue

12

pop. This Derrick, from all accounts, was a first-rate hangman. Leastwise, none of his customers ever came back to complain."

The flask went around. The company rule had yet to be invented that could keep a roustabout from his whiskey. A fertile ground for tall tales was the way men like themselves who had tapped into luck, spent their millions. "Thomas P. Wendell now, he had this thing about being buried alive. It came from working the Howard well. When she blew there was a crater two hundred fifty feet wide. You couldn't even find the derrick. Tom was part of the cave-in, went in with the rig on top of him. Never did get over it. And when he made his pile, he put it in his will that they run a telephone line to his crypt. The lid of the coffin was to be open and the phone within easy reach. Not only that, he left millions more for someone to sit at the other end of the line, you know, to monitor it in perpetuity."

"Creepy," Ted said, "sitting at the other end of a phone that never rang."

"How do you know it never rang?" McNulty asked.

The men ragged him. But Ted didn't mind, he was accepted, no longer the kid who sat on the sidelines. As a token of his new status, he was included in the Saturday nights at Fanny's place. The prostitutes were on the scene as soon as they spudded the first well. Fanny herself broke Ted in out of consideration for his youth. Thereafter he chose for himself. The girl was called Dimples, a provocative name, since with clothes on, no dimples were discernible.

Two men took charge of his life. When he graduated high school, his dad pointed him to Princeton. "The way I figure, Ted, we're expanding all the time. Eventually, it's going to take brains to run this outfit."

What the old man had in mind were business courses, but Ted gobbled up geology, mineralogy, vertebrate paleontology and something set down in the catalogue as metamorphic petrology.

After his sophomore year Ted spoke earnestly to his father about marine sediments and anticlines. The old man chewed him out. "Might as well use a divining rod," he said. Ted walked up the road to sulk and

13

wonder why he'd been sent to college in the first place.

McNulty, who always knew what was going on with any member of his rig, explained it to him. "Your old man's right, Ted. I could give you a list of oilmen as long as my prick that have gone broke listening to geologists. But," he added, "times are changing." The kid had stood up well. You never got a complaint out of him. The brawny youngster had undergone a number of McNulty tests. And the main thing that came from it all, fancy schools or no fancy schools, he had the making of an oilman. Andy took him off cleanup detail and set him to logging mud. "This will give you a chance to use your education. Water weighs eight pounds to the gallon—right, College Boy? Now, you keep the mud at ten and a half, and let me know if she goes an ounce either way."

For years Ted had watched other men fill their gallon can from the return circulation and weigh it with a spring scale, now it was his turn. "Some jokers won't bother," McNulty said, "but it's the only sure way. You can't go by the way the pump sounds or the look of the stuff. There's always the chance gas could be leaking in and lightening it, and the next thing you know, it's hell at the other end of an exhaust pipe. So remember, a difference of a half pound can start a gusher."

Ted was determined to measure up to this responsibility. He always felt challenged on a field, and walked lightly with a sense of what was underneath. The new job was a way of looking directly in and down. The drilling fluid, thickened with clays and iron oxides according to a secret recipe of McNulty's, was pumped into the pipe and emerged from holes in the cutting tool to flush away the chips and bring them back to the surface. Ted sloshed around in spillover from the sump, fishing bits of rock out of the strainer, trying to identify them by color, hardness, texture, even biting into them. He began to visualize the slanted, irregular slabs of stone their feeble needle was piercing. And always he remained alert for a glint of oil on the brown muck.

The third summer McNulty watched him speculatively. Trouble was building between the kid and the Old Man. Ted was up to something. For one thing, he

14

was keeping his own records of the core tests and pestering drillers at other sites to let him copy their logs. McNulty knew the signs. Every oilman, like every horse-player, has to have a system, something that tells him where to lay that twenty-to-one bet.

McNulty was right. Ted was working on a project. He had mapped the subterranean geology of the entire field from the drilling history of the wells and dry holes that had been bored into it. Surface features and drillings logs indicated the dip of the strata, and his samples collected over two years enabled him to calculate porosity and permeability coefficients. Gradually in his mind there built up a picture of a vast structural trap, with the present wells only nibbling at the borders.

The apex, that's where they ought to spud in, and quit kidding around. That evening he stayed out of the crap game and took a walk down the road to settle himself. Midway he changed course and headed for the doghouse.

His father was labeling samples. Tacked over his head was something labeled SCHEDULE:

11:00 a.m.	Get up
11:30 a.m.	Sober up
Noon to midnight	Work like hell
Midnight to 3:00 a.m.	Get drunk at Fanny's
3:00 to 3:30 a.m.	Beat hell out of them that's got it coming
3:30 a.m.	Bed

Next to the last word was a hefty nude. "Can't you see I'm busy, Ted?"

"This won't take a minute. I just want to tell you I'm not going back to Princeton."

The Old Man set the samples down in front of him. "The hell you say."

"I have some ideas on where we should be drilling." He was prepared for his father's loud groan and continued unfazed. "The way I see it, we're only tapping the perimeter. I'm dead sure about that."

"If you don't mind my interrupting," the Old Man

15

said, "you are going back to New Jersey for the start of classes. This happens to be your senior year."

"I know, Dad. But I'm learning more on the job."

"Then you're fired." Angstrom returned to his samples as though the interview were over.

Ted stood his ground. "I'm experienced now. I can sign on anywhere."

The Old Man knew this was true. He changed tactics. "You're within a year of graduating. Think what that means, a college man."

"I have thought. That's part of the bargain I want to make with you. I want you to stake me. All the costs are here, everything. I've broken it down. The derrick and equipment will run $2,856. That doesn't include salaries, of course. Or the new hydrodynamic pressure tests I'd like to try out."

"Hold on, hold on! Let me get this straight. What costs? What figures?"

"For the new hole."

His father became absorbed with his pencil. He drew it through his fingers a couple of times. "Hydrodynamic pressure," he muttered, then looking up. "I think what you're saying is, if I drill some particular hole, you'll go back and get your degree. Is that right?"

"Almost right," Ted grinned at him.

"What's almost?" Dealing with his son was like arbitration, you took what you could get.

"If I'm right, I want to be a partner."

The Old Man leaned back and laughed his deep belly laugh. "And what if you and those high-powered professors you listen to are wrong, and I'm out five thousand bucks? Do you still expect to be a partner?"

"Yes. And I'll work the debt off."

"At the kind of wages I'm paying you?" Again the rumbling laugh. "Come on, partner, let's buy ourselves a drink."

McNulty, seeing the two Angstroms roaring through town later that night, thought—the kid's got a way with him. Then he thought—but he's not his own man the way he thinks. And those that have anything to do with him will feel it, because the oil was there first. McNulty

16

had seen oil consume men. And he'd seen certain men fight back. But it was a contest that was never done.

Ted was back on the job after a night matching his dad drink for drink, he was checking the muddy fluid with its burden of cuttings, watching it drain into the settling pit, following the progress as it was laundered and allowed to overflow into the pickup sump. This was the point at which he weighed the sample. He judged they would soon be at sufficient depth to bail, removing bottom water so they could bring her in. He had brought his own life in last night too. He considered himself an oilman. This conclusion was premature.

It began with an earthquake. Ted thought that's what it was. The ground lunged under his feet and the air roared.

"She's blowed!" someone yelled, pointing at the horizon where oil gushed like a bottle of warm beer with the cap knocked off.

The men grabbed slickers. McNulty threw him a hat. "Come on!" They charged across the open field, past producing wells toward the plume in the sky. A truck full of men screeched by. In the distance he saw his father's car, bouncing crazily over the ruts. From every side people were converging on the gasser. A column of oil spouted two hundred feet, thundering to earth, blowing in under a pressure of possibly 3,000 p.s.i. A high wind carried the black jet, covering everything with a coat of oil. Men slipped about, hauling sandbags, dodging catapulted rocks. A perimeter ditch was being dug. The earth rumbled again and slid. Mud hogs and engineers ran for their lives. The noise was deafening. McNulty tore some felt from his hat and indicated by sticking pieces in his own ears Ted was to do the same. Now they were on top of it, the hissing from the mouth of the hole was so loud they no longer heard the noise itself, only the reverberation. Men were handling lengths of iron pipe as though they were babies. They were so hot that a spark from any one of them could ignite the gas. So far, thank God, she was blowing cold.

A drill pipe shot fifty feet into the air, sections of it spinning through the sky like pinwheels. A geyser of gas towered above the rig. Another twenty tons of pipe tore loose. Rocketing steel struck the crippled derrick, twisting and wrapping itself around the structure, tearing large chunks away.

"What happened?" Ted yelled into the ear of a dazed machinist.

"A little gas was showing, that was all. We were hauling up the bit, I don't know, maybe we moved it too fast. Suddenly the whole works is shooting up around us. There's all hell to pay."

Ted caught sight of his dad on the derrick floor. He was holding to the framing as though riding out a storm. McNulty was trying to persuade him to come down. Ted ran up to them keeping his head lowered, debris of all kinds was hurtling past. His ears were ringing as the air around him exploded. He slipped in the oily mess and was down. The palms of his hands were scalded as he pushed himself to his feet.

"We've got a problem," his dad yelled calmly. "The end of a cable has fouled the master gate. We can't get the son-of-a-bitch closed."

Ted slid through one of the pried-up boards on the floor to inspect the top of the casing that led to the master gate. He found the wedged cable. It had to be removed so the valve could be closed and the runaway gas shut off.

Ted stuck his hand up through the gaping board and waved it, indicating he needed a tool. A bolt cutter was slapped into his palm. He winced, feeling pain for the first time. He ducked back under. Everything was heaving. He located the cable again and knelt down only to be pitched onto his face. Metal seared his cheek. He must have landed on some goddamned tool or other. He tried to wipe his eyes and for a moment completely encrusted them. His father was yelling at him to get the hell out of there. "If she catches fire, you're a goner!"

Mud was popping, potholes of it, and he repeatedly scraped it off so he could see the cable. He positioned the open bolt cutter and brought all his force to bear, snapping the cable clean. He took a deep breath to keep from passing out. Now to pull it free.

His hands no longer closed. It was impossible to grip with them. McNulty jumped down beside him. "Ted,

18

get out. I mean it, out!" He hauled on the extruding cable and it came clear. "Got it!" he yelled up to Angstrom. "We've got her gagged!"

In answer there was a terrible rending, the crown block blew straight into the air and fell through the entire structure. The floor subsided and the slatted sides of the rig buckled. Irv Angstrom dived under the flooring. The three of them huddled, waiting.

After a minute they looked at each other. They grinned. There was a cutback in noise. The men must be screwing the valve closed, securing it with turnbuckles and chains.

The Old Man asked the question out loud that each had been asking himself, "Well, are we all right? All in one piece? Give us a hand here!" he called.

They were pulled out into daylight and Ted looked at his dad. His face was smeared with sweat and oil, his lips cracked and caked and he was smiling. Ted laughed back. The raw power that flooded and spurted from the core of the earth was capped. The massive casing head was being fastened back, the lugs screwed in place, and cement poured over everything in sight to hold against pressure.

They had battled a force, a black force out of the earth, subdued it, channeled it, got it running in tubing and pipelines. Ted felt a surge of unadulterated joy. He'd beat back the oil.

Then he began seeing what was going on. A bogged-down ambulance was standing by. No one could get it to run. They were loading the injured into a horse-drawn cart. A man next to him was holding his head and moaning, his eardrum broken.

"You're next," his dad said to Ted.

"Me?" Ted replied in astonishment. "I'm fine."

"Fine? Just look at yourself, the skin on your hands is hanging in strips."

Ted looked.

"And your face," McNulty said, "Good God, your face."

Ted was conscious of a thick viscous fluid rolling down his cheek into his collar which he assumed was oil. He felt with the back of his hand and it came away

19

blood, a brackish blood, as though what he had thought as a child was true and inside him oil coursed.

"You must have landed on a pair of pipe tongs, or maybe they breezed through the sky and hit you," McNulty informed him cheerfully. "This is a brand you've carried a long time. The only difference is, now it's marked you for the whole world to see."

Ted once more raised the back of his hand and felt gingerly along the raised welt that followed the angle of his cheekbone. "Goddamn," he said, "you're right." He was still laughing when they shoved him into the cart.

His dad came to visit him in the infirmary. The Old Man tried to put it in perspective. "Do you know you got a hundred bucks coming? That's right, she was spitting out thousands of dollars a minute. So I offered the men a hundred smackers if they could contain her before dark. She's pumping good now," his dad continued. "Waking or sleeping that well means twenty dollars an hour to us."

The explanation bothered Ted. The things he remembered had nothing to do with the twenty an hour they'd earn for the life of the well. What he remembered was the battle, flinging himself into it. Had he risked his neck, been scarred for life, fought with his last strength, not feeling his own pain, for twenty dollars an hour?

Twenty dollars waking or sleeping. Great! But what about the man with the broken eardrum and the fellow with the head injury?

The answer lay deep as the well. They fought, all of them, in oil-drenched mud, pitting themselves against a monstrous roar, against an earth that sent shock waves through its crust. Overstrained arms jerked with spasm, backs could scarcely straighten. Ted's hands would be useless for months.

But the scab had a dressing on it and the well was running smooth. Sure, when you thought about it afterward, money was the reason. But not at the time. The inside of the earth had burst out and they'd stuffed it back in. Now he had the right to call himself an oilman.

The pipe tong scar which ran the length of his left cheekbone was a badge of honor in the oil fields. At Princeton it set him apart, as did his graphic speech and explicit cussing. Jason Talbolt liked him for this. Ted pretended to despise Jason. But how could you despise somebody whose main fault was trying to be friends? That's what it amounted to.

"Then you'll come?" Jason asked.

Ted was being asked as a last minute replacement to a weekend party at the Long Island estate of Jason's aunt, Lillian Grenville. Ted knew there were a dozen possibilities ahead of him on Jason's list, but that he hesitated to ask any of them on the spur of the moment. Ted Angstrom might not quite pass muster with his aunt, but he was the best that could be got on short notice.

Ted understood and while his pride bristled, a canny instinct told him this was a chance that might never come again to get a look into the inner circle, the New York Four Hundred.

With twenty wells on the pump, he and his dad could probably buy and sell the Grenvilles and the Talbolts a dozen times over. Nevertheless, these aristocratic noses sniffed and smelled black goop. Ted's nose, broad and thick like the rest of him, drank up the acrid smell, unlike any other. It stank, and he loved it—and rubbed the noses of his fellow Princetonians in it whenever he could. The way he saw things, it took two or three generations with money laundered and neatly packaged in unbreakable trusts and conservative securities. He was confident his children would look down noses every bit as refined and delicate as Jason Talbolt's. The notion tickled Ted and he laughed the hearty laugh of a man used to space around him. Jason looked inquiringly at him. "Then you'll come?" he repeated.

"Why not?" The drawling tones of a dragged about childhood, the brawling country talk of Pennsylvania, Texas, Oklahoma and California had given way to an Eastern accent become second nature. But the laugh would not be corralled, the laugh remained free and untrammeled, loud and boisterous. Jason laughed with him. But Ted was not fooled, he saw the slight twitch of disdain in the over-refined beak.

Ted was angry with himself. Yet he looked forward to writing his dad casually—*"By the way, spent the weekend . . . etc., where I met . . . etc."* He hoped the list would be long and distinguished, and expected that it would. He knew Old Man Angstrom prided himself on the gentleman son he was turning out.

Ted was less sure. At home in the pool halls and beer joints of oil towns in half a dozen states, he was about to demonstrate an equal ease in the drawing room. Or was he? He wondered, and kept on wondering right to the door of Jason's shiny blue Daimler, what the hell he was doing.

The car cleft the mild summer stirring it up and dividing it into two airslips. Fields blurred, pollen and dust mingled into a warm smell. Ted found it difficult to sustain the brooding mood in which the trip had begun. Jason talked incessantly about a beautiful, winsome and utterly delightful girl called Evelyn Popper whose father was a retired admiral. "She is smashing. Absolutely smashing. But I want your word, right from the beginning, Ted. She is my private preserve. No poaching. I hope you've got that. Because if I find out otherwise. . . ."

Ted grinned. "You'll have me barred from the floor of the Stock Exchange. Who else is going to be there, and by that I mean girls?"

"Well," Jason stretched his long legs, and since his foot was on the gas pedal the effect was to drastically accelerate. "Let's see. Evelyn, of course. And Peggy Gould, a luscious bit of woman from Smith. And Cora Anvil, watch your step there. What a tease, and it's pure come-on, you never get to first base. Then there's that stuck-up bit of baggage, Brillianna Grenville who's insinuated herself with my aunt, moved in, so to speak. Poor as a church mouse, but never lets you forget she's a Grenville. She's a prig and a waste of time. But Sally Vale now, there's a dish. What a pair of boobs. I was madly in love sophomore year, but she beat me at tennis once too often."

It was pleasant breezing along, talking girls. Ted began to feel less harshly disposed toward himself. In fact by the time they reached Long Island, he was quite mellowed, the bumpkin Ted had been totally banished and Theodore Angstrom lounged beside his friend, unabashed by the wrought iron fence that stretching for blocks marked the perimeter of the estate. Neither did the twenty foot gate with its annunciator intimidate him, it was the kind of portal through which he expected to pass. Halfway up the drive Jason stopped the car and jumped out. Ted followed somewhat less agilely and was introduced to his hostess who paused looking against the sun. She held a croquet mallet in her hand. Nevertheless she took time to size up Theodore Angstrom. He had seen arrows fitted like her eyes with four intersecting razor blades. It was a quick, merciless coring process he was submitted to. The smile was charming, the words gracious, but the eyes sliced, dissected, and you were sectioned, stained and classified in a second. You couldn't retard the judgment, you couldn't say, "Wait, I have qualities, talents, thoughts you don't know about." Too late, the decision had been rendered.

He was introduced to the other croquet players but was so disconcerted by Mrs. Grenville that the only name he could recall afterward was his own. He depended on Jason to clue him in later.

They drove up to the Tudor house where they were taken to one of the wings and given adjoining suites. Ted's impression was of richly textured but dark rooms. Pulling back heavy drapes he discovered a narrow balcony. From this he looked out trying to get his bearings. It would be pleasant to take a walk before dinner, limber up a bit after the long drive and explore the estate. His mental route lay through a copse which opened onto a formal garden.

Jason was chatting to someone in the hall, so Ted turned the other way. He wrapped himself in a kind of introspection which he hoped would ward off a casual word or conversation. He was lucky, most of the guests were gathered in the salon for tea. He successfully skirted this area and escaped by a side door. Being outside always restored him to himself. Exercise, even something as mild as walking, put him into communication with his body. It was a good body, forceful, active and alert. Why had he let Mrs. Grenville scissor him up like that?

As he moved it began to work. He was Ted, not Theodore. And remember, he told himself, the black goop they despise is what got you the invitation. Your money and the money it's rolling up fascinates them. What they didn't see was the gamble each time you sank a hole. And they knew nothing at all about the follow-through, refining the crude, cracking and separating into different grades with a battery of stills, each one the junction for a tangle of pipes; then into the marketplace, selling your barrels, finding outlets, that was adventure too. Hell, that was the world out there. He'd been trying to sell this picture of a total operation to his dad. The Old Man thought in terms of bringing it out of the ground. He couldn't visualize all the aspects Ted saw. But Ted was working on him.

He looked around. Only the rich and the insane were shut away from the world behind ironwork gates. The world was what Mrs. Grenville sensed in him and recoiled from. Rough? Sure. It was a working world. It produced. It spawned what his dad called new energy.

The power he hoped to control would make the world over in its image. He knew it. And he knew what it would bring. A house like this, more than one, perhaps. And a sense that he belonged. He had been walking at the edge of the trees where they bordered the garden, laid out in the form of crescent waves frozen in more colors than he had ever seen. At the center of the garden was a gazebo where six paths met like the spokes of a wheel.

Standing in the hexagonal frame was Evelyn Popper. He recognized her immediately from Jason's description. Day and night met in her as they did in this moment. A dropped sun and a white moon showed together in the sky. The same duality seemed imposed on her. From this slight reed of a girl he felt strength, as though it were by her will the magic meeting of day and night occurred. The piled dark hair contrasted with great blue eyes. Moats of sun burned about her, accomplishing subtle transformations of rosy hues. It was an intrusion

24

to watch her bathe in the last of the sun. Damn Jason. What rotten luck that this young woman should fall to him. She belonged to herself, completely to herself. She was the first human to stand and contemplate the universe.

Ted took a backward step. He didn't want to be caught looking at her. He didn't want to speak either, or have her speak. What he experienced was direct and not to be tampered with. He walked back the way he had come remembering the girls he had been in love with. He'd had whores since he was fifteen, but he also had visions. Once, riding a bike, he saw a girl lean out of an upper story window. She was a storybook princess and he loved her and would always love her although he never saw her again.

Perhaps he reacted so strongly because of the book. His mother died without leaving much for her only son to remember. The few things they had shared were lost in the roving days that followed with his dad. For a while there had been a dull green book with a cloth cover whose back was broken and thready, through which you could see bound pages knotted together. The book was one his mother read to him and which he sloppily colored, pressing the crayons hard, breaking their points. One page he hadn't colored. He didn't want it changed. It showed a princess in a long gown. Her hair was dark, had her eyes been blue? The girl at the window was that page come to life. It had nothing to do with sweaty thighs and panting kisses in an upstairs parlor. Unconnected and not touching his life was the page he left uncolored. Until the girl in the window, he thought the picture was of his mother. Then he identified it with what his father referred to as the "right girl."

He'd just seen the right girl standing in the middle of a gazebo watching a sunset, and she belonged to someone else. Or did she? Perhaps she didn't share Jason's feelings. In that case. . . . Hell, in any case. Was he going to let Jason Talbolt or anyone beat him out? She was for him. The immediate problem was to avoid the agonies of meeting over supper and being forced into making banal comments.

He found his way to the correct room, dressed

25

quickly, then told Jason he wasn't ready. He could not allow Jason to introduce them. He loitered until the last minute. When he did go downstairs there were so many people gathered that he imagined his entrance was entirely unnoticed.

This was not the case. "My dear," Mrs. Grenville could not be said to speak more loudly, she simply brought more timbre to her words so they carried, "may I present Jason's friend, Mr. Theodore Angstrom?"

Ted turned and was riveted to the spot. The girl in the green cloth book, the girl in the window, the girl in the gazebo were one. He looked into Evelyn Popper's eyes. They were blue, but not exactly, more a blue-gray. "My niece, Brillianna Grenville."

What! His princess of the sunset, his peerless beauty, that stuckup snip, that bit of baggage who thought too well of herself? His wits were utterly scrambled. He said to her, "You're not Evelyn Popper?"

Brillianna looked amused. "Whatever gave you that idea?"

He recovered himself. "Jason told me she was the prettiest girl here. So the mistake was natural. As for him, all I can say he's a dense fellow with no eyes in his head."

"That was a nice retrieval," she said. "I wonder what cousin Jason said about me? But I won't embarrass you by asking." She extended her narrow hand which he accepted into his with a sense of awe and wonder.

Dinner was announced and she was claimed by someone else, one of the croquet players. Jason came over and introduced him to Evelyn Popper.

There were placecards, and Brillianna Grenville was at the far end of the table. Ted was seated beside Jason who arranged to have Evelyn on his other side. Ted's partner was the well-stacked, tennis-playing Sally. Her hair was bobbed and she posed a great deal in an effort to outdo the movie flappers. There were many lulls in their conversation. During these Ted attempted to pump Jason about his cousin.

26

Jason answered reluctantly or pretended not to hear, for each time his attention strayed, Evelyn and the young man to her right found things to say to each other.

"Jason."

"What?"

"About your cousin, about Brillianna. . . ."

"She's not my cousin. Other side of the family."

"Yes, I just met her. I can't believe it was the same girl you were talking about."

"Have you been treated to the story of Armagh yet? No? Well you will be. Armagh, bastion of Protestantism in northern Ireland. And the Grenvilles, lords of all they surveyed." He turned to recapture Evelyn.

Ted persisted, "The name's French, isn't it?"

"Norman," Jason corrected him. Evelyn was chatting like a magpie with her neighbor. "Remember the battle of Hastings? That's how far back they go. They were given most of Ireland as a fief. And when the potato famine came along, and her grandfather, the old baron, didn't modify his style of living, the peasants trussed the family up in the carriage house and burnt the manor to the ground. I say, Evelyn, have you tasted these crab-apples?"

But Ted gave him no peace. "Was it completely destroyed?"

"They looted first, and what they couldn't carry away they burned. The old baron died a few weeks later and Brillianna's father inherited the ashes. Instead of making a stand, he decided to emigrate. After four hundred years a Grenville turned his back on the title, the property, everything. He brought the whole family to America. Now for Christ's sake, man," he added under his breath, "have a heart, will you?"

Ted nodded, trying to digest what he had heard, the granddaughter of an honest-to-God baron. No wonder she reminded him of the princess in his tattered childhood book. It was the way she was put together, the fineness, the delicacy of her features. She was all magma and igneous. He was the granite of which mountains are formed. She was bred, he forged. And it was oil that put him in the same room with her. While they might be in the same room, he knew they were not of the same world.

He poked Jason in the ribs.

"Now what?"

"What happened to the family once they got here?"

"Come on, Ted." But Evelyn was again engaged to her right. "Her old man became a druggist. Anyone who would walk out on family holdings has the soul of a druggist. Now will you shut up about Brillianna?" He gave Ted a shrewdly malicious look. "Why the interest anyway?"

"She's damned attractive."

"She's a bore. She's conceited. And all you'll ever get out of her is *Armagh*. That's her main pastime, poring over old albums of the place. She talks of nothing but the past glories of the Grenvilles. It's ridiculous. And all the time she's living here on my aunt's charity."

"Why do you hate her? She turned you down, huh?"

Jason rolled his eyes toward his dinner companion. "Keep your voice down, will you!"

"Okay," Ted said, "just wanted to get things straight."

"All the same," Jason hissed in his ear, "if you take a tip from me, you'll steer clear of Brillianna Grenville."

Ted fell into a reverie and Sally Vale was forced to repeat her question as to whether he liked playing net.

After dinner he gave Sally the slip, managed to circumvent Mrs. Grenville and wound up standing by her niece. "Hello."

"Hello," she said.

He remembered that although he had seen, indeed studied her, and taken the trouble to learn something of her history, that she knew nothing of him beyond his name. He probably should ask if she cared for coffee, which was being served along with brandy for the men. Instead he stood like a clod, which, he told himself, was what he was beside her. Even her name inhibited him. Brillianna, undoubtedly a family name, which like the surname went back hundreds of years. This young woman knew who she was and who her people were. Ted felt stripped of his usual defenses.

Ted Angstrom was rarely unsure of himself. He had always been able to draw on his power to charm and persuade. Tonight it deserted him. Distress showed in his eyes. The eyes did not match the rest of him. They were those of a dreamer. "I'm hoping I can take you out of here," he said without preamble. "Could we walk in the grounds?"

She hesitated a moment, then allowed him to lead her from the room. Once outside she filled her lungs with night air. There was a look of mischief about her that he had not seen before. "You're wasting your time on me, you know. I'm the poor relation."

"I know who you are."

"Then why bother? My cousin Jason must have told you all about me, that I'm scheming to catch a rich husband."

"No, I swear, he never said. . . ."

"But it's true," she said serenely. "I am."

"All the better then, because I'm rich."

"Very rich?"

"Yes. And I plan to be richer."

"Oh? How are you going to accomplish that?"

Her low, modulated, unhurrying voice touched some deep nerve in his body. "By vertical integration."

"Vertical integration," she repeated, liking the sound of it.

"It simply means getting into all phases. You see I'm in the oil game." Unconsciously he used his father's terminology. "And a first step would be to build our own refinery. In size alone it's like a university complex, which makes it quite an undertaking."

"That's where the oil is separated into different grades?"

Her clear eyes shading from gray to blue reflected a keen intelligence. He realized he could talk to her. He said eagerly, "It's all run through a condenser and several qualities of gasoline as well as dozens of lubricating oils pressed out. We'd process kerosene, benzine, naphtha, tar, paraffin wax. . . ." He stopped himself. "It's crazy talking to a girl about naphtha and paraffin wax," he said.

"No, I'm interested. I'm always curious about what other people are interested in. Generally they don't tell you. Small talk, polite observations, that's the proper way to converse. The only reason you and I don't follow the rule is that we're both misfits."

He looked at her with amazement. "I may be. In fact, I am. I've been thinking of myself as a sort of spiritual gate-crasher, although actually I was invited . . . last minute of course."

She smiled. "Of course."

"But that's not true of you. This is your aunt's house. This is where you belong."

She shook her head in denial. "Do you know where I belong? In very small, dingy quarters over a pharmacy in Newark, New Jersey. My father stands all day, patient, resigned, waiting on customers, grinding his pestle to fill their orders." Her hands clenched at her sides. "It was to give everyone else a start, all his brothers and sisters. They've each made something of themselves. They are doctors, professors, one is a lawyer, Brian married Aunt Lillian and plays polo. Father did it all standing in his shop, grinding and grinding. If you could see his hands, long, slender, busy with prescriptions and bottles, labels for Johnny's cough or Mrs. Wilson's sciatica! He is in exile. We all are. Our true home is Armagh, but they burned it down. There's nothing to go back to. Armagh is a state of mind."

"Isn't everything?" Ted asked, feeling his own state of mind somewhat unhinged by her. She had brought the conversation to Armagh as Jason predicted. But he found a strange fascination in the Gaelic name.

She made a place for him beside her on a bench and began to speak in a rapid undertone. "What I told you before about growing up in the pharmacy isn't true. In a way I grew up in Armagh. It was a game we played, my sister Elizabeth and I, but it was more real than anything else.

"You see, as long as I can remember my parents talked of the past, of what we had, and lost. Why, I knew my grandmother's matched bays as though I had stroked their muzzles and fed them sugar. As for the house, even now I could draw it for you. The room I liked best was the third-story playroom with its window-seat looking out over the estate. And among the staff my special favorite was a redheaded freckle-faced girl named Mary Frances. One day she dropped the cocoa pot and was dismissed. That's because the pot was part of the Limoges china Grandmother collected. The set was dated and each piece signed by Haviland himself with a great green flourish. A few remnants were recovered and brought to this country. Mama once placed a candle behind one of the plates. The porcelain was so delicate we could see the shadow of her fingers holding it."

She seemed wrapped in that other time. "Anyway, the china is gone with everything else. Mama sold it a piece at a time. I never heard my father lose his temper before. When he discovered it was gone, he said, 'You'd no right.' That's what he told my mother. 'You'd no right. The Limoges belonged to Elizabeth and Brillianna.' It wasn't even a set. He felt so strongly because it was the last reminder."

She turned to Ted and he was astounded to see tears in her eyes. "The game," he said urgently, in an effort to distract her.

". . . Yes, the game. It was always late in the afternoon with the blinds pulled down. Mama insisted on a quiet time. That's when Liz and I played it. *Where are you?* we whispered across the bed from my side to her side."

"Where are you?" Ted repeated, baffled.

"Yes, don't you see? We were back in Armagh playing hide and seek. *Where are you?* That would be Liz. And I'd answer, 'In the oratory.'

"Then I've caught you. I'm in the study. That's what she'd say. I knew she'd jump out at me from the alcove on the stairs. But I remembered the back way that led to the kitchen." The excitement of the old game brought color to her cheeks, as it must have as a child when in the quiet time she wandered the ancestral grounds and played up and down the staircase and through the great rooms.

Ted was touched by the strangeness of what she said, and that Brillianna would confide such corners of her life. He recalled how alone she looked when the sunset like a prism cast its colors over her. Was she lonely? If so, that was something they shared.

Brillianna guessed this when she referred to them both as misfits. He wanted to question her further. But she insisted on returning to the house saying her aunt would be looking for her.

That weekend there was always an activity in the way, tennis, riding, cards, formal luncheons and teas. A picnic was planned for the day of their departure. Ted's bag and racket were packed and loaded into the car. The entire party drove to the country and spread their lunch by a stream. Ted had given up, deciding there was no use trying to get Brillianna alone. When surprisingly there she was at his side asking if he'd like to walk along the water.

"Yes. Yes, I would."

She smiled over her shoulder, and he hastened to catch up to her. They walked in silence neither knowing quite how to begin. Ted stopped and hunted for a flat stone to skip. She applauded when it skimmed and hopped four or five times. "You're good," she said.

"At some things. I haven't been very good at catching up with you."

"Have you wanted to particularly?"

"Of course I've wanted to. There are all sorts of things I want to know about you. And now it's the last day, I'll never find out."

"Find out what? What do you want to know?"

"That's the trouble, I'm not really sure. Crazy things like, how come you're you."

"That's easy. I grew up poor, everyone else here grew up rich."

"That doesn't explain it. I've known tons of poor people."

"The game is what made the difference," she said gravely. "I told you about our game. When I was sent on an errand it wasn't the grocery store or barbershop I passed, but the stables and carriage house. Beyond was a rock wall you could climb and run off into the moors."

"Yes, that's part of it, of what makes you Brillianna." But he felt another part eluded him.

"My parents never did think America a civilized country. When we children went to school they were

32

heartbroken. The Irish peerage speak a pure English, and they considered our diction hopelessly corrupted. My parents disapproved of a great deal they saw about them, especially the moral laxity." She laughed. "The only recreation suitable for young girls was to spend the Sabbath in the cemetery. We had regular Sunday outings with Liz and me playing among the tombstones."

Ted shook his head, "I should think you'd be marked for life. Like me."

She reached her hand out impulsively toward his cheek but didn't touch it. He wanted to catch her hand and place it where it had wanted to be.

"Perhaps I *was* marked, I don't know. Our other diversion was Mama's reading from the Bible. I still love Bible stories. They are the only ones I knew, besides those my parents told of Armagh."

"All this only confuses me more," Ted protested. "You ought to have grown up peculiar. You know what I mean, but you didn't."

"That's because I'm a wicked girl. At least that's what Mama always says."

"Are you wicked?" Ted drew her down on a log. "I would like to believe that."

"Why? What would you do?"

In quick demonstration he leaned over and kissed her. They were both surprised. "Brillianna. . . ."

"Yes?"

"Nothing. I just like to say your name. It's like you."

She spoke in a whisper, very quickly. "I'll tell you two scandalous things about myself. But I'll only tell one of them now."

"How will I find out about the other?"

She stooped to pick a wild daisy and he saw down the neck of her dress. Her breasts were nestled close to the edge of the material.

"Well," she said, "that will be up to you, won't it?"

"Don't worry, I'll manage to get back here."

"How?" She twirled the flower in her hand. "My aunt doesn't like you."

Ted put his arm on the other side of the log. This could be interpreted as either resting his arm there or

33

having it around her. "She doesn't like me because I like you."

"That's one reason." She pretended not to notice the arm.

"And I'm not her idea of a gentleman."

Brillianna clapped her hands in agreement. "She says you have rough edges. So how will you manage?"

"Jason."

"Jason?" she asked dubiously.

Ted grinned. "At your aunt's, it's Evelyn Popper. But at Princeton there's someone else."

"How absolutely low of you," Brillianna laughed.

Ted assented cheerfully. "On your account I've resorted to blackmail. So I'm pretty evil too. Now tell me the first scandalous thing."

"All right. But for you to realize how really awful it is, I'll have to explain more about my family. Elizabeth and I were always bathed in a big copper kettle. And because Mama insisted that the good Lord saw everything, we were washed inside our nightgowns."

Ted looked incredulous.

"It's true. And there is nothing feels worse than a soggy nightgown clinging around you. So you know what I did?"

"Took it off, I hope."

"But you can't know what stepping out of that nightgown signified. It meant I was unruly, rebellious and altogether shameless." She laughed flinging her arms over her head. It was a gesture of abandonment and he pictured throwing himself on her in the present but also in the past when she stepped from the bath naked.

"It was such a marvelous sensation to be free and unhampered, to lather and rinse every inch of my body. And afterward to rub myself into a glow. Mama tried to make me feel guilty and sin-ridden, but I didn't. Not in the least. And I never wore that muslin nightgown in the tub again."

His arm was around her now, all pretense of resting it on the log forgotten. "Was that the awful thing?" he asked, slightly disappointed.

"Of course not. I told you that so you'd see why I

had to get away, understand why I did what I did." She hesitated. "You may hate me. Or. . . ."

"Or what?"

". . . Understand how impossible it looked. My father was worn out and there didn't seem to be any future for Liz and me."

"Didn't any of the brothers or sisters offer to help?"

"No, not one. Not until Aunt Lillian wrote. She and Brian have no children and I suppose she wanted companionship. Mother and Father assumed Elizabeth would be the one to go. But Aunt Lillian hadn't specified which of us it was to be. Actually, I don't think she remembered our names." Brillianna's laugh was short and self-conscious. "I thought about it a great deal and I just knew it would mean more to me than to Liz. You'd have to know Elizabeth to understand what I mean. She accepted things as they were, which I never could. And she wouldn't play the games anymore. So I took her place and came instead."

Brillianna seemed to be looking past him. "I guess that's the worst thing anyone could do to anyone else. Sometimes when I'm dancing or having a good time, I think . . . it should be Elizabeth." She swallowed in rapid succession and turned her eyes on him. They were wide and still as though she expected a judgment. "Now I've told you. You have a right to despise me. But I can't let anyone be my friend, really my friend, unless they know me. The bad things too."

"How did you manage it?" Ted asked. He shifted slightly so his leg was against her skirt. He could feel the warmth of her skin through it. She seemed unaware of his subtle movement.

"I thought about it a long time. Then I asked to borrow Mama's Bible. Poor Mama, she was pleased. All the same, it mystified her. But I'd remembered that every family date of any consequence was on the flyleaf. Marriages, births, you know the kind of thing."

Ted nodded, "I still don't see. . . ."

"It didn't need much to tip the scale, just something, anything. So when I saw Lillian Hartley Grenville was born July 15, I sent her a letter. And in it I mentioned what a coincidence it was to have the same birthday and it must be an omen of some kind."

Ted laughed immoderately as he always did. Since he refused to pronounce judgment on her, she pronounced it on him. "I don't think you should laugh. It wasn't a nice thing to do, to cheat your sister out of all the good things, the wonderful things that have happened."

"I only laughed because you're so unpredictable, the most unpredictable person I know."

"But you agree it was a terrible thing to do?"

"I'm sure your Aunt Lillian would think so and your parents. Elizabeth certainly would. But it strikes me it's like wildcatting, where you send out some private person to buy up the land you're interested in, because the minute anyone gets the idea a company is involved the price goes sky-high. I don't think the others here have ever had to do things like that. But I've done them and you've done them." His hand, having found its way under her skirt, was feeling her thigh.

She jumped up. "I knew you'd despise me," she said, pushing past him and making her way back to the picnickers.

Ted followed, but she saw to it there was no opportunity for a word in private. He stood looking uncomfortable and a bit ridiculous. This Grenville world was a size too small for him. When she said goodbye it was with formality, as though he had never stroked beneath her dress.

Ted was confused, miserable, and did brilliantly in his examinations, which he went at frenetically studying non-stop. But when it was finished and grades posted, he was unable to let up. Or sleep. He went over it until a groove was worn in his brain. How could a girl confide such intimate things to someone and then brush him off? Or did she really believe he despised her?

To interrupt the cycle he tied one on, pulled the chandelier from the frathouse ceiling, and since he was under it, was cut in a dozen places and ended in sick bay.

A sedative sent a slender ghostlike companion into the beyond of his dreaming. She beckoned him past rigs and bore holes laid out in checkerboard fashion across the world, and pirouetted in a shower of oil. The black drops splashed her like rain, but left her untouched. When he attempted to grasp her he discovered he was completely blackened and oil-daubed. She turned away in disgust.

He woke shouting for Jason and was released to his roommate's custody. Jason was allowed no more peace than himself. "When are you going to your aunt's?"

"Will you do yourself a favor and forget that girl?"

"Number one, I can't forget her. Number two, I don't want to."

Jason gave ground reluctantly. "I don't see how I can just show up with you."

"Why not? Why the hell not?" Ted got his way.

His forwardness did not score any points with Lillian Grenville. "How nice to see you again, Theodore." She smiled the half-smile that caused no wrinkles. "Who are you staying with this trip?"

Ted's smile creased his entire face, but his skin was young and resilient, all lines disappeared the next instant. "I'm staying with you," he said easily. "Jason invited me."

"How neglectful of him not to have mentioned it."

"If it will be an inconvenience. . . ."

"What an idea." It was Brillianna coming to his rescue. Was he forgiven then for hearing her secrets? Or had she forgiven herself for telling them? "Aunt Lillian is marvelous at tucking people away in odd corners. She'll find a place for you, won't you, Aunty?"

Mrs. Grenville, seeing herself outflanked, gave in graciously.

When they were alone, Brillianna tilted her head to look at him. "I think I behaved very foolishly last time we met. We both did. Do you want me to apologize? Or should we both apologize?"

"No. As long as you know that I could never think badly of you."

She inclined her head and a wayward wisp of hair shook loose. "So," she said, her blue-gray eyes suddenly alive with merriment, "you managed Jason after all?"

"There's more I want to know about . . . Armagh."

"Armagh? Why it's just a heap of ashes."

"Then I guess I really came back to talk to you."

Narrowing her eyes she scrutinized him for what seemed a long time. "Do you want to know why you came back? I mean really? It was because I put a spell on you."

"You're a witch then?"

"No. This was a garden-variety spell. I counted on your curiosity to bring you back. Remember, I told you one wicked thing I had done. And next time we met I said I'd tell you the other."

Ted was uneasy, remembering how the first confidence had ended. "Are you going to?" he asked.

"If you want me to. But if I do, I'll never see you or speak to you again."

"What!" Startled and horrified, he knew she meant it.

A group of young women came over and laughingly informed Brillianna she was needed to make out dance programs for the evening. She called to him over her shoulder, "It's up to you."

He was sorry he had come, yet he stayed. The party that night was even more painful. When Brillianna entered the room he approached her only to be shown a card dangling from her wrist on which other names appeared ahead of his. He sulked on the porch and avoided the young ladies he was supposed to convoy around the floor. He kept track of Brillianna as best he could and of the dances, until he was her official partner. He claimed her with sullen anger. After all, she had made out the cards.

"I love dancing," was her opening remark.

"That's too bad, because we're not going to dance." He half pulled her across the room and out the door. She wrenched her wrist from his grasp and went to sit on the glider. He followed.

"That was quite an exhibition," she flared at him. Yes, flared, like one of his own wells, when gas topped it.

"Have I ever pretended to be a gentleman?"

She rubbed her wrist and refused to look at him.

"You talk of Armagh and a manor house," he said bitterly. "I've lived in a dozen lean-tos and shanties up and down the country. Your father gave away a title. My dad's claim to fame is that he knew Drake when my grandfather worked for him. That, and the fact that he wildcatted as far as Mexico. So, I may not be up to your games, Miss Grenville. But I know when you're playing them."

"Oh, I'm playing games with you?"

"Aren't you? You knew I'd come back. And when I did you fixed it so I wouldn't see you."

"You're seeing me now, aren't you?"

Ted threw back his head. "And a fine job I'm making of it."

"What do you want?" It was a taunt. "Your story? You were promised it by a young witch and all young witches are brought up to keep promises."

He was on his feet and shouting at her. "Am I some kind of joke to you?"

"Don't be angry." Brillianna was all at once subdued. She took his hand and pulled him down beside her. "I can't tell you. Not now. But I'll make a bargain. In ten years I'll tell you. No matter where we are, I'll write it, or cable you, or. . . ."

"Damn it, I don't want to know. I don't want stories. I'm not a child and neither are you. All I want is to be able to talk to you again."

Her face became white and resolute. "That's what I want too."

"Is it?"

She nodded. The rough edges her aunt remarked bothered her not at all. She made sure to get him back with her games and stories. Now he was here she was dizzy with excitement. His strength was a force like oil itself, its visible scar lay on his face. His vitality, the restless landscape behind his eyes, made her call off the game. Begun so lightheartedly, she knew now she would never reveal the second secret.

Brillianna placed her hand midway between them where he could find it. "Who was Drake? You said your father knew him."

"Colonel Drake, they called him. He was a railroad

man. He had the idea that you could drill for oil the way you do for salt. He put down the first well in Pennsylvania." He stopped and looked intently at her. "Brillianna," he said, "I don't want to give you the impression of immense wealth. It could turn out that way. But every oil pool in the world is different. Each one is a riddle."

"You'll guess right," she said complacently, because it had to be. It wasn't a game in her mind any longer but actuality.

"You see at the moment we're at the crunch. We're putting it all in the hopper, our own capital, everything. It's an all or nothing proposition. We're even going public to finance the refinery. That means if things turn turn sour, we lose the fields. But if it goes right, we parlay it into something big, control the entire operation."

"Vertical integration," she whispered, leaning closer. In a moment he would say it.

Ted raced on, "The action is in the California fields. They've sunk to seven hundred feet. Can you see it? Joint after joint of steel casing lowered, the engine laboring, a great chain pulling the rotary table, and all the time the pumps are driving a river of sludge to the bottom. That's where I want to be, fitting the rubber packer over the casing."

She didn't know what a casing was or a rubber packer, but that's where she wanted to be too.

"Dad is there now, in the Long Beach fields. He's the kind of guy your aunt wouldn't let through the front gate. I barely made it myself. But Dad was in the right place at the right time and had an instinct for what was happening. I'm proud of him. And you'd have to see it my way, be proud too. Otherwise being who you are, it wouldn't work."

"Are you asking me to marry you?"

"You went out and made your future," he found her hand and was squeezing it, "and I want you to go the rest of the way with me. If we can read the puzzle, we'll found a dynasty. Yes, I'm asking you to marry me."

A dynasty. He'd said what she was thinking. The Grenvilles reconstituted—Angstroms. Her breath caught in her throat. But because she had brought up the subject of marriage herself, she made him wait for her answer. "About the mining, I don't quite understand. You mine, you take out oil from the earth. But what do you put back?"

He looked at her with total incomprehension.

"When you farm," she explained herself further, "you take crops from the earth. But you put something back, you seed, fertilize, mulch, water. You always have to put something back. What do you put back when you mine?"

"Nothing. Not a damn thing." He forgot to watch his language. "You just take. And when it dries up one place you take from another."

Brillianna knew there was always a payment to make. But she was willing to make it. "What is California like?" she asked.

"Lots of space. An ocean. . . ." He stopped himself. "I never heard you say yes, Brillianna."

"Then you just weren't listening."

He'd had whores since he was fifteen, but he'd thought so long about this second kiss that he bestowed it awkwardly. Brillianna had the better of him. She was the only person who did.

There was a struggle with Aunt Lillian. Gaily, radiantly, Brillianna handled her.

Tough, wily and charming, Ted let his father know the refinery would be just the thing for a wedding present. Later he argued for a chain of gasoline stations to have an assured outlet for at least one phase of their product. But Brillianna's instinct had been correct. Oil was taken and consumed, and what they fed back into the reamed earth was the current of their lives.

The couple were married at the Grenville estate, July 29, 1923. They moved immediately to California. Brillianna took one look at Long Beach and rented a movie star's home in Santa Monica.

The young wife and Old Man Angstrom were antagonists from the start. Irv Angstrom never called Brillianna by name, referring to her as *She*. He felt constrained

41

by her proper manners. She fended off his boisterous stories and earthy humor with a ladylike politeness against which the old man was helpless.

He whispered to his son. "How is her thin blue blood going to keep you warm nights?" Ted only laughed and continued to indulge his wife. In the living room of the beach home Brillianna confided her plans to him, at least partially. "This is a magnificent place, of course. But it doesn't feel right to me. If I were building, I'd do so many things differently. In fact," she hardly dared look at him, "we should think seriously about building our own home."

"Why not?" he said carelessly. "Look around for some property."

She had seen what she wanted in Carmel. The ocean resembled the moors, stretching without boundary. She had become used to the ocean and waking to its moods.

"You know," he said, pursuing the thought, "I think it's a great idea. Keeping up a front is a big part of the oil game."

She kissed him with passion, opening her lips softly. "Thank you, Ted. It's my dearest wish to see Armagh rise again."

"Armagh?" He drew back flabbergasted. "Who said anything about Armagh? We're not building any god-damned castle."

"A manor, Ted, with dignity and gracious lines. The home I never had. The home you deserve. Who else will have anything like it?"

"You're right there," he said, allowing himself to become persuaded. "In fact you're always right. It's a fantastic idea. You match me move for move."

His moves were vigorous. No detail escaped him. He scanned the guest lists for social weekends as though going over a bill of lading. Their parties were an anomalous assortment of Brillianna's relatives, any of the New York crowd who happened to be on the West Coast, combined with oilmen, prospective angels, backers, and cronies from the old days.

It was this latter group Brillianna found trying. They were apt to appear in loud sport shirts, and one bantam cock was addicted to diamond rings, ostentatious, large, real. This type of guest she came to recognize as dating from the East Texas days in Beaumont. She came to know the stories too, and to wonder if they would be served with the meat course or wait for the chocolate mousse.

"There was Mrs. Slop," her father-in-law's voice boomed the length of the table. "I kid you not, that's what we called her, Mrs. Slop. And the reason she was called Mrs. Slop, she was the garbage lady back in Beaumont. Besides being the garbage collector, she had a little pig farm. Well sir, when Spindletop blew, she was knee deep in oil. She leased that pig farm for thousands and went right on collecting the garbage."

Then there were the jokes, tried and true, told over and over. Like the dude who, looking out at the desolate Texas landscape, asked, "What does this country grow?" The answer: "Men."

Or the fellow who wanted to know who made the world. He was told: "God did. But it was organized by John D. Rockefeller."

The laughter was of a particularly bitter nature as many of those present had come away bloodied from encounters with J.D., whose stranglehold on transportation allowed him to dictate policy and dominate the market.

This was the cue for Irv Angstrom to recall a letter written by Governor O.M. Roberts of Texas, who appointed a committee at the turn of the century to investigate the possibility of mineral resources within the state. The committee made a six month survey and reported there was no indication of resources of any kind in all of Texas. Governor Roberts replied, "Gentlemen, I accept your report and discharge the committee. But I say to you that every word in your report is a lie. I repeat, it is a damn lie. Do you think God Almighty would create a great country like Texas and not provide for it?"

Brillianna's parties, which she feared would be a laughing stock, became celebrated. People wanted to hear at first hand about the time oil was cheaper than water. "Yes sir, I remember when oil sold for three cents a barrel, but water had to be trucked in, you paid five cents a glass for it. Those were the days the world moved into East Texas. People slept on pool tables and in barber chairs. The first gusher flowed for nine days. Dudes poured in from everywhere. Kids took off their shoes and waded in the stuff. Talk about speculation: oil leases were hawked on street corners like patent medicines. The old hotel, Crosby House, that was the trading center. An acre of land sold for one million dollars. But you got to remember that the first six wells brought in produced as much oil in one day as all the wells at that time in the entire world."

The easterners and the movie people loved it, they ate it up, they wanted to know what the prospect was for California oil. That's when Old Man Angstrom looked at the company severely, like a belligerent Santa Claus. "Good. I'd say the prospects are good. And this time they're not going to catch me with my capital down a dry hole. I know, I was in on the East Texas thing. Experience told me that where there's salt domes, you got oil. But I drilled four hundred and forty feet through a kind of quicksand and came up empty. I was trying to arrange financing when Spindletop blew not eighty miles away. I got my financing all right, but I was stuck with partners. The Mellons got in on the third strike. That's Gulf today. Bought up half the concession for a million and a half. I know. I was there. Well, not quite there. Eighty miles away."

He was gently led back to the question, "So you think there's a future in California oil?"

"It's not me, it's not what I think. Why when I was a young man, some Yale professor, he said so."

"That was Silliman," Ted put in, "professor of geology and chemistry, Yale University. He was interested back in 1864. You know about the Ventura gusher, turn of the century? They say there were so many wells that tools lost down one would turn up in another. And of course Doheny made his famous strike at the La Brea tar pits in Los Angeles. There's oil all right, up and down the coast. Offshore too. The question is, will it be easy to take?"

Before they could come by any particulars of the Long Beach site, Old Man Angstrom treated the company to a eulogy of Colonel Edwin L. Drake. "When he was a lad they used to call it snake oil, doctors of healing and naturology sold it from their buggies. It was known for its curative powers." That always got a laugh from the table.

"It fouled water wells and salt mines. And when the Pennsylvania Rock Oil Company saw samples of oil skimmed off a spring on the land of a Titusville doctor, they sent Drake in to investigate. Drake's idea was to drill the way they did for salt, with a wood tower to house the machinery. But the rocks were water reservoirs. They spent more time bailing than drilling. My dad was one of the crew. I grew up on his stories of Drake. At the end of a year the hole was only down forty feet and had cost the company over two thousand dollars. So they told Drake to quit. But not him. He kept going, scrounging food and credit. At one point he was so needy that a neighbor gave him a sack of flour. He drilled on for two years, and discovered the invention that made oil a business, drilling inside a pipe."

"About the Long Beach wells," one of the guests interposed.

Irv Angstrom rode over him. "And the amazing fact is, even though the company long ago quit paying him, he considered it the company's well. So after making the most famous strike in history, he left the oil business and became Justice of the Peace in Titusville."

One night Brillianna continued the account with a bright smile. "And would you believe, twenty-one years after Drake's death an oilman erected a tombstone to his memory. Correct me if I am wrong, gentlemen, but I believe it said, 'He shook the bough that others might gather the fruit.'"

Her husband sat back in his chair and applauded. One old-timer laughed until he was pounded on the back, not so much at the story as at Brillianna stealing Angstrom's punchline.

While the Old Man complained directly of her snobbishness and the cool manner which drove away old friends, Brillianna was more subtle. She praised his father to her husband. But she was determined that when she rebuilt the three-story manor in Carmel, everything

45

would be lavished on it with the exception of spare bed-rooms. They would be there, but under different guises. The top floor was to contain the master bedroom, drawing room, nursery, and oratory; the middle floor, a massive library, music and billiard rooms; the first story, dining room, ballroom, living room, study, kitchen and servants' quarters. Her coup de grace was to outfit a replica of the carriage house as a guest bungalow, elegant in its decor and well removed from the main establishment.

When he heard of it, Irv Angstrom was furious. "She's put me out in the stables," he bellowed.

In revenge he lured Ted for days at a time into the fields. Ted was in his element. He loved nothing better than to slosh around in the black ooze on which their empire was founded. But it was more than that. Down a few hundred feet was the life blood of the modern world waiting for Ted Angstrom to tap into.

Such power staggered him. He moved among his crews as though inebriated. The men thought he'd had a nip or two. They didn't know he was drunk on the awe-some idea that a laboring engine was sending probes into his future.

Brillianna was intoxicated too. She drew the plans herself, from which she insisted the architect must work. She corresponded with her father asking for the remaining albums without letting him know the reason. Part of her triumph would be when it was shared. It was the home her father was born in, where Grenvilles had been raised for four hundred years. Prince Charlie, the young Pretender, had gone falconing on the estate. Historic documents and religious proclamations were signed there.

While Ted was in Long Beach, Brillianna was in Carmel. The day the structure was framed she walked through its bones, like the lofted ribs of some ancient forgotten beast. She peered out at the sea which marched and marched without approaching closer. When the enormous cage was enclosed and the facade bricked over, she ran lightly up the staircase, her hand following the curve of the polished balustrade. "You won't catch me now," she said. All the same she peered into

46

the shadowy corners of the alcove. She alternated between radiant delight at what she had wrought and strange contemplative moods as she moved from room to room.

Ted, when he was permitted to view the new Armagh, complained because there was no furniture and hardly any place to sit down.

"You don't furnish Armagh from a catalog or a department store," she replied tartly. "It's a matter of tracking down each piece."

"Well, I'd appreciate it if you'd track down some chairs first."

She looked at him almost shyly as though she were giving him herself. "You do like it? You are pleased?"

He kissed her fervently. "It's the most extraordinary place I've ever seen. And it cost the most money, and I don't give a damn if there aren't any chairs."

While Brillianna furnished Armagh, she had several other projects going forward. One was to marry her sister Elizabeth to the senator from North Carolina. This accomplished, her conscience was at rest concerning her. A great deal of her time was also spent in commissioning an agent to retrieve the family china which her mother had sold. Not content with this, she determined to have the entire collection, including those pieces that had been looted a quarter of a century ago. Barclays Bank was contacted, advertisements placed in the Dublin and local Armagh papers. Antique dealers cooperated, a door to door campaign was mounted. The collection which had been her grandmother's pride was painstakingly got in hand and shipped to California.

Brillianna's delight in unwrapping, handling and arranging the ancient porcelain was an odd mixture of tactile and psychological satisfaction. She passed a candle on the far side of the china as her mother had done to see the outline of her own fingers. The motif was a wisp of flowers, the scalloped edges embossed in gold. On the day the set was complete, dinner plates, salad plates, cups, saucers, serving platters, and finger bowls all restored, she wrote her parents inviting them to visit. Armagh was ready for inspection. The last detail had been seen to. Ted would be in Long Beach, which was as it should be. This was a Grenville affair.

Brillianna sent the car to the airport. She elected to greet her parents from the front steps of the new phoenix. When she heard them in the drive, she stepped outside.

Her mother pressed her hand to her chest. Her father stood as though at attention. Brillianna ran down the stairs into his arms, kissing him, hugging him, and then her mother, trying to tell it all at once: the two years it had taken in building, the research that had gone into it, the authenticity, the overseeing of each detail so that it was an exact replica of the original.

Room by room they made their way through the house. Bemused, her parents followed her like children. Sometimes Grenville merely stood and nodded. Sometimes he suggested a piece be moved slightly. "The armoire was more to the right, I believe. Closer the door." Before the tour continued she had it placed where he designated. Her father halted at the staircase and looking up, "It was here," he said, "just here above our heads that my brother Charles and I tied Sophia over the drop by her sash. A blue sash it was. Well, well." He shook his head.

The moment came. Brillianna ushered them into the formal dining room. Her father saw the table appointed with the Haviland dishes he remembered from his boyhood and fell utterly silent.

To give him an opportunity to recover, Brillianna recounted the story of her efforts, how each piece had been discovered and repurchased.

Grenville grasped her hand and raised it to his lips. "A daughter of mine has put the family back together. This is something I struggled for all my life, but was unable to achieve."

Brillianna lowered her head.

When she looked up from this victory she saw she had left Ted too much to his father. They were constantly gone, surveying new holdings, or bringing in a well somewhere. She pondered the situation and decided to give her husband a son, and herself an ally. It was time, she felt, to found the dynasty.

Ted had been hinting the past year that they should settle down to raising the next generation of Angstroms. Mentally she corrected him. *Grenvilles*, born to the new Armagh. Lords in this infant democracy. Ted's wealth and her lineage assured it. And for what other reason had she rebuilt the old home?

He was back several nights later and she snuggled into his arms, listening docilely while he pursued the topic.

"How about it, Kiddo? We've got the goddamnedest, biggest house anyone ever had. What do you say we start filling it up."

She responded by stretching her body against his. "I want him to have your eyes," she whispered.

Like most young women when they stop taking precautions, she expected to be immediately pregnant. At the end of three months she consulted her doctor as to the probable cause of infertility.

"If I asked Ted to submit to a sperm count, he'd truss me up and stick me down one of his black holes," Dr. Terrell said. "Give it a few more months, Mrs. Angstrom. Keep on with the temperature chart. And remember, half the world is trying, and the other half is trying not to."

Aunt Lillian was more helpful. Brillianna mentioned the problem casually in a letter. But Lillian understood at once—that single sentence was the reason for writing. Only barren women gather as much lore on the subject as she possessed. But before imparting it she wrote acidly, "Of course, it may be your husband's fault. In which case there is nothing to be done. The bull that roars loudest does not always perform. I should know. However, you have not been trying long, and these hints may help. A woman's fertile period is just before the rise in temperature, or roughly two weeks before menses. This is the time to concentrate on, morning and night for three or four days. I recommend foods high in vitamin E. Oysters are extremely efficacious, as well as raw eggs, especially if you can locate one which has been fertilized. You can determine this by the small

49

blood spot at its center. Also a pillow under the hips is helpful. You have gravity working for you."

Whether it was gravity, timing, or choking down raw eggs, a child was conceived. The infant was not the son they hoped for, but a daughter, christened Brilli. Ted found it hard to accept, hard to let go of the picture he had formed in his mind. It had to be a boy so he could take him into the fields as his father had done with him, explain the thrill and pursuit of oil. It was a man's world, and a man's son was part of him. The boy would have his grandfather's humor, his own drive and sense of adventure.

For Brillianna's sake he gazed down at the small Grenville, beautiful, fashioned like a doll. The child was born into an atmosphere of anxiety. The world was stunned by the events of October 29. That Tuesday, 14 billion dollars were lost on the New York Stock Exchange. Two weeks later 26 billion more in stock values evaporated. President Hoover in an address to Congress maintained that the economy was fundamentally sound.

"That's it," Ted said. "Now I know we've had it."

"But we're not heavily invested," Brillianna reminded him. "It's mostly paper profits. We're not hurting the way a lot of people are."

"I'm not thinking of the market," Ted retorted. "I'm thinking oil."

"I see." Brillianna became still, a knack she had, as though looking inside her own mind. "Now I do see. A depressed economy, steel output practically nil, the automotive industry going bankrupt, factories closing. Those are our customers."

Ted paced the forty foot living room. "I've got to go to Long Beach. I've already laid off men. Now Dad's come to it. I can't let him do it alone. Some of them are old friends, been with us since I was a kid."

Brillianna nodded, this was not the moment to tell him Aunt Lillian was stranded on the Riviera and had cabled for funds.

Ted left and the phone rang constantly. That's when she discovered the memo pad with a list of cancelled contracts. Another notation informed her that four of their gas stations were in foreclosure. Until that moment she had not realized the income from the wells went to meet the obligations on the refinery, the processing plant, the trucking operation and the string of filling stations. She saw how overextended Ted was, and that Armagh II was built on sand with no solid foundation.

In the past the sight of the fields cheered Ted. But these monsters chugging faithfully away were impotent as long as prices were at rock bottom. The shed was still his dad's office. Their partnership had been dissolved at the time of Ted's marriage, the concession divided, and each went his separate way. The Old Man did what he knew, he pumped. Recently it was a struggle keeping a jump ahead of quit-claims, mechanic's liens and overdue notices, taking out ten-day options on a list of tracts, paying five percent of the land purchase price and sinking a test well. But Long Beach was oil rich, and while there were plenty of jinx holes, enough came through to keep up the scramble. He's in a hell of a lot better shape than I am, Ted thought.

Angstrom sat at his desk with a pile of papers impaled on a spike in front of him. More papers littered the surface. Through the window came the steady sound of the pumps.

"Good of you to come down, Ted," his dad gripped his hand, "but there's not a damn thing you can do."

"I can be here," Ted said grimly. "How drastic is the cutback?"

"Another twenty percent. The stockholders love that figure. A twenty-percent rollback, that really gets 'em on their hind legs dancing."

Ted didn't comment. "Where's the list?" he asked.

"List. What list?"

"Your twenty percent."

"You think I need a list on paper?" He tapped his forehead. "It's all up here, Ted. These are men I've worked alongside of forty years. I don't need a list to tell me who they are."

"Well, I do. I thought I'd talk to some of them."

51

"What the hell good is talk when you got the pink slip in your hand?"

"It's better than being kissed off without a word."

Irv nodded and scribbled some names. "Well, there's Monty Ewell, with me in Oklahoma when a gasser caught fire. And Tony Warfield, he goes back, my derrick man in East Texas. Andy McNulty, now that's one you may want to handle yourself." He avoided looking at Ted.

"McNulty? Why McNulty?"

"Because, goddamn it, I can't carry him any longer. I've got shareholders breathing down my neck, checking over the books. I've had McNulty down as age sixty-four for seven years. I can't get away with it anymore. He's out."

"Yeah," Ted murmured. "What about benefits? He got anything coming in the way of benefits?"

"You talk like some union organizer punk. Where would I get funds for any benefits?"

"What about compensation? Has he ever been injured on the job?"

"Are you kidding? Same as the rest of us. Couple of dozen times."

"Maybe I can write it up so the insurance company will pay something."

Irv snorted. "That would be a first."

"But you can't just let Andy go. He'd never get another job."

"Ted, you worked with Andy. I've worked with every man out there."

Ted nodded. "Where will I find him?"

"He's working Number Five."

It was toward the end of the day, McNulty was packing up his gear. Night work was a thing of the past. He hailed Ted, "You old son of a rooster, how are you? I see you still carry the pipe tongs on your face. I don't know how the devil we got through that one. Lord oh Lord, was she ever a gasser."

"You're looking good, McNulty."

"Ornery as ever. What brings you this way? Haven't seen you around lately."

"No, well you know how it is."

The light eyes peering from the weather-beaten face shot him a keen look. The dark visage had the swirl patterns found in oak paneling. "Sure do know how it is. The depression don't play any favorites."

"That's right. My dad's had to lay off a lot of good men."

"And I understand more heads are due to roll."

"Yeah, that's right. Andy. . . ." The smell of oil was suddenly noxious. He felt sick.

"You know," Andy said, "it's a funny thing. I was thinking of going in and seeing the Old Man." He called him that although Irv was ten years younger than himself.

"Andy," Ted said again. The fumes had got to him. He must get this over with.

"Yes sir. I was saying to myself just this week, Andy, with the depression on and all, it ain't right you holding down a job some young fellow might need. I been thinking of retiring."

Ted could hardly believe his ears.

"Yep. I been giving it a lot of thought. I've piled up a few bucks in my time. Never struck it rich, but while there's life, well, you know what they say. I been thinking of throwing in the towel here and doing a bit of prospecting on my own. I know this area just over the border in Baja."

"You really think you might do that?"

"Think? Hell, I've decided. Got my mind set on it. Maybe you could break it to your dad."

"Sure, Andy, if that's the way you want it. We'll miss you around here, you old buzzard."

"That goes both ways. It's been a few years."

"I'll send you your back pay and a bonus. You know after all this time you're entitled to a bonus."

"Is that a fact? I didn't know that."

"It won't be much," Ted said. It sure wouldn't be as it would come out of his pocket. "Just a token. I'll enclose it with the check."

They were walking slowly from the field. "My car's over there," McNulty indicated a nearby lot. "So tell your dad I'll be dropping by now and again just to jaw

53

about old times. As for you, keep your nose clean, hear?"

"I'll try."

McNulty walked off in the direction of the car. The next thing Ted knew people were running. He turned in the general direction of the commotion. They were gathering around McNulty's old heap. "No!" Ted shouted, not knowing what he meant by it. He pushed his way through to kneel over McNulty, who grabbed his chest with both hands. He was frozen in that position, his face contorted, but he recognized Ted. "Remember, old hangman Derrick?" the words gargled in his throat. "I told you about him."

"Don't talk. Just lie back." Ted slipped his coat off and doubled it under Andy's head.

"His customers never came back to complain. That's me, I won't be complaining none."

"Sure you will, loud as ever. We'll find something for you. There's always something. Night watchman. How about night watchman?" He was talking to a corpse. He tried pressing McNulty's chest, working his arms and slapping his face. Ten minutes later he walked away. He avoided the office. It wasn't his dad's fault, but he didn't want to see him. "Prospecting in Baja," he said aloud. "Yeah, McNulty, you do that, you do that."

He returned to Carmel, but he was still there in the fields. Brillianna couldn't get him to talk about it. That night when they turned in, his shoulders started to shake. "Baja," he said and rolled against the wall.

Brillianna had never seen him like this. He seemed unable to communicate what was bottled up in him. During the morning he went for another of those lonely walks on the beach that were becoming a habit with him. Brillianna took the opportunity to phone her father-in-law.

"You?" he yelled in surprise.

"Look, Irv, I have to know what's going on with Ted. Are things very bad down there?"

"Bad? They're worse."

"What happened yesterday?"

"What happened was there were layoffs. We got by-laws. I mean, I can't pick and choose. He was sixty-five, sixty-five hell, he was seventy. There was no choice. That's the way the Articles read. When you're sixty-five, whammo. But this was a double whammo, because he died."

"Who died?"

"I'm telling you. Andy McNulty walked off the field but he never reached his car. It was his heart. He was dead before the ambulance got there."

"Was he a friend of Ted? Did he know him well?"

"You might say that."

"Thank you." She hung up slowly. The easy win streak was at an end. Ted's confidence was badly shaken. Not only did he hold himself responsible for McNulty, but the death of the oilman was a sign. He had killed him, oil itself had killed him. The black goop never quit, it flowed up the pipes day and night, but it was a drug on the market. The black commodity he kept pumping had no outlet. And on top of that, someone called Andy McNulty dropped dead.

Brillianna sat down and quietly looked at a quiet sea. They had been married six years and her husband had never needed her before.

By the time Ted returned from his walk, the servants were dismissed with two weeks' severance pay and she was busy moving into the downstairs study on the first floor. "What is going on?" Ted asked.

"We've got to retrench. The house is the size of a hotel. So to cut utilities, I thought we'd move in here. Just you, me and the baby. It will be rather cozy, don't you think? Sort of a lark, like camping out."

"You mean, close off the rest of the house?" It would never have occurred to him to ask this of her.

Brillianna prepared the first meal she had ever cooked for her husband. "Do you realize I don't know my own kitchen," she said setting supper before him. "Isn't that amazing? It's as though it belongs to some other woman. I'll have to rearrange everything, I still haven't been able to find the measuring cup."

He nodded. He even smiled. Perhaps this was the moment to introduce a lighter note. She told him about Aunt Lillian. "She's stuck in Nice. It will take four hundred dollars for her to get home."

"Send it," Ted said with satisfaction.

"But. . . ."

"Send it."

They would have been all right if not for the phone. He included her now in his walks on the beach. The sand below their home was white. Back traveling waves met oncoming combers and the crash sent spume six feet into the air. By the time it reached their feet it was a froth of pearly bubbles. But when they got back the phone was ringing.

Brillianna answered, recognizing Mr. Taylor, an attorney for John Paul Getty.

She handed the receiver to Ted and going into the kitchen tied a tea towel around her waist. Ted came in a few seconds later and sat heavily. "The buzzards are circling in."

"Another offer to buy you out?"

He nodded glumly. "They smell blood."

"Well, don't think of selling."

"There's no way I can hold on."

"It's time for the Cantor show," she said, jumping up. They had met the creator and writer of the comedy hour, Dave Freedman. And when the hotel clerk asked the stockbroker if he wanted the room for sleeping or jumping, Ted laughed. Brillianna sent up a silent thank-you for Dave's offbeat humor. "When it's a dagger in the heart," he once told them, "that's when it's funny."

Ted hadn't understood what he meant. He did now. For him, that laugh was release after weeks of watching the plants he supplied cut back production or close outright. Suddenly he was able to confide in her. "The simple fact is, I'm not able to pick up my options. I stand to lose every lease I have."

"That won't happen." She spoke so decisively that he was heartened. She rose and began to clear.

He followed her to the sink, forgetting to bring his plate along. "The word is out, I'm up for grabs. Another corporation that thinks I've had it is the Southern Pacific Railway. They've helped themselves to more than a billion in oil lands, calling it their *right of way*. I heard from their lawyers, too."

"You mustn't sell, Ted.

"Let everything else go," Brillianna said, "but don't sell the wells." She continued fiercely, "I married an oilman. You told me no guarantees. We've lived in a wildly lavish fashion. But don't forget I grew up poor. I know economies you wouldn't believe."

"Saving on toilet paper isn't going to help," he said roughly. "And how do we keep afloat? My God, I'm incorporated at forty million dollars and I don't know how we're going to live."

"Trust me," Brillianna said. "I don't like being poor. But I'm experienced at it. And for your information, it does help to economize on toilet paper."

Ted first heard of Quentin Thresher from his father in the summer of 1932. The Old Man drove up twice a month on Fridays to spend the weekend and discuss conditions in the fields, which had not improved. Gradually, Ted sold off his subsidiary operations or abandoned them to lien-holders, paring back until only the wells were left. Finally, his back was to the wall. As a stop-gap measure and to avoid losing it altogether, he mortgaged his Long Beach concession. He felt physically sick, and to overcome the sense of frustration went out and purchased a fancy new mailbox. He did this in defiance of his wife's stringent economies, for the old one brought nothing but trouble and bills.

Shamefacedly he explained the black and silver presence to Brillianna. It would, he claimed, be a roosting place for better luck. She looked at him in amazement. At that moment the expenditure for the mailbox seemed to her the culminating disaster. Like a fisherman with a new fly, he hoped to lure luck to their side by laying out two dollars and ninety-five cents.

His dad understood and tried to console him. "It's the goddamned limited market, Ted. The lousy prices."

"No. I was spread too thin. In normal times it would have worked. But with the price of oil going nowhere. . . ."

Irv nodded glumly. Without outside business obligations to meet, without a family, without Armagh II, he was barely holding on.

"I wish to God there was some way we could have saved your operation. But everything I can lay my hands on goes into lease money." The only hope he could hold out was, "I can't live forever. It will all come to you eventually."

Ted didn't answer.

His father was deeply concerned at his apathy. He thought of offering to take him back into partnership. But he didn't trust Ted not to get involved again in some chancy enterprise which would drag them both down to bankruptcy. Ted refused to face facts and Brillianna was as bad. Here they still sat in their castle. It's true they occupied one room. But what of that, there were taxes, weren't there? Until they came to their senses, anything he gave Ted would be down a sinkhole. So the Old Man dredged in his mind for an anecdote, something to lighten the atmosphere, and he remembered Quentin Thresher. "I had a strange experience the other day. This character comes into my office with a document. And I mean a document, seal and everything. Claimed it was signed by an Arabian prince." Irv laughed the belly laugh that Ted inherited. "Well, just out of curiosity I did a little checking. He'd been all over with that damned paper, New York, Texas, everywhere. Of course he didn't get any place with the majors. So now he's after small fry like me. Just thought I'd tip you off in case he gets in touch with you."

"Why should he do that? I'm running my field for creditors."

"Well, just in case. I put him down as a crank. No use wasting time."

Ted was weary. He wanted to get to bed, pull the covers up on another day.

That same week a Mr. Thresher was on the phone to him. Ted expected a fast-talking promotor, but the man came across as low key, almost diffident. Ted had nothing else to do, so he made an appointment for that afternoon, choosing a time Brillianna would be on the beach with Brilli.

There was something prim about Quentin Thresher.

58

He looked about him, much impressed. "Unusual spot you have here."

Ted had opened the library for the occasion. "We like it," he said.

Mr. Thresher presented his credentials. "I am an engineer. I was working on the construction of a bridge and highway in Yemen when I was contacted by Mr. John Eustace Nichols, the renowned traveler and explorer. As well as being a close friend of the King of Arabia, Ibn Saud, Mr. Nichols is an expert on the country."

Thresher fascinated Ted. It seemed he belonged to a different century, speaking of kings and exotic lands.

The man spread his hands almost apologetically. "I accepted a commission to assist in an effort to find additional water supplies. Of course every drop of water in Arabia is precious. And the king hoped there might be artesian springs. The exploration consisted of tapping the limestone layers in certain areas and was carried out under the most difficult circumstances. After months of investigation I was forced to conclude that the possibilities for water on a significant scale were poor indeed. The King was immensely disappointed. His main revenue, you see, is from the pilgrim trade to the holy city of Mecca. He badly wanted a more reliable source of national income, which he hoped might come from expanding agriculture."

Ted laughed. "He asked for water and you gave him oil. At least I take it that is the gist of this meeting?"

Thresher was without a vestige of humor and could not be hurried. "I mentioned in my report that the sedimentary formations of limestone and sandstone in massive beds could indicate oil. The King was interested in bringing in foreign capital to explore and develop such possibilities. I explained, of course," Mr. Thresher sounded so impeccably correct it was impossible to believe he had not used these exact words to the King, "that I was not the person to handle financing. However the King was insistent. He doesn't understand business arrangements, Western style. But I would be less than candid were I not to mention that I will receive a reward from the King if I can bring him a signed deal."

The idea of Mr. Thresher and the King of Arabia doing business tickled Ted.

"I brought a copy of my mapping report." Thresher unzipped an attaché case, taking out papers and a folded map. "The Arabian desert, as you can see, is an enormous trapezoid. It is the eastern edge of the country along the Persian Gulf that I found of particular interest." His finger marked the area. "Here, near Dhahran in the Hasa, there is evidence of igneous activity and strong deformation with associated faulting."

"What about salt domes?" Ted asked, bending over the charts.

Thresher nodded. "Throughout this entire area we have domes, lime and gypsum. The limestone hills are capped with ferruginous chert sediment."

Ted examined the map closely. It was an article of faith with him that any salt dome was worth drilling.

"The Dhahran is composed of folds and uptilted strata. The underlying sedimentary rock is porous. Picture a ribbon of crepe paper sixty miles wide in places." Because Thresher did not add, 'an ideal bed for oil accumulation,' Ted thought it.

"The concession area that I recommend consists of five hundred thousand square miles," Thresher concluded blandly.

Ted was nonplussed. That was a quality of Mr. Thresher's, coming out with the most astonishing propositions as though he were commenting on the obvious. "Half a million square miles?" Ted repeated bemused.

"That is my recommendation." Thresher dug around in the case and extracted a document on high quality bond. "I have here a letter of agreement. It states that I am authorized to represent Ibn Saud in all phases of negotiation for the Hasa area." He passed the typed contract to Ted, who looked at the signature: 'Abd al 'Aziz Ibn 'Abd al Rahman al Faisal al Sa'ud, Grand Cross of the Bath, Grand Cross of the Indian Empire, King of the Hejaz and of Nejd and all Arabia.

"That is a rather unique signature," Ted admitted, and the next moment found himself asking, "Do you have rock samples with you?"

Mr. Thresher lifted his case and placed it on the desk. Inside were rows of neatly labeled small sacks, the kind marbles come in. Ted opened one after another, fingering the contents—rock chunks and finely ground sediments. He saw a picture of Arabia quite different from Thresher's trapezoid, which seemed to him completely artificial, arbitrarily cutting up the earth's crust into kingdoms and spheres of influence. In actuality, Arabia was a tableland, tilting down from its high border in the Hejaz at the Red Sea, falling steeply across the peninsula to the low, shallow waters of the Persian Gulf. Gravity would pull the oil exactly as Thresher said, to sea level along the eastern shore of Saudi, the Hasa.

The map, spread and positioned with an ashtray, showed three bodies of water and enormous slices of desert. All were inconsequential. The real mass, immense, static, and caught in the interstices of porous formations, began at the Bahrein Islands and was trapped by the great anticline of Arabia. It underlay man's boundaries and nature's. A mile under the Gulf, two miles, six miles, as deep as Everest was high, tides were pinioned in black oil-soaked crevices.

A bore hole into the earth would reveal it. A pipe, such as he could sink, would reach the largest oil fields in the world under their blanket of sand. The vision exploded in his mind.

And this man Quentin Thresher was talking five hundred thousand square miles. How many wells could you sink in that?

The question itself staggered him. How many barrels could you take out?

How many cupfuls of water could be dipped from the sea? Luck, that had turned her back on him for three years sent Thresher to him, uncapping hope, releasing it from deep fissures.

Contrapuntally to his enthusiasm, reality intruded. In fact, it drummed him into the ground. At this moment, when he had been handed a chance of a lifetime, five hundred thousand square miles of oil land, there was no way he could come by even a piece of it.

Brillianna felt things were not the same between them. Ever since Ted mortgaged the Long Beach fields she had to suffer his black moods.

She didn't mind cutting corners, or that they continued occupying a single room of the house. She never complained about this. In return she felt business worries should be kept separate from their lives. She stood by Ted waiting for the day things would turn around. What else could she do?

Did he expect her to sell Armagh, was that it? He had never suggested such a thing. Had he thought it? Did he really expect her to give up her home?

Why weren't they able to discuss it? Why weren't they able to discuss anything? He had stopped confiding in her. Was he in danger of losing the wells altogether? She didn't know. She didn't know herself what she would do if it came to that. Armagh was not just a property. Armagh was a restoration. Someday it would provide a setting for Brilli. Ted must see that.

Somehow, for some reason, she felt she satisfied neither her husband nor her daughter. Brilli was a sturdily independent two-year-old who squirmed out of her embraces.

Brillianna turned to her own childhood. She wrote her parents asking them to come for a visit. It would mean opening up another room, but only for a week. The reunion, she felt, would renew her ties with the past where perhaps answers lay.

She waited for her mother's reply impatiently. Mrs. Grenville wrote that they were sorely tempted to see their grandchild, that it was hard to make do with snapshots and letters. But in these times it was impossible for them both to leave the pharmacy. It was decided she would make the journey alone. She could scarcely wait to see little Brilli, and of course Brillianna and Ted.

Brillianna scurried around making things as comfortable as their limited space and means allowed. Her sense of well-being told her she had done the right thing. She hummed as she worked.

It was a shock to see her mother. One never expects people to change. She had attempted to prepare herself by saying, she'll be a little older. But she was unprepared for a sharp birdlike quality which she didn't remember. Mrs. Grenville cocked her head to one side and asked if Brilli was "trained." Brillianna admitted there were still occasional accidents. Already she was wondering how wise this visit would prove to be.

Mrs. Grenville, of course, did not mention their reduced circumstances but took everything in. She told them several times how well the senator from North Carolina was doing. And she continued with her own schedule much as though she were at the pharmacy.

After supper she asked for the Bible as she did at home. The first night Ted escaped and Mrs. Grenville read aloud to Brillianna and little Brilli, who fell asleep. The second evening she suggested that the Bible reading was an activity that should involve the whole family. "Stay with us, Ted. I know you'll be glad of it."

Ted relented, and Brillianna shot him an amused glance. Actually he needed a quiet moment. He had things to think over.

"Exodus," Mrs. Grenville announced in a clear voice. She had finished Genesis the night before. "Chapter one. Now these are the names of the children of Israel, which came into Egypt; every man and his household came with Jacob. Reuben, Simeon, Levi, and Judah. Issachar, Zebulun and Benjamin, Dan and Naphtali, Gad, and Asher."

Ted fidgeted. He ran his hand over his scar. It occurred to him that he might be able to take out an option on the Saudi concession after all. It would mean scrounging a down payment. That would give him six months to work something out. In that length of time he could come up with partners, sell off a part interest.

Caution suggested to him that Thresher had failed in a similar attempt; the majors didn't take him seriously. This, of course, was the very circumstance that gave a small operator like himself a chance. However, even to come up with an initial payment would mean borrowing on his insurance. It was too wild a gamble.

Still, oilmen were a gambling breed. He remembered

a time his dad couldn't meet the Saturday payroll. He dropped by the rig and shot craps with the crew. Two hours later he had enough to pay their wages.

Brillianna fixed him with a reproving glance. He tried to bring his mind back to the children of Jacob. "And the King of Egypt spake to the Hebrew midwives, of which the name of one was Shiphrah, and the other Puah."

Ted surrendered. He might as well admit it. Al Hasa was a dream, an *Arabian Nights* fairy tale. "Therefore God dealt well with the midwives: and the people multiplied and waxed very mighty. And it came to pass because the midwives feared God, that he made them houses."

Ted's decision left him with a sense of loss. He had gone so far as to look up the great dun-colored peninsula when he got home, studying at leisure the change in altitude from the Red Sea as the land gradually sloped toward the Persian Gulf. He made an effort to corral his thoughts, allowing Mrs. Grenville's voice to touch him with monotony.

"And there went a man of the house of Levi; and took to wife a daughter of Levi. And the woman conceived and bare a son; and when she saw him that he was a goodly child, she hid him three months. And when she could not longer hide him, she took for him an ark of bulrushes and daubed it with slime and with pitch and put the child therein. . . ."

Revelation, like a burning bush, flamed up and brought him to his feet. "Did you hear that? I'm asking, did you hear that?"

"Ted," Brillianna whispered, "Mother's reading."

"Brillianna, my love, she's reading words. I am seeing a vision. *Pitch*, that's what it said. And pitch means *oil*."

"What is he talking about?" Mrs. Grenville asked, bewildered.

"For heaven's sake, Ted," Brillianna admonished, "what is it?"

"The Good Book has backed Saudi. Moses's cradle was smeared with oil. And I bet Noah's ark was caulked with it!" He swung her off her feet.

Mrs. Grenville dropped the Bible, its pages sprawling.

"Ted!" Brillianna protested, "have you gone mad?"

"You can bet your bottom dollar on it. As a matter of fact," he laughed uproariously, "that's what you have bet."

Ted tried to express his gratitude to Mrs. Grenville. "You said I'd be glad if I stayed and listened."

She waved him away, evidently thinking her daughter had married a madman. After a long-distance telephone conversation she found it necessary to cut short her visit.

Brillianna always needed time to mull things over. And the more she thought about this newest venture of Ted's the more it disturbed her.

"Is this Mr. Thresher the man your father warned you about?"

Ted tried to sidestep this, persuade her it was no hunch he was acting on, but a certain thing. "The oil is down there."

"Ted, be reasonable. The Arabian peninsula is across the world. You've never seen it. So how can you know? How can you be so sure?"

"Because, damn it, I'm an oilman."

"What will you use for money?" she shot at him.

"I'll raise it."

"How?"

"That's my business." He slammed out of the house continuing the dialogue in his head. He had already decided to hock the policy he'd taken out when Brilli was born.

The following day he and Thresher met again in the library. There was new urgency on Ted's part, he had to keep Thresher from going to anyone else. So far the men who knew oil, the experts, had been put off by Thresher's fanciful descriptions. The man was an engineer, not a geologist. They considered him, as his dad did, a crank. But when they woke up to the territory he was offering for exploration. . . . He must conclude. He'd phoned the bank that morning and they were only prepared to lend five hundred on his insurance. But such minor troubles he dismissed as so much water seeping into the casing.

Ted cleared his throat and moved in on Thresher. "I assume you've contacted the majors?"

"Yes." That was one thing about Thresher, he was painfully honest. "I must admit to a negative reaction in New York. I had a slightly better reception in Texas, but nothing definite."

Ted drummed his fingers on the desk. This action, meant to fluster and intimidate, spurred Thresher to loquacity. "The King wants it quite clear that active production is spelled out in the contract. If oil is discovered in commercial quantities he would count heavily on royalties."

"Just out of curiosity, what closing figure does the King have in mind?"

"The King's terms are straightforward and simple. A thirty-year loan of fifty thousand pounds sterling, repayable at six percent."

"Fifty thousand pounds sterling." Ted began figuring on his blotter, and frowning at the numbers he produced. This was more mumbo-jumbo, a technique he had from his father. It added to the opponent's tension and uncertainty. "I make that roughly a hundred and sixty-five thousand dollars," he said looking up.

Thresher, unfazed by his performance, nodded agreement.

"You realize I am an independent," Ted said. "If I make an offer it would be contingent on participation. I would need to bring in partners."

Thresher hesitated, but a covert glance at the magnificent room and the palatial setting beyond the window seemed to reassure him. He settled his gaze on Ted. "I take it you are interested in the King's proposition?"

Ted leaned back. "I tell you what I'd like to do, Mr. Thresher. I'd like to give you a binder, say a thousand dollars to show good faith and tie up the concession for six months until I've had a chance to put out some feelers."

"Well, I don't know really." Thresher's voice expressed genuine uncertainty. "I hadn't thought in those terms."

"Look," Ted said, "You've been to New York, you've been to Texas. The majors aren't interested."

"But a thousand dollars, that hardly seems adequate. I don't know how the King will react to that."

"Come now," Ted laughed, "you have his proxy, you have the authority. And when you consider I'm not buying anything but time. . . ."

Thresher placed his fingertips together and looked at them. "Still. . . ."

"You drive a hard bargain," Ted said. "Fifteen hundred." And before Thresher quite knew what was happening he was shaking hands.

"I'll write out the check." Ted's mind was racing ahead. This was Friday. He'd hang onto Thresher until the bank closed, which gave him two and a half days to cover the amount.

Ted tore up the first check; he wasn't able to get the King's name on the line. He started again, his writing cramped and small, *'Abd al 'Aziz Ibn 'Abd al Rahman al Faisal al Sa'ud. . . .*

Thresher came around and looked over his shoulder. "That will be sufficient, it is not necessary to enter the King's titles."

Ted nodded and turning the check over wrote on the back: *This sum secures a six-month option on the oil concession known as the Hasa, Arabia.* He looked up at Thresher a bit dazed. He had just concluded a deal with the King of Arabia.

In fact he had just paid the King fifteen hundred dollars which he didn't have. He folded the check in two and handed it to Quentin Thresher.

"When I walked in this door," Mr. Thresher said, "I never dreamed. . . ."

"No," Ted said. "Me neither. This calls for a drink."

"I'm sorry. I've gotten out of the habit. Arabians are strict Muhammadans, you know. They don't indulge in alcoholic beverages, or cigarettes, for that matter."

"How about women?" Ted asked. "They're not so strict about women, I hear. Tell me, Thresher, how many wives does this Ibn Saud 'Abd al 'Aziz whatever have? Fifty? A hundred maybe?"

"Four," Mr. Thresher replied. And then because he was a scrupulous man, added, "at a time."

The banks had been closed fifteen minutes when he allowed Thresher to depart. Immediately the jovial air he had adopted fell like a pugilist's guard. He sank down behind his desk. Fifteen hundred dollars. With the five hundred on his insurance, that left a thousand to go.

The figure was branded into his brain. A brief rummage in a bottom kitchen drawer turned up his bank book. He and Brillianna had a joint account. He ran his finger down deposits and withdrawals until he came to the total:

Thirty-five dollars.

He dropped the book back into the drawer and slammed it shut. Ted believed in luck. He believed it was something you made yourself. When he was in school taking exams he used to flip a coin to find out how he'd done. If he didn't like the result, he called two out of three. That way you forced your luck. All you needed was a small edge. If you played with the house you never lost. And the way he looked at it, *he* was the house, with his own pipeline to a special kind of luck.

Of course there were times when he guessed wrong. But that was when it was a *guess*, not like now, when he *knew*. He could smell that oil. And for a paltry thousand dollars he wasn't going to let it go.

A thousand dollars: a few years ago that was a boat charter for a weekend's fishing off Baja. He used to throw that kind of money away, not even count it. Now. . . .

Now he closed his eyes, mentally conjuring up people he had done favors for at one time or another. He spent the next hour on the phone. McKay's wife had just had a baby. Nothing there. Phillips was in Argentina. Hubber had a bankruptcy pending. Tolle's number was disconnected. Hart Curry was willing to have a drink if they could meet in Daly City. "Well, look, that's quite a drive. I'll tell you what it's about. I have a chance to close a deal. But it's going to take a bit more cash than I have on hand. I thought maybe. . . ."

Sure. Hart was willing, good old Hart. He'd chip in a hundred bucks. Ted upped him to two hundred and drove to Daly City. He and Hart had a couple of beers. Hart was his kind of guy, a loner, wildcatter. He was interested in offshore drilling in Mexico. Ted said nothing about his deal except that it wasn't firmed. Hart operated like that, he understood. No questions, the two hundred on the table.

But that was it. End of line. There was no one else he could call on except. . . .

The drive back to the house gave him a chance to consider how to approach his dad. Irv Angstrom was his best bet. His wells were free and clear. Ted was thinking past the eight hundred dollars he needed Monday. He was thinking his dad might come in with him. If he was willing to put up Long Beach, Irv Angstrom could swing the Arabian concession. That would be something, he and his dad, partners again with half a million square miles to wildcat. They'd have to bring in someone else to get on the pump. But with the lease money paid, there'd be no hanging back. The trick was to get the ball rolling.

Long experience of his father taught him that it was important to start out on the right foot. He was crusty, and it was easy to get on the wrong side of him. But how often he'd said, "You got your gambling blood from me, son." It was all a question of approach. The right moment. . . . After dinner, when he was relaxed, he'd get out the scotch.

He didn't see his car in the driveway. He looked in the garage for the slightly beat-up Buick his dad drove up every other weekend. He was regular as clockwork. Was it possible. . . ? Could it be that for some unaccountable reason he had decided not to come? That would be a catastrophe, bad in itself, but worse for the crack it would create in the luck he was building. Anything that interfered could cause the whole tenuous structure to falter. If it once did that, it was like a plane whose engines conked out; without propulsion, without thrust, it spiraled toward earth and he with it buried under the wreck. "Hi!" he said, letting the door slam. "Dad here?"

"You're late," Brillianna said.

"I know. I couldn't get away. How come Dad isn't here?"

"He'll be here tomorrow." She looked at him questioningly.

"Why tomorrow?"

"Tomorrow's his Friday."

Panic clawed his gut. "Today is Friday," he said, trying to stay calm.

"It's Thursday. Come on, let's have dinner. Everything's overcooked as it is."

He followed her in. Thursday. Seven o'clock, Thursday. How could he make such a mistake? What was he thinking of? He had until tomorrow morning to make good his check. He didn't know what he ate. He went through the motions so as not to make her suspicious. "I'll skip dessert tonight." He pushed his chair back from the table. "I have to go out."

Brillianna made no comment, a bad sign. Nevertheless, there was nothing for it but to fly to Long Beach. He drove to the San Francisco Airport, waited with eight other passengers at the Century Pacific gate, and spent the two and a half hours in transit silently conversing with his dad. Setting down in Los Angeles, he went directly to a pay phone and put in a call to Dan Williams, arranged to borrow his car, took the bus, and walked the rest of the way. What a miserable shunting about this had turned into. Dan urged him to come in but Ted muttered something about a family emergency.

His dad lived in a bachelor apartment, which meant there was no bedroom. The living room couch did double duty opening into an uncomfortable bed.

Ted ran up a flight of stairs and knocked. His father wasn't there. Ted knew where to find him. He glanced at his watch. It was crucial, absolutely necessary that he borrow eight hundred dollars for deposit in the morning.

He decided not to mention Arabia or a partnership.

This wasn't the moment. He couldn't risk drunken recriminations or a fight. There just wasn't time.

Mulligan's was dimly lit, but there was no mistaking the barrel-chested old man who did his drinking standing up. "Hi, Dad."

No grin, no affectionate clap on the shoulder. The old man acknowledged his presence curtly. "So you're in my bailiwick, are you?"

"Yeah. I had to see a fellow down here. I thought maybe you'd fly back with me tonight."

"That's mighty nice of you. Do I know this fellow you came way down here to see?"

"No. I don't think so."

"I don't think so either, because he doesn't exist."

"What are you drinking?" the bartender asked Ted. He indicated his dad's glass. "I'll have the same."

"That's gin," the old man said. "Gin. Not classy enough for a man who can't stay in his own bailiwick, who's got to go to hell and back to pump air and water."

Ted cursed his luck, the old guy was smashed.

"So," his dad went on, "in spite of what I said, you let that phony lease hound, Thresher, get to you. I told you to throw him out on his dandified ass. But no, you want to pump in the Arabian peninsula. Don't look so surprised. It was a coup for Thresher, he was on the phone to half the companies in the country telling them you had a corner on King Solomon's Mines, is it?"

"Dad, will you wait, will you hold on?"

"Hold on? While you make a joke of the Angstrom name? What's wrong with your own country? What's wrong with American oil? Long Beach oil? It's proven, it's there for the taking. I'm bringing it up steady."

"Nothing's wrong with it, Dad. It's dependable. As you say, it's there. But I've got a lease on half a million square miles. You always said, if you want to find oil, throw away the books and go into the field. You're the one who told me H. L. Hunt proved you drill enough holes without going broke, you're bound by the law of averages to hit."

"You're quoting back at me what I said all right. But the words that didn't seem to get through to you are, *without going broke.* Seems to me you're already broke. Except you got some hidden assets I didn't know about?"

Ted straightened. This was the price.

"I don't understand you, Ted. I swear I don't. Getting mixed up in a wild scheme like Arabia! You and the King! Boy, oh boy, will I take a ribbing: 'Hear your son's buddy-buddy with the King of Araby,' 'How's young Angstrom's pal, the King?' Jesus Christ, Ted, haven't I dinned into your head enough times, schemes like this are the oilman's undoing? I can't believe you'd fall for it."

Ted recognized they had changed positions. When he was in college he wanted to call on geologists, do seismographic work. But the old man pooh-poohed all that, refusing to drill on scientific recommendations, preferring to put down four wildcats at a time. "I can't understand your reasoning, Dad, now that I've come around to your way of thinking."

"Who says it's my way of thinking?" Angstrom bellowed. "I don't think 'concession' if I haven't two cents to bless myself with."

"The way I look at it, if I pump anything at all, I pump a fortune. Oil can be brought to market well below present costs, using Saudi labor."

"Saudi labor, my behind. A bunch of goat herders, that's what you have, inefficient as hell. To say nothing of getting the equipment in. Every goddamn bolt, screw and nailhead has to be floated up the Gulf. Pilferage will run you forty percent. You got to have armed guards. And you got to pay for armed guards. You got to pay for everything, and how the hell are you going to do it? That's what I want to know." Angstrom overrode Ted, not allowing him an entering wedge. "You forget to order something, some simple thing, you don't just run down to the hardware store and pick it up. The whole operation grinds to a halt while you go through Cairo to London and back and up the canal, paying salaries all the time. Paying men to stand around."

"Dad," Ted put in, "if you'd seen the geologic samples. I held them in my hand. There had to be oil where they came from."

"And where was that? Arabia? How do you know that creep Thresher didn't pick them up on my Long Beach site? Don't tell me you fell for the oldest con of all?"

"You don't want to listen," Ted said.

The lobes of Angstrom's ears turned red. "All right, let's have it."

"Have what?"

"The touch. You're going to put the bite on me, aren't you, boy? You didn't fly down here to ask me to dinner."

Ted's lips barely moved. That was not surprising as his heart barely pumped and all vital signs dropped to just about zero. "I don't want anything from you." Then getting louder, "You think I came down here to borrow money from you? I wouldn't borrow money from you, not a red cent, not if I was starving." He slammed down a buck for his drink and barged out.

When he hit the cold air of night, cold reason woke. What had he done? In any circumstances he hated fighting with his dad. In the past, with nothing to win or lose he had gone a long way to avoid it. But tonight with everything at stake, he stuck his chin out, allowed himself to be baited.

He'd been off balance from the first. Damn Thresher's hide, he hadn't waited to broadcast their deal.

The deal. The fifteen hundred dollars. The check.

There was no use going over it. A mental paralysis, which he mistook for calm, settled in. He retraced his route, dropping off the borrowed car, catching the bus to the airport in time for the milk flight, which besides stopping at Bakersfield and Fresno, put down in Santa Maria and Salinas. This time the Lycoming carried only two other passengers. He picked up his car at the other end and drove home. The whole sequence seemed completely unreal. Except for the fact that he was exhausted he wouldn't have believed any of it.

He didn't go into the partitioned-off bedroom. He couldn't risk waking Brillianna. He flopped on the couch, kicking off his shoes. He thought of sneaking in and getting the clock.

That would be a stupid thing to do. Let them come

and get him. What would the charge be? *Larceny? Grand larceny?* He wondered if he should deposit Hart's two hundred dollars, but he couldn't see that it would make a difference. If the check didn't clear, it didn't clear.

Brillianna woke or rather roused him at the usual time. "I'm not getting up," he said.

"Are you sick?"

"I'm sick."

She tiptoed out.

Why do people tiptoe when you're sick? He could hear her shushing the baby. A desert burned like a fever into his imagination and trapped sediments soaked in oil at extraordinary depth. In a matter of seconds a complete fantasy unfolded in his head. He saw his father's Long Beach stock in the safe-deposit box. They were lying with a rubber band around them, next to his. No, his were gone—he'd pledged them. But all he had to do was remove his father's stock, cover the option and control the entire Saudi concession. This was a crime, he told himself. But the real crime was that he could see what other men could not.

Brillianna came back and set tea and toast beside him. "My goodness," she said, "you're soaking wet. I'll bring a towel and fresh pajamas." He waited for ten o'clock. Thresher was a ten o'clock man. He'd be at the bank as soon as the door opened.

At first he'd think it was an oversight. There'd be a telephone call. He was glad he had collected a few hundred dollars, it would pay a lawyer. No, his wife and kid would have to have that for eating money. He could picture Brillianna's attempts to extricate herself. She would try to borrow on the insurance only to find he already had. In desperation she would ask Aunt Lillian for a loan. It wasn't only Thresher. He didn't give a damn about Thresher. It was Brillianna and Brilli he had robbed. He was everything his father said he was. Besides being an idiot, he was a thief. And this was the day everyone would know it.

Brillianna came in, looked disapprovingly at the cold tea and toast, gathered them up and told him Mr. Thresher was on the phone.

"What time is it?" Ted asked.

"Ten o'clock. Why?"

"Nothing. Tell him I'm sick."

Brillianna was back once more. "I'm sorry, Ted. This time it's your father. I told him you weren't feeling well, but he insists on speaking to you." Ted rolled against the wall. She went away.

There was a pinstripe in the wallpaper. Funny, he'd never noticed that before. Brillianna was bending over him. "Ted, I have a message for you. Your father says to tell you it's covered."

A pinstripe of gold and tan and. . . . "What?" He pulled the covers into a tangled pile and jumped over them racing for the phone. "Dad?"

"About last night, son. I was a few sheets to windward. When I sobered up a bit, and got thinking about your flying down and all, it seemed to me that maybe you were in a bind. So I phoned a couple thousand bucks into your account this morning. . . . Ted? Are you there?"

"Yeah."

"*She* said you were under the weather?"

"Oh no. No, I'm fine." From across the room his wife sent an inquiring glance in his direction.

"Just tuckered out after the trip last night?"

"That's all it is. Listen, that was pretty decent of you. Thanks."

"How many sons do I have, anyway? Only one that I know about." He laughed.

Ted laughed with him. He could have kissed the old buzzard. And he could have broken his neck. Why did he have to put him through a night like last night?

He called Thresher back. Thresher wanted to chat about Saudi Arabia and King Ibn Saud. Ted was disposed to let him. Fifteen hundred dollars had bought the King and the Kingdom. He owned them both for six months.

When Ted was ten he played Parcheesi for the first time. He was completely caught up in the idea that you could have so many things going for you, that your luck with a pair of dice made it possible to skim around the board, at the same time halting your opponents. This was like real life, you got going and nothing could stop you. This was what his father called the system, the way things worked.

He was entranced, moving his men, doubling them up. The only thing that galled him was the other players, men on his dad's rig, slow, slow to think, slow to move. He saw instantly the advantages and disadvantages they pondered.

He started explaining, even though it was against his interest. His explanations slowed the game even more. Finally he skipped them, saying: "You can't double up there, you'll block your own man." They grew used to following his judgment. They knew he knew best. They resigned the fate of their cardboard pieces into his hands. Soon he was arguing with himself versus himself as Tim or Mr. Emmons.

Eventually he told Mr. Emmons he'd won. Mr. Emmons was pleased. Ted felt odd about it though.

It was like that now. The other players were slow to realize. He wanted to reach out his hand and move for the other parties, consummate the deal so they could get going, sink that first well, go down, bore a hole where only the hooves of camels trod and an occasional Bedouin fire marked out the brief hours of night. He would open the earth, folded into a fault that once stood by the sea. Downward-warping sand beaches stuffed into deep graves. Fine-grained sediments accumulating in Interglacial silled basins. Shields of Pliocene rock anchored in geosynclines, with oil settling like molasses between them and seeping into porous carbonates until they bled black. The drill rips open the epochs, splits the Miocene, bores past the Oligocene to the Paleocene, cuts into the Mesozoic. Oil from Triassic foraminifera flows into the pipe. But the bit strikes deeper, taking from the Silurian, the Ordovician, from shelled creatures in the shoreless seas of the Cambrian, trilobites, mollusks, brachiopods. The steel turns, the bit drives to the beginning, primitive bacteria, blue-green algae, pressed into oil three-quarters of a billion years ago.

The revelation first felt when Mrs. Grenville read aloud filled his senses, he brought it with him to meetings and to lunches. Thresher was no salesman and didn't pretend to be. Ted felt his own presentation would bring in partners. The Arabian desert floated on oil. Was that so difficult to understand? There must be some way to impart this vision directly. But it was given to him alone. So he marshaled figures, data, contour studies and spoke in terms of them. No one else saw it. He was unable to evoke it for them. He just wasn't getting through. After an initial contact he would wait expectantly for a follow-up that never materialized.

The months began to evaporate and he was no closer to concluding than he had been on day one. He began avoiding Thresher and ducked his phone calls. Thresher was demanding such things as concrete plans and timetables.

With barely a week to go, Ted made the decision, the only decision open to him. He sat a long time thinking about it. His luck, which had blazed momentarily, was back in hiding. No matter how he pursued, it remained elusive. This was the moment to redouble the bidding with an act of faith.

An act of faith was demanded, a total and complete wager of his future. It began with buying a gun. He dressed conservatively to make the purchase, attempting to look the solid citizen. The clerk started filling out a form. He repeated the question. "For self-protection, sir?"

"Oh yes. Self-protection." Another way to put it was protection against self. It was either his father's wells or Armagh. Armagh made more sense. His money built it. He'd be within the law. But Armagh was sacrosanct. Armagh was Brillianna.

He began to act out the fantasy, the one he'd had on and off for six months, the one that allowed him to look with X-ray vision into the safe-deposit box. He phoned the Long Beach bank and asked for the names of the officers, making an appointment with someone to whom Irv Angstrom was just a name. With the exception of

77

the manager, none of them knew his father anymore. That made it possible.

Had he really been planning to do this from the beginning? When had he realized his father never went there anymore? Had the thought germinated after that harrowing trip to Long Beach? Or was the knowledge simply dormant in him?

It was a local branch where he and his father kept their accounts in the old days when they were still in partnership. Now the Bank of America handled his dad's payroll and shared his line of credit with Security First. All that remained in the old bank was a checking account with a few dollars and the safe-deposit box with his father's stock. They both had keys to it, just as they had to each other's cars and houses, much to Brillianna's annoyance.

Ted spent the evening practicing Irv Angstrom's signature then drove all night. At ten in the morning he was at the Long Beach bank. He cleaned the stock out of the box, and courteously waited until the loan officer was free. As he walked toward the desk, someone hailed him.

"Hello there, Mr. Angstrom."

The pores of Ted's skin engorged and sprinkled his body. This was the one man he had counted on avoiding. The manager turned to the loan officer and urged him to take good care of him. "The Angstroms date back a long time. I guess I'm about the only one here who remembers the beginning of the Long Beach operations."

The loan officer pumped his hand. A genuine smile replaced the banker's smile. He said what an honor it was. He discussed the depressing state of the market and trends in oil shares. Luck was riding on Ted's shoulder. The accidental collision with the manager had put him in solid. "I'd like to apply for a personal loan, secured by stock in my company. Here are the papers. And I might as well bring my statement of net worth up to date."

Ten minutes later he had signed *Irving Angstrom* seven times and mortgaged his father's wells, for which he received a certified check in the amount of a hundred and fifty thousand dollars. Seven times. Seven. Lucky seven.

He went to a tourist court and checked in so he could be sick. So he could throw up and not have anyone ask what was the matter. With his head in an alien porcelain toilet bowl he brought up everything he had in him including breakfast and his soul.

Until now he had regarded the problem from a single point of view. What he saw at this moment was theft.

Was it possible? He had gone to Princeton. He was married to a Grenville. He himself was Ted, that is, Theodore Angstrom. Which brought him step by step to what he retched and gagged on.

Ted. He was *Ted* who signed *Irving*. How could he have done that? To steal, that was one thing. But to steal from his dad. If it ever came out it would be the same as killing him.

His father wouldn't believe it. No father and son were closer. Someday he would do for a son of his what his old man had done for him, take the boy into the fields. Give him a taste and smell of oil. Then educate him for the responsibility he would assume. How proud his dad had been of his good grades, his college degree. The old man had given way a bit too. He never really believed that the geologists Ted hired could tell more by analyzing and matching and computing than he could by feeling rock between his thumb and forefinger and getting the lay of the land. But he acquiesced, shrugged and took it as a sign of the times.

The early success in Long Beach was every dream the old man had come true, the mansion at Carmel, even the ladylike wife he called *She* and *Her*, the stories he still told when he came up weekends, of Drake and the old days. If it could have ended there. What a heartwarming saga. A devoted father, a loving son.

Maybe it could still end there. This alter ego, this other self inflamed by visions, who believed in blind luck, whose eyes penetrated to the back of time, who X-rayed the earth and bank vaults with equal certainty; this modern day Columbus who hit Ferdinand and Isabella on the head and said: I have discovered a new world, a continent of oil! This crazy fellow didn't reckon with the other crazy fellow who bought a gun and put it in the glove compartment under a map of the city. In case he had to stop himself. In case it hurt too much.

Ted went out to the car and looking around to see if anyone was watching, quickly slipped something into his pocket. He turned back to the motel room, took out the weapon and looked at it. He had never handled a gun before. You could shoot yourself.

He saw where it was hinged and opened it. The chamber was empty.. He had forgotten to bring in the bullets, they were still in the glove compartment. He went out to the car again. Everything should have special significance. He knew significance was there. He just couldn't think what it was.

He spilled the bullets on the bed and loaded them into the hollow chambers. What was the action of a bullet? It spun, he knew that. A deep clean bore didn't seem bad. But he didn't like the thought of a rotating, tearing passage. Of course that was the idea.

- He knew there was a kick, but he didn't know how to allow for it. Did you aim lower, figuring the gun to jar upward? How much lower? It would be terrible to make a mess of it.

Sitting on a bed—rented for a night by high-school kids quaking to find out what it was all about, by salesmen falling into it dead beat, by married couples with a crib in the room—he wondered had anyone ever swallowed a handful of pills or splattered his brains onto the freshly made-up linen?

Go down a few feet, break open the crust of another age and you could smell the mold of old agonies and crimes. Agony and crime hadn't shells. Only shells survived. His own charade would be quickly acted out. Brillianna, summoned to identify him, would have to look at him. But he wouldn't have to look at her.

Or at his dad.

The mess deterred him, the pulpy, bloody mess. And suppose they pulled him through? It seemed better to face them without the added indignity of tubes for drainage and glucose.

He got up, unloaded the gun and drove around. It

was a stage toward going home. It was like going home, but without the people.

"You've been late every night this week," Brillianna said, then she looked at him. "Ted, my God, I know you're in trouble, but it can't be that bad."

He thought he had himself under control but he didn't trust himself to speak. She saw through him immediately. Would he be offered a last cigarette before the blindfold was positioned? How would she start, with a question, or an accusation? He didn't wait to find out. "I'm afraid I haven't acted according to Grenville standards. Your father, the druggist, would not be happy about all this. Oh, I know you've never stopped comparing me to that failure in shiny pants, mended coat and a tie with the spot removed, but the cleaning fluid ring showing."

"What are you talking about? Calm down please, you're frightening me."

"Well, I'll tell you something, there is no energy in the man. None. Everything he does is proper, correct, honorable and absolutely useless. . . ."

She pushed him gently into a chair and stood in front of him with a glass of brandy. "Sip slowly."

He knocked it out of her hand. "What do you know, you or your father? I was tracking, the same as any hunter, following the spoor. The earth shifted, rocks fractured, they dammed a continent of oil. You only understand what it is to be stuffy and honorable. You don't understand what it is to be an oilman."

"Just tell me very simply what you've done."

"I stole one hundred and fifty thousand dollars." He looked up because there was no reaction. "I stole it from Dad. It was pretty easy actually. I went to the bank in Long Beach and signed his name, and kept signing it. Irving Angstrom. Irving Angstrom."

"So the payment on Saudi has fallen due?" She looked out the window. The sea could be heard crashing below on the beach. In the old days floodlights played over the water, now it was totally dark. "You may not believe this, Ted, but I understand. Do you remember when you were courting me and I was egging you on with games and foolery? I said there were two

81

terrible things to reveal about myself and I would only tell you one? The other I couldn't tell you," she smiled benignly at him, "because by then I'd decided to marry you. But it's time you knew." She came and stood beside him.

"The secret was that I was prepared to marry anyone who would build Armagh for me." She had his attention now. "That's the truth, that's why I married you. I can tell you now, Ted, because somewhere between then and now that silly girl grew up. You come first with me, Ted. And I'm ready to prove it. We're going to sell Armagh."

Ted's shock showed in his eyes. "I'd never ask that."

"Then you do know what it means, that it's a part of me. I thought I would do anything to protect it." She threw herself down beside him and began to tremble because she felt the outline of the gun in his pocket. She drew it out gingerly and let it fall from her fingers. "So my wonderful Armagh has become a place where my wonderful Ted wants to kill himself?"

"I was out of my mind. That's the only way I can explain doing what I did to Dad. You know how I feel about the old guy."

"You'll put the stocks back in the morning."

"But then . . ." he said haltingly, "there won't be enough money to cover the option."

"That's right, Ted. You'll have to give up the Hasa, just as I've given up Armagh."

He knew there was no appeal. She placed Armagh fervently, lovingly in his lap. Stripped herself for his sake. Yet he was marked before he met her. Oil had laid its stamp on him. It was impossible to be grateful. Damn it, her magnanimity was on her terms. And she was spelling it out.

"We're sure to realize enough for a down payment on a modest house. And Ted, you'll redeem not only your father's fields, but a portion of your own, maybe the whole thing. You're still an oilman and always will be!"

What did she know? Trade the dream for the sure thing, settle for being able to check the loading rig, see to it that the lumber was delivered, be on hand when the water string was run down. Sure, he'd enjoy sloshing

around in mud, oil and water. He'd missed the camaraderie of blasting men, drillers and riggers. And the
Angstrom tradition, to be on hand himself for the state
inspector's visit. Ted had a way of pushing things
through. When the final liner was down and the dynamite charges set, it was he who made the last check. He
knew when he had shut-off. But an inspector could foul
you up. So he made it his business to be there with a
glad-hand, a drink from the thermos, a couple of jokes.

Then with the permit in his pocket, the last bolt tight,
the disk bit was ready for the journey into the earth. It
was like launching a ship. Crews from nearby jobs
funneled over, old friends got wind of it and turned up
to pay their respects to the machinery and drink to a
strike. It was your beer, but what the hell, you were
paying for the case out of the gusher that might lie
beneath your feet, down a mile, down where fifty tons
of steel strained to lift it.

It had been great. But that wasn't what he wanted
now. She offered him the old game, when he saw a new
one opening. Besides, Armagh, which she so bravely
renounced, was his anyway. Bought and paid for by him
and him alone. She had simply convinced herself and
him and everyone else that it belonged to her, that
Armagh II, was in fact, Armagh I. But the original had
been outside Dublin. This was Carmel. Where did she
get off dictating terms?

"I only ask one thing of you," she spoke ardently,
"your solemn promise that you will buy back Armagh.
No matter at what cost, no matter what it takes. You
see, Ted, I have absolute confidence in you."

He laughed. "Except when it comes to the Hasa."

"That was always a crazy scheme. Even your father
says so, and every oilman you've talked to."

His hand wandered to the jagged scar on his cheek.

Armagh was thrown open as though for a celebration. Rooms that hadn't been used in years were aired
and dusted. Brillianna did it all, bit by bit. She employed no one. It was as though she were laying out the

dead, with such loving care did she go over every inch of the mansion.

When she was ready a discreet advertisement appeared with the heading: PRINCIPALS ONLY. She would not have realtors marching through making a field day of it, satisfying their curiosity as to what lay behind the gates. She preferred to conduct well-screened prospects herself through the house and grounds. Her manner was aloof and severe. If a prospective buyer had the temerity to ask what the maintenance was, he was crossed off her list. Even in bad times, or perhaps especially in bad times there were people with money. When questioned about the furnishings, she replied coldly, "As is."

The astounding view, the glamour of the house, the fact that it was a replica of a baronial manor, finally brought her her price. There was an additional cost to Brillianna: the purchaser insisted that "as is" included the Haviland china.

The day the papers were signed she shut herself away. Everything was gone, wiped out by their joint signatures. She ran her hand across the meticulously matched paneling. Brillianna Grenville's existence was suspended. Brillianna Angstrom set her course. It was a detour. She renewed her vow, her pledge to return. This was the home in which Brilli would be raised. Armagh was hers, the roots reaching back into generations of her family.

In much the same way the Arabian peninsula was an interior part of Ted's life. He read up on the history of the area in back issues of the London *Petroleum News Service*. A couple of Belgian geologists poked around in 1923. Shortly afterward a Major Holmes appeared on the scene, posing as a collector of rare butterflies. He concentrated his attention in the Dhahran area. Eventually it came out he was a representative of the Eastern and General Oil Syndicate.

"Butterfly collector," Ted muttered shaking his head. However the man concluded a deal on the Hasa, Ted's present leasehold. In 1925 it lapsed due to lack of funding. Well, that wasn't going to happen to him.

A small section of his map folded to Dhahran had

been pierced with a thousand pencil points on a thousand different occasions when he sat late indulging this new form of wakeful dreaming. The points converged on the Dome of Jabal. This was the spot. It was here he would drill.

Ted's initial remorse had simmered down to a troublesome twinge that surfaced in unguarded moments. As God was his witness, he had stayed clear of Armagh. It was Brillianna herself, who unwittingly brought him that eighty thousand dollars. She was doing the right things. The reasons were wrong, but women didn't understand business. Selling Armagh was her decision, admittedly to secure the old, safe, plodding life. But why piddle around in Long Beach when there was a continent waiting to be tapped? You couldn't go wrong with oil. It was the future. American companies were opening up South America. They were in ahead of him there, but on the Arabian coast he would be first. Top dog.

For him it was the only game in town. He didn't look too closely at the stakes. It was simply a loan his dad and wife didn't know they were making. The stocks would be returned with the old boy none the wiser. And Brillianna would have Armagh again. All he had to do was keep the balls in the air, just keep the balls in the air.

Ted opened an office in San Francisco from which to run his affairs. Brillianna was pleased that he evinced so much interest in the old fields. With an easy mind she set herself to carrying out the next phase of the project, to find an inexpensive home near the office.

The real estate lady who whisked her away in a Pierce Arrow had the tough veneer of her profession. Her excessively blonde hair was growing out and fear showed. It was a difficult time for real estate ladies. "You can pick up some buys," she told Brillianna.

Brillianna mentioned her ceiling price of fourteen thousand to Mrs. Wycoff.

"Of course I can show you several homes in that range, but nothing imaginative. You know the kind of thing, with one bath."

"I'm afraid that's what it will have to be."

They pulled up in a drab neighborhood, the paving was cracked, the grass yellowing. Brillianna made no move to leave the car. "It seems a shame with that sparkling bay out there, not to look at something with a view."

"No view. Not at the figure you mentioned," Mrs. Wycoff said firmly. "However," she consulted a book of listings, "there is one, I haven't seen it personally, but they specify *partial* view."

"What does that mean, over roof tops and past telephone wires?"

"Probably." Mrs. Wycoff put the car in low and started up a steeply ascending street. They passed a corner laden with shrubbery. The house, set well back, had a *For Sale* sign in front. Mrs. Wycoff didn't slow.

"I suppose that's out of my bracket?" Brillianna asked.

Mrs. Wycoff smiled.

"Let's stop and look," Brillianna said impulsively.

"Mrs. Angstrom, have you any idea what the house costs?"

"Let's see it anyway, just for the fun of it."

It was not Mrs. Wycoff's idea of fun not to make a sale. "Thirty thousand dollars," she said implacably.

"That's an asking price," Brillianna pointed out. She knew all about asking prices.

"They're certainly not going to come down sixteen thousand dollars."

"I know."

"Oh well. Why not?" Mrs. Wycoff had decided this young woman would not buy a house today. She relaxed her saleswoman-client attitude; she opened up, confiding how dreadful things were, properties just weren't moving. She hadn't concluded a sale in four months and had an application in with every department store in the city, as well as with the telephone company and insurance firms. She hadn't heard from any of them and didn't expect to. They were laying people off, not hiring.

Still, one shouldn't leave a stone unturned, didn't Mrs. Angstrom agree?

They climbed brick stairs and followed a path back to a wide veranda with a startling view of Alcatraz and Angel Island. The water twinkled, a million cut diamonds gleamed. Brillianna thought, I've grown used to living by the sea. I could almost feel at home here.

"Now this is what I call a beautiful house," Mrs. Wycoff bubbled. "It belonged to an old man, they say he was ninety. It's a death sale. That is, his lawyer, as his executor, is handling the sale for the estate." She unlocked the large realtor box fastened to the heavy door and they entered.

How civilized to have a vestibule, Brillianna thought, and stepped into the living room. A stone fireplace, parquet floor, and a garden bursting in through casement windows. There were five bedrooms, each with its own bath and private entrance, and all looking out on the water. "It seems an odd arrangement of rooms. Why so many exits?"

"This old man, besides being enormously wealthy, was enormously peculiar. Eccentric even. He insisted his family live with him. But none of them were on speaking terms, so he built the house giving a suite to each. And the day he died they all moved out. Well, I may as well tell you, since we're just looking. He was murdered."

"The old man?"

"Bludgeoned to death. They found him around back. He must have heard a burglar and gone to investigate."

"Or else it was one of the heirs." Brillianna speculated.

"Well, it does make the property difficult to move."

Brillianna took an envelope out of her purse and began to figure on the back of it. "I'm making a cash offer," she said, looking up. "Twenty-four thousand dollars."

Brillianna was acutely conscious that she was over budget on the new house, not slightly, but by ten thousand dollars. However she had a plan which justified the expenditure, and she hastened to explain it to Ted. "We'll take in roomers. I figured it to the last penny. The roomers are our bank payments. And because of the layout of the house, we'll never see them, never be bothered by them."

Ted gave her no argument but nodded absently. She was surprised and somewhat disappointed. She thought of the acquisition of the stately old place as a coup.

When Ted inspected it, he was pleased. He liked anything well constructed. He tapped the solid walls as they walked through the rooms. He stopped before a picture window. "Look at the lights across the bay. You know, Kiddo, this would make a hell of a nursery."

"You mean for Brilli?"

"I don't mean for Brilli."

She pushed him away. "Oh Ted, this isn't the time."

"Why isn't it? That son we've always wanted. Just think, he'd be the fourth generation in the oil game. That would make it an Angstrom dynasty."

"Our son is going to be raised at Armagh. I see him expanding on what you build."

Ted snorted, "You don't want him to get his hands dirty, and that's the whole idea. To understand oil, you've got to get into the fields."

"Almost getting yourself killed?" she chided, touching his cheek.

"Even that's part of it."

She turned from the subject. "We'll talk about it later, when things are more settled."

"Sure," Ted said cheerfully and had her in bed more often than before. She obstinately douched out his sperm. It was a contest between them.

Ten years after coming out in New York society, Brillianna Grenville Angstrom was running a rooming house, dunning tenants for the rent, learning to put in washers and repair faulty electrical fixtures. She did not find her life incongruous. This was the path back to her husband's self-respect and to her spiritual home, which would always be Armagh. The life she currently lived, that took place in the sturdily-built house behind flowering acacias and live oaks, utilized her energy; and under her guidance things ran smoothly.

It happened unexpectedly. There was a phone call from a neighbor of her mother's. Her father had died in the night. Ted was involved, as she believed, at the Long Beach site. He was sympathetic. He couldn't get away, but he was sympathetic. She packed up the child and went back herself.

It surprised her that the house was still there over the pharmacy as in her childhood. She recalled how she had hated it and schemed to get away. She remembered superimposing the faded glories of Armagh over this dinginess. She had even succeeded in making Armagh a reality . . . for a time. She saw again her father's face when he followed her through the rooms of his boyhood. Every detail was perfect. He could not suppress his emotion when he entered the dining room and took in the Haviland table setting. She wished now she had not sacrificed it. She had given up everything for the black substance her husband pumped. Her parents did not comment when she sold Armagh. Perhaps her gesture in building it had been enough. A strong sense of futility overcame her.

She wanted to beat her fists against the sky, shred space. Why should that immensity, that great pile of nothing be there and he be gone? *Gone*. She hated euphemisms. He was *dead*. She tried to get herself together to deal with her mother. Her mother was sunk in on herself, as though by making herself small and stooped, misfortune could not find her. She was confused, not realizing she was already robbed. She talked to her husband as much as to Brillianna. Her other daughter, Elizabeth, arrived. Both young women rejected in the calcium of their hard bones and the hormones of their health the deterioration they witnessed. It was difficult to accept the non-being of the parent who fathered you, but impossible to have empathy with the erosion of will and person they found in their mother. Revulsion was a symptom of the fear opening in both their hearts. Were their days—full, busy, constructive—hurtling them toward this?

89

Each daughter wrung from her mother a promise to visit, and left. The old woman cleaned her house, washed her clothes, and when all was in order, sat down in her rocking chair, Bible in hand, and died.

Once again the sisters met in the old home, the temporary home, where they had dreamed of Armagh. All these years their parents had lived over the pharmacy. They visited Elizabeth in North Carolina, admired the house built in Civil War days, inspected the barns and tack house, and returned to the pharmacy. They visited Carmel, exclaimed at the amazing replica, the dazzling setting, and Brillianna's success. But on the second trip her mother had not stayed, and she never invited them to the rooming house. She loved them and they loved her. But she allowed them to love her from the pharmacy in New Jersey, and for her part, thought kindly of them now and again from California.

A black tarn opened in her. There were all sorts of things she wanted to know: about the family, about them as *people*, what was the content of their world, real and imagined? Too late, too late. The lament washed over her like a dark sea.

Grief instilled in Brillianna what Ted had not been able to. Death demanded replacement. She now wanted the child Ted wanted. She needed the warmth of a baby in her arms to counteract the cold hollow sensation of two deaths. A rapacious mouth at her nipples was a refutation. In her body she would bring life back into her world.

She conceived.

Ted was ecstatic. He began with the usual talk. "Imagine, explaining it all to him. Your own flesh and blood. The big changeover to rotary drills, the square kelly. Did you know the cone type rolling cutter rock bit was patented by Hughes? It's what tamed those howlers, the runaways. We'd gag them with a master gate. But if you didn't get those valves fitted just right, if a piece of cable got stuck, or anything else, wow! It went wild. McNulty used to say, like an exhaust pipe connected to hell. Funny, I haven't thought of Andy McNulty in a long time."

"Just remember, if it is a boy, he's also a Grenville. He may not have your interest in all that."

Ted shrugged. Women in her condition were notionative. His real plans for his son he kept to himself, a partnership in the Saudi Arabian continent. He had taken out a ninety percent mortgage on the San Francisco house as well. He needed it for a down payment on equipment. He was running a check on the order. It was easy to tick off the big stuff—hydraulic drilling rig, a gate valve capable of holding five thousand pounds, lumber, strings of pipe, cement, cables. It was the small items that were driving him crazy—the 9 inch collars, the 9-by-2 nipples, the die threads and the 1-by-2 packing gland. Each time he counted these, he came up with a different number.

The strain of concealing everything from both his father and Brillianna was constantly with him. They had to be kept apart; his main fear was that Brillianna would blurt out something about regaining the Long Beach concession, which his dad knew he had not done. At first the new house was the excuse, moving and then settling in. Ted started dropping by to see the old man periodically, so he wouldn't feel cut off. Brillianna's pregnancy was a godsend, it provided a further excuse to. . . . *The balls were in the air.*

Brillianna was having more difficulty with this pregnancy than the previous one. Everything was a bit too much. Brilli crayoned the wall above her bed and Brillianna collapsed in tears. The tenants complained, she fought with them. As a consequence, two roomers left. She didn't care, lethargy invaded her limbs . . . and still demands were made on her. Ted wanted to bring some oil executives to dinner. Next the plumbing backed up in the downstairs shower. On top of all this, more likely because of it, she began spotting.

Terrified, she waited for Ted to come home. "Ted, I have a small show. What do you suppose it means?"

"It means you should get into bed."

"How can I do that, with an active three-year-old and. . . ."

Ted cut short her objections. "We'll get someone in."

"We can't afford it."

"What we can't afford is to take chances with this baby."

"You should have heard the way Lucille carried on about the shower. I told her I was nobody's maid."

"Of course not," he soothed.

"Nothing's going right, Ted. Nothing."

"You've been doing too much, that's all. But we'll make some changes around here. We'll hire someone starting tomorrow."

Ted got her to bed and called the doctor who confirmed his common-sense edict that Brillianna stay in bed with feet elevated. He hired temporary help. Maria and Tomas worked out well. The crisis passed. And Ted decided to conduct the final Saudi negotiations, which were to take place in London, himself.

He delayed telling Brillianna until the last minute. He needed an excuse that would hold up and invented a convention. She put out a hand, grabbing a chair to steady herself. "I can't believe you'd spring something like this on me. Are you saying that you're leaving for London in the morning?"

"I didn't want to tell you earlier, because I wanted to make sure you'd be all right."

"I find it hard to believe you would choose this time to go anywhere."

"I didn't choose the time," he said as patiently as he could. "It's important to keep current with what's going on, new patents, new techniques. It happens the convention is now."

"What do you expect me to say, 'Have a nice time'?"

"Look," he saw a way out of their quarrel, "why not come with me?" His mind was racing ahead. He could deposit her somewhere . . . a good hotel. She needn't know about the shaikhs or Thresher. As far as she was concerned, it was a convention. "I mean it," he urged. "You're not that far along. It will be a great trip. You and me, like the old days."

"Really, Ted, there are times when you are so like your father. You live in your own world. A lovely world where all the facts are arranged to suit yourself.

I can't go to London now. I couldn't stand the trip. But you go, Ted. By all means, go. You might as well be there as here."

"All right. It was only a suggestion."

"Is your father attending the convention?" she asked.

It was an innocent enough question but he hadn't prepared an answer. A good oilman keeps his hole full of mud at all times to pack down the seething pressure he has tapped into. Ted sensed he had not done this. As quickly as a torch of gas can turn to flame, she knew.

"There is no convention. It's Saudi, isn't it?"

"Brillianna, I. . . ."

"I know, Ted. You were waiting for the right moment to tell me. When the Dome of Jabal or whatever it is, comes in. You were going to decorate the Christmas tree with thousand dollar bills. Right? You were going to give me back Armagh. Right? Oh my God." She sat down heavily. But she didn't take her eyes from him. "You never put back your father's stock. And you let me sell Armagh." She had been speaking dully, apathetically. Now she was on her feet. Blows fell on his chest, she hammered at his face. "Liar. Thief! Thief!" She collapsed against him with a strangled sound, then realized it was he she was leaning against. She tore herself away and headed for the closest chair. The struggle now was with herself. When she spoke to Ted, it was slowly as though careful diction would make a difficult communication possible. "What you did to your father was something I could never understand. That man loves you, you are his only son. But you did it. All right. I made it possible for you to undo everything. Instead. . . ."

"Look, I'm aware of the sequence of events."

"Their sequence, yes. But are you really aware, do you really know what you did in taking Armagh and tossing it into the pot, that jam pot you think Arabia is going to turn out to be? And don't say I did it myself. Of course I did, *for you.*

"You remember the state you were in the night you took the money. You even had a gun. It had come to that. You couldn't live with yourself. Armagh meant your self-respect. It meant your own wells redeemed."

She looked, not at him but into him. "You didn't re-deem them, did you? I'll tell you what you did, you sunk every cent into Saudi. It didn't matter to you that the price was Armagh. And what about the other costs, which I bore? I took in roomers, I did all sorts of menial tasks, I worked past my strength, I almost lost the baby, the son you wanted. Why? I wouldn't spend the money because I thought it was going into Long Beach, into a new start.

"I don't know how much of all this you saw. You were so engrossed in dealing with a king, in playing big shot. My parents died, Ted. Do you know that? Brilli learned to button her shoes. Do you know that? I don't think you have a family at all.

"You're playing a game. You always told me that. But I never knew what you meant, or realized that I was just one of the moves. Through me you acquired the background you wanted. When things were going well, I was the hostess you needed. When they were going badly, I was your servant. You didn't hesitate to lie, cheat and rob me. And for what? A crazy dream.

"The Hasa! No respectable oilman will go near it. Thresher is a laughing-stock, a pompous buffoon who wouldn't recognize oil if it were under his nose. And you handed him everything we have. Will Armagh buy the King another dozen wives for his harem, do you think?"

"It's funny," Ted said, "it's almost a relief that you know."

"But I don't know. I don't know at all. I know what you did. But I've lived with you ten years and I don't know you at all. I know a laugh, I know a smile, the quips, the easy-going person you seem to be. But that isn't you. It may be what you'd like to be, but it isn't what you are."

"Is it going to do any good to call names?" Ted asked. "Do you think I don't know them? They make quite a list, beginning with ruthless, dishonest, son-of-a-bitch. Okay. But what you lose sight of is that I did it for something."

"For me?" Brillianna asked, "for the child you almost lost?"

"Yes." Ted spoke it with conviction. "Of course for you. And Brilli and the child too. But also for the oil itself, which is bigger than the desert it lies under. Do you know what it's as big as? Our whole friggin' civilization. That's right, it's going to determine how people live their lives and fight their wars. It is power. Inconceivable power."

"For you?"

"For me. For this family, the dynasty we're founding. But it reaches beyond us, beyond everything that we standing here can know."

The Grenville eyes opened very wide. "You're a madman. How can one reason with a madman? Ted, can't you see, it's a dream, a romance, a completely wild gamble that no sane man would take. You've stripped us of everything."

"I had to do it," he replied.

"I believe you. And I'm sorry for you. But I don't intend to watch you destroy yourself. And I don't want to be on hand when your father finds out what you've done to him. So when you return from London, Brilli and I will be at Aunt Lillian's." She left the room and he made no attempt to stop her. Having your wife walk out on you went with the territory. It was part of what he had become.

But he'd never been those things before. Thief, liar, cheat. And he'd never had his wife leave him before either. Ted was as horrified and amazed at himself as she was. *Did the accused know right from wrong?* Of course he did.

That was the worst of it, he felt Brillianna was right to walk out. Given a little more time he could have carried it off, returned with the deal signed, ready to signal the development of his concession. But the many balls he had been so dexterous keeping aloft had crashed. His luck crashed with them. He was denuded, naked, with only tickets left. Tickets to New York and London. Even the cash he was negotiating with had been transformed from physical wells and two actual houses into fluid assets which had already left the country.

His only hope now was to catch up with his confidence the other side of the Atlantic. Perhaps his luck had merely taken another train, made connections for a berth on another boat. That was his one chance. There was no further drop to squeeze from the bare rock he left behind. He himself had leached everything dry. What do you put back, Brillianna had asked at the beginning. Then he answered confidently . . . nothing.

The word acted as an electric goad. Why was he accepting her evaluation? Had he scooped and taken with both hands to feed a dream? The Hasa was no dream. And he no ordinary thief. It would take money to tap those oil soaked sediments.

All right, he bellowed with no one to listen, *I took*. If you knew what he knew, you had the right. Oil had no morality. It was older by eons than any system of justice, older by eons than *homo sapiens* who invented those systems. No rules applied because he drilled past them. At the same time, he tapped the future where rules were still to be written. And when they were, they would be written by him, a man marked by the Jurassic Age. He went to find his wife to try and explain this.

She was in the bedroom standing before her full-length mirror. She must have heard him because she turned as though studying herself. She had changed into a filmy nightgown and robe which displayed her body. As though unaware of this, she began languidly to brush her heavy rich brown hair.

Ted caught the aroma of the perfume he had given her on their anniversary, a signal between them. Relief overwhelmed him. This was her way of making up the quarrel. It couldn't be done with words. Only like this.

He moved in. Elemental and basic, her anger could not seep away. It demanded further contest. He slipped the sheer material down her arm, kissed her bare shoulder.

"Don't you listen? I'm leaving you. I've had enough. All I can stand."

He paid no attention to her words. Even pushing him away was a deliberately sexual act. He caught her in an embrace whose meaning was clear, pressing her in a slow revolving caress.

Brillianna struggled, but sensually, rubbing her body along his. Ted brought her down on the carpet the Saud family had sent. The jardiniere of flowers undulated. Its sapphire heart throbbed and the stylized scimitar thrust against the octagon field. The pattern of dropping pears floated through all the shades known to the weaver.

Brillianna jumped to her feet and with a backward glance that dared him to follow, dashed ahead of him through the house, discarding her robe, then pulling the nightgown over her head and flinging it at him.

He caught her on the stairs. There had been tumultuous lovemaking there before, especially when they first moved in and he declared he would have her in every room, "even on the floor of the goddamned vestibule."

He set her above him and probed. Moaning, she pressed against him and he ejaculated into the hidden fertile region. He felt her stiffen and knew she caught her breath. "Are you all right?" he asked.

She nodded.

"You'll be here when I come back?"

"Yes."

He carried her into the bedroom, turned the covers down and placed her beneath them. "I'll sleep in the other room so as not to disturb you. I've got to be up early. Will you wish me good luck?"

"No, Ted."

"But you will be here?"

"I said so."

"Thanks. I'll make it up to you."

"With oil? With an Arabian king? With Mr. Thresher? And another thing, Ted, don't thank me." She turned to the wall.

Ted phoned his father from New York. "This is it. I'm meeting Saudi's minister of finance in London. I'll have the initial concession agreement in my pocket in less than two weeks."

Wires strung the length of the country hummed. "Dad?"

"Yeah. I'm here."

"Well?" Why did he need his dad's good opinion and good wishes? What perverse demon made him hunger for both? "Well, what do you say?" he persisted. After all the old man couldn't know the proceeds from his stock were in a London vault.

"What does your wife say? That's more to the point. You must be doing this on Armagh. How does she feel about it?"

"She'll feel great when we tap into oil."

"Yeah. Well, go make your mistakes." The old man cleared his throat, relenting somewhat. "And son, don't get outsmarted, especially by a king."

So that was that. Things were wrapped up. He didn't know exactly how he stood with Brillianna. She was a bit too much for him to figure. But she'd be there. And when he came back he'd lay a fortune in her lap.

The first negotiations took place February, 1933. Present were Theodore Angstrom, his lawyer Karl Duncan, and Quentin Thresher. For the Arabian government the minister of finance, Shaikh Abdullah Sulaiman al Hamadan, acted as the King's personal representative. His consultant was Shaikh Hamid Ibn Julwi, dark-complected even for an Arab, voluble in his own tongue but speaking grudgingly and sparely in English.

Ted was taken aback by the long robes and flowing headgear. He assumed they would adopt Western dress at least while in London. However, he forgot his embarrassment in the tussle which developed over the naming of the proposed company.

Ted suggested Cal-Saudi Oil. Shaikh Sulaiman was displeased that the name Saudi did not precede the other. "As in a camel train, the most noble beast goes before."

Ted looked for help to his lawyer. But Duncan was having difficulty controlling his facial muscles.

Ted gave way. It was the Saudi-California Oil Co. which was described as seeking the concession of al Hasa on the eastern seaboard along the Persian Gulf and extending inland a journey of three days by car from Hofuf with the sun between the two eyes the first day and on the right shoulder thereafter, which was understood to be five hundred thousand square miles of territory. The preliminary exploration was to be of an area consisting of one hundred square miles.

At the end of the session, the shaikh announced that a journey to Cairo had been arranged. "For the entire group," Thresher said, obviously not believing the guttural sounds he translated.

"I don't understand," Ted said. "I thought things were ironed out. Why go to Cairo?"

Thresher enquired of Abdullah Sulaiman and returned the answer. "Ibn Saud wishes it."

The party went to Paris, by rail to Brindisi, and boarded a flying boat to Alexandria. Egypt. Land of the Bible. Ancient, yet part of his time and life. They made their approach directly into azure, bright water, the heat reached up and sucked at them. When the hatch opened, they were enveloped in a steamy vortex reminiscent of a Turkish bath. "This has got to be the hottest place on earth," Ted exclaimed.

"The Saudi climate is much warmer," Thresher assured him. "But one acclimatizes."

This remark did nothing to lessen the annoyance that had been building in Ted. Even in California, Thresher had taken his commission from the King with painful seriousness. Here, he was an authority ready on the slightest provocation to lecture on the people, culture, customs, history and religion of Arabia, Egypt, Yemen or Palestine. His precise recounting managed to make everything dull from the black pearls taken in Bahrein and sold in the suqs, to his stories of Jinn, Afrait and Shitan, creatures which the Koran tells are created from

99

fire. Ted could well believe it. Everything in this part of the hemisphere was fire-created.

They continued by train to Cairo, where rooms had been booked at Shepheard's. Ted arrived feeling more dead than alive. But a short nap refreshed him. That evening the party at their table included, much to Mr. Thresher's discomfiture, several dark, full-fleshed women. When Ted leaned toward Nuri, he discovered the clefts of her body were rubbed with aromatic oils and blends of perfume dizzying to the senses. Thresher, pleading work, excused himself. But Ted felt removed from the orbit of Grenville codes. For ten years he had wanted no other woman than Brillianna. Now he was embarked on an adventure in a strange land and opening Nuri would be like uncorking an unknown wine.

Later, in Ted's room, Nuri told him Egypt's troubles were due to Farouk's undersized penis. "I entertained him," she said. "But he could not entertain me. It was quite sad."

Nuri was squatter than an American woman, and fleshier. Her body, a constantly revealed surprise. There were lines of scent under her heavy breasts and along the most intimate folds of her anatomy. She asked permission to bathe and prepare him in the same way.

Their lovemaking was languorous, the sweet oils made penetration easy. He felt half suffocated rolling on the soft seas of her flesh. "What about Ibn Saud?" he asked. "Is his equipment all right?"

She laughed. "In his young days, I have heard, there was no virgin left in the Empty Quarter. His nurse, they say, when he was an infant, set him in the courtyard on a shawl of cambric and turned to a task. When she came to fetch him, she saw a she-goat suckling on the baby's member which was enlarged and firm as a man's."

"Marvelous," Ted chuckled. "I don't think we have such a wealth of detail about our government officials."

She inclined her dark head. "It explains much."

"I'm sure it does. George Washington in terms of his libido. Freud would agree."

"I myself," Nuri continued, "do not go with Arabians. They are a nation of syphilitics, born with the worm that eats the eyes and the genitals. The King himself is blind in his right eye, and it cannot be treated. It was in the womb with him from his father."

The next day the shaikh guided them around the residential section of the city. Police clubbed a group of beggars that broke out of the alleyway attempting to solicit alms. Ted suspected there was a Cairo he was not shown.

They were entertained sumptuously that evening at the Geziral Club and Shaikh Sulaiman explained to Thresher that they would drive to Suez City in the morning to make connections with their ship.

"Ship? What ship? I thought we were going to sign the agreement here," Ted protested.

"No," Thresher said. "In Jidda, a city so old, they call it the Grandmother."

"The King again?" Ted asked.

"No. It was I who insisted this time. The shaikh is starting to renege on the agreement."

"Renege? What do you mean, renege?"

"Just that, haggle, change things around. It's perfectly customary, it's the way things are done out here. The British call it shaky-do. We are going to need help, someone on our side who understands their psychology. Only one man fits that description, John Eustace Nichols. He's lived in Saudi most of his life. As a matter of fact, he is a convert to Muhammadanism. He's rather an eccentric, with a craze for baboons. I'd be safe in saying he is one of the great explorers, comparable to Lawrence and Doughty. He is also the dealer for Ford cars and has sold the King two hundred of them. I understand it is his enterprise which is responsible for introducing baby carriages to the ladies of Jidda. It was Nichols who brought me into the picture, so I'm returning the favor really."

"All right. If that's what it will take to close." Ted added thoughtfully, "I suppose we'll have to offer him a piece of the action?"

"No, I think not. He'll let us know what he'll require when the time comes."

"I'd like to know, damn it, what this whole thing is going to cost me." The burst of anger helped ease his general sense of frustration. Duncan absolutely refused to go on to Jidda. He promised to stay in Cairo and go over contract wording by phone. Shaikh Sulaiman informed them this was quite possible. Ted had the feeling Duncan was the only prudent member of their party. If he had the sense God gave him, he too would call a halt.

It was a short drive to Suez City. They were greeted on the quay by an agent of Ibn Saud, the Shaikh 'Abd al Aziz al Qusaili who after conveying to them the King's pleasure, which, according to him, grew as they approached his land, and having ceremoniously inquired as to the rigors of their trip and the state of their health, gestured toward a large sambuk or dhow with an ornately carved stern anchored dockside among the booms and jaulboats. Ted rather liked the look of the craft, it had the golden cast of well-oiled teak. Scattered on the water were dugout canoes from which men were fishing with circular nets. Farther out at greater depth they held hand lines.

'Abd al Aziz al Qusaili approached Thresher and spoke to him at some length. Thresher turned to Ted. "He wants you to know that he is the owner and also the captain of the boat which is to take us to Jidda, where our Mother Eve is buried."

"You don't say?"

"He says he is a pearl merchant. But just between us, he looks like a slaver to me."

Ted's jauntiness disappeared. "You mean that seriously? They actually have slaves?"

"It is quite legal. Many pilgrims pay for their journey to Mecca by bringing along a child for the marketplace. There are still raiding parties along the East African coast, and a number of stolen Caucasians as well, valued, both girls and boys, for the beauty of their light skins."

"Well, I think we're ugly enough to be safe." Ted's quip covered a profound sense of unease. These prospective business partners were not civilized as he knew and understood the word.

The two shaikhs held a long whispered conversation, for which Thresher apologized. "They would think it poor manners to burden us with the details and arrangements for our comfort."

"If it's my comfort they're concerned with, a Budweiser with a big head on it would go good just about now." Ted said this mainly to annoy Thresher, who had lectured him on the strict alcoholic abstinence of the Wahhabis, Ibn Saud's family and clan.

The shipowner broke off his talk with Sulaiman and smilingly motioned the party aboard. The boat seemed small, standing high in the water. Its poop, Ted saw, had been redesigned as a lounge for passengers. It was spread with Persian rugs and silk cushions in a wild array of colors.

The crew were mostly East Africans who flashed white smiles as they tossed luggage and provisions in the waist of the ship. Part of the provender was a live sheep which they staked out. The captain stood looking on, telling amber prayer beads.

MGM and Fox Studios are trying to make me think I'm on my way to Arabia, Ted thought. Actually he was aware of no dislocation. The fact of black men in flowered gowns, their heads bound in cloths and turbans, or a fringe of palms beginning to move past, held little reality. Reality for him could not be seen. It was subsurface, a continent of oil carrying hot, dry sand on its back. It seemed completely logical that he was here, leaning against cushions, being served coffee in handleless cups.

Each of the crew members came up to them and saluted. The captain suavely explained to Thresher they had defiled the carpets by stepping aboard with their shoes on, and according to custom owed the offended parties the price of a sheep.

"How come you didn't know that?" Ted asked Thresher irritably. "And what is the price of a sheep?"

Thresher shrugged. "It is whatever they say it is. I will take care of it."

"Well, use their money, those *riyals*."

They were standing well off from shore, and as they slipped through the water they caught a slight wind which alleviated the intense afternoon heat. The movement of the dhow was pleasant. They were brought sugared dates. "Damascus," the captain said, indicating their place of origin.

Ted received the impression that the Shaikh Abdullah Sulaiman was too far above the captain in status to condescend to discuss more than the most immediate business. At any rate 'Abd al Aziz al Qusaili seemed to enjoy chatting with Thresher, who translated pertinent bits of information. "Our cargo is tea, coffee, shark oil, and pearls. The ship is just back from an eight month voyage to Uqair on the Gulf."

Ted nodded, his eyes searched the shore continuously. In biblical times this land was already old. Men wandered here thousands of years and it was still the same. Now two Americans from a parallel world, sailed up this humid sea to wake this waste region from its slumber.

It was prophesied the desert would bloom. A strange flowering it would be, he mused. Not palms and the tamarisk tree, but power poles and derricks reaching skyward. Not airborne thistle, but planes; not trackless sand but stretches of macadam binding towns together. He had a quarter of a million dollars in equipment ready to ship into the Hasa, a fleet of trucks, generators, mixers, shovels, steel cables, wire, electrical switches, and the big stuff, heavy cats for road building. They waited in warehouses and docks.

Sand dunes stretched hundreds of miles. He was seeing with his own eyes the escarpment of limestone shafted into the Arabian peninsula that he had studied on topographical maps. Great ridges were swept bare, lying exposed like the ribs of some felled giant. A giant whose blood marrow he would pump.

The flat-tailed sheep last seen tethered and protesting appeared in mounds of rice served with syruped figs. Thresher reiterated he was to employ only his right hand in forming the food into slightly greasy balls.

After the first day the journey took on a somnolescent quality. Thresher told him again about his installation of a windmill in Jidda to pump water into the city's conduits. "It is sixteen feet high."

Ted was more interested in John Eustace Nichols. "What about those baboons of his?"

"He has an enclosure behind his house, where he keeps them. But one or two are tamed, they wear collars with precious stones and have free run of the house."

"And you really think this man can be of help to us?"

"He is a good friend of the King's. And his partiality toward Americans is well known. In fact, he adopts quite an anti-British stance."

"He's anti-British in spite of being British himself?"

"Decidedly so. His attitude reflects his antipathy to colonialism."

There seemed to be several peculiar Europeans who floated occasionally into the Arabian scene. Thresher mentioned Major Holmes, the collector of rare butterflies.

Ted nodded absently shading his eyes. "I read about him. How do you disguise yourself as a butterfly collector?" Nothing moved on the land ridges or on the sea but themselves. Miles of space produced an uncanny feeling. Time was a dimension of the landscape. He understood the excitement among the crew when on the third day they sighted a speck in the distance.

An hour later the shadow of a large sailing vessel fell across them. A babble of greetings was climaxed by each sailor choosing a counterpart on the other ship, hitching up his skirts, exposing himself and acting out mimed movements of copulation, with much eye rolling, grunts and high-pitched laughter. This diversion lasted as long as the two boats were in sight of each other. After which things settled down.

Ted once more watched the shore. In the old days, the riches of Araby had been in her pearls, musks, spices, antimony, gold, wrought silver and the skins of panthers. While all the time, all through the ages, a deep and unsuspected seepage was penned against impermeable rock.

He closed his eyes to ward off Thresher and indulged in the type of daydream peculiar to him. He was determined to try out seismic refraction. He had seen it used in Texas to survey subterranean formations. A dynamite charge was set off underground, and the difference in arrival time between reflected and refracted shock waves plotted as a function of surface distance from the shot point. He remembered as a college kid mapping the subsurface geology of the Long Beach fields. All those pages of figures, elaborate calculations based on wild estimates—today you simply recorded shock waves in opposite directions and that gave you the slope of the layer.

By the time they approached Jidda toward the end of the week, Ted had new respect for their captain. It took a constant watch to detect the many hidden reefs, whose presence was attested to only by the eddies of current breaking around them.

They came about amidst hoarse cheering from the sailors, and headed for port. A line of water made a distinct demarcation from deep blue to a tawny shade. It was so shallow he could see bottom sand as they rode in across the ripple of waves.

Quayside, a party of notables stood in sweeping headkerchiefs and robes. "Al Emir." Sulaiman spoke with satisfaction.

"The one with the camel stick in his hand," Thresher whispered.

It was a busy port, fishing scows putting in, and larger sailing boats loading and unloading. Hundreds of camels were crouched for packing. Ted and his hosts debarked, to be welcomed by the emir, in the first of what would blend into a dozen such ceremonies. The captain parted from them as though they were brothers. He seemed to be really grief-stricken.

Two Ford cars waited. Their hosts motioned them in and entered after them. The Arabian chauffeurs drove as though they were urging camels forward, careening over rocky, barren hills to meet a more trodden path. From a distance the town had the look of ivory with protecting walls lying mellow in the sun like an old cameo. They passed a group of soldiers lounging by the wall. Their eyes ringed with kohl made their appearance fierce. However as the Fords with the foreign guests raced by, they fell to giggling. Arabian men did a great deal of giggling, Ted thought.

They were escorted to an inner wall, past the market place, which was covered against the molten orb that all but melted the city. He glimpsed a bewildering number of narrow streets winding off from the converging center of the market square. The stench was overpowering. It penetrated every mud brick, as though sewage seeped through the walls of the houses. The labyrinth web of streets was used as latrines by men, camels and herds of sheep.

Hovering over the immediate smell was another, less definable odor. He decided it was decay, the crumbling of centuries. Houses were not allowed to fall down but were patched with fresh mud while balconies of rotted wood were braced in various ways. He wondered about the diseased eyes he saw everywhere and remembered what the Egyptian, Nuri, had said. Syphilis, trachoma, he didn't know, but it affected a large portion of the people who were also encrusted with dirt and numerous scabs. He noticed camels decked with bells and blue beads to ward off the evil eye, but there was no protection against the camel-stick used to urge and beat the creatures on. Their rickety frames were shamefully overloaded, and he guessed their Bedouin masters sold them for transport or meat without inquiring.

Ted was amazed to see the British flag in front of an administrative building. They passed a mosque of lacy mortar and tile, and then larger residences before coming to more open country. Here he saw palm gardens buried in sand. The topmost fronds waved tattered in the wind. Farther along, a date grove adjoining an attractive pavilion had been dug out. It struck Ted there was something unnatural about the fertility of an oasis. The palm trees offered little shade. It seemed to him it was hotter passing under them. Water stood in ditches forming a green scum. With the parched desert encroaching on all sides it was particularly repulsive to have it wasted, allowed to stagnate. He wanted to protest to someone. *Write your congressman*, he told himself wryly.

They entered the grounds of a palace, planted with

papayas, pomegranates, fig and date palms. He noticed a covey of doves and small yellow-throated migrating birds. The party was taken along a corridor of deep arches to the second story where quarters had been prepared. Here, servants removed their clothes and persuaded them into a steamy bath, pouring ewers of water over them. After a vigorous toweling, they were handed robes of a soft gray material.

Thresher had wisely refrained from mentioning that native dress was mandatory for foreign visitors. Ted was incensed. "They can't be serious." And after a brief struggle with the yardage, "Which is the front and which is the back?"

Ted was almost compensated for the indignity by the sight of Thresher.

"Mind the stairs," Thresher cautioned, picking up a corner of his skirt. A Nubian bodyguard appeared to escort them to the Viceroy of the Hejaz, Faisal, the second son of Ibn Saud.

"This is an honor," Thresher said. As they hurried past crowds of suppliants waiting to see the viceroy, Thresher mumbled a few more words about Faisal. "He is the most capable of the King's sons, and the most experienced in war. He captured Jidda, as well as Medina, from the Turks. He is more sophisticated than most Saudis, and the King chose him to lead a trade mission to London at age fourteen. So watch it, he may understand English." This was to forestall Ted venting his spleen, a practice he indulged more and more.

They were received at one end of a large undecorated room divided by a line of pillars. The sun was in their eyes as they approached. They could be seen but not see. Ted strained to penetrate the gloom of the diwan and the men reclined there. Their host rose to receive them, and coming forward, Ted's hand was grasped by a hawk-like young man with intense eyes who wore a wisp of a beard on his chin, under his lip and in the angle of his jaw. The majlis consisted of their constant guide, the Shaikh Sulaiman, and the emir who met them at the pier.

Faisal made the usual elaborate salutations: "My day has brightened since Allah sent thee," "From the sea has come good," and so on. All the while sharp eyes were sizing them up.

Thresher replied in kind. The guests were waved to the diwan and entertained with sherbet and coffee. Each was served three times. Faisal informed them that the King cabled greetings and congratulated them upon the completion of their journey. The only oblique reference he made to the reason behind their visit was a quote from the Koran: "The profit of the earth is for all." This was said directly to Ted with a courteous inclination of the head.

Thresher translated and Ted pondered the pronouncement, wondering how to take it.

They were not allowed to depart until a censer had been swung back and forth a few times, and rose water from a long-necked bottle sprinkled into the palms of their hands.

The much-needed rest Ted was looking forward to did not materialize. Their hosts had no idea of providing them with privacy. A coffeemaker set up his hearth, hanging brass pots in gradated sizes and responding to shouts of "Qahwa!" by serving his ware. The coffee brought an invasion. Scores of people squatted on the floor, waiting their turn for an audience. Others came to transact business among themselves.

The muezzin's call to evening prayer sounded through the room via a loudspeaker. Five times a day slave and master, buyer and seller, suppliant and shaikh faced Mecca. Sometime after morning prayers Ted received a letter from Aunt Lillian. It was a surprising thing to receive out here in the middle of nowhere. It was surprising to receive any mail at all at such an ungodly hour. He decided to read it and go back to sleep. If it had been from Brillianna, he would have torn it open eagerly. But the most he could muster for a missive from Lillian Grenville was mild curiosity. It turned out to be an extremely vehement letter. In fact he couldn't make head or tail of it. Apparently Lillian had come to keep Brillianna company. That part was fine. A good idea. But the rest was incomprehensible, exuding spite and venom. Ted couldn't believe Brillianna would mention their quarrel or the reason for it to Lillian. Yet how to explain. . . ?

He couldn't get back to sleep. No, that wasn't it, he *was* asleep but feeling tired and dispirited, as though nothing he did had meaning. "Fighting your way out of a paper bag," that was one of Dad's expressions.

He thought he was traveling in troughs of desert dunes which crested above him. Their hollows shaded, but at the same time if the wind blew, the massed sand could topple and bury him. He plowed on at the bottom of the mound, making no effort to change course, although he saw the muasar gathering. The dancing funnel of fine sand syphoned upward. It bowed and salaamed, courting before engulfing him. He was caught in a rain of stinging granules. The veil cast over him turned to lashing words.

Aunt Lillian's words. He had a shimmering picture of Aunt Lillian, heightened like a mirage at noon. In his own living room she brushed past him with a glance of such scorn and distaste that he was shaken.

The mirage wavered. Brillianna, keeping up a forced conversation, Lillian not addressing a word to him. A door closed in his face. He felt himself in a desolation outside time. He was still in the San Francisco house but it was a landscape without demarcation. He plodded on, passing the bleached bones of a camel. Nearby was a cairn, a few stones piled one on the other. How lonely, even for the dead. In a domain where sun ruled sand, he felt the Egyptian harlot's breasts like half moons, pendulous over him. Of his wife, he remembered only her perfect carriage. He breathed heat into his lungs. The blistering air watered the desert where no water was. It became impossible to brood about shut doors in California. It seemed to Ted the last word he heard was again the first, the cry, "Qahwa!" The coffee-maker was busy.

Ted felt in his sash for Lillian's letter, hoping it was part of the nightmare. It was there. He took it out and read again, "I want you to know that I hold you responsible for Brillianna's mental and physical state. Your actions regarding your wife were despicable. I

110

consider you an absolutely selfish and egotistical man, which bears out my opinion of men in general."

What did she mean, mental and physical state? Should he try to place a phone call? What would they say to each other? Aunt Lillian was an hysterical female. And it was disloyal of Brillianna to confide in her. If he'd gotten Armagh money under false pretenses, that was between them. What kind of letter would the old busybody write if she knew about the stolen Long Beach funds? She'd probably arrange for the California Highway Patrol to pick him up at the palace. When he wound up his business here, they'd sing a different tune. If he ever did, of course.

A note delivered by hand, distracted him. John Eustace Nichols, Esq., invited them to breakfast, asking that they kindly place themselves in the safekeeping of his servant. They were becoming used to doing just that. Ted figured if he was destined to wind up in an alley with a knife in the back, it would have happened before this. They followed the salaaming black to a parked Ford.

Nichols' residence was a somewhat dilapidated two-story house not many blocks away. Once inside the door a latticed courtyard provided relief from the pervasive sun. The man Thresher introduced as, "the well-known British explorer" looked more like a salesman of baby carriages and Fords. In this capacity Ted admitted to himself he would have to be considered a super salesman, ready to trek through the Empty Quarter or cross the entire peninsula.

It was a short man, rather too plump, who wrung their hands enthusiastically. "Sit down, sit down. I have chairs. A table too. A few amenities, as you can see. Well, well, well, it's good to see you, Thresher. And of course, you're Angstrom. We've not had many Americans turn up in Jidda. There was Crane, of course. Have you told him about Crane?" he asked Thresher. "Fine chap, interested in bringing boy scouting to Iraq. Scion of an old American family. His father made a fortune with flush toilets, I believe. But be that as it may, if you succeed in getting a concession on al Hasa, Mr. Angstrom, you will have pulled the rug from under us

English. We've been in here with subsidies of one kind or another for years. Never got much out of it either. For a while we paid the King to leave his principal enemy, the Sherif Hussein, alone. But after a while, we didn't care about that anymore. Please, make yourselves at home. We are having a typically Arabian style breakfast. It's the only kind you can get here." He chortled appreciatively at his witticism.

The food was delicious, freshly baked bread, goat cheese, fruits in syrup, buttered eggs, dates, apricots, and warm milk slightly colored with tea. "I rather imagine you've had all the coffee you can accommodate for a while," their host remarked. "Although as you probably know, at the time of the Prophet, there was no coffee. When it was first introduced into Arabia, the Wahhabis denounced it, especially the ulema. But they became addicted and relaxed their scruples. Of course, the list of things opposed by the ulema can be headed *Everything Western*, or in their parlance, *inventions of the infidel*."

"The Wahhabis, that's Ibn Saud's family, isn't it?"

Nichols nodded. "He is descended from Ishmail, son of Abraham, if you want his account of it. By the age of twenty he reestablished his fanatics. When the first lorry was seen on the street of Jidda, a group of holy men, ulema, charged it, as they say the buffalo did your iron horse in the old West. They kept coming, hurtling their bodies at it. I want to tell you, there were a lot of mangled and dead ulema that day.

"You can imagine their opposition to the wireless stations the King directed me to install, and the network of telephone communications. Ibn Saud finally won their approval by secretly recording a prayer and broadcasting it over the entire town. No machine that repeats the word of Allah could be evil. So that round was won. But a few years ago there was an assassination attempt, he had to raise an army against the more extreme faction of the Wahhabis. They folded rather quickly. You see, they are used to obeying the King.

"As a small child he was stuffed into his father's saddle bag when the men of his family escaped from Ibn Rashid. At ten he took part in the butchering of the

112

enemy clan, including their retainers. Those who didn't die fast enough were thrown down a well. That gives you some idea of his seasoning. To this day he believes the earth is flat. I am the only person to ever contest this point with him. But even I do not press it." Nichols regarded his guests with baby blue, slightly watering eyes.

"What else can I tell you? Ibn Saud is an enemy of communism, but not for the usual reasons. Someone once told him that communists sleep with their mothers and sisters. In dealing with him even at second hand, you would do well to remember that he views his kingdom as his personal estate. His law is from the seventh century, the law of the Koran and Sunna. He has forty-four sons. Their education is complete at the age of twelve when they have mastered the holy books.

"I am not defaming him when I tell you these things. This man is my friend. He is, I believe, thoroughly honorable. And it is unfair to judge him from our Western point of view. In his personal habits, if we except women, he is austere. He neither smokes nor drinks. He dresses simply. The only distinction between his thawb and that of any Bedouin is, his is clean. He allows himself a single ring of silver and carnelian on which his name is engraved. He lives in a rambling mud palace at Riyadh and sometimes takes advice from men whose faces he likes."

Ted did not blame Nichols for attempting to play up his friendship with the King. That was what he had to contribute, access to Ibn Saud. But the deal he had initialed in London was fully worked out. It was merely a matter of obtaining signatures. A few thousand dollars should purchase a word in the King's ear, and that, Ted felt, was the extent of Nichols' usefulness.

Unaware of this summation of his abilities, Nichols made a far different evaluation of his services. "I am in a rather delicate position," he said. "As a friend of the King, I must bring him what I truly believe to be the best deal possible."

"The terms of the agreement were set in London," Ted pointed out. "We are simply here to ratify it and iron out minor details. The only way you can help is to smooth things with the King, explain the advantages we are offering." This was the moment to clear his throat and get to business. "It seems to me in exchange for that service you should be on the payroll. After all, a man ought to be compensated for his time."

"No one disputes that," Nichols conceded.

"Say, five thousand dollars on the signing of the Hasa contracts, if you have the opportunity to speak to the King."

Nichols' face took on an owlish expression. "Five thousand dollars. Very well, although naturally I'll submit an expense account as well. My participation might involve traveling to Mecca or even Riyadh."

Ted had the distinct impression that Nichols was working both sides of the street, collecting from the King as well. Still for a small graft, the man would put in a word. Ted felt he was buying good will, salting the bird's tail. "I don't see any objection to an expense account if it's kept within reason."

That satisfied Nichols. "I'm convinced you'll need a spot of help with the King. He is totally unrealistic in business matters, changes his mind every other day. He is especially suspicious of foreign interests. It is understandable. At one time Britain divided his kingdom between itself and Turkey, on paper of course, but it was a plan Ibn Saud's spies got hold of. The southern half of Arabia was to go to Britain and the northern, including the Nejd and al Hasa, were to be Turkish. Another British treaty guarantees the Shaikhdoms of Muskat, Oman, and Abu Dhabi their independence. This also rankles the King, as he feels by right it is his territory. But the British have concession agreements there they will never give up. Which is why you have a better chance of concluding, being American. Still, he will ask advice of his slave, his chamberlain, and he will ask me."

Ted felt he had better spell it out for Nichols. "You realize of course, that you are not part of the negotiating team. You are to act in a strictly unofficial capacity and keep in the background."

A golden baboon ambled in and perched in Nichols' lap. He stroked it absently. He didn't respond to Ted

114

but followed his own will-o'-the-wisp. "In a way, I suppose, Ibn Saud is an anachronism. In 1901 he gained control of Riyadh. With fifteen commandos he got over the wall of the city, forced an entrance to the governor's house, only to discover the governor was not there but at the fort.

"He waited all night to murder him, drinking coffee and praying. At daybreak the governor returned home, stopping to inspect his horses. The assassins dashed out, cut his throat, entered Masmak Fort and announced to the citizens that Wahhabi rule was returned." Nichols' round eyes fastened on Ted. "His grandfather had been governor of Riyadh, you see. His father was driven out, and he reinstated his family's reign.

"His Wahhabis were the scourge of the peninsula, brutalizing and terrorizing the land into submission. In spite of being forced to move against them five years ago, they remain the core of his personal troops. They are committed to the destruction of the infidel, especially backsliders among themselves. The ulema flog people publicly in the streets if they have been reported lax in their religious observances, or caught smoking or drinking. Also it is possible you will see an occasional hand or foot hanging in a prominent place in the market. The penalty for stealing is prompt decapitation. Years ago I saw the head of a man I sold coal to, on a pole."

"Well," Ted said uncomfortably, not knowing quite where this conversation was leading, "let's hope he's mellowed since then."

"The point I am about to make, is that he is a desert fighter, but the modern world is lapping at the periphery of his desert. He knows this. He knows the price he must pay for his kingship is to submit to new ways. He has hitched his destiny to the star of the West. You will find last week's *New York Times* in his library. There is a five kilowatt wireless station at Mecca and another at Riyadh, which I helped set up, as well as half-kilowatt stations for the provincial capitals and four mobile units. There is a telephone system from Mecca to Jidda to Riyadh, with a line to Cairo. We are in the process of enlarging this in spite of Wahhabi pressure. No, you

115

will find him anxious to deal. He has no choice. His only source of income is the pilgrim trade which has fallen off drastically since the depression."

Ted was surprised. "You mean the '29 crash was felt out here?"

"No spot on earth escaped the effects of it. The pilgrims are staying home in droves. And the few that come, don't spend. The King is desperate for another source of revenue."

"What is he like personally?" Ted asked, keeping an eye on the baboon who had left Nichols' lap and was scratching himself on the carpet.

"Ibn Saud is the most contradictory man on earth. Childish and unreasonable one minute, charming and urbane the next. He knows the Koran and he knows Arab history. He reminded me once that if they had not been defeated by France at the Battle of Tours, the Arabs would have crossed the English Channel. What else? He's tall for an Arab, about six foot three, and he rides a tall camel, selected from the famous Mulair breed. His people refer to him as Ask-Shuyukh, which is the plural of Shaikh. His hour-by-hour activity is reported on loudspeakers in every oasis village: Ask-Shuyukh are dining, are coming, going, receiving, hunting, as the case may be. He is or was married into every important tribe in the kingdom, and has ties of blood through his many children with all the noble households. In this connection there is an amusing story. They say the last veil he removes from a woman is the face veil. You know the Arab saying: *A woman is a full moon with a wisp of cloud passing across her*. Anyway, the story goes, that if the woman doesn't please him, he simply doesn't bother to remove the face veil."

Ted laughed. "Never?"

"Never. And although at present he is fifty-five, suffers from, they say, glaucoma, and his hearing is impaired, in spite of these infirmities he rides his camels and his favorite mare." Nichols smiled. "The Arab believes that in all animals but man, the female is superior. . . . But the thing I most want to stress, the man is aware of the outside world and determined to be part of it. He owns four airplanes and a fleet of Fords and

116

Chevies. His hospitality is lavish. Don't let it lull or fool you. He is shrewd, informed, and will drive a hard bargain."

Ted left pleased with the way things worked out with Nichols. For a sum of five thousand dollars plus expenses, he could count on Nichols' favorable interpretation should he really have the King's ear. It was important not to overlook any opportunity to weight the scales.

He and Thresher were meeting later that afternoon with Shaikh Sulaiman. Thresher invited him to inspect his windmill, but Ted declined. An idea had taken hold of him. Here he was on the Arabian continent. He found it tantalizing that the Hasa lay the other side of that blinding desert. If he could only stand where he had stood a thousand times in his mind, take in the features of the Gulf one by one. He broached the subject to Thresher. "You know if Nichols makes a trip to Riyadh, I might go along and continue on to Dhahran."

Thresher was genuinely horrified. "Out of the question. The King has not invited you to Dhahran. He has invited you to Jidda. In Jidda you stay."

"I just want to look at the merchandise. Is that so unreasonable? I'm pouring my life's blood into it."

"Impossible. His Majesty's honor would be impugned. You would wreck the deal."

"I'm not trying to force my way into his harim. I'd just like a look at what I'm buying."

Thresher was adamant. "Be realistic. What you want to know is how far down the oil is. You can't tell that by standing there, only by sinking a hole."

Ted gave way reluctantly. All his previous business dealings had not prepared him for negotiation with an absolute monarch out of the seventh century. There was nothing for it but to capitulate. "Okay," he said. "I think I'll look over some figures before the meeting. It seems to me we're not too far apart."

Back in his palace rooms he rechecked each item. The finance minister wanted a down payment of £50,000. In London, Ted suggested an initial payment of £30,000 as a loan, plus a second loan consisting of the remaining £20,000 to be paid eighteen months

117

later. This had been the substance of the "in principle" contract they had signed.

What remained to be worked out was the additional loan Sulaiman indicated would be required if oil was discovered in commercial quantities. The question of royalty per barrel was also not settled. Ted hoped for a tax exemption clause and permission to build a small on-site refinery.

He was deep in calculations when Thresher returned in a state of shock. "Something terrible has happened. I think someone has been playing a double game. I just left Major Holmes outside the British Consulate."

"Major Holmes—you don't mean the butterfly man?"

"Who still represents Eastern and General Syndicate. That's the outfit. . . ."

"I know, that held the concession on the Hasa. But it lapsed years ago."

"That's right. Holmes lost the lease in 1925. Nevertheless, I am disturbed that he seems to be in the picture."

Ted leaned back to take in the agitated figure of Thresher. The thought crossed his mind that Thresher had joined Nichols in cooking up something, but he dismissed the idea. "You think there's an effort to get outside bidding going?"

"I do, yes. And you haven't heard the worst of it. Holmes told me he heard in Cairo that Mr. Longstreet is due to arrive this week. He is the agent for Anglo-Persian, the Iraqi outfit."

"I don't like this," Ted said, "I don't like it at all." Was it Nichols who had given the pot a stir? Or perhaps Sulaiman? With competitors actively in the field would the King back out?

Ted attended his meeting with trepidation. The minister of finance salaamed, thanked Allah who had brought them to this fortunate hour, and went through the ritual of requesting information as to their health, their sleep, their food. Ted waited warily for the axe to fall. Hedged with formality, the pace of these conferences was interminably slow.

Finally he cut through the verbal exchange, asking

118

the shaikh if he was prepared to sign a firm agreement along the lines initialed in London.

"That?" Shaikh Sulaiman seemed incredulous. "That was what we termed 'in principle.' The principle is still well with us. It is the amount which is insufficient."

"The amount? Are you questioning the two payments?" It was Ted's turn to be incredulous.

"No, it is the overall amount that is not satisfying to the king. Together, the payments come to only fifty thousand pounds. His Majesty says one hundred thousand pounds and the concession will unquestionably be yours."

"Shit," Ted replied.

Thresher did not translate.

"Look," Ted tried to keep his voice from shaking. "Tell the bastard we agreed fifty thousand pounds total. Sulaiman had the King's proxy, he initialed for the government. I initialed for the company. The amount is no longer open to negotiation."

Thresher and Sulaiman went at it for some time. "It's no good," Thresher said finally, "A hundred thousand pounds or they won't deal."

"All right," Ted stood up. "Tell him to go see the butterfly guy. I can't do business like this."

"You can't walk out on the King of Arabia's finance minister." Thresher was in a panic.

"I just have." He plunged down corridors and through archways until he was in the street with the sun scorching his eyeballs. He pushed his way past townspeople and Bedouin, who seemed to him not picturesque but consumptive, malnourished, and, judging from the splashes of discolored stench at his feet, suffering from dysentery as well.

He walked waist deep in shade waiting for it to creep up and cover his head. He should never have come himself to Jidda. He should have sent someone to represent him, a Major Holmes or a Longstreet. He needn't have gotten involved. He was mad, out-of-his-mind-insane to be here. Thresher told him, 'A stranger is a guest in any tent for three days.' That's right, three days and then they plunge the knife in. He found Nichols' house. He

119

didn't think he'd be able to, but he was standing in front of it.

He was stopped at the door by an African who seemed seven feet tall. He raised his voice. He shouted. "Nichols, are you here?"

Nichols emerged looking pink in the face and affecting a puzzled manner. "I must say, is that you, Angstrom? Come in and sit down."

"No need for that, I'm here to tell you I'm cashing in my chips. I don't sit in on games where people wander in off the street and join."

"If you're speaking of Major Holmes, I'd no idea when I spoke to you this morning that he would turn up."

"Or that Longstreet from Iraqi Oil is en route?"

"I'd heard the rumor, but when you've been out here as long as I have, you don't pay much attention to rumors."

"I think you should pay attention, Mr. Nichols, because those are the men you'll be dealing with. Let's see if they'll come up with a hundred thousand pounds sterling."

Nichols pursed his lips. "Does that mean Shaikh Sulaiman doubled the ante on you? No wonder you're upset. It's typical shaky-do, of course, that's all it is. They got in touch with Eastern and General and Anglo-Persian figuring if they were on the spot higher stakes could be forced on you."

"They are friggin' well mistaken."

"Of course, of course," Nichols soothed. "It's childishly transparent."

"What was the point of London?" Ted fumed, "What point is there in further negotiations of any kind if they don't feel themselves bound by an agreement?"

"You're right. You're absolutely right. I will undertake to get the shaikh back on the track. And I think I can perform a bit of legerdemain as far as the Major is concerned."

"Like what?"

Nichols' smile was bland. "Like causing him to disappear."

Nichols was as good as his word. By the end of the

week Major Holmes left Jidda to buy a hat, as he expressed it. Thresher was enchanted by the atmosphere of intrigue. Ted too was curious to know how Nichols had accomplished the rout. At the same time, he was frustrated at not knowing what was going on. It was obvious he had misread Nichols. His entire Saudi deal seemingly depended more and more on this fey character, this salesman of baby buggies, this admirer of baboons.

A second meeting was set up with Shaikh Sulaiman, who was as blandly courteous as ever. Nothing was accomplished, but Thresher pointed out a hopeful sign. The King chose this time for his annual pilgrimage from Riyadh to Mecca, bringing him only forty-five miles from the negotiations at Jidda. Nichols, as a Muhammadan, had the distinct advantage of being able to travel to the holy city. Thresher whispered that in British circles it was believed he converted simply to have this edge on European competitors. However that may be, Nichols departed in a jaunty mood telling Ted he wanted to sound the King out. "Make sure we're in the ballpark, as you Americans say."

This was fine with Ted until he heard from Thresher's contacts in the city that Mr. Longstreet of Iraqi Petroleum had arrived on the S.S. *Taif* and gone directly to a desert encampment outside Mecca.

"What's going on?" he demanded of Thresher, who could only shake his head.

"Whatever it is," Ted said bitterly, "we'll be the last to know." He was more worried than ever. Too much depended on Nichols, who seemed a frail reed to lean on. His eccentricities were a byword. No one could predict what fancy he would indulge next. Also it began to dawn on Ted he had not bid high enough to command his loyalty. He was acutely conscious that five thousand dollars plus expenses were hardly adequate for consummating the largest oil deal in history. Ted recalled with chagrin that he had refused him a place on the negotiating team and told him to keep in the background. Background, hell! He was running the whole show. And what was to prevent him tossing everything to Longstreet, or even fetching the Major back.

Ted brooded on the situation for forty-eight hours, at which time he was summoned to the telephone. It was Nichols, who was back in town. He asked Ted and Thresher to drop around to his office.

Nichols greeted them affably with Arabian flourish. This irritated Ted, but he set his jaw and waited. Nichols indicated to his secretary, or maybe it was his slave, that he could withdraw. Turning to Ted he announced, "I think I can close."

"What about Longstreet?" Ted wanted to know.

"Longstreet's no problem. The King had to hear his proposition, of course. I don't know precisely what it was. I had a talk with Longstreet myself. He asked me to act for him. I turned down his rather considerable offer." Nichols paused to let this sink in. "I then had a crucial talk with Ibn Saud. I was able to persuade him that the Iraqi Company had no intention of developing new fields. Its sole interest in the Hasa concession is to prevent competition with its own oil. Since the King wants a royalty of four shillings per ton, it is vital for him to have a guaranteed rate of production." He gave Ted one of his owlish looks. "Which makes you the favored candidate."

"What about the hundred thousand pound loan?" Ted asked. "Were you able to shake him on that?"

"I'm authorized to bring you pretty much the deal outlined in London. The King agrees to a loan of thirty-five thousand pounds, payable within thirty days of signing. Five thousand pounds to be considered as the first-year rental on the land. The money is to be repaid only out of royalties."

"In other words: no oil, no repayment?"

"That's it. Now at the end of eighteen months, a second loan of twenty thousand pounds is due. If you subtract the land rental, which I admit he just dreamed up, we're back to your original fifty thousand pounds. Juggling it around this way is merely a face-saver, it allows the King to close without seeming to back down."

"Let's close then before he changes his mind again."

"There are two other conditions."

122

"Oh? What are they?"

"Well, three actually."

Ted waited.

"The King wants a free supply of gasoline and all petroleum products for the entire country."

"Done," Ted said. "What else?"

"He insists on being paid in gold."

"In gold?" Ted was stunned. "You mean, *gold?*"

"Bullion, correct. The King doesn't understand checks or paper money. He is used to Sulaiman's piggy-bank methods of hearing the coins drop in, and the ones he likes best are gold."

"Well, I suppose it can be arranged," Ted conceded. "It will be awkward, take a hell of a lot of manipulation. But okay. I agree. Payment to be made in gold. And the final condition?"

"In view of the fact that I had to travel to Mecca, and various unforeseen difficulties involved, that the itemized expense account I submit is not open to question."

Ted raised his eyebrows. "Now I'll make a condition."

"What's that?"

"That you tell me why Major Holmes decided to go to London for a hat."

"I should tell you in any case. That's item III." He cleared his throat. "If you recall our agreement, there is a small payment due me, as well as the expense account. The expense account begins with item I: my recent trip to Mecca in which I canvassed the King's wives, through household eunuchs, of course, and made valuable gifts, noted herein." Nichols took out a document and waved it under Ted's nose. "Also noted here are monies paid by me to discover which slave would be serving the King when the contract was read. A gift was made to him of a Ford car. A second automobile to the King's chamberlain. All told, the Mecca trip can be charged off at two thousand pounds.

"Item II: the fact that I was able to persuade the King of my point of view, namely, that Mr. Longstreet and Iraqi Petroleum would not actively seek oil in al Hasa, is worth to your company—another two thousand pounds."

"I begin to get the drift," Ted said. "Major Holmes and his hat . . . is another two thousand pounds."

"Precisely." Nichols rubbed his pudgy hands. "And worth every penny. Although actually it was a simple ploy. I merely told Holmes that the King expected him to make good on the default of Eastern and General Syndicate before he would be allowed to enter the bidding. Since the Syndicate defaulted in 1925 and we are presently in 1933, that would mean eight times the lease monies of two thousand pounds a year, or upward of fifty thousand dollars on the table before negotiations could start."

Ted agreed Nichols had earned his expense account. If this man had ever sold baby buggies to Jidda housewives, there must have been quite a markup.

But Nichols was not done. "A bonus of a thousand completes the tally sheet."

Decision time was fractional. Ted would conclude now or never. "Right! The bonus to be paid in dollars." He knew the Englishman was thinking in pounds sterling. But each man had pushed the other to the limit.

"Of course," Nichols gave way gracefully, and to lighten the atmosphere, added, "I don't require gold. Your personal check will suffice."

They shook hands on it.

The session with the Minister of Finance was a formality. Shaikh Sulaiman stated through Thresher the demands which Ted, through Nichols, was prepared for. He agreed to a payment of fifty thousand pounds when oil was discovered in commercial amounts, and an equal sum to be paid the following year. He agreed to the royalty. He agreed to the rental. He agreed to pay in gold. He agreed to everything.

The Saudi-California concession was ratified. Mr. Duncan, whom Ted contacted by telephone in Cairo, insisted the King himself be a signatory. This was Duncan's sole and total contribution. But Ted recognized its value. It was worth keeping Duncan in Cairo cooling his heels at considerable expense.

Nichols set out with the document for Mecca. He rang up on the palace phone later that night. It was a bad connection.

"Well?" Ted shouted.

"I read the contract to Ibn Saud."

"So, what did he say?"

"Nothing. He fell asleep. I didn't know quite what to do, but I kept on with it. When I finished there was rather a strained silence. I think that's what woke him."

"For Christ's sake man, did he sign or didn't he?"

"He interrupted himself in the middle of a soft snore, sat bolt upright, turned to Sulaiman and said, 'I put my faith in Allah,' and signed."

Ted grabbed off his headgear and threw it into the air with a wild cheer. Thresher started pumping his hand.

It was April, 1933. The United States declared an embargo on gold. Ted's office phoned via London, via Cairo, with operators breaking in on them in three languages. "Ready with your call, sir." "Cairo, can you hear me? This is London."

"No," Ted gasped. "I don't believe it."

"I'm afraid there is a complete gold embargo. Everybody says we're going off the gold standard," his secretary reported as the London operator asked again, "Have you reached your party, sir?"

"Wait," Ted said in desperation. "What was the date, the exact date the embargo was signed into law?"

The answer came without hesitation, "20 April."

Ted couldn't breathe, it was the same day the Saudi-California contract was signed by the King in Mecca. "The hour," he called into the phone. "I need the hour. I'll hold." There was an outside chance their agreement had anteceded the U.S. embargo. When his secretary came back on the line, this slight hope was demolished. "We went off the gold standard Thursday April 20 at twelve noon."

Ted hung up the receiver limply. Ibn Saud had not signed until six that evening. He turned to Thresher, "I don't care if they flog me through every street in Jidda, I've got to have a drink."

He discovered that for a price, contraband liquor and cigarettes could both be had. Liquor in that climate bore straight to the brain. He was feeling fuzzy when he received word that Shaikh Sulaiman requested an immediate interview. "Tell him I'm sick," Ted mumbled, "indisposed, drunk."

The man went away. "He'll be back," Thresher said.

"So he'll be back. Am I responsible for FDR and the U.S. government?"

Thresher called for a bath and a massage. Ted was steamed, rubbed, pummeled and anointed. Somewhere during this process his head cleared. "The time difference!" he shouted at Thresher. "Mecca is eight hours ahead of Washington. Ibn Saud signed at ten in the morning Washington time, two hours before the embargo was law."

Three weeks later Quentin Thresher counted £35,-000 in pieces of gold laboriously into Sulaiman's hand. By then Ted was home.

Brillianna opened her eyes. Ted was standing over her. For a moment she looked at him tenderly. Then she remembered. He was the enemy.

She drifted again, coexisting with distant pain and hazy, sporadic memory. She knew it wasn't Ted who was there. It was a different face, nothing like Ted's. Ted's face was changed. It was hard and incised like the rock he mined. Besides, Ted was gone. When the cramps started tearing at her uterus, he was in a pullman on the way to New York.

The spasms knotted like birth pangs, bringing sweat out on her forehead. She remembered the effort to reach the telephone. It was by the bed, she had only to pull herself toward it. Agony slipped over her senses. A wild scream started in the upper region of her head. The unformed infant emerged in the amphibian stage, looking like a large chrysalis with its eye buds migrated, arms still pinioned and legs rudimentary.

It was a monster lying on the bed in its blood and hers. But it would have been normal and it would have been a son. She saw now that it was Dr. Terrell and not Ted who bent over her. Brillianna smiled at him. There was no color in her lips. They were undifferentiated from the rest of her face. The smile bothered Dr. Terrell. "You came through the surgery very well."

126

She nodded and seemed to drop off. Then her eyes opened wide. "Surgery?"

"You were hemorrhaging when they brought you in."

She tried to think back. She must have reached the phone. At some point she resigned her body into the hands of others. Teams of experts did what needed to be done. Moved her, admitted her. Then the injection that caused consciousness to reel away. Dr. Terrell brought his face closer. It was a soft face, a gentle face. How could she have thought it was Ted's? Ted's face was granite. Nothing made an impression on it. Almost nothing.

The doctor was speaking in a sympathetic tone, she tried to pay attention. "You see, there was no choice. You were bleeding profusely. Ordinarily we like to get the husband's consent. But I knew Ted was on his way to London. No possible way to reach him. And no time. I performed a hysterectomy." He patted her hand. "But you're luckier than some, you have a child. That little Brilli is more like you every day."

". . . a hysterectomy?"

"I'm sorry."

She struggled to sit up, to fight him. "No. It was a miscarriage. A simple miscarriage."

"I'm afraid not. There was a great deal of tearing. As I say, medically there was no choice."

She fell back against the pillow.

The doctor continued. "I explained that spotting such as you were having could lead to a miscarriage."

"A miscarriage, that's one thing. But what you've done is ream me out, hollow me of everything that makes me a woman."

"I left the ovaries," Dr. Terrell said. "That will keep the hormones flowing. Keep you youthful, as beautiful as you are now."

A high keening sound escaped her, she meant it as a laugh.

"What precipitated the episode?" Dr. Terrell asked. "I did warn you about intercourse."

"Yes, with your kind face and kind mouth and understanding eyes, you put it into my head. And there it was when I needed a weapon. Well," she shrieked at his bewildered expression, "I don't have a gun in the house.

127

And the kitchen knives are in the kitchen. Don't you see what he did? He took Armagh and threw it away. So I wanted to throw away something too, something he valued. I fought with what I had, myself."

The doctor, alarmed at this incoherence, nodded to the nurse who administered a sedative.

"He didn't care about a child," the woman on the bed said frantically. "He wanted a son to put into the fields, to be himself all over again." Her speech began to blur. "Do you want to know something funny, Dr. Terrell? Mama never spoke to me about sex. Not until the very day of the wedding. The wedding was on Long Island . . . Long Island. She was helping me into my gown when, out of a blue sky, she said, 'Brillianna, are you able to bring yourself to use this man's toothbrush? Because what happens tonight—is much—more— intimate.' That's funny. Don't you—think that's funny? Ted's teeth are thick and even and beautiful. So I said yes. And Mama hugged me. She never hugged me, but she did this time and said, 'Pray God you will be a happy and dutiful wife.'" Brillianna took a long and quivering breath. "I am neither. And God has punished me—because there will never be a chance now. Never."

When she woke she was tired. Very tired. She knew she had won something but she couldn't remember what it was. She had a dream that upset her. Her pillow was wet with tears. She tried to recall what the dream had been.

Eating. That was it. She had been eating and eating, trying to fill an empty space. What a stupid dream. Suddenly she screamed. She sat up in bed and screamed.

Brillianna wanted a fairer trial than she could give herself. She wrote from the hospital asking Aunt Lillian to come and stay with her. While she waited for her aunt, she tried to figure out what life had left her.

Not much, it seemed. What Ted had not taken, she had taken from herself. He plundered her, she had completed the job.

Now what? Divorce? She was a Grenville. She could not become a castaway creature importuning for alimony, or a Mrs. Wycoff, the desperately insecure real estate lady. Or a secretary one passed as though she were an attachment to a desk. That was not the route back.

Once before she had started with nothing and built Armagh.

It would happen again. And it would be through Ted. Painfully she traced the emotional thread of her life. She fell in love because she believed in his genius. Even when she despised and hated him, she never doubted. Somehow he would pull out of this Arabian venture. It might mean bankruptcy. But pull out, he would, by fraud, lies, deceit, only this time it would not be at her expense. His methods and his oilman's knowledge had gotten her Armagh. If she stayed with him she would have it again.

Lillian Grenville found it difficult to recognize the high-spirited young girl she had sponsored in this wan, withdrawn woman. She waited for Brillianna to confide in her. It was Brilli who established the old comradeship between them. Lillian adored the active youngster. "She's Grenville, down to her fingertips."

Her mother had reservations on this score. "I don't know," she said, "her eyes seem to me Ted's."

"No, no, those great sweeping lashes, definitely Grenville."

But the expression was Ted's, both the dreaminess and the stubborn resolution which no pleading could shake.

Lillian took her knitting from her bag as she watched the self-absorbed play of the child in the sandbox, busy with cups, pail, and cookie molds. "She's going to be a beauty," she said with satisfaction.

"At least," Brillianna said, "she'll never know the grayness of my childhood."

Lillian shot her niece a quick look of sympathy. "If only I'd known about you earlier."

"My parents were good to me in their way," Brillianna mused. "I think maybe it's difficult to be the right parent for certain children. I sometimes wonder how good a mother I am."

Lillian was shocked. "I've never seen anyone more devoted."

That was true. But she recognized it was to fill her

own life rather than for the child's sake. Brilli was extremely contrary where she was concerned. If the little girl dropped her pail, rather than accept it from her mother's hands, she would pick up one of the molds or cups. If Lillian returned the plaything, she accepted it happily enough. Brillianna couldn't explain this. She kept hoping the child would relent and come to her, imagining those round arms spontaneously about her neck, and that comfortable little person on her lap.

Was Brilli's reticence her fault? Did she herself not know how to show the child affection? She had never been demonstrative with her own mother. The comparison, however, seemed not to be valid. She provided a far more normal environment for Brilli, who did not need to fantasize a life. Everything would be lavished on her, she was determined on this. In a few years there would be a select private school. There would be friends home for the weekend. Little girls making fudge and divinity in the kitchen. . . . Brillianna wondered if she was falling into Ted's ways, building dreams? She gave herself over to them. . . . And when the time came there'd be boys.

Not a Ted Angstrom, she would see to that. She'd know by the faraway look in a boy's eyes he was the one to avoid. If he stood painfully mute in the midst of conversation and pulled you off somewhere to spill into your ears a confusion of hopes, he was the one Brilli must turn her back on.

It was the third day of Lillian's visit, a pleasant morning, the bay danced and sailboats bobbed on the clear expanse of water.

"I not only lost a child," Brillianna said without preamble, "I had a hysterectomy."

Lillian could think of nothing to say.

"We had intercourse," Brillianna went on fixedly, "and I'd been spotting."

"But didn't you realize the chance you were taking?"

Brillianna said huskily, "Will you watch Brilli?" and left the porch. It was then Lillian wrote the letter Ted received in Jidda.

Lillian had been disappointed in the marriage, of course. Ted was new money, his background not at all

130

what she had in mind for her niece. That mysterious quality *breeding* was absent. He was attractive, the dreamer's preoccupation coupled in him with a bright, mercurial streak. It was *that* Lillian mistrusted. And now her intuition was amply vindicated. But even she had not imagined the complete egocentricity of the man. To force himself on his wife at such a time was inexcusable.

The women met for lunch, each waited, each held back. Lillian asked for Ted's address, and Tomas was sent to post a letter. Maria served them home-baked corn pones, a tossed anchovy salad and iced tea. Brillianna leaned back in her chair and regarded her aunt with curiosity. "Aren't you going to say?"

"Say what?"

"The letter to Ted, of course."

"It may have been none of my business. However," Lillian patted the corner of her mouth on which no crumb was discernible, "I told Theodore what you should have told him yourself. That what he did was unthinkable. Everyone knows a woman must have consideration at a time like that. I'm sorry, Brillianna, if I took too much on myself. But I simply couldn't let him get away with it."

Brillianna appraised the older woman thoughtfully. "Dear Aunt Lillian," she barely breathed the words, "don't you know that Ted isn't capable of anything like that? Only I am."

"You? What do you mean?"

"There were two needs. His drove him to the Arabian peninsula. Mine, I made a gift of. But he cheated me, Lillian. He promised . . . never mind what he promised. You see it took me all these years to realize that everything, his life, my life, even Brilli's, had to be fed into the pumps. He believes this. It's part of the mystique. In some obscure recess of his mind is the certainty that it won't gush or thunder unless everything is in the pot. When he took Armagh I finally understood that he wouldn't stop there. My future was forfeit, and Brilli's, and the child's I was to have. Don't you see, I had to stop him. I fought back with the only arsenal I had. Ted didn't know when the battle really began. I was the only one who knew." *That's enough*, she told herself. *Stop right here.*

Instead she poured more tea. "You've been married to a Grenville for thirty years. Don't you know us at all?"

Silence fell between the two women and extended itself. "I've known for a long time, of course," Lillian said slowly, "that we have different birthdays."

Brillianna couldn't let Aunt Lillian remain with the picture of a submissive woman, mistreated, abused and rendered sterile. She had to speak. "Can we use the word *sex?* I think we can. That was my instrument. I smiled at him when I hated him. I led him on. I ran through the whole house, shrieking, throwing my robe at him, pulling my nightgown off, tossing it backward. It caught on his shoulder.

"I was naked. I intended to be naked. At the top of the stairs, that's where he caught me. I was terribly afraid. Physically afraid of penetration. But I didn't shrink back." She recited this in a monotone as though trying to get through it.

"But you were spotting. Surely the doctor. . . ."

"Of course he told me. That's what gave me the idea." She drew a succession of shallow breaths as though she were crying, but there were no tears. The tear ducts were sterile too. "I meant to hurt him, that's all I could think of. I couldn't be sure it would work, I couldn't be positive it would happen. But I wanted it to happen. You see, I never dreamed. . . . I thought there'd be other children someday when Ted settled down and accepted responsibility, when. . . ."

Her aunt replied in a self-contained and distant manner, "At the time I discovered the little ruse about our birthdays, I put it down to high spirits and the capriciousness that was such an attractive part of your girlhood. I think I liked you the better for it."

Brillianna was heartened by this reaction. She said impulsively, "I count on you, Aunt Lillian, to tell me how to fill my life. You've always been such a vital person. Your life has been so full. Everything around you was always so much fun."

"Really? Is that what you think? Then why did I

bring a niece who wasn't even my flesh and blood into my home, treat her as a daughter? Did you ever think what lay behind that? Rounds of doctors, of tests, nights of prayers, tears, and finally facing the fact. In Roman times they stoned barren women. I stoned myself, drove myself through a wilderness of meaningless activity.

"Look at me, Brillianna, I want to say this to your face. I regard what you did as a crime. A crime, no less. You have willfully voided yourself as a woman, turned yourself into a shell, empty of your own future. I shall never forgive you. Try to fill your life. I dare you. I challenge you. For me it was charity affairs, fund raising benefits, art, music. So much trivia. The basic stuff isn't there. Oh, you're lucky there is Brilli. But one child is not a family. To be revenged on your husband, to deprive him, you have mutilated your life. I am sorry for you, my girl. And I am sorry you had to tell me. I am the last person you should have told."

Brillianna was shocked by what she had brought down on her own head.

Lillian rose from the table. "You might apologize for me to Ted. He may have done much to be condemned for, but he is not the monster I told him he was."

"But I am? Is that what you're saying?"

Lillian left the room without answering.

The rift with her aunt was extremely painful for Brillianna. She lost not only her confidante, but, since she was not close to her sister, the last ties with her family and her girlhood. Her instinct led her to reason: if she is my friend, she must accept me, understand what I did and why I did it. This was impossible. And she knew it. Why had she insisted on a truth that would alienate them?

Looking back, she continued to be uneasy and not understand her confession.

She didn't sleep well. Each morning she stepped from her shower and looking into a fogged mirror rubbed the surface with a corner of her towel. There she was. A young, vigorous-looking woman. The surgeon had left the ovaries and the facade remained, what Ted called her good bones.

Ted didn't write. Perhaps he didn't know what to write. But he sent a present. It arrived in an enormous wooden box. Tomas uncrated it on the lawn, prying up the boards while Brilli hopped up and down in excitement and Brillianna and Maria watched.

Inside the box was another of cardboard, and when that was ripped open, mounds of excelsior were disclosed. Brilli joined Tomas and the two of them shredded the stuff letting it fly where it would.

Something odd was being revealed. At first Brillianna thought it was an enormous cauldron of red clay, but the shape was wrong. Maria crossed herself.

"It's a god!" Brillianna exclaimed.

"That's what it is," Tomas agreed. "But I fear he did not stand the trip. As you can see, he is in two pieces."

"Lift him out," Brillianna said.

Tomas freed the terra cotta idol from the last shreds of excelsior and attempted to fit him together. But a narrow flake had broken off and been pulverized. It was impossible to balance the head on the torso, let alone glue it back. Tomas gave up trying.

"Too bad," Brillianna said. "We'll put it out with the trash."

The child Brilli had been staring into the brooding featureless face. "Oh no, Mummy."

Brillianna decided her daughter was right. It might be impolitic to throw out Ted's present. Besides, Ted would be convinced that throwing out a god with garden cuttings was bad luck. He would feel that was no way to treat a god, even a broken one. So the red clay figure in two pieces was hauled to the hillside garden. The larger section crouched in the honeysuckle with the sprinkling system striking it about the haunches. The head, placed slightly above in the rockery, watched.

Brillianna invited a neighbor, Professor Belmont, from the archeology department at Berkeley, to have a look at their acquisition. First the professor examined the head, tapping it occasionally. Then he peered at the massive mid-section. "Definitely East African. Extremely primitive. Most likely belonging to a tribe known as *Obstacle of Enemies*, studied principally because they smeared their arrows with the grub of a certain beetle."

Brillianna could not overcome a feeling of uneasiness. With any shift in light the planes of the face suggested yet another expression. "You don't suppose it has the evil eye, do you?"

"As far as I can tell, he doesn't seem to have an eye of any kind," the professor remarked.

Brillianna shivered slightly.

"Too bad it was so severely damaged. I believe it is a replica of Kumju. Yes, indeed, what we have here is a somewhat crude facsimile. There is a much finer example on loan at Princeton which has the traditional tusks, lacking here."

"A replica! That makes me feel better," Brillianna declared. "I didn't like the idea of an actual god, that people prayed to, sitting in the honeysuckle and geranium ivy."

It was no broken, clay-pot replica of a god who punished her, but the Lord Jehovah Himself. And Brillianna was fearful. Ted had been gone three months. The rooms belonged to the tenants, not to her. Her section of the house was empty. No matter what he had done, there was zest to living only when Ted was part of it.

A god, wasn't that just like him? Sending her a god! Crazy, impetuous. He undoubtedly saw it in a bazaar and thought . . . just the thing for Brillianna.

He did think of her then. Did their quarrel weigh on him? Did he remember what happened afterward? Did he think of that last night? What would his reaction be when he saw her and she was not pregnant? Her life was frozen around that moment in time.

When he knew there would never be a son, would he want a divorce? She shook her head. She would fight him once again if she had to, this time for himself. She would enter the field with an appealing face, a body he found attractive, a will as strong as his. She was thirty-two years old. Dr. Terrell had left the ovaries. On the illusion of youth and fertility she must build new strength. She set herself a task. She must learn to forgive. She must forgive herself and she must forgive Ted.

135

That made it possible to stay where she belonged, his wife, mother of his child, mistress in her own home, Mrs. Angstrom.

A cablegram from Cairo reached her. She scrutinized the impersonal words. Ted's itinerary and arrival time made up the message which was signed, LOVE TED.

The word *love* pierced her defences. It was a conventional signature. Still, it hadn't been necessary to add. He hadn't written, not once. But he thought of her, missed her, wanted, and perhaps even needed her.

She bought a new suit out of the household money and a feminine blouse, ruffled at the throat. Brillianna didn't generally go in for ruffles. But she wanted to impress him with a femininity she no longer possessed.

Ted stepped from the train into his old life. He changed worlds almost as casually as he changed from his Arab dress. Black clouds of smoke swirled past. She rushed toward him through the clank, snort and whistle. "Did you get your lease?" she asked coming up to him.

"I'm home," he grinned, pulling her to him. Then he moved back to look at her. "Brillianna . . ." he said.

"I didn't know how to write it.".

"What happened?" He continued staring at her flat figure.

She reached up and kissed him. "It's good to have you back. It was terrible going through it alone. Come, let's get the bags into the car. I'll tell you about it on the drive back." She twined her fingers in his. He'd forgotten how attractive she was. Put together in a way to fire a man. "God, I'm sorry, Kiddo."

She put her hand quickly over his.

"How's Brilli?" he asked.

"She's fine. She wanted to meet you, but it was past her bedtime. You'll see a change in her. She's quite a little lady."

"Is she still pretty like her mother?"

Brillianna led the way to the parked car. Ted settled with the redcap and slipped behind the wheel. "Did you get the god I sent you? East African."

"Yes, he's splendid. He didn't survive the trip in one piece though."

"He didn't?"

"No, but it doesn't really matter, we've set him in the garden. Both his head and his torso. He looks imposing. We've got two gods instead of one."

He turned onto the highway. "Now tell me."

"It was right after you left, that same morning. It was terrible. There was no one to help me. I could hardly reach the phone."

He seemed to be concentrating on his driving, but he was thinking back. "Did it have anything to do with. . . . ?"

"Please don't feel guilty, Ted. It was my fault as much as yours."

Space intruded into their conversation. There was too much space between them.

"That explains the letter from Aunt Lillian. She really chewed me out and I couldn't figure why. God, I'm sorry. I expected you to be sticking out a foot." Again, one of those pauses. "Was it a boy, or . . . could they tell?"

"It was a boy."

A groan got past locked teeth. "I'm a clumsy fool, an idiot. But the spotting had stopped, you said it had stopped."

"Ted, it's nobody's fault. It happened." She placed her hand on his arm, and he patted it. She was comforting him when she should have been kicking him around the block. This was the son he had waited for, the son he was building an oil empire for. He asked himself how important the trip had been. What was the purpose of an oil empire if there was no son to take over?

Ted tried to rouse himself from the moraine of self hate that rolled over him. There was Brillianna to consider. As bad as it was for him, it must have been hell for her.

They reached the house and he pulled into the driveway. "There'll be others," he said to cheer her.

"No."

There was a finality in her voice that chilled him. "What do you mean, no?"

They sat in the car, neither of them making a move to get out. "It was necessary to do a hysterectomy."

137

That wasn't possible. It was a time of new beginning, an auspicious moment. His life was in ascendancy. His fortune, like the world, revolved a hundred and eighty degrees. It alone was free of the physical laws that bound everything else. The sun rose, but it also sét, while his prospects continually mounted. What she said wasn't possible. It didn't jibe, it didn't fit.

Brillianna was holding herself stiffly away from him. The posture of her body indicated more than her words. What she said was true. Ted felt a sudden revulsion. It was as though when they used the scalpel on his wife, they scraped him bare of the years he had loved her.

The first step in exploring his vast concession was a letter to Ibn Saud to ensure the safety of his geological teams. It read in part: "Men of the new Saudi-California company propose to look under the kingdom's floor. These men are dear to Theodore Angstrom. Theodore Angstrom is dear to the Saudi-California Company, having set his name to the agreement. The agreement is dear to the government of the United States." Ted was well aware that there was no justification for the inclusion of this last line. The government of the United States took no interest whatsoever in his dealings with Ibn Saud. But damn it, they should.

The King, on receipt of this document, assigned a dozen of his soldiers to each pair of exploring Westerners, ostensibly as guides. In fact, to see they did not roam close to Wahhabi villages. The first surveys were made by air, and likely sites marked for detailed investigation. Spelunking geologists dropped into fissures and caves, picking up samples of shells and rocks. Wildcatters crisscrossed the country, staying in touch by radio. A pier was built at al Khobar to bring in shipments of men and supplies.

Arabia has been described as a land waiting for something to happen. Exploration went on month after month under the worst conditions possible. Shade temperature in the summer reached 120 degrees. The nearest safe drinking water was often a spring miles from camp. Motor vehicles gave the most trouble, axles broke in the rocky wadis, radiators steamed dry, cylinder blocks cracked. Jeeps and trucks were constantly mired in the dunes.

Ted got through to Nichols in Jidda, having recalled that Fords were surprisingly good on sand. Nichols had a better idea. It seemed the British in Egypt used a large, soft, spreading tire, much like a camel's hoof. Ted ordered these shipped up the Gulf, and until they arrived, suggested that the men in the field let the air out of their tires, taking the pressure down to make them flabby. "Like a camel's hoof," he yelled into the black face of the phone.

Two years of formation mapping produced a number of possible test well sites. A decision had to be made. Front money was running out, Ted was up to his ears in unpaid invoices, and his credit had come to an end. One of the surveyors jubilantly cabled that existing maps were inaccurate and the concession actually included several thousand more square miles of territory. Great, Ted thought, just what I need. More sand.

He consulted his intuition and chose the Dammam Dome. At least it was near Dhahran. On April 30, 1935 they spudded in the first test hole, Dammam I, with a cable-tool rig transported piece by piece from the States. With no dynamite available—the shipment was tied up in Cairo customs—they broke up the rock by the primitive method of heating it with wood fires and then drenching it in cold water. The driller had a single word of Arabic for communication with his Saudi crew. This meant "up." His only way of expressing "down" was to bellow "up!" while shaking his head *no* and cursing a blue streak. It became clear that the nomadic Saudis hadn't the vaguest idea of a work day. More Americans were needed to man the operation, but they were difficult to come by. Ted settled for Italian labor.

Dammam I came in at 1,977 feet with an initial flow of 6,000 barrels per day, which made Ted's week and enabled him to raise new funding. But the next cable reported a drop to a mere 100 barrels average, which might be satisfactory in California but not halfway around the world. Ted ordered Dammam I plugged with cement. They started rigging up for Dammam II.

The Texas backers Ted had conned with the first news on Dammam I were beginning to pull out and the banks were closing in when, in May 1936, fourteen months after the first derrick had gone up, Dammam II started to give encouraging indications. All it took now was no sleep, continual phone calls, and meetings around the clock. By the end of June, Dammam II was flowing at a commercial rate, 160 barrels an hour.

A pay horizon! This was it, his vision was vindicated. His luck gushered. Ted turned his face upward when he heard, and laughed. He could almost feel the drops spill over him. Nothing could stop him now. Texas Oil bought in as a half partner, bringing marketing facilities east of Suez, three million dollars cash, and a promise of eighteen million more out of oil produced.

Ted lost no time redeeming the Long Beach fields, both his and his father's. For three years he had lived with the fear that his dad would take it into his head to visit the old bank and look over his stocks. There was no reason for him to do this. But he might. The pay horizon on the Arabian anticline saved him from this nightmare.

Ted had always known. In his mind it was a question of *when*; and would he have the capital to continue drilling. From the first moment the knowledge of a province, a netherworld of oil, was seared into his brain. It was as though he could look out of the drill bit with a mole's eye at the impregnated rock.

Brillianna's response to the strike was to repurchase Armagh. She paid an exorbitant price for it. Ted said nothing. But he felt it was a betrayal. She was an oilman's wife. She knew the three million was not for them personally, but must go into refinancing, exploration, and equipment. That three million was working money. She should have waited. Instead, she insisted on keeping the San Francisco home as well. Brillianna didn't like parting with houses.

It had taken over three years to accomplish the return to Armagh. She inspected every inch of the property with a deep sense of satisfaction. Everything was the same. The sea washed the white sand as though there had been no hiatus in their watching. The horizontal pines leaned away from the wind. Everything was the same, yet they were two other people.

Ted insisted the broken god purchased in Cairo move with them to Armagh. It was lucky to have a god. Ted needed luck right now, for at 3,200 feet the pay zone petered out. They sunk another test well. There was oil, but in disappointing amounts.

Brillianna, with a complete disregard for this fact, began picking up pieces of signed Limoges. Taste, that was something she did have. She had decided to offer patronage as Lillian had done. She could think of several instances where collectors had achieved the status of celebrities themselves by reason of their discrimination. J. Pierpont Morgan did not fit this description, having bought up Renaissance manuscripts; rare drawings by Fra Filippo Lippi, Fragonard, Brueghel and William Blake en masse; as well as an entire collection of incunabula. Some of the pieces were of unparalleled rarity and beauty, but that was due more to the size of the collection than to the unfailing judgment of the connoisseur. More flair was demonstrated by Gertrude Stein, the American expatriate people were talking about. Without the unlimited means of a Morgan she made each acquisition a separate gem in the overall tapestry of the post-impressionists.

In the face of his wife's extravagance, Ted remembered his father saying, "That one is too good for us, Ted. Too high and mighty."

To take his mind off his troubles Ted began making regular visits to the Long Beach fields. He took his daughter with him, whisking her into the car. She slept the entire way, to wake in a hotel, and after breakfast accompany her father into the land of skeletal derricks.

It was the old dream, and it sent a chill through Brillianna. Pretending to sleep, she would listen to them leave. Through the walls she heard Ted's excited, joyful whisper. He returned to the fields with such zest that she wondered if life with her was an exile. To wallow in mud, smell oil, hear the creak of pumps, was a release. He forgot his Texas partners, the incompetent Saudi sands, the importuning Ibn Saud. Had he forgotten too, that the little girl was a substitute, standing in for a shadowy figure that had lost definition?

As though to make up for any hidden unfairness, Ted loved Brilli with fervent dedication. He took the fastidiously dressed child by the hand, guiding her past the clanging scrapers and grading machines, showing her the rotary table and strings of casing waiting to be run in. The mud line jumping like a snake frightened her and she clung to her father's hand.

Ted tried to give her a sense of what she was seeing. "The derrick has to be high because it contains the hoisting equipment that we use to raise and lower the drill pipe. The bit wears down quickly, you can see that, pulverizing rock the way it does, then it's got to be hauled up for repair." This Grenville daughter must become an Angstrom son.

"Everything," he told the little girl, "everything you see here will belong to you. And other fields. *Al Hasa*. Remember the name."

She nodded, looking with round solemn eyes at the derrick swinging its arms. On the ground, men were grappling a ninety-foot length of pipe, while strapped into a harness stories above on a small platform, the derrick man guided the rope that would lower it into place. Her father left her with an engineer and began climbing a ladder nailed onto the side. There was a higher one. He climbed that too until he stood beside the derrick man. They talked a moment. Her father wasn't tied into a harness like the other man. He just stood there.

To Brilli it was magic. The men were blackened trolls, changelings out of the earth. The lofty rig, a fairy-tale tower. While at night with electric lights strung on the structure it resembled a Christmas tree.

"Some of these men," her father told her, "are third generation, like me. You now, you'll be the fourth generation coming along."

He tried to make it a story so she would understand. "You know what energy is? It's what lets you do things, hop, skip, run, jump. Well, all the energy in the world comes from the sun. Plants store what the sun gives

142

them, animals eat it, and we eat the animals and in that way come by their energy.

"At first men used their own muscles, then draft animals, then winds and streams, and finally coal was burned. The burning released energy. We used it to power ships and machines.

"But this is a new age. It began with Great-grandpa Angstrom and oil. Oil does the work now. It makes things run. The whole world depends on it." He recited all the ways he could think of in which it was used. She nodded her six-year-old head.

Her father showed her the spot where they were about to spud a well, he took her to one that was bailing, and past the score drilling. She watched the boss carpenter himself cut mortise joints in the sills, drill through them and set them with bolts. She watched the welders at work, the tool pushers, mechanics and superintendents. The engineer conferred with her father, unrolling a blueprint.

When things went wrong her father's voice took on a new timbre. The men jumped then. A tool lost down the hole, a botched cement job with water seepage that could ruin the whole lease, and he pitched in, grabbed a hard hat, working alongside the crew. She understood what was going on. The oil was trapped in layers of rock, against which gas pushed. Gas could cause the well to blow, and a water-tight channel had to be made for it to flow up. That's what they were doing, setting the block of cement at the bottom, weighing the mud, making every crevice solid, tight. It had to be filled inside and outside the casing.

Someone yelled. There was a rupture in the pipe. They pulled up four joints at a time until the leak was found. Her father reached in with a device called an overshot, which looked to her like ice tongs. He jiggled this about until it caught on the drill stem. Then up it all came, the broken piece was unscrewed and replaced by a sound one.

Work started again. Her father returned to her completely blackened. It was more than grime, a shiny black mask was smeared over his face, distorting his features, making his eyes a popping white expanse and the inside of his mouth cavernous red.

She screamed.

It was the only time he ever struck her. "That's what I am, Brilli, *OIL*. And don't you forget it."

The Dammam Dome in Dhahran was the sure shot that failed. It was an imperious rock cap forming an anticline resembling the roof of a house. The search for oil was still a search for anticlines.

Ted convinced his partners. Dammam IV was drilled, followed the next year by Dammam V and VI. They stayed dry.

To add to his frustration, there was a tug of war over Brilli. Until now she had attended public school. Brillianna felt boarding school was more appropriate. Ted was baffled. What was wrong with public school? He had a business appointment in Dallas. When he returned Brilli was gone, enrolled in Melbourn.

He missed the noise of a child around the place. Brilli being an aeroplane, Brilli playing jacks, Brilli splashing in the pool, hitting wrong chords on the piano, laughing up and down the walks. Besides all this, their forays to Long Beach were effectively terminated.

"She needs the companionship of other children," Brillianna said with no qualms, looking brightly at him.

Well, perhaps a woman knew better how to raise a girl. He supposed, after all, oil fields were no place for Brilli. The old dream crumpled. He didn't need it. He followed the progress on the Dome of Jabal.

It was a fair weekend with the wind off the sea. Brillianna was in San Francisco. She wanted to see the gold swatch against the undelivered orange and tan divan she had selected for the library. Ted was devising a system of shadow bookkeeping. The stated costs to be consulted for tax purposes, and something called Real Costs, so he would know where he stood.

Tax credits for royalties received abroad had been pushed through Congress, thanks mainly to the Speaker of the House, who was from a swing state. Then there was the representative from Louisiana, whose family subsisted on oil royalties; he simply turned his back if the discussion failed to toe the line on oil depletion allowance. The stage was set. They simply had to go deeper in Saudi.

Ted's attention was distracted by a trespasser on the beach. The front of the estate was protected by a scrolled iron gate and fencing. But there was a state law that limited ocean-front property to the mean high-tide line. This meant that the beach in front of your house didn't belong to you and anybody could walk through one of the vacant lots farther up and simply make their way across the sand. You pay a quarter of a million dollars for a place, Ted reflected, and you don't even own it. Of course if an interloper came up past the high tide mark you could call the cops. He decided to mosey onto the terrace. At the sight of him the beachcomber would probably scurry off. He opened the double doors and strolled out. In the pleasure of his first deeply drawn breath he forgot the trespasser.

The sea was a surface reflecting the sun's light. He moved to the edge of the low stone wall for an unobstructed view. There was that person, almost directly below, loitering, as he could see now.

It was a girl. She seemed to be examining the tide pool by the cluster of rocks. What should he do? Call to her? Motion her off? That might seem churlish. He elected instead to amble down the path to the beach. It was a broad swath cut into the cliff with landings at suitable intervals. Sections of it were built into stairs whose risers were massive railroad ties.

The young woman looked up. She must have seen him, but she returned to her study of the pool. She was wearing pants rolled to the knee and she ventured into the water. This was not the behavior he anticipated. A trespasser of any sensibility, on seeing the owner approach, would move on. This young person dug in, so to speak. Entrenched herself by wading into the pool.

Seen and ignored, Ted had no intention of beating a retreat. It was his place, damn it. He approached the tide pool carelessly, as though it was whim alone which

145

caused him to meander in this direction rather than another.

The young woman was not fooled. "I suppose you've come to throw me out?"

Her face was surprising, dominated by dark eyes that followed the line of her cheekbones, which gave them something of a slant. He saw now that she was very young, a student was his guess. "Of course not," he protested. "Why should I want to do that?"

A strand of dark hair blew across her face, she brushed it away and motioned toward the house reposing regally on the bluff. "When you own *that*, I suppose you don't like miscellaneous people coming by."

Ted smiled slightly. "Are you a miscellaneous person?"

"I'm Sara Rosenfeld."

She's Jewish, Ted thought. Although he wasn't sure exactly what was entailed by the observation. "How did you get here?"

"Walking. There's been no one on the beach all morning except some skimmers feeding."

"And why are you poking around in this particular pool?"

"It isn't only this one. I've been investigating every one I pass. There's a whole microcosm in every small trapped puddle. Diatoms and bacteria floating here by the million."

"You're a science major?"

". . . and other things." She smiled at him in an unfriendly way. "I'm someone concerned with what's happening in Spain. And I don't like the Peel Commission Report that wants to partition Palestine, or the Japanese taking over China. So I walk on the beach and say to myself, that green sponge doesn't worry about such things. The tube worm never heard of Spain. I remind myself there are worlds coexisting with ours which have no knowledge of us or our problems." Miss Rosenfeld gave him the same smile, even less friendly than before. "There are even *people* like the tube worm and the mollusk."

"And you think people who own houses along this beach are in that category?"

146

"Yes."

"That's rather cliché thinking for a student," Ted reproved. "Because I own a house in Carmel, you jump to the conclusion I have the social conscience of a mollusk."

"That isn't just a house," the girl said. "It's a Versailles."

"And you convict me on it?"

She hesitated, troubled for the first time, "Not necessarily."

"How do you know that I, too, have not been giving the Peel Report a good deal of thought?" He saw her eyes were not black, as he at first believed, but a dark blue, with spokes that carried a deeper color from the rims. It was quite extraordinary to see them lighten as her expression changed.

"You've studied the Peel Report?"

"Yes, I'm quite in accord with it. I think partition will bring stability to the area."

"Stability?" Her eyes gathered blackness and storm.

"Of course. You give the Arabs a section of Palestine, namely Transjordan, and they're satisfied. Give the Jews the coastal strip and they're satisfied."

"Are they? With an area insufficient for immigration and impossible to defend? As for the Arabs, those who are given Transjordan may be satisfied, but what about the others?"

"Come up on the terrace," he said. "I'll give you some lemonade for the walk back and we can argue it."

"No. Why should I play games? I am a Jew and it matters to me."

"Are you also Spanish?"

"No."

"Well you said the uprising against Franco mattered to you too."

"You're right," she said with decision. "We are two human beings. We should be able to talk. I would like lemonade. I was thinking awhile back about going up to one of those great homes, knocking on the door and asking for a glass of water. But I thought before I ever got that far someone would run me off or apprehend me. And they say there's no class system in America."

They started toward the path.

"So you're a student?"

"No. I am Sara Rosenfeld, who is currently studying."

"I understand the distinction you make. But again we seem to have opposite views. I slapped my daughter's face once because she couldn't see that I *was* what I did."

"You actually slapped her?"

"Yes. I don't know why I told you. I'm ashamed of doing such a thing. As a matter of fact it's bothered me ever since."

"You were indignant because she didn't see you as you want to be seen?"

"That's it."

"There is no one way I want to be seen. I want to live a dozen lives, all totally different."

"That's because you're very young."

"I'm nineteen."

"Very young," he repeated. They were winding their way up the path. He elicited more information. She was a junior at Berkeley, majoring in biology with a love of art and poetry.

She turned for a view of sea from the vantage point of height. "What is it like," she asked, "to always have the best of everything? The best view? The best house? And all the other *bests* you must have?"

"It's nice," Ted admitted.

"I suspect," Sara went on, "to react to an ocean with enjoyment is to respond to a primordial mystery in a superficial way. That's another world out there, sustaining billions of organisms."

"But you do feel pleasure in it?" Ted challenged her.

"I do, yes. But I think it's irrational."

"That's the trouble with an education," Ted said. "You learn too damn much."

"Too much? Can you learn too much?"

"I think you can, if it interferes with your enjoyment."

"Enjoyment is a hedonistic value. It exists for rich people more than it should."

Ted laughed, breathing in sea air and expelling it. He liked sparring with her. "I can call names too."

148

"Oh? What names?"

"I could say you are full of prejudice and intolerance." She swung to confront him, but swallowed her denials and laughed just as he had done a moment before. "You're right, of course. You're absolutely right."

"Now that we have insulted each other, let me introduce myself. I'm Theodore Angstrom." Why did he say Theodore? To put the proper distance between them? To emphasize his status? Why in the world hadn't he said Ted? Perhaps unconsciously he wished to point up the age difference. She was nineteen. He, pushing forty. Was he telling himself something? He found her lean-hipped, boyish body attractive, and began to speculate. She was uninhibited on a verbal level. Was she free and easy sexually? He didn't think she had a bra on under her shirt. He didn't know much about young girls these days. Being a coed made her seem independent, but it was possible she was a virgin.

He could see she was bright. In a woman, he considered that a fault. However Jews were bright. There was a Jewish boy in his class at Princeton, very bright. Ted hadn't tried to know him, he seemed arrogant, aloof, preferring his own company. This girl had something of that quality. She thought well of herself. And was not the least abashed by the sight of the swimming pool, the dressing rooms, and bricked patio that led to the opulent three-story home.

Ted seated her at a table and rang. Tomas appeared almost immediately. "It doesn't have to be lemonade," he said to his guest. He no longer thought of her as an interloper.

"Lemonade will be fine."

"A beer for me, Tomas."

"I'm Sara Rosenfeld," she said, introducing herself to the servant.

"Yes, miss," Tomas replied.

Ted watched this interplay with an amused expression.

"He's a person, isn't he?" Sara caught the look and fired up. "Existing in the same time slice as myself."

149

"I don't think I'll send my daughter to U. C. Berkeley."

"Why not?"

"I don't think I could take it."

"I think your daughter will go to Bryn Mawr or Vassar. How old is she?"

"Seven."

"Well, you don't have to worry about her turning out like me for awhile. Anyway," she looked at him with frank interest, "you are the one who is behaving unconventionally. You are the Lord of the Manor," she gestured at the far flung property, "and you invite a trespasser to have a lemonade on your premises and talk."

"You think that's unconventional?"

"For someone like yourself, yes."

"Why do you say that? Do you think you know me?"

"Well, you have to be a certain type person to have all this."

"What type?"

She remained mute.

"No, I'm serious. What type?"

"You have to be brought up to believe any American boy can be president. That means you believe in the work ethic. Work hard enough and it's yours. But is that really the way of it? I suspect your family had money, position. That's for starters. Next came the right schools. And the right marriage. Those are perhaps the externals. I recognize you have to have a lot more than that. Things like drive, ambition, single-mindedness. Perhaps—I'm only guessing—ruthlessness, or disregard of people if they're in the way, or don't fit in."

Ted laughed. "I'll give you an A for courage if not accuracy. It seems odd to me a person as sturdily independent as yourself should make me out a *Daily Worker* caricature. The truth is that in '29 when everyone was mired in an uncomfortable present, I was involved in the future, planning for it, working for it. I had some of the things going for me you suggest. But mainly, I saw what other people didn't."

"You're saying imagination brought you all this? That's odd. My grandfather was a poet. But his imagination didn't bring him even a living. He had to sell boot-leg coal. When I was a small child I was bathed in a round copper pot because the bathtub was where the coal was kept. It was stolen. Our whole family was employed in stealing coal. So what I'm saying is, imagination didn't do a thing for us. I wonder, was it because my parents were immigrants, spoke with an accent, and had no capital to invest, that you are the host on this very sparkling day and I the intruder?"

Tomas came with the drinks on a tray. "Thank you," Sara smiled more brightly on him than she had done on Ted. But when he withdrew, she turned to continue her thought. "I don't believe your version. I don't think you are an imaginative person. Are you, for instance, contributing to the International Brigade?"

"Is that some sort of criterion? To me it's leftist politics."

She nodded as though his reaction was the one she expected. "I think you're a kind person. You knew I had a long walk and a long walk back. You gave me a lemonade. That's nice of you. I think if you hit a dog on the highway you'd get out and do something about it. Yet you know people are being destroyed for resisting tyranny, and it doesn't touch you at all. You are completely insulated. If you were more imaginative, you would feel something, empathy, compassion."

"If I had your orientation, your particular bias. Life has more facets than you seem aware of, my girl."

"Sara Rosenfeld," she corrected him.

"Sara Rosenfeld," he said, inclining his head, making a gesture toward her. "Perhaps I do have a social conscience. There is more than one way of demonstrating it. You, apparently, think in terms of political action. I am concerned with power. Not personal power, you understand. I'm speaking of the raw power in the earth that will decide how populations live. Getting the power to service the world will have more impact ten years from now on the people in Spain than the outcome of the present conflict."

She was puzzled. "Power? Do you mean coal?"

"Oil."

151

She sat back in her chair as though the riddle of the man in front of her was read. "You're an oilman?"

"I don't like the way you say that."

"But oil explains all this. And also some of the attitudes you hold about yourself. Does your oil come from the Argentine?"

"There are large commercial fields there. But I'm exploring in Saudi Arabia."

"Arabia?" she exclaimed. "That's all we Jews need. Surely God couldn't have loaded the dice that much? He couldn't have given the Arabs oil. It would be too unfair."

"How do you sleep at night," he inquired, "worrying about all these remote corners of the world?"

She was preoccupied and answered with a question of her own. "Do you really think there are significant amounts of oil in Arabia?"

"Iran, Iraq have been producing for some time. Now, hopefully, there's Bahrein, Oman, Abu Dhabi and Saudi."

"It's David and Goliath again. In population, in territory, and now oil. Oil means money and in that part of the world, money means guns." She looked huddled and disconsolate.

"Have you family there?"

"I do, yes. My brother Dov and his son. But I'd feel this way whether my brother was there or not," she said, "because I'm a Jew."

He smiled. "We had this conversation on the beach. I asked if you were also Spanish."

"And I said I was a human being."

"Implying at the same time that, in your sense of the word, I am not."

"I hope you're not offended. You've been very nice. And I'm sure by most standards you are a fine person."

"But not by yours?"

"Why should you worry about that? I'm nobody important. What I think doesn't matter. There." She set her glass down on the table. "That was refreshing. I enjoyed sitting up here on top of the world and being very elegant."

"I enjoyed it too," Ted said. "The whole experience. You are something of an experience, Sara Rosenfeld. Talking to you is a bit like the bull sessions we used to have in college."

"Yes. I punish myself thinking that. I do nothing concrete. I talk. As you say, a bull session. Well," she stood, "thanks again." A small mocking smile involved a muscle at the corner of her mouth. "I can find my way out." She ran down the steps, a slight figure in rolled up pants, splashed and damp, bare feet and a boy's shirt knotted carelessly around her middle.

Ted reached out a hand to delay or stop her. Might as well attempt to corral a nimble drop of silver mercury, it eluded all grasps. Sara Rosenfeld was gone.

For the next few days Ted did a great deal of his work on the terrace, glancing up from compilations of paper and reports, letting the sea soothe his mind. He was coordinating data on Dammam VI, which was beginning to give more hopeful signs. But his mind jumped from the waterless sands of Saudi to the coastal sands below him. He found himself peering in the direction from which Sara Rosenfeld had come.

It didn't seem remarkable to him that he discussed the Spanish Civil War, Palestine, oil, his own attitudes, and sea life with a young woman trespassing on his property. Perhaps Sara Rosenfeld was not unusual at all, but simply representative of the generation which had grown up since he had been in college. It seemed to him that she was someone of deep innocence, who did not know the proper, distant kind of conversation employed between strangers. *Ingenuous.* That was the word he was searching for, the word which described her. He kept looking up from his work, half expecting her to appear again. She did not.

He supposed while she seemed spontaneous and original to him, he must have struck her as stodgy, conservative and middle-aged. The contributions he made to their discussion were of a routine sort. She would not have found him interesting. He had given her a look at wealth and she had not been impressed. So why should she walk along the beach again?

Ted picked up the engineering maps of a proposed road from Dhahran to the seaports of al Khobar and Ras Tanura. But he could not concentrate. He felt as he had on a short excursion from Jidda into the desert. His sense of direction was befuddled. It was impossible to tell if the horizon was five miles away or on top of him. It was the same now. He didn't know where his mental horizon was. He had the same feeling of unease experienced then, at the lack of demarcation. The only substantial landmark was age. He was thirty-eight, exactly twice her age.

He was still a youngster, something of a prodigy in the oil business. Head of his own company. When Dammam VI came in, he would be an *immortal*, so designated by Stephen Field, in a Supreme Court decision which gave to corporations the rights that the Fifth and Fourteenth Amendments had intended for private citizens. A company or corporate conglomerate, under this ruling, enjoyed the prerogatives of an immortal person whose assets and holdings would go on in perpetuity, increasing, growing, multiplying.

He was a young man to have reached the point he had. He was aware of the qualifier: *to have reached his present position. Young* he no longer was.

Sara Rosenfeld was young. He saw himself with her eyes. Time had touched him with fifteen pounds on his frame, with gray in his sideburns. But more than that, he had scarcely looked up. He knew about the backlash over sending scrap metal to Japan. He was familiar with the causes of the Spanish Civil War. But these various crises were so much print, another story to peruse with orange juice, coffee, and toasted muffins. He had no opinions or attitudes regarding them.

Ted wondered how much of the world had passed by while his nose was to the ground sniffing out oil like a goddamned bloodhound. In retrospect the meeting with the girl irritated and annoyed him. In an exchange of ideas, he had come off badly. Why had he told her, an absolute stranger, that he had slapped his

154

daughter? That was hardly calculated to put him in a good light.

On the other hand, that was the whole point, an attempt was made to say who and what they were. She said she was not a student, but studying. He said, as he had to Brilli, *I am oil.*

Was that as sad a statement as she seemed to think? Delineating? Narrowing? He was a specialist, with the nerve to back his insight. But that didn't prevent life rushing by. Another generation had grown up, were in college, already at work questioning his values. That seemed the principal business of the young, questioning the premises on which you erected your life and finding them creaking, obsolete, outmoded, and inadequate.

They didn't give credit either, these kids, for what it had taken out of you along the way. They just looked at you from opaque dark eyes and made offhand judgments. Who the hell was Sara Rosenfeld to disturb his tranquillity? A street-smart radical. Book-smart too. Probably most of what she said came out of books. Books. . . . Berkeley. Sara would have returned to Berkeley. That's why she hadn't marched up the beach again. A tremendous joy burst his skin and he emerged more himself than he had been.

Decisions on the Saudi operation had piled up, he tackled them with vigor. He okayed a landing strip. At the moment survey planes were setting down in gravel flats. It would mean a sizable bank loan but it was important to be ready. When oil gushed was no time to start paving airfields or wondering where to lay the pipelines. He decided to run the pipe to al Khobar, where barges could move the crude for refining at the Bahrein facility. He studied the map again. It seemed to him Ras Tanura made an excellent terminal site. Within fifteen minutes he finished his work and took the path to the beach and the tide pool below.

At the bottom he removed his shoes and socks and rolled up his pants. The hot granules shifting place under his weight felt good. Sensations long forgotten, woke. A montage of childhood memories stirred: a fort with shell doors and apertures washed by an encroaching sea, drip castles of wet sand dropping from

155

between his fingers, a run and a long jump landing with heels dug in.

Gulls that had flown at his approach, circled and landed. He stared into the pool. A light green sea lettuce floated, spreading its leaves. Anemones with shells and bits of stone adhering, fastened their disks against the rock. A hermit crab scuttled under its plundered dome. Patches of waving moss and barnacles grew in clumps.

He felt that Sara Rosenfeld saw a great deal more. The longer he stared the more creatures were revealed. He thought he might pick up a book to learn their names. He was sure she knew them. That was the advantage of being in school. But so much didn't stick. By the time you were his age. . . .

He studied the tracery of tube mollusks on the rock. When he finally heard Brillianna's voice, he realized she had called his name repeatedly. She was standing on the terrace, waving, but the wind carried the words away. She turned in the direction of the beach path. Ted didn't want her to come down and stand where he was standing. To forestall this he bounded up the path, meeting her halfway.

"What in the world were you doing?" she asked.

Looking into myself and finding a dormant, stagnating Ted Angstrom, was the reply that came to mind. But since one didn't say things like this to Brillianna, he modified his thoughts suitably. "Nothing. I just took a break." And then he forged ahead, implementing a decision he didn't know he had made. "I noticed in looking over my contracts this morning that I don't have everything I need. Some papers are still at the office. I thought I'd go in and pick them up."

"Mind if I ride along?"

He did mind. But he could think of no good reason to put her off.

Brillianna sensed his hesitation. "I won't be in the way. You can drop me at the house. I want to check over the garden, see whether Iggi got the double petunias in."

"Sure," he said. She seemed so pleased, he felt guilty. She returned to the house for a sweater, meet-

156

ing him on the circular drive. On impulse and by way of recompense he invited her to the theatre. "You'll be by a phone, so get tickets for this evening. Anything you want to see. We'll make a night of it. Dinner and a show, how's that?"

"Marvelous. I'd love it."

"I've been so involved, I let too many things I'd really enjoy doing go by the board."

"I envy you," she said, "being wrapped up in your commitments. Nothing seems that important to me. Oh, there's you and Brilli, of course. But Brilli's at school and you're so busy. It seems I ought to be more independent."

"I should think with two households to run and keeping our social calendar straight, you'd be busy enough."

"Why should that be enough for me? It's not enough for you."

"Other women . . ." he began.

"What do I care about other women? Let them take lovers or devote themselves to needlepoint. I want to do something that counts. What would you think of my collecting?"

"Collecting?" He didn't understand exactly what she meant.

"Yes, collecting. If you're astute, you can do quite well at it. And I have a good background in art history. My father was interested in Chinese art and had a special fondness for T'ang horses, if you remember."

"Hmmm," Ted said. He had never admired his father-in-law. "It sounds expensive."

"Oh, it is. And prestigious for the wife of an oil millionaire."

"Yes . . . well, hold off a bit. You know Dammam VI is down three thousand feet and we've struck out."

"But you were so certain. And you've never been wrong about oil."

"I don't know," he said, "it's the third winter." Seeing her worried expression, he relented. "Go ahead, buy your pictures or whatever. It's a business, right? There will be a sizable tax write-off."

"I'm not ready yet. I thought I'd decide on a period.

157

I'm doing some reading on the post-impressionists. They called them Les Fauves, which translates something like raging beasts rampaging through canvases."

Ted nodded. He didn't know anything about art. But he was inclined to be tolerant of anything that kept his wife occupied. He dropped her and instead of proceeding to the resplendent new company quarters in San Francisco, drove to the university campus and went directly to the registrar's office, where he looked up *Rosenfeld, Sara* in the directory of students. The address was within walking distance so he left the car parked and proceeded on foot. The place he was looking for proved to be a turreted old mansion cut up as a rooming house.

The doorbell didn't work, but he heard voices inside. After standing some seconds he pushed the door open. The room was full of sprawled young people of both sexes, reading and eating. One young man was doing a scale drawing on the floor. Several people looked up but no one acknowledged his presence in a formal way or inquired what he wanted.

"I wonder if you could tell me—" he said to a young woman chewing an apple, and then stopped waiting for her to look in his direction.

"You want something?" she asked with her mouth full.

He suddenly felt what kids they were, nothing but kids. If Sara were here, she'd be one of them, another kid. He had an impulse to turn and walk out, but he was embarked on it now and felt obligated to continue. "I'm looking for a Miss Sara Rosenfeld."

The eyes flicked over him for the first time. "You won't get her in. She's at work."

"Would you mind telling me where she works?"

"You a friend of hers? I mean, it's funny a friend of hers wouldn't know that."

"For Christsakes," another girl cut in, "why make such a big deal of it? You think he's FBI, or what? She works at the cafeteria."

"Thanks," Ted said. It was a relief to get out of the place. He knew if he stopped to think about it, he'd go back to the car and pick up Brillianna.

·He continued walking. The cafeteria was a place to avoid, as the sound level bordered on audiomania. When he opened the door several stray dogs entered with him. He glanced around but didn't spot her.

The least conspicuous thing to do was to grab a metal tray and get in line. He picked out a sandwich and a cup of coffee and maneuvered toward a table against the wall from which he'd have a good view of the room.

He ate his sandwich without tasting it, dividing the room into quadrants: a pair of chess players, but mostly solitary students gulping food, chewing absently with open books propped in front of them. There were several gregarious tables at which friends met by pre-arrangement, and a few couples.

"Why Mr. Angstrom, what in the world are you doing here?"

Somehow while he looked for her, she had walked up to him. Of course he was subconsciously peering about for an elfin figure in rolled up slacks, while the bus girl at his table was completely swathed in a white apron meant for someone of more ample proportions. "I was looking for you."

"Looking for me? Why? Are you going to serve me with a subpoena for having trespassed on your world?"

"Don't be hostile, Sara Rosenfeld."

"You remembered my name."

"And everything about you. Can we talk somewhere?"

"What about?"

"Tide pools," he said and immediately felt he had made himself ridiculous.

She picked up his plate and empty coffee cup and placed them on her tray. "I don't understand," she said.

"I can't explain. At least not here."

"Try."

"It's something I realized, that we'd been able to talk. I saw I'd been cut off from that kind of thing. Look, it's impossible here. When are you finished? Can I wait for you?"

"I'm almost through. I'll meet you out front in ten

minutes. Okay?" Without waiting for his reply she moved to another table and began clearing. Her movements were swift and deft. She knew the people at the next table, three young men. She stood there a moment talking and laughing. It was a natural thing to pause and laugh with friends, why did it sour his stomach to watch it? Abruptly, he got up, tilting the table as he did so. Outside he paced around, keeping the cafeteria in view. It was a day in March. A warm wind gusted, sweeping clouds before it, leaving great tracts of blue sky.

She had been surprised to see him. He was the last person she expected to see. But now she had seen him, what was she thinking? He told her he wanted to talk. But he hadn't thought what to talk about. He didn't know what he would say when she appeared. In fact if he had any sense at all he wouldn't be here when she walked through that door.

At the same time he knew it would take a major force to remove him. Why? Why had this overly intense girl become the main source of his speculations? When he saw or reacted to something, he asked himself how Sara Rosenfeld would see and respond to it. No person had ever held that kind of place in his thinking. He accorded her almost as much time and thought as Dammam VI.

Divested of the apron, she was coming toward him, dressed neatly in a navy serge skirt and tuck-in white blouse. He suspected it was the same blouse she had worn on the beach. He made the guess that it was the only one she owned.

For the first time she seemed ill at ease. He was so anxious to change this that he forgot he had nothing to say to her. "I had some business on campus."

She looked surprised.

"Yes, at the engineering library, and I remembered that you were not a student," he smiled at her, "but studying here. I also remembered I hadn't talked like that with anyone in years, where you open up and say things on your mind or what comes into your head. I got to wondering about you. What kind of person you are."

They were walking along campus paths randomly. "And you found I don't spend twenty-four hours a day staring into tide pools. That I am one of six hundred thousand people that the NYA is helping to work their way through college. I'm afraid on the beach the other day I tried to make myself out some fascinating kind of person. I wanted to impress you because you had all that. I didn't want you to think that someone just passing by, like me, might not be interesting too. I'm afraid, Mr. Angstrom, I consciously tried to say unexpected and arresting things. Sara Rosenfeld cocks her head: 'The Archbishop Ussher in his book *Annales Veteris et Nova* states the world was created precisely at eight p.m. Saturday, October 22, 4004 B.C.' The wealthy and important Mr. Angstrom is properly amazed at this erudition from a nobody, a trespasser. What I am saying is—" she looked at him as though trying to assess how he was taking this—"is that it was a pose. I'm not like that. I'm an ordinary person trying to decide what life to live. And resentful that I have to choose. Because the minute you do, you lock yourself away from ninety-nine percent of it."

"What are your options?" Ted asked.

"Oh, I suppose nursing. That's a good career for a girl who has to make her own living. I'm pretty easily appalled though, if things go wrong with people. One thing I know," she smiled ruefully, "I'm not going to be a waitress. I thought of librarian. I'd like that. But there don't seem to be positions open. Same goes for teaching. Besides a teacher's career is over if she marries."

"Are you thinking of getting married?" He attempted to make the question casual, but like a child was holding his breath.

"No. I don't think so. But I don't want anyone dictating to me, especially not a school system."

"Well, you have another year before you have to make up your mind."

"You remember that?" She shot him a rather odd look. "You remembered I am a junior."

"I told you, I remember everything."

They stopped walking.

161

"That's odd, isn't it?" she asked.

"I don't know."

"I mean, it's odd because, so do I."

He put his hands in his pockets so as not to wrap them around her. "Can I get you a cup of coffee someplace, not the cafeteria?"

"Let's walk some more. I want to know about you too. Were you always sure what you were going to do? Or did you ask yourself, why lead one life rather than another? Why this rather than that?"

"I always knew. I was born into an oil family. My grandfather was with Drake in the old days. When I was a kid my dad used to take me into the fields. But I suppose one of the reasons oil can be exciting, it doesn't box you in. There are so many phases. Exploration, getting into the field. Then there's the business end, marketing, selling. Or transport, distributing, and a totally new field is opening, developing oil products, creating a demand."

"But none of it has much to do with people, has it?"

"It has everything to do with people. As I told you when you were having your lemonade, oil is going to determine the quality of human life."

"You sound so pious when you say that. But you've skimmed the top off for yourself. Don't you feel guilty up there in your seventeenth century castle, when a third of the schoolchildren in the country don't have one hot meal a day?"

"That reminds me of my mother saying, 'Eat your breakfast, the poor in China are starving.' That never made good sense to me, not even then. It makes less now I understand something of how supply and demand work."

"You needn't lecture me." Almost instantly she took his hand in a gesture of contrition. "I'm sorry," she said, and as quickly dropped it.

He was glad touching him made her self-conscious. "That's all right."

"What I'd really like to be is a kind of Pierrette, a gay-sad clown dancing through life, tapping people on the shoulder, waking them from their dull, plodding lives, telling them to have courage."

"You think that's what people principally lack? The courage they need for their lives?"

"Don't you?"

He didn't answer but remained thoughtful, sunk in himself.

"Another function of the clown is to question and tease those who are certain and righteous, until they question too."

"I think you make a good gadfly. I think you have been successful."

"With you? I didn't mean you."

"Maybe not. But until you stuck a toe in my tide pool I hadn't realized my life was becoming more and more shut away from people, what they believe and do and think. Everything raced by and I didn't know it. I wasn't aware of it. Not until I met you." He reached for her hand and put it deliberately between his. She did not withdraw it. He felt he held a wild bird. "Sara."

"Yes?" She looked straight into his eyes.

"I don't want to lose you."

The hand panicked, worked its way out of his. She began walking fast, back the way they had come. Ted overtook her. "Sara, don't just walk away."

She shook her head, her hair bounced across her face into her eyes. She walked faster. She began to run, but erratically, almost colliding with other pedestrians. He felt it utterly wrong, inconceivable even, that she was running from him.

Sara's flight had in some manner stripped him of himself. He was on the outside looking at an ego recently vacated by Ted Angstrom. Some moments passed before he recalled that he was midway through a day in which his participation was a foregone conclusion. He had a wife to pick up. He had invited her to dinner and a show. Afterward they would drive back to Carmel. A busy schedule for someone to whom schedules were a framework to hold up a nonperson.

Is that what Sara had run from, the emptiness that showed through? "You're quiet tonight," Brillianna said, touching her wine glass to his and smiling across the flickering candle-lit space between them. She was lovely. It hurt him that she had taken extra care with her makeup, her hair, because it didn't matter. It would never matter to him again.

She had spent the afternoon at Madame Duchamp. In spite of the French name, she explained, the entire staff were Hungarians, specialists trained in the art of the facial in Vienna. She had been rubbed and massaged into a youthful glow, steamed with preparations of herbs. Blends of creams brought the texture of youth. "It is so utterly a feminine sanctum," Brillianna said, "deep pile rugs, mirrored walls, the hush of modulated female voices speaking French. But if anything is dropped or misplaced there's a sudden babble in excited Hungarian. You are reclined in a chair and covered with a flowered chintz which matches the drapes. Your hair is bound back, cotton placed over your eyes and the girl starts kneading your shoulders. You give yourself over to pure sensation and complete relaxation. I almost fell asleep."

He followed part of this, enough to nod in the right places. He had gone too fast, been too outspoken in his approach. Perhaps he disgusted her? He remembered the boys in the cafeteria, boys her own age with whom she stopped to laugh and joke. Perhaps she was in love with one of them, involved with one of them? It seemed to him incredible he hadn't bothered to ask, but taken for granted her life had been lived to this time in hiatus waiting for him. How egocentric, how ludicrous he must seem. It would never have worked. He closing in on forty, she nineteen.

"A gold and white striped paper," Brillianna was saying. "I knew the minute I saw it that it was perfect. Do you realize it has been twelve years since we built Armagh? And do you know what Armagh II has over Armagh I—the bathroom! The view from the john is the best in the house. That's why it's so much fun redecorating it. Do you like a gold and white motif?"

"It sounds nice."

"You'll love it," she said, sparkling like the wine.

It was no use. Ted was thinking of the way Sara's hair covered her face and the uncoordinated way she had run from him.

The flush in Brillianna's cheeks was becoming. She leaned across the table, traced the veins of his hand with her fingertips. "Do you know what I was thinking this afternoon? It made me laugh out loud. Do you remember that shirt I bought you for Valentine's Day?" He had heard the story before, which was fortunate. It allowed him to analyze his interview with Sara and still maintain the proper look of amusement. "I got it in one of those little boutiques. I didn't have my glasses and I thought the design was a series of hearts, which was somewhat wild, I admit. But I decided it would be attractive for the beach. And when you tried it on, you couldn't believe it. . . ." She was laughing, tripping over her words. He joined in. "Apparently it was one of those shops that cater to, well you know, *that* clientele. And the shirt was actually pornographic. What I thought were hearts and flowers actually were bare buttocks disappearing into shrubbery. And since it was an overall pattern, the scene recurred about a hundred times."

Ted laughed again. It sounded forced and discordant to him. He couldn't find the hole in the fence. He wanted to, but he couldn't. There was no way back to his old life.

Ted counted the days. He had to give Sara time. That had been the trouble, going too fast. So he held off. It was agony to wait. What he had blurted out was quite true, he couldn't lose her. And yet asking himself the logical next question, how could she fit into his life . . . he had to admit he didn't know.

He was thrown completely off stride. Nothing got done while he remembered how her eyes changed shape when she laughed or the feel of her hand in his. When he was with her he was alert and excited as though embarked on some sort of adventure. He had to see her. But it was impossible to go to that rooming house again and face those kids. Behind their indifference he was sure they were laughing at him.

Did he appear ridiculous to Sara? No, he was sure

165

of that. Sara never felt or thought in any standard mold.

While he would not go to the rooming house, he spent hours cruising and walking the streets around it. Sooner or later he would see her.

He never thought past that. Would a glimpse be enough? Was it enough to keep tabs on her, know she was alive and well and in the same world with him? He knew the answer was no. He wanted more than her hand in his. He wanted her with a hard-on need. He pictured her submitting, and provoking him again. He remembered the shape of the white blouse. Her breasts must be wide as well as full. He wanted to lay his head there, wanted her nipples hard and firm, and her mouth seeking his. She would be an active lover, he knew it. He could tell. She wouldn't lie on her back and wait. There was a time when Brillianna . . . there was nothing there for him anymore. She was a dry well.

But Sara would be a runaway, uncapped. Sara was the woman he wanted to know him. He would dazzle her with stories of Arabia, of Jidda the grandmother city, of the women whose veils he had lifted. And casually during the course of the conversation, mention that his partner was a king. Sara didn't really know him at all.

A paralyzing thought occurred to him. He might not recognize her. He was keeping a strict lookout, but it was entirely possible he might not recognize her face.

His panic subsided. He had come to know her better in a matter of minutes than Brillianna with whom he had spent fourteen years of his life.

When he saw her coming out of a small grocery it was a continuation of the scenes going on in his head. Only he had not imagined the packages.

He parked and crossed the street. "Here," he said, "let me help you with those."

The eyes had been caught unaware, the eyes were glad to see him. But she snuffed their greeting. "I can manage, thanks."

"Might as well give me something to carry, I'm going in the same direction."

"Okay." She handed him a bag with three grapefruit, and shifted the other parcels.

"How've you been?" he asked.

"Fine. How have you been?"

"Fine." This was not the dialogue which had proceeded in such scintillating fashion in his mind. "There's quite a few grapefruit here for one person."

"I'm on a grapefruit diet. That's all I eat."

"But is it good for you?"

"I don't know. I lost three pounds."

"You're not . . . I mean, I don't know why you want to lose weight. As a matter of fact, if you want to know, you look as though you could use building up?"

Sara smiled for the first time. He had been right about her eyes, they squeezed into an almost oriental slant.

They were approaching the rooming house, but she was headed for the back door, the kitchen door he supposed. That wouldn't be so bad. With any luck they wouldn't meet anyone. "I'll just help you in with these," he said when she turned on the porch to retrieve her sack. She walked in ahead of him holding the screen door with her foot so it didn't bang in his face. "Well, where do these go?"

"I thought I'd eat them now. Want one?"

He shook his head.

"If you leave anything lying around in this kitchen it disappears. You see, it's communal." She helped herself to a grapefruit and started peeling it. "Tonight is my night to cook. So what I do is just get the essentials, try to use everything up."

"Good idea."

"Tonight I'm making stew."

Ted looked through the scant packages, "I don't see the meat."

"A vegetable stew. It's cheaper."

He nodded.

"It's really very good. And healthy."

"But you're going to stick to the grapefruit?"

She nodded. "If you want to help, you could cut off the carrot tops. The knives are in with the silverware, second drawer to your left."

167

Among the hodgepodge he located a knife and began cleaving at the carrot greens.

Sara was rummaging below for a large pot, which she brought up triumphantly and filled full of water. "Odd our happening to meet like that."

"We didn't happen to meet."

"Now you can run some water into the sink and soak everything."

"There are dirty dishes in the sink," he objected.

"Take them out. We're certainly not going to wash them. Everyone is supposed to clean up after himself. What did you mean," she asked without a change of voice or expression, "when you said we didn't happen to meet?"

"If I tell you, you'll run away again. Or, since this is your place, shove me out the door."

"I see." Her look was disconcerting, direct.

Had she thought about him? Perhaps not in the same unceasing manner, but however glancingly, had some picture or memory of him crossed her mind?

"Could you. . . ?" he hesitated. She wouldn't help him, but continued watching with a calm expression as though she were removed in time.

A redheaded girl came in, looked at the counter and then at Sara. "I left a peanut butter sandwich right here. Then the phone rang."

"Have a grapefruit," Sara said.

"No thanks." She turned in a huff. "The call wasn't even for me."

The door slammed behind her. Sara shrugged.

"Is it always such a madhouse around here?"

"Usually."

"Look, Sara . . ." he dropped his voice in case someone should come in again. "Do you think we could be lovers?" He was horrified it had slipped out that way. No sophisticated dialogue, no King of Arabia.

Sara concentrated on the vegetables, removing them from the water and shaking them. She took the knife with which he had topped the carrots and began slicing parsnips, green pepper and onions. "I wonder what gives you the impression that you can walk in here and say that to me. But then of course, I suppose that's part of being Theodore Angstrom."

"Ted," he interrupted, "Ted, who loves you very humbly and very truly. You may not believe that, Sara. I didn't myself at first. But you're part of everything I do, everything I think. We've held all sorts of conversations. . . ."

"In which, no doubt I was far more agreeable than I am now." She turned on him. "In the first place, I don't believe your 'very humbly, very truly.' I grant you the words have a nice ring. But you don't know what they mean, not humbly anyway. You've never been humble in your life."

"I am now, waiting for you to answer me."

"And what kind of answer do you expect? For the man who has everything," she too whispered but with a held down quality as though the words might escape her control, "it would be a new experience, wouldn't it, a Jewish mistress." Her breath came quick. "Do you need that? Is your wife frigid? Or perhaps she doesn't understand you? The answer, Mr. Angstrom, is no."

He walked out, found he was worrying about that stupid grapefruit diet and came back to talk sense into her.

Sara was crying.

"Sara!"

"It's the onions. For God's sake will you go away!"

Ted obeyed. He went away and he stayed away. At the end of a week he raced back to the rooming house. The bell had not been fixed. It was still out of order. It probably had been for years. He pushed on the door and went in. It seemed to him the same students were there, lounging in the same positions. He picked someone at random to address and asked for Sara Rosenfeld.

"Sara? She doesn't live here anymore."

"What?"

"That's right. She moved out. She's getting married. Isn't that right, Sylvie?"

Sylvie was not interested enough to look up from her book. "Yeah, that's right."

"Married? But. . . ." He tried to hold himself together. James Cagney with a bullet in the gut. He had half a reel to lurch through before the end of the picture. Hands spread where the bullet penetrated to keep his insides in place. He walked out feeling he was playing a scene, that it wasn't happening. It couldn't be happening.

Sara Rosenfeld, who had poked a bare foot in the tide pool and discussed the world, who had sipped lemonade and regarded him with great serious eyes, was going to be married. His sinuses were blocked. Sinuses hell, he was crying. Out in the public street tears had come into his eyes.

"No," he said out loud, "no."

He walked to the cafeteria and sat scrutinizing every face. When he left he took the exact route he had taken with her. "Why are you doing this, Sara?" Several people and a dog looked at him. He came to the place where they had stopped, where she left him.

"Why?" This time the cry didn't leave the orifices of his head. On the way home he was in an accident. He sideswiped a car making a left-hand turn. The paint was scraped off both automobiles. The other driver was shaken but unhurt. Ted had a mild whiplash.

He acknowledged he was at fault, left identification, and went on. He didn't go directly to the house but down to the beach. He sat on the rocks, trying to ease the pain in his neck by rubbing it. Now his head was aching. He got up and took the path to the house. His mission was to find some aspirin. But no painkiller from the medicine cabinet could help the fact that Sara was getting married.

Ted lost the hardy instinct which made survival of his company preeminently essential. Correspondence with personnel in Saudi collected on his desk. He took long walks in which he tried to come to terms with his desire for this young girl. Was he already at that pathetic state where an infusion of youth was needed?

Perhaps it was not a question of Sara at all, but a matter of biology.

The business reports he waded through, instead of being a source of fascination, seemed interminable. He kept losing his place or, what was worse, reading entire paragraphs with complete noncomprehension. He knew Brillianna worried about him. She told him he was working too hard and tried to get him to break for longer lunches. On pleasant days they took these on the terrace. As she leaned forward to renew the iced tea in his glass, Brillianna gave a small exclamation of annoyance.

"What's the matter?" Ted asked.

"Someone down there by the tide pool. Really, it's too much. People today have a total disregard for private property. Look at that, cool as you please. Ted, do something."

At her first words he turned, trying to anesthetize anticipation.

Memory fitted the distant figure. He saw her face with the darkly blue eyes, although she was too far away for this kind of detail. But what was readily apparent were the rolled up pants and blowing dark hair.

He rose from the table. His behavior was compulsive, moving him along the terrace to the path. Brillianna was disconcerted, his emotion seemed out of proportion to the offense. Still she had called his attention to the trespasser and asked him to do something. She watched with concern as he ran down the path. She moved to the parapet for a better view of what was happening. Ted was making his way over the sand. The young person showed no indication of leaving, but turned and waited for him to approach. It struck her as curious. She couldn't say why.

"Sara," he said looking into her face.

"They told me at the house you were looking for me."

"You went back there? You didn't. . . ."

"Get married? No."

"We can't talk here. Walk away, back the way you came, to the headland. That puts you out of sight. I'll take the car and meet you in ten minutes."

She nodded. There were fine drops of mist, of rainbow spray caught in her hair. She passed him by without looking at him, walking as he indicated, toward the headland.

He stood watching her, wondering at the fondness that centered on that slim figure. How did it happen he felt this way about someone he scarcely knew? But he did know her. She revealed herself to him as no other person ever had. She was at home with him, able to talk freely, intimately, as though they had known each other a lifetime.

"Who was it?" Brillianna called.

He gathered his wits as he walked up the path. "No one. Just some student. I sent her off."

"I hope you explained this is private property."

"Yes." He followed her to the table. "Brillianna, there's a special delivery from Thresher I'd like to pick up."

"But you haven't finished lunch."

"I've had all I want. Thanks. I won't be too long." He moved toward the side of the house and the garages. That had gone better than he hoped. He took the sports car, waving away Tomas, who liked to putter with it. His heart hummed and raced with the motor. He turned off at Three Arch Bay, the picnic area.

She was perched on a rock staring out to sea. When he sat down beside her she didn't turn her head. The sea was ruffled and bright. "Sol has a hardware store," she said, as though they had been discussing the topic. "It's very middle-class and Jewish. I wouldn't expect you to understand. My father is broken up. A chance of security, a home. Poor Poppa, he has my interests at heart."

"*I* am what is best for you," Ted said.

"You? Do you know what my father would do if he knew about you? He would go to the synagogue, put on his prayer shawl and recite the prayers for the dead over me."

"Do you think it would be that bad?"

"I don't know. You're Gentile, rich, older, you can't marry me. My father would hate everything about you. But I knew all of a sudden that I couldn't marry Sol."

They watched the sea being playful. It tossed white waves that rolled in as bubbles around their feet. "Was that your wife on the terrace?"

"Yes."

"What's her name?"

"Brillianna."

"That must be a family name."

"Yes."

"She must come from a fine old family. She must be very suitable for you."

Ted could think of nothing to say.

"What does she call you? She calls you Ted, doesn't she?"

He nodded, he was beginning to feel miserable.

"You're right," Sara said, as though he had voiced his misgivings. "It's better if we don't talk about her. I don't like the name Ted anyway. Theo is more like you, more like who you are."

"No one's ever called me that."

"Good. Then I will."

He put his hands on her shoulder and turned her toward him. "That means you have decided to be with me."

She began speaking very fast. "I don't know what I'm going to do, Theo. But one thing, I'm never going to accept anything from you. You'll never have the satisfaction of thinking you can buy me. No setting up in a fancy apartment, no gifts, nothing like that. I'll move back to the house and continue school. Sometimes we will see each other. Do you agree to that?"

His reply was to take her in his arms. He pressed her with authority against his body and kissed her with a kiss that explored and tasted her.

Cool and virgin, before this moment she had never wanted a man. She had allowed kisses as evidence of her favor. But she granted and received without passion. Now she allowed her body to swing into his, outlining herself against him, wanting him to know her, wanting to discern what manner of man had roused her.

"Don't be afraid," he spoke into her hair.

"I'm not afraid because nothing's going to happen."

"Yes it is."

"No. I haven't decided."

"Yes you have."

"But. . . ."

He slipped his hand under her shirt and cupped her breast. Fighting her, he carried her to the lee side of the rocks where he set her down in the warm sand. His mouth and his hand quieted her impulse toward escape.

He could hardly believe the beauty of her body. He bent over her to kiss the pulse of her neck, the pink soft nipples which his lips brought to hardness. She was a conspirator in her ravishment, passing her hands over him, guiding him to the moment of entry. His demand fired her and she gave herself wholly to the act. A series of contractions occurred deep within her. This man had made her woman, discovered her to herself.

When it was done he raised himself. She kissed him deliberately and fully on the mouth. Without passion this time, as though she set a seal upon their love.

It wasn't practical for Sara to go back to the campus house. They needed a place where they could be together. Ted took a small apartment in the Berkeley hills. He was against her continuing to work as a bus girl, but she was adamant. "If I take anything from you I'm your whore; this way I'm your lover."

She returned to school, and visited her parents weekends, when he found it hard to get away. Afternoons were theirs. Theirs was a love full of sunlight. They spent hours on the deck, shrouded in privacy by eucalyptus on either side. They drank lemonade like children and devoured each other's bodies. She treated him to her theories on the sexuality of furniture, broad, squat Victorian pieces with skirts and thick bowed legs. Or the aggressively utilitarian look of modernistic chrome. "Its concern for reality carries over into architecture. Do you know the chief engineer on the George Washington Bridge left out all the masonry the specs called for on the towers? He wanted the structural supports visible. I think that's great."

"I think you're great."

Sara was a subscriber to magazines. She had lost count of the number of boys she was putting through school and helping win prizes. The result was *The New Masses, Consumer Research*, and the relatively new *Life*. She was impressed by its photographic journalism, similar to the technique John Dos Passos brought to his novels. She read sections aloud to Ted.

She deviled him to take her into San Francisco. They went twice, both times to see Marc Blitzstein's musical *The Cradle Will Rock*. Ted was reluctant to venture out. But she persuaded him that occupying gallery seats they would hardly run into anyone he knew.

He had a marvelous time. He forgot he was an oil tycoon. He felt young and radical, and his sympathies were with the downtrodden. He had even given up trying to buy Sara a coat. The lining on the one she had was cut from an old gray blanket. One day, sitting on the deck overlooking the bay, Sara said, "Did you ever hear of the Nuremberg Laws?"

"Vaguely," he said, idly tracing the span of the Golden Gate Bridge.

"Vaguely," she reiterated. "They were enacted September 15, 1935. Can't you tell me anything about them? Try, Theo, just one thing."

He squinted and the Golden Gate blurred. "Well, let's see. They'd be German of course. And since you sound upset, they'd have something unpleasant to do with Jews."

"It's disappointing that you don't know. I don't mean that against you personally, Theo. But it just seems, well, that the only people who know about them are Jews. The Nuremberg Laws deprive Jews of their civil rights."

"Really? Can that funny little man, what did you tell me his name was, really do that?"

"Schicklgruber. And yes he can do it. And did do it. That's the reason sixty thousand Jews emigrated to Palestine last year. They have no legal status in

175

Germany, no recourse in the courts. They aren't citizens anymore, they're serfs."

"Tell me," he said with curiosity, "are all Jews everywhere as concerned as you?"

"Tell me, are all Gentiles everywhere as unconcerned as you?"

She fumbled a lithe arm beneath the deck chair and came up with a copy of Sinclair Lewis's *It Can't Happen Here.*

"Wow," he said, "you've brought up some big guns."

"I don't want you to think I'm paranoid. Just because nobody persecutes big blond men by the name of Angstrom who look something like polar bears, doesn't mean the practice is going out."

"But what about the other side? With all these Jews flocking into Palestine, what about the Arabs?"

"Oh, so you've heard about the Arabs? In fact I seem to recall you do business with Arabs. You didn't know about Nuremberg, but you know about the poor dispossessed Arab. Do you know why? Because Hitler's propaganda machine is working night and day to see that you do. The Germans and the Arabs have become buddy-buddy. There are chairs in Arabic and Iranian at Heidelberg University. And Orde Wingate, a British official in Palestine, claims that the Grand Mufti of Jerusalem receives ten thousand pounds in sterling annually from the German government, that's thirty thousand dollars a year to buy arms, print propaganda, and just generally foment trouble. Raiders are imported from Syria and Iraq to make forays against undefended farm communities.

"Recently the attacks have been against their own, Palestinian Arabs who advocate coexistence, or who haven't contributed heavily enough to the Higher Arab Committee. The Arab mayor of Hebron was assassinated by terrorists. And there was an attempt on the life of the mayor of Haifa."

"Still, you can see the Arab point of view. They don't relish the idea of being a minority in Palestine."

"Yes," Sara shot back, "because they know how they treated Jewish minorities inside Arab lands. Besides Palestine was never Arab. It's been Turkish for centuries. Why did it never occur to the Arabs to claim the land from the Turks?"

"On the other hand you can't deny that there are half a million or so displaced Palestinian Arabs."

"And the number is growing by leaps and bounds. I'm not denying it. That fact is kept constantly before us. But the Shaw Commission. . . ."

"Good God, you're a walking encyclopedia. First it was the Peel Report, then the Nuremberg Laws, and now something called the Shaw Commission."

"Which you have also never heard of."

"I admit it. I never heard of it."

"Well, it was a British commission set up in 1931 to examine this particular problem: namely, how had Jews acquired Arab land. And it established that ninety percent had been purchased from absentee Arab landlords with large holdings, at exceedingly good and sometimes fantastic prices. It was the Arab landowner who pocketed his gains with no thought for the thousands of Arab tenants that he, *he*, not the Jews, dispossessed." She turned his face up to hers and leaning over, kissed him. "Theo, do you know why I tell you all this? I want you to know me. Being Jewish explains a lot."

"That's right. The Russians back a Popular Front, and right away you think: how will that affect Jews?"

"It's true," she said.

"I know it's true."

"But it is terrifying to think if things become worse in Europe, all those people may have no place to go."

"I don't think we need assume things will get worse. Dictators have put their unemployed boys into uniform before. That's one way to solve the problem."

"And put their factories to work making arms. Perhaps it is good for the economy, but those arms are going to be used."

"On Jews?"

"I don't know. On everyone. At least that's what my brother thinks."

"He thinks there will be war?"

"Well, Dov believes the hope for peace is pretty

177

fragile, with the Axis trying out their weapons in Spain, Japan entrenched in China, and Italy in Ethiopia."

"How did he happen to pick up and go to Palestine?"

"His wife died. He was David then. He couldn't seem to get his old life going. So he packed up little Louis, Lev now, and went where he felt he was needed. They took Hebrew names, and live on a kibbutz, Ein Harod. It's a hard, primitive life, like America in its pioneer period. I think it's satisfying to him."

"He's an idealist like you. Waiting for a cause to come along and exploit him."

"That's unfair."

"It's the way of the world," Ted said. "Things have never been any different."

"But they *could* be." She pushed him to a sitting position to look into his face. "You and me, that's private, Theo. No strings, no politics, ever. I know you have dealings with the Arabs, but remember, I don't ask anything of you."

"Sara," he laughed, "you exaggerate my influence. I've never even met Ibn Saud."

"It's so odd," she mused, "about Dammam VI. If it comes in, you and he both feel you have a right to that oil, *personally*. A product of nature should belong to the world. Did you ever doubt your right to be rich, Theo?"

"Nope."

"But. . . ."

"Look, I searched for it. I invested my money. If it's there, I'll transport it, refine it, distribute it. It's mine."

"I know you *think* so. And I'll admit you've more right to it than Ibn Saud. From what you told me, his grandfather ruled the Hasa, and his father lost it. His only claim to all those potential millions is based on assassinating a Turkish governor."

"That's all it takes sometimes. From then on he was able to sign a written paper for his warriors to present at the gate of heaven for admission thereto."

"Really? Did he really do that? Tell me about his wives."

"The Koran allows four at a time. Plus four slaves and four concubines."

"And instantaneous divorce. Right?"

"That's right. A man has only to say three times, 'I divorce you,' and it is done."

"Supposing you could say it three times? Would you?" Sara threw herself against him. She seemed to be crying. At least she wouldn't let him see her face. "I'm sorry. I'm sorry," she murmured against his throat.

"You are like Monaiyir, the most self-willed of Ibn Saud's hundred and fifty wives. He divorced her and forced her to marry one of his cousins. But he was miserable without her and made her second husband divorce her so they could remarry. He had seven sons with her."

"I'd like to have a son by you."

To distract her from this line of thought, Ted teased, "You wouldn't want one like the Saudi princes. They have the reputation of being not only venal but stupid. There's a story about one of them who drove his new Cadillac until it was out of gas. He figured it was broken. So he left his custom Cad in the middle of the desert for the lizards, and bought another."

She laughed, but in a preoccupied way. "We're so different, Theo. Such different persons. The only thing, the only solitary thing we have in common is that we love each other." She rocked him in her arms, tightly, as though she were afraid.

The first anniversary of their meeting came around. They couldn't believe they had known each other an entire year. "And yet," she conceded, "I can't believe there was a time when I didn't love you." She made a special dinner. He brought champagne and tying a dish towel around himself embarked on a flambé dessert with bananas and batter soaked in brandy. He set it aflame and they watched the blue blaze run about in the pan.

"Elegant." She clapped her hands. While they spooned up the dessert he told her about the oil-rich Huntington Beach field. "It was bought by an enter-

179

prising door-to-door salesman of the Great Books series." Oil was very much on Ted's mind. They had started on Dammam VII which was already at a deeper level than his Texas partners had been prepared to go. "It's possible," he explained to her, "to drill right past paying oil sands and not know it. You see, if a hole is drilled four thousand feet and deviates three degrees from perpendicular, it could bottom anywhere within a three-acre circle."

The dark blue eyes surveyed him and made judgment. "Theo, you're worried."

"We're drilling the seventh dry well in Saudi. I can't keep it up. Sometimes I feel I should be on the spot. So many things can go wrong—like how you read the drill-stem tests, whether to punch into the side or go deeper. It's down there, damn it, I know it's down there."

This seemed the moment to bring out the gift she had for the occasion, a chess set. Surprise and pleasure passed over his face, and as quickly, disappointment, even anxiety.

"You don't like it," Sara said.

"It's beautiful."

"It was made in Mexico. The pieces are alabaster. A friend of mine picked it up for me. I asked her to find an especially nice set. But something is wrong. Are the pieces too large for the board?"

"No. It's the tusks."

The rooks were carved as elephants and she looked at them in puzzlement. "I think they're handsome."

"They are," he hastened to agree.

"But something's wrong with the tusks?"

"They go the wrong way."

"What do you mean, the wrong way?"

"They turn down. That's bad luck."

Sara rocked back on her heels to look at him. "Are you serious?" She saw that he was. Spilling the chess pieces out of his lap she flung herself on him, laughing and kissing him. "You're crazier than I am. *The tusks turn down!* Really, Theo, you're too much. I shall give them away. They'll make a lovely present for someone I don't like very well but want to impress. Maybe one of my professors."

He agreed this would be an excellent way to dispose of the set. Then he mounted a defense of his theory of luck. "It's real. It's there. Most of the things that influence our lives can't be seen. Like atoms, they're just a theory. No one's ever seen one. They know they're there by the way things happen around them. That's the way it is with luck. You're part of my luck, Sara, and you're going to bring me more."

"How do you know? I brought you elephants whose tusks go the wrong way. Maybe I'll bring you bad luck."

He covered her mouth with his. Then drew back. "I know what you've brought me, a youth I didn't stop to taste. Love, when I thought it was too late." With the last glass of champagne he told her stories of Ibn Saud. Perhaps because of her radical, socialist upbringing, she loved these tales of the autocratic King that came by way of Thresher and John Eustace Nichols.

"He never learned to use a knife or fork," Ted said.

"Like me. I hate to see a long line of silverware by my plate. I always wait for someone else to start."

He told her about the American explorer Charles Crane, who had a disastrous first meeting with the King. "Gift giving is an extremely important ritual. Ibn Saud presented Crane with two matched stallions. Crane gave the King a box of dates he had brought from California. Since dates are just about the one thing that grows in Arabia, it was pretty much bringing coals to Newcastle. The King turned to the lowest slave present and asked him if he liked dates. The poor man stammered something or other and the King gave them to him.

"Then there are the hospitality stories. A classic one is told of a poor Arab who had only a fine mare as his chief possession. A wealthy shaikh from another tribe passed by, saw the animal, and in the course of a few days sent word offering a handsome price for it. When he arrived at the poor man's tent, he was received with honor and was served the prize mare for supper."

181

Sara thought about that for some time. "They're living in another century."

"The seventh," Ted confirmed.

"That explains the repression of women. What happens, for instance to the wives Ibn Saud casts off?"

"Oh, that's an honor, one they carry all their lives. If they were fortunate enough to bear a son, the King builds a mud palace for them in Riyadh, and they are renamed for their male child."

Sara was horrified. "You mean they don't have their own identity anymore, but are simply Mother of so-and-so?"

"That's right, it's extremely prestigious."

Sara made a face. "What if they don't bear a male child?"

"Then they are looked after by their nearest male relative. It is the King's custom to divorce the wife he likes least before starting a trip, so that he's free in case some interesting possibilities come along."

"You sound as though you like the idea." Sara squeezed her oddly set eyes into two suspicious slits.

Ted laughed. "His favorite wife, Monaiyir, was a European."

"What was her real name, Patricia Smith or Anne Davis?"

"I don't know. But I do know he built a separate house for her. Nichols says that about eight hundred people crowd into the palace every night."

"I can see that Pat Smith would like a bit more privacy. Is she still married to him?"

"No, she and her son died in the flu epidemic after the war. His second wife, though, held on. She is the mother of Prince Saud who will succeed him. And although they've been divorced for thirty years, she still runs his household. But I don't know how much time Ibn Saud spends with his wives. He once told Nichols he had never seen a woman eat or drink."

"I suppose," Sara said, stuffing more banana into her mouth, "they don't do such vulgar things."

"Each of Ibn Saud's sons is given a black slave boy as companion, and after infancy the princes have nothing to do with their mothers, for, as the Arab says, 'How can a woman teach a boy to be a man?' "

"How indeed?" Sara asked. "We don't know whether the knife goes in directly over the heart or a quarter of an inch to the side. Thank God I was born a good Jewish girl whose father is a schoolteacher and whose grandfather was a poet."

"That's right, you did say once he was a poet."

"He would have been famous, except he wrote in Yiddish. As it is, he is well known among Jewish intellectuals. As a matter of fact when Einstein spoke at Yeshiva University he sent my grandfather a complimentary ticket. This created a tremendous crisis in my family. Grandfather felt he was too old to benefit from the lecture, and my father didn't have sufficient background in mathematics. So all the cousins and nephews were interrogated to determine who should use it. I guess Grandfather thought some of the magic would rub off."

"And did it?"

"I don't know. I even forget who went. But my grandfather was a wonderful man. He looked like a prophet, white beard, sharp eyes. Once we sat on the moon together."

"How was that?"

"Well, he lived in New York, and my folks used to take me to visit every summer. They had a big amusement park at Coney Island. Grandfather read that on a certain day anyone dressed in a costume was allowed in free. So we fixed ourselves up. I went as a gypsy in my mother's petticoat and Grandfather was Sir Isaac Newton in a wing collar and string tie, as he attempted to explain at the gate. I began to have a suspicion as we approached the gate that something was wrong. Could it be that grandfather was the only person in the entire city to have spotted that item in the paper?"

"There weren't any other costumes?"

Sara shook her head. "And next to being stark naked, the worst thing to be in a crowd of soberly dressed citizens is in a costume. Grandfather had gotten the date mixed up. So we had to pay. But that was all right, he made me forget about being self-conscious.

We went on the gaudy rides that spin you and turn you upside down and ended up sitting on a half-moon and having our pictures taken."

"He sounds like quite a guy."

"A mensch, we say in Yiddish. He was. He used to say, 'It is death to mock a poet, to love a poet, to be a poet.'" She placed her arms around Ted's neck. "In a way you remind me of him. You're obsessed the way he was. You are completely absorbed by that black stuff you syphon out of the earth. You think of oil as imprisoned in rocks waiting for you to come along and free it. You have to be a poet to think like that."

They made love on the couch. It started slow like the pulse in his throat which she kissed again and again. Like the pulse it quickened into maddening rhythm. Her genitals ached to receive what was expelled into the skin of a condom.

Afterwards she lay without moving in his arms. . . .

"What are you thinking?" he whispered.

"About the elephants."

"I knew it." He swore softly.

It seemed impossible that while they in their eyrie watched lights gleam in outline of the bay, events moved the world closer to war. When he read that Germany appropriated the Sudetenland, Ted began to think that Dov Rosenfeld's fears were not so ill-founded. He worried about his concession in case of a full-scale European conflict. Would Ibn Saud remain neutral? What about Cairo? Who would control the Suez Canal?

He was more than willing to have his mind wrested from such thoughts when Sara put on her coat lined with the blanket, and said she was taking him to a socialist meeting. He was frankly curious. He wanted to get out and hear what people were saying.

Militant young people, emulating tough Hemingway characters, gathered to hear the poems of Bialik read in Hebrew. Afterward there was wine and talk. He had never heard so much talk. "Americans love Mussolini.

You know why? He got the Italian trains to run on time."

One Hemingway hero buttonholed him. "Are you aware that seven point three out of every hundred men who work in oil fields are maimed or actually killed on the job? What responsibility does your company take for that? What compensation benefits are there?"

He brushed the young man aside and went in search of Sara. He found her sitting quietly in a corner undergoing psychological testing by a graduate student. When she had responded to the questionnaire he declared she most closely approximated the category *Delinquent Girls*. She loved that.

"Delinquent girls, did you hear, Theo? Isn't that marvelous?"

His head was beginning to swim. The politics of "that cripple in the White House" were discussed. Sir William Beveridge's "cradle to the grave" security, analyzed. Many there knew students who had followed Theodore Dreiser to Kentucky in his investigation of conditions in the coal mines.

"Another Theo," Sara whispered. Ted was sure she'd had more wine than was good for her. "Theodore Dreiser is doing a series of interviews from Harlan County. The mine owners are trying to discredit him, of course. They've accused him of adultery."

"I don't quite see . . ." Ted began.

"But he held a press conference and declared he was impotent!"

He let it pass. He wanted to bundle her up and get her out of there. Someone else was asserting that last year at election time a well-known baby powder company slipped notes into employee pay envelopes to the effect that if Roosevelt were reelected, they would lose their jobs. "It's a fact. My brother works for them."

The most important thing about anyone seemed to be his politics. An individual with a shaved head, whom Ted decided was a double agent, asked him which of the people present he considered to be merely progressive, and which pinko, or party sympathizers.

Ted worked Sara toward the door, through talk of Roosevelt's alphabet soup, the PWA, CCC, AAA,

NRA, CWA. A redheaded youth captured them with Churchill's statement that Palestine was not to be a Jewish home, but that a Jewish home was to exist within it. A plain, serious-looking girl asked Ted directly, "Will there be war, do you think?"

"It doesn't look good," he replied.

"But surely Europe won't go to war over the Sudetenland?"

"I judge by other barometers. The Germans have assembled vast amounts of oil drilling equipment on the Rumanian and Polish borders."

"You didn't tell me you thought there'd be war," Sara said as they were walking home.

"I don't think we'll be involved."

"Not America, perhaps. But I heard a very disturbing thing in there. Something they are calling *Kristallnacht,* or the week of broken glass."

"What does that mean?"

"Apparently a seventeen-year-old Jewish boy whose father was deported to Poland in a boxcar, went a little mad. He murdered a secretary of the German Embassy in Paris, Ernst vom Rath. That seemed to be the signal the German government was waiting for. Troops went on a rampage. Over twenty thousand Jews have been arrested." She shivered. Her hand in his was icy.

"There'll be more applications for visas to Palestine," Ted observed.

"You've spent an evening with my friends, Theo. Tell me what you think of them. Be honest."

He had been thinking he wouldn't care to go through another such evening soon. Those kids with the pitiless stamina and enthusiasm of youth put him through an emotional wringer. He felt, he must admit it, old. And he wondered if he seemed so to Sara. At her age you could seize the world by the tail and toss it over your shoulder. One of her friends had called him *sir*.

"They're a good bunch," he said, "no harm in them. They talk a lot," he said as an afterthought.

"That's a Jewish failing." For a while, her hand tucked in his, she spun some thought of her own. "Did you know," she said suddenly, "that the cross is thousands of years older than Christ or Christianity?

Actually it's a solar device representing the arms of the sun."

"That's interesting."

"Interesting? You don't care at all that I just took your sacred symbol away from you?"

He looked surprised.

"You are a Christian, aren't you? Oh Theo, do I seem strange to you? Is my nose too big? Would you know I was a Jew if I hadn't told you? My father says I'm not a Jew at all. I don't believe in the Jewish faith. So what is different about me? I'm afraid, Theo. I'm afraid of what is happening in the world. And don't tell me it's happening over there. It's happening inside me. The broken glass from those Jewish homes has struck, shards of it, in my heart."

Ted put his arms around her. He didn't know what to say.

To please her he began letting her take him to the cluttered rooms of local artists, which she referred to as studios. Sometimes, for lack of canvas, entire walls were painted.

Sara was well informed as to happenings in the art world. "Diego Rivera was brought to New York by Rockefeller, John D. Jr. He painted Lenin prominently on the walls of Rockefeller Center. Then he did a portrait of John D. with a bulbous nose and leering expression." She laughed. "I don't know which he resented more, his nose or Lenin. Anyway, he had everything scraped off. Archibald MacLeish did a great satire on it, 'Frescoes for Mr. Rockefeller's City.' But they still hadn't enough. Edsel Ford, hearing that the great Rivera was in the country and he wouldn't have to pay his transportation, got him to do a mural for Detroit's Art Institute. Diego chose for his subject a Marxist view of toil inside an automobile factory. He portrayed Henry Ford fondling a ticker tape with one hand and a woman with the other. And he did the Christ Child as a fat ugly baby being vaccinated, presumably with a lot of moralistic nonsense." The artists

187

she showed him were not Diego Rivera, but Albert Gross and R. Fineman.

One thing to be said for proletarian art, it made sense in a storytelling fashion. After this preliminary exposure, Sara felt he was ready for something more abstract. In one attic room, where paints and soup simmered side by side on a burner, were odd geometric shapes in primary colors.

The artist himself, a stooped young man whose arms hung out of his sleeves, explained they must not be distracted by the figures. "It is the space between I am concerned with. The spacetime continuum is what created balance in the world. In the modern world, there is neither. So I re-create it here."

Sara whispered it would be nice if Theo would purchase a small painting. "I know he is hungry."

Ted bought an egg dangling in space for thirty-five dollars, and won a squeeze on the arm and a devoted look from Sara. "I've never had an original before," she said. "Where shall we hang it?"

"I'll leave that to you." He bought her lunch in a student haunt with sawdust on the floor. He was uncomfortable in these noisy, strident places. But he ran no chance of being seen or recognized. He talked about what was uppermost in his mind. "Even George Washington was interested in oil. It is recorded that he acquired a tract of land in western Pennsylvania because of a bituminous spring. They say it was of a highly inflammable nature, and that he used to pour alcohol on it to watch it burn."

"It's funny about that word, inflammable. Flammable means exactly the same, doesn't it?" It was plain she was following her own thoughts. "Do you remember that graduate student who analyzed me at the poetry reading? He told me a lot about you too."

Ted frowned. "Let me see if I can guess. He said I was too old for you. You don't have to be a psychology major to know that."

"All right. If you don't want to hear."

"No, go ahead. I'd like to hear. What did he have to say?"

"You don't need to be so defensive. He thinks you're

a very deep person. And he finds this interesting in view of your speech pattern."

"My what?"

"Your speech pattern. He says you speak in a series of clichés, but you don't think in them, they simply act as placemarks, sort of parentheses, a way to keep a thought isolated until you have time to take it out and look at it, examine it at your leisure."

"Look Sara, no more, huh? No more fund raising for your brother's kibbutz." He laughed shakily. "I finally learned to pronounce it. No more protesting scrap metal to Japan, no more subsidizing impecunious artists. Out in the world we have to accept the world's evaluation of us, two people from two different generations and two different walks of life. We have to seem incongruous and strange from the outside. It's only when we're alone that the differences disappear, that we think alike and feel alike. From any other perspective it's impossible to understand what we have. It's magic, Sara. You don't fool around with magic."

Sara nodded, but what she said was in disagreement. "You're saying it only works in our own little eyrie, all alone. That it can't work in the world. I say it can. You have to have faith, Theo. None of these people can come between us. None of them wants to. They are worthwhile, involved human beings with a social conscience. We shouldn't turn our backs on them completely. We should live in the world, Theo."

"And do those grubby kids constitute the world? I'm sorry, Sara. For me they don't."

"I see. They wouldn't be accepted at your club. You forget, neither would I."

They stared at each other hostilely a moment before Sara was in his arms. She made a list of her faults in penance. And he agreed to take her to another art show. This featured Klee, Kandinsky and Marc Chagall.

Theo found himself enjoying the whimsy of Chagall who introduced animals unexpectedly into his scenes. Kandinsky's canvases were explosions of lines at cross purposes and red suns tying worlds together. Klee was the most difficult to understand, his lines spidery webs that seemed spun in his own mind. A purple glove fell on his arm. He turned and looked into Brillianna's face.

Everything he had and everything he was seemed to slide down a deep hole, probably Dammam VII. It was the deepest grave man had yet dug. The Pharaohs built high; he, Angstrom, dug a mile down.

Brillianna managed her usual smile. A charming smile, extended to him, and to the girl at his side in a dirndl dress. "I never expected to run into you here, Ted." And then almost without a pause, "May I meet your friend?"

"This is Sara Rosenfeld."

Brillianna searched her face in what appeared to be a benevolent manner. "Yes, of course. How very clever of you, my dear, to get him to this exhibit. I myself should never have tried. It is marvelously exciting, isn't it?" She slipped her purple gloved hand through Ted's arm. "It was pleasant running into you, Miss Rosenfeld. And now, if you'll excuse us, there's a little tea shop around the corner that I've been wanting to try."

Ted stood his ground. "I can't, Brillianna."

She whispered in his ear, "The owners are friends of mine. Please don't embarrass me." Then directly to Sara, "Perhaps Miss Rosenfeld would join us?"

"Thanks," Sara said nastily to Brillianna. "I wouldn't know which fork to use." She rushed past them without looking at Ted and disappeared in the street. Down the hole with water seepage and the bit pounding.

"She seems a lovely girl. Sweet face. How old is she?"

"I don't intend to talk to you about Sara."

"I see." They left the gallery arm in arm.

"What about Thurston's? They have a delicious smorgasbord."

"I'm going after Sara."

"Do you think that wise or even kind?"

"You don't understand, Brillianna. This isn't some casual pick-up."

"I didn't suppose it was."

"I'm sorry," he said. "Shall I call you a cab?"

"No. Tomas drove me. Remember there are dinner

guests tonight. Mr. Douglas, among others. Don't be late." She kissed him on the cheek and crossed with the light. Her gray suit clung in fashionable lines to her slender frame. She looked like Mrs. Theodore Angstrom. She was Mrs. Theodore Angstrom. They were gambling together on the biggest oil empire in history.

She was co-founder of his world. He knew he would not be late for dinner. But he must find Sara, square things, explain, if that were possible.

World had impinged upon world, and the private small one he crept into with Sara was endangered, perhaps destroyed.

He drove vertical San Francisco streets, nosed the car over the bridge, finally angling it against a curb. Jumping out, he took the stairs two at a time. Of course she wouldn't be here yet. He had the car, she would have to use public transportation. He went inside and waited. The place was somehow different. He had never been here alone before. It felt bare. He looked idly at the room, a print he'd bought, a pottery vase he'd given her, and the Egg prominently displayed. He smiled.

It was growing dark. He peered at his watch. She should be here by now. He began to imagine alternatives. She could be walking around, she did that sometimes when she was angry or upset. Suddenly he knew. A cold sensation swept him. He realized Sara was not coming back. He called her. "Sara," he said into the empty room.

He snapped on the lights and went into the bedroom. Pulling open the closet door he saw her few things and some of his own hanging side by side. But things didn't mean anything to Sara. She wouldn't bother to come back for them.

He went out onto the deck. The cushions still held the dent of their two heads. Abracadabra, the rest was gone.

He remembered the dinner party and his promise not to be late. Brillianna had behaved well. She had not been angry, but shown pity, charity even. She carried things off. But the kind of feeling he had for

Sara was not something one could be polite about. It was a deep vein where their lives ran side by side. They should have stayed here high and safe.

He knew it was wrong to venture out, he felt it, but he'd been unable to explain it to her. She thought he resented her friends, but it was this he feared. Their eyrie abandoned and Sara gone, taking Theo with her, condemning him to be Ted.

His attempts to find her were frantic but useless. She had not moved back to the campus rooming house. And he was unable to locate a Rosenfeld in Berkeley with a daughter by the name of Sara. The hunt must be expanded, he called in a professional agency. He was terrified she had married the hardware store owner. He would not accept that she had the right to walk away, to give what they had to someone else. The touch of her, the sound of her, the taste of her was uniquely his. When he showered alone he remembered the water spraying down on them both and how he would take her still wet, slippery with soap, and laughing.

No, he was not late for the dinner party that first night, nor those thereafter. Brillianna set up a series of golf dates with his partners from Texas. He played golf with the top men in Gulf, Mobil, Standard of New Jersey, Royal Dutch Shell, Texaco, and British Petroleum. They talked of the likelihood of war and what it meant for oil. Admiral Nimitz was quoted as saying it would be "a battle of oil, bullets and beans."

Italian East Africa was important because it constituted a threat to Middle East oil through the Red Sea. They speculated whether the British could maintain control of the Suez Canal. Turning to Ted, an international oil magnate asked if Ibn Saud would allow British men-of-war to continue to ply the Gulf.

Ted said with a practiced grin, "Top secret."

Actually he knew no more than they. Although traditionally Saudi was in the sphere of British influence, there was much pro-German sentiment in the King's cabinet. In case of war he had no assurance

192

that Ibn Saud might not throw in with Germany and immediately confiscate the Hasa concession. Another possibility was that the King might take advantage of the general uncertainty to nationalize the fields.

As though to balance the bleak news out of Europe, Dammam VII blew through its nose. Into the sky it shot, and black rain fell on the sands below that seethed and boiled. The phone didn't stop ringing. Cables poured in, wires of congratulations. Old Man Angstrom grabbed Brillianna around the waist and began an Irish jig. Brillianna tossed her head, hairpins flew in every direction and her well-groomed tresses gyrated madly on her shoulder. She held out a hand to Ted, who swung into action. The old man dropped out wheezing. "I can't have a heart attack today. Not today!" He pushed Brilli toward her cavorting parents. But the child remained firmly planted on the sideline, her eight-year-old face set in a censorious expression. This kind of exhibitionism was rejected as not in good taste at the Melbourn school for young ladies.

Ted guided Brillianna faster and faster in a tightening circle. She was laughing helplessly, tears on her face. Ted was wobbling, disaster imminent. He chose an arm-chair to collapse into. They continued to laugh in short explosions, unable to catch their breath.

"Are we rich then?" Brilli asked.

"Rich? Your daddy just invented the word, Baby."

She disliked being called Baby, and went into the garden to talk to Kumju who understood her.

"Do you know how far down we drilled that hole?" Ted said. "Forty-seven hundred and thirty feet."

"Nobody, but nobody would have stayed with it. Only you." Brillianna hugged him. "Everyone wanted to pull out. Oh, Ted." Brillianna kissed him full on the mouth, something she had not done recently. "You had the vision. You held out when everyone was for throwing in the sponge, including your own Texas partners."

Ted laughed. "Especially my Texas partners."

"And your old man," his dad said. "But thank the good Lord you never did listen to me since you were fifteen years old and I told you to stay away from women."

Ted abstracted one of the cables from the pile on the table. "Look at this. From Cairncross. He estimates we're pumping two to three thousand barrels a day. We're in production! We're over the top."

Old Man Angstrom shook his head. "And another half million square miles of it. East Texas, Pennsylvania, Oklahoma, they weren't in it, not with that kind of oil. They just weren't in it."

The house filled with cut flowers, plants, anthericum flown in from Hawaii. Booze kept arriving, cases of champagne and a cannon, an actual cannon, filled with Courvoisier. Ted was exuberant, but some small part held back from the general euphoria. It had looked good for Dammam II.

However, the following month a cablegram arrived which convinced him. He tore it open and turned to his family. "What do you know? The King of Arabia would like to meet me. We are invited to a celebration at his palace in Riyadh. And don't tell me you have nothing to wear," he said to Brillianna, "because they'll put you in one of those burnouses and veil you from head to foot."

She was laughing uncontrollably, and looked so beautiful that he forgot all the things he held against her. He wanted her. For the first time since Sara, he wanted her.

"Ted . . ." he had pulled her from the house, along the flagged path and into the car. Her face was rosy and flushed, she let her hand fall against the upholstery. "Where are we going? Where are you taking me?"

"Quiet, my girl. It's a simple case of kidnapping. Remember that old hotel in Sausalito?"

"Gothic? High in the hills? Surrounded by trees?" She hugged him. "Don't tell me we're going there?"

"The Alta Mira. Six months ago, I think it was, you said you wanted to have breakfast on the terrace and look out over the bay."

"I remember. But that you should!"

"I remember everything you do and say." He hadn't intended these words to cast a pall over her mood. But instantly memory was with them, a passenger in the car.

After a moment she moved closer, snuggling against him. It hadn't been spontaneous. She considered and then did it. Ted was hard to fool.

The room had an old-world elegance with a tiled Dutch stove taking up one wall. Ted ordered a bottle of Mumm's.

"I don't have any night things," Brillianna said.

"Good." He began to undress her.

When the champagne arrived she hid in the closet. "Come out, come out," he called, "wherever you are."

She emerged laughing, with a towel around her. Brillianna responded passionately to his embrace, her body seemed to swell as she turned in his arms. It had been a long time. The encounter was a lusty hair-pulling, on-the-bed, off-the-bed lovemaking. It was like their first days.

They lay naked together, he absently stroking the smooth flank that moments before he had pinioned. "Tell me about Arabia," she whispered.

"Nichols writes that the King just inspected the new facility at Ras Tanura with great festivity and no comprehension. The first tankers will be loaded by the time we arrive. Winter is the best time of year. They say the climate then is like the Mediterranean."

"I feel as though I'm living the *Green, Blue, Red,* and *Yellow Fairy Books* all together. It's fantastic, Ted."

"Everyone's got a talent. Mine is a nose for oil."

"And what's mine?" Brillianna asked.

There was a wistfulness in the question that escaped Ted. "Being my lady. Sitting on my left hand. On view, envied, emulated."

"I can't imagine this ceaseless rain of money. In a way I'm afraid, the shower of good things might be too much, it might drive us apart again. Ted," she placed her hands on each side of his face, "I've missed you. It isn't the trappings I care about. It's you."

He made a mental note to call off the agency that was looking for Sara. He was home, years of misunderstanding and mistrust were cleared up. Brillianna was the woman he needed beside him. He hardly understood the alienation. He didn't want to remember. It was past.

A week later she walked into his study with an envelope in her fingers and dropped it on his desk. Fury blanked color from her face. He knew two things instantly: that he had reckoned without the Grenville pride, and that the letter was from Sara. "That's finished," he said to his wife.

"And you don't know where she is?"

"No."

"Then burn this." She turned the envelope over so the return address was not visible.

"Brillianna," he said, "you can't dictate to me like the headmistress of Brilli's school. You can't say 'burn it.' I don't intend to see Sara again. But I certainly won't burn her letter."

"Very well." Without leaving the room she called her maid, ordering her to unpack the clothes she had spent the last several days collecting for the Saudi trip. "You can take your mistress with you."

"I will." He was caught in the funnel of a storm. It paused directly over him. Other places Brillianna was shouting, a door slammed, a blind banged with ocean wind. Where he was it was quiet.

He looked in wonder at the charade he had been prepared to play. Important people weren't important. A wife with the proper background was not important. Even the great waterfall of money. All that meant was that Ted Angstrom had gambled big and the chips were raked in and stacked in front of him. But even that was nothing without Sara. For no reason there came into his mind her habit of brushing her teeth with salt to save money on toothpaste. And he was destined to be one of the richest men in the world.

He didn't know if the quiet he had found was a retreat or a storm center. But he knew Sara shared it.

Her note was conventional. She had read of his success. "Dammam VII. I'm glad." She signed it, *your young friend*.

He sometimes called her that in despair over the

196

difference in their ages. She never understood this and simply accepted that besides being his lover, she was also his friend. The thought pleased her.

The address, which he had no trouble finding, was another cooperative around the corner from the first. He was sent upstairs with a curious look and told, "Third door on your right." Sara, sitting on an overturned garbage can that was scrupulously clean and undoubtedly sterilized, was studying in poor light with a pile of books and a carton of milk beside her. She bit her lip when she saw him and swallowed hard.

He didn't come any farther into the room. "Sara, I found out there isn't time for quarrels or being apart, or even making up. I want to be with you from now on, whatever."

She slipped off the green upside-down garbage can and rushed into his arms. He held her against him, feeling her not as woman but as child, as love.

She spoke against his chest without looking at him. "When some great catastrophe happens, like an earthquake, people call the police. I don't know what they say, 'Please, Sergeant, the earth is shaking around my house, will you send a squad car over immediately?' I felt like that, Theo. I wanted someone to see that my life was flying about, shaken to pieces. And I wanted them to do something about it. But no one even thought I looked wan or pale or thin. They thought I looked just fine. Only Papa said once I should not skip breakfast. But breakfast wasn't going to help, or getting eight hours' sleep.

"At first my days were formless. Life has form and shape and color and purpose. Grief has none of those things. It's like that time before night when you have to peer to see things, to make them out. So, you know what I did? I asked your advice.

"Remember, Theo, one day you told me about the water buffalo you saw in Egypt. They had tied a blindfold across its eyes so the poor beast couldn't tell it was walking endless circles as it pumped water from the well. I decided that was the thing to do. Not try to go anywhere. Tie on a blindfold, study, take long walks and study some more."

He turned her face up to his for the kiss that meant a renewal to both of them. Her hands flew along his neck and shoulders, assuring themselves. "Oh Theo. You're just the same."

"No."

"That's right, your well came in. It must mean you are very successful, very rich. I always knew it would come in. Was it wrong of me to write? I wrote right away. I wanted you to know I was glad. But I didn't mail the letter. It sat here and I looked at it every day. I shouldn't have put a return address. I didn't think you'd come. But I wanted you to know where I was in the world. I wouldn't feel so lonely then."

"You knew I'd come," he said simply.

"Did I? I suppose I did. You see, you do that for me. You don't let me lie to myself."

"What's the idea of a green garbage can?"

"Oh that?" she laughed. "Someone was moving out and it was cheaper than a chair. Also it reminded me not to be puffed up, that probably everything I was doing was garbage."

"Well, you're going to take a term off anyway. We're leaving for Saudi to see Dammam VII."

"Saudi?" She held herself at arm's length and looked into his face. She remembered the purple glove possessively on his arm and the tailored gray suit. "What about your wife?"

"My wife is my wife. That says it all."

"But Theo, you went out of the gallery with her. I watched from across the street. And it looked so right, you and her. We are the mismatched ones."

He shook his head gravely. "Only by certain standards, which I don't have time for anymore. I'll tell you something, Sara, I don't have to conform. And neither do you. The world will conform to us."

"I want to know who will go to Saudi. Will your wife go?"

"No. As a matter of fact she suggested I take you."

"She did? It is the kind of thing I would do if I were miserable and terribly bitter. But I can't be sorry for Purple Gloves. She has so much and I have only you. If I do have you?"

"Sara, let's get one thing straight. I've never left you. You've always been the one."

"I know, I know. I'm afraid of so much good luck. I'm afraid to be too happy. And in the gallery, you looked so right together. You were Mr. and Mrs. Angstrom, and who was I? Sara Rosenfeld, guttersnipe."

"Stop thinking and talking of yourself like that." He kicked at the green garbage can and it fell over and rolled across the room.

"Are you going to give me a new image? Will you make a lady of me?"

He laughed. "What, for the King of Arabia? He deals in quantity, not quality."

"And how will you introduce me?" she challenged him.

"As Sara Rosenfeld, who else?"

"I don't know, Theo. Remember when I dragged you into my world? You tried, but you didn't fit it and it didn't fit you. And when I insisted, that was the end for us. There was that gallery and there was your wife. I think if we had been content to stay high in the hills, just like you said, nothing would have separated or harmed us. Perhaps we should do that now. Go by yourself, Theo. Look at Dammam VII. Meet the King. And when you come back I'll be here. It will be our world and we'll never venture out of it."

"No, Sara. I thought about doing it that way. But I don't want you to take up a corner of my life. I want you to be the most important part of it. I can protect you now, Sara. I am an immortal person, not in myself, but in my company. The money I make is not ordinary money, it is upper bracket, bypassing the income tax. The world has never seen such power from Power making power, making more power. There *aren't* assets like these, the greatest kings in the world don't have them. Governments don't."

"But you do? Theo, the idea terrifies me. It's outside you now, an independent entity. Your immortal person, and I suppose there are others, the automobile industry, steel, drugs, the electric companies, I wouldn't begin to know them; they are simply self-perpetuating sovereign empires."

"Step into the new world, my young friend. It's never existed before. Oh, it had a sort of murky beginning with coal, and the barons of the industrial revolution. But governments were still run by individual men. No more. The *immortals*, the new conglomerates, they elect, crown, put in office, and perpetuate in office. And it starts with raw black crude. I'm going to show it to you, Sara."

"When?"

"We'll be in New York on Tuesday and sail the next day for London. Here are the tickets." He tossed them at her.

She read slowly: "Mr. Theodore Angstrom. Mrs. Theodore Angstrom. A deck. Cabin 16."

"What do you care what it says? It's going to be a shipboard romance."

"We could stay in our cabin the whole crossing. Never come out." Before he could object she said penitently, "I didn't mean that. You came into my world. I'll come into yours."

Their bodies were hungry to touch and explore and have each other again. It was a cot with a broken spring. It was Ted cupping her nakedness in his hands. It was Sara moist before he touched her. They became the act. No Theo, no Sara, but a deep opening and closing, a probe that quickened. When their bodies released them, they clung together. "You are my home," she whispered, "I'll never leave again."

He kissed her, not insistently now, but gently. She was many things to him. "When we've seen the oil gush and dined on goats' milk and wild honey, I have a surprise for you."

Immediately she was absorbed trying to guess. "Big or little?"

He shook his head.

"Heavy or light?"

He laughed outright. "You're not even warm."

"You've got to help me. Is it a person, place, or thing?"

He grew serious. "The first two."

"A person and a place? Now I'm really baffled. I can't guess. You'll have to tell me."

"From Saudi it's a short hop in a company plane to Palestine, to your brother and his boy."

"Dov? You'd do that?" A spasm crossed her face, contorted by sudden tears. "I could see my brother and Lev?"

He nodded and she beat him on the chest. "And we were playing games, heavy or light, big or little, odd or even! How can you be so evil!" Her arms were around him. "You just gave me something I never dared wish for. I thought our letters would have to be enough. Am I really going to see Dov and all because you are this marvelously, impossibly, fantastically evil, evil darling? Really Theo, the land of milk and honey? The holy land, the land our teacher Moses was not allowed to enter?"

"You want to go then?"

"Don't pretend you don't see what it means to me. I haven't seen Dov for eight years. Lev was a little boy. And the land, I want to see it too, that bit of land that looks so small on maps, the homeland repromised."

"And where would you like to go next? Paris? Rome?"

She shook her head. "I think I'll ask Ibn Saud to give me one of those pieces of paper he hands out to his warriors. I think I'll be ready for heaven. I think maybe I'm ready right now."

It was odd in a way, Brillianna thought. Armagh was what she so desperately wanted and Armagh was what she had, as though some sardonic genie granted her wish at the expense of everything else.

As mistress of Armagh there was a great deal to busy herself with. That was one thing about a house, something always needed doing. She held to these things, mistress of Armagh, Mrs. Theodore Angstrom. *A will as strong as his.* She needed it to keep things in proportion.

Other men had mistresses. Especially men in Ted's position. It was true that most did not flaunt their women as he did. But she would not allow this to drive her out. Divorce? Pack up the emotional baggage of years and vacate the new success? Leave what Ted called the upper bracket money to him? Why should she do that? He might even marry his Jewess. No. She would stay where she belonged, his wife, chatelaine of Armagh; and to give herself full title, Mrs. Angstrom, who commanded respect.

She would wait. But not passively. She decided to redecorate her bedroom and dressing area. She started with the framing around the panel of mirrors, for which she chose a gold paper with butterfly design. There weren't enough butterflies to please her so she cut up an extra roll and with a paste-pot appliquéd additional ones to the wall.

Setting the items back on her dressing table it startled her to see the number of pictures and snapshots she had collected in an assortment of frames. Brilli as a baby, the usual bear rug picture. What a plump, jolly infant she had been. And there she was looking out with a solemn glance on turning five. Brillianna stared at an enlargement of the three of them, Brilli riding Ted's shoulders. And Ted and herself, the formal wedding picture. How young they looked. She felt tears gather for all they'd had to face. Unknown then in those brave smiles.

It wasn't Sara Rosenfeld. If she were honest—and she struggled to be—nothing had been the same since the operation. The mystery, the secret ingredient that brings lovers to the edge of the world and shudderingly back again, had been absent for a long time. She was given a chance the night at the Alta Mira. But the gay leopard Dante wrote of, the sin of pride, tripped her up, made her rage at Ted, giving him an ultimatum while her hold on him was new and fragile.

Of course she lost. She must sit alone with her Grenville pride to keep her company during the long nights. She had as good as handed her husband to that avaricious young person. Now she must wait. At thirty-seven she must be abstemious as a nun.

What was she supposed to do? Grow a hymen, wither, shrink, dry up? She could not take a lover. Ted was her lover, lusty, demanding, insatiable. Glancing at her too wide bed, she went over in her mind the times they had each other there. She sat on the edge of it and grabbed a pillow against her. She was lying, lying, lying! She had never had a chance. The hysterectomy finished things. Since then Ted's lovemaking was routine, based on routine need. And when Sara Rosenfeld appeared, even that stopped. The Alta Mira—she clung to that, the old Ted loving her as he had once done. That was no lie, it happened. She had thrown it all away for the gay leopard whose haunches were dry.

Brillianna got up, smoothed her dress and continued to rearrange the photographs. Her parents were on her dressing table, smiling, not knowing they were dead.

Why pretend? She was dead too. Her life might as well have a silver frame around it. It could be placed behind glass and dusted by the servants.

Cabin 16 was filled with flowers, champagne, telegrams. It didn't matter that she didn't know the names on the cards or the signatures on the wires. When she opened the closet there was a complete wardrobe. Nothing had been overlooked, dresses, suits, coats, nightgowns and robes.

"All right, just for the trip. So I won't disgrace you. But you must help me," she added in panic. "What do I put on first?"

"For a promenade around the deck, the tweed skirt and a sweater."

Before this could take place Sara's things had to be stowed, and an old satchel filled with books tucked under her bunk. "They're mostly library books. I'll have to pay a terrific fine. Some are my grandfather's."

He idly glanced at a title, "*Arabia Deserta*, volume II. What in the world?"

Sara seemed a bit embarrassed. "I thought I should know something of the country and the people. You know how I am, Theo. So full of prejudice and middle-class Jewish intolerance. Look at the way I behaved with you when we first met. It's a wonder you

203

ever wanted to see me again. But I have a real opportunity to shed all that and see for myself."

"How many of these tomes do you expect to get through?"

"I don't know. I'll read a little each night." She adjusted the tweed skirt Ted suggested was appropriate. "You see I have two pictures of the Arab. One is a dauntless Rudolf Valentino. The other, terrorists who leave bombs in the marketplace that maim women and children. Somewhere in between there's got to be a better evaluation."

Ted grunted. He was impatient to show her off. This was part of the new Ted Angstrom who could do as he liked. The oil flowing from Dammam VII meant rules no longer applied. He was treading not only on American sensibilities, but Wahhabi, forcing Ibn Saud to play host to his Jewish mistress. Teasing the tiger. Baiting his Arab partner. Sara's presence emphasized his equality. It was a standoff. He was another king.

A promenade of the ship represented one thing to Ted and quite another to Sara. His idea was to keep circumnavigating A deck. Hers was to plunge to B Deck and past uncarpeted steps to C, and finally down a cast iron companionway to the hold. Here she discovered aliens being deported: a felon, a man with forged papers, and a grandfather separated from his family, sent back because in the screening at Ellis Island they discovered he was tubercular.

Sara talked with everyone, was at home with everyone. The elderly Smyth couple on C Deck had lived thirty years in America but were returning to finish their days in the land of their birth, England. When Ted inquired what part of England, they replied, Manchester.

"That should finish them off pretty fast," he commented to Sara.

During another turn on A Deck, Ted ran into people he knew. One of the ladies, flashing an assessment of Sara asked, "Is Brillianna not making the trip with you?"

"No," Ted said. That was the end of it. They were invited to make up a table of bridge. Sara declared she didn't know the game, which shocked Mrs. Carleton far more than that she shared Theodore's cabin.

At a buffet luncheon that afternoon Sara helped herself to three chocolate mousses, an eclair, and several brandied Napoleons. These she took below deck and distributed to the children. Ted refrained from comment.

Dressed for dinner the first night out, Ted paid wondering homage to the dressmaker's art. Sara might have passed for a debutante except for unexpected eyes whose Tartar slant lent an exotic quality to her appearance.

There were place cards at the captain's table. Mr. Angstrom to the captain's right, Mrs. Angstrom at his left. Ted picked up the card with his wife's name and handed it to the steward. "The name is Miss Sara Rosenfeld." Captain Dunbar bowed over Miss Rosenfeld's hand.

A Mrs. Rodgers felt unwell and retired. That was the only defection. Sara accepted the partying, never failing to ask Ted to name a cocktail, so she could sound fluent when asked what she would have, and always leaving it somewhere.

The real thrill of the trip for her was to wander in the bowels of the ship. She was amazed at the cargo it was carrying, automobiles chained and blocked along with bulldozers and heavy machinery. Packing cases of assorted sizes stamped with dozens of labels intrigued her. She discovered a foundry and talked endlessly to the smith as he threaded pipe and brazed flanges on a broken stanchion. Deck officers were sent after her, but it was soon recognized that her will constituted a force much like the weather. It was best to bear with it and ride it out.

Three fine days of sun and calm seas prevailed. Then they ran into gale conditions. The decks were swept clean of passengers. Ted gave up the pretense that he was not seasick and lay down with a towel over his face. Sara was immersed in her books. "Do you know," she said, "that Ibn Saud made it a law that no one may cut down a palm tree. Now a man who will make a law like that can't be all bad."

"Hmmm," Ted said.

Sara was totally absorbed. She was being offered a unique chance to see and perhaps learn to know the Arab in his own land. She hoped, with her reading as background, that once actually in Saudi, the character of the people would become clear. What if she could come to her brother, Dov, with ways to approach the Arab in friendship. Jew and Arab were both Semites, once fellow tribesmen wandering the same desert region. Their languages had common roots. She learned that Christ spoke Aramaic, a dialect from which both Hebrew and Arabic derived. She read on, fascinated. During the diaspora Jews found sanctuary from persecution in Moorish Spain, where they were honored for their learning and valued for their knowledge of silver and goldsmithing. At one time both peoples dwelt side by side in peace. She wanted to tell someone. "Theo," she said, but he was asleep.

A day out of port the weather subsided, and passengers who had been invisible most of the trip reappeared. The glimpse of London was exciting, but their schedule allowed no sightseeing. A Fairchild was waiting to fly them via Rome and Athens to catch a night's sleep in Beirut and refuel for the flight to Baghdad and the Persian Gulf.

Syria was an arid bleak land to fly over, but proceeding south into Iraq, Sara was soon staring down at the Tigris River and the lush valley spreading to either side. "The cradle of civilization. Or is that the Nile?"

"It depends on who's calling the shots. Valleys, rivers, countries, land ridges, are so many fences. Beneath, where it counts, there is no demarcation. The porous sedimentary layers, the sandstones, limestones and clay, they are the guardians of oil. Men say Iraq, Iran, Arabia, Bahrein, Oman. No. It is just one enormous black rock sponge without division where the earth's blood is trapped. We didn't know it had blood. It has, the kind of blood in living bone, a deep, inner, pent-up plasma. This changes the character of the earth, of the way we think about it."

"But you didn't make the oil, Theo," she protested.

206

"The sun did. And billions and billions of untold creatures."

"True. But I, and men like me, and like my dad, oilmen, *found* it. Who owns the diamond mines and gold mines? The men who staked out claims."

It was an old argument by now. But they pursued it hotly. "They should have a reward. And *you* should have a reward. A dog is lost and is returned to its owner, there is a reward. But it is not right to keep the dog."

He never ceased to marvel at her quaint attitude which would have made a poor man of him. She came up with more amazing statements. "Did you know there were Jews in Medina in the 6th century? That's right, and in the northern Hejaz, at Khaibar, there was a Jewish kingdom."

"That's one thing I didn't know. I didn't know Arabia was Jewish."

"Well, if you don't believe me, the waterworks can be seen to this day."

"Okay, okay," he said laughing.

"The first scientific expedition was sent in 1759 by the Danish court. It was headed by Carsten Niebuhr."

"Not Nieberg?" Ted pretended surprise.

"Don't laugh. He was the only one of his party to survive."

"I expect we'll fare better."

"The first mention of the Saud family is in his diary. He tells of a religious revival that gave rise to the Sauds of Daraya in Central Arabia. Muhammad Ibn 'Abd al Wahhab was educated at Damascus and returned in the early 1700s to gather an army. That's the Wahhabis, whose code was purity through force of arms. They sound a bit like the Christian Crusaders. Anyway, by 1803, I think it was, his son 'Abd al Aziz was master of Arabia. About this time there is a record of a European traveler, a Swiss, Johann Ludwig Burckhardt."

"Probably the first Swiss banker," Ted said. The books she quoted were not those he would have recommended to acquaint her with Arabia. They had nothing to do with sediments, sulfur deposits or oil exploration.

Sara had a concentrated expression on her face.

"Then came Giovanni Finati, an Italian deserter, who joined the Egyptian army. And finally, you won't believe this, but here goes. . . . Ali al Ablassi, a Jew who traveled lavishly and was believed to be a spy of Napoleon's."

"You made that up," Ted said, "about his being a Jew."

"Honest Injun. And now comes Theodore Angstrom of the United States of America, and another Jew, also traveling lavishly. Do you think they'll suspect me of being a spy, too?"

"A regular Mata Hari. But don't kid around, Sara. I don't want to walk into a market and see your pretty little head on a pole."

"Tell me again how to recognize the Wahhabis."

"They usually wear large white turbans or sometimes just a white band in the headkerchief."

"I'll remember not to ask them the time."

"You do that."

"Although I don't want to fall into the trap of prejudging. They're probably mostly just holy men and teachers."

"Don't you believe it," he said.

They passed the confluence of the Tigris and Euphrates, and shortly afterward the Persian Gulf opened under them.

"There's no color at all," Sara exclaimed, "either in the water or on the land. It's all such brightness you can hardly stand it."

"Actually the Gulf is quite shallow. Look how low-lying the land is." He pointed from the porthole showing the Arabian peninsula inclining toward them.

"It seems to stretch out fingers, as though they were trying to grasp the pearl reefs."

"Those fingers are mud flats called sabkha. It's hard to tell from up here, but some of them are fifteen miles in length. And the crust varies from a few inches to over a foot in depth. In most cases it will support a car."

"Do they ever get stuck?"

"All the time. But there are generally camels or trucks or people to pull you out."

The Shaikhdom of Bahrein, a group of flat islands, came into view. It should have been beautiful with palms and a fringe of gentle waves. But looking down, she saw derricks, pumps, and storage tanks.

Ted was excited and craned to keep it in sight. "It's only fifteen miles off the Saudi coast, halfway between the Quatar peninsula and the Hasa. The largest island is Muharraq. Manama is the capital. They're mostly British owned."

It pleased Ted to see that the Dhahran airstrip was well graded and paved. They came in smoothly, stepping into a blazing flat world whose every tiny granule of sand seemed cut to reflect sun. Several cars at the far end of the field rolled forward to meet them. From these stepped men in loose gowns and flowing headgear.

They approached and salaamed to Theo, who returned the bow and shook hands with his old friend, Abdullah Sulaiman, the minister of finance. Sara stood to the side watching with interest. Finally Theo took her by the arm and brought her to the group, "My traveling companion, Miss Sara Rosenfeld."

Dark, keen eyes met hers. She was quite sure they were not used to women in a vertical position. She did not offer her hand, but neither did she drop her eyes. It was they who looked away from her naked face, and then looked again covertly.

She smiled, saying through her teeth, "I think you could sell me to the highest bidder."

"Shut up," he whispered, not knowing how much was understood.

A discussion ensued which was handicapped by a far from fluent translator. Ted turned to Sara. "The Emir of Uqair hopes that our shade is never less and offers us the hospitality of the Dammam fort. But we've got some prefab housing, where I think you would be more comfortable."

"I vote for the Dammam fort."

"That would please them. But I have some business to go over with my people here." The minister and the emir salaamed and withdrew so they could hold a conference with the company personnel who formed a small knot a few yards away, not daring to break in on the Arab welcoming committee. Now they rushed over, men in pith hats, who had adopted British style shorts, shaking hands vigorously, their unmistakable American features burned dark as the Arabians.

"Congratulations! Congratulations, sir!" Blue eyes out of rough-hewn faces, exulting at another man's success. "A bonanza!"

They called Dammam *Lucky Seven*. Ted said, "The Hasa is known for its black pearls. We just went down deeper and found the goddamnedest, biggest, blackest of all."

The eyes under the helmets traveled several times to Sara. Cairncross, the engineer in charge, came over. "We have quarters prepared. I wouldn't try the fort, if I were you, Mrs. Angstrom. You'll be more comfortable here with us."

Ted stepped to her side. "Excuse me, gentlemen. This is Miss Sara Rosenfeld."

Hats were doffed in the heat. There were outstretched hands, more than she could shake. There was new interest in her and in Angstrom.

"We'll dine at the fort, so as not to offend our Arab hosts. And plan on getting back."

Sara was amazed that he had not asked to be taken immediately to Dammam VII, which was after all, the source of his fortune and the reason for this trip.

It was Cairncross who said, "I expect you'd like to see Dammam VII."

Sara admired the nonchalance with which Ted said, "Sure." He didn't give her the option of retiring to bathe and rest, but twining her fingers in his, piled her into the car their compatriots had provided. They bounced over roads more marked out than actual, toward the Dome of Jabal.

A caravan of camels approached and Sara wanted a picture. Ted explained the camera was considered a form of evil eye and suggested it would be better if she mentioned the encounter in her diary.

"How amazing," she said, gazing after the retreating beasts, "to meet them outside a zoo. They seem quite overloaded. What are they carrying?"

"Provisions, a tent, and those skins roped at their sides are water bags." But his real interest was in the composition of the surface rock. "Miocene deposits. And running inland, Eocene, where great granite veins are swept bare between Salwa and Jal-Rin." He broke off.

"Is that it?" Sara followed his eyes. "Is it the Dome of Jabal? Oh my goodness, there it is!"

The sand dunes sprouted wells, pipelines, tanks. A turbaned Sudanese pedaled a bicycle lethargically. The imported laborers carried on their work in slow motion. Italians, Indians, Africans, and a few Arabs from the local villages stopped to stare. The car passed the first of the six nonproducing wells. Each had held Ted's expectations, to each he had entrusted his dream of getting out the oil these sands, this whole country, rested on. But the monsters were quiet and in disuse.

Number VII you could hear clanging. Sara watched his face for some sign of transformation. A release valve long shut off should open. She expected him to jump from the car, be all over the machinery. Wasn't it necessary for him to know that well viscerally, tactually, climb up on it, run his finger around the flowline and the casting line, bring the black smear under his nose to smell?

Ted was the last out of the car. Climbing down he picked up some core material, pressing it between thumb and forefinger, feeling texture and grit. "How many barrels are you taking?" he asked the foreman, and nodded at the answer, staggering even to him.

He was tapped into the largest oil deposit in the world. "The crude smells sour," he said. "Watch out for H_2S in the wadis."

Sara smiled at the offhand way he spoke, as though he were not personally involved, as though it was not his life's blood that was being transfused into containers at ground level. He did not climb the derrick, tap the underside of tanks and pipes, or investigate the soundness of every foot of machinery. At this most important moment in his life, he chose to play it as though it were another man's well. But he didn't fool Sara. She saw his hand travel the length of his scar, and watched his eyes, avidly alert to every detail. Nothing was too trivial, nothing too complicated to escape his attention.

This operation was an extension of Theo. And she worried about him, while secretly reprimanding herself. It was crazy and Jewish to worry when things were not only going well, but extraordinarily well.

What happens next, she found herself wondering. Not many people she knew realized their dreams, in fact, no one. But here were Theo's metal arteries pumping. Was he feeling the thick viscous stuff in his veins? He was actually on the site of Dammam VII on the eastern edge of Al Hasa, crown of Arabia. He was not yet forty years old. What happens the rest of his life? The conquest was made. America discovered. What now? Would he take up golf? Buy a yacht, travel, attend his wife's parties?

The other half of the question nagged her mind, would he retain a small corner where he could run away and be with her? She was watching his triumphal entry through the streets of Rome. Caesar himself had ordered the arch built and, tossing his jacket to someone, his tie loosened and finally yanked off, he rolled back his shirt sleeves and, young and fit, marched through it.

The populace loved him. They took their cue from him, kept it low key, but it was obvious they loved him. They crowned him with leaves of laurel.

And then?

Historians never recount that. Once it was over, could he go back to being Theodore Angstrom? While her Jewish heart worried, her pride in him surfaced. When he singled one of the men out to speak to, it was something they would talk about, remember, write their families. The man she loved was not an easy man to understand. He was a poet whose ink was oil and whose tablet the stern rock face of nature. He was an adventurer, a dreamer, whose dream was larger and more impossible than any man's before him. To him it was reality from the first. To her, only to her had he confided the gamble. Everything he had. Everything, his wife's home, Armagh, his family, integrity, man-hood, his life wagered against this moment.

The men gathered around him, anxious to tell him how it had been. He heard the stories from those who were there. Dammam VII had blown oil and mud, the wind catching it, drowning everything, men, animals, and structures. The Arabs ran howling into the desert, claiming they had dug into the abode of the Afrit, the black tears would be followed by black curses, black rain by black wind.

But the Americans and the Europeans leaped into it, bathed themselves in the shower, washed each other down with the black goop until only the whites of their eyes showed. They got drunk on smuggled whiskey, and it was impossible to get anyone back to work.

Ted roared with laughter. It was his coronation they were talking about. Of course they got drunk, bathed in oil, danced in oil, fell down in it, sloshed around on their hands and knees unable to get to their feet while their buddies roared and were pulled down in turn. An orgy of slippery sliding Calibans, of drunken satyrs, shouting and cursing in a dozen languages. Understanding each other. At that moment oil transcended everything. They didn't need a common language, only joy, success, and drink to know they had done this together, brought in a well the world would talk of for a hundred years.

No. Sara had not seen anyone get what they wanted before, not completely, not totally, not all the way. She watched Theo. He shook hands when they were extended, listened to the stories, his matter-of-fact attitude creating an aura from which the men stood back. For six years he had known it would happen. For six years he had tried to tell other people. Now let them tell him.

Ted's expert eye never ceased scanning, judging, his mind making assessments. Sara, following his mental progress over the field, understood fully why she loved him.

She sensed his power, his tremendous pent power, that could hardly be expended. In everyday living how do you come by a day like this? He was a Niagara caught in snapshot, ready to plunge, but not plunging. It was all held back. And now, when he had every right to funnel oil-bearing cuttings through his fingers, he refrained. How could a man live with such incarcerated power constantly held in check? There were divisions, phalanxes drawn up in battle formation, that wanted to move. Instead he had dinner with his wife or went to a Zionist meeting with her. She hadn't understood him, not until now. He could have gone to jail. He had told her everything, the whole miserable business. But there was no disgrace in Theo's future.

He was feted, and would be the rest of his life, acclaimed for his insight, his tenacity, and yes, she allowed the word, *genius*. A modern genius, working in a new media. Modern, because he would make the world modern, bring it to a new era.

If he hadn't been successful they would have branded him a criminal. She was afraid because she was so unlike him. She clung to the security of everyday things. She couldn't imagine daring past what other men dared, a gamble with everything in the balance. Yet was she not standing on the Dome of Jabal in Dhahran, with dazzling sand underfoot, raining in her face when the wind blew?

Tom Mercer was the man in charge on the field. Both he and Cairncross explained to Sara that they had a couple of generator trucks, their own kitchen and refrigerator cars, water tankers and vans with both air-conditioning and heating units. Mercer added, "We've set up on the edge of the shore. The view is really magnificent."

"We'll be back as soon as we can get away," Ted said, "but I know Sara is anxious to get a taste of Arabian hospitality." That's the way it was left. Arab slaves escorted them in a procession of cars to the old fort.

"It must be frustrating," Ted teased her. "The first slaves you have ever laid eyes on and you haven't two words in their language to tell them about Abraham Lincoln."

"I don't know," she said. "They look better off than the camel drivers."

They passed Uqair, the principal port, where hundreds of white and brown camels crouched for loading and unloading. There were pearling dhows at work in the shallow water, but dominating that part of the Gulf was a British naval vessel.

Sara was watching Ted's face. "You don't like the idea of British ships, do you? You see this as an American preserve."

"Did you know that this fort was once bombed by the British?" Ted evaded, and then decided to answer. "With war a possibility in Europe, Britain is a bit too interested in my concession."

"I suppose oil makes it essential that this part of the world remain neutral. Will that be hard to manage?"

Ted sidestepped the issue. He was well aware that the British could always trade the Palestine Jews for neutrality. "I don't know," he said.

They were escorted to the upper story of the fort where they were passed on to a new group of servants in bright robes and sashes. Veiled women with fluttering gestures and small shrill sounds separated Sara from Ted and took her off to the ritual bath.

Her clothes were taken from her and passed about with much interest. Naked, she was led to a slatted floor, and water from handsome ewers poured over her. She tried to convince herself that this was not an indignity. After all, were they not giving her their most precious possession, water? This was true Arab hospitality. Liking it was another matter.

Afterward she was rubbed with herbs and blends of perfume. A gossamer robe belted with black pearls was slipped over her head, and a shawl and veil set on her hair. The women clapped their hands. Tinkling laughter proclaimed their satisfaction at the result, which transformed her into a princess of the East.

She was again taken by the hand to a section of the dining room partitioned from the majlis by a fretwork screen. There were many dishes, and the trick was to work a mouthful into a rice ball with your right hand. She avoided the meat, which might be mutton but which she feared was camel, and turned instead to candied fruit in syrups and flat bread.

215

The main amusement at her table was peeking through the lattice at the men. The emir and the governor sat on cushions around a low board spread with food. They ate quickly, helping themselves from brass tables. She watched Sulaiman lean toward Theo.

"Allah the merciful, who brings the blessed rain and causes the desert to flower, has brought again the bloom of your presence. And our great Kings, 'Abd al 'Aziz Ibn 'Abd al Rahman al Faisal al Sa'ud, Masters of the Hejaz and supreme rulers of the Nejd, would set eyes on their brother Angstrom and clasp to their bosom one who has caused such a wonderous crop to be taken from where men knew not it existed. Therefore, my worshipful friend and his concubine Sara Rosenfeld will be guests tomorrow at the palace at Riyadh."

Sara choked at the description of herself as a concubine, then said in a slightly raised voice, "Pick me out a comfortable camel."

"We are honored," Ted spoke loudly to cover her remark. The ladies on the other side of the partition were not intended to be heard.

"When you have rested the night, it happens Their Majesties the Kings have their personal plane waiting to fly you as the assis migrant bird across the great desert." Sulaiman bowed.

Ted bowed. The translator bowed. The governor bowed.

On their side, the women bowed and Sara bowed. They were sprinkled with rose water. Dinner was over.

Sara sat in a corner of the van and worked on her diary. A vice-president of Standard of New Jersey was holding forth.

"Esso wants a piece of the action out here. An infusion of new capital, and things will really take off. We are thinking in the neighborhood of thirty percent. In order to attract American workers, we need a multi-million-dollar complex."

Ted seemed to go for the idea. "California type bungalows, a clubhouse with pool, golf, dining room. We'd set up a clinic, a health center, hospital, and staffing."

Sara looked up. "Would that be for everyone? Or just company employees?"

Standard of New Jersey coughed. "It's not our country," he said.

Ted was impatient at the interruption. He saw a resort town, a Palm Springs or Las Vegas. "Here in the Hasa, within five years, possibly four. That's why Sara and I are making the trip to Riyadh. I think it's important to soften up the King. Or as a Sulaiman puts it, the Kings. After all, we've got to have a cinema and booze. What else is there to do in the middle of Arabia? He's got to keep his Wahhabis in line."

That night looking out at night-fishing on the Persian Gulf, Sara moved close under the American blanket and silken Arabian cover. "Do you remember the game we used to play, at least I think all children play it? King of the Golden Mountain? That's you. I thought that, because I pictured you standing up on the highest derrick platform on the dome. But no one else guessed. I was the only one who knew you wanted to climb the rig and slither under the tanks, trying handles, tightening turnoffs."

Ted only laughed.

"Oh Theo, it's been a glorious day." A scarab, set high on long dainty legs, watched their lovemaking from a corner of the silk coverlet. When Sara discovered it, she would not allow it to be squashed, but insisted Theo edge it gently outdoors where it could rejoin others of its kind.

In the morning two groups came to see them off in their AD9. Sara noticed there was no commingling. There were the Arab representatives, and the Americans, standing distantly on the same field, each with farewells to say.

Much to Ted's relief they had a British pilot. "March is the name, sir. I come with the plane."

"I was afraid we were in for an Arabian who would try to fly the thing with a camel stick."

They were airborne and the walled town of Hofuf soon under them. When it disappeared, the emptiness, the utter loneliness of the land was a sisterhood with infinity. The sands ran north and south through the

217

middle of Arabia. The northern sand sea was the Nafud, the southern, Rub'al Khali, the Empty Quarter. Below them the desert of the Dahna and the stone range of the Arma began the ascent to the Nejd plateau.

Five years before, a journey such as this would mean crossing two hundred fifty miles of barren waterless waste, and not as the crow flies, but trekking zigzag from oasis to oasis along ancient caravan routes. Camps and settlements were tucked between the Tuwaiq mountains, that bleached backbone blown bare of sand from which the land hangs to either side. In the folds were the fertile oases. What they passed in forty-five minutes would have been several days' journey and a steep descent into the Wadi Dawasir. Beyond the thrusting barrier of the escarpment was a blazing desolation.

"I don't see how men live, or even animals," Sara said with awe.

"It's a bleak existence. The Bedouin spend their lives looking for pasture. It springs up in the most surprising places after the rains."

"I wonder," she mused, "how it will be from now on? I noticed Arabs among the work crew. Not many, but some."

"It's happening. Those who work for the Company have a higher standard of living. They aren't hungry. They can afford houses, more wives." He shot her a look out of the corner of his eye.

"Of course," she agreed, "the better things of life."

Once they saw a black tent spread in the emptiness, a couple of camels staked beside it. "A poor family," Ted guessed, "camped well away from the main routes to avoid the hospitality law, the obligation to feed strangers."

Crest after crest of sand. In the troughs scrub grew and camelthorn bushes. They could see steeply rising mountains in the west. He told her that Riyadh meant "the gardens," and she was delighted to point out date groves which were their first sight of Ibn Saud's stronghold. Another landmark was a giant freestanding stone. "The Needle's Eye," their pilot called back to

218

them, "known as Wakhrouq." The wireless station was also a prominent feature, if not picturesque. They flew over Ramah, an important well lying northeast of the city. It started to rain but their pilot set down with no difficulty on a gravel field outside the walls.

"I didn't realize," Sara said, "how shut in he is. Shut into the desert and shut into his town."

A shaikh of the royal house stepped forward with his madi, or body of servants to greet them. "Your coming is green," he said. "To come with rain in our land is auspicious."

March translated somewhat hesitantly, and they walked toward a parked Cadillac. Ted noticed Fords had been replaced by the more opulent limousines. He wondered if his old friend Nichols had a franchise on these as well. The word at Dammam VII was that Nichols was at Riyadh, and he looked forward to seeing him.

They took off at full tilt toward the most amazing walls. From a distance they looked like an unbroken column of men standing shoulder to shoulder, which was undoubtedly the impression they were meant to convey. Their pilot, who was allowed to drive only airplanes, explained, while holding on to the door handle of the car as though ready to jump, that this was the famous architectural feature of Riyadh. Stairs had been torn out and a ramp installed to allow cars to drive to the second floor of a semidetached and re-mote part of the palace. Here they got out and pro-ceeded by foot along corridors with deep Nejdi arches. Figures in dark robes squatted in shadows telling prayer beads and recounting religious epics.

No one looked up as they passed, but Sara felt eyes on their backs. Adjoining rooms were assigned them. "I suppose I'm going to be bathed again," she whispered.

"You are if we're to dine with the King."

She made a face and whispered back, "When do we give our presents?"

"Now." Ted indicated to the servant that he was to take the California saddle he had brought to Ibn Saud.

It was authentic Spanish, heavily embossed with silver, which showed effectively against the black polished leather.

Sara brought as her gift and private joke the rejected alabaster chess set whose elephant rooks had down-curling tusks. She felt a bit ashamed of the present now that her hope was for rapprochement, but consoled herself that Ibn Saud would be unlikely to share Theo's superstition. In any event she had nothing else to give. The King's chamberlain dismissed the servant and himself swept everything into a shawl brought for that purpose. "Al durahman al tabaishi," he said.

"That's either a very long thank you or his name," Sara hazarded. Veiled women circled her, and with a backward look she was led off.

Her Western clothes were again set aside. She was given more scrupulous attention than before, even the lips of her vulva were spread and rinsed with heated water. This forwardness angered her. She had read enough to know they were checking for signs of menses. A menstruating woman could not be admitted to the male presence, let alone that of the King. At the moment, Sara reflected, she was quite pure. But she felt sorry for these poor women who cooperated in their own degradation. She was toweled and anointed with musk, sandlewood, and amber. Her eyes were outlined with kohl. The women murmured at her beauty, unaware that they had humiliated her, and laid gauzy filaments of sheer cloth over her body and head, for draping across her face. Sara made an effort to discover whether the veiling of women and confinement in harim was Koran law or a practice developed by custom. But her sign language was not sufficient to the occasion. She was served coffee with great ceremony and learned that *della* is coffee pot, and *finjal* a cupful.

She thought the Arabian way of taking you by the hand and leading you off as though you were a child, delightful. The women did that now, taking her to Theo that he might admire the wonders wrought.

"Is that you, Sara?" He was quite bedazzled.

"In a bedroom culture," she said, "there are certain things they do very well."

"Yeah. You stink good."

She privately thought the dove-gray robe of fine cambric and mantle that fell to his sandaled feet pre-eminently romantic. The headgear emphasized his aquiline features and the blueness of his eyes.

An enormous black entered in the livery of the royal household, a scarlet robe trimmed in lemon flowers with heavy embroidery and gold fringes. He salaamed, motioning Ted to follow. Sara was again taken in charge by the women who led her through a maze of crumbling passageways mottled by the setting sun.

A bell tolled to announce the muezzin's call to prayer. For some minutes everything stopped. The tableau held as the name of Allah was invoked. After-wards they continued by their women's route where many feet had worn holes in the stone, to a sitting area with low tables laden with an array of succulent dishes. She inhaled the fragrance of orange blossom jam.

From her place of honor Sara was able to look through the lacy partition directly at Ibn Saud. He reclined in his majlis with his sons about him, along with governors and emirs from other provinces. She was surprised to see several Europeans present.

Theo entered with a somewhat rotund Englishman, who she guessed was Nichols. The talk broke off. Ibn Saud rose and stepped forward to greet them with the formal inquiries Arab etiquette demands. He led Theo to a place on his right hand.

In repose the King's face was grim and forbidding as he fixed his guest with his good eye. In that one glance Sara saw the hand-to-hand fighter on camel and horse-back. They said he ruled by proving he was able to kill, then bestowing unexpected clemency and often inviting rebel chiefs to join his army. These men were among his staunchest supporters.

Many of his subjects, on kneeling to him, said, "Turn your eye away from me that I may speak."

221

Theo was obviously surprised, and she thought disconcerted, by the presence of other foreigners. They were introduced as Mr. Creighton-Jones in charge of locust fighting and his team.

"Locusts? What happened to the butterflies?" It didn't take Theo long to discover they were trained geologists.

Creighton-Jones assured him locusts were a considerable problem. "During the winter they're not so bad. Little boys gather them and once the wings, heads, and legs are removed, they can be rather tasty fried in butter. But when they begin to come in clouds, look out. They feed on anything edible. The swarms are so great that those behind eat those in front. If they hit against any obstacle they pile up in great numbers, decaying with a loathsome smell. But you were saying something about butterflies?"

Theo did not enlighten him. He spoke instead with the King's second son whom he had met in '33. Sara saw her chess set in the lap of the Emir Faisal, which was evidence that the gift found favor. Theo's Spanish saddle was also reposing with a high official, so the first hurdle had been passed. The gifts would not be mentioned, that was bad form. But they could expect gifts themselves when they departed.

Lantern bearers began to walk among the guests, then censer bearers waving golden filigree pots of incense. Slaves slid an entire camel across the floor on a low raft; inside its slit belly was a goat, which in turn was slit to accommodate a hare. Inside this creature reposed bay leaves, fruits, and herbal salads sprinkled with coriander.

Sara sucked honeycomb from the tips of her fingers. The women beamed at her enjoyment. She was wondering what a feast such as this cost. Many items, the crab legs packed in ice, partridge, and stuffed oysters, must have been flown in from Cairo, Paris, or even London. And in the United States, among her college friends, the burning issue was whether to marry on fifteen dollars a week.

She was fascinated by Ibn Saud. He dwarfed every man in the room with the exception of Theo. They were different builds. Theo solid, Saud lean, his beaked nose giving him the look of a fisher bird. He resembled, she thought, the German propaganda pictures of Jews. His one eye was a drowned sea, floating between his lids it could congeal on the instant in sudden concentration. She understood the threat of being brought before him would frequently make a guilty man confess. He was sternly paternalistic, and his people said, "His judgment is like lightning."

She felt his charm too, as he inclined his head to listen. He seemed in great good humor. Why not? Theo estimated he would see seven million dollars from this single operating well within the next few months.

The King was discussing the sacred herd of al Mulair; the camels were his special pride. On them his personal troops were mounted. He seemed completely at ease and she judged that, aside from the foreign guests, he was surrounded by members of his household. According to Theo, he liked to see the same faces around him, and when a man received an appointment, it was generally for life. That spoke well for him, she thought.

Theo, in a relaxed mood repeated the joke he liked best. Thresher saying to the King, "You asked for water and I gave you oil."

Ibn Saud's expression did not lighten. Apparently jokes did not translate well. Or it might be he would have preferred to find water.

Theo wisely proceeded with a description of what he had seen in the eastern Hasa. "High gravity oil. Proved resources. In the neighborhood of four trillion barrels."

These figures obviously meant nothing to the King, although they caused a stir among the English. Nichols translated nobly, but it was doubtful if the Saudi language contained words for such concepts as "trillion." Sara guessed Nichols used some analogy: endless pens of sheep, or camels kneeling in a line from here to Hofuf.

Theo tried again, picturing the blessings of wealth flowing into the kingdom. "Schools can be set up, clinics, doctors, brought in."

223

The King was displeased. "The family Saud have long possessed medical knowledge."

Nichols, translating, could not refrain from adding, "Camel urine. Taken orally or rubbed on the exterior, depending on the nature of the complaint."

At that moment two guards until now hidden in shadow, stepped forward. Armed with curved scimitars they escorted a dirty, ragged Bedouin. Hair matted, face pocked, smelling of his camel, he was led before the King. Ibn Saud held up his hand for silence. With eyes on the ground and in a crouched position the man poured out a lengthy tale of grievance.

At the King's command food from the table was wrapped and handed to the suppliant and three gold pieces counted into his palm by the chamberlain.

It impressed Sara that Ibn Saud held himself open in this manner to the lowest of his subjects. They could demand and receive an audience at any time. Their problems of stolen goods or an injury done took precedence over the affairs of state. The wild-looking fellow bowed his way out calling on Allah to witness the heart of this noble King.

Ibn Saud emitted a great cry. Sara thought he had been stabbed by one of the scimitars. But the cry was for coffee. The warlike sound was taken up by every slave and soldier in the room, and carried to the distant recess where the coffeemaker sat in readiness.

Theo had been briefed on the coffee ceremony, which took a slightly different form with the king. Ibn Saud was served first. He grandly waved the aromatic beverage to his guest, who must not fail to decline and send it back to the King. Ritual demanded the King make another offer. This was to be accepted.

The King asked if Theo had inspected Ain al Saba, the largest and deepest spring in al Hasa, from which seven conduits led. "It lies green in its bed of rock. It is my hope, with the equipment the company brings in, more pure water may be found."

Ted was amazed to realize the main thing on the King's mind continued to be water. No wonder he had not appreciated his sally. The King didn't comprehend that everything he hoped to produce through agriculture could be bought with oil revenues. He explained to Ted that the water table at Riyadh was steadily declining. Nichols added, "This is not surprising, they use water power to run generators that light not only palaces and homes, but the date gardens as well."

"We will try with our equipment," Ted assured the King.

Ibn Saud quoted the Koran. "For verily, God changeth not that which is in a people until they try with that which is in themselves." He emphasized each word with his camel stick.

Ted attempted once more to interest him in oil. But the King considered there was nothing further to say on the subject. It had gushed from the Dome of Dammam as Allah, in his infinite wisdom, willed. "My British friends," he bestowed a smile on the chief of the locust team, Creighton-Jones, "assist in the search for water. They do this freely without asking us to repay them. You Americans are too much business. Not enough is done in friendship, from the heart."

"With all deference to Mr. Jones," Ted purposely and offensively omitted the Creighton, "no government gives from the goodness of its heart. The British, in fact all Europe, are menaced. The Persian Gulf contains the British concession at Bahrein. If war should come. . . ."

"It will come," the King said knowingly. "It is the natural condition of man to war. This is understood by the German leader who calls himself Fuehrer. There is an ancient path of blood which must be followed. The Germans know this and have gathered, so the wireless tells us, the most powerful army in the world. Of course, the sea protects both the countries of Britain and America."

Creighton-Jones and Theodore Angstrom announced at the same moment that they needed no seas to protect them. In an attempt to ease the situation Ted turned to a discussion of alternate plans for a pipeline. He mentioned the port of Haifa, which was geographically an ideal terminus and would save billions of dollars annually in transportation.

The King glowered. "Not Haifa," he said. "The Jews are attempting to steal Palestine. It may be they will succeed. We shall not make them rich in their port of Haifa. Rather we shall push them into the sea."

"But the Iraqi terminus is already there. It is the most direct and logical route."

"I quite agree with the King," Creighton-Jones put in. "Haifa is the last place for your oil port."

"I thought your expertise was locusts, Mr. Jones. I suggest you go fry yourself some."

The King demanded a translation and Mr. Nichols' powers were hard pressed.

A moist embroidered towel was brought Sara. The women daintily touched their finger tips to it. But Sara scrubbed her hands in an effort to rub off the hospitality of her enemies. Because they *were* her enemies, and it had been stupid, childish and naïve to think otherwise. She had seen herself meeting her brother in Ein Harod, with the wisdom and insight necessary to bring Jew and Arab together. Seemingly they complemented each other's needs. The Jew with his technical skills, the Arab who needed them and had oil money to purchase them. But the interchange at dinner utterly discouraged her. The bitterness was too extreme, suspicion and hatred a current that ran deep in Arab nature.

The King announced a hunt had been organized in their honor to begin tomorrow when they had rested, prayed, had coffee, bathed, and breakfasted. Nichols expressed their appreciation at this unexpected thoughtfulness, and the banquet was over. Everyone bowed to Ibn Saud, more florid thanks poured from the practiced Nichols on their behalf and they walked backwards out of the room. Ted tripped over one of the Persian carpets laid everywhere, and this made Sara feel better.

Outside she was introduced to John Eustace Nichols and Creighton-Jones. Jones said, "You are certainly among the first half-dozen foreign women to set foot in the capital, Miss Rosenfeld. And one of those became his wife."

"I don't believe Ibn Saud and I have much in common," Sara replied tartly. Whereupon Nichols related

226

the story of a mountain sage, a holy man known for his piety throughout the land. Eventually the King too heard of the wise man and sent an emissary inviting him to his court as an adviser.

"The wise man declined with thanks. And when the emissary departed, he washed out his ears and also the ears of his donkey."

Theo laughed, "I take it you are anxious to return to Jidda?"

They left Creighton-Jones at his quarters and walked to the Palace Qasr Faisal, named for the King's grandfather, where Nichols was staying. "Things are heating up in the Middle East," he told them. "Damascus is seething with Arab xenophobia. The Grand Mufti of Jerusalem is in Berlin as Hitler's guest. An Arab likes to hear what he believes. The Mufti believes in a takeover of Palestine, and will return with the funds to accomplish it. This means a continued pinning down of part of the British army. We have at least twenty thousand men stationed there. And although I didn't dispute you in front of the King, I rather agree with Creighton-Jones regarding the inadvisability of a Haifa pipeline. The Kirkuk-Haifa line has already been sabotaged."

"I hadn't heard," Ted said thoughtfully. "Thousands of miles of pipe are certainly vulnerable. Which brings us in a roundabout way to our friend, the leftenant of the locust brigade. What the devil are they doing here?"

"Pretty much what you think they're doing here," Nichols said, "and incidentally ridding the country of locusts."

"What are they after in particular? Concessions, refineries, pipelines, transport? And how will they pay? They weren't able to come up with hard cash in '33."

Nichols glanced at Sara. "There are other currencies," he said.

"Such as restricted Jewish immigration into Palestine?" she asked.

"Such as *no* immigration into Palestine."

She gasped. "But the Balfour Declaration. Britain can't turn its back on that."

"In times of national crisis, my dear girl, there is

no such thing as national honor. The Higher Arab Committee has had frequent talks at Whitehall."

"But the mandate?" She ripped off the veil and used it loudly as a handkerchief.

"There are men of integrity, but when the tempest breaks who knows how far the reed must bend?"

Theo and Sara went back through the date gardens. The women assigned to her saw Theo and withdrew, but not without subdued loquacity regarding the missing veil.

When they were alone he wrapped his arms around her. "Don't worry, the Arabs are so disunited they can never agree on any policy."

"Not even killing Jews? I thought that was the one point on which they reach unanimity. What a hateful old man he is. Did you hear him say, drive them into the sea?"

"It's rhetoric, Sara. They love bombast, the flowery phrase. He is interested in two things: water and oil. He is not really interested in Palestine. It's too far away."

"Do you think so?"

"I know it. He is the original Midas. He's not concerned with anything that doesn't immediately turn to gold. Did I ever tell you that I had to pay him in actual bullion for the concession? He also demands gold from the religious pilgrims that come to Mecca. Nothing else will do. They sell their children to lay a gold piece in the hands of his minister. As for the British, neither they nor their butterfly collectors or locust fighters are going to get a foot in the door of my concession."

But Sara was upset on other grounds. It all poured out, her crazy dream of finding a common denominator that would unite her people and the Arabs. "Dov says many Palestinian Jews think it is *British* policy to foment trouble so they can hold onto the mandate. Because traditionally there is a history of friendship that lasted into the Middle Ages. But I saw tonight how impossible it is. The preset in that man's mind, and probably in the mind of every Arab, is unshakable." She crept into his arms.

Ted was touched, but could think of nothing to

comfort her. "I'll tell you what, I'll forget the locust fighters, if you forget the King."

She nodded and slept. Toward morning he made love to her, and she responded, hardly aware what rhythm had gotten into her sleep.

The call of the muezzin was piped into every room in Riyadh. It startled them awake before first light. Next they heard the coffeemaker grinding his beans.

In what appeared to be a parking lot of kneeling camels, the hunting party assembled. There was much commotion as the animals were loaded with every kind of equipment. Racing in and out among the camels were several dozen automobiles gunned through the area by wild-eyed boys of ten or twelve. They took devilish delight in making the beasts bray and roll their eyes. Only the fact that they were hobbled kept them from bolting.

To add to the confusion a mobile wireless was in the process of being mounted on a truck, and a refrigeration van piled with crates of perishables. Nichols came up to them panting slightly. "The court is moving into the desert for a week of hunting."

"A week?" Ted said. "We hadn't planned to stay that long."

"Plan on it," Nichols retorted. "You are the guest of honor, there's no backing out."

"When he said he was arranging a hunt, I thought he meant for the afternoon."

"Who are those kids driving around like maniacs?" Sara asked indignantly.

"Princes of the imperial household. Spoiled brats. They're given Cadillacs the way boys elsewhere are given bicycles."

Ted gathered that Nichols did not own that particular franchise or he would have been more tolerant.

The desert air was still cold from the night, giving energy to man and animal. Nichols indicated the mounted wireless. "Saud's chain of on-the-spot information. It keeps his three-and-a-half million subjects in hand. He knows what's going on in any sector of his kingdom instantly. There's something sad about the old King, at least in my eyes. To bring in this enormous oil revenue he sold out his own creation, the Wahhabi state. He needs to keep tabs on them, and he does. He also subsidizes the desert tribes to keep them loyal. By means of this combination, communication and largess, he maintains complete control of the peninsula."

A car was assigned to them, and Sara had her first experience chasing along with mares and camels over dunes and plunging into hollows on low pressure semi-flat tires.

"Would it be possible," she asked after an hour of this, "to get out and walk a while?" This they did, and it was a relief from the breakneck pace and wild jouncing of the car.

"When I was first in this country," Nichols reminisced, "there were panthers and monkeys in the uplands. But Ibn Saud introduced motorized hunts. I have seen herds of gazelle reduced by two or three hundred animals in a day. The effect is disastrous, of course. The desert ibex is all but extinct, and the few gazelle that remain have taken refuge in the mountains. Nothing moves within a hundred miles of Riyadh, except a few scorpions, rats, horned vipers, and a peculiar double-beaked white spider."

"What they'll do is drive the game down from the mountains, then?" Ted asked.

"The beaters started out last night." Nichols was fatigued and suggested riding again. Sara was sorry to be cooped up once more in the car. But she enjoyed Nichols' stories of how the King was dealing with his new-found wealth.

"It's still Sulaiman and his piggy-bank methods. There is an entry I have seen with my own eyes, entitled *Riyadh Affairs*. It is an allotment for the royal household, and it is exactly four times the total budget for the rest of the country." Sara gasped. That was too much for her socialist conscience. "When the King wants to hide a particularly flagrant expenditure there is something Sulaiman devised called *General Development*. This is 12.5 percent of the total budget for the entire kingdom. Another whopping 10.4 percent goes for security. This is not a military expenditure, it's for the maintenance of his private bodyguard. And this is the man who started out a Wahhabi puritan," Nichols concluded.

"Is there any allotment whatever," Sara asked, "for health or education?"

Nichols smiled. "On paper, five percent. But this has been absorbed by the royal household. You see, the King cannot conceive of any but the royal family receiving an education or calling on the services of a doctor."

"You sound bitter, Mr. Nichols." Sara spoke gently.

"I've given my life to this land. I don't like the way things are going. It's inevitable, I suppose, but I don't like it."

"Have you said so to the King?"

"I have. And been threatened with exile. I do not stand in high favor these days."

They camped the first night by a well of sweet water, at which a camel turned the water wheel. There were several houses nearby, fallen into ruins. But a city of a hundred tents rose magically. The King's pavilion was three times the size of the others and had, besides, an extra tent pole. The green standard of his family was planted in the sand before it.

Prayers like the sustained note of an organ were chanted, sounding eerie in the wilderness. The King decided on the spur of the moment to entertain his guests by races. Sons and nephews threw their swords, points quivering, into the sand. And mares were ridden past the King's tent, each contestant in turn saluting. Then, with fierce whoops, they flicked their horses to racing speed. He who was first to seize the haft of the sword, pull it from the ground, and return to the starting point to bury it anew, triumphed.

While this diversion was in progress, slaves and servants set up massive cauldrons, and the aroma of their efforts floated over the camp. The King awarded prizes to all winners and everyone gathered about the low tables which had been spread with an amazing variety of food.

Caravaneers from many areas had been called to the hunt. Unkempt, wild looking, they carried, besides the thin camel cane, a dagger at the waist. Nichols explained it was useless to inquire what tribe they were from. "Tradition forbids a truthful answer. If someone offends you, he assumes you will take revenge on his entire family or even clan. They usually know among themselves by the way the hotta is worn, or whether or not the hair is braided, or by a beard shaped a certain way."

Around the campfire that night, Nichols told them the story of King Solomon's mines. "It was called the Bani Sulaim gold mine, and was first worked by order of King Solomon. It was operating until the end of the tenth century. By then, under deplorable conditions. They herded slaves into the mouth of the cave, giving them neither food nor water—these were bargained for when sufficient ore was brought up. The mine lay dormant a thousand years, as things can in this country."

"And a good thing too," Sara interpolated.

"In 1935, an American company began working it again."

By this time Sara was drowsing on Ted's shoulder, so they went into their tent. It seemed they had just dropped off when they were waked by the imam's call to prayer. Sara didn't need the white turban as identification, she knew by the stern expression he was a Wahhabi. "I couldn't be the follower of a God who gave me this little sleep," she complained, and downed three cups of coffee to set her up for the second day's journey.

Ibn Saud sent for Ted to breakfast with him. His enormous tent billowed in the wind, as did the standard whose flutterings marked the house of Saud.

The King relaxed against his camel saddle as he ate. When he finished, he asked that the Western woman be brought to him for conversation.

Ted was nonplussed. He had not foreseen this eventuality. Sara could almost be counted on to say the wrong thing. Suppose, for instance, she brought up the Jewish question? He should never have risked teasing the lion who reached out now with tentative paw.

Perhaps he could forestall this fancy on the part of

the King. He protested through Nichols that it was too great an honor. The King took this as customary politeness and, waving his words away, sent servants to escort Sara to his tent. Ted privately vowed to stick by her side and coach her on what to say, or, at the least, see to it that Nichols' translation did not reflect Rosenfeld remarks too closely.

Sara arrived, flanked by blacks of the royal household. She slightly inclined her head.

"I am the King," Ibn Saud said through Nichols.

"I am Sara Rosenfeld," she replied.

"You look well in the garments of our women," the King observed. "Do you find them comfortable?"

"All but the veil. I find that a bother." She successfully avoided Ted's eye.

"You don't like it?"

"No. And I don't suppose any woman does."

The King thought upon the matter. "Arabian women are used to it."

"Tell me, is it decreed in scriptures they must wear it? Is it so stated in your holy book, the Koran?"

"There is no mention of it in the Koran. It is a thing of not that much significance."

"Well, if it isn't holy law, then it's merely a matter of custom. And so great a King as yourself could abolish it."

Ibn Saud was astounded at her words. "And become known as a profligate?" said the man who had known a hundred and fifty wives. He decided they would speak on another topic. "Do you find beauty in the desert?" he inquired.

"Yes. Especially at night. The stars are so much larger and brighter, as though I am looking at other worlds."

The King was pleased with this answer. "You are well spoken for a woman. Know that the wasm come with the rise of the Pleiades." He contemplated her with interest. "How many years have you?"

"Twenty-one."

He shook his head in commiseration. "I should not have thought you so old."

She laughed at his remark, which somewhat be-

233

wildered and thoroughly charmed the King. "This day your camel shall ride beside mine."

"But I have never. . . ."

"I have said it." He turned to the men. Sara was so nervous at the thought of a camel ride that she ate little breakfast. "I thought I was joking when I said I wanted a comfortable camel," she said when Ted joined her. "Do you suppose they have such a thing?"

"I'm not worried about the camel," he said lightly. "It's the King. He's taken a shine to you."

She laughed. "No, he hasn't. He thinks I'm too old."

"You know, Sara, you said a number of impolitic things. Like criticizing the veil."

"Theo, please don't lecture me. This may be an opportunity. Do you think I will be able to speak directly to the King?"

"For Christ's sake, Sara. We're here to smooth the way for an American compound. Don't gum up the works."

She considered what he said. "I'd never do anything to hurt you, Theo. Still. . . ."

A servant in the livery of the royal household salaamed before her and led her toward the kneeling, impatiently groaning rows of camels. She was handed onto a white one, prettily caparisoned with bells and beads.

The King was already mounted. His height and his camel's height set him well above other men. She was glad to see Nichols also made up the party. Ted stood obstinately beside her although he had been assigned a car. He said to Nichols, "Tell His Majesty I would prefer a camel."

Nichols transmitted this information to Ibn Saud. The King looked down at Ted from his great height and replied that the camels were taken.

Sara's beast lurched to its feet. Once up, the gait was not unpleasant, something like a rocking chair. Their group formed the heart of the procession. Soldiers ringed them with automatic weapons slung from their saddles.

Ibn Saud turned his one eye like a searchlight on Sara. "This is my camel corps," he told her through

234

Nichols. "Crack troops. I am also building a mechanized battalion."

"That's too bad," Sara called to Nichols who rode between them, although slightly behind. "I hope the oil does not bring you trouble."

"Riches invariably bring trouble," the King shouted at Nichols, his eye fixed on her. "But it is a man's destiny to preserve what is his. The Koran says a man's possessions and his children are his enemies."

"I agree about the possessions. But children?"

He smiled down at her tolerantly. Nichols, raising his voice, gave his reply. "By extension, all one's subjects are children. They come at the beginning of summer for the annual gathering to make known their requests, to complain against their neighbors. The Qadis deal with matters of Koran. I, with civil law. When it is appropriate, I honor them with a bag of rice or, if they are nobly born, a mare of worth."

"It seems to me," Sara said, "the poor man should have the mare of worth. He would need it more."

The King thought on this. "You have a strange tongue for a woman."

She caught the reins tighter in her hand. "A Jewish tongue," she said.

"Do you think I should translate that?" Nichols asked.

"Yes."

The King rode in silence after hearing Nichols out. "You are a Jew?"

"Yes," she said to the King directly. He understood the word.

"I have heard that the women of the Jews are beautiful," he said with courtesy, then waited for translation and embarked on a story. "There was in our country in the sixth century A.D., an Arab Christian saint known as Aretas. He was governor of the Abyssinian Kingdom of Aksum. He and the people of Najran were converted by the Nestorian, Phemion. It was a sad thing, Saint Aretas and the other Christians were slaughtered by Dhu Nuwas, a Jew."

There was a pause on Sara's side. "I didn't happen to know him," she said.

"Do you jest?" the King asked via Nichols, but turning his single beacon on her.

"Do you?"

Nichols wiped his brow.

The King replied severely. "The Jewish people are being misled by bandits, the Irgun Zvai Leumi and the Stern Gang."

Sara caught the gist of what was said, recognizing key words, *Irgun Zvai Leumi . . . Stern Gang.* She did not wait for it to go through Nichols. "The Arabs too are being stirred up by fanatics such as the Grand Mufti of Jerusalem."

"This is getting sticky," Nichols protested. He repeated her words, but in a deprecating manner which implied: she says it, not I.

The searchlight, the single eye glared. "You speak of one with whom I have shared hospitality."

"I'm sorry he is a friend of yours. The Jews also have friends among Arabs. Almost twenty years ago King Faisal of Iraq gave his approval to the reestablishment of a Jewish homeland, and urged his people to welcome returning Jews. He even signed a treaty of friendship with Dr. Weizmann." She waited in suspense for the effect of this.

"No one could foresee in those times in what numbers they would come. They descend like locusts. The character of the desert is such that even the most obscure individual is known. In this way each person has importance."

"That's nice," Sara said, "where it is possible. But I understand it is an edict of Your Majesty's that not even a palm tree may be cut down. And I thought, a man who will not cut down a tree will surely be merciful to people in need of protection and help them to their ancient home."

Ibn Saud reined in his al Mulain camel and spoke at length to Nichols. "He says," the Englishman repeated, "I do not discuss politics with women. If I did, I would point out that Palestine is the home of the Arab. I have been informed by Radio Berlin that America has many Jews residing in it, including the

236

president, Mr. Roosevelt. But I was unaware that Mr. Angstrom's favorite wife was a Jewess."

Sara jumped to Ted's defense. Mr. Roosevelt must fend for himself, that job was quite beyond her. "I am not Mr. Angstrom's wife. Only a concubine. And he never listens to me."

"Then he is a sensible man." The camels were still stopped and Nichols edged closer so the King would not need to shout. "That you are beautiful," Nichols said, speaking for the King, "I find pleasing. That you are a Jew, I find displeasing. That you speak as you do, I wish to think on. If you are to ride with me again, my servant will fetch you." He laid on the camel stick and instantly was forward of her surrounded by a band of his guard.

"Well, I had my chance," Sara said glumly. "I didn't do much for the cause of peace. In fact I muffed it."

"Don't be too sure," Nichols said. "My heart was in my mouth the whole time. The King has been known to take his ire out on the one from whom he first hears the idea, regardless of where it originates. He is an antagonist of the Jews. I have seen him literally foam at the mouth when he gets going. He was surprisingly restrained with you. He may even consider what you said. I think the palm tree and the Jewish people got to him. Where did you hear that?"

"I read it on shipboard. Probably some journalist made it up."

Nichols laughed. "You must be quite a handful for Angstrom."

"I hope I didn't hurt his effectiveness with the King."

"It's better to have it come out this way than any other. Although I am surprised Angstrom should run the risk of impairing his position with the King by bringing you."

"He feels he and the King are equal partners. And that what he does or does not do is none of the King's damn business."

"Still, the King is a king, with a kingdom, and oil in his backyard. All Ted has is a piece of paper."

"Then I am a liability?"

"An extremely charming one."

"And Ted was aware of it when he took me along?"

"Of course."

"He is an impossible person," she said.

"I agree. It is why we are friends."

Nichols was the recipient of a dazzling smile which the veil of gauze could not entirely hide.

Camp was made earlier than on the preceding day. They reached a spring with well-tended apricot and pomegranate trees. There were seven mud houses and near these the tent city was erected.

Sara dismounted, glad to be free of the rolling gait of her beast. She saw him watered, however, before looking for Theo. Although Nichols assured her a camel in his prime can go six days without drinking. "There is moisture in the camel-thorn bush they munch. A horse is a different matter. In summer they must be watered by midday."

Actually, although she had not been willing to mention it to the King, the face veil was some protection against the fine grit that settled over everything. The skins of water strapped to camels and cars alike for the second evening provided the royal family and their guests with baths. The same ladies who served her at the palace performed the toilet here. The water poured steamy and scented over her.

Refreshed from the journey, the company repaired as on the previous evening, before the light was lost, for games and sport.

"Whatever happened between you and the King?" Ted demanded, coming up to her.

"Well, he didn't ask me to be his hundredth and fifty-first wife, if that's what you're implying. What you really want to know is did I put my foot in it, say anything that might endanger your precious oil city. Let's see. For openers, I told him I was Jewish."

"Was that necessary?"

"I thought it was."

"What else?"

"What do you mean, what else? I don't have to report to you. Besides if you're so worried about my Jewishness, why the hell did you bring me along?"

238

"I'm sorry, Sara. Of course, I've no right to fire questions at you."

Her anger vanished. "Oh Theo, all I told the King was that a man who protected palm trees would surely protect a people returned to their ancient home. That couldn't hurt you, could it?"

"No, of course not. Forgive me, Sara, just . . . just forgive me."

The contest this evening was falconry.

"Every Nejdi household has its falcon," Nichols was again at her side. "They depend on them to catch bustard and hare. But the truth is, the Bedouin don't know much about their birds and are forever losing them. It's different with the King's falcons. They are imported from Iraq and given excellent care and training. As a matter of fact, each royal falcon has its own slave."

Sara shuddered. "Theo told me slavery is legal here. I find it hard to believe."

"And the trade is not just in blacks. There's a small but brisk business from the north in Georgians, Armenians, and Circassians."

A Nubian in the King's service salaamed to Nichols, inviting him and Ted to the King's side. Sara did not know if it was unseemly for a woman to be present or if she was out of favor. However she was content to watch from a distance, as the death of small birds did not appeal to her.

The royal princes and the male guests gathered about the King under the green pennant. A bird was released into the sky while the still hooded falcon waited on Ibn Saud's gauntleted arm. When the prey was considered to be at a suitable distance the chain and hood were removed. Sara was amazed at the duplicate profile. King and falcon looked incredibly evil with their curled beaks.

The falcon's talons gripped, its purpose evident as it launched into the air, fanning with enormous wingspan the King's draped kaffyeh. It made straight for the small bird for whom there was no escape. Sara turned away her eyes and did not look until the falcon rested once more on its master's glove. It was made to regurgitate by means of a small gold band around its neck and rewarded with other fare, entrails hand-fed by the King.

She was glad of the sustained note of the imam who called them from their sport. She found she was not ready for another meal of iced dishes and syruped fruits.

That night something prowled near their tent. In the morning Theo told her they found wolf tracks. Later she discovered a thief had been apprehended and his hand severed at the wrist.

It was the morning of the hunt, and the minor incident of the thief a prelude to excitement mounting through the encampment. The beaters sent word they had discovered gazelle and were driving them from the mountain onto the plateau. The King, with a dozen of his grown sons and chief ministers, had taken to jeeps. Ted and Nichols were included in this company.

Slaves held unpleasantly lean dogs who strained at their leashes. These creatures resembled greyhounds and were called saluqui. To Sara's surprise, the falcons were also riding the arm of the King and his cohorts.

At a blast from a horn the dogs were set free. They streaked across the scrub desert like emaciated shadows. The jeeps tore after them creating tracks with their splayed tires on the seamless sand. The din was ferocious, baying hounds, jeep horns, and guns fired into the air as the company disappeared in their respective dust clouds.

Sara clapped her hands and cried, "Qahwa!" Her women brought not only coffee but a Persian carpet. Thrown on the sand it was smoothed and spread by the side of the tent. She lay on her stomach drinking the strong brew and amused herself watching an army of dung beetles rolling along balls larger than their bodies. She must have drowsed, because she thought of going inside the tent and sleeping. But when she opened her eyes, she was in the same spot. The day's shade had stolen over her, and she felt chilled. The sound that roused her was the hunting party returning.

The horns were distant, the yapping of the dogs closer. Making straight for her was one of the most beautiful creatures she had ever seen. It was traveling in graceful leaps, its body flowing from one bound to another, but as it got nearer, she saw it was chased by the King's falcon. It had plucked the eye from the gazelle, and the hole in its forehead ran red. Swooping again, the bird pecked at the other bright orb. The gazelle evaded with a quick, contorted movement. The falcon countered the feint, descended on the creature's head, and ate out the remaining eye.

The jeeps were in sight. The blinded thing, blood pouring over its face, rushed directly at one of them. A blast of the horn sent it at another. The royal princes stood, laughing, aiming, but holding off. The dogs bayed expectantly. The gazelle could still outrun them, but the circle of horns tormented and confused the creature, which turned first one way, then another, until the released saluqui brought it down. A scream fastened in Sara's throat. She had seen the Arab at his play. She huddled on the ground where she was. She had never uttered a Jewish prayer, yet she found herself saying quickly, over and over, "Sh'ma Yisroel. Hear O Israel. God of my fathers, save your people. Save them."

The blast of guns rang out over her prayer. The gazelle was slung with two dozen other blinded animals in the rear of the jeeps. They had their night's feast of fresh meat.

Ted looked rather shaken when he came in. "Did you know," she asked him, "did you know what it would be?"

"No. Of course not."

"Albert Schweitzer said, 'Man can hardly even recognize the devils of his own creation.' So that's Ibn Saud who makes the journey to Mecca every year presumably to earn grace. How do you think he'll take to the golf links? They may be a bit tame after this."

"Sara, get hold of yourself. After all you can't judge the man by Western standards."

"But Theo, he is your business partner. The man you will have dealings with for the rest of your life."

"Sara, the women are waiting to dress you for dinner."

"Dinner? You think I'm going to eat those poor

blinded creatures? If anyone asks after me, which I doubt they will, please say I have a headache."

"Sara!"

"Oh Theo, can't you see it? They are going to throw my people to this man and other barbarians like him. We are to be blinded, tormented, set upon and dragged down by dogs, shot at for sport. Theo, I am sick. I want to go away from here. I must get out. I feel trapped in these wastes, pursued by falcons. Please let me go to my brother, to Palestine."

"Travel alone? You're mad, Sara."

"I'll meet you. You'll come as soon as you can. And when you join me I'll have all sorts of marvelous things to show you, Jewish things, that will convince you Jews were in Palestine before any people that still walk the face of the earth. Theo, you must say yes. I am so afraid of how these Arabs play."

He tried to calm her, but she was beside herself, past reasoning with. He decided she was right. The sooner she left Saudi the better. He made an excuse for her through Nichols to her ladies.

The King, on hearing Sara Rosenfeld was indisposed, sent from his own plate a gazelle heart to strengthen her.

Nothing could hold her in that desert. She was the small bird released into the air, the gazelle running without sight, confused by horns and the laughter of men. "I must leave *now*, Theo. Tonight."

"You'll have to have the King's permission. You're a guest. It would be unforgivable to leave so abruptly."

"I don't ask you to leave, just me. I have to get out of this tent, out of this sand, out of this terrible desert."

"But what will I say?"

"Say anything you like. Tell him I've got the curse."

She turned her back on him and squeezed herself into a small knot on the silk cushions. Ted sought out Nichols. "Sara has to return immediately. She is really quite ill."

"Hmmm," Nichols said, "figured she might be." They walked together toward the large tent with the extra pole. "You're a rum one, Angstrom. Bringing your Jewish mistress. Even I wouldn't have thought of that. You know she had me in something of a quandary. That was quite a conversation they had, the King and Sara. I didn't know whether I should translate accurately all she said. However I did. Enjoyed it too. Miss Sara Rosenfeld is the only person besides myself, so to speak, to tell Ibn Saud the world is round."

The news that the gift of gazelle heart had not improved Miss Sara Rosenfeld's condition put the King into a bad mood. He was suspicious that she was malingering, worried she might be really ill, and thwarted in the decision he had arrived at to have her ride at his side once more. He had even toyed with the idea of taking her as a wife. There was room for one at the moment. But his Wahhabis would make a fuss at a foreign woman, and if it were discovered she was a Jew, it would put her in danger of an ulema assassin. Besides, he was unsure as to protocol, uncertain how to approach Mr. Angstrom on the subject. Until all these matters were decided in his mind, he did not wish her to leave. "I will send my physician," he said, brightening at the solution. "The man is a Syrian. He has treated my family for years with the small black pearl of al Hasa ground to an efficacious powder."

"And camel urine," Nichols added on his own.

"I thank Your Majesty," Ted stuttered over the words, "but in her fever she longs for water and green hills."

The King pondered the problem. "We ardently wish for the recovery of Miss Sara Rosenfeld. To that end I shall arrange for her and her ladies to return to the palace at Riyadh. By means of the wireless a plane will come within the hour. The Syrian doctor will be in attendance. When she is recovered she will choose which white mare of the stables of Saud shall be hers." The King issued an order and they were dismissed.

Ted turned to Nichols. "I want a Company plane to meet her at Riyadh and fly her to Palestine."

"I am convinced the King expects to see her in Riyadh on his return. Otherwise how is he going to present her with a white mare?"

"Fuck the white mare."

Nichols shrugged. "Very well. It just means borrowing the wireless for a few minutes. The plane will be there when she arrives."

"Do you really think he is taken with her?" Ted asked.

"The King is taken with every woman if she is not pock-marked, scarred or cross-eyed. And Sara Rosenfeld would be quite a new experience for him. It would be different if she were your wife, but he is aware she is merely your concubine. And it is as well the relationship was explained to him in these terms. The punishment for adultery is quite biblical—stoning."

Within an hour, a light plane landed. The King sent a gift of a robe for Sara's departure. And the King's translator begged her to notice that as a result of her conversation with his royal master, a veil was not included. She was carried to the plane accompanied by two ladies and the physician. Playing her part, Sara lifted a languorous hand toward the green standard under which Ibn Saud sat. When Ted bent over she winked. Once stowed aboard, the takeoff watched by all, they seemed to fly directly into the sun.

By the time Ted arrived in Palestine, Sara had been there two weeks. They were to meet at the King David Hotel at four-thirty, and she was late.

He was late too, for that matter. His plane bucked headwinds, customs was slow, the taxi had taken forever, which made it doubly inexcusable that she was not here. He had traveled across Arabia and the whole Middle East. All she had to do was be here.

He went into the bar and ordered a double scotch. Ten minutes later there was a light touch on his arm. He turned, looking into a sun-browned gypsy face. Her hair was caught back in a kerchief the way the Jewish women he had observed wore theirs. He didn't like her looking like a Jewess and smiling in such a radiantly happy way. He felt the cool look of several British officers on them.

"Oh Theo, I've been reborn. I couldn't stay here, you can see that. I mean, it's so stuffy and British. So I went to the kibbutz Ein Harod in the Jezreel Valley to be with Dov and Lev. I wouldn't have known Lev. He's fifteen. So serious and intelligent. The life is hard but I think Dov has adjusted. In many ways he seems the same, older of course, sterner. . . . But I haven't asked you how your trip was?" And before he could answer, "You'll never guess what I've been doing. Picking oranges."

"You've been what?"

"Picking oranges. That's why I was late, the truck broke down."

"Truck? You came by truck?"

"Well, I don't expect *you* to go by truck, darling. So don't look cross. I've got a perfectly wonderful sightseeing schedule worked out for you. First we'll have dinner. . . ."

"Right here," he said.

"Oh? Do you think so? Dov and Lev are anxious to meet you."

"Here."

"Of course."

"You did bring a change of clothes, I hope?"

"Actually, no. I didn't take much, if you remember. And the people are so poor."

"You mean you've given every blessed thing away?"

"You'd have wanted me to, Theo."

He reached into his pocket. "Go get something that you can appear here in." Then relenting, "And something for later on too, you know."

"Yes, I know." She brushed his cheek in a kiss and was gone. That evening he might have been escorting a Parisian model, exquisite in a broad-rimmed hat and pearls that set off a simple black dress. He ordered her favorite, Bristol Cream sherry.

"Ibn Saud was extremely annoyed at not finding you at Riyadh."

"Not our first night. Please Theo, let me tell you about the marvelous itinerary I've worked out."

"What is it?" he asked.

"I thought you'd want to see the agricultural settlements. Degania is the oldest, with over twenty new ones established since. It's really remarkable what's been done. In 1930 there were 15,000 acres in citrus. Today, 50,000. Then I want to take you to the chemical plant where they mine deposits from the Dead Sea. They dig up these chunks of salt, dry them, and turn them into potash. And knowing you, high priority has been given to the terminus of the Kirkuk-Haifa pipeline."

Ted found himself laughing. This was a different Palestine than he would be seeing if Brillianna had him in tow. "What happened," he teased Sara, "to the road to Calvary, the Church of the Sepulchre, Gethsemane, the Mount of Olives?"

"They're here too. That's what so strange about Palestine. It's all here, the old and the new. The dead and the living."

"And you want me to see the living first?"

"It didn't occur to me that perhaps you would like it the other way round. But we'll do it in any order you want, Theo."

He took both her slender brown, slightly roughened hands. "We'll do it your way."

They started out the next morning. "Don't look at the tangles of barbed wire thrown up in front of the Mandelbaum Gate, or the British officiously scrutinizing passes. You need a signed pass to get into the old part of Jerusalem. Imagine that! David, king of the Israelites, established the Ark of the Covenant there. And Solomon built a great temple that stood until 586 B.C. when Nebuchadnezzar destroyed it and carried the people into captivity. Theo, it's so *old*. Remember the Songs of Zion? '*If I forget thee, O Jerusalem*' . . . they were written then, in captivity. But the point is, *they made it back*."

Ted observed that the city stood on an elevated rock spur, probably of basalt.

Sara was telling him how Jerusalem was lost a final time. "In A.D. 66 the Jews revolted under the Maccabee brothers. Revolted against the Roman Empire. That's like Pismo Beach, California, rebelling against the entire country. And then the long exile until the year I was born, 1917, that's when the British signed the Balfour Declaration promising us the land God promised us. But recently it seems they're not anxious to let us have it."

Ted pointed out a wall standing on Crusader foundations. The narrow cobbled streets led past Arab coffee houses which, as in Saudi cities, was where business was transacted.

"Yes," Sara snapped, "the business of carrying out terrorist attacks and killing Jews."

Ted deplored such statements. He felt at home in the Arab section. The open air markets overhung with thatch reminded him of Jidda and Riyadh. Sara told him that when they sold to Jews, the Arabs soaked the fruit in water to make it weigh more."

Ted laughed. "Do you really believe that?"

"If only it would remain at such a level," she said. "Things are bad. Worse than Dov wrote. The Mufti is back in Lebanon where he has drawn up a murder list of Arabs friendly to Jews. So far, Arabs have killed more Arabs than anyone else. The terrorists are brought over the border from Syria and Lebanon and billeted in Palestinian Arab villages. Many times these Palestinian Arabs beg the British for protection against their 'guests.'"

Ted related the Islamic lore he had from Nichols, according to which when Allah created the earth, Murder and Dissension took up their abode in Syria.

"You must tell that to Dov," she said. "It is still true."

They took a taxi to the kibbutz Ein Harod. Ted had reservations about this family meeting. Who was he anyway? The guy who slept with this guy's sister.

But Sara had her heart set on it. "He knows, Theo. Dov was the only one I could confide in. I couldn't tell Poppa. I never have. But I wrote Dov. The main thing in his life was Becca. So I knew he'd understand about us. He saw that I was happy and kissed me. He once said being happy was a form of prayer."

"He sounds like your brother, all right. And the boy?"

Sara hesitated. "I don't know. Times are so unsettled. You don't know who your enemies are. Some say the British; some, the Arabs. Hagana, the principal self-defense organization, has an official policy, *havlaga*. The word means restraint. But it's hard to persuade a young boy who sees the harassment of his own settlement, to be moderate. The agricultural communes are targets because of their isolation. Crops are tended with carbines as well as ploughs. Fawzi Kackji make almost nightly raids, burning fields, uprooting young trees, and firing indiscriminately at anything that moves. If you're a Jew, whether you're six months or sixty, they want you dead. Dov is afraid Lev has joined one of the underground organizations. The British have a policy of stop and search. If you're found with a weapon it could mean a death sentence."

"But the kid is only fifteen."

"That's just the age, isn't it? He leaves after supper every night without saying where he is going. Dov thinks he is drilling as a soldier of the Irgun or the Lehi."

"He's probably meeting a girl."

"Maybe." Sara sounded unconvinced.

"Well, why doesn't he ask him? After all, he is his father."

"I think perhaps because he is in sympathy with Irgun philosophy himself. It seems odd for a man as gentle as Dov to take such an aggressive position, but he is beginning to feel that Arab terrorism must be met head on."

It seemed to Ted a bleak and desolate land to fight over. Its topographical features were uninteresting, and the soil impoverished. As the taxi passed a cluster of rocks, it came under fire. A fusillade of shots rang out all around them.

Sara's reflexes were instantaneous. She pulled Ted to the floor, squatting beside him. The driver pumped the accelerator and wheeled the car crazily down the road. The crack of small arms fire continued sporadically.

"We could go back," Sara whispered, "and call for a British escort."

"How far are we from the kibbutz?"

"Five or six miles."

"Any other good ambush spot along the way, high ground, rocks?"

She thought a second. "Not near the road. It's pretty open."

"Keep on!" Ted shouted to the driver, who replied in voluble Yiddish.

"He says he has to anyway. There isn't enough gas to go back."

They were out of range and resumed their seats. "You'd think they'd have tried to shoot out the tires," Ted commented.

"They probably did. They're terrible marksmen. If they'd aimed at the sheep, we'd have had it."

"Don't the British do anything about these ambushes?"

"The British," she said bitterly. "And oddly enough, it's you, Theodore Angstrom, who almost got yourself killed in this miserable excuse for a taxi, you who are responsible. It's the oil, Theo. It has changed the political picture. The Arabs have something the British need. So No. 10 Downing Street looks the other way when they pour down from the hills. It's especially embarrassing that most of the captured weapons are of English make."

Ted said nothing. He didn't relish being shot at, but he understood the dilemma. The British were in a bind: sacred pledges were all very well, but oil could easily mean survival.

Ein Harod was seen first as a narrow string of wire whose bulbs illuminated the neat outlines of furrowed saplings. They were challenged by a girl who stepped forward rifle in hand. She recognized Sara and waved them into the settlement. Ted approved the irrigation system, pipes laid out geometrically with periodic sprinklers. The King of Arabia would give half his kingdom for this.

It was the dinner hour. Workers were trudging in from the field, implements over their shoulders. A modern tractor headed for the barn. The buildings which formed neat modern complexes were made from ancient soil. It was odd to think of sand trod in biblical times being poured into the concrete hopper. But to settle here meant maximizing whatever was at hand.

Sara gave the order and the taxi came to a stop. A

palaver ensued because the driver would have to spend the night at the kibbutz. It became acrimonious, and Ted was certain the question of the fare was at issue. He sided with the driver—being shot at, in his book, demanded more than a ten-percent tip.

From one of the small, semidetached bungalows a man and boy stepped out. The light of the room was behind them, it was hard to see their features. The man was of middle height, the boy slender, half grown. Ted shook hands with Dov Rosenfeld who said simply, "You are welcome." The boy said nothing.

They went inside to a room bare of articles. There was a homemade table and two benches. The table was set for four. "I am the chief cook and bottle washer," Dov said. "You'll find it very simple."

A pot of thick soup was the main course, and a neighbor sent a loaf of freshly baked rye bread. "The raw vegetables are from Lev's garden," his father said.

The boy had an arresting face. There was a resemblance to Sara, the prominent cheek bones forcing the eyes to a slight angle. A dark, brooding quality settled over his features which seemed at variance with his years.

Dov was easier to know, a mild man, Ted felt, a just man, who weighed everything in a balance of his own. Not only did the son not resemble him, but the boy possessed a smoldering, implacable quality. There was another attribute Ted felt in Lev, discipline. Even sitting with his father and young aunt, he gave the impression of being in control.

Sara was happily recounting the sightseeing she planned for Ted. "I want to take him to the copper refinery. Theo will like that. He likes knowing how things are run."

Lev spoke for the first time. He looked at the potato peelings in his soup. "Then why not tell him how things really are. That on every border in Europe there are transit camps where Jews wait for permission to enter Palestine. The Nazis are yapping at their heels. And we are forced to negotiate—not with the big powers, they wash their hands of it, your Roosevelt, all of them. No, we deal with the consuls from certain

South American countries to grant visas to Jews." Lev looked at Ted. "The condition is, that they not use them to enter South America, but simply as a ruse to get into Palestine. Even this the British are trying to stop. They connive at bringing Iraqi murder squads over the border so they can say the country is too unsettled for immigrants to enter."

"Son," Dov spoke quietly, "we don't know there is British connivance. It may be simply poor intelligence or, at worst, indifference."

"How can you justify them? They have a mandate to protect us."

"Yet Ben-Gurion stated the other evening in the paper that our only hope is to preserve common cause with the British."

"The British have turned their backs on us. Anyone who suggests collaboration with them is a traitor to our people." He walked to the door.

"Lev," his father called, "where are you going?"

"Out," was the reply.

Ted agreed with Sara, this was an old refrain between them.

When he was gone, Dov said by way of apology, "He has seen terrible things for one so young. A friend, only a little older than he, was found with a concealed weapon. The British flogged him. Because of his age they were lenient, eighteen lashes."

Sara said suddenly, "Why don't I take Lev back with me for a while to America? He was born there. It's his country too."

"It doesn't need him. This land does. You heard him say *our people*. It is too late."

"Where do you think he went tonight?" Sara persisted.

Dov said, "It is better not to know. It is for my sake he does not answer."

"It is terrible to be so bitter," Sara rejoined.

"It is worse yet not to react." Dov turned to Ted. "It is the young, the sensitive, who feel injustice the most keenly. Take Avraham Stern, the leader of the Lehi, the extremists. All sorts of stories are told about him, that he moved from country to country on

251

a Red Cross I.D. card. Yet this advocate of violence and retaliation is a poet. It is true Lev worries us. But we must ask what worries him. He thinks of the transit camps, the human misery, the fear, the conditions of crowding, lack of sanitation, disease. Yet even there, is hope. Hitler is setting up camps of another kind for the non-Aryan, the inferior people, Slavs, Jews, Poles, those who disagree with him. There—is no hope."

The talk turned by common consent to more ordinary topics. "You must take Theo to Mikveh Yisrael," Dov said. But the shadow of the absent boy hung over the evening. Before they turned in on the narrow cots Dov had borrowed for them, he opened a cupboard and took from it a bottle that had evidently reposed there for some years awaiting an occasion.

Dov rubbed it with the tail of his shirt, pulled the cork and poured out three glasses. He raised his to Sara and Ted. "L'chaim."

Ted remembered Sara employing the same toast. He recalled it meant *Life!*

Ted found an apartment across the bay from San Francisco in a small place called Tiburon, in Marin County. The attempt at old world elegance, with a balcony overlooking the water, was nullified by an electric barbecue and wet-bar.

He watched Sara thread shishkebab with utmost concentration. A slice of lamb, a round cut of bell pepper, pineapple ring, and baby potato. It annoyed him that she accepted the luxury with which he surrounded her with the same serenity she would have shown had he dumped her back at the rooming house co-op. "You would have been perfectly happy to stay at Ein Harod, wouldn't you?"

Sara balanced the skewer and looked at him in amazement. "Why should you say that? Why should you even think it? I'm an American. As much as you are. That doesn't mean I'm not interested in what Jews are doing there, or that I'm not concerned or proud. I'm all those things. And I'll always be grateful that you took me, especially that I saw Dov and Lev. But as for wanting to stay, that's nonsense. I'm as American as apple strudel."

They tried to keep things light, to love a lot and laugh a lot. He had the feeling it was all piling up, not just on him, but for the world of men. In March the cry "*No pasaron*" was silenced. Madrid fell, the Quince Brigada decimated. The Germans and Italians shipped their machines of war home. A malignant quiet settled over blackened olive trees and torn stone walls. Ted thought of the earth, the earth had known such times when cataclysmic upheavals brought abrupt change.

Spring broke over the world—Hitler disregarded the Munich Pact and took Prague—morning glories sent out tendrils and opened—Prime Minister Neville Chamberlain and Premier Daladier—lilacs hung in fragrant bunches—agreed to come to Poland's aid in case of attack—birds set up a twittering—animals began to have their young. Puppies and kittens and calves and human infants came tumbling into the world. Female breasts swelled with milk. It seemed, yes it seemed. . . .

"Damn!" Sara said and waved her finger in the air.

"Go put butter on it. I'll take charge."

"You always overcook things."

"I won't this time." She was back in a moment. They had agreed not to cast a pall over their barbecue by discussing the German-Italian mutual assistance pact. But the situation was so grave that Ted found himself talking around it. "You know, Standard of New Jersey just sold the butyl process to Germany. I argued against it, but. . . ."

"You told me once, but I forget, is that the process for making synthetic rubber?"

"Right. Standard thinks it pulled off a coup. It claims Germany hasn't the necessary oil reserves to make use of it. But if they march into Poland, they'll have 3,300,000 barrels. Austria and Moravia have already given them 800,000 barrels."

"Theo, for heaven's sake take the shishkebab out of the coals. Let's get them onto the plates."

Ted knew it as Command 6019. He read a draft some months before it appeared as an official proclamation. Issued by Malcolm MacDonald, British Colonial Secretary, it became known as the White Paper. The 1933 White Paper had been a disaster for Jews. But it was nothing to the edict of May 1939, according to which the Balfour Declaration was all but dead.

The Arab delegation meeting in London demanded an end to Jewish immigration into Palestine. The British felt pushed to the wall. On the brink of war, they had to have access to oil in Iraq and Iran, as well as Bahrein and Kuwait, Oman and Abu Dhabi. England agreed the Jews would remain a minority in an Arab Palestine. They agreed to prohibit them from buying land except in western Palestine which was already largely in Jewish hands. They agreed on a new immigration quota whereby 15,000 persons a year would be allowed into the country until 1944, when the gates would close forever. They agreed, they acquiesced, they concurred. While, in true civilized fashion, leaving the door open a crack. It was stipulated that if, after ten years, Jew and Arab had learned to live in peace, two independent states would be set up, with Jewish taxes supporting both.

Ted rushed to the apartment in Tiburon. He found Sara quiet, composed: "Any day Hitler will march into Poland. Then they will have to rescind the White Paper. Otherwise, what would all those people do? There is no alternative."

"You mean the Polish Jews? If it's a question of oil versus a raggle-taggle of displaced persons——." He was sorry he had spoken. Now she was really upset, trying to convince herself the British were too civilized to abandon innocent people to destruction, but remembering Lev had told her the British were capable of anything.

It was a disastrous weekend. Her agitation communicated itself to him, his attempts to avoid the subject were as unfortunate as his attempts to deal with it.

The symphonies she put on the record player failed to soothe either of them. When he returned home, Ted found there had been two transcontinental calls from Cairncross at Dammam VII.

That meant trouble. Getting back to him wasn't easy. The call went through Paris and Athens, both cities in a state of war alert. Finally, Cairncross's voice came in over considerable background static. "The British have teams of geologists and diplomats swarming all over. Some are guests at Riyadh. You know about the drought? There's very little grazing land left. And the pilgrims are staying away, afraid of war. There's talk of the British helping the King with subsidies."

"But Ibn Saud took in seven million dollars this year."

"It's spent, and more. You've no idea of the excesses, the extravagances. He is counting on the British and their promises."

"Why should the British subsidize him?"

"Exactly," Cairncross said. "And there's more."

"Well?"

"I don't want to offend you, Mr. Angstrom."

"Spit it out, man."

"Well, the British are putting it about that the Company opposes the White Paper. You know, the Arabs listen to Berlin radio, and they think half of America are Jews. And again, I'm sorry, Mr. Angstrom, but I feel it's something you should be informed of."

"I said, get on with it."

"To put it bluntly, the King is persuaded that to placate Sara Rosenfeld you personally are working against the provisions of the White Paper. That may be all that's needed to tip the balance in favor of the British. The feeling here is he may give them some part of the concession."

Ted was stunned.

"Our limey pals seem very cocky and sure of themselves," Cairncross continued.

"But the agreement. . . ."

"Again, in strictest confidence. I, Mercer, a few others who have seen him, feel the King has gone

255

downhill, aged a good deal. Things seem to be slipping from his control. He ranted and shouted at me for inquiring about the British delegation, and wound up yelling, 'You are a company. I am the King!' Meaning, I take it, that he can scrap any agreement that no longer pleases him."

"What do you suggest?" Ted asked.

"A letter, sir. An immediate letter stating your backing of the White Paper in the strongest possible terms."

"I can't do that."

"Mr. Angstrom—"

"I can't support a sellout."

There was no reply. Ted was aware he'd gone too far. He tried to adopt a lighter tone. "Anyway, as an American, what do I know about the ins and outs of British diplomacy? Even if I wrote such a letter, what would it accomplish?"

"It would satisfy the King for the time being. Give us a respite. Give the lie to British-spread rumors. I wouldn't have phoned if I didn't feel things would explode in our face."

"I appreciate that, Cairncross. You did the right thing. I'll get back to you in the morning."

Ted hung up. He found he was continuing the conversation with Sara. "It won't make one goddamned bit of difference whatever I do. We both know that, not as far as Command 6019 goes. And if I don't comply, I could lose the Company."

The Sara of this imaginary dialogue didn't reply. He could think of nothing for her to say. He began to draft the letter.

There is a desert wind that blows for fifty days. Ted did not experience it in Saudi, but in Carmel. He told himself Sara was synonymous with disaster. The roots of catastrophe were inherent in their relationship. To continue would be fatal.

This conclusion changed nothing. He raced to their apartment and allowed her to tell him how tired he looked.

"You mustn't worry, Theo. The Saudi fields will be all right."

"You think that's all I think about? Give me credit

for sharing your worries. I don't like this damned White Paper either." He stopped, aghast. What had possessed him to say that?

But Sara was smiling. She had clipped a statement by Ben-Gurion. "We shall fight in this war as if there were no White Paper, and we shall fight the White Paper as if there were no war."

"I like his spirit," Ted mumbled.

"My people will survive this, and worse."

"I feel a change in you, Sara," he said uneasily. "You're sort of entrenched in yourself."

"That's what you do during a war, entrench. But you're there with me, Theo."

"That's right. You can count on it."

Like Prometheus on the rock, each day he plucked out his own liver and ate it. Each night it grew back: and again and continually he disemboweled himself.

September 1, 1939, the Polish air force was destroyed on the ground, and a new word entered global vocabularies. It was teletyped, wired, phoned, cabled around the world: *Blitzkrieg*.

Three days later Britain and France declared war on Germany. Events continued to unfold with unreal rapidity. The British navy yard was infiltrated and a moored battleship, *The Royal Oak*, sunk. Russia invaded Finland.

It was hard to realize—only that winter Ibn Saud had indulged his flair for the spectacular, issuing invitations to Ted and party for the celebrations at Riyadh.

The war in Europe made such excursions anachronistic. The hedonist life was cordoned off by a membrane of human suffering, as people fled and armies marched.

Saudi oil production was disrupted. It became U.S. policy that no American tanker be sent on the now hazardous voyage to the Persian Gulf. The tremendous enterprise in the Hasa that had taken six years to bring to present levels of a million tons per annum, ground to a halt. Ibn Saud, so quickly adjusted to a grandiose scale of living, was totally cut off from royalties and partnership earnings. This, of course, nullified the agreement, which stipulated that the company keep pumping.

Abdullah Sulaiman cabled Ted that in view of the world crisis, the King would continue to honor the concession agreement if the company paid six million dollars per year over a five-year period. Ted knew from his people in the area that the drought in Saudi continued. Men and camels died scratching for moisture near the traditional springs. Everything dried up at once, the oil, the pilgrims, and the land.

Ted cabled back that coming by such sums in these times was difficult, but he would manage to send the King three million and attempt to raise another three. Sulaiman's reply, when stripped of fulsome Arabic phrases, was plain enough. The King required the full six million, not a penny less would do. In the meantime, the board of directors turned down Ted's request for the initial three million, pointing out the company had already spent $27.5 million on development of Saudi oil, which there was now no prospect of moving.

The only good news of the week was that three British cruisers damaged the *Admiral Graf Spee* to such an extent that the pocket battleship limped into port at Montevideo and was scuttled to avoid capture.

Sara phoned. She was crying.

He couldn't understand her. "Hold on. Count ten. Okay. Now what's that about the Irgun?"

"I'm sorry, Theo. I'm so worried about Lev. The Irgun is smuggling people by the thousands into Palestine. I know he's involved. When I read about it, his face got in the way of the print. I *saw* him. I remembered that determined look. He could be imprisoned or even dead, and there'd be no way for me to know."

"I'll come right over," Ted said.

"You don't have to. I feel better, talking to you, letting it out."

"I'll be there."

There was no trace of the storm of tears. Somewhere in the three years he had known her she had grown up. She was a beautiful woman. The curly hair

258

was brushed severely away from her face emphasizing the contour of upswept eyes. She was in control but her mood was bitter. "I find it hard to take all this enthusiasm for the British. They haven't relaxed their blockade of Palestine at all. In fact, they've brought pressure on the Turkish and Greek governments not to carry Jewish passengers into the Mediterranean. You'd think that was their particular duck pond."

Ted tore at himself. "The British are a threat to me too. But you've still got to be on their side. The alternative is Hitler."

"I know. I know. All I complain about is this Anglophile euphoria. Their political policies remind me of Saudi when the beaters drove the animals toward the falcon waiting to pluck out their eyes. Then those terrible dogs will be unleashed."

He put his hand to her shoulder. Words couldn't combat her mood.

She made the effort herself. "You shouldn't have come tonight, Theo. Usually I can fight this kind of depression. But tonight I feel as I did in the desert—trapped."

And tore again.

He received another cable from the Saudi minister of finance. The King's fleet of cars and lorries was out of commission due to lack of spare parts. Would the Company lend its transport to take food into the central desert for distribution to the King's people? The courteous Arabic ended with a clear demand for money.

Ted leaped into action. A show of good will was necessary as he still could not arrange funding. He cabled Cairncross to instruct his skeleton staff to put every available Company car, truck, jeep and plane at the King's disposal.

But something nagged at the back of his mind. Where was the food coming from that the King intended to distribute?

Ted made discreet inquiries, and traced the source of the bounty to the British, who had flown in wheat from Egypt and Canada, as well as rice from India.

Alarmed that Britain had increased its foot-in-the-door maneuvering, Ted turned to the powerful oil lobby. Three million dollars was raised and sent to the King. Sulaiman cabled back, "Where is the other three million by means of which the children of Ibn Saud may continue to count as dear their American friends?"

Ted temporized. Denmark fell. Norway was invaded. Denmark officially accepted German protection. Norway declared war and King Haakon VII slipped across the channel to form a government in exile. The following month Luxembourg was invaded with no resistance. Belgium and the Netherlands declared war on Germany. The war lasted four days. Queen Wilhelmina joined King Haakon in London, also forming a government in exile. Ted saw the oil-rich Netherlands Indies left undefended.

On the back page of the *San Francisco Chronicle* he noted that leaders of the Irgun had been rounded up by the British and sent to Acre prison to join their comrades Raziel and Stern, taken earlier. Ted did not wait for Sara to call. He dropped everything.

"Their only crime," Sara said, "is a demand for open immigration. They must allow it, Theo. The Germans are setting up forced labor camps. Sometimes, I must confess it, sometimes Theo, I hate myself for being safe and comfortable when the world is in agony."

Dunkirk.

The British evacuated 360,000 men by sea in sloops, in yawls, fishing boats, cruisers, anything that would float.

Ted and his father had heated debates before Ted realized the old man was discussing a different war. His war was World War I. But they agreed on one thing. A war was won or lost on oil. "Take Verdun, 40,000 motorized transports brought in fresh troops and munitions, saved the day."

Ted, after initial shock at the old man's failing, hardly listened. He had been poring over the London *Petroleum News Service*, which was already a month old. Based on statistics there, he concluded that oil was Hitler's Achilles' heel. "At the rate he's moving

260

his armies," he told his father, "I figure a deficit of two hundred thousand tons. He picked up eight hundred thousand crude in Austria and Moravia. Poland brought over three million, two and a half million, and Albania nearly one and a half million. Rumania accounts for most of the captured oil, with a whopping forty million plus. But he plans to go a long way on it. It's clear he wants all of Europe, and intends to invade England."

Old Man Angstrom shook his head. "Hitler's got all the coal and lignite he needs. They'll synthesize petroleum. That's what they did in the Battle of the Somme. To say nothing of the sea battles. I remember stories of this captain, forget now which side he was on, but when he sent his dog down from the bridge, that meant an engagement. Didn't care so much about his men, but when it came to this dog, Labrador, I think it was. . . ."

Ted was still engrossed in his calculations. "If I were Churchill I'd bomb the bejesus out of the Ploesti fields. And if I couldn't reach them with the planes I had, I'd build new ones."

"The Ploesti fields?" Brillianna joined their game, looking up from the afghan she was knitting. "Those are the best defended, best fortified in the world."

"It would shorten the war," Ted said. "We agreed this is an oil war."

"But you couldn't order that kind of low bombing mission, the kind you'd need to knock out Ploesti. It would mean the lives of thousands of airmen."

"It's what makes sense. Without those fields Hitler is crippled."

"If I were in his place," Brillianna said thoughtfully, "I'd lay a pipeline to the Danube and ship by river."

"That's pretty much what's happening. Nichols got a letter through last week. He wrote there's been a twenty-five percent cut in the use of petroleum for cars, truck and home heating in Germany. And that traffic and commerce have shifted to canals, rivers, and rail."

There was a new camaraderie between them. The

Saudi fields had become important to Brillianna as the warp that held the lavish tapestry of her life together. She kept informed, and he needed someone to try his ideas out on. He found he enjoyed the conversations this led to. She was encouraged, confident that the long wait would pay off. Sara Rosenfeld must be quite a liability these days.

"Just thought of another example," Irv said. "Aisne, the Battle of Aisne. Couldn't have been won without oil. You don't have to take my word for it. Lord Curzon, that's right, Lord Curzon said, 'The Allies floated to victory on a flood of oil.' His exact words. As I recall, the Germans were especially short of lubricating oil. And they'll have the same trouble the second time around."

The battle for France began June 5, 1940. The Germans attacked along a hundred mile front. Paris fell nine days later. Hitler invited Great Britain to surrender.

But it was the shock of Italy's entry into the war that brought Ted's Princeton German back to him. "Drang nach Osten."

"What did he say?" Brillianna asked Brilli, who was home for summer holidays.

"Drive to the East," Brilli answered without hesitation.

Ted came out of his reverie. "It's an old idea with them. Probably goes back to the Crusades. Germany first entered the Middle East oil picture about 1900 through two railroads, the Anatolian and the Baghdad, for which they were granted oil rights amounting to twenty-five percent. This was assigned to the Deutsche Bank when the Turkish Petroleum Company was formed around 1912. After World War I, the French got the concession. Now it's up for grabs. I see a pincer movement, Hitler aiming at the Suez from Libya and the Italians coming out of the Sudan and East Africa. Hitler will take the wells of Iraq and Iran. Italy will take mine."

"Ted, please calm yourself." Brillianna was alarmed because he was calm. It was unnatural for Ted to repress his fury and frustration. Yet there was no way for him to let it out. He was across the world from his fields. Who was to protect them? The madness of men and nations had not entered his calculations.

He continued in the same frozen voice, "The Nazi propaganda machine is run from Teheran. They all listen to it. The King's closest advisers are pro-German. So it will go one of three ways. Either my wells will be seized by the Italians, or if I don't come up with three million additional payment, the King will nationalize them. The third and most likely possibility is that he will hand them over to Britain, which seems willing to subsidize him."

Brillianna was able to think of nothing to comfort him. The Saudi fields seemed vulnerable no matter how things went.

Ted mounted a grim watch on the situation in the Middle East while events on other fronts held world attention. The flags on his map represented oil fields; arrows, the Axis armies threatening them. Ted's war differed from that reported in the papers, whose main concern was the daily pounding England was taking from the Luftwaffe.

It was news when the United States, in defiance of its official neutrality, on September 27, 1940 transferred fifty over-age destroyers to Great Britain in return for air and naval bases.

On that same September 27, Japan signed a pact with Germany and Italy to create a "new world order."

"I wondered," Ted said aloud, "who would wind up getting the Netherland Indies' oil and France's Indochina fields." He placed new arrows across the Pacific and the South China Sea.

In October, the first peacetime conscription was voted by Congress. America was arming. Plans called for a two-ocean navy as well as an air force of 50,000 planes. The action heartened the French who formed an active underground. None of this had much to do with Ted's war.

The Italians bombed Dhahran. Dhahran! That was him, Theodore Angstrom! A cry tore from his solar plexus. He saw the wings of the planes tilt as they came in low over his fields, diving, dropping their explosives. Ted erupted along with his wells, "Idiots. If they can't have them, they'll destroy them. What kind of imbecile reasoning is that?"

Brillianna looked at him wonderingly. "I believe you'd rather they seized them than bombed them."

"My wells are on fire. Have you ever seen an oil fire? Waste! Waste of a prodigious kind. Energy, finite energy roaring into a vacuum, consuming itself, when it could power the war."

Actually the bombing of Dhahran was a more violent signaling of the scenario Ted had predicted, an attempt to break Britain's blockade of the Mediterranean from Gibralter on the west to Suez in the east. Ted's fury, like his wells, burned and smoldered. The Germans drove through southeastern Europe. Greece was menaced and the British ousted from Libya. The campaign for the oil of the Middle East was on schedule.

But something had changed. They had attacked Ted personally. This gnawed constantly at the center of his being. And as he brooded, it became clear to him that with the U.S. destroyer deal isolationism was dead. He could raise the three million Sulaiman was dunning him for. Washington would have to listen. In demanding the money he was speaking in the national interest. For it was certainly in the national interest to protect an American oil concession, which happened to be the largest in the world. Three million was small potatoes to ensure a permanent supply of fuel toward the day when the U.S. entered the war.

If he could command government monies, it would enhance his prestige with the King and automatically curtail the threat posed by the British. Theodore Angstrom was batting in a new league. He no longer needed to go through his brother-in-law the senator from North Carolina. All that was required was to pick up the phone. The American government was at the other end. He was a man with open sesame to top people, people whose names, until now, he had merely read in the paper.

After a private talk with Jesse H. Jones, administrator for the Federal Loan Agency, who would ultimately have to approve the release of funds, Ted was put on the agenda at the next meeting of PAW, the Petroleum Administration for War. He set forth the case for money necessary to satisfy Ibn Saud, emphasizing that an American resource was threatened on all sides by the belligerents.

He convinced Jones, who saw to it that there were several impassioned speeches in the Senate on assistance to Saudi Arabia. Not content with the pace at which bureaucracy moved, Ted buttonholed him again, "I'm telling you, Jess, the British want their finger down our wells and up our ass at the same time." Jones promised that he would go to the top. A week later he showed Ted in strictest confidence the reply from President Roosevelt: "Jess, will you tell the British I hope they can take care of the King of Saudi Arabia. This is a little far afield for us! FDR."

"Why won't he see? Why will nobody see? This war has got to be run on Saudi oil. And without government help I can't do a damn thing to protect it."

Ted continued to write conciliatory letters to Abdullah Sulaiman. These became difficult to compose, he had run out of half-promises and hints of forthcoming money. He kept close tabs on the news, hoping something would come along to help him. His luck was due to turn, he knew it. If only he could hold.

Early in 1941, Britain announced it would be unable to pay for the war materiel it had been purchasing from the U.S. Then it came, the change in luck, from a totally unexpected and unprecedented source. The United States Congress gave the president authority to "lend-lease" arms and supplies to those democracies whose defense he deemed important to the security of America.

Lend-lease!

What a beautiful solution. Ted was on high. What a concept! He had to admit that in this case Roosevelt was inspired. Or what was more probable, had listened to men who, for a change, knew what they were doing.

Ted set to work through a Cabinet member, who laid the suggestion before the president that Saudi be maintained in the American camp through the vehicle of lend-lease. But the report which filtered back to Ted was negative. "Sorry, Angstrom. The Man says there is no legal way it can be done."

"But why not? I don't see that."

"The language of the bill specifies aid to democracies." His go-between gave a rueful chortle. "And there's no way Saudi Arabia can be considered in that category."

"It's a technicality!" Ted bellowed. His high had been short-lived. It was a long way down. He went back to monitoring the news. In a communication from Cairncross he learned that his friend Nichols had been interned in England as a pacifist. That figured. He wondered what happened to the baboons. He could guess what happened to the jeweled collars. The Nazi drive for the Mediterranean began in force. Based in Yugoslavia, the assault on Greece was stepped up.

Ted stood for hours in front of his map of the Middle East. Greece capitulated. Enemy planes now blocked British use of the Suez Canal.

Ted saw another way, a possibility of entering the war personally. In his mind, the government's transfer of destroyers to Britain rescinded the order against American shipping. Without authorization of any kind, he contacted Cairncross and Mercer, who were still on the job, pumping a few barrels. The dispatch Ted got through ordered them to load whatever oil there was on small tankers. *Make a run for it around the coast of Africa* were his instructions.

He felt buoyed up by this action. Especially as he got word back that some of the Americans were hitching a ride home. It was only a trickle, but he was moving oil, getting it out. Hardly more than a gesture —still at the right time in the right place, it could forward supplies or allow a blockade to be run. He even pictured a battle won with Angstrom crude. He felt victorious, invincible. He felt good. He had taken a stand.

America too, adopted a more forceful policy. A steady stream of U.S. materiel began to be convoyed across the Atlantic. The press came up with an alliterative phrase: *Bundles for Britain.*

Several things happened in quick succession. The United States took Greenland under its protection and U.S. naval forces landed in Iceland. In spite of these newly acquired bases of operation almost two million tons of shipping were lost to German U-boats in the first half of the year. Among them Ted Angstrom's tankers.

He spotted the loss himself, reading the fine print of the shipping news, *"with all hands."* He felt as though he were being punched senseless. His ego had sent these men to their deaths. He proved they couldn't keep Angstrom oil bottled up. And for that display of arrogance, seventeen of his employees were dead.

"Make a run for it around the coast of Africa."

Ted walked along the beach squinting at the sea. Rolling in at his feet scalloped and bright, it was hard to imagine it had enfolded his men and his ships. How had it happened? Torpedoes ripping hulls, explosions and flames wrapping men. They jumped. But the flames followed, an oil fire can't be doused by water.

Two small tankers.

Something intruded into his self-flagellation. He couldn't be sure, but he thought—he looked up at the bluff. His daughter was calling, running nimbly down the steps.

"Didn't you hear me, Dad?" She came up to him breathless.

She was only eleven but he felt a certain shyness at her physical maturity. She was a handsome girl, with a charm unconscious of itself. Part Grenville, part Angstrom. Her restlessness was like his own. He wondered what dreams lay behind her wide-set eyes.

"So, you're home for Easter, are you?"

"You don't have to do that," she said.

"Do what?"

"You know, make conversation. I just want to walk."

He nodded and they marched along, their footprints washed out behind them by the tide. His men, catching a ride back to their families. Families they wouldn't see grow up. There hadn't been much time for Brilli. He resolved to make time. His little girl, whom he remembered taking onto the fields, was now this vigorous, long-legged preteen.

She peered several times into his face. "You shouldn't worry, Dad."

"I'm not worried."

"Yes you are. But you shouldn't be. My own philosophy is, don't. Especially about things you can't do anything about."

A communication signed Theodore Angstrom, and sea-wrinkled, oil-burned bodies washed bloated in tropic waters.

Brilli continued blithely, "That's one category, things you can't do anything about. The other things not to worry about are those you don't *intend* to do anything about."

The girl intrigued him. "Like what?" he asked.

She laughed, "The report I'm supposed to do. I'm not going to do it. Otherwise it wouldn't be a vacation. Oh, I hate school."

"Be more precise," he encouraged her. "You don't hate school, not the brick and mortar buildings anyway."

"I hate them too."

"What's this report you are so strenuously not worrying about?"

"Can you guess? Geology. That's what I got assigned because I'm an Angstrom. So it's your fault. And as far as I can see, geology is just a bunch of eras, and you've got to memorize which came first, and the names are about a mile long, Mesozoic, Paleozoic, Proterozoic."

"Okay. Right off, each of those names end in *zoic*. What do you suppose that means?"

"I don't know."

"It means life. The front part, that tells you how old the life is, at what stage of development. Geology carries you back to the beginning when chemical elements gathered into organic compounds. The way we set the hands on this prehistoric clock, is by rocks and sediments. The core of the earth is highly compressed nickel and iron. Around this is a layer of heavy igneous rock. What's igneous?"

"It means hot, doesn't it?"

268

"Right. Formed from magma and volcanic flows. The outer crust is largely composed of sedimentary rocks. Limestone, for instance, indicates the region was under the sea at one time. That's why often when you find limestone, you find oil." And the bodies of men. He remembered their sun darkened laughing faces when they told him about Dammam VII. He hurried on, "Sandstone, shale, conglomerate, those were once mountains, worn down. Igneous wells up from below, pushes into cracks in the earth's crust. The earth is so warped from internal heavings and displacements that you can't tell which layer is older. That is, you can, but not by which lies on top."

"I know," Brilli became animated, "you tell by the fossils. Maybe I *will* do the report. I've got an idea for it now. I'll write about fossils and the sea."

—The sea. Fathoms down where no light finds its way. Cold, dark. Perhaps a personal letter of commendation signed by him. And pensions for the widows. That was it, the Company would see to it.

Sara would say he was buying his way out. What would his Angstrom daughter say? He felt she might have done the same thing, assuaged the restlessness.

His guilt behaved like the sea itself. Other preoccupations forced themselves on him, and the guilt was swept from him. Just when he thought it gone, it would wash over him in a fresh wave. He tried to rationalize. These men were among the first to give their lives. Countless Americans would follow.

Ted's war, which all along was fought against the British as much as the Germans and Italians, now shifted to his own government. His anger at the administration's indifference to his oil fields became rage when he learned that the British were following Roosevelt's advice to "take care of the king," and using American lend-lease money to do it. Ibn Saud's every wish was granted. The three million he kept demanding was paid into his coffers by the British with the assurance of an additional six million per annum over a period of the next five years.

Ted called Jones. He called his cabinet contact. He called his brother-in-law. He explained to anyone who would listen that it was disadvantageous in the extreme to allow England to pay those sums to the King. Or if, in fact, this was the only way it could be done, someone highly placed in government should make it clear to Ibn Saud that the British remittances were *American* money.

In his heart Ted knew the King would never follow this explanation. He wouldn't make the effort, it would bore him. And if, by some miracle, he did understand, he wouldn't believe it. Why should the American government give Saudi Arabia such a generous subsidy through British intermediaries and not seek credit for its own generosity? Ted found difficulty explaining it to himself. It would be impossible to convince the King.

Those officials he trapped into meetings were far more concerned with the fact that Germany had invaded the Soviet Union. Ted placed a flagged pin on the Baku oil fields by the Black Sea, and turned his attention to the theater that threatened him. While Germany was attacking Russia, British forces in Egypt struck into Libya, hoping to open a passage to the Suez Canal.

On the Russian front, the Germans in rapid succession took Smolensk, Kiev, Odessa, and Rostov. The Russians counter-attacked, retaking Rostov and driving toward the Ukraine.

The opening of the second front convinced the Japanese of an Axis victory. Under German prodding, the Vichy government handed over its bases in Indochina to Japan, which lost no time occupying the territory. Ted had already inserted rising sun flags in this area. He chuckled morosely when events caught up to his prediction.

In spite of the building tensions between the U.S. and the empire of Japan, on November 26, the secretary of state announced full American economic cooperation with Japan, asking in return for a withdrawal from China and a break with Axis powers.

December 6, President Roosevelt appealed directly to Emperor Hirohito to work for peace.

December 7 was a Sunday. The voice of the president reached almost every home in the country, recounting in tragic tones the American losses in the attack on Pearl Harbor. In two hours, 2,800 Americans were killed. The base was struck by submarine and carrier-based planes, which accounted for eight American battleships sunk or hit, an undisclosed number of cruisers and destroyers lost, and six air bases heavily damaged, with most planes destroyed on the ground.

The president of the United States spoke, the Zenith radio vibrated with his voice, recounting the grisly casualties. But comprehension failed to follow. A deadness, a lapse occurred, a void in which each person, after his own fashion, began to put it together. The magnitude of what had happened sank in slowly.

Ted kept shaking his head, arguing, mumbling. Was the conversation with Jesse Jones, with his brother-in-law, with Roosevelt or with his own drowned dead? He stared malevolently at the bulky radio, which he refused to turn off for fear of missing some fresh catastrophe. "We had to get in. But this way? It doesn't make sense. Where in hell was everybody?"

Two and a half hours after the attack, the Japanese government declared war on the United States and Britain. Britain retaliated the following day with its declaration, while the U.S. Congress announced that a state of war had existed with Japan since December 7.

December 8, Britain declared war on Japan.

December 9, China declared war on the Axis.

December 11, Germany and Italy declared war on the United States.

The Latin American countries came in on the Allied side, while Bulgaria, Hungary, and Rumania declared they were at war with the United States. Hitler took personal command of the German forces.

Brillianna and Brilli were preparing for Christmas. The usual ornaments were unavailable, and broken decorations were replaced by silver paper foil. But from a distance the tree looked as gaily festooned as ever.

"Come help," Brillianna suggested.

"What can I do?"

271

"Test the lights for one thing, and see that they work."

Ted made an effort to get into the Christmas spirit. This was difficult in spite of the eggnogs with cinnamon sticks Maria brought in. In what he considered his own bailiwick, Axis air power continued to block the Suez Canal. Oil supplies for Allied forces in Egypt, the Near East, and India were rerouted around Africa. Ted hoped they would fare better than his small armada.

The stalemate was broken in January when Field Marshal Rommel initiated a drive to seize the Canal. It was a direct bid for Ted's fields. The British crumpled and Bengazi fell. Ted was glued to the radio. The British dug in and stayed dug in. "They've stranded themselves," he declared. "Their supply lines won't be able to catch up. Their oil is exhausted. Do you know what's going to happen?" He turned on his wife as though she were personally responsible. "To hold their positions, the British are going to help themselves to Dhahran."

"No," Brillianna said staunchly. "We're allies. They won't do that."

"You're damned right they won't." Ted flew to Washington. He hounded old contacts, made new ones, and saw to it that his Texas partners put pressure on Congress. Finally Ted managed to get to Cordell Hull, who promised to consult with the secretary of the interior, the formidable Harold Ickes.

Ickes was unexpectedly sympathetic. He agreed with Ted that at all costs American oil must be prevented from falling into British hands. The result was an historic document sent by Roosevelt to Winston Churchill, in which the president expressed concern about the British desire to "horn in" on the oil concession in Saudi.

Somewhat reassured, Ted looked up from his private oil war to see that things had deteriorated elsewhere. The Allies, now consisting of twenty-six nations, were hard pressed. The Axis arrows were closing in. Guam and Wake had fallen. Hong Kong was the next to go.

Ted turned from his duel with the British to his other chief foe. Rommel was on the move again. In a purposeful thrust he met the British head-on at Tobruk. New "I" tanks were rushed to defend the desert front. It didn't help. In what Ted considered the most disastrous event of the war, Rommel's crack Afrika Korps moved into Cyrenaica.

It was at this low ebb, when Ted conceived things could not possibly be worse, that events he himself had set in motion struck like a boomerang.

It started innocuously enough. Secretary Ickes was made director of PAW. Ted was delighted. He had a friend at court. And ammunition fell unexpectedly into his hands. A British effort was made to open a bank in Jidda, which would put Saudi in the sterling zone and make it virtually impossible for an American company to conduct business.

President Roosevelt lost no time. By executive order No. 8926, lend-lease was extended to the government of Saudi Arabia. "I hereby find that the defense of Saudi Arabia is vital to the defense of the United States," read the document that was slipped to Ted.

"If he'd been able to," his confederate said, "the Man would have made Saudi Arabia a democracy by executive order."

It had taken three years to put through. Ted thought of it as his crowning achievement. His personal war, the oil war, was won.

And lost the next day.

Theodore Angstrom was summoned to a meeting at the White House. It was presided over by the director of the Office of War Mobilization, attended by the secretary of the navy, a representative of the State Department, a technical expert from the War Department, and Ted's friend Ickes, secretary of the interior.

It was Ickes who had the floor, and he lost no time in exploding the bomb. "The first order of business of the government's Petroleum Administration for War should be the acquisition of a participating and managerial interest in the crude oil reserves of the entire United States."

Ted couldn't believe it.

"This acquisition," Ickes went on blandly, "will

273

serve to meet an immediate demand by the army and navy for large volumes of petroleum products, and will also counteract certain activities of a foreign power which are presently jeopardizing American interests in Arabian oil reserves."

Ickes continued to quote the substance of previous conversations with Ted, bringing out that in most cases it was governments rather than private companies who owned oil concessions. He referred to his notes, scribbled in Ted's presence, rattling off the 56 percent the British government owned in Anglo-Iranian, the 50 percent in Kuwait, the 25 percent in Iraqi Petroleum.

When he finished there was consensus. It was agreed that "steps should be initiated looking to the acquisition of an interest in the important Saudi Arabian fields."

Ted stumbled out of the meeting. Ickes spotted him in the hall. "You do see the necessity of this, Ted?" he said, catching up with him. "American reserves are being consumed at an alarming rate."

"It's the wrong way to go at it," Ted mumbled, "the wrong way."

But the project of government acquisition was in the works. The wheels were turning. The Joint Chiefs of Staff submitted a report to the president describing the dangerous depletion of American oil and pressing for the adoption of measures that would guarantee a supply outside the United States.

The State Department followed up with a memorandum to the same effect. Within two weeks an interdepartmental committee representing the Departments of State, War, Navy, and Interior arrived at a unanimous decision to recommend acquisition, interest, or ownership in petroleum reserves outside the continental United States, and to finance, retail, develop, export, or lease such reserves.

Ted flew home and lay low, but kept himself informed. The correspondence with the White House which in due course crossed his desk, said in part, "The interest to be acquired by the U.S. government in the Saudi-California Company shall be the ownership of 100 percent of the stock of the corporation."

What particularly incensed him was that the PAW members voted themselves directors of the corporation which they expected to be in their hands shortly. Ickes was designated for the presidential slot.

Disheveled, looking like a madman, Ted burst in on Sara.

She listened in consternation. "Oh my darling, I don't see what you can do. Maybe your lawyers can write in a proviso that after the war the company be returned to you."

"That's not what they want," he bellowed. "They want to steal it from me."

He sought out his dad. When he had finished, the old man poured himself a drink. "There's a war on, son. I'm turning over every drop of oil I pump to the government."

"Yes, but they're your wells. Nobody is trying to move in on you."

"Ted, the whole country could go down the drain. Where are your precious fields then? Roosevelt is commander in chief, every last man jack of us is responsible to him. From the kids dead with their faces in the mud to General MacArthur, we take orders. Anything else is rank insubordination."

"Why not say treason? That's what you're implying."

His dad said slowly, "I would consider it treason for you to buck the head of the armed forces during wartime."

Was that what he was doing? Was that what he was contemplating? He just wanted to keep control of his own company, that was all. He was as patriotic as the next fellow. But damn it, he was an oilman.

Brillianna was in her sitting room working on the afghan. She listened attentively to everything he had to say.

"Are you asking my advice?"

"Yes. Yes, I am."

"You have no choice, Ted." His head dropped heavily forward. But he had not heard her out. "You have to fight."

He snapped instantly to attention, staring at her composed Grenville features. His brain reeled. "Do

275

you realize you are telling me to pit myself against a wartime president with wartime powers granted by the United States Congress?"

"My dear Ted, the United States is not some little banana republic. No industry has ever yet been nationalized in America and I don't see why they should start with you."

He bent and kissed her. "Sometimes you scare the living daylights out of me."

"That's because I'm more yourself than you are. When you realize that, you'll stop going to Tiburon." She threw that out in passing, so casually that he didn't think about it until later.

"What are our weapons?" he asked. "What do we fight with?"

"The weapons provided by the country: a free press and a congress. Also you are a wealthy man. But use discretion, Ted."

"You're the only one who understands, who really understands," he said.

"Of course," she replied quietly. "Oil is your life's blood. Your deepest allegiance lies there."

"That's true. It may be wrong, but it's true."

"Nietzsche speaks of beyond good and evil, of what is in the man, the person."

"But he's a German philosopher."

She smiled. "Only during the war, and that won't last forever."

"You're a remarkable person, Brillianna. Thank you."

She looked deeply into his eyes, "When I ask you to fight, I'm asking you to fight for me too." She returned to blocking out her afghan.

The proposed takeover began with a telegram. Ted returned to Washington and had lunch with Ickes. Ted considered appearing with his lawyer, but decided against it. He wandered into the restaurant, was shown to a secluded table and shook hands with the president's hatchet man. It was said that while Roosevelt glad-handed and grinned, this man did his dirty work —the smiling face and the frowning face, like masks in a theater. The two men shook hands. Ickes didn't bother to trade even a few jokes but plunged into a gloomy summary of the war to date. He spoke of every man's patriotic duty. He spoke of thousands of Americans dying in the field or in watery graves. In fact he sounded very much like Irv Angstrom. But when he mentioned one hundred percent ownership in Saudi-California, he ran into a stone wall.

Ted adopted a patient tone. "You know it won't work, Harold. Government has never been efficient in operating business."

"That's one of the things we hope to rectify. Production is practically down to zero."

"That's not my production operation. That's the Afrika Korps and the bombers."

The two men parted without pretense of amicability.

Ted stalled on the second meeting. He conferred secretly with lobbyists, as he was not too sure his Texas partners would go along with this kind of log-rolling. Ickes became pressing on the subject of another get-together. The meeting could no longer be put off. The secretary of the interior had time to think things through, and, for the sake of expediting negotiations, informed Ted that he was in a position to make a firm bid for seventy percent of Saudi-California, leaving Ted, as he pointed out, thirty percent.

This sparked no visible gratitude. It was however evidence that his trip to Washington had been effective. God knows it had better have been—a good deal of money had changed hands, and if the old curmudgeon probed, there was quite a bit he might uncover.

"We can go a number of different ways," the secretary was saying. "The present owners could receive a percentage of the oil produced, or, at the option of the government, be paid off in currency."

Ted evinced no interest in being paid in one or the other. This time he had not been invited for lunch, which made it easier to break away.

There was an unaccountable tumult in the press, opposition to government control of private industry, and cries of nationalization. Editorials appeared denouncing expropriation of private business. "What be-

277

comes of free enterprise," one article expostulated, "and why are we fighting this war?"

At the third meeting Ickes said, "Look Angstrom, this is it. I'm bringing you the best offer our government can come up with, a fifty-one percent for us, forty-nine for you."

The affability on Ted's face did not waver.

"We are even taking under advisement having you manage the company," the secretary continued. "With the clout of the United States government behind you, you'd be in a very different position in dealing with Ibn Saud. And of course there'd be no question of foreign powers sucking about."

Ted nodded politely, keeping bottled his fury at being offered a managerial position in his own company.

Negotiations dragged on. The noticeable coolness in their relationship increased. Mr. Ickes stated publicly that it was his belief "the company was reaching certain members of the Senate and House." He increased the pressure on Ted. Time was running out. The secretary indicated the government was annoyed at the intractable position Angstrom had assumed and might withdraw its favorable terms if the business were not concluded immediately.

Ted had pulled out every stop. In desperation he said that under certain circumstances he might be willing to give up thirty-three and a third percent of the total holding. Ickes was plainly dissatisfied with thirty-three and a third percent of Ted's life blood. They agreed to a further meeting.

The break Ted was looking for:

Midway.

The Imperial fleet was turned back and Japanese expansion was at an end. In North Africa, however, the situation was critical. Rommel took Tobruk. The British 8th Army contained him at El Alamein in what seemed to be a standoff. General Montgomery was named field commander. Ted felt his luck ran on this Britisher. If El Alamein was lost, so were his Saudi fields. Neither he nor Ickes would have a percent of anything.

No. 10 Downing St. was drawing plans for a November offensive, but Montgomery moved the date up to October 23. Rommel was convalescing in Austria, leaving his command without leadership. Montgomery ordered a bayonet charge in which infantry literally hacked an opening for an armored breakthrough. A day later British tanks were deploying six miles past the front forcing the Germans out to defend the invading wedge. By the time Rommel returned, two days later, half his armor was destroyed. After a week of heavy fighting, he retreated to Fûka. Hitler countermanded this maneuver, losing Rommel his chance to regroup. By stages he was driven 1,300 miles into the desert.

Allied troops entered Tunisia. Lieutenant General Dwight D. Eisenhower secured strategic points in Algeria and Morocco. If Montgomery and Eisenhower had only known—they battled for Theodore Angstrom and private enterprise. With the enemy near collapse on all fronts, Congress would never sanction the nationalization of a taxpaying American corporation.

Ted put it to Ickes this way: "With Rommel chased out of North Africa, we won't be needing you guys at PAW. But thanks anyway."

He didn't laugh. Not until he hung up the phone. Then he allowed himself to picture the secretary's taciturn sallow countenance. So, he had imagined himself president of Saudi-California. Well, he had another think coming.

The war was not over. But it was over as far as Theodore Angstrom was concerned. Down came the map, and the dozen flags were tossed into the wastebasket.

Arriving unexpectedly at the Tiburon apartment, he had to let himself in with a latchkey. He was amazed to find Sara there. She was lying face down on the couch.

"Sara," he said, going over to her, lifting and turning her. "You're ill."

"They're exterminating them."

"What are you talking about?"

"They have a name for it. It is called the *final solution*."

"Sara, you're not making sense. What is?"

"The official German policy is to kill Jews."

He rocked her in his arms. "Where do you get these ideas? It's not true."

"Yes, yes. They do it in trucks, gas them."

"Believe me, it's an atrocity story. You always have these lurid accounts, partially as justification for what the country has been through."

"Everyone, the children, babies, everyone in the trucks."

He shook her, but gently with compassion. "Sara, you're a sophisticated person. How can you be taken in like this?"

"It was a smuggled letter. Someone my father knows received it."

"It's always the same toward the end of any war. There were stories in 1917, some of them printed in the paper. Belgian children nailed to barn doors. Responsible people investigated—the rumors were completely unfounded. No children had been nailed to anything."

"Really, Theo?"

"Believe me."

In April 1943, Ted was invited to attend a conference in Bermuda, held jointly with the British to establish guidelines for rendering help to Jewish refugees. Ted was mildly surprised by the invitation. Sara's hopes soared. If the conference were composed of men like Theo, something at last would be done.

A select group of American representatives were taken aboard a U.S. cruiser. Conscious of their mission, the atmosphere was at first subdued, but as they slipped into southern waters and fish jumped, there was trolling from the deck, iced drinks, and conviviality developed.

They met their British counterparts during a day of acclimatization on the incredibly white sands of Bermuda's famed Elbow Beach, and were lodged at a bougainvillea-covered villa, from which a kidney shaped pool and warm surf were both accessible. There was a golf course, and rum drinks served by barefoot servants on rocky promontories against which waves gentled and idled. That evening both contingents met in formal attire. After an admirable meal beginning with the island's specialty, sauteed flying fish, they got to business.

British intelligence briefed them. A Major Harris spoke, reporting that Nazi high officials meeting in the Wannsee suburb of Berlin had arrived at the "final solution" of the Jewish problem.

Ted had just heard those words, *final solution*. He held her in his arms and told her it was impossible, that she wasn't making sense. But Major Harris of British Intelligence presumably was a man who made a great deal of sense. Their information was that the decision first surfaced July 31, 1941 in a directive from Goering to Heydrich. It took eight months to implement. Mass transportation to the death camps began. Systematic extermination of all Jews became the official policy of the Third Reich.

The room took on stillness, absorbed it. The space between the walls and the joists under the floorboards filled with it. The stillness was like a gag, it choked him. Yet he didn't choke, or move or look at his neighbor. His was one of a dozen closed, controlled faces, that stared at the speaker.

He must stand up, speak, shout, denounce.

Then it hit him. He had wondered why he was chosen as part of this delegation. It seemed an odd honor to bestow. The reason was suddenly obvious, it was in the hope of some such outburst. He must shut up, stifle his impulse to protest. He could only listen and observe. His attitude would be reported directly to Ibn Saud by the omnipresent British, or possibly by some of the American oil interests present, who would like nothing better than to step into his shoes. He must keep his own counsel.

He looked back on the fight he had put up for his concession. Somewhere during all this, Sara's Theo had slipped from his grasp. He wanted to be that Theo, honest, loyal, and open. But he was riding two horses and they would not stay at the same pace or even on the same course.

Lord Moyne, high commissioner for Palestine, was mildly criticized by an American delegate for refusing refugee ships permission to land anywhere along the Mediterranean. He described the tragedy of the *Struma*, which, after waiting three months in Turkish waters to discharge its human cargo, was finally towed out of the harbor where it blew up, killing all aboard.

The British in their turn expressed surprise at this criticism. That particular decision had been in accordance with the guiding principles laid out fully in the White Paper of 1939.

Another day of sun, of bathing, of tall rum drinks. The Allied delegation felt more in tune. The tide of war had turned strongly in their favor. They discussed strategy and troop deployment in Tunisia, and dealt with a request from the Jewish Agency to allow Palestinian Jews to make parachute drops into the camps where it was rumored the killing was being stepped up.

The Colonial Office deemed it ill-advised to permit such a drop by insufficiently trained men. The matter was disposed of before lunch.

After a siesta it was decided, in further exploring means to assist the Jews, that it was mandatory not to relax the White Paper policy or lower U.S. immigration bars. Ted applauded with the rest. But the last rum punch had not agreed with him.

When he returned to Carmel, Ted gave his attention to increasing production in Saudi.

He was interested to see that an action he advocated at the outset of war was finally undertaken at this late date. American planes raided the Ploesti Oil Field in Rumania. As far as he could gather, 178 B-24 Liberators flew 2,400 miles round trip from a base in Libya. The loss was 54 planes. Results: unknown.

Ted shook his head. What they needed was a low-level attack, pound the bejesus out of them.

He did not let Sara know he was back. He had neither the will nor the courage for this continual deceit. He was feeling so low he was positive things could not be worse, when a call came through on his special phone. This line was only used by Saudi representatives, his partners, or Washington.

It was Lynch, one of his Texas associates. "Say Ted, the word is you didn't take an active part in the Bermuda Conference. That didn't sit well at Riyadh."

"You're leaning on me, Lynch. What's it about?"

"The British have convinced the King that your, shall we call it, nonparticipation at the conference is proof that you have been working against the White Paper. He is in a vicious mood, and it will take reassurance from you personally to calm him down."

"Let me tell you something." Ted meted out his anger evenly. "I've had it with the King. I've calmed him down, coddled him, wheedled, borrowed, and scrounged money for him. He can go to hell."

"Look Angstrom, yell at me. But reassure the King. You were set up in Bermuda. Now, let's not go through a war to lose the concession at the very end."

"All right," Ted said wearily, "what will pacify His Majesty?"

"A letter, stating your personal backing of the White Paper and your pleasure at the manner in which the Bermuda Council for the Jewish Refugees proceeded."

"It seems to me I wrote this letter four years ago. Maybe I can dig it out of the files and copy it."

"It's got to be sincere suit, Ted."

"Yeah, yeah."

"And the bottom line has got to read bully for the Refugee Council and Lord Moyne."

"Sure. Why not? And Tom, I didn't mean to sound off at you. I'm glad of the tip. I figured maybe I had friends there."

"You did. So make it good. We want off the meat hook."

"Will do, ol' buddy."

He sat at the typewriter. His fingers stiff, unused to the keys. He made so many mistakes on the first draft that he balled it up and threw it away. No matter what he told himself, or how he rationalized, each time he depressed a key he was doing something unspeakable to Sara.

Two more drafts followed, each crumpled with sudden distaste. But at last he had a well-punctuated, typo-free document on his best bond paper, which said that the Malcolm MacDonald White Paper agreement continued to represent his own thinking on limiting Jewish immigration to Palestine. He stated that it had always been the policy of his company to back the proclamation and he personally vouched for the powerful oil lobby in the United States taking the same affirmative stand as in the past. He extolled the recent Bermuda Conference and its conservative go-slow approach to Jewish immigration.

He folded the letter, slipped it into an envelope and wrote across it *Air-Mail Special Delivery*, then took it himself to the post office for weighing and to insure security. No one could be trusted these days.

How true. Brillianna heard his private phone ring. She was concerned. She lingered downstairs listening to Ted at the typewriter. It had been years since he had done his own typing. Yet his hunt-and-peck method was unmistakable. It was clear to her that he entrusted this particular business to no one. Neither secretary had been called in.

When he went out, she entered. Checking the wastebasket was elementary. Almost immediately she noticed that balled rejects which she took out, carefully smoothed and read, one after the other.

She picked up the phone. She knew Sara's number although she had never used it.

"Hello?" sounded the light airy voice.

"Miss Rosenfeld, this is Mrs. Angstrom. I must see you."

There was a pause. "Are you sure? Are you sure you want to? It won't make any difference you know."

"I wouldn't be phoning you after all these years, Miss Rosenfeld, unless something rather extraordinary had come up."

"Very well. Do you have my address?"

"As a matter of fact, yes."

"I'll be here the early part of the afternoon," Sara said.

"Goodbye then."

"Goodbye."

284

Brillianna took a great deal of care with her costume and her cosmetics. It was distinctly unfair to be fifteen years older than your husband's mistress. Still, the line of good bones prevailed. Weekly facials, an array of creams and lanolins kept her skin toned and young. She was a handsome woman.

For all that she didn't like herself lately. They were little things, of no consequence, yet indicative perhaps. She found herself making demands for personal attention from maitre d's and waiters. She craved recognition. She was Brillianna Grenville Angstrom. She wanted people to know it, give special service, debate with her over the wine list, help her choose from the tray of French pastries wheeled to the table. She could see how impatient this made Ted.

"Why do you bother?" he asked. "You'd think you were establishing an alibi for murder. The only thing you didn't ask him was the time."

She was ashamed of this compulsive behavior. Why aggravate Ted, when what she wanted was to win him to her side? She made progress when she backed the decision he wanted to make, to fight the government, the Department of the Interior, and PAW. When he won, she won. He was grateful to her. This showed in a dozen ways. He adopted a more intimate, carefree manner. He told jokes, cleaned up, for her and Brilli. She waited for him to come to her bed. He did not.

She patted her perfectly arranged hair a final time. All that was about to change.

She decided on a taxi. It would be a terribly long ride. She thought of the times Ted took it. Settling back, she tried to relax. Had she the strength to outface Sara Rosenfeld? She opened her purse and was reassured as her fingers came in contact with the heavy bond. She had the ammunition. All she needed was to make this effort. Force her energy, force her mind and her will. She had it within her means to banish that girl who had for so many years taken her husband's love.

The car ate up the miles. She closed her eyes. Society had become permissive. Everyone knew Ted had set his fancy woman up in an apartment. They thought none the worse of him, but allowed themselves to pity his wife. She had endured sympathetic and knowing looks, while behind her back they murmured, "Poor dear, do you suppose she knows?"

Her strategy all along had been to hold on. If you held on long enough things fell out your way. She learned that from Ted. She also had the continuing strength to go on year after year. And today she would taste the fruits of the long battle. Today she would gobble one entire young lady and savor each morsel.

They drew up in front of the apartment. The sumptuousness of it angered her, terraced private gardens, a spectacular bay view. She instructed the cabbie to wait. Mounting the steps she rang and was told through the annunciator to come up.

She took the elevator. At the second floor a door opened and she had her second sight of the young woman. Sara Rosenfeld had grown up. No wild gypsy lass, but a young woman in a simple dress, hair tied back, stood there. What strange eyes she had, like a Tartar's.

"Come in," Sara said. The room was a young room, yellow and white, with a Chagall and a Picasso on the walls. Were they originals? Had Ted lavished those on her? The bay danced and the balcony was a hanging garden, verdant with shrubs, alive with flowers. Armagh seemed sterile by contrast. The period pieces she collected with such care made the house stiff and old. Ted didn't want old things about him. He wanted youth. He wanted this young face and body. The sudden anger she felt on the street was with her again.

The anger gave her strength for what she had to do. "I don't want you to ask me to sit down, or offer me tea or a drink, or make conversation. I didn't come to know you. I never want to know you. But I do think, since you are wasting your youth on my husband, that it is important you know him."

"I do know him," Sara said serenely.

Brillianna took out three crumpled sheets of paper. "I'm going to leave these with you. In his defense I'll say that I really don't think they left him any choice. He's very afraid, you know, of losing the Company." She walked toward the door. "I'd be sorry for you, except I don't think you were sorry, not in all the years it was going on. Still, let me say one thing. You're young. You'll get over him."

Sara watched her close herself in the gold cage and press the down button. Brillianna Angstrom swept into her life to make the pronouncement that it was over. She left documents on the table as proof.

Sara set her mind. No matter what terrible things those papers contained, she swore they would not accomplish what Brillianna so confidently expected.

What could be written down, typed, she could see now the pages were typed, what conceivable thing could be typed on three pages that could change what they were to each other? They were in love. They had so much to say to each other, or nothing, and it didn't matter which. It had been that way from the beginning.

She picked up the pages. They were all more or less exact copies. Not reading word by word but in a general purview she understood what they said.

Now she read carefully, a word at a time. Poor Theo. Brillianna' was right. He had no choice. They told him he would lose Dammam VII. She'd been there, seen that it was his, belonging to him in a special way. No one had believed in Saudi. No one gambled, not as he had.

So did it really matter that he affixed his name to this fawning letter? The White Paper was not initiated by him. It was British policy whether or not it had Theodore Angstrom's approval. His letter addressed to 'Abd al 'Aziz Ibn 'Abd al Rahman al Faisal al Sa'ud made not one whit of difference. It was not one bit more real because Theo endorsed it.

How totally miserable he must be. Miserable, ashamed, and guilty about the farcical conference in Bermuda. He would blurt it out to her, not sparing himself. They pressured him. He folded. It was that simple. Already she was pondering how to lessen the harsh judgment he must have made of himself. She would remind him of their agreement from the first days—not to let anything from the outside impinge on them. And her own resolution, not ever, but ever, to take advantage of who he was. Oil was his life. She knew it at the beginning. She knew it now. In the world that placed them on opposite sides, his wife would have been right. But they didn't live in the world. They lived in their own eyrie. They lived in each other.

He was late, which was fortunate, as he had not run into Brillianna. That possibility hadn't occurred to her, she had been too taken aback by the phone call. Later when she did think of it, it was too late to reach Mrs. Angstrom. So she simply prayed that her first date with Theo since the conference would not be ruined by an encounter with his wife. But sometimes you didn't know what to worry about. She had worried about the wrong thing, a trivial thing. The conference, that terrible conference could not be dislodged from her head.

Sara made sure none of the internal travail showed when she greeted him. Even so Theo's performance outdid hers. He seemed not only in control but completely at ease. He had himself well in hand. Only a touch of breeziness in his manner indicated he was under any kind of stress.

He kissed her lightly on the cheek and poured them a drink. She waited. In his own time. In his own way.

"Well, that was a great conference in Bermuda," he said and pledged her in the Jewish toast she had taught him. "L'chaim!"

She raised her glass silently and drank.

"I took the floor, addressed the meeting that first evening. I decided I had procrastinated enough, delayed too long. It took a certain amount of firmness, that was all, but I've worked out something that will turn this whole White Paper declaration around. I came out for a pipeline to Haifa. You see what that does?"

. . . He told her once, 'Never put water on an oil fire.' Why was that? She tried to remember.

"A line terminating in Haifa will bring tremendous opportunity for employment. Instead of fighting to keep people out, they'll be needing them."

. . . Oh yes, you're feeding the oxygen, feeding the flames. It was better to dynamite, he said.

"There will be workmen needed to lay the line, to guard it, more men to set the refinery up. Arabs won't do, they'll need architects, engineers. There'll be scores of jobs for men who can read blueprints. To say nothing of the transport part of it. Not only loading and unloading, but records, that means clerks, white collar workers. It stands to reason they're going to need people. They'll have to reverse the White Paper. You'll see, immigrants from all over Europe will be pouring in."

"Sometimes," she said looking him full in the face. "it means losing the well."

"What?" He took a step back from her.

"It was all yours, Theo." The opaqueness was massive, it seemed to swallow the words. "All yours. Free and clear. I didn't ask for an effort on your part I knew you couldn't give." She shoved the typed pages toward him.

"What's that?" he said, recognizing them.

"I could even understand that to hold onto Damman VII you had to write what you did."

"Sara. . . ."

She saw tears in his eyes but she didn't stop. "You lied and schemed for something you already had, that was freely given. You had my love, Theo. You had my trust."

"I was trying to hold it together, Sara. I've been trying to do that since the beginning of the war."

"John Eustace Nichols told me I was a liability. A pretty one, he said."

That added, inconsequential sentence terrified him. He felt her decision was made and she wasn't even here for him to argue with. "I didn't care about that," he said urgently. He took her hand but it lay limply in his and he let it fall. He faltered and reached wildly for another tack, honesty. "Taking you to Saudi was a blunder, a bad one. The King's been suspicious ever since. He thinks I'm a Zionist or something. It's made things more complicated, that's all. I've had to eat some crow, like that letter."

Sara nodded her head. "Yes, I can see that. I've been . . . a jinx well, isn't that what you call it?"

"You've been my life, that's what you've been."

She listened to everything he said, but in an odd

way, as though he were reading a letter intended for someone else. "I'll remember you said that."

"Sara, stop talking like this." He was losing ground. He was losing Sara. He flayed about. "I couldn't speak out in Bermuda. I'm sorry. And I'm sorry I can't be your idea of a hero."

"Just a person, Theo. A person I can trust."

He tried to keep his voice steady, nothing else was steady. Even his vision blurred. "You're going to do it, aren't you? No matter what I say, you're going to take six years of our lives and walk out with them."

"Yes, Theo. When you came in here, so jaunty, so glib about the things you were doing for that sad, betrayed handful of humanity that is part of my blood, I knew there was no way back. I'm gone from your life like the Jinn." She looked calmly, remotely back at him. "There aren't even footprints left."

He went out and had four wisdom teeth pulled. It was something he'd been putting off. He had it done under local anesthetic. Good God Jesus how it hurt. The throbbing and the ache were at an unbearable level for days.

Gradually it subsided. No more gnawing, no more festering. After the pain there was numbness, when that wore off there was relief. It had become so difficult to love Sara Rosenfeld.

He began to take an interest in the closing phases of the war. His radio informed him that three savage days of low level bombing knocked out the Ploesti target at the cost of 2,277 American airmen and 270 planes.

"They should have done it at the beginning," Ted muttered at the newscaster.

In 1945, a high priority call came through on his special line. He took it without trepidation. He had won and he had lost all that he was going to win or lose.

State Department credentials were verified via code. Wallace Murray was on the line. "You know of the Yalta Conference? It's in progress now. The Man has agreed to meet in secret with Ibn Saud. I'm not at liberty to tell you where this is taking place. But you are invited to the party. A navy lieutenant will be at your door and properly identify himself in about twenty minutes."

"Do I have anything to say about it?" Ted asked.

"Be ready," Murray told him and hung up.

Ted asked Brillianna to pack for him.

"What will you need?"

"Damned if I know."

"You weren't told anything?" She shook her head in vexation. "Well, I'll start with socks and a change of underwear. You'll need that anywhere." When Ted told her of the conversation she realized things between them were taking on an everyday kind of normalcy. He never asked if it was she who brought Sara the discarded letters. He must have known, but if he blamed her, he put that behind him too. Brillianna had smashed the glass and stepped through the silver frame.

The lieutenant arrived on time, presented credentials, and escorted Ted to an unmarked car.

He knew he was going out of the country. Ibn Saud never left his kingdom. On the other hand, he couldn't imagine an ailing president, who had just undertaken the grueling trip to the Black Sea, traveling on to the King's stronghold.

They drove to Travis airfield. Here he was met and taken in charge by a Colonel Gale. "Do I get a briefing?" Ted asked.

"Sure. Once we're airborne."

Ted's best guess was Cairo. But Jesus, bombs were still falling there.

After takeoff, Gale said, "My orders, Mr. Angstrom, are to deposit you at Jidda harbor in Saudi Arabia. This is not your destination. It is simply a rendezvous point. I am to see you board the destroyer, the U.S.S. *Murphy*."

Ted still was not comprehending any of this. "Why me?"

"It seems the King of Arabia is taking a trip and he wants to be surrounded by friendly faces."

"Mine?"

"Apparently. My orders are from Captain B.A. Smith, countersigned by Commodore John S. Keating. By now they are paying their respects to the King. Embarkation is 3:00 p.m. tomorrow, February 12. By that time the King will have struck his tents and gone aboard."

"Is President Roosevelt aboard the *Murphy*?" Ted asked.

"I wouldn't know. I was told only five people in Arabia are aware of what's going on. The King is supposedly leaving for Mecca. Instead he will dispatch a telegram in code to the crown prince, I believe that's the Emir Saud, in Riyadh, instructing him to carry on in his name until further notice. And he will inform Faisal, his second son, so he can take charge of Jidda and Mecca in his absence. He has a list of those who are to accompany him by motorcade 'to Mecca.' The U.S. government allotted the King four guests." Gale grinned at Ted. "I understand they are trying to keep it to twelve."

Ted grinned back. "He probably wants to bring his harim."

"Believe it or not, that was part of it. The King claimed he couldn't travel in state without his family. But the commodore persuaded him that sufficient privacy could not be guaranteed aboard ship."

Ted chuckled.

"Anyway," Gale continued, "upon entering his limousine, the King will instruct the chauffeur to drive to the pier. Not until that moment will the members of the party know anything out of the ordinary is taking place."

"And who makes up this party?" He was glad to hear his old adversary Sulaiman, the finance minister, was included. William Eddy, the first U.S. minister to Saudi, was to serve as official translator. The other guests were Yusaf Yassin, the foreign minister; Hafiz Wahab, minister of state; the King's private physician, Dr. Pharaon; the King's younger brother, Abdullah; his third son, Muhammad; and his sixth son, the Emir Mansur, minister of defense.

His court, that was understandable. But why the

King should want him present was difficult for Ted to fathom. It is true he had partaken of hospitality, known the palace, tents, and coffee of Ibn Saud. Making a journey for the first time among Westerners, perhaps it was reasonable he think of his guest and partner. Because the King liked and remembered his face, he was about to be flown over a war.

Some hours later he was issued an antiflak jacket. "You probably won't need it," Gale said, "but you never know."

Ted didn't bother to put it on. His belief was they couldn't kill a dead man. Meeting a king and a president wasn't going to infuse life or restore the vigor of the old Ted Angstrom. For a long time now it had been a matter of getting through in good form, carrying on with what style he could muster. And, at times, enjoying it.

The skies were quiet over Suez, although he detected rumbling from the ground. There was a refueling stop, and dropping to within sight of the Red Sea, they proceeded along it to the airport at Jidda.

Navy men were waiting, and Colonel Gale turned him over to them. They traveled to the harbor by jeep, and he was hurried aboard a motor launch. The U.S.S. *Murphy* was there just as Colonel Gale said it would be. It loomed large and gray, an incongruous sight in these waters.

Captain Smith was on deck to greet him and assign quarters. There was some sort of commotion going on. Ted poked his head through a companionway and saw two dhows tied alongside. Herded into them were perhaps a hundred live sheep. A rather portly shaikh was attempting to bring them aboard. The situation was considered critical enough to disturb Commodore Keating. Even so it was a standoff until the arrival of William Eddy, who was called to interpret.

The shaikh was Yusaf Yassin, the King's foreign minister, who embarked on a long speech. Mr. Eddy turned to the commodore repeating Yassin's words. As the complicated preamble went forward, two other dhows pulled alongside loaded with tons of vegetables and sacks of grain and rice. Into the confusion stepped

Ted's old acquaintance, al Shaikh Abdullah Sulaiman. Ignoring the hundred braying animals, he strode to Ted's side, embraced him as a brother, and began the lengthy inquiries as to his health and the fatigues of the journey that Ted recalled so well. He then presented the overheated Yusaf Yassin, who interrupted his account of the King's provender to salaam deeply.

Mr. Eddy outlined the commodore's position, which, simply stated, was that there wasn't room for a hundred sheep on his destroyer. He thanked the King for his thoughtfulness, but they had lockers full of frozen meat.

"Frozen meat?" Yusaf Yassin was shocked. "You mean *old* meat?"

"It's perfectly good." The commodore turned to Eddy. "Tell him it is what I and my men eat. We have sixty days' provision in lockers on board. Plenty for all."

Yassin, Sulaiman, and Eddy huddled. The reply, when it emerged, was that not only was it unthinkable the King eat old meat, but the King desired to slaughter daily from his finest herds so all might taste of his bounty.

The commodore was a resourceful man. "Tell them it is navy regulations. My crew has to consume their own rations."

Yassin was greatly perturbed. Sulaiman himself began to bargain for the King. "It is necessary for the maintenance of the good health of the Kings and the Kings' retainers that seven Nedji sheep be brought aboard."

Seven was not a hundred. The commodore agreed. "Although how four people are going to consume seven sheep in the space of two nights and a day, I don't know."

"I believe we agreed on twelve people," the captain reminded him.

When the King appeared it was with an entourage of forty-eight individuals and water bags from the sacred wells of Mecca. The captain again felt unequal to the situation and again the commodore was summoned.

The King, skirts whipping in the wind, was handed up without mishap. His face lightened on seeing Ted, he went immediately to his side and took his hand. Mr. Eddy interpreted the string of panegyrics the meeting brought forth in the heart of the King. "My long life has brought a final good in your coming, Mr. Angstrom." This from the man who dunned him for money, threatened to nationalize his fields, played footsie with the British.

The intervening seven years told on him, harsh lines were cut into his narrow face, but the one good eye was as keen as his falcon's. He gets off his camel, Ted thought, steps into a limousine, onto a motorboat and finally a destroyer, having skipped the intervening ten centuries completely.

Captain Smith was asking Commodore Keating what should be done about all these people.

"Who are they?" the commodore asked. Mr. Eddy stepped in. "They are the royal princes, ministers, the King's bodyguard, personal servants, the coffeemaker. . . ."

"The coffeemaker?" The commodore's face brightened. "That's one we can jettison."

Both Ted and Eddy were so horrified that they spoke together in an effort to give a picture of the man's importance.

"Very well," the commodore said. "Let him stay. Let them all stay. But explain there aren't quarters for everybody. They'll have to bed down where they can."

This seemed perfectly reasonable to the King. He had been assigned the commodore's cabin. The commodore was temporarily bunking with the captain.

The King with great pomp was taken below past sailors standing at attention, their eyes popping. The little coffeemaker was appareled in a sumptuous flowered robe, while the King lent dignity to an unadorned garment of woven camel hair.

Upon inspecting the commodore's quarters, the King declared loudly that he could not sleep there. "I am desert bred. I cannot be so confined. My nature rebels."

Yusaf Yassin suggested half the ship from deck to

keel be curtained off so that the King might establish himself there.

The commodore replied rather patiently that it would be impossible to operate the ship under those conditions. A compromise was reached and canvas spread over the forecastle converting it to a tent. Oriental rugs instantly covered the deck. The King's favorite chair, which had been transported, was set in the center so he might sit as usual and hold his majlis. Ted noticed, among his other infirmities, that the old King limped badly, and his physician was never far from his side.

They had been underway a short time when the King and his chief astrologer, Majid Ibn Khataila, entered into an intense consultation. The King dispatched a slave to the commodore requesting the presence of the ship's navigator. Mr. Eddy explained it was imperative for the King to know the exact position of the ship, as the hour for evening prayers was approaching, and Mecca must be precisely located.

The two professionals, the astrologer and the ship's navigator, Lt. Fowler, got together, heads bent as Majid Ibn Khataila unrolled his charts. Mr. Eddy was called upon to interpret these hieroglyphics to Lt. Fowler. He then gave a short lecture on the compass to the King's astrologer, who watched the needle with interest, verifying Western knowledge against his own mystical observations. Oddly enough, they arrived at a consensus.

The King was fascinated by the moving needle and himself asked for an explanation of this modern invention which tallied with ancient wisdom.

The exact compass bearing for Mecca was rechecked against the scrolls a final time. At the appointed hour the King was able to face the holy city and lead the entire company in prayer. Mr. Eddy rerouted a sailor who was hurrying to the bridge. The shadow of an unbeliever must not be cast between a Muslim at prayer and Mecca.

Another catastrophe was averted when the coffeemaker attempted to set up his charcoal heating pan on an ammunition rack.

Two of the seven sheep were slaughtered in preparation for the evening meal. The shaikhs assumed that the black messboys were slaves and commanded them to assist in preparing the meal. They continued to address them in Arabic even after Mr. Eddy explained they were Americans and crew members.

"Not slaves?" Yassin asked.

"Citizens," Mr. Eddy replied firmly.

The plan, as Ted learned from Captain Smith, was for rendezvous at 10:00 a.m., February 14, in the Great Bitter Lake in the Suez Canal, with the U.S.S. *Quincy*. "The president made the trip to Yalta on her, and on the way back this meeting was arranged by Mr. Roosevelt."

His own presence began to make sense to Ted. The King was no doubt fond of his face. But he suspected it was the president who had requested his attendance as an oil expert. Ted thought it likely that Roosevelt was curious to meet one of the few men to have bested him, which he had certainly done during the negotiations with Ickes. From being an opponent, he was now a proponent of the U.S. government. Certainly his name was familiar to both leaders.

If the schedule was to be met, it would take two nights and a day to negotiate the Red Sea, very different from his leisurely trip by dhow twelve years before.

The King sent word that the chief officers, as well as Mr. Eddy and Mr. Angstrom, were to join him at his meal. The commodore agreed provided he was allowed to collaborate on the supper. The King and his shaikhs ate the lamb and rice cooked by his servants, but were persuaded to try apple pie topped with a double scoop of vanilla ice cream. The King vowed he had never tasted anything to equal this and wanted to know how it was made. A recipe for the American dessert was translated into Arabic, but it remained a puzzle, as the principal ingredients, apples, were unknown to them.

A basket of apples was brought and passed about. The King, biting onto one, declared it delicious. He was told that was its name, Delicious. Becoming enthusiastic, he asked about the possibility of planting apple trees in al Kharj, the agricultural experimental farm.

The King's habit was to retire early. Arabs were to be found bedded down in gun turrets, in the scuppers, at the bottom of the look-out bridge. Sailors had to step carefully, as the King's entourage rolled themselves in their robes and bunked where they were when the notion took them. The crew of the *Murphy* repaired below for their nightly movie.

At one bell, shortly before dawn, the navigator and astrologer again conferred, took joint bearings, and the Arabs faced what was certainly Mecca. That first morning a messboy served the King an American breakfast consisting of fruit, coffee and eggs, the bacon being omitted.

The King, after rinsing his mouth with American coffee, which brand is lost to the annals of history, spat and cried, "Qawha!" for his own more potent brew. That was only the beginning of the repast, the messboy entered with hotcakes and maple syrup. The King waved them away. He was replete. However he caught the sorrowing look in Yusaf Yassin's eyes as the pancakes were taken past. The King relented. "I believe our brother Yusaf needs this additional food to sustain his extra weight."

Yassin reached for the platter. Not understanding permission had been granted, the messboy whisked them out of his reach. "These pancakes are for the King and ain't nobody else going to have them." The party of Arabs was greatly amused at Yassin's expense.

While the King posed cheerfully for snapshots with the commodore, the King's third son approached the captain. News of the movie, which was forbidden by Wahhabi law, somehow leaked to Muhammad, who employed a spot of blackmail. His father the King would surely hear of these ungodly goings on, if he and his brother, Mansur, were not invited to the movie the second night. The prince had the officer over a barrel and it was so conceded.

During the afternoon, demonstrations of military power were carried out for the King's entertainment.

Antiaircraft fired at smoke deployed for that purpose, depth bombs were discharged at targets towed behind the ship. The King was much impressed, especially by the noise. He was also pleased by Mr. Eddy's running commentary on the death and destruction these weapons were capable of.

That evening the King let it be known he was to host twenty-one officers in an Arab-style feast. No apple pie tonight. The entire group sat cross-legged on the deck under the canopy around the King. Ibn Saud was in the best of humor. He related anecdotes of his many battles and held up one of his fingers broken years ago by a fragment of a Turkish cannon ball.

After supper it was suggested rather diffidently by Commodore Keating that while he understood movies were forbidden as a general rule, they had selected an *educational* film, which by no means could be classified as entertainment, for the King's special viewing. This being so, His Majesty's gracious permission was asked to show it. The King huddled with the minister of finance, the minister of state, the minister of foreign affairs, and the minister of defense. From the beginning there was no question as to the decision. They were immensely curious to see this Western abomination.

The film was shown on deck. It was a documentary of an airplane carrier. The crawl announced it as *The Fighting Lady*. Ibn Saud watched transfixed. At the conclusion he felt impelled to make a preachment against it. Such wonderful diversion was not for his people. They could easily become addicted to these pleasures and neglect their religious duties. All the Arabs were in vocal agreement. But when the old man was in bed, the Emir Muhammad and the Emir Mansur were in the first row watching Lucille Ball loose in a men's dormitory, in the course of which her dress was ripped off. The King never learned of the orgy.

At four bells, 10:00 a.m., the rendezvous on Bitter Lake was accomplished. Before debarking the King made gifts of Arab costumes and daggers to the commodore and captain; costumes and watches with the King's name inscribed were handed to each officer; and over the loudspeaker it was announced that fifteen pounds sterling would be distributed to each petty officer and ten pounds sterling to each seaman in appreciation of their courtesy and hospitality.

Commodore Keating and Captain Smith called Ted into consultation. They had no gift for the King and the occasion obviously demanded something. The result of Ted's cogitation was that Ibn Saud was presented with two submachine guns and the commodore's navy field glasses.

The transfer to the *Quincy* was successfully made. The King, three princes and two ministers, Theodore Angstrom, and Mr. William Eddy crossed the gangplank to meet the president of the United States.

Mr. Roosevelt was seated in a wheelchair, a plaid steamer robe over his legs. At sight of him Ted was appalled. The cordial world-famous grin could not hide the man's pallor or the crinkling smile obliterate lines of deep fatigue. The stress of war had made him a casualty.

However he exerted every charm. He was a spellbinder and Ted almost forgot the evidence of his eyes. Roosevelt took Ibn Saud by the hand in a natural and courteous gesture. "The United States government speaks in friendship to you, Saud of Arabia, through my lips."

The King, obviously touched, replied, "Allah gave Arabia the true faith, and gave the Western world iron." By which it was understood he meant technology. "We come in friendship to learn."

Theodore Angstrom was presented to Mr. Roosevelt along with Mr. Eddy and the royal delegation. The president turned a keen glance on Ted and said, "Well, well. So you're Angstrom." Then in an undertone, "Stick close, I may need you."

The King and Roosevelt spoke for an hour and a quarter on deck. As a guest, Ibn Saud initiated no topics, although he reiterated several times that he had made this historic trip seeking friendship. FDR was a witty conversationalist, the time did not flag. During their discourse he expressed himself confident of a speedy Allied victory. The King concurred that such was indeed Allah's will. He then mentioned rather

300

diffidently that Mr. Winston Churchill also sought a meeting. "I have returned him no answer, waiting to ask my principal host," he bowed in Roosevelt's direction, "if he deems it appropriate."

"Why not? Mr. Churchill's a very decent chap. I've always enjoyed him. I'm sure you will."

Lunch was announced, to be served below in the private dining room set aside for the president. "Because of the awkwardness of this chair," Mr. Roosevelt said to Ibn Saud, "I will ask you and your party to allow Admiral Leahy and Mr. Eddy to escort you in one elevator. Mr. Angstrom and I will take the other."

Ted, appreciating the honor but somewhat wary, wheeled the president's chair to the designated elevator. No sooner had they entered it than the president pressed the red emergency button, bringing them to a lurching stop. Mr. Roosevelt immediately took out a pack of cigarettes. "Smoke?" he asked Ted.

Ted accepted and they lit up.

"I didn't think I could make it," the president said. "I'm an incurable chain smoker. Even my wife's failed with me."

"I think it commendable of you, sir. And wise, not to smoke in the King's presence."

"Yes, I was briefed on his attitude toward alcohol and tobacco, but it's pure murder." He puffed a few moments contentedly. "Well, Angstrom, you're a hard-nosed s.o.b. Gave us a devil of a time over your Hasa concession. Beat us hollow."

"Sorry about that," Ted muttered, "but I have strong convictions, sir, about government in private enterprise."

"I understand, especially when the enterprise is yours. That's all right, Angstrom. I admire a tough opponent. That's why you're here. I want you to see for yourself that it is official U.S. policy to allow no foreign domination in the area of the Saudi concession. My purpose is to make this perfectly clear to the King. I think I have. You heard him ask my permission to accept Mr. Churchill's invitation. Lord, Winnie won't appreciate that." He laughed. "Well, well, we'd better be getting on down." He pressed the button a second time and doused all evidence of his cigarette.

A light luncheon was served, after which the atmosphere became more intense. "Now that the war is drawing to a close," Mr. Roosevelt observed, "there is a good deal of concern in many quarters in the United States as to how best to rehabilitate the Jews in Central Europe. We all know they have suffered quite indescribably, and as an important power in the Palestine area, your thoughts on the matter would be of great interest to me."

Ibn Saud spread his hands as he sometimes did in his majlis when disposing of a thorny matter. "Give the Jews and their descendants the choicest lands and properties of the Germans who oppressed them."

Mr. Roosevelt enjoyed this reply, but evidently felt the subject should be pursued in a more serious vein. "Understandably the Jews might hesitate to accept such a proposition for fear of being set upon a second time."

The King replied, "No doubt the Jews have good reason not to trust the Germans. But when the Allies, as they surely will, destroy the Nazis, they will be able to protect the victims."

The president coughed into his hand. "I think we're on a wrong tack. The problem to be solved, is really the question of Zionism."

"The enemy and the oppressor should pay. What injury has the Arab done that his lands should be taken? It is Germany who stole their lives and property. It is for Germany to pay."

"But if we take as a premise," Roosevelt probed, "that it is impracticable for the Jews to be returned to Germany, in that case, what should be done? I ask, since you are a neighbor to the situation."

The King seemed somewhat out of patience. "I am an uneducated Bedouin, but it is Arab custom to distribute the survivors and victims of battles among the victorious tribes in accordance with their supplies of food and water. Your great country has the most food and water. Besides which, have you not twenty-six Allied nations? Palestine has already more refugees than its small area and poor land can sustain."

"I quite agree," the president soothed. "I neither

ordered nor approved of the immigration of Jews to Palestine, nor is it possible, in view of our understanding, that I should approve it."

Ibn Saud was mollified. And the president again assured him that nothing would be done which would disturb the status quo in the Middle East. "Yet Mr. Angstrom and Mr. Eddy are witness to the fact that I did solicit your opinion on the subject of the disposition of the Jews. I promised certain senators that I would explore the matter with you. I have done so. And I might add that I have learned more about Palestine from Ibn Saud in five minutes than I learned through all my years in government."

When this was translated the King salaamed deeply. Roosevelt had an instinct for handing back to the Arabs their own particular brand of bull. This conference aboard the *Quincy* reminded Ted uncomfortably of Bermuda. At three-thirty the captain arrived to say the ship must prepare to sail.

The King was thrown into a state of consternation. "It is impossible. You, Mr. Roosevelt, and Admiral Leahy, and others of your choosing must board the *Murphy* and partake of Arab hospitality."

The president handled this by saying, "To my regret the security arrangements of the convoy are inflexible, due to wartime conditions. The schedule must be maintained to the minute."

The King retreated from his position, but only a step: "Then must you drink coffee with me to cement our friendship and the friendship of our two nations, and to bind tighter the agreements between our peoples."

Roosevelt's affable smile bespoke his agreement. The coffeemaker was sent for from the *Murphy*. He arrived resplendent in a robe of many-colored silk and squatted over the brazier which he set on the floor. As he fanned the charcoal into fire, the King said to Roosevelt, "We are twins, of an age, heads of state, with grave problems. At heart we are both farmers. You have told me of your desire to return to Hyde Park. And Allah in his wisdom has given me oil to farm. There is yet more resemblance. We both bear severe infirmities. You are obliged to move only in a chair, while I, because of old wounds, walk with difficulty and am unable to climb stairs."

The president replied, "We will bear our infirmities. We will bear the burden of age, and we will farm. However, as a twin you are luckier than I. You can still walk, and I have to be wheeled everywhere I go."

The King gave the handleless cup to the president, who, knowing no better, drank from it.

The King, overlooking this breach in etiquette, replied urbanely, "I think you are the more fortunate. Your chair will take you to your appointed destiny, and you will get there." He drank off his cup at a single quaff.

Roosevelt said, "If you think so highly of this chair, I will give my twin the twin of it, as I have two on board." The order was given and the chair was wheeled across the gangplank to the *Murphy*. The King salaamed. "This is my most precious possession, the gift of my great and good friend."

The King and his party then took their leave. The discussions had been in progress five hours. The president was ashen, and when he let down his guard, near collapse. The U.S.S. *Quincy* weighed anchor for Port Said.

It amazed Ted that everyone played his role. The president, who should have been at home in bed, expended his last strength. Ibn Saud, likewise, and to Ted it seemed quite purposeless. The pomp and circumstance alone were real, and the belief of the participants that history watched their every move. But why should any of this surprise him? He had even less excuse to be here. This ship and these people had no direct bearing on his life. In fact, his life was a strange and alien thing. Continuity was gone from it. Like the rest he went through the motions expected of him.

It came as no great shock to read eight weeks later that Port Said was only a first stop for Roosevelt. The destiny to which his chair took him was death.

Ted scoured the papers, trying to guess which way the world was going, looking for events to tack his life onto. There were a good many: the Russian entry into

Berlin, the suicide of Hitler in his bunker, the unconditional surrender of Germany. But it was the blast over Hiroshima, equivalent to 20,000 tons of TNT, that fired Ted's imagination.

Now that was power.

It ended the war. There was time again to remember the day his world blew apart. He hadn't articulated her name in two years. But he had a code way of thinking about her. He remembered a coat with an old gray blanket for a lining.

To give his life impetus, he kept himself informed about the work proceeding at Los Alamos. The atom was split, releasing energy in quantities previously unknown. Theodore Angstrom realized the potential was incalculable. It was a new power source, unfamiliar to him. But then his own life was unfamiliar to him. He was not at home in it.

He had gone through a war, a personal war. He had gambled, and he had won.

He had gone through a war, a personal war. He had gambled, and he had lost.

When the AEC was formed, Ted placed one of his key people on the board. For a man who needed to make his own luck, to be busy, to turn outward, it was a good time. Power was about to take new forms.

"I hate my mother. I hate her. I hate her. I hate her. Dad too," she said as an afterthought, "but not all the time."

This anger was poured out to Kumju. For a dozen years the red clay god in two pieces had reposed at Carmel where he occupied a garden in company with trees whose serrated leaves seemingly grew at the end of twisted rope. His flat, unindented face stared out from jonquils and fuchsia.

Brilli threw a handful of pebbles at Kumju because you might as well at a clay pot. That's what he reminded her of—a red clay pot. She threw more pebbles. If he were any kind of god at all he could have stopped her mother. Now it was ruined, the secret life she hid in with Chris discovered and torn up.

They had made a warm, two-people world and snuggled into it. What kind of world did Brillianna Grenville Angstrom intend to replace it with? What did her mother have in mind for her? And why couldn't she leave her alone?

What was possible now? When she was at school, she thought the world must be somewhere else. When she came home for vacations, it wasn't here either. The war ended and horizons expanded, it was Locarno for water sports, and skiing on Monte Bre. Or they'd stop at the Hotel Formentor where the pines reminded her of Carmel. Acapulco was fun too, especially at Christmas with fireworks and crowds. She learned to sail there when she was nine and had to relearn at Newport Beach, because Mexican sailboats weren't rigged like regular boats.

She was a good sportswoman, taking trophies in riding and tennis. But the world she was looking for was in none of these places, nor in any of these things.

Not swimming from rocks on the Riviera, or hunting souvenirs in Casablanca.

Where was the real world that other people found and did things in?

When she was at school, she tried an exercise in remembering. She couldn't remember what her parents looked like. But one thing came back, distinct in her mind. She remembered being taken onto producing fields when she was very young, hearing the rhythmic clang of pumps, smelling the smell that made her sick to her stomach.

Her father had gotten away from that, *the crude* they called it. It still flowed in pipes somewhere in Arabia. It was the base, the foundation of the new consortiums, she understood that. But in 1946 her father was a different man. She thought of him as tall and rectangular as the buildings he owned, where commodities no one ever saw were traded and sold, where ticker tapes and computer banks were housed.

Before the hatred, before the clouds of anger, in fact only days before, if she had tried to picture her mother, it would have been as a blur of activity: philanthropies, functions, dinners, and a mania for collecting. Away from her parents, she remembered them only in this absurd fashion. There were times when she could not remember herself at all. Then she would dash into the bathroom to stare at herself in the mirror.

She wasn't as delicately made or as fine-boned as the Grenvilles. To her mother's dismay, she reached her height of five foot five and grew an additional three inches. The Grenville and Angstrom strains warred in her. There were the dreamy eyes behind which she knew how to hide her thoughts. There was the patrician, tilted Grenville nose, but the mouth was her own with its seasons of discontent.

At school she had managed to reach the eleventh grade without friends. To impress the girls she told them she had a god in her garden. She became known as a liar. So she made up a story of a large family of brothers and sisters and cousins who all joined together during the summer. They liked her better then. The trouble was, now she did not care for them.

308

She did not apply herself to her studies and, as her teachers put it, failed to measure up to her potential. But she was fond of reading, uncritically consuming anything that came her way. The time she felt most free and most herself was when riding. She loved horses. Their largeness made her think of Angstroms, and she liked the idea of controlling them.

She was a patient trainer. One of the horses at the school was stable shy. No one could get him to the barn because of an overhanging roof between it and the tack house. Brilli knew she could do it. It was a Saturday, so there was no objection to her working with the animal, a shiny black quarter horse. Her method was to ride him around the corral in expanding rings, bringing him gradually closer to the overhang.

It required the better part of the afternoon, so slowly did she increase the perimeter. Finally she rode Paco through the dreaded area. There was no rearing, no bolting, he was peaceful and as quieted as a rocking horse. The stableboy, who was shoveling layers of manure to dry and then pitchforking it into a compost heap, left his labors to sit on the whitewashed fence and watch.

"That was a pretty thing to see," he said.

Brilli didn't answer, but moved toward him quickly so her sunstreaked hair flashed. "I want Paco every time I ride."

"You know we're not allowed to reserve horses."

She turned an imperious look on him.

". . . but I'll do what I can."

It wasn't only the control she exercised over the creature, making him step high, holding him to dressage, proud and slow. Part of it was the headlong dashes, kicking him out of a canter into a gallop that lathered his sides and left them both breathless.

And the jumps. She loved to jump. Her mother insisted she wear a riding helmet, but she left it at the rear of the closet in her dormitory room. She liked her hair to fly with his mane. She kept raising the bars. Chris, the stableboy, watched her. She knew he did. She didn't care. It was what was between her and the horse that mattered, a shared sense of danger and excitement.

She took to grooming Paco herself, examining his hooves for stones, watering him, brushing him down, smoothing the steaming flank. She sneaked him oats, which he adored. It was a special treat. Brilli began to come to the stable before classes and rake down his hay. There were fine bridle paths around the school, one led to a waterfall and both horse and rider enjoyed plunging beneath it and drenching themselves. They were a good deal alike, horse and girl, spirited, half wild and highly bred. They recognized these qualities in each other. Brilli felt less alone, there was a companion with whom she could ramble, look at Queen Anne's lace, while he cropped a velvety bit of forest grass.

For the most part, Chris didn't like the arrogant young ladies that took out horses and didn't care if they returned them lame or saddle sore. Many times the horses' mouths were inflamed from the bit—that angered him. These rich spoiled girls were afraid and pulled back.

Billy, he thought that was what they called her, was not like that. When she returned Paco, she went over him meticulously. She managed the saddle herself. When she used one, it was always the light English. Mounted, she was part of the animal.

Chris was more tongue-tied and stupid around her than the other girls. And more aware of his shortcomings. This was a girls' prep school. Prep meant preparatory, preparing for college. There was no chance of college for him, not even the two-year community kind. He was a high school dropout, and acutely conscious of his ungrammatical English. Pronouns in particular loused him up. He would say, *himself, herself, myself,* to avoid having to choose between *he* and *him, she* and *her, I* and *me.* Mostly he kept quiet and said nothing.

"You're not much for talking, are you?" Brilli challenged one afternoon as they were rubbing down the horses.

"Oh, I don't know." He didn't look at her. "How come you got a boy's name?"

310

"I don't have a boy's name."

"Don't they call you Billy?"

"Billy?" She thought this was funny, but she didn't let on. "You're right, that *is* my name. My parents wanted a boy."

"You ride like a boy," he said.

"I ride better than a boy. What's your name?" she asked, knowing it was Chris.

"Chris."

"I bet I ride better than you."

"Maybe," he said.

"Look," she spoke rapidly, "tomorrow I'll get up early. Five in the morning. I'll meet you here. We'll race to the waterfall. No one will know."

"If they found out, I'd lose my job."

"And I'd probably be expelled, made an example of. So forget it."

"No." He made up his mind. "I'll do it."

"But I get Paco."

"Sure."

"Who will you ride?"

"Chalky."

"Chalky?" She laughed, "I'm sure to beat you."

"Maybe not. I've been working with Chalky."

She walked away, still laughing.

At five in the morning, color was withdrawn from the world, flowers were black and buildings gray. She ran all the way and arrived out of breath. Chris was already there. He was getting out the saddles.

"Let's ride bareback," she said.

Morning was beginning to show them to each other, it had not returned color to things yet, but cast a strange new look over the world.

"The sun is in the wrong side of the sky," Brilli commented. "Good old Helios." She tossed that out because he wouldn't know what it meant and it would remind him that he was a stableboy even if he won, which he wouldn't. She threw herself across Paco and then got a leg over. She scorned getting up by the fence like the other girls.

Chris swung himself up on Chalky. Brilli gave him a conspiratorial grin that said, "We're in this together."

311

Then with tennis-shoed feet urged Paco out of the corral. The horses tossed their heads and neighed at this unexpected, early-morning freedom.

The animals knew the way and went from a trot into a mad gallop. They tore along the forest trail, the smell of wet mulch under their hooves reached the nostrils of horses and riders. The dew hung in spiders' webs, branches cracked. The world was young this morning. The sun had never risen before, it swirled in concentric spectra through the trees. They drew the smell of loamy earth into their lungs. Chalky's dappled sides pressed Paco's. They could hear the waterfall. They leaned forward for a sight of it.

The low angle of the sun struck with prismatic colors. "Look," she said, "a rainbow!" And plunged into the heart of it. But like everything else, when she reached it, it was gone.

"You won!" he called.

She didn't care about that anymore. She wanted to be part of the rainbow. "It's gone," she said.

"No, no, it's still there. I can see it."

"Can you?"

"You're right in the middle."

"What color are my eyes?"

"A band of green. And then lavender, I think, fading into blue."

"And my nose and my mouth?"

"Tints of rose. And the rest of you is a sort of yellow."

"Yellow? That's because I'm made out of gold. Pure gold."

He urged his horse in too. The water plastered his hair along his cheek, and washed away the smell of stables and animals. He was a boy laughing with her. He was her friend.

"Have you ever had a shower here?"

He shook his head.

"I haven't either. I was afraid someone would come by. But it's too early. No one's up yet." She kicked her tennis shoes into the stream and pulled her middy blouse with the school's insignia over her head. By

312

some acrobatic hitching about, her riding breeches and underpants were off and thrown over a bush.

Chris dismounted, stripped, and stepped from the pile of dirty clothes, beautiful and male to Paco's side. Paco was excited by the smell of him and lifted his front legs in the air, but Chris was already up behind Brilli.

He caught her around her slippery waist and hung his head on her shoulder to look and fondle. She had witnessed a stallion mount a mare and stared with amazement at the long tool used on the female. When Chris pushed her forward, she knew what was going to happen. She wanted this joining onto another human being.

He was fumbling. She raised herself as though she were posting and he forced an entrance. The horse bucked and they slid to the ground, he still positioned, not willing to retract for fear he could not find the hidden spot again. They continued on the ground, accomplishing the act from the rear. Neither knew there was another way. "Billy," he said.

She couldn't tell him that wasn't her name, not after what they had done and felt. Every atom in her quivered.

He pointed in alarm to blood between her legs. But she was already a woman and used to blood. She cleansed herself under the waterfall. He watched her splash and turn her head into the spray. He came in with her and they played until they were roused again.

This time he held her face to face. They didn't think it was possible, but she leaned against a flat rock and he penetrated. The smell of human semen put the stallion into a frenzy, he pawed and reared and muddied the water.

Chris would not let her ride Paco back. She was glad. Chalky was not such a broad horse and she ached at the center of herself. But at least she had found out where the center was.

Brilli was on time for her first class. She looked at the schoolroom of young girls with new eyes. She felt superior, knowing the secret into which they had yet to be initiated. She had carnal knowledge of a man.

She thought in those terms because of daily attendance at chapel where she sang, "I'm the child of a king. With Jesus my savior, I'm the child of a king."

It was an Episcopal chapel. Her father's people had been lowly Methodists, but the Grenvilles were, in Henry's time, among the barons who brought the Church of England into being.

It was hard to know if her mother had married beneath her. In many ways she had. The great wealth, of course, was Angstrom. But then there was Grandpa Angstrom, still pinching the maids on the rump and making them squeal. Still talking in what mother called "his earthy language," letting out a string of expletives from time to time that greatly enhanced her own vocabulary. The money, she supposed, made up for his lack of social graces. And of course, Dad was a Princeton man. What would the family do if she turned up married to Chris? Mrs. . . . here she had to stop, she didn't know his last name.

A boy from another walk of life, her mother would say. No use to argue we're Americans, equal, and all that. "There is still such a thing as breeding. Who is the boy? Who are his people?" Brilli laughed out loud in the middle of geometry.

Of course she couldn't march in with him. It would be a year and a half. But once she was eighteen. . . . She thought it was eighteen, but it differed from state to state, she'd have to look up California law. If it wasn't legal here, they'd go where it was.

The family would be terribly shocked. Mother especially, horrified every time he made one of those dreadful faux pas, *irregardless* for *regardless*. Mother always lifted her eyebrows over that.

Chris was the first person she had ever met who didn't have plans for improving himself. He loved animals. He loved being around them. He was at home outdoors and knew all sorts of fascinating lore, such as which grubs could be fried and eaten and what berries to pick on a walk. She never saw him with a book. But he knew things. He had the art of being still. He took great pleasure in watching animals and birds. He was curious about their habits and instincts. He could

314

lie so quietly that field mice would scurry over him, or jays pick up bits of nearby straw. Running counter to these periods of intense concentration was his enjoyment of hard physical exercise. He did much more around the place than he was asked to. He shoveled, raked, mended and painted fences, re-roofed the barn. He also had a small subsistence garden which he tended.

Sometimes she would see him tear off into the woods at a dead run for no reason at all. Once, giving him an hour's start, she took Paco and followed. When she caught up with him he was lying stretched out, his arms extended like a crucified Christ. He ran until he fell down, and there he lay utterly exhausted.

Except for occasional chance-taking, they met only before dawn. Their love was illumined each day by first light. She thought of it as a holy thing. It amazed her that most of the time they did different things in different places. The law of their own bodies decreed them one. Sometimes she would skip her shower for the pleasure of smelling his ejaculation dried against her thighs.

Her breasts grew large. When she went home at Easter, her mother said she was filling out and insisted they go shopping for new bras. They were custom fitted for uplift, firmness and modesty. She did not enjoy being patted into the garments and surveyed by the saleswoman and her mother. The first thing Chris always did was free her breasts and let them spring out.

Her body hungered for him. She moped around the house and wouldn't be nice to the young men who were invited for parties, sons of women in her mother's set, rising executives in her father's companies.

They were not put off by her curt manner. Howard Knolls was particularly attentive. He seemed to turn up everywhere—at the club, where she beat him roundly in tennis; at dinner, where he managed to sit next to her. He was tall, reasonably athletic, he golfed, sailed, and was a research associate in one of her father's firms. Mother said that Father "had his eye on him."

He did not walk with animal rhythm, but the way a

man in a Brooks Brothers suit and a forty-dollar pair of shoes walks. His hair did not fall in shaggy curls, it was neat, trimmed, and he used some sort of goop on it. There was the scent of cologne on his body too. One night at the club, he drew her into the shadows and kissed her. It amazed her that his sex organs remained passive, hidden inside trousers and jockey shorts. Nothing could prevent Chris from rising to pinion her. She even probed Howard Knolls a bit with her thigh, not from desire, but with curiosity, to make sure it was there. She allowed her body to swing into his. He immediately released her.

She laughed. To him she was the boss's daughter. Only to Chris was she Billy.

What most disturbed her on this visit home was Grandfather. The old man's failing health had not been mentioned in letters, nor had she been told of the series of small strokes. It was sad to see what had been a great bear of a man, shrunk and fallen in on himself. Scoliosis drew his neck forward, cutting inches from his height. His skin hung loose and pleated in heavy gray folds. He was the death's-head that stalked their festivities.

> "It is an ancient Mariner,
> And he stoppeth one in three."

That's what an education did for you, made you draw back from your own grandfather.

In these days when he was chilly and his life at low ebb, Irv loved his granddaughter for her red blood, the life coursing through her. Angstrom blood. Angstrom life.

"It's his fault," he told Brilli, "that gas is four cents at the pumps." He was referring to Herbert Hoover, whom he thought was president. "But Roosevelt would be worse. He listens to that idiot Maynard Keynes. *Spend your way to prosperity* indeed, whoever heard of such a thing?"

Another time she observed him sitting alone on a stone bench looking out at the sea, the great Eternal he was about to join. Out of pity she went to him and put her hand on his shoulder. She withdrew it almost instantly. It was like rattling dried bones. Neither the sea nor his own demise preoccupied the old man. He was worried about the lease men he'd sent out in the thirties to buy up tracts of land cheap. "I tell them, take the lease out in your own name. Make the down payment with a cashier's check, conceal the fact that you represent a company."

"Was that how you got your Long Beach concession, Grandpa?"

The old man nodded. "We took out a lot of barrels in my time, a lot of barrels."

"Do you remember when I was little, Dad used to take me into the fields? Do you remember that? The creak of the pumps was a kind of music. And at night when they lit up the derricks, they looked like giant Christmas trees."

"Yes sir, we used to string lights to keep working by. Imagine you remembering, you were such a mite of a thing. I thought then you were going to take after your mother's people, turn into a Grenville. But you grew out of it, grew tall like an Angstrom. You've got the look of my mother. She was a handsome woman, bore seven children, been dead fifty years. But you got the look of her." His shrewd turtle eyes in their bed of wrinkles had never succumbed to glasses. They surveyed her with unaccustomed keenness. "You got yourself a man, don't you?"

Brilli was startled into the truth. "Yes, Grandpa."

The old man laughed silently, his shoulders heaving. "Well, don't let *Her* hear of it, your ma."

"I won't," she said fiercely.

"Or your dad either. He's always been too much under her thumb. You'd find yourself married off before you could say Jack Robinson, to one of these bloodless, career-minded, mealy-mouthed, uppercrust dudes."

"Oh Grandpa, it's so good to tell someone. That's exactly what I'm afraid of."

"This lad of yours now, he's got plenty of juice in him, I'll warrant?"

She smiled. "That's true."

317

"And he's no company man or ever will be?"

"How did you know? Oh Grandpa, you're wonderful."

"Well, you don't get to the end without having gone through the beginning."

"You're not at the end, Grandpa. You've a long ways to go yet."

He corrected her. "From where you're at, death is something you don't think on, except to worry about. But the closer you get to it, the less bothered you are about it. Which ain't to say I'm not going down fighting. I've been a fighter all my life. And this is no time for a change. Don't you change neither. I'm glad you've got a fellow. And when they find out and the roof falls in, fight the whole goddamned consortium. That's what they call themselves these days, consortiums."

It was the last talk she had with her grandfather. He got bronchitis and had to keep to his room.

Brilli was back in school six weeks when she was called out of class to the office of the headmistress. Her first thought was they had found out about her and Chris. The office was a place she generally went to hear a lecture on *applying oneself*. You didn't go there to hear your grandfather was dead. But when she saw her mother sitting there, she knew. Brillianna had death written all over her. She even smelled of death. The death of a sperm whale. Her black suit was chic, but it was black.

"He was a very old man," her mother said, "in his eighties."

"Did he fight?" Brilli asked.

Her mother looked at her in some concern, not knowing what she meant. "We'd like you at home for the present, Brilli. Mrs. Melbourn had kindly agreed to private tutoring so you won't lose your class standing."

"No," Brilli said.

Her mother continued as though she hadn't spoken.

318

"Your father feels the loss very deeply. You know how close they were."

"No," Brilli said again.

"She's upset," Mrs. Melbourn said to her mother.

"Of course she's upset. But she must think of other people, of her family. Brilli dear, at a time like this a family draws together. You don't need to pack. We'll send for your things."

"I told you no. I'm not going."

"Brilli, I think you've treated us to enough hysteria. Your father needs you."

"My father has never needed me."

"Brilli, I know this is a shock, that you are upset. But please save this kind of thing until we're alone. The funeral is tomorrow."

"I'm not going to the funeral."

"Brilli, for heaven's sake, get hold of yourself."

She stared at her mother with Angstrom eyes. "I'm sorry you had the trip for nothing. I refuse to go back home. I simply won't."

Her mother and the headmistress exchanged glances. "I think," Brillianna said, "this is something we must handle in private."

"Why not step into the study?" Mrs. Melbourn suggested.

"I don't need to step into the study, or anywhere else," Brilli said violently. "Stepping into the study isn't going to make me go home." Nevertheless she followed her mother into the book-paneled room.

Her mother exclaimed over the stained glass window although she had seen it before. The headmistress left them. "Now young lady, what is this all about?"

Brilli stared back, defiant but silent.

"It would be a disgrace not to attend your grandfather's funeral."

"Grandpa wouldn't care."

"There is such a thing as respect. And there is your father to consider."

"All right." It was a technique she had employed with her mother before. A tantrum, then a partial giving-in usually brought her what she wanted from the beginning. "I'll go with you and stay for the

319

funeral. But I want to come back to school. I'd miss my friends. And I hate the idea of being tutored. May I come back, Mother?"

"We'll see. I'll talk to your father about it."

"No. I'm not leaving here unless you tell me I can come back."

"I won't be forced into a decision, Brilli."

"Whose idea was it anyway to take me out of school, away from my friends, away from my studies?"

"It was my idea. It would only be for a short time. I thought you would be glad to do that for your father."

"You never put me first. You never think what would be best for me."

"That isn't fair, Brilli, and it isn't true. To be perfectly honest it never entered my head you would oppose me on this. But since you feel so strongly, I suppose it would be no good having you glooming about the place. The whole idea is to cheer your father up, take his mind off things a bit."

"I'll stay over the weekend," Brilli said. "And I *will* cheer him up. I want to." Suddenly she was hugging her mother, clinging to her, "Honestly I do. It was just the thought of being kept home. I'd hate that."

"All right, dear." She patted her somewhat awkwardly. "It won't happen."

"Promise?"

Her mother nodded and Brilli sat down in a chair and started to cry. "Did Grandpa fight hard?"

"You mean, did he suffer? No. He went in his sleep."

Brilli looked up with something like satisfaction. "That's the only way they got him. They sneaked up on him."

Brillianna shook her head. Her only child was a complete enigma to her.

Ted did not need cheering up. He needed to be alone to work it out. But Brillianna always attributed to others what she would have preferred for herself.

Irv Angstrom's death in a way was Ted's death too.

It was the death of the California strike. It was the death of the early days in the fields when he had hung around trying to avoid college. The Long Beach wells, like Irv Angstrom himself, were finished.

When the maid came screaming, having found the body, Ted didn't go in at once. Crazy things caught in his mind, like that plane flight to Long Beach, how his dad had chewed him out, and then covered for him. Irv Angstrom knew the blood that propels you forward, lets nothing stop you, lets nothing get in the way. What he hadn't known—he was the victim.

Suddenly Ted wanted to talk to Sara. If he could justify himself to Sara——He preferred not to think of her as she must be now, but of the Sara who was nineteen with rolled-up pants, a shirt knotted around her middle, and spray caught in her hair. She'd probably married whoever he was, with the hardware store, had a kid, and forgotten all her radical notions. The old man never knew Sara. He knew about her though. And joked about her, letting him know he'd been a hellraiser in his time.

What did that mean? That you had your share of broads, wealth, and booze before the maid rushed in and said you were gone.

Gone?

What the hell was *gone?*

A few men, for a short while, would remember. He went in to see his father. Automatically his hand went to the pipe tong mark on his own face. The old man was laid out stiffly, his eyes closed. "You never knew it, Dad. But I gave you a royal screwing. Took your Long Beach fields, used them as collateral for the Hasa.

"Once when we were having a few together, I almost told you, 'Dad, your son is a true Angstrom, a true son-of-a-bitch.' I wonder what you would have done, grabbed your heart and had angina? Or would you have said, 'You know, I did the same thing to my old man.' You grew up not knowing how to use your knife and fork, but you recognized the main chance. You were *my* main chance, Dad. —Dad?"

But it wasn't his dad anymore. This on the bed had

321

stopped being Irv Angstrom. It was a facsimile of Irv Angstrom, lately a human being. It was an indeterminate stage, before the cells and atoms, bones and corpuscles became provender for the earth. Perhaps in a million, million years some part of him would be put on a pump and come up slow and black.

Justice took a long time. That's why in human terms there didn't seem to be any. We're not around long enough to see how it works. Ted walked from the room absently. You didn't say goodbye to yourself, or ask forgiveness of yourself. Irv Angstrom was his foundation. That foundation was gone, like so much else.

It made no difference to him that his daughter was home. He barely remarked it. Brillianna, however, was uneasy about the girl. Her temper tantrum at the school, something secretive in her manner decided her to take action.

Brilli in the past had not been devoted to school, nor had she ever brought any of the girls back with her on holidays as her mother frequently suggested she do. Her refusal to leave was so unexpected and surprising that Brillianna, acting solely on her own responsibility, made inquiries.

Brilli and Chris had not been as unobserved as they imagined. There were times when she lingered later than she should, and one or another of the girls noticed her return. Since she had no close friends, Brilli was unaware of the speculation and gossip.

The headmistress in her turn took much the same steps as Brillianna. By the time Brillianna had the facts, Chris was discharged. As the mother of a sixteen-year-old, she tried not to panic. This was a problem many parents had to deal with. Looking back she could not blame herself.

Perhaps it was the Angstrom strain, uncaring as to price. Or what was more probable, it was random, like a lottery. A certain percentage of girls got into trouble. Brilli, unfortunately, was of this number. She blamed the school. With an enrollment of over two hundred young ladies there should not have been an eighteen-year-old stableboy.

A stableboy. A shudder passed along her frame, which

she repressed. I can't make myself ill over this, she thought. She was canny enough to bide her time. She gave no indication that she knew, but arranged for Brilli's yearly medical checkup, an examination from which her daughter emerged rather flustered.

The diagnosis: no pregnancy.

'Thank God for small favors.' It was an expression of her mother's that popped into her head.

Her next move was to arrange for Brilli's admission to a select girl's school in Geneva. She debated whether she need confide in Ted. His natural inclination was to give into the child. Unless he knew, Brilli would twist him around her finger.

Ted's reaction was a bellow. Brillianna had taken the precaution of closing the door, but he could be heard through the entire house. "What are you telling me? I send her to some fancy school at fancy prices, and neither they nor you can keep the girl in hand?"

"There's no use ranting, Ted. It's not the end of the world. In fact it could be a lot worse. It's established that she's not pregnant."

Ted groaned.

"Families handle this kind of thing all the time. I've arranged for her to go to a fine Swiss academy. It is quite rigid and authoritarian. After a year there, she will be glad to come home. She will 'come out' as I planned, and she will be married. My purpose in going into all this with you is that she will certainly attempt to circumvent me and get together with this boy. I want you, for once, to back me up."

"She needs a hiding, that's what she needs. In my day a sixteen-year-old who overstepped the mark was whaled within an inch of her life."

She knew he was blowing off steam, but it infuriated her. "And how old was the young girl you seduced?"

"What are you talking about? I never seduced anyone in my life. And she wasn't underage. But this, this is statutory rape."

For the first time Brillianna became alarmed. "You wouldn't make a case of it, Ted? I mean, to be revenged on the boy would absolutely ruin Brilli's future."

"I'd like to get my hands on him."

"Well, you can't. He's gone. Fired."

"A stableboy, you said? Is she crazy, or what?"

Brilli was making plans to return to school. She had more than kept her part of the bargain: come back for the funeral, been on hand all week, and now she was restive. Missing Chris was not a passive thing. Her eyes demanded the landscape of his face and form, her fingers wanted to run the familiar course of him. Her flesh demanded his.

She snitched a perfume from her mother's dresser and rearranged the bottles so it wouldn't be noticed. She would ravish and delight his senses. She began to imagine their first encounter . . . when her mother came into the room. There was a purposeful look to her that Brilli didn't like. Perhaps she had noticed the missing perfume.

When there was something unpleasant to do, Brillianna lost no time getting at it. "Brilli, you are not going back to Melbourn. The whole unsavory thing has come out. Your father knows, I know, Mrs. Melbourn knows."

"What unsavory thing?" There was still an edge of possibility that her mother was talking about something else.

"The unbelievable episode between you and—" she couldn't bring herself to say stableboy—"that hired hand."

Brilli pressed her hands against her stomach as though she would be sick. "It was a trick. You tricked me into coming home. You never intended to let me go back."

"No. I simply thought your behavior most peculiar. And I investigated."

"You investigated me? Your own daughter? Does that mean you went to an agency, hired some grubby little man to ask questions?"

"What choice did you leave me?"

"Well, I don't care what you found out. I'm going back."

"You could hardly expect Mrs. Melbourn to accept you under the circumstances."

"She knows too?"

Brillianna nodded.

Fear grew somewhere in the roots of her brain. "Where's Chris? What's happened to Chris?"

"There will be no criminal charges, if that's what you're afraid of."

"Criminal charges? Mother, what are you talking about? We love each other."

"Legally, he committed rape."

"Rape? Are you out of your mind? I'm in love with a boy. He's in love with me. Now where is he?"

"Gone. Dismissed."

"Gone where? Where is he? How will I find him?"

"You won't, Brilli. I want you to listen to me very carefully. You are leaving for Geneva to attend an excellent academy. You will be strictly supervised. There will not be an occasion for another such indulgence."

"I won't listen to you. How can you use such terrible words to describe something so beautiful? Don't you know the difference between indulgence and love?" Her eyes opened wider, as she stared at her mother. "You don't, do you? Now that I am a woman, I can see that you're not. I'm going to my father."

"You have a true instinct as far as it goes, Brilli. If you were a son, your father would clap you on the back. But you're a daughter and more apt to get it on the backside. Your father is a man who has accepted all the clichés because he hasn't had time to do much living. Wives and daughters are chaste. He won't understand anything else."

"He'll understand love."

"With a stableboy? This is a man who is building an empire."

"My father loves me, even if you don't."

Brillianna ignored the charge against herself. She merely said, "I advise you not to go to your father over this. But of course, you may."

"Don't advise me. Not any more." She ran out of the room and through the house, a maid scurried out of her way. She pushed open the massive door to her father's study. He was speaking long distance, making a reservation.

He looked up, annoyance on his face. This was some-

325

thing he expected Brillianna to handle. An incoherent daughter seemed about to throw herself on him. "Brilli, let's understand each other. I am disappointed, as any parent would be, at your behavior, your lack of judgment, lack of restraint. But you will hear no more from me on the subject. So be a good girl, listen to your mother and things will work out for the best."

He had arrested her somewhere between the door and himself. Because she had been screaming at her mother, her voice didn't come out properly. In a hoarse whisper she said, "So the plan is to keep me in Switzerland in a minimum security facility. Or is it maximum? And then you'll bring me home and marry me off?"

"All that's your mother's province. She is a very sensible woman. She'll get you out of this scrape and none the worse."

"Father, haven't you ever loved, really loved someone?"

For a moment she thought she had broken through, the muscles of his face relaxed and he seemed about to speak to her as a person. But it didn't happen. "You listen to your mother, girl. She's the only one who can get you out of this fix."

"If you know where Chris is, please just tell me that."

"I don't know," he said grimly. "And a good thing for him."

"Why are we all acting out these ridiculous parts, irate father, distraught mother, sinful and unrepentant daughter? Can't you see how unreal it is? Please Dad, don't let Mother play this game."

"If it's a game, my girl, it seems to me you're the one who began it."

"Oh my God, I can't talk to you either." She rushed from his study. She turned corners and doors slammed.

One of the maids was waiting in her room with a letter. It took five dollars, most of her allowance, to get it into her hands. Brilli tore it open violently. The illiterate scrawl shocked her. The misspelled message ran between wide blue lines in childishly formed letters. Chris suggested they meet in a drugstore. How stupid!

Again she ran, this time into the garden where she

326

poured out invective to Kumju's no ears, no eyes, no face. "I hate my mother. I hate her. I hate her."

"Dad too," she said as an afterthought.

As she looked more deeply into Kumju she knew she hated them, not for their high-handed methods, but because they were right. The storm had passed. The ache was still in her, but Chris wouldn't do. Almost anyone else would, any man whom her mother could be counted on to disapprove of.

Brilli cleared out her savings account into which fond relatives put money on birthdays, and took a taxi to the airport. Arriving in New York, she did not leave the terminal but waited for the new pressurized *Constellation* to London. Shortly after takeoff she went into the small toilet and locked the door to read OCCUPÉ. Each step had been thought out. She began by pulling her blouse over her head, turning it around and undoing the top three buttons to give a décolleté effect. She placed her oxfords in the paper container and, taking from her purse a pair of high-heeled shoes, slipped them on. Then she went to work on her hair, sweeping it into a French twist. She dug deeper into her purse for her mother's purloined makeup, applying it dexterously and sparingly.

The image in the mirror changed from schoolgirl to well-groomed young woman. Pleased with the result, she returned, but not to her seat. As the plane was far from full, she moved back to tourist class.

The stewardess came by, she brought Brilli a magazine and asked if she desired a cocktail. Conscious she had passed the test, she ordered a gin and tonic. She had sampled them before under the covers at Melbourn, but never at twenty thousand feet.

Her father had business in Jerusalem and Cairo later in the week. She'd heard him on the phone making arrangements to stay at the King David Hotel. She would simply wait for his arrival. And when they met, it would be different. Her mother wouldn't be there, for one thing. And after she had been missing four days, he would be so relieved to see her, he wouldn't force this Switzerland

327

thing. She had *had* it with pimply-faced adolescents who earnestly questioned who they were.

She knew who she was and where she was going and not going.

The city of Jerusalem was an armed camp bristling with soldiers. Brilli discovered that the King David Hotel housed British HQ. Guards demanded passes, and didn't like being shown a passport. By the time she reached the main lobby, she had run a gauntlet, explaining a dozen times who she was. "I'm meeting my father here." Each set of soldiers, convinced by her American accent and air of confidence, passed her along for someone else to cope with.

A British major finally approached, introduced himself, looked at her papers, and escorted her to the desk behind which several women were at work, filing. "Look after this young lady, will you, Miss Grey?"

Miss Grey glanced up. "Yes?" she asked crisply, not caring for the cosmopolitan elegance she saw before her.

"I'm with the Angstrom party," Brilli said. "I believe Mr. Theodore Angstrom is booked in here."

"May I have your papers please? As you see, this is British headquarters. The hotel as such, is closed to the public. However there is a wing for diplomatic missions, VIPs, that kind of thing. If you'll wait a moment, I'll check."

"That's all right, Nina, I'll do it." A young woman with an air of authority moved opposite her on the other side of the desk. Slightly oblique eyes regarded her intently. Brilli felt more uneasy under their quiet appraisal than enduring the stares of the soldiers.

The woman spoke. "You did say the Angstrom party?"

"Yes, I did."

"That would be Mr. Theodore Angstrom." It was not a question so Brilli said nothing.

The woman turned to consult a file. "Here it is." She removed the card. "Angstrom, Theodore. Party of one." She looked severely at Brilli.

"We arranged it at the last minute." She found her

328

aplomb deserting her. "I guess he didn't have time to notify you."

"I see."

It seemed to her the woman did see, perhaps too much. Her continued inspection was disconcerting. Finally the woman said, "According to this, Mr. Angstrom has canceled his reservation."

"Canceled?" Panic was injected into the word. "But are you sure? I'm his daughter. I've got to find him."

"I'll see if there is a message for you." She examined the pigeonholed wall behind her. "I don't find anything."

Brilli had been holding her breath as though by some miracle there could be a message. "There's obviously been some mixup," she said, trying to put a good face on things. She hadn't money enough to leave Jerusalem.

"Could he be staying anywhere else in the city?" the woman asked. "With friends, perhaps?"

Brilli shook her head.

"I don't want to presume, Miss Angstrom, but your father is well-known here. The hotel will take the responsibility of telephoning your home."

"No," Brilli said sharply.

Before replacing the card, the woman turned it over. "We're in luck." She sounded relieved. "He can be reached at Shepheard's, Cairo. I'll tell you what we'll do, Miss Angstrom, we'll arrange a room for you here for tonight. For the moment we'll call you a foreign envoy." She looked at Brilli brightly. "When you've had a bath and ordered up dinner, you can place a call to your father."

"You've been very kind," Brilli said, and added, "I can't help feeling you are doing this on your own. Is it because we're fellow Americans?" The woman didn't answer at once and Brilli went on. "It looks like a dead city out there. I had no idea the country was in a state of siege. Are you trapped here too?"

The woman replied, "I am a Jew."

Brilli drew back at the implied rebuff. "I didn't mean anything personal."

She's Grenville too, Sara thought, this sixteen-year-old trying to pass herself off as a woman of the world. And succeeding, this beautiful, sophisticated Brilli. The Angstrom admixture bowled her over, the measured way she spoke, especially when she was upset.

Sara found an excuse to busy herself with the cards, to turn away from Theo's eyes. Dreamer's eyes, in this too pretty, too petulant face. The girl had run away, that much was clear. She had come across the world to find Theo. How he must adore this only child. She was tall like the Angstroms, but with an imperiousness that did not belong to them.

Theo had been uncomplicated, single-minded. That was the secret of his power, it was focused. It had never been possible to help Theo. Sara prepared herself to look up. "If you'll follow me, then."

"Thank you," Brilli said. The woman led her toward an elevator. They got out on the second floor and walked endless corridors to a separate wing. Her guide carried a ring of keys from which she selected one and opened a door. Standing aside, she waited for Brilli to enter.

"It will do nicely," Brilli said, surveying it. "Has it a private bath?"

The woman laughed. It was a harsh, desperate sound, which she checked immediately. "I'm sorry," she said. "Yes, it has all the amenities."

There was a pause. "I suppose you think I'm awful," Brilli said. "I mean, just riding through the city I saw barbed wire strung everywhere, lower-story windows boarded over, buildings burned out and gutted, military police. There must be a good deal of suffering here, and all I can think of is a warm tub."

"It's not your war, Miss Angstrom."

"Please don't say that. It's true, of course. But I do sympathize with the people here."

"They're called Jews."

"Yes, of course, with the Jews. And I can't help having the feeling, Miss. . . ?"

"Mrs. I am Mrs. Baruch Adron."

"Thank you, Mrs. Adron. I feel so strongly that if you hadn't intervened, I would be sitting on my suitcase somewhere, not knowing what to do."

Quite suddenly Mrs. Adron smiled, and the stony pattern in which her face habitually locked, broke into delightful planes of mischief, gaiety, and a girlhood not

330

too far receded. Brilli knocked ten years off her age.

"Why don't we have dinner together," Brilli said impulsively, "since the hotel is temporarily footing the bill. As you can see, I'm alone. And I really would like someone to talk to."

The flicker of response was repressed. "I'm afraid as an employee, that is not possible."

"What about one of those little Arab suq? I think I could stand their prices."

"Miss Angstrom, the city is under martial law. It is unsafe to be on the street. Since I have to a certain extent intervened in your behalf, I want your promise that you will not go wandering around. Please wait right here in this room until your father can be contacted and make arrangements for you to join him in Cairo."

"Suppose he's moved on again and I'm stranded?"

"Why don't we try to reach him now?" She placed the call with the hotel operator. It was routed through Athens to Cairo, and seconds later Shepheard's was on the line. Mrs. Adron handed Brilli the phone. She was informed Mr. Angstrom was expected Thursday.

She left a message. "Tell him it's his daughter. I'm at the King David Hotel in Jerusalem." She hung up, looking at Mrs. Adron. "I'm afraid you'll have me on your hands a couple of days."

Mrs. Adron smiled. "I think we can manage that." She opened the door to the bathroom and started running the hot water.

"You don't have to do that," Brilli said.

"Of course I don't."

"But then. . . ." Brilli started, only to stop mid-sentence. "I was wondering, did you perhaps know my family in the past?"

Again the smile made her face young. "I'm afraid, Miss Angstrom, we traveled in different circles."

"Well, it's awfully good of you to take so much trouble with me. I didn't realize I was landing in the middle of a war."

"Don't the papers . . . no, I suppose not. The fate of a few Jews isn't that important."

"Oh, the papers say, 'Middle East hot spot,' things

331

like that. But you're totally unprepared for roadblocks and those great hoops of barbed wire everywhere."

"Well, your tub's full. Enjoy your bath."

"And dinner?"

"You're hungry, are you? I'll see it's ready in half an hour."

"You're an angel, Mrs. Adron."

"You mustn't make snap judgments, Miss Angstrom."

Brilli laughed, "My father says those are the best kind."

"Does he?" Mrs. Baruch Adron looked at her as though she were seeing someone else, and closed the door.

While Brilli splashed in warm suds, Sara leaned against the wall of the corridor. It was happening again. They called it *Black Saturday*. She, Dov, and Lev had turned in. Her sleeping senses were penetrated on a dozen different levels. Searchlights, car headlights, a bullhorn issuing commands in English and Hebrew. Dov reached out and seized her hand at the unmistakable rumble of tanks.

The inhabitants of Ein Harod were ordered to come out, hands in the air, without weapons, and walk a mile down the road. The compound remained quiet, as though hoping the tanks would go away.

The command was repeated. Lev walked into the harsh glare of concentrated lights. He couldn't see past them, so he spoke into them. "You are committing an act of aggression against a peaceable community."

A British voice replied: "You were given an order."

Lev then asked what they were accused of.

The amplified words of the bullhorn filled their ears. "You have four minutes to comply."

Lev came inside unhurriedly, leisurely. Once inside, he rapped out commands. "Get everyone into the dining hall. Lie flat on the floor. Hold hands. Sing!"

Sara fled out the back. She could hear Lev's voice. He had returned to stand in the light. "It is our Sabbath," he said. She knew he was attempting to gain time.

"Three and three-quarters minutes," was the reply.

At the end of the stated time the tanks moved in and began the work of demolishing buildings. Walls caved in. The armored division moved to encircle the dining room.

Sara's eyes were closed. She could hear the boots, they entered the dining hall. Flat on the floor, holding hands, their voices raised, *"Yesh banu ko-ach. Our strength is within us."* A heel crushed her wrist, her hand fell open. Twelve-year-old Yeva, whose hand had been in hers, was yanked to her feet. She saw a man, David she thought it was, spring forward. He was felled with a rifle butt.

The women and girls were dragged to the stables. The mass rape continued all night. Their female parts were handled, roughly penetrated. The accompanying words and jeers, Sara understood. Soldiers lined up to relieve themselves in the bodies of the women as though they were toilet bowls. When there was light enough to see, the shame of the women was increased. The men who had taken their turn gathered to cheer on their buddies. At nine-thirty they were called off. It had gone on for eight hours.

They had been so misused and brutalized that few could stand. The Jewish men that had not been arrested, hastened to the stables. The women begged them not to come in, but to bring water, buckets of water, and clothes.

As she leaned against the wall of the hotel, Sara recalled washing off semen and her own blood. It was still uncertain if she would need an abortion. And she and Baruch had wanted a child. But only a monster could be born of such a night. . . . What had been the cause of the attack?

Three months before, the British decided at the urging of President Truman to accept a hundred thousand of the remnants of Hitler's death camps into Palestine. But Prime Minister Clement Attlee made this conditional on disarming all clandestine Jewish military groups. The Irgun responded with an outbreak of sabotage. They destroyed bridges, dynamited roads, dismantled rail ties.

The British government, at the urging of Ernest Bevin, retaliated by breaking off a section of mandated territory and granting a state to 300,000 nomads. It was called Transjordan. Within what was left of Palestine, the Hagana went underground, joining the resistance. The orders were, no casualties. There was to be no loss of life, a protest only.

The British flew their wives and children to Cyprus and on to England. Attlee issued a statement of policy, suggesting that "displaced persons could best help in the restoration of Europe by staying where they were." A joint commission with the Americans was hastily announced, for the purpose of studying the problem further. Curfew was instituted, detention camps set up, hundreds arrested, and armored attacks against outlying settlements such as Ein Harod became official policy.

Sara remembered in her body. It was a special kind of memory, visceral, hot, and present. She remembered Theo Angstrom like that. She had been married. She had loved again. And it had been torn up again. Her husband went out with Lev. Lev returned. He tried to tell her how it happened.

She knew how it happened. Baruch was not young or agile like Lev. He had served as a cryptographer during the war. When they came to Palestine he trained with other middle-aged men in an olive grove at night, with sticks at first because they hadn't guns. Sara did not ask him not to do these things. At a time like this you had no right to protect one person and keep him safe.

"We'd planted the charge," Lev said. "The bridge was blown. It was just a question of getting away. I tried to cover him."

Sara nodded. "I know, he was slow." She patted the sleeve of Lev's jacket. "You did what you could."

And that was true now. You do what you can even when time sweeps over you and pulls you backward like an undertow. You look into a girl's face and feeling overpowers you, as much with you as it had ever been.

When the soldiers were zipping their flies, she said loudly and distinctly in cultured British English, "You bloody bastards." They looked around, startled, not knowing which of the women spoke. And they made for the barn door, they couldn't get out fast enough.

She still douched night and morning trying to wash away what they had done. But the shock of searchlights, bullhorn, tanks, and rape was no greater than a girl's voice asking for Mr. Angstrom.

Angstroms were no good for her. Faced with another Angstrom, memory burst open everything she repressed.

334

The Angstrom worried her more than the Grenville. The Grenville she could deal with. But there was a side of the girl that pierced her defenses. She went down to the kitchen of the Café Regence and ordered Brilli's dinner.

She caught her usual ride to the kibbutz with Moshe who hired out with his decrepit taxi during the day. The job at the King David dated from the time she and her husband lived in the city. After his death she decided to move to Ein Harod. But Lev persuaded her to keep the position on a part-time basis. Her English was a valuable asset, one the British paid well for, and the commune was desperate for money. So she retained the small apartment in the city and divided her time between it and Ein Harod. The three days spent at the settlement were home, the four in Jerusalem an exile. It was her contribution, one she was uniquely qualified to make. It was called consorting with the enemy, and for it they paid money into her hand.

Then the barn. Some had fumbled for her breasts, most drove up her with no preliminaries. One woman, Becca, had, after repeated entries, been roused to respond sexually—the Tommies made a ring around her. Their taunts and laughter seared her own organs and kept them dry.

"What do you mean," Lev said, "you're not going back? You must go back."

"To work for them? Are you out of your mind, Lev? Or are you such a child that you don't know what it was?"

He regarded her with hard twenty-two-year-old eyes. "I know what it was."

"I forgot," she said caustically, "you were in the British army."

"That's right. And you are now in the service of the Jewish army."

"What are you talking about?"

"It's simple. You have a position we can make use of. You have a card that allows you to enter the King David. Your address, as far as they know, is the Jerusalem apartment. There is nothing to connect you to Ein Harod."

"Nothing. Absolutely nothing."

335

He ignored the note of hysteria. "You hold a U.S. passport. You are, if not exactly trusted, at least permitted to work for them."

"If I heard a British voice or saw a British uniform, I'd scream or vomit or kill. . . ."

"You'll do none of those things, Sara."

"Why do you keep calling me Sara? I'm your Aunt Sara."

Lev replied, "You have received an assignment." He took out a miniature camera and put it on the table in front of her. "You are to photograph the guest registry each week."

Sara shook her head as though denying what she heard.

"Sara, you don't live in America any more. It's not comfortable. It's not pleasant. People get hurt, people die."

"You think I haven't found that out?"

"Then why are you here? The only reason is to fight for Eretz Israel, for the land. What does it take, Sara? They killed your husband, they. . . ."

"Don't talk about it, I forbid you."

"If you won't fight, get out. You're useless to us."

Sara was trembling. "Dov would never forgive you if he heard you say that to me."

Lev walked out of the room.

"Take your goddamned camera with you," she yelled after him. But it was she who stretched out a tentative hand to touch and finally take it.

"You're quiet tonight, Sara," Moshe, the driver, was speaking to her. Had she fallen asleep in the taxi during one of her nightmares? That was an evasion, calling them nightmares. Everything had happened, and she remembered and would remember.

"Just tired," she said.

"Who isn't?" Moshe responded, glad of the chance to philosophize. "Even this old jalopy. The shocks are tired. And the tires, we're riding on patches, held together by more patches. Did you know you were late? I waited almost an hour."

"I'm sorry, Moshe. I ran into. . . ." She was unable to finish the sentence. Brilli wasn't an old friend, or anyone she even knew. It was her eyes she knew. Angstrom eyes.

336

They were on the coastal route to Afula, having been stopped at Lod and now at another checkpoint south of Kfar Sava. The officer here was not satisfied with their papers and told them to get out and lean against the side of the cab for a body search.

"Hey mates," Moshe said, "I was with you at El Amein."

"All right, all right," the sergeant waved them on.

"Bloody bastards," Moshe muttered.

She should have stayed, had dinner with Brilli. What pleasure to sit across from her and watch that young face. But she didn't trust herself. Suppose she jumped up and kissed her, or started to cry, or worse yet, laugh and not be able to control it.

What a willful child she must be, spoiled and unruly. Got up to look twenty and traveling of all places into a guerrilla insurrection. Sara found solace in the fact that she was looking for her father. She must love him very much to feel he would understand. Was she running away from school, was that it? She could imagine the kind of school Brillianna would send her to. Latin wouldn't suffice, they'd teach Greek too, and decorum. The charm didn't need to be inculcated, it was already there.

Five miles out of Afula, with Mount Tabor blotting out the stars to the north, the engine coughed and quit. Moshe roused Sara and had her step on the starter while he poked under the hood. "As long as it's not the fuel pump," he said, and checked the distributor, the battery, the gas tank, and blew out the lines, but it was the fuel pump.

"Can you fix it?" Sara asked.

"That's what's the matter with it. I tried to fix it, when I should have bought a new one." The only thing to do now, he informed her, was for him to walk the five miles back to town and hope he could roust someone out of bed who would sell or lend him a fuel pump. "You stay here."

"In the middle of the road?" The Valley of Jezreel was dotted with Jewish settlements but bordered north and south by Arab terrorist strongholds.

"I've got a gun under the seat. Can you use it?"

"Yes," Sara said. Lev taught her to shoot a gun, to

photograph and develop prints of hotel registers, to rejoice when the Irgun carried out a mission and fought terror with terror. Was it better to go humbly to the gas chambers, crying on the name of the Lord?

The gun, Moshe said, was under the seat. She should find it, cock it, and prepare to blow the head off the first Arab to come by. She was falling asleep when she should be alert. Nightmares again were crowding at the edge of darkness. She should be on guard. But against what? Why did she think of that girl almost as a daughter, that tall, arrogant Angstrom?

When Moshe finally returned it was daylight. And then the fuel pump had to be installed. By the time they arrived at the kibbutz, the men had been in the fields several hours.

Sara was pulled from the car, her hand grasped in a mailed fist. That's what it felt like, as Lev brought her into the room.

"Where the devil have you been?" He mouthed the words so they were scarcely audible.

"Where the devil do you think I've been? At a ball or something? What's the matter with you, Lev? And will you please let go of me."

He dropped her hand and stepped back from her. She could see now that he was pale as though in shock and the pupils of his eyes were expanded leaving only a rim. "The taxi broke down," she said. "Moshe had to hike into Afula for a fuel pump. I spent the night in a ditch somewhere. He gave me his gun."

Lev closed his eyes and sat down on the bench. He put his hand over his face.

"Lev? What is it?"

"It's nine o'clock, Sara."

"So it's nine o'clock."

"You don't understand. I was going after you."

"But. . . ."

"My God, Sara. I thought you'd stayed in town and decided to go to work today."

"Why should I do that?"

"How should I know? All I knew is that you didn't come home and at twelve thirty-eight the King David blows."

The pause was fractional. "What? What are you saying about the King David?"

"That the Irgun is blowing it up."

"The King David Hotel?"

His lips moved, he was speaking fast, but not above a whisper. "It means breaching their headquarters, police station, a half-dozen agencies, all at once. It will be a sensation."

Sara stared at him in disbelief. "It will be a holocaust."

"No. There'll be a warning. We have our wireless plugged into the switchboard. The operator will receive the message in plenty of time to notify everyone. They will have half an hour to evacuate."

She wasn't functioning, not coming to grips with it, still trying to get her bearings. "Suppose something goes wrong?"

"We're giving it to the papers at the same time, as a double safeguard."

"How can you talk about safeguards when you're blowing up a building full of people?"

"I'm telling you, no one will be hurt. But imagine penetrating the heart of the entire British operation."

Sara picked up her purse from the table. "When did you say this device is going to go off?"

"Twelve thirty-eight. . . . What are you doing, Sara?"

She hurried past him to the door. "A friend of mine is there."

Lev looked incredulous. "Who?"

"Never mind. I've got to get her out."

Lev stepped in front of her. "Aunt Sara, I can't let you into the center of that mess. Can you imagine what it will be? Every Jew within miles will be rounded up."

"Let go of me, Lev."

"No."

"Lev. . . ." She started to struggle with him, but silently so that neither Dov nor any of the others outside the open windows would hear.

"All right, if your friend has to be got out, I'll do it. I planned the escape route. I can get through."

Sara nodded. "South wing, second floor. Room 216. Brilli Angstrom."

"Angstrom?"

"It's his daughter. Swear to me, Lev, you'll find her. That you won't come back without her. Swear it."

He nodded briefly, grabbed his old army cap and jacket and took the jeep with the license that flipped to British plates. Sara knew what that meant. He was going to drive the direct route through Nablus and Ramallah. That was the southern anchor of what was known as 'the triangle,' or center of Arab guerrilla activities. If he were recognized as a Jew he'd be pulled from the jeep and hacked to pieces. I can't let him do this, she thought, and did nothing to stop him.

Lev glanced at his watch. At eleven, the assault unit, disguised as Arabs, would deliver cans of milk to the basement. The dynamite and detonators were concealed in the containers. The crucial part would be to get by the Arab help in the kitchen. There were about fifteen cooks and waiters. It would be an easy matter to fool the British, but an improperly tied sash or sandals from the wrong part of the country could mean discovery. In this eventuality, the kitchen help were to be held hostage until "Gideon," the code name for their commander, set the timing clock. At that moment the Arabs would be released and the general alarm given. A warning smoke bomb would also be lobbed.

This should be happening in about an hour and a half. The mobile telephone unit would call the switchboard, and reporters from the *Palestinian Post* converge on the hotel, which would be evacuated. By the time he could reach it there'd be a lot of hardware in sight, people milling about, but he could probably spot an American girl in the street.

He was racing time. He sat the jeep as straight and tall a target as he could make of himself. He roared down the center of the main dirt road of Nablus leaning on the horn. Hens fluttered from his path and an ancient Arab tugged his goat to the side. The British always drove like this, the arrogant bastards, spraying Arab and Jew with their dust. He knew, he'd been in the 8th Army tank corps.

Think like a Britisher or they'll have your balls between your teeth and your hide in strips. Straight. Tall. As conspicuous as possible, Lev Rosenfeld ran the triangle.

340

At twelve-thirty he turned into Julian's Way and abandoned the jeep. The hysterical crowd he expected to see overflowing onto the curb was not in evidence.

Everything was quiet, normal.

He could hardly take it in. Had they fouled up? What had gone wrong? The planning stages seemed perfect. When "Gideon" asked, "Questions?" there had been none.

And there wasn't time to ask himself any now. Perhaps the operation had been betrayed, the bomb never triggered. Or perhaps the British received the message and refused to believe it. His job was to reach the second floor and get out before twelve thirty-seven.

He knew of a service entrance and walked casually past. It didn't appear to be guarded. He heard a British voice asking what was the meaning of that bloody smoke?

If the smoke bomb had been thrown, then the incendiary device was planted, and for some reason, which he could not think of, the warning disregarded. Why should the British be so foolhardy as to ignore it? Was it Sandhurst and Lord Nelson and *going down with the ship* and all that claptrap? Or did they simply refuse to believe that a bunch of tailors and merchants and pawn shop owners could penetrate their defenses? Arrogance was the more likely answer.

Lev sauntered up to the service elevator just as the guard returned. Each was surprised, but Lev recovered first. He was well-trained and by the same army. He pressed his thumbs into the man's carotid before he had time to level his gun. When he was dead weight Lev lugged him to a broom closet and stuffed him in. Seizing a white towel, he tied it around his waist, hoping to pass as a waiter. He kept the gun and took the fire stairs to the second floor. Against all regulations the door was locked.

He ran up the next flight and pushed identical double steel doors. These opened. He then ran down a flight, passing unnoticed. The white apron made him invisible.

"Will someone do something about all that smoke?" a voice demanded in aggravated tones. Lev walked on. When he was opposite 216, he knocked.

"Yes?"

341

"A message, Miss Angstrom."

The door opened. There were impressions. She stood almost his height, light hair and eyes. "Brilli Angstrom?"

She nodded.

"Come with me, hurry. I'm a friend of Sara's."

She tried to close the door on him, but he had her by the wrist and pulled her into the hall.

"What is this?" she demanded. "I don't know any Sara."

"Well, she knows you."

"Mrs. Adron?"

"Yes. Now will you hurry!"

"But. . . ."

"They're going to blow up the hotel." She kept up with him, raced the hall into the stairwell. As they emerged on the ground floor he told her. "Now, slow down. We're walking out. Walking together. Natural."

"Stop!" someone yelled at them. And at that moment a flash, illumination, a surface-contact blast and ground shock. A hammer blow from the air, a rush of hot wind. He imagined the milkcans, projectiles hurtled from the basement through the roof, cleaving the south wing of the hotel in two. Chandeliers and wall brackets crashed to the floor, stairways collapsed. A dust plume rose, fine particles and incinerated flakes were carried in a strong updraft. The rubble was a mixture of walls, ceiling, tile, arms, legs, bricks, animate and inanimate objects. A new cement, a new mortar, dust and blood, sifted to the ground. Pressure sucked the air from around them. A second shock wave pushed the first, the air decreased, pulled away from them, tremendous heat remained.

Brilli gulped, her lungs scaled. The blood vessels in her ear had ruptured. There was no sound. At least no sound reached her. It was all a deadly pantomime. The young man had been thrown to the floor and because he had not let go of her, she too was on the floor.

The building swayed, lath and lintels wavered and crashed. Framing and plaster were enveloped in flame, cracked cement crumbled on top of them. A section of stairway stood with nothing to either side of it. She could see now that a portion of wall had fallen on the young man, that he was hurt. I could get away, she thought.

People were rushing around, some crawling, others lying still, the mortar gray on their bodies making it seem they had been dead a thousand years. Because she could not hear, she didn't know if the screams were in Hebrew or English. She couldn't even tell by the clothes. Grime and silt covered everyone. Mouths opened and nothing came from them.

The young man lifted his head and heaved himself from the debris. Then he caught his leg, low at the ankle. He set his teeth, one row against the other, and tearing a strip from the apron around him, bound the ankle. He said something to her. She understood she was to help him up. She still thought of running. But he had said he was from Mrs. Adron. So she bent over him. There was something wrong with her equilibrium, she stumbled into him. He placed his hands on her shoulders and pulled himself up. Once again her hand was firmly in his. They continued, she lurching uncoordinatedly, he limping. They had to stop every few feet to lean against the walls. Lev entered one of the rooms whose door lay on the floor and pulling the counterpane from the bed, covered her, including her blonde head. They left the hotel.

They were bringing people out and parts of people. They were trying to do it decently, but it looked grisly to see a stretcher with an army issue blanket, and all it covered was an arm still bleeding at the stump. "You left most of the person," she wanted to say. But perhaps it was the largest fragment they could find.

Men were opening and closing their mouths like fish taken from water. Some of the wounded were being taken to the YMCA across the street. Others ran about distractedly, sometimes back into the building from which colonnades of black smoke rose, interlaced with bright quick flame. The air was hot on her skin, especially the skin of her face. She drew the bedspread closer around her. The young man had her in a death grip. He limped ahead of her. She expected him to fall at any moment, what looked like a piece of bone protruded through the skin of his ankle. He left bloody marks. She tried not to step in them.

He knew the city like an Arab. Perhaps he was an Arab. Would that be better or worse? He spoke English, but with a strange inflection. Probably he did know Mrs. Adron and she should continue to follow him.

Then it occurred to her—what did she know about Mrs. Baruch Adron, except she had run a bath for her, ordered her supper, and let her stay? She had also suggested the phone call to her father, which made it appear she was someone to be trusted. But then, all that might have been a ruse. Brilli didn't like being dragged along winding, narrow, smelly streets. They weren't really streets but alleys, turning and twisting like a maze. A cart and donkey were tethered outside a confectioner's while a delivery was made. The young man indicated she was to get in.

She climbed up, and he threw a burlap bag over her, swinging himself onto the board-rigged seat and lifting the reins. They were fast, but not fast enough. The irate owner dived into the street, waving his arms. His mouth, too, flapped like an expiring fish. For a while he chased them, then gave it up. They avoided anything that resembled a main thoroughfare. She thought they were in the Jewish section of Jerusalem. Contingents of British troops were already on the streets.

The young man abandoned the cart, and led her to the basement of a house. The walls were of dirt, shapeless in places with protuberances of fungi from which she snatched back her hand. This connected with another section, more like a tunnel, broken by strange elbows, ascending and descending illogically. She could hardly make out the hopping form in front of her, its absurd gyrations grotesque, deformed.

The rock and dirt of the walls seemed to change shape as darkness filled them. Wooden beams shored them up, running vertically. Her hand came in contact with the cicatrices on stones, like keloids that would not heal. An entire underground network of blind arches had been dug under the city.

Her guide fell and she tripped over him. If he were dead, how would she find her way out of here? But with his hands against the earthen wall he got up and they continued the dreadful journey. She thought he had fallen again, but he was sliding down an apron of rock. She, crouching, followed. It was no longer possible to stand.

They rested in the tunnel, perhaps slept. She tried to wrap herself in the bedspread, but somewhere it had been lost. She knew her hearing had returned because she heard him groan, but her ears still ached and seemed filled with fluid. The air was foul. She clambered over him and reaching back, pulled him after her. "Come on. If we don't keep going, we'll suffocate." She asked his name, as she had done before. This time she made out the response. Lev. She thought he said Lev. Everything was distorted down here, covered by slimy growth. Time did not exist. It might have been hours since the explosion. It might have been a day. It was all blurred—fiscal, school, calendar year. What time did one go by buried in a catacomb?

The vault under which they made their way on elbows and stomach was a running course of granite. Subterranean veins of gloom penetrated her mind. Her father would have identified madrepore. Thin, alternating veins of schist tore her flesh. Wriggling forward had become automatic. The air freshened, there was a flash of light. She was unprepared for the sudden drop and fell, letting go of Lev, clutching at the sides of the bank. But her fingers found no grip in the hard calcareous layers.

Her warning shout kept him from plunging after her. She had fallen into a clay spring, an abandoned well. Above her a patch of sky, and light striking the rim twenty feet above. She picked herself up and explored the gallery into which the tunnel opened. It was a sort of web, with a great sheet of water lying at a lower level near her. This trickled from green sandstone between layers of limestone and chalk.

"Are you all right?" His voice came weakly from above.

"Yes. I think I'm in a well."

"We took a wrong turn somewhere."

"There's a pool of water. But farther to the side, where the shaft is, the water has almost dried up. You can see the sky."

"I'm going to put my arm over the edge. See if you can reach it."

She stood against the rock on her toes, feeling for his

fingers. "No. But if we can figure some way of protecting your ankle, you'll land in fairly soft clay."

"I'll hang by my hands and try to jump down on my good foot."

"Perhaps I can catch you."

"No. Stand clear."

She was amazed that he was able to cling to the ledge by his fingers and lower himself. His left foot scrabbled for a hold, he found it, rested, lowered himself again. The right leg hung useless, the left began exploring for another crevice. Brilli took him around the waist, staggered, and with her back against rock inched herself and him to a sitting position.

She couldn't remember what he looked like. She had seen him in the door of the hotel, but they had been blown into another chunk of world since then. She looked at him now and laughed. He was completely blackened, coated with earth and grime. A fine white powdered patch on his forehead extended into his hair, graying it.

"Shut up," he said. "We could be in an Arab quarter."

"I'm sorry. How's your ankle?"

"As far as that goes I'll live. But not if you keep making noise. The Arabs build their houses over cisterns such as this."

"Well, I have no quarrel with Arabs. And if there are any up there, I want them to get me out."

"You forget," he said, "you're with me."

"That's bad?"

"Bad enough to get you shot."

"Well, thanks a lot. I thought you were supposed to be helping me."

"I got you out of the King David, didn't I?"

"But hardly in the nick of time." She regarded him with widening eyes. "How did you know it was going to happen?"

"Miss Angstrom, you have guessed it. You are in the company of a terrorist."

"You planned to blow up all those people?"

"No, not that. I don't know what happened. They were warned to evacuate. I suppose they just didn't believe it. They didn't believe we could do it. British arrogance."

346

"And exactly why did you do it? It seems not only a terrible thing to do but stupid as well."

"You don't really want to know. You just want to argue. Why don't you wash your face?"

It hadn't occurred to her until now that she must look as blackened and bedraggled as he. Besides, she was thirsty. She leaned over the spring where it ran clear, and drank, then plunged her face into the water, allowing her hair to trail in it. It felt marvelous.

She should do something about what's-his-name, *Lev*. She turned and looked at him. He was still huddled where she left him, bent over his leg as though that was what he had become, that's what he was, a leg. She didn't want to have anything to do with that broken ankle. She hated pain. She decided just to clean him up. He'd feel better, she was sure, once his face was washed. He still had that ridiculous strip of towel around him, ragged where he had torn it off and filthy from the push through the excavation. Nevertheless, it seemed the best thing to use. She untied it.

He was completely unresisting. In fact, almost toppled over as she pulled at the knot. The sweat on his face reassured her, small beads of moisture were coagulating the dirt. "You look like Tom the chimney sweep," she said. And then realized he wouldn't know who that was. Too bad to be a Jew—cut off from everything everyone else was interested in, interested in what no one else gave a hoot about.

She took the cloth to the stream and rinsed and twisted and squeezed the dirt out. Finally, when only clear water dripped from it, she returned and gingerly began to mop his face. It was almost like uncovering a painting encrusted with patina. She was curious to see what was there. First she freed the forehead into the roots of curling hair. The hair reminded her of Chris, unruly, falling forward into his eyes.

She went back to cleanse her cloth and returned to free his eyes, gently in the hollows, gently under the up-sweeping lashes. Then she cleaned the prominent cheek-bones that pushed the eyes into an exotic frame. Another rinsing was necessary before she was satisfied. When she rubbed the rag across his lips, they opened for the moisture. Of course. He was thirsty as she had been.

She returned to the freshet. Making the cloth as wet as possible, she wrung the water into his mouth. This seemed to revive him. She did it several times more until he was sated. Then she went to work on his hands. She liked his hands, long, slim fingers, but powerful and sinewy. She remembered how they had lowered the weight of his entire body.

"My shoe," he said. "Take the shoe off."

She had enjoyed cleaning him up, bringing him back to a semblance of a human being, but she didn't want anything to do with the injury. "Let me wash your hands first."

"No, no, get the shoe off."

Unwillingly, she undid the laces and began to unthread them. Even this small displacement brought a smothered groan. "I can't," she said, letting go.

"You gutless American bitch, do I have to do it myself?"

"Then keep quiet." Widening the shoe from the tongue as far as it would go, she slipped his foot out. Fortunately, there were no socks to take off. The makeshift bandage was not hard to remove. When it came away, a pulpy mass of discolored flesh was released, and she could see what she feared, the end of a bone sticking out. "It's broken," she confirmed.

"I didn't expect to dance the hora on it. Or what is it your president plays, the Missouri Waltz."

"Very funny. But what do we do?"

"Set it."

"I can't do anything like that. I don't know how. The best thing is to get you to a doctor."

"A prison doctor? Or are you thinking of getting help from the Arabs? Look Brilli, is that what they call you? It isn't difficult. I'll tell you what to do. I'll draw you a picture. Did you ever take biology in school?" She nodded. "All right. It's not human blood, it's a frog. If you faint, you get an F. You make a nice job, you get an A. First, we look the situation over." He had been fumbling in his pocket and finally extracted a packet wrapped in plastic and bound with rubber bands. "My first aid kit. Standard terrorist issue." He spread it out on the ground. "The codeine is for me, the tranquilizer is for you. First you'll shake this powder into the wound. Get closer, it's not catching."

He himself leaned forward to inspect and diagnose the injury. "If you look away," he said to her, "how are you going to know what to do? That's better. The thing sticking out, that's nothing bad, only the end of the fibula. That's what's come out of its joint. This knob, that's the external malleolus, that's what you're going to push on. Because there's a place on the other side that it's got to fit into. Like a ball and socket." He drew a diagram in the clay with his finger. "Don't even think of a frog. You're fixing your sewing machine. No, you wouldn't be fixing a sewing machine. You're fixing the clasp on your diamond brooch. You push the ball in the socket, click, it's done. Then you tie it all up." He looked around. "We need a splint. See if you can find a couple of flat sticks, pieces of boards, anything to hold it once you've got it into place."

"There's nothing like that down here. Only rocks."

"How do you know until you've looked?"

Reluctantly she began to wade about on the slippery moss and root in the clay. "Nothing."

"All right. We'll make our own. Pull off my other shoe."

"Why?"

"Will you do it? Will you just do it?"

She pulled it off, and he went to work on the soles, ripping them from each shoe. "Now tear the cloth once more, lengthways."

She obeyed. So far she had done everything he asked. Her mind remained with the present task, refusing to speculate on what these preparations were leading to.

Lev looked up at her. He smiled deeply and she smiled back. "Now," he said, "take the smaller strip and tie my hands behind my back."

"What? Have you gone crazy?"

"When you have done that, I will wedge my body between these two boulders as tightly as possible. Since we are running out of material, a bit of cotton from your dress is required. You will first put a plug in my mouth and with a longer piece bind it so that it completely covers my mouth and tie it behind my head." He pointed at the swollen, purple mass that was his ankle. "What's the name of that knob?"

"The malleolus," Brilli said, through clenched teeth.

"Good girl. The *external* malleolus. That's what you're going to push on. It won't be hard. You'll have plenty of leverage if you immobilize the foot." He handed her the soles of his shoes. "One of these goes behind the ankle and one in front. As I said, the first thing is to dust the wound with streptomycin, your hands too, everything in sight." He wedged himself into position. "Okay, put one sole against the external malleolus and push up and in. If it doesn't go in, try something else. You got to get the ball back in the socket, you got to fix the clasp on the brooch. Understand?"

Brilli backed away. She sat at the other side of the cistern as far from him as she could get.

Lev methodically laid out strips of linen on his lap, along with the soles and shoe laces. He waited.

Brilli ignored his maneuvering. "I wonder how long we'll be down here before somebody finds us."

Lev said nothing.

"I mean, we could be down here for days without anyone finding us."

"We have water," Lev said. "You can go a long time with water."

"But I'm hungry."

"That's just a sensation. People can survive weeks without eating. Like camels, they live on their fat."

"I don't have any fat. And neither do you."

The pause between them lengthened.

"You're going to have to do it, Brilli."

"But how do I know I'm strong enough to move the bone?"

"You're strong enough."

"How will I know when it's aligned?"

"You'll feel it slide in. If nothing happens, change the direction slightly. It's got to go in. There's no other place for it to go. Then hold it in place while you tie the bandage over the leather. Use the shoe laces for good measure."

"What if you die?"

"People don't die from a dislocated ankle, but they can be crippled for life if it isn't set."

"Set properly," Brilli amended.

"You'll do a good job."

"How do you know that?" she asked belligerently.

"Because I know your father. You're just like him."

"You knew my father? That's not possible."

"In 1939, just before the war."

"But that's when he went to Saudi."

"He came here too. Sara wanted to come."

"Sara?"

"Mrs. Adron. She was Sara Rosenfeld then. Your father's mistress and my aunt."

"Oh," Brilli said, struggling not to show surprise.

"I hope you're not shocked. I thought you knew. I mean, it went on for six years. I thought everyone knew."

"Of course. I just didn't make the connection, that's all. Why did they break up?"

"Look, my foot is killing me. They broke up over politics, all right? He was doing business with the Arabs. She was a Zionist. She married shortly afterwards in the States and they came out here when the war ended. Baruch was a nice guy, everyone liked him, even the bastard British who killed him." He caught his breath sharply. "The reason I told you this—I expect a hell of a lot from an Angstrom. You're his daughter by the look of you. You've got his guts or you wouldn't be here. For God's sake, Brilli, I don't want to be a cripple. Line it up, no matter what. If I pass out, keep going. Remember, nobody dies because he broke his ankle. Into the socket, girl. I beg you, get it into the socket."

She bound his hands behind him, stuffed the material in his mouth, then wound the gag around it and pushed him farther into the wedge of rock. "Okay, Lev. Don't you dare fight me." She straddled him and inspected the wound, trying to satisfy herself as to what she must do. Dabbing away the congealed blood was easy, so was sprinkling the antibiotic powder. She could no longer postpone using pressure. "Now," she said, and pushed with the palms of her hands.

Lev's body arched into a bow. The irises of his eyes

rolled slowly upward, only vacant white slits showed. Brilli pressed harder against the shoe leather. Like a ball into a socket, he said. But it was guesswork. There was nothing to guide her, no change in resistance. The physical effort was tremendous. Sweat rolled into her eyes. She kept blinking so it wouldn't obliterate her vision. The bone must have moved because it wasn't sticking out any more. Blood and serum were leaking, covering her fingers. His head fell back. It was done. She wound the bandage, her hands trembling uncontrollably. She could hardly tie the shoelaces that held the whole soggy mess in place.

Lev was unconscious. Leaning over him, she unknotted the gag and removed the wadding. His teeth had bitten and ground it to shreds. Rolling him on his side, she released his hands, then dragged him from the rocks to the soft red clay and scooped a pillow for his head.

She tore another piece from her skirt and wrung it out in the stream as a compress. Then she sat beside him, not knowing what else to do.

Her name was Sara. A biblical name.

Had her mother known? She was sure to have. It had gone on six years. Suddenly she didn't hate her mother anymore. Her heart was released from that particular pain. She had always thought of her parents as Father and Mother. She never thought of them in bed together. Perhaps her mother functioned best as Mrs. Angström, the companion with whom he was seen, who entertained the Washington inner circle and the oilmen, no longer a wild and woolly breed, but cultivated, invading the highest posts in government. She wondered sometimes why she had no brother or sister, why she was the only one.

Was Sara the reason? A few years ago the face had not been rigid and set. She had caught a glimpse of that younger, carefree Sara, a disarming laugh, a playfulness, tenderness even, in the way her face softened.

Sara Rosenfeld and Theodore Angstrom. How had they met? "We moved in different circles," she had said. Brilli took that as a denial that she knew him. It was not a denial, but intended to throw her off, prevent her from learning about that secret life, away from her and her mother.

She found she was an ally of her mother, a Grenville, censuring, passing judgment. Then she remembered the sweetness with Chris, the taste, the feel of him. And she felt close to her father and sorry for the proper Brilliannas of this world. She was an Angstrom. Lev sensed it. Lev had said it.

Lev opened his eyes and tried to wipe dust from his vision. "You can taste the sand. I think I'll always taste it." He grabbed her arm. "There. Do you see it? Do you know what it is, sun-dried bodies, twisted into a knot, fallen on each other. Just like their lorries. These two-man baby Eytie tanks got no armor at all. They're death traps. They look good, nice lines. But the traverse of the turret is too small."

Brilli didn't know what to do. She put a cool hand on his head.

"Fighting in the desert is something you've got to adjust to, your stomach number one, then your eyes, and finally your bowels. I don't think I'm ready for the whole goddamned Italian army. But there it is. Look at that, someone lobbed a shell into the lead truck, it's knocked clear across the road. We're going to be fighting in a goddamned traffic jam. I can't believe their staff cars, ordinary Fiats, just four cylinders. And those huge diesel trucks, must be ten tons. They're too heavy for this sand, they're already bogged down. Their artillery, I'm telling you, old fashioned infantry rifles. Charity from the Germans, they must be left over from the last war. It would be a disgrace to be killed by one of those."

She wet the rag and put it on his head again. He spoke quietly of two crack Panzer divisions, the 15th and the 21st, that Rommel threw against Tobruk. "Six hundred Mark IV tanks, with 88-millimeter guns on pivotal mounts. The motorized stuff alone is about a hundred and twenty-five thousand machines and vehicles. The little mobile Eytie tanks come in at night and repair the German hardware we maul during the day. We have it as bad as the Italians, fighting out of these shitty U.S. *General Lees*. High-turreted, perfect targets. They're engineering monstrosities. The Germans can out-gun and

353

out-maneuver us. The gun and observation mounts high on the starboard make it easy for them to pick us off. Don't look around. Don't look. The German *Tigers* are fighting *under us* from the wadis, sleek, underslung, they're shooting out our bellies, knocking off our gunners. We're taking high muzzle velocity fire. They're blasting us into blazing infernos.

"Don't be dead, Tim, don't be dead and I'll tell you a joke. The joke is: our stinking air-conditioning isn't working. So it's no worse if we get blasted, do you see? We're roasting anyway. Listen, Tim. Do you hear that? Biplanes, Gloster Gladiator fighters and some old Bombay transport planes with machine guns strapped on. Look at them swoop in. They're giving us a chance to get out." In his excitement Lev leaned forward, but sank back immediately.

"We're disabled. I can't move her. Come on, Tim, get your blanket and water. We'll make a run for it." Lev stopped rambling and looked directly at Brilli. "I keep forgetting Tim's dead." He recognized Brilli and continued speaking in a more conventional way. "I lay rolled up in my blanket in the depression of a wadi most of the night. But I was watching more than sleeping. And I noticed a curious thing. Once it was dark the Germans and Italians were sent out to collect oil rags from the stalled tanks."

"Of course," Brilli said. "They could be processed into synthetic crude. The Axis was running out of oil. The crankcases of planes shot down over Libya showed they were using inferior blends."

Lev stared at her. "Angstrom's daughter," he said. "But you're right, that affected the efficiency of the mortars."

She nodded. "That's what my dad always contended. How does the ankle feel?"

"Better. Ball-socket?"

"Of course ball-socket. And that was very silly about the diamond brooch. I never had a diamond brooch in my life. But I did do a good job. Nothing sticks out. You'll be right as rain even if you did just fight the battle for Tobruk."

"That was a mess. My mate was killed, and I hiked

354

out. All I remember are the sand flies and how cold the nights got. Half the men were down with jaundice or fever. No wonder, we slept on the ground beside slit trenches, ready to roll into them. They were like graves. They were graves for a lot of us."

"Best not to think of it," she said, imitating her mother's cheerful voice.

"And it will go away? I don't think those things go away."

"You seem a hundred years older than me. You've been through so much and I haven't been through anything. In fact my life is so dull, I have to invent things to happen in it. How old are you, Lev?"

"Twenty-two."

"And when you joined up?"

"Eighteen. The British took us all right. In 1942 they were taking anyone. But they never acknowledged in any official way there were Jews serving. When we were wounded or died, we were designated simply: Palestinians."

"That doesn't seem very sporting of them."

"From the beginning of the war we wanted two things. The first that the RAF bomb the rail lines between Budapest and Auschwitz. That would have stopped the movement of their cattle cars to the ovens. The RAF could have done it from their base at Foggia."

Brilli said slowly, "I think I begin to understand what happened today. The King David. I don't condone it, but I begin to see it goes back a long way and is mixed up with all this bitterness and injustice. And the fact that you fought with them."

"As the Germans fell back, word got out that the killing in the camps was accelerated. Since the RAF would do nothing, the Jewish Agency formally petitioned Britain to allow Jewish paratroopers to raid concentration camps and save Jews from extermination. The plan was approved by the British military authorities. But the Colonial Office set up some sort of meeting with the Americans in Bermuda. The rescue effort was vetoed." He raised his voice, accusing her. "Oil dictated the final cremations in Treblinka, Dachau, and Auschwitz. Oil!"

She met this charge with Angstrom coolness. "What

was the other thing? You said there were two requests."

"Our own brigade, a Jewish brigade fighting out of England."

"Why wouldn't they allow it?"

"Who knows? Maybe they were afraid we'd steal ammunition. Or maybe they didn't want any Jewish heroes. Then, late in the game, September 9, 1944, the British War Ministry set it up, the very thing we'd been begging for, our own brigade. It was pitted against the Italians, and I transferred into it. By that time the Nazi war machine was creaking at the joints. And when the death struggle of our people was over, we were compensated by being allowed to march into Berlin with the other Allies. Yes, Lev Rosenfeld entered Berlin under the Star of David. And the Germans kept to their houses and peered through shuttered windows and were afraid. We sang *Hatikvah* and got drunk and fraternized with the Americans. And I never felt worse in my life. The role of conquering hero that the German enjoys so much made me feel like a lead toy soldier. I wanted to get away from frightened faces. At Ein Harod there were furrows to plough, saplings to plant."

"And you came home to this? Another war?"

He nodded. "What the Nazi didn't finish, the British seem intent on destroying. And in typical British fashion, without animus. They've nothing against us. It's simple appeasement. In their clubs they call it *the season*, meaning open season on Jews."

"For the Arabs too?"

"Of course. They were supplied and let across the borders."

"It's Ibn Saud and his dollar power. I don't see how the Jews can fight it. The Saudis made ten million dollars in oil revenues this year, and production is just starting to climb back. My father says by 1950 it will be at least two hundred and forty million and no one can guess where it will go. One Saudi Prince buys Chanel No. 5 in quart bottles and uses it to bathe in. Mother and I were with Dad last year in New York when he had another royal son in tow. We took him to the Waldorf Astoria for dinner and do you know what he said? 'Sometimes I wish

I were an ordinary American and lived right here at the Waldorf.' "

Lev didn't laugh. "We have a saying that it is foolish to underestimate fools, Miss Angstrom. . . ."

So, she thought, he has taken charge again. When he needed me, I was Brilli.

"Miss Angstrom, I see no point in your remaining in an abandoned cistern. You did a good job on me. In a couple of days my ankle will be well enough to put some weight on it, enough to get out. But you're able-bodied. You shouldn't have too much trouble scrambling to the top and reconnoitering. If you hear Arabic, get back down as fast as you can. The British have evacuated their women, so you'd be taken for a Jew. It wouldn't be a pleasing way to end up. But chances are you will run into a British patrol. They must be out in force by now. All you have to do is explain who you are, that you were in the King David when she blew, that you experienced shell shock, and ran and kept running. And hid until you were reassured by the sound of English voices. Although it will probably be that incomprehensible cockney that you hear. And that's it. Your father will be contacted and you will rejoin him."

She smiled at him sweetly. "Do you know what a ranunculus is? A little flower that looks like it's made of crepe paper with its sides all ruffled. They come in every autumn color. I was wondering if they could be grown in Palestine."

"Brilli. . . ." He was back to Brilli again. "Don't be more exasperating than you need. Stop talking about flowers and get up that rock face."

"Mother always said, think of pleasant things at the dentist. Being down this well with you is a bit like being at the dentist. So I'm imagining ranunculus. And the other thing I'm imagining is chestnut vendors in New York. You buy a bag, steaming hot, their shells split at the top. It's part of Christmas, like ice-skating at Rockefeller Center."

"Will you please stop? Believe me, the situation is serious."

"Or camellias. Your Aunt Sara would know about

them. Camellias are as much a part of San Francisco as the Mark Hopkins or cable cars."

"I think we are in an Arab village. Most of the occupants are in the hills with the terrorists, some have just cleared out. But others perhaps, remain. You will have to go carefully. But it's gotten dark, it should be easy to keep hidden. Then all you have to do is wait for a British patrol. Well?"

"How can I leave you? You've nothing to eat."

"I never saw a girl whose mind runs so on food. I told you I can hold out a long time."

"With your bad ankle you may not make it up. Or it might get worse. Infection could set in."

"Not a chance, not with all the antibiotic you poured in."

"But the point is, I wouldn't know. The Arabs might find you or the British throw you into prison and hang you when they discover you were in on the King David bombing."

"Well, then what do you propose?"

"I'll get out and take my bearings. You will give me Mrs. Adron's address, not written down of course. I'll memorize it. Then I'll contact her and she will have your friends come for you."

"What? Twenty men for one? That's not good arithmetic. Besides, you must not be involved. My aunt would skin me alive."

They both laughed. "You're more afraid of her than of the Arabs."

"Much more. Now Miss Angstrom, let's not have more discussion. I have already picked out the ascent. You will start there, from that boulder, then look to your right, a good purchase for your hands. You can reach it and pull up so that your feet are resting where your hands were."

"I can't do it. I'd fall."

"The worst that can happen is that you break an ankle. And I'll set it for you."

"Thanks." She started at a run for the granite slab and scrambled on top of it.

"Bravo," Lev said.

"I can do without your encouragement. I'm not a

358

child." But she adhered to the route he picked out. It was difficult, facing inward, her face plastered against the side. One advantage was, she could not see the widening drop below. There were a few desperate scramblings with her feet, her fingers caught the stone edge, smooth, laid by men.

But what men? And were they still around? She pulled herself over the side and lay flat, her heart gyrating.

The silence was absolute. It occurred to her she should move from the well. If she were found there, Lev would be discovered too.

She explored a few feet at a time. It was a house, or had been at one time. Only one wall stood and part of a second. She was in what seemed to have been the courtyard. There was an Arab kiln for breadbaking, which had not been damaged at all. She stopped where she was. Along the road were the headlights of a convoy and voices.

British voices. She crept into the stove, drawing the door after her, but not completely. She watched as they passed. Searchlights mounted on the trucks played over the countryside. It enabled her to see as well. It was an Arab village with many of the houses intact. It had the look of having been recently evacuated.

When the military vehicles moved on out of sight, she darted across the road and began a systematic ransacking. She found cellars stocked with roots, a sack of coarse flour, and bottles of arak. The most important discovery was a brazier with charcoal and a blanket. She loaded everything into the blanket and dragged it across the demolished courtyard. "Lev," she called down. "Ahoy below. Don't let any of this land on your head." She threw it down the shaft and undertook the descent, sliding the last five feet.

Lev was in the same position. He hadn't moved. "It is an Arab village?"

She nodded.

"And there were no British patrols?"

She crossed her fingers for a white lie. "I think one had just passed through. Anyway the houses were deserted, and I was able to liberate some much needed supplies." She placed her hand on his forehead. "Just as

359

I thought, you have fever and you're shivering. So here's a blanket to wrap up in."

"Probably has fleas," he muttered.

"Don't look a gift camel in the mouth." She stretched it on the ground and rolled him into it. "There, that feels better. Admit it."

"Admitted."

"And there's going to be dinner. Some rather grubby looking shriveled vegetables. And some sort of dough, which will either make library paste or bread, I'm not sure which." She was collecting the pieces of charcoal which had scattered.

"You'll have to figure some way to shield the glow of the brazier. It could give us away."

"What about putting it under my stepping stone, the one I got up by?" When she was through with her preparation, he was asleep. She chewed on a tough untasty morsel remembering the eggs Benedict that Mrs. Adron—Sara had sent up just last night.

She decided not to douse the coals, but to leave them for warmth. She slid over to Lev and tried to free a corner of the blanket for herself. She crept close to him in her attempt to loosen a fold. She wasn't able to unwrap much and pressed against him for warmth. Why had she not waved and called out to the British contingent? She would be in some decent hotel by now, all her wants looked after, meeting her father with high tales of adventure, and wresting a promise from him—no more school.

She would get a job. Lots of girls did. Something with one of his companies. But for the moment she was content to snuggle against the hard young body of this soldier of the Irgun. He was more exciting than Chris. A man. He thought nothing of killing, strafing, dynamiting. What did he think of women? How did he treat them afterward? She unbuttoned her blouse and got out of her skirt. Certain things Chris liked to do himself, he liked to reach in and release her captive breasts. He sometimes tore off her underpants or just pushed them aside.

Stealthily, without waking him, she unbuttoned Lev's shirt and ran her hands over the hair of his chest. She opened her mouth and set it against his, forcing her tongue between his teeth. She mounted him, assuming the male position. He let her ride him, tormenting herself. Then turned her over unsheathed for entry.

She died into eternity. The procreation of the world took place in her body. "Lev, Lev."

He threw her off. In anger he said, "I'm twenty-two, in good physical condition, aside from an ankle that's a bit far from the action. Self-gratification, *a good lay* as you Americans say. You and I had nothing to do with it."

"A thrill ran through every part of you. I felt it. But you're afraid. We Angstroms are too strong medicine for Rosenfelds. I'm a package tied with a red, white, and blue flag and sixty million dollars. Lev," she turned his face toward her. "We can be together. You'll stop this hole-in-the-wall running, hiding, vengeful existence. What's in it for you but dangling from a rope in a British prison or being hacked to pieces by Arab women? Lev, my father will be so glad to get me back, he'll agree to anything. We'll go back...."

"Stop right there. You are tethering the wrong camel. You see us married. You see me being vice-president of one of your father's corporations. Well, before you go any further, let me tell you I took part in blowing up the oil refinery at Haifa, and trained with Dov Gruner. We carried out the assault against the police armory at Ramat Gan. They only captured Gruner because he was wounded, that's the only reason. And you know the British, they intend to hang him, but in the meantime they've operated twice on his jaw."

"How do you know they'll hang him?"

"Because he refuses to recognize the right of a British court to try him. He offers no defense. Don't you see, don't you understand? This is no *sweet land of liberty, of thee I sing*. This is a country where any soldier, any policeman, any immigration officer can arrest you on sight without cause, without a warrant. You can be held without trial, without even speaking to anyone. For harboring a murderer the penalty is three years. For concealing an 'illegal,' one of those skin and bone, hollow-eyed leftovers of Hitler's atrocities, eight years.

"The Hagana has finally issued a call to arms, and we have joined with them in a declaration of war against the British until they give over the mandate and are driven

361

out. In reprisal the British are trying to paralyze Tel Aviv, parts of Jerusalem, and three weeks ago they came into Ein Harod. How can I describe it to you? Do you know what terror is, or rape, or beatings, or jail? On top of this they are starving us, no produce trucks are allowed to move. The British call this an 'operation.' It is even commanded by a general, General Gaines.

"That is what the bombing of the King David proves, that we are not contained. And there have been six hundred and eighty activities in other zones. We stormed three British camps with mortar and machine gun fire. We blew up the Officers' Club at Goldschmit House in the center of Jerusalem. Eighty men were killed or wounded, armored vehicles destroyed. We mined roads, jeeps, held up a British army pay train like wild west bandits. We almost succeeded in digging a tunnel from a potato warehouse across from British headquarters. We carried the dirt away in potato sacks. They discovered the tunnel, but didn't get any of us. So we raided the British camp at Sarafand, disguised as Arabs and using arms purchased from British soldiers, or not turned in at the end of our tour of duty in the British forces."

"All right, all right." She forgot to keep her voice lowered. "You've made your point. I don't think you're exactly what Daddy would call vice-presidential material. The 'human factor' he's always talking about is a bit overactive, like in thyroid trouble. You're a violent man. You've grown up in violence, been trained in it, but you're much more vulnerable than you pretend."

"Yes," he said angrily. "That makes you happy, doesn't it?"

"It does." She smiled without opening her mouth, which made what she was thinking secret and unknowable.

"Being an Angstrom," he said, "you like to win."

"That's part of it," she admitted.

Four days passed. It was the height of summer. They were uncomfortable in their rocky cistern and hungry. Neither cared much. Brilli made nightly forays scrounging for whatever had been left. Then one night as they lay together, he grabbed her wrist tightly. "Listen."

The sing-song of Arab voices carried to them. She looked into his face, stricken.

"It had to happen."

"I know."

"The plan is the same as before. You climb up. Hide. Wait for a British patrol. Run out in the street waving your arms. Tell them the story about being at the King David, who you are, that you are an Angstrom. That you've been in a state of shock."

"I know. I know all that. I don't want to leave you, not ever."

"Yes you do. You choose men that can't possibly fit into your life."

She had told him about Chris. "That's not true. Or if it was true, it isn't anymore."

"Well, if you think I am fool enough to ask you to desert your family, stay here with me, get shot at, fight British, fight Arabs, you're crazy."

"You don't even give me a chance to say no."

"That's right. Remember it, Miss Angstrom."

"You hate me because of your aunt."

"Don't be childish. My aunt was raped three weeks ago by thirty-three Tommies. Do you think I want that for you?"

She threw herself on him. "Then you do love me."

"Is it a victory for you if I say yes? Very well, Brilli Angstrom, I say yes." He kissed her severely on the mouth. "I love you. Now will you get the hell out of here? Hide in that old kiln."

"What about you?"

"I assume your father is here looking for you. After you've met him go to Ein Harod. It will seem natural that you say goodbye to Sara. She looked after you, contacted your father. It will arouse no suspicion. I'm stronger now. I can get out with the help of one man and the jeep at this rendezvous point. See, I have drawn a map, only x's and lines. Memorize it and repeat it to her."

"All right." She left him and walked slowly to the rock.

"Brilli," he raised himself, his weight on his good foot. "That first night when you went up, I thought I heard trucks."

She didn't turn around, she didn't look at him. "You

363

did, Lev." She began to climb the overhung rock face. She hid, as before, in the kiln and had not long to wait. When she saw the headlights of the lead car, she scrambled out and, running to the center of the road, waved the convoy to a stop.

They suspected an ambush. She was taken to the staff car, a gun trained on her as she told the story she had rehearsed. She laughed nervously. "My hair isn't combed and my face needs a good wash, but it's me."

"I believe the young lady is telling the truth, sir."

The colonel was the go-slow type. "Some of these saboteurs speak perfect English."

"I know, sir. But there's a missing persons out on a Brilli Angstrom."

"You think they don't pick up on our wave length? Besides, four days seems a bit long to be in a state of shock."

"Are you a medical doctor?" Brilli asked pertly, and then in a more conciliatory tone, "A call to the American consul should convince you. There is an American consul, isn't there?"

"You are going to HQ, young lady."

She sat primly beside the colonel and the sergeant and did not say another word.

They stopped in Julian's Way, which was strung with bales of barbed wire. A single path led through to the hotel. Brilli was taken inside and turned over to intelligence.

It developed that her father and mother were both in the city. The duty officer placed a phone call.

"Brilli, is that you?" Her father's voice went quite hoarse. "Brillianna, they've found her!"

Her mother took up the phone. "Thank God. Are you all right, Brilli?"

"I'm fine."

"You don't know, you can't imagine what we've been through. They've been sifting the rubble for bodies. There were more than two hundred dead and wounded. They haven't all been identified yet. It almost seemed after four days—but we tried not to let go of our faith, not to give up. And now you're here."

Her father took the receiver. "We're coming to get you."

364

"Thank you, Daddy."

Both her parents arrived by taxi. She was hugged and kissed and her disheveled appearance not commented on. The grinning sergeant said he guessed this was a proper identification.

In a suite of her own with bath and dressing room, she began to remember who she was. After she bathed and shampooed and creme-rinsed her hair, she appeared in her mother's robe and answered questions without answering them. They were so relieved to have her back, they didn't notice.

Her mother at last retired, declaring herself exhausted, also there was packing to do if they were to get a plane out tomorrow.

Her father stood up too. "No, wait," Brilli said. "I didn't tell it all because of Mother. Do you know someone called Sara?"

"Sara?" His face went tight. "You throw a name at me like that. Sara who?"

"Sara Rosenfeld, who lived with you for six years."

He sat again heavily. "Is Sara here?"

"It's she who was responsible for getting me out of the King David. She sent her nephew Lev. He got me out."

"My God," he said. "Sara."

"She lives at Ein Harod with her brother and Lev. And tomorrow, first thing, I must go and thank her. If not for her I'd be part of what they're still sifting out of the rubble, and you'd have to identify me by Dr. Auck's fillings."

Theodore's mind had taken another tack. "Is she well?"

"Do you mean by that, how does she look? She looks great. Sunbrown, confident, but I don't imagine she's the same person you knew."

Her father seemed uncomfortable with the next question. "And she told you about us?"

"No. Lev did. She just sort of took charge of me. Got me a room when I had no money. Found you in Cairo, helped me place the call." Brilli paused. "She married, you know. Her name is Mrs. Baruch Adron."

"I'm glad she didn't marry that hardware store fellow. I never met him, but I never liked him either." Shadows

365

gathered in her father's eyes. He looked old. He looked weary. "When did she marry?"

"Several years ago, I think. They came out here together."

"Is she happy? Did she seem happy to you?"

"No. But I don't think Sara needs to be happy."

"Did you meet him? The husband?"

"He's dead. Some scuffle with the British."

"Poor Sara."

"Oh, I don't know."

"She carried her fate with her, it was sealed up in what she was and who she was."

"Do you want to ride out with me tomorrow to Ein Harod?"

"No." He went out, not to his wife's room, but into the street.

Brilli fell right to sleep.

At breakfast, which was served in the adjoining sitting room, Ted said, "There's a woman responsible for saving Brilli from the bombing, getting her out of the King David. Brilli wants to see her before we leave. I thought I'd ride along."

Brilli looked up sharply at her father.

"But of course," Brillianna said, "we should all go. Someone who saved Brilli's life."

Ted said, "It was Sara."

"Sara?" Brillianna turned ashen. She set her fork, its contents untasted, on her plate. "All the more reason," she said. Then to her daughter, "Of course if she warned you, she must have had some sort of advance information."

Ted intervened. "We're outsiders. We can't begin to understand the ins and outs of politics in this country."

"Well," Brillianna said briskly, "there's not much time. We have to be at the Lidda airport by three-thirty. I'll have the bags sent directly."

While her father settled the account, her mother phoned, making arrangements for a motorized escort. Brilli didn't love her mother, but she was proud of her.

The Angstroms rode behind a British car with red flags attached to either side. They sped along, passing donkeys, sheep, bicycles and military vehicles. There was no

366

ordinary traffic, no lorries or trucks with produce. Lev was right. The Jews were at war with the British. How could a handful of men fight the British Empire? Then she thought of Sara, and of Lev, especially Lev, the set of his mouth, his hard body and hard mind.

The guard at Ein Harod was not anxious to let them in. Brilli intervened. "Tell the escort car to stay here, Dad. There's been trouble recently. We'll go in by ourselves."

The officer was reluctant. "I can only give you twenty minutes, sir. If you're not back by then, we'll have to come in."

"That's plenty of time," Ted said. Time, he thought, was an odd thing, galloping on without much meaning. And then there were twenty minutes.

Brillianna sat back seemingly relaxed. But the thought that Ted would be seeing Sara consumed her. To be indebted to that woman was to her, preposterous, an utterly unreasonable quirk of fate.

The taxi rolled up to a building which looked as though it had been shelled. The whole place was pock-marked by heavy fire. There were a dozen people, men and women at work, mixing cement, patching walls. They looked up at the approach of the cab. Brilli spotted Sara and jumped out. She ran up to her and kissed her.

Sara straightened, handed the stick with which she was mixing mortar to someone standing by her. "Lev?" she asked.

Brilli hurriedly recited the map of lines and x's.

"Repeat it," Sara said.

She listened intently. "I know where he is. We'll get him tonight."

"He says send only one man and the jeep. But the village is occupied again, be careful."

"Why didn't you come earlier when they were still in the hills?" Her thick wavy hair was pulled from her face by a kerchief, her hands were gray with mortar, and there was a light streak across her cheek, but her eyes were keen; they looked and saw. "He is a soldier of the Irgun. Battle tested. He fought at Tobruk against two Panzer divisions. God knows what he has done here to drive out the British, but there are things we Rosenfelds have no

367

defenses against. In some ways he is a child, younger than you."

"You want to know if we had an affair," Brilli whispered hurriedly. "Yes, we did. An uncomfortable one on hard rocks and an Arab blanket with lice. His ankle is badly broken, he'll probably never walk without a limp. It was terrible for him and terrible for me. Yet if he'd let me, I'd stay with him."

Sara regarded her steadily. "Eighty people died in the south wing of the King David."

Brilli couldn't answer. If she opened her mouth, tears and sobs and she didn't know what, might come out.

Sara reached up and kissed the tall young girl on her forehead. "Mazel tov, Miss Angstrom." It wasn't until that moment she saw Ted and Brillianna getting out of the taxi, coming toward her. She stood waiting. They were on her ground, her turf.

Brillianna reached her first. "There is no way to say thank you for a daughter's life."

"There is, Mrs. Angstrom. Don't make her run away again."

Brillianna nodded, accepting the rebuke. "May we shake hands?"

"If you wish." The women shook hands gravely, unsmilingly. Brillianna returned to the car.

Sara turned to Ted. "I'm not up to this. I'm not up to shaking hands with you too."

"Sara. There must be something we can say to each other."

"I don't think so, Theo. There's no bitterness. It's gone. I'm glad you have your daughter safely back. She's a rare person. I'm glad I had a part in it." She turned away. There was a great deal that needed doing. Almost everywhere she looked was a task, if not today, tomorrow, if not tomorrow, the day after.

Ted saw her efficiency, her almost soldierly bearing. The slightly thickened, upright figure picked up the handles of a wheelbarrow and trundled it off. Had this woman been the same who shared his life, even to his thoughts? Was it possible that for six years he continued an affair with this rather plain, determined person? He returned to his wife and daughter in the waiting car.

They were unusually quiet on the ride out to the airport. Ted felt he had been robbed, but of what, or by whom, he didn't know.

Brilli had an impulse to stop the car, tell her parents she couldn't leave. But eighty people dead in that blast. And Lev, whom she taught to love, and who could be tender in his passion, who told jokes and funny stories, had known it was going to happen. He helped plan it. He said so. This was the boy she wanted to run to. "I don't think your father would consider me vice-presidential material." She struck a balance between laughing and crying by being absolutely still.

Once at the airfield her father took charge. A company plane was waiting to fly them to Athens. From there they would return to the U.S. via London. No Geneva. No girl's school. She had won hands down. They boarded and took off.

"I wonder," Brillianna looked down at layers of clouds under which was Palestine. "Do you think there will ever be a Jewish state?"

"No," Ted said with conviction.

"Yes," Brilli replied at the same moment with the same conviction.

When Brilli discovered she was to have Lev's child, she said nothing. It was her secret, at least for the moment, and it made her happy. When it became apparent, it was late to do anything.

"An abortion now is out of the question," the doctor told her mother.

Fuss, fuss, fuss, why was it women fussed so?

"I don't understand you, Brilli," her mother concluded.

Brilli smiled at her. "I don't understand you either. When I was fifteen I asked you about sex. And do you know what you told me? Really, it was quite unbelievable. You started talking about toothbrushes. You said that's how you knew you loved a man, if you could bear the idea of using his toothbrush. . . . Lev passed that test, mother. He threw back his head when he laughed. And his teeth were perfect, every one of them."

"Oh, there's no talking to you." Brillianna drew up lists of eligible young men from the Company and its subsidiaries, as though she were giving a party.

They came to lunch, they came to dinner. They played tennis, badminton and ping-pong. Some paid open court to Brilli, others were embarrassed by the situation, but none withdrew.

"Pick one of them," her mother told her, "and be quick about it."

Brilli read that the Arabs drove three trucks filled with explosives into the center of Jerusalem. The charge killed 175 people. One American tourist was listed by name. She read that 251 Irgun members were rounded up and deported in RAF planes to exile in Eritrea. She remembered he said to her, "If we become a state, we must not depend on foreign promises or international guarantees. We must make it happen ourselves."

Two Jewish terrorists, the morning of their execution, blew themselves up with a grenade smuggled to them in a scooped-out orange. This time there were names. Neither was Lev.

"All right," she informed her mother. "Tell Howard Knolls. I don't know whether he has won the princess or the pumpkin."

Her mother kissed her. "I was hoping it would be Howard. He is an extraordinary young man in a sensitive position with the AEC. Your father thinks he will go far."

"That's nice."

"Besides he seems a very understanding person."

"I don't remember him. Which one is he?"

Her mother simply gave her a look which said, don't try that one with me. "Oh yes," Brilli brightened, "he wears two-tone shoes. Very sporting."

"I noticed you talking to him half the evening."

"We did talk some."

Howard Knolls insisted on talking further. "I know," he said, his fair complexion reddening, "what it is on your part. Pressure from your family, that kind of thing. And I'm glad because it is my only chance to win out."

"Win out?"

"You know, marry you."

"Oh, I see. I'm glad you think of it as winning."

"I've always been in love with you. I don't want you to think there's any other reason. I hold an excellent position. I don't need your father. And I won't accept promotions simply because I'm his son-in-law."

She smiled. "You're one of those. You prefer to think it's your own hard work, brains and talent. Who knows, in your case it might even be true." Her smile broadened. "But you'll never be sure, will you?"

"Do you despise me for wanting to marry you?"

"Not at all."

"And you do believe that I love you?"

"Does it matter that I believe?"

"Yes."

"Well, then, I think it's more palatable for you to love me than not to love me."

"I swear, I don't know what to make of you, Brilli."

"Let's keep it that way, shall we?"

"After the baby is born, if you want a divorce, I'd stand aside, I wouldn't contest it. That's a promise."

She looked at him for the first time with interest. "Howard Knolls, I suspect you may be a very decent person."

He kissed her, and another man's child squirmed between their bodies.

Her father was delighted at the news. "You couldn't have chosen better. Not only is he a fine man, but as a scientist he has already made a name for himself in atomic energy. It's exciting to think that the family will dominate, not only oil but all forms of power."

"I'm glad you're pleased, Daddy." She herself considered Howard Knolls a perfect choice. Since she couldn't remember what he looked like when she was not in the same room with him, it gave her a lot of extra time for remembering Lev.

The wedding was at Armagh. The San Francisco house was a gift to the young couple. Engraved invitations read: *Family only.* And the child nobody wanted. "Hush, hush," she whispered, "little Irgun fighter."

The morning of the ceremony there was an attack on Acre, which the British considered an impregnable fortress. It had resisted Napoleon's artillery only to be penetrated by a band of Irgunists. Forty-four political prisoners were released in the gun battle. Five of the attack force were captured, three sentenced to hanging. Trailing her antique satin wedding dress behind her she went into the bathroom and threw up. Her bridesmaids glanced at each other: morning sickness.

Brilli rinsed her mouth and looked at her reflection in the glass. It was true, what her mother said. She made a beautiful bride. The cunningly designed drapery of her gown concealed her condition, or at least diminished it.

Smile, she told herself, this is your wedding day.

Since the war there was difficulty getting the amounts of steel needed to lay the tapline, officially known as the Trans-Arabian Pipeline, which for political reasons was scheduled to cross the Arabian Peninsula, Syria, Transjordan and Palestine, winding up at Sidon, Lebanon. This worked well enough in theory but in practice Ted's people had to negotiate with old enemies. The Petroleum Reserve Corporation was reconstituted from the disbanded PAW, which had never forgiven him for failing to turn Saudi-California over to them. They now balked at taking steel out of the country, declaring it would drive prices up and cause shortages in the U.S. Their solution was the familiar one, that the American government undertake the laying of the pipeline and the building of refineries.

Ted fought back. He brought in Standard of New Jersey, which paid half a billion dollars for forty-percent participation and provided the additional muscle to obtain the huge amounts of steel needed.

After the merger, an export license for 20,000 tons was approved by the Department of Commerce on the grounds that it would serve "American strategic, political, and economic interests."

The Petroleum Reserve Corporation countered through the Senate Small Business Committee, repeating that such depletion of American steel would lead to soaring inflation. Several meetings were held before the Company found a way to overcome this patriotic argument with a super-patriotic one. In return for the steel needed to lay

372

the pipeline, the Company agreed to transport *at cost* for a period of ten years substantial quantities of oil for the national military establishment. Once again the Company beat out the government.

But there were other governments to deal with. And the newest cost estimate was a staggering 200 million dollars, which could only be considered a starting figure. Now began the heat from the Arab states: 310,000 barrels of oil must be carried a distance of 1,040 miles. Ibn Saud wanted 250,000 dollars annually for the laying of pipe across his desert. Lebanon asked only 18,000 dollars as it would have the terminus. Sir Alan Cunningham, realizing that the end of British rule was at hand in Palestine, saw no reason for the Jews to derive any revenue. Consequently, he allowed free passage of the line through Palestine. Syria's demands, on the other hand, were so outrageous that Ted threatened to have the terminus in Haifa after all. That brought Syria into line.

A son was born to Brilli toward the end of March. From the beginning he was a quiet infant, who seemed intent on trying to figure out what kind of world he had been thrust into. He was brought home from the hospital and no one could think what to call him.

In a household of blond, golden people he was dark and alien. When he turned his strange up-swept eyes on his family, they felt uncomfortable.

His grandmother could hardly bear the sight of the child. No hint of Grenville or Angstrom there. It was that girl and her people. There was only one member of the family to whom the baby was a source of joy. A rapport existed between grandfather and grandson from the first. When Ted looked down at the small new bundle he said, "Well, well."

The child brightened whenever his grandfather was in the room, giving ingratiating toothless grins reserved for him. And for his part, Ted didn't mind when he was spat up on or came away soggy.

"You'll spoil the baby," Brillianna said, signaling her disapproval. Ted only laughed. This was what she had denied him. What he had waited for so long. It made no difference that he didn't have the Angstrom name. He had the Angstrom blood. And he could have been *her* child, so strongly did he resemble Sara.

Ted finally named the boy. He called him Lev.

Brilli was furious. "You might consider Howard. How do you think that makes him feel?"

"How Howard feels does not concern me. A two-million-dollar trust goes with the name."

That shut them up.

Howard's feelings had recently become important to Brilli. She found her husband more dominant than she had supposed. He was not susceptible to her whims but single-minded in his purpose, which was to get her into bed. It was impossible for Brilli to sleep with a man without being in love.

In the midst of an affair with her husband she became pregnant. She turned Lev over to a nursemaid, finding it uncomfortable to be reminded of four days and five nights down a cistern with a wounded Jew.

Ted invented games with little Lev. One of which consisted of saying to him in a mock-stern voice, "No laughing is allowed in this house. No laughing, I say." Although he was too young to understand the words, this sent the child into paroxysms. No one could see why. His daughter's second pregnancy did not interest Ted.

It was Baba the boy first crawled to, and with encouragement, pulled himself up by. It was Baba he walked to. Everyone knew Baba was not Howard Knolls.

For Lev's first birthday Ted invented a new game. He pushed the one-year-old in the swing, and when by laws of motion and gravity the swing returned, he yelled, "What are you coming back for? Stay away!" And gave the swing another shove. Lev went into peals of laughter. His gruff Baba didn't fool him.

There was a cluster of Carmel pines lying to the ocean side of the estate, windswept, twisted almost horizontal within a few feet of the ground. These became known as dropping drangles, because Lev dropped from them. He was agile and fearless, and disdained a boost up. Maneuvering his way along the bark, with a whoop he would let go. It was a feat they were both proud of.

But there wasn't time enough. Iban Saud suggested that the Company build him a railroad. He had ridden on one in Cairo after his visit with Mr. Roosevelt. He enjoyed it very much. He would like his railroad to run from Dammam to Riyadh. Ted put his experts to work pricing his toy. The figure they came up with was 160 million dollars. The King's ministers pointed out that the Company had been operating within the kingdom all these years without paying income taxes.

"So, he found out about that," Ted growled and initialed funds for the railway.

The next communication out of Saudi was a flowery epistle to the effect that Arab armies had joined in brotherhood. If the proposed Jewish State were to be voted in the U.N., they would march and crush the infant reptile.

The identical missive was received by secretary of state George C. Marshall and under secretary Robert A. Lovett, who met with American Jewish leadership and made it plain that there would be no American military aid if statehood went forward and the Arab horde descended.

May 14, 1948, as Brilli nursed a blue-eyed replica of herself, the State of Israel was proclaimed.

President Truman accorded *de facto* recognition eleven minutes later. Brilli wondered sleepily if Lev Rosenfeld was celebrating this day. Irgun spokesmen announced they would no longer be soldiers but builders in Eretz Israel.

Brilli had not known the man she married. For a short time he was Ahura Mazda, god of light, handsome in a tall, blond, Protestant manner. An aloof man, even their lovemaking was kept on a certain plane. She was his "little one," never accepted fully as a woman. Not even when their daughter was born, named the first day, Brill. She was enchanted by this second baby who so closely resembled her, and nursed her a full year.

Gradually Brilli came to realize that what her husband told her before their marriage was true; he could make it without her father's influence. She admired his brilliance and watched with pride as he moved up quickly in the

375

tightly structured hierarchy of the Atomic Energy Commission. To do this meant, he explained to her, a sacrifice on both their parts.

She wanted to cooperate. "I understand," she told him. But she didn't, not fully, the loneliness that began to mark each day. She tried to draw closer to him, even preparing questions to ask about his work.

He brushed these aside. "You wouldn't follow it. It's too technical."

"I guess that's a polite way of saying you have a stupid wife."

"You're far from stupid, Brilli. Actually, you are quite bright. It's just that you never apply yourself."

"That's what they told me in school."

He took to bringing a briefcase home, bulging with documents. She attempted to detain him with stories of the children, "Lev was so funny. You know how Mother slaps his hands when he picks up one of her knick-knacks? Well, I caught him picking them up anyway. And when he set them down, he slapped his own hand."

He listened to her account and, at the first pause, took his briefcase into the study. It swallowed him up. That was the last she saw of him. After four years his appetite and hunger for her were satisfied. She was not absolutely sure that the figure in the twin bed on the other side of the night table, who now restricted himself to sex with her regularly and therapeutically, was Howard. Sometimes she pretended it was not, that it was someone else. She was afraid it was Lev who had crept back into her nights. She banished his young, hard body and said to herself, 'It is not Howard. It is not Lev. It is someone else.' For a year this someone else was faceless, nameless.

When she went out, it was usually to a show with her parents, or a dance at the country club. One Saturday night when she returned home and the gray figure came around from his side of the nightstand to her bed, she imagined a specific person. She always danced with her eyes closed and was surprised when the music ended to find a brightly lighted room and many people. More and more when she opened her eyes, it was Eric Tildon's face she looked into. She danced the last dance of the evening with him. It was he who worked her to a frenzy, but it

376

was her husband who withdrew too soon. To get relief she went into the bathroom, locked the door and masturbated. It was terrible to cry quietly. She wished she could cry noisily like her children.

Tildon was a widower. Because he was in politics the affair was carried on discreetly. They became adept at slipping away from parties separately, to meet at his apartment. This evening he was moody and preoccupied. "Brilli," he said suddenly, "will Howard give you a divorce?"

She looked at him without answering.

"I've been appointed to a post abroad. I want to take you with me. We'd be a family. Would you like that?"

"You mean a real family, with my children and your children?"

He grinned. "You wouldn't be turned into an old woman in the shoe. My two boys are pretty well grown. They are away at school most of the time. I think it would give them a sense of stability though. Mainly of course, it would be your two little kids."

"Three," she corrected him.

"What?"

She nodded.

"Mine?"

"Of course yours." She laughed, "I've had migraines every Saturday for months. Howard's so busy, I don't think he even noticed."

"Let me feel the baby," he said.

She took his hand and placed it against her body.

"What were you going to do?" he asked. "Were you going to tell me?"

"I hadn't decided. I don't decide things till I'm up to the wire. What would you like? Place your order now, a boy or a girl?"

"A girl," he answered without hesitation. "Everything with you is a first. I've never had a daughter." He fell silent, and then asked, "Can you handle Howard?"

"No problem. When we married he said he wouldn't hold me to anything. It was our understanding."

"That was a long time ago. He may have changed his mind."

"No, it will be all right. Basically, Howard is a nice person."

Nevertheless Brilli prepared carefully for her interview with her husband. She dressed soberly so he would take her seriously. She rehearsed her admission of guilt an entire day, and waited until Saturday afternoon. He relaxed from the week then, with a round of golf. When he returned from the club, she intercepted him. "Howard, I've been wanting to talk to you."

The urgency in her voice attracted his attention. "You have been out of sorts lately. Is anything wrong?"

"Yes." She felt as though she were plunging beneath icy water. "Yes, there is. I want a divorce."

"A divorce?" The forward movement toward the study was deflected. "Come, it can't be anything serious. I don't even remember quarreling."

"I'm in love with someone. I'm having an affair." This wasn't coming out the way she had planned. Her statements were too bald. She meant to edge into things more, soften the blow.

"An affair? Well, I suppose that's a crisis for any marriage. But you are my wife and the mother of two children. I don't think it can be too serious."

"It is." She stood her ground. "It is serious."

"In that case," he came toward her and took her hands, "the reason is not hard to find. I've been busy. The whole thing is my fault as much as yours. I won't ask who it is. Okay? We'll start over again. A second honeymoon. I might even get away for a week or two."

This was not what she expected. She scarcely knew how to handle this leniency. "Howard, I don't want to be forgiven. I want to be free to marry."

"I'll never let you go, my darling. I'm in love with you."

"I'm sorry Howard, but I can't allow you to back out on a bargain."

"I'm aware of no bargain."

"The reason I agreed to marry you was because you said you'd release me if I wanted. Remember? You promised me."

Howard smiled at her. "A young man desperately in

love will say anything. You can't hold me accountable for something said six years ago."

"I do."

"But my darling, that isn't fair. I'm more in love with you than ever."

She looked at him oddly. "I don't believe that," she said.

"I've forgiven you, haven't I?"

"Is that a mark of love or indifference? Howard, I am carrying his child."

That seemed to catch him off balance. "Really Brilli, there are ways and means, was it necessary to get pregnant?"

"Now you know why I want the divorce."

"My poor, impulsive girl. I stepped into this same situation once before. I am perfectly willing to cover for you again. The child you are carrying will be my child."

"No."

"That's a peculiar response. You are not behaving in a very mature way."

"Let's stop the games. I don't want this marriage any more. I don't want you. All I want is for you to let me go."

"I won't do that."

For a full minute neither of them moved or took their eyes from the other. "What do you want, Howard? I know it isn't me. Is it money? You know when we were married, Daddy settled a million dollars on me. It's yours."

"I am a scientist," he replied coldly. "Money doesn't interest me."

She continued to scrutinize him. "I see. Of course. Why should you settle for a million, when eventually you will have a piece of one of the largest fortunes in America? My pure abstract scientist is not as other-worldly as I thought." She dashed past him.

"Where are you going?"

"To my father."

"Your father? Who do you think arranged the match?"

She stopped where she was. "I decided myself. No one pressured me."

"Of course not. That's not the way Angstrom works.

379

We had a conference in which he explained to me you were a highly emotional, idealistic girl. It was his idea, that touch about giving you your freedom. He's a shrewd old boy, I must give him that."

"I don't believe you. Why should my father care who I married?"

"Don't be naïve. You're not just anyone. You're an Angstrom. But I wasn't just anyone either. I was already a research consultant to the AEC. He wanted a man he could count on in that operation. He needed me."

"Liar," she screamed at him. "Liar!" She fled to the car, backed the length of the driveway at top speed, and headed for Carmel. She drove with the top down and her hair was a tangled briar patch when she pulled up at the estate two hours later.

She raced through the house. Her father was on the long-distance telephone. She deliberately depressed the switchhook, breaking the connection. "I hope that was the King of Arabia."

"Brilli, what in the world? Have you gone out of your mind?"

"Just about. I came here for an answer. One answer to one question. Six years ago I thought I decided to marry Howard Knolls. But he tells me the marriage was engineered by you, that your main concern was to buy the loyalty of someone in the AEC."

Ted leaned back in his chair. It was some seconds before he answered. "I believed Howard would make you a good husband."

"How convenient. Two birds with one stone."

"Look Brilli, you knew Howard was with the AEC. You knew my interest in this type of energy. There's nothing new in all this. I don't see what you are so exercised about."

"You will in a moment. Because I am about to find out what my happiness means to you." She sat on the edge of his desk. "Dad, I'm in love with someone else. I am pregnant by him, and he wants to marry me. But Howard won't give me a divorce, even though that's the trick he used to make me decide on him in the first place." She looked at her father shrewdly. "He says the idea was yours. . . ."

"Now wait just a minute. This is coming at me too fast. You are in love with someone else?"

"A fine person, Daddy. Someone you would approve of."

"And you're having his child?"

"Yes."

"Howard knows about this?"

"I just told him. It's the money, Dad. It's too big for him to let go of. I want you to buy him out. Whatever it takes, give it him: shares, stock, cash, anything he wants."

"Let me say right off the bat, I will never give away what I've worked for. The money goes to you and to my grandchildren. And to Brillianna, of course, should she survive me. Howard will get his share under community property laws. And if you want my opinion, I think you should get down on your knees and thank God for a husband who is willing to forgive your indiscretions. He's treated you a great deal better than you deserve. Most men would whale you within an inch of your life."

Her lips drew back over even white teeth. It was not a smile. "What all this really means is that you are forcing me to continue with Howard, knowing I love another man and am carrying that man's child. I see now that Howard is not a liar. Everything he said was perfectly true. You never thought of me. All you thought about was a way to bind Howard Knolls to the Company. You took a leaf from Ibn Saud. Too bad you have only one daughter to manipulate and use, and not forty-four sons."

"Brilli, wait. Don't go flying off like that." But he couldn't stop her.

She drove straight to Eric's apartment and leaned against the door, ringing the bell repeatedly.

"Good God," he said when he saw her. He brought her in and made her sit on the couch while he got a glass of water. "Catch your breath. We'll talk in a minute."

"Eric, none of it worked. But I don't care. It doesn't matter. I'm coming with you. He promised me, Eric. He did, he promised me." She tried to compose herself. "But

I have it figured out. I won't be an embarrassment to you, I swear it. I have my own money. I'll come to Paris and take my own apartment. We can see each other."

There was a pause. Perhaps he counted to ten slowly. "What about your children?"

"Yes, that's what I've been thinking all the way here. But they'll be well taken care of. They won't want for anything."

". . . except you."

She put her hand across her mouth and seemed to sink into the soft cushions. Then, making a deliberate effort, pulled herself upright, set the glass on a low table and straightened her dress. "I can't let you go without me. Loving you is as necessary to me as breathing. I'm stifling in this marriage. The children . . . " she leaned forward and made a pattern with her finger on the frosted glass, "the children are part of me. And I love them in the same way I love myself, a much more calm, taken-for-granted way."

She put his arms around her, and they tightened there. "I need you. Otherwise I'll become my mother. My mother waited for my dad to turn to her, and when he finally did she was dried up emotionally, and I suspect physically too. She forgot how to communicate, if she ever knew. She's a symbol—wife, mother, grandmother. But there's nothing there to love, Eric." Her kisses were frantic. "Save me from that. I have so much love and no one to take it, until you. If you don't let me love you, it will all back up in me and stagnate the way it did in my mother."

"Of course you're coming with me," he assured her. "But we will have to be careful. My sons are at an age . . . well, you know. What about Howard? You were so sure he'd allow you to divorce him. Is there no way to move him?"

She shook her head.

"I'm worried about you. A new assignment means I'll be busy until things shake down. But every moment I can steal is yours, except for holidays. I have the boys then."

"I understand. That's when I'll visit my own children."

"Will the family allow it?"

"Allow it? They're my children," she said fiercely. "Besides Howard doesn't care anything about them. He might like to punish me. But he'd never cross Dad. And at least where the children are concerned my father will stand by me. So will Mother. It's mostly Mother who will be responsible for them."

He kissed her gently. "What about the little one? Ours?"

"I think I'll come home to have it."

"Perhaps when Howard sees you really mean to leave him, he'll give in, let you go."

"I don't want to talk about him. Can I use your bathroom?" She sat on the upholstered vanity settee and stared into the mirror. She saw the face of little Brill. It was odd how alike they looked. At first the resemblance fooled her. She's just like me, she thought. But she wasn't. She was amazingly precocious, with a mind that functioned in a totally logical manner. The two strains, Angstrom and Knolls, never met in her. It was as though children starting at opposite sides, tunneled through sand to reach and feel the other's hand. This meeting didn't happen in Brill. There was an area of her nature that no one reached. Words seemed to get into the five-year-old head whose meaning she didn't know. The child made up stories, insisting that Kumju told them.

Lev, only thirteen months older, had grown tall and straight and looked at the world from his father's eyes. You could count on Lev. And she would have to as he grew up.

Could she really dissect herself this way? But the alternative was always present in the form of her mother. That was what not being loved did to you. Her mother tried. But she couldn't draw close even to the children. It had been too many years since she had been close to anyone. She had lost the knack. Brilli had a deep fear of ending up like her mother.

Ibn Saud died. There was no reason for Ted to be affected by his death. They had never been friends, in fact the King's ingenious ways for wringing money out of him

383

had infuriated him for twenty years. The King knew instantly, it seemed to Ted, when he bought into the Argentine fields. He was aware when any other government received a percentage higher than his own, and was never averse to veiled threats of nationalization.

During the war he flirted with both sides, joining the Allies at the end when victory was certain and he might share in the spoils. They met only twice. Once during that ill-conceived 'entertainment' in the desert that had driven Sara to flight, again aboard the *Murphy* and the *Quincy*.

No, they were not friends. They were contemporaries. The old King's passing was a reminder of his own mortality. 'Abd al 'Aziz Ibn 'Abd al Rahman al Faisal al Sa'ud by the end of his life received three million dollars oil revenue a week. There was still no banking system or method of investment at Riyadh. Carpenters were simply set to work making more boxes to hold it all.

There were no public works instituted in Saudi as in Iran and Iraq. The two thousand royal princes, cousins, nephews, and in-laws were given excessive amounts of cash to spend. Inflation jumped forward in a crazy spiral. Ibn Saud's solution was to demand that the Company double wages. They reluctantly complied. This, of course, made things worse. The aged King shook his head. He didn't understand.

Ibn Saud's last child, a girl, was born when he was sixty-seven. He lost his potency. It was this more than blindness or old wounds that preyed on his mind. He became increasingly sedentary, and, in a final rebellion against time, dyed his hair.

Most of old Riyadh was bulldozed away, giving place to concrete Mediterranean-type villas, boulevards, ornate offices, and palaces. The first of the new palaces at Nasiriya, just outside Riyadh, was filled with swimming pools, fountains, imported plants and floodlit gardens. Costing twelve million dollars, it was a monument to poor taste. The King himself grew tired of it, razed it to the ground, and replaced it with one costing thirty million. This was, if possible, more garish than the first. The American presence created a great desire for material things, and the orgy of extravagance and mismanagement Nichols had written about accelerated.

384

Many of the new palaces and apartment houses under construction in Riyadh fell down before they were complete, the contractors having mixed too much free desert sand into the concrete. This effort to plunge into the modern era was frustrated at every turn. Fuses blew, and nobody mended them. Refrigerators froze, and instead of being defrosted, were discarded. Rats got into the ducts of the air-conditioning and small pellets were spewed into the rooms.

The overtaxed wells in Riyadh were failing. The Saud family waved problems aside. They had a corner on the world's money. "We will pipe water from Iraq."

Many of the old King's sons were drunkards, two were murderers. One son, having been asked to leave the home of the British consul during a disturbance at a party, returned and shot the consul dead. Another gave a feast at which some of the guests died of poison. What was perhaps worse, women were present. These scandals were not capable of being hushed up. The King passed death sentences on both sons, imprisoned them for a while, and reprieved them.

Riyadh was filled with salesmen, each with a novel scheme for separating the young millionaires from their money, and the princes cooperated. When traveling, they reserved not rooms but floors, not compartments but entire trains, not first class but the airplane. Waiters were tipped in hundred dollar bills.

In Kuwait where the British government acted as adviser, schools were built, hospitals constructed, and the shaikh was the biggest investor in the London stock market. Ibn Saud spent none of his money on public works. Plans were under way toward the end of his life for a hospital at Riyadh and an enlarged pier at Jidda to handle a greater volume of pilgrim trade. It was the Company that decided in the name of public relations to plow back some percent of the profit into the establishment of free hospitals, schools and sanitation. It seemed strange to Ted that he was finally doing what Sara wanted.

He was anxious for particulars of the King's passing. It seemed he died of a heart attack in his sleep. The year was 1953, but who would remember? His body was buried in an unmarked grave, as was the custom. Few knew where it was. Few would visit it.

Ted pulled himself from lethargy. He must think of the future. The King's eldest son Saud would succeed. He was then a man of fifty-one, not so tall as his father, nor so capable as his brother Faisal. In fact, the task he inherited was quite beyond him. It was, Ted thought, an explosive situation. Saud had as many sons as his father, lived in as vast a palace, and was always accompanied by an entourage.

The man he leaned on and whom Ted would be dealing with, was Faisal, the hawk-featured second son. Ted speculated whether Faisal would be content with executive power minus the title. As Ted read him, he was an ambitious man.

While Saud inaugurated his reign with shows of pomp, Faisal made policy and quietly gathered power. Faisal was not cast in typical Saudi mold. He had experience of the modern world. Even his family life was quite Western. He had only eight sons. They were at Oxford, at the Royal Military College, at Sandhurst, and several were in the United States at Stanford and the Ivy League schools.

Ted thought the proportions interesting. Saud had forty sons. Faisal, eight. And he, Theodore Angstrom, one grandson. Such odds pleased an Angstrom.

Brilli returned to Armagh for the birth. The baby was a girl. Variants on Brillianna had almost been exhausted. The dainty mite whose eyes took up a third of her face was called Bea Anna. She affiliated with her brother and sister from the beginning, knew that though a lesser being without their accomplishments, she was of the same genre. The baby was never as happy as when the children were in sight. Their play delighted her, and their rough and tumble brought gurgles and coos.

Brilli tried not to go back to Paris, to stay and make the three youngsters the content of her life. But she could not endure the cold politeness her husband meted out to her. And she missed Eric, even though a large part of her time was spent waiting for him. It wasn't a satisfactory life. It was lonely. But when they came together, the ache she carried with her was soothed. She devoured her children with her eyes, hugged them, played their games in an intense, hectic manner.

"Two little birdies sitting on a hill.

"One named Jack.

"One named Jill." These were two tiny scraps of paper stuck with a bit of sputum to the index finger of each hand.

"Fly away Jack."

Jack flew away by the simple process of substituting fingers. Brill bent her blond head, Lev his dark one, to watch. It was Jill's turn to disappear.

Next it was Brilli who was gone.

Nearly three years passed and the Knolls children continued to live at the Carmel residence during the week, spending the weekends in San Francisco with their father.

Bea Anna, never able to pronounce 'Grandmother,' or perhaps not caring to, tried for Brillianna and came up with the combination that stuck. *Grandbee* was how the children came to refer to her. Brillianna rather liked the title, the family name now worked its way through three living generations from little Bea to herself.

Grandbee was a remote figure in the children's lives. Slender, elegant, she exerted tremendous authority and was the final arbiter in all decisions concerning them. Lev had tried since he could remember to circumvent her. And kept from her information that he gave freely to his sisters and grandfather. On the Carmel property he discovered three quail, gray with flat tails, a red squirrel family and a gray squirrel family, as well as a blue jay of a surprisingly light color, who aggressively kept the other tenants at bay.

The San Francisco house had its attractions as well, a sycamore with a hollow place for leaving messages, and a cat known as Tabby.

Lev was, as always, his grandfather's special ally, and shared his most important treasure with him. He showed him the hummingbird nest the size of a quarter with minute eggs reposing in it.

Ted nodded appreciatively. At fifty-seven he was looking more and more like Old Man Angstrom, and was called that behind his back by younger colleagues. Politics in 1955 and 1956 meant oil, and Ted was deeply involved. The British Empire, shaken and collapsing, had withdrawn its last troops from Egypt two months before. In an effort to protect oil interests, a pact was negotiated with Iran, Iraq, and Pakistan, who also had no means of shipping if the unpredictable Nasser should decide to close the Canal.

Egypt saw the Baghdad Pact as an attempt to isolate her. Shortly after, England withdrew from the Aswan Dam project, and the United States, in spite of political pressure brought by the oil industry, also reneged. Predictably, Nasser's reply was nationalization of the Suez Canal, barring it to Israeli shipping. This action cut Israel's eastern supply lines. The Port of Elat at the tip of the Gulf of Aqaba was useless since the Tiran Straits at its entrance were controlled and heavily fortified by Egypt on one side and Saudi Arabia on the other. Israeli access to the Red Sea, essential for trade with East Africa and the Far East, as well as for receiving needed oil from Iran, was entirely cut off.

In the midst of Ted's preoccupation with these events, Brillianna started in on him about Brilli. She had never reconciled herself to the irregularity of the life her daughter led in Paris. "Ted, I think if you wrote again. The children are growing up. They are starting to ask questions. What can I say to them? Please, Ted. You still have influence with her."

"She has a husband. It's not my place. What can I phone, cable, or write at this late date to make her change her way of life?" Nevertheless he was drafting a stilted letter along the lines Brillianna suggested when Israel joned forces with Britain and France. Striking at the Canal itself, Israeli troops took the Gaza strip and the Sinai. The letter to Brilli was forgotten. Ted lent active support to American-Russian intervention in the U.N. By November the triumvirate withdrew. Israel secured a guarantee of passage through the Tiran Straits in exchange for the return of captured territory.

It was another eighteen months before Brilli came

home. By that time Lev was eleven and he began to know. Or had he always known how oddly he fit into this golden clan? A dark Caliban. Especially beside Mother who was the most golden of them all. Mother had returned, an older sister to play with them. They swam in the pool and had picnics in the garden. Brill, looking up at the god in two pieces, wanted to know how Mother knew his name was Kumju.

Mother said an anthropologist identified him.

"Did he tell you stories when you were little?" Brill asked. "About the Crocodile People, and a tribe deep in the jungle whose dogs don't bark?"

"Of course not. And I wish you wouldn't make them up, Brill," Mother said.

"But I don't," the ten-year-old shook her long blond hair, "Kumju tells me. He lived along the salt route. They traded shells for salt. People had to have salt or they died."

"Where do you get such notions?" Mother asked uneasily.

"I told you. Kumju knows about things taken from the earth, like salt and copper and fire."

"And oil?" Lev asked.

Their mother interrupted with a laugh. Eric Tildon had married. Their stolen time had not added up to enough. He wanted a home for his sons. Brilli kissed him lightly and said she understood. She understood that the consuming love she gave was not returned. She came home to her children to find the two eldest almost grown. She pursued the subject of Kumju because Brill's odd insistence that she communicated with the god worried her. "Oil? No." She tried to keep it light. "I don't think he's kept up with the times. I don't think he is that modern."

"I checked on him at the library," Lev said. "He's awfully old. He was worshiped by Kashta, King of Kush. Kush was campaigning in Egypt when Rome was founded. Mansa Musa believed in Kumju too. That was at the start of the Hundred Years War in Europe, during the reign of Edward III of England and Philip VI of Spain."

"Kush?" Bea said and laughed.

"Kush is by the first cataract of the Nile." Brill knew other things but she kept them to herself. She seemed to

389

remember a temple to the sun at Mesoe. And she understood that women were tied by ties of blood, and men by ties of water. And that Kumju himself was made of both. Kumju, who had known other times and other peoples, had turned his seeing on her.

"What's cataract?" Bea wanted to know.

"It's a waterfall."

Brill asked Lev, "Did you really look all that up in the library, or did Kumju tell you?"

"What do you think? I read about it."

"But he might have told you if he'd wanted to," Brill insisted. She hooked her arms around her knees and with a faraway look said softly, "His stories always end in a special way. . . . You are as the baobab tree, you are as a well of sweet water."

For Brill he appeared in many guises, as a misplaced star, or an interred fire lapping over buried gas gurgling in subterranean streams, leaping to cataclysmic force in ruptured rock. His turbulent spirit forced a path to the upper world where he translated the earth.

Kumju whispered things about Mother too, or maybe it was Maria and Tomas she overheard. They were things Brill didn't want to know, things she didn't want to understand. They all agreed it was fun when Mother was home. She was always laughing, playing tennis, swimming. But there was something unreal about it. Perhaps because they knew it would end abruptly.

"She was called away," Grandbee said.

Called away? Where? By whom? For a few days the children listened up and down the paths for her voice, her easy laughter. But she was gone and their own play silent and subdued.

The family's efforts to locate Brilli proved extremely embarrassing. The police were called in. They discovered her in Monterey with her tennis coach. She returned light-hearted but driven—to stay a matter of days. This became a pattern. The visits were now more frequent but disquieting to the children.

Lev waited for a chance to talk. Once he found his mother stretched on a towel sunbathing by the pool. When he approached, she jumped up. She smiled as she passed him. "Look how lazy I've been." He smiled too, but he knew she left to avoid him.

Another time she was sitting on the rocks below by the tide pool. When he saw her there he turned back guiltily.

"Lev," she called, looking up at him, squinting a little with the sun in her face, "you're so like him." This utterance seemed to startle her.

Lev said what he'd been wanting to say. "Don't go away again." She turned her head, but not before he saw a gleam through her lashes. Was it a tear? Was his mother, who was always laughing, crying?

"I owe you that. That's one thing I can do for you." At first he wasn't sure she was speaking to him. "You see, some people are good at putting things together, making them work. But I get the pieces in upside down or backwards or sideways." She shook her hair which the wind was whipping around her face. "Well," she said briskly, "Grandbee tells me you're quite a handful, Lev. Try to take more responsibility. Especially for Brill."

"Yes, ma'am," was what he said. What he wanted to ask was, why Brill?

"Now, run and play." She was always telling him that.

The family took a waterfront place at Newport Beach over Easter vacation, which instead of a front yard had its own mooring and the bay. But much of the pleasure was gone because their mother was once more "called away."

Lev and Brill received a Lido 14 as a parting gift. "I had one like it when I was your age," the card in Brilli's handwriting said. Everyone looked for the card later. Lev had taken it. It began, "Dear Lev and Brill—" He put his fingers over the place that said *Dear Lev.*

After a few lessons they handled the small craft as though they had done nothing else their whole lives. Brill, fond of pretending, insisted, "We are above the first cataract. I am Mansa Musa and you are the black Kashta." But for Lev it was enough to hear the slap of the canvas as she came about. The gentle pitching of the boat was a rhythm he loved.

Why pretend to be anyone but Lev? That was a good person to be. They stood on the dock arguing. Brill would not give up the King of Nuba, or the cataracts of Egypt.

As Lev unwound the rope to cast off, she gave a tremendous heave with the oar against the side of the pier, sending the ship out of reach of this dangerous dark enemy. The sailboat bobbed with yards of water opening between them. Lev crouched, took his bearings and jumped.

He made it, after a fashion, crashing headfirst into the stone anchor. He lay with no blood on his face, but perfectly still.

Brill crouched beside him, "Lev, please don't be hurt. I don't want you to be hurt. I don't care if you're only my half brother. It doesn't make any difference. It doesn't matter. Please, Lev. Kumju will make you well, you'll see. Kumju! Kumju!"

Brill's harsh screams brought her father, who carried the boy into the house and laid him on the couch. He notified Angstrom before calling the doctor.

Lev was floating in the boat, far out at sea. All sorts of strange memories and ideas occurred to him. He remembered Grandpa's stern voice, "No laughing in this house. No laughing, I say," and the hilarity that followed.

He and Grandpa. Grandpa talking, he listening, learning all sorts of things that had no relation to anything, but which he treasured because Grandpa entrusted them to him. He learned about Walgreen drugstores where you sip sarsaparilla sodas or phosphates. He never asked what those were, but imagined the taste and smell for himself.

He learned there was no elephant graveyard. But a graveyard of red salmon on top of certain waterfalls, up which they fight their way to spawn and die. His mind shifted from the word. It was a word he had just heard in this room.

Was he going to die? Was that why Brill was crying? Or were they blaming her? That was stupid when it wasn't her at all, but the noble Mansa Musa. He remembered what she said in the boat, "I don't care if you're only my half brother."

That was an odd thing to say. Lev mused over the idea. How could you be half a something? Half a brother? Half a Lev? It was another of Brill's strange ideas and it floated away caught on sunbeams. The sun derives its energy by converting hydrogen into—he couldn't think. The sun was on his closed eyelids as he rocked in the boat. He wanted to dive over the side. You weren't supposed to, but it was only for a moment, then you clambered in, dripping and cool.

If he jumped now he might not be able to get back. He felt hot, and motion was making him sick. It sent his brain crashing into the side of his head, and the jar sent it crashing back. The pain was a series of explosions, regular, even. There was no way out.

Perhaps he should jump. Fantasies receded. Thought wasn't in words anymore. It was a buzzing in his head. He was falling away from himself, disconnecting. Some one was chafing his hands, liquid was being forced into his mouth. It ran down his chin. Grandbee must have come because all these things were happening. Then he heard her voice. "You think, doctor, that the boy's mother should be notified?"

"One never knows with head injuries. It might be a good idea."

"Yes, I have an address for her somewhere. Maria, will you bring the book upstairs by my telephone? I'll send a cable."

"That's probably wise. I don't want to move him tonight. In the morning we'll check him into the hospital and run some tests. We'll know more then."

The voices became indistinct. Lev slipped around in places strange to him. When he opened his eyes next his grandfather was sitting beside him holding his hands. His grandfather was away on business, it was funny he was here. "That's better, son. You had a nasty fall. Everything will be all right now."

The other people were still in the room, Grandbee and the doctor, and Maria by the door. They must have sent Brill out. The doctor lifted his wrist and took his pulse, checking it against his watch. Lev could feel the beating too. It scared him, he didn't like to think of things working away inside, in case they stopped.

"Better," the doctor said, "more regular."

"His color's better too," Grandbee observed.

"Don't let him out of bed tonight. Do you have a urinal in the house?"

Grandbee had everything in the house, bedpans, enema bags, ace bandages, they always came along on vacations.

Grandfather whispered to him. "Your mother will be coming to see you. You'll like that, won't you?"

He tried to answer, but the words came out backwards.

Grandbee followed the doctor into the hall. When she returned it was with instructions for Maria. "Prepare him for the night, and leave a bell by his side. You won't mind sleeping down here in the study, will you?" Grandbee always knew what to do. For once Lev was grateful. Everyone left but Maria, who washed his face and hands, wrung out a fresh compress for his head and made him urinate in the jug. He couldn't with her looking, so she spread the sheet over him.

He felt drowsy. Mother was coming. Maybe this time she would stay, although of course he knew she wouldn't.

He slept until a small sound woke him. The door to the living room where they had bedded him down, clicked into place. It had been opened very quietly.

"Lev?"

It was Brill. She crossed the room to him. The light from the marina showed them to each other. "You okay?"

"Yeah," he said but without making the sound.

"I brought you something to keep your strength up."

He smiled, she sounded just like Grandbee. Brill laid a Babe Ruth candy bar on his chest. That was hardly the nourishing broth Grandbee would recommend.

"Later," he still could not articulate the word.

"But aren't you hungry? You didn't have dinner." She threw herself down beside him, hugging him and trying to cry quietly. "I got scared when they cabled Mother. Did you know they did that? That's what they do when people die. If you die, Lev, I'll die too."

"I won't die," he said with his lips.

"Anyway, Mother's not at the address she gave Grandbee. They can't reach her. The hotel said she's gone on to Greece."

"Mother." This time he spoke out loud. He began to turn his head from side to side. "Mother."

She laid her face down by his. "It's all right, Lev. We don't need her. I'll take care of you. I'll tell you stories."

The lights snapped on. Maria stood there in a long

nightgown, her hair in a shiny black braid down the middle of her back. "Brill, you are a bad girl to wake your brother who is sick." Maria was such a mild person that she never managed to sound angry, even when she scolded. "Come to bed before the grandmother hears you."

Brill slid the Babe Ruth under Lev's pillow. "I'm coming."

From the moment he entered the hospital Lev mounted a campaign to be let out. Since there was no fracture, he was released after several days. His symptoms were intermittent headaches. But he was rather proud of his face. It was discolored from the bruise but also from a blood clot whose dark outline was clearly visible on his cheek. "Now I look like you, Grandpa."

Ted laughed. He had left all his affairs to be with his grandson. The two of them lay on deck chairs under a beach umbrella. Little Bea made sand pies from a blue and red pail and sang all the time. She could hear something once on the radio and sing it. "I try the music on," the five-year-old said.

Grandbee decided it would be good for them all to stay another week in Newport. She engaged a tutor for Brill so she would be well up in her classes.

It was his grandfather who filled Lev's days trying to tell him who he was. As he talked, Lev's mind kept leaping back to something Brill said, leaning over him in the boat, "I don't mind if you're only a half brother." He wasn't absolutely sure he'd heard it. But even if she said it, he somehow could not ask her what it meant. He thought of asking his grandfather, but he couldn't do that either. Still he listened carefully to the rambling peregrinations, hoping for clues.

"You know, son, it takes a long time to grow anything large. I say, *grow*, because I think of the Company as a living thing. Once I thought it was mine, that I owned it. But that's not the way of it. Here I sit with you, yakking away, sipping a cool drink, and the Company goes right on being the Company. It doesn't depend on one man

395

now, or a dozen men. It's too big, Lev, too rich, too diversified. It's a pluralistic system—professional managers, they're in charge now. But even they aren't important. Part of their job is to reproduce themselves, groom men to take over, who in turn groom others. It's no longer the son, the son-in-law, or even the grandson. You'll usually find some of them in top jobs, but they no longer exercise autonomy, or even much authority, no more than would normally go with their position.

"You, Lev, I'll expect you to come into the business, some aspect of it, certainly. And as an heir and scion you'll be expected to exert moral leadership. But no Rockefeller or Angstrom of your generation would dream of telling an oilman what to do. If they work for us, they *know* what to do.

"Presidents today usually started out with the companies they head. You don't leave a company where you're looked after as we look after our people. Not only do we pay top wages, but you might say we're our own government operating within many governments. We take care of our employees, cradle to grave—health insurance, stock dividends, retirement. That's the way you attract the best, by putting them in the six-figure bracket. The year you were born our assets were a hundred and fifty million dollars. I couldn't begin to compute it for you now. A man who can tell you how rich he is, isn't rich. Remember that, Lev."

Lev nodded. This was information you couldn't learn in school. You could only learn it from a few people, and his grandfather was one of them.

"I think of the Company as a living cell that divides, and subdivides, compounding itself. And it spews out whole new sections. When I was active, it was called *selling*. Now it's *marketing*, and that's a science in itself. Then there's *distribution, merchandizing, pricing and volume, design*. Development, figuring out new petroleum products, drugs, chemicals, synthetics.

"*Policy making*, I still retain a voice there. There's something called a Steering Committee that sets up channels of communications; and an office that integrates research with operations and puts everything on computers. And that's just within the central hydra. We've reached out and sucked in other businesses. We have profits to invest. We're into hotels, factories, shipping, utilities. Profit is a bookkeeping device now. You spread it around like butter, the stockholders get theirs, the employees, the suppliers, and . . ." he laughed, "sometimes even the customers."

Lev had a quick mind. He understood a great deal of this. "Oil is the fuel, isn't it, Grandpa, for rockets?"

"Damn right. It's the fuel that will take us into the future. And if other forms are developed, it will be under our aegis. We, you and I, are part of a self-perpetuating system designed to be immortal."

"Immortal," Lev repeated, "that's going on forever. It's kind of like a beehive, the bees die, but there is always a hive."

"In a way. But you're oversimplyfying. We've become sophisticated, we've taken a lot of our principles directly from government. We employ a system of *checks* and *balances* based on the Constitution. It's a useful model, helps us cope with organizational sprawl. The hundred biggest companies are all self-perpetuating, self-regulating. As I said before, private governments on the international scene.

"And remember, profit is no longer slicing a melon. It's a way of providing the good life. And with your brains, son, I hope you'll do more than jet-set through it. I hope you'll play your part, be an example, take your place in the future. Your great-grandfather was the past. And me, I'm sitting in the middle, astride past and future. It's a grand place to be. The only trouble is, you're not there for long, they topple you."

"Who does, Grandpa?"

"Never you mind, son. Never you mind."

The boy's eyes clouded from deepest blue to obfuscating black. The old man was vulnerable to those eyes and that face, with manhood in it waiting to be manifest. "And I belong?"

"You are an Angstrom."

"I don't just half belong?"

The old man looked at him sharply. "Now what do you mean by that?"

"I don't know," Lev said. He closed his eyes, sud-

397

denly tired. His grandfather sat a moment pondering the boy's face, then left quietly, placing each foot carefully so as not to wake him.

Lev heard the phone ring. It was an overseas call from Athens which Grandbee took from the study. The French doors to the patio were open.

Lev listened, knowing it was his mother. He was angry with her. He could have been dead days ago, and she just got around to inquiring about him. He was glad Grandbee's voice was cool.

"Is that you, Brilli? How are you? The boy is much better. We didn't know at the time, of course. . . . No, no, he is no longer critical. In fact he's up and about some, doing quite nicely—I'm sorry, I can't understand you. Try to calm down, Brilli. I told you, he's making a good recovery. There's no need for you to come. . . . Of course the decision is yours. Of course he's your son." There was a brittle quality to Grandbee's words. "But it's my feeling that these sudden on-again off-again visits are truamatic for the children. . . . Suit yourself. I'm going up to open Armagh, and the children will be with Howard. If you wire your time of arrival, someone will meet you. . . . No, I'm not holding anything back. He's much improved. . . . Of course you can talk to him. Lev!"

Lev kept his eyes closed.

Grandbee, trailing the telephone cord, came to the doorway. "He's sleeping, Brilli. I don't like to wake him."

The family broke up the following day. Maria had already been sent ahead. Ted flew off to New York, Brillianna left to oversee a professional cleaning crew at Carmel, and Tomas took the three children and a Raggedy Ann doll by plane to San Francisco. From the airport they went by cab.

Maria was standing in the circular drive, her eyes red and swollen. She said, "Mother of God, have mercy. Go to the study, children. Your father waits to see you."

Brill took Lev's hand.

Howard Knolls, tall and Nordic, a latter-day Viking,

looked at the children. They were five, ten, and eleven years old.

"I want to talk to you," he said. And remained silent. Brill looked at Lev.

"Yes sir?" he asked.

That seemed to bring Dr. Knolls back to his task. "As you know, your mother was returning from a vacation in Greece." That's what the family always said, vacation. Dr. Knolls began again. "On a flight into Rome, there was an electric storm. The plane went down. There are no survivors."

Bea continued to play with Raggedy Ann. The silence made her look up. Brill kept swallowing air as though there wasn't enough around her. Suddenly a terrible wrenching sound came out of Dr. Knolls. "My poor little girls," he said, sweeping them into his arms. "My poor babies, Mother is dead."

Lev watched. The three were one, convulsive in their grief. He stood quietly watching his sisters cry and went out of the room.

He passed the kitchen. He could hear the servants. "I got it on the radio. It was terrible. Bits of bodies strewn about for miles over the countryside. There won't be enough of her to bury." They had all taken planes. It might have been the one he was on. He wished it was, and then took back the wish because Brill and Bea were on it too.

He walked outside and up to the old sycamore. He leaned against it, put his head against it. Then he put his hand in the bowl. It was in this hollow place that they sometimes left messages for each other, he and Brill and Bea. Maybe Mother had left a message in there for him. He knew that was nonsense, that it couldn't be. But it upset him to find it empty. She had wanted to talk to him. Yesterday she asked to talk to him. And he kept his eyes closed. What was she going to tell him—*run away and play, Lev.*

Why was she uncomfortable when he was "underfoot"? He put himself to sleep nights imagining she would steal into his room. When he was asleep, that's when she would kiss and hug him and smooth back his hair. He had observed other mothers do this with their sons.

He knew he wasn't being fair. His mother was dead because she was coming to make sure he was all right. Was it his fault then, because he had fallen? Brill's fault because she shoved off in the boat without him? Or Grandbee's fault for sending the cable? It was all a muddle in his mind and his head was pounding.

—What did he know about his mother?

She was unhappy. How did he know this? Because some part of her beat in him. She had never been able to open her arms or her heart. He knew she was preoccupied with Brill, that her storytelling and flights of fancy upset her. She used words like *precocious* when she spoke of her. And there was a wariness in the way she approached her, as though she were afraid. He remembered she said to him, *especially Brill.* But whatever it was she felt about Brill was not enough to keep her home. She delegated that responsibility to him.

Why didn't she stay home? Or write? She never wrote. Once in a while there was a postcard showing mountains or water. She had drawn a tight circle, and was not able to let anyone into it. The circle was drawn not to keep him out, but everyone.

Why was that? Why had she done that? Was it a safer way to live, not to let anyone at you? It must be, because when she wanted to see him, that killed her. Why hadn't she said just once, "Lev, I love you"? Perhaps she would have said it on the telephone. But he knew she couldn't. She lived in a lonely, empty hollow, like the place in the sycamore.

Why had he pretended to be asleep? He hoped God would punish him in some terrible way for that. But he grew afraid and asked Mother not to let it happen.

If only Brill would come looking for him. Or Grandpa. Then he remembered Grandpa was out of town. He began to strike at the sycamore tree with both fists until they were bloodied.

Grandbee arrived. She had powdered heavily. She looked like a clown with all that powder. She found Lev and kissed him perfunctorily on the forehead. He pulled away. He was not used to having women touch him.

"Whatever happened to your hands?"

He hid them as well as he could.

400

"Go and wash up, Lev."

"Yes, ma'am."

Ted flew in. His blood was congealed. It was a kind of jellied consommé, a broth his heart had difficulty pumping. He found it impossible to be charitable to his son-in-law. Why the devil hadn't he been able to handle her? If he'd kept the girl in line, this tragedy would never have happened. The two men shook hands silently. There was not much to say.

It was hard to think that the woman flaunting her lovers in the night spots of Europe was Brilli, whose small hand he held when he showed her the Long Beach operation.

The doorbell rang. A Western Union boy stood there. He handed the telegram to Tomas, who handed it to Ted. He tore it open. "Arrive S.F. flight 44, 6:30 p.m. your time. See you then, Love, Brilli."

Brillianna took the wire from his hands. Her womb ached as though she carried a red hot coal in it. The fruit of her body turned to ashes. "If only I hadn't cabled. But when she phoned back, I told her not to come. I told her Lev was all right. It didn't seem to matter, she sounded completely frantic. It was guilt, I suppose. She'd been on a yacht party, that's why she didn't get the message, not until she returned to the hotel." When they were alone she said to her husband, "It isn't right. It isn't natural, when the child goes first."

"No," he said.

Brillianna was doing penance for sins remembered and unremembered. "She was so unhappy."

"As far as I can see, it was her own fault. Why did she have to make such a mess of things? She had three children and an upstanding husband. What else did she need?"

"A husband who was not too busy for her." Brillianna saw it all so plainly now when it was too late. "Brilli needed love. More love than any of us ever had for her. I suppose that was the explanation for what happened when she was in school, and then again with that terrorist. It worked for a while with her and Howard, I know it did. But his job was too demanding. *I* know how that can be, but I am made of different stuff. She was like you, she went looking, gambling on a strike. And it degenerated into one sleazy affair after another."

"Don't," he said. "Don't hurt yourself."

"I know. I can't believe she's gone, that I can't scold her or talk to her, or tell her my feelings about things. Oh Ted, there'll just be silence from now on. Just silence."

"At least she was coming home," he said.

They slept in each other's arms that night. Two people who had gone through a life together drew comfort from each other. There was no need for words, just body warmth.

The children had been returned to their grandparents' home. In the morning, on Angstrom's side of the bed, was Lev. He had brought a blanket and laid it on the floor beside his grandpa.

When you're starting to feel old, Ted thought, more is demanded of you than you can give. He picked the boy up and carried him to his own room. The child's thin arms wound around his neck. "Mother's dead, Grandpa."

"I know, son."

He was able to cry against the old man's chest, and Ted rocked him like an infant until he slept.

The morning of the funeral Maria dressed the girls and laid out Lev's clothes on the chair by his bed. When they went downstairs Grandbee was there to see they ate breakfast. After pushing his food around his plate, Lev stood inspection with his sisters. Grandbee straightened his tie, and told him, tie, buttons, and belt buckle must always line up.

Lev nodded mutely. He didn't understand any of this. What were they burying? Nothing had been sent home. Yet the large polished black limousines began arriving, parking one behind the other in the drive.

"The Family" were ushered to the first car. The door was held for them and the children climbed in the backmost section. Lev realized it was not actually the first car. Parked fifty feet ahead of them was the hearse. He could see sheaves of flowers behind heavy plate glass.

Brill took Bea on her lap. The child looked as though she would cry, not from understanding, but because of the solemn atmosphere and severe faces. "Let's sing 'Alouette,' " Brill said, and immediately the little girl's voice piped the rhyme. Lev enjoyed hearing their light voices. Why did the grown-ups need these little birds for their grim rite?

The procession began to roll, car after car. Great-aunt Elizabeth and the senator followed with their married daughter and son. Then came executives, presidents, vice-presidents, board chairmen, members of the boards of directors, lawyer, bankers, and friends who stopped by for tennis or a drink.

Bea Anna fell asleep in Brill's arms. Brill turned to him. "Do you think you'll cry, Lev?"

"Why should I cry?"

"I mean when the coffin goes into the ground."

"Mother's not in it."

"She isn't?"

"How could she be in it? The plane blew up."

"Kumju said some little piece of Mama will blow around the world, and she'll be there watching too."

"Think of that, Brill. And when they put the coffin in the hole, don't look. Look at me. And we'll both think that."

"All right Lev. Don't forget."

"I won't."

"Promise."

He nodded and her hand sought his.

They rolled through the cemetery gates to a garden of statuary and markers laid out evenly. For each headstone, cars had come, people stood, and gone away. No one comes back. Except they had to. Lev thought of Grandpa's joke about "dying to get in." He whispered it to Brill, but she returned him a blank look. Why was it he always did and said the wrong things with his family?

They drew up before a fieldstone chapel. The family assembled outside, a small group: Dr. Knolls, the Angstroms, and the Knolls children. The other cars disgorged mourners, who held back out of deference, yet pressed as close as they felt proper, to watch, to murmur in low voices and offer comments. "Three beautiful children."

"All quite different looking."

"But didn't you know? They all have different fathers."

They began to move forward into the chapel. The front pew was roped off with a velvet cord. An usher lifted this and the family filed in. Before them was a coffin of silver and black covered with a blanket of woven garlands. Even the pulpit was decorated. It looked, from the wreaths banked everywhere, as though all the flowers in the world had been stripped from stalks and bushes and brought to this place of death.

The minister, high-church Episcopalian, gestured gracefully, the lace of his sleeves moved as though in wind. He spoke of Brilli Grenville Angstrom Knolls, beloved wife of Dr. Howard Knolls, noted scientist; daughter of the great industrialist giant of modern times, that was Grandpa, and of Mrs. Grenville Angstrom, daughter of the hereditary Baron of Runnymede and mother of this vibrant young wife and mother, taken so suddenly, by God's will; taken at the height of radiance and beauty, spared perhaps unknown sorrows, but leaving, sorrowing, her three motherless young.

It went on and on. Bea announced she had to go to the bathroom. Brill whispered with the usher and took her out. The minister didn't say what the woman outside said, that each child was by a different father. Of course, that fit, *half brother*. He was eleven years old. He was capable of figuring things out. Dr. Howard Knolls, whom he had been taught to address as *sir*, was Brill's father. That meant he, and probably Bea, were illegitimate. *Bastards*. He felt pleasure in thinking that word, especially here in church, where the minister was extending his lace sleeves over all of them in a super-holy way.

And what did that make his mother, Brilli Grenville Angstrom Knolls? There were words picked up at school, picked up from Grandpa; words for women that went with men, did sex with them. Pushover, tramp, whore, nympho, hot pants. One girl whose brother he knew had been pointed out to him as "easy."

Who was his father? Did *she* even know? Had it been what the boys called a one-night stand, an accident, a broken condom in the back of a car? No wonder Dr. Knolls kept him at a distance, and Grandbee was remote but correct.

His mother too. "I haven't time now, Lev." Or, "We'll talk about it later." But time had gobbled her up. Later was *now*, and ended for her.

404

The service was over. Everyone remained standing in their pews while the family filed the length of the church. All the people looking at him knew. It was a thing everyone knew. He walked past their collective gaze, tie, buttons, and belt buckle lined up.

Once again they entered the cars and drove a short distance to the grave site. It looked quite festive, a pink and white striped canopy erected so they could stand comfortably in the shade. More tiers of flowers artistically arranged. The coffin, still flower draped, rested on short stanchions, you had to peer down very closely to see the earth to every side was excavated, that the coffin rested atop a meticulously carved abyss.

Grandbee stood thin and straight as a pole. Her eyes were dry. Beside her was Grandpa. He looked soft and marshmallowy. His big chest had caved in. He did not try to hide the tears that rolled down his face. It was hard to remember that his mother had been Grandpa's little girl.

It was of this little girl Ted was thinking. He kept reverting to the times that he had taken her, a bit of a thing, into the fields. He remembered once he had slapped her. He couldn't remember why.

Lev looked across at Brill who held her father's hand. What did Dr. Knolls feel? He didn't look as though he felt anything much. He looked as though he would be glad to get out of here. Lev liked him a shade better for that.

Maria held onto Bea, the other visible proof of his mother's indiscretions. *"Man goes to his long home."* They began turning a ratchet and the flower-laden casket started to sink into its precision-cut hole. He felt Brill look at him as they had agreed.

Why should he look at her? She had somebody. Her father, who was holding her hand.

He felt Brill's eyes on him, waiting, expectant. Why should he play that stupid game? She was always playing stupid games and believing them. A part of their mother blown around the world to be with them, to comfort them. Brill was sort of crazy.

"She's the deep one," Grandbee used to say. Was it deep or even sensible to have such nutty ideas? Brill's gaze was insistent now. She insisted he keep his promise, his part of the bargain. Why should he? He wasn't even her brother. Just a half brother, a bastard. Why should he look at her? It was only a box, an empty box. Everybody knew it. Grandpa knew it, so why was he crying?

The coffin disappeared and then the flowers, and now the rectangular hole, *man's long home*, showed itself. Brill fell on the ground under the pink striped canopy, in a dead faint.

Lev sprang to her, was leaning over her before anyone else. "I'm sorry, Brill. I'm sorry."

They pushed him away.

She'll never forgive me, he thought helplessly. He had broken his word. He had not stood by her as he promised, not helped her though those last desperate moments.

The children were confused, but everything around them continued in the same pattern. They lived with their grandparents during the week, visiting their father weekends.

Brill hunted out Kumju. She stood before him in the garden of horizontal trees. "My mother is dead." She said it over and over, a sort of chant.

Kumju replied in an odd way. He said, "You are as a spear balanced for throwing. And I will arm you with the spur of a white cock."

Brill looked with double seeing. Kumju showed her vaulted earth lying deeper than graves, lying past the igneous that dammed her grandfather's oil. When the earth shuddered, turning on end, the clay that made Kumju lay exposed. And when his great haunches were formed, it was of earth. Earth was his belly, earth the flattened head. And it was the earth that called him to a new task. "In the third generation," he told her, "is born one of the priestly caste."

Brill understood, and from that time brought him some small offerings. Sometimes she sat quietly, watching a line of ants gather to feed him.

"My brother Lev promised me. He promised me, Kumju."

"Forgive him, Mem Brill. He is as the king of Tekkur, whose official executioner never left his side."

She didn't understand that. But she made a treaty with Lev. "Do something extraordinary. A wonderful feat, and I'll believe in you again."

Lev walked light-footed on top of the seawall without looking down at the jagged cliffs that fell seventy feet to a pounding sea. Brill smiled. He knew it was not enough.

He stole the Maserati out of the garage and drove her around in it. She kissed him on the cheek.

Lev prepared for the ultimate test. With Brill watching, he climbed to the roof of the three-story mansion, a rope slung over his shoulders. His plan was to descend by means of it to the ground. He fastened it securely to the chimney and let himself over the side of the roof, paying it out as he went.

The venture was boldly conceived. However, an oversight was incorporated into it. He had neglected to measure the rope. He was past the top story when he saw that far from getting him to the ground, he would not be able to make it to the second level. Grandbee's study was located there, surrounded by a narrow balcony with decorative iron posts.

Lev swung at the end of the rope and took aim for the balcony ten feet below. He dropped directly onto one of the ornamental cast-iron spears which went completely through his knee.

Impaled, he hung there. He could see Grandbee at her desk. It was a cardinal rule of the house that when Grandbee retired to her study, she must not be disturbed. All the children were aware of this. Lev arched his body, catching hold of the post, in his attempt to pull his leg free. Pain swelled over him and he let go.

Brill hopping around on the ground beneath him, dashed in search of Maria. Maria fetched her husband, and the trio entered the balcony from the adjoining room and set silently to work to extricate Lev.

Grandbee glanced up from her correspondence. "What on earth is going on?"

The spike, the cement, his leg, Brill, the servants, were covered with blood. Maria and Tomas stood mute and apologetic, the boy dangling between them.

"I didn't mean to disturb you, Grandbee," Lev said through twisted lips.

Another convalescence began. He didn't mind too much. He gathered his sisters around him. "We have the same mother," he told them. "Half our blood is Angstrom blood."

"We have different fathers," Brill said. "I heard the servants. Dr. Knolls is *my* father. Who is yours and Bea's?"

"We don't know. And it doesn't matter. We are a different kind of family. There is just us. From now on, the three of us, we are the family."

Brill said Kumju must be told. Lev leaned on her shoulder and she helped him hobble to the distant garden. Bea trailed after them.

Brill had told the story many times. There was a special tone of voice in which all Kumju stories were told. The language was strange too, as though there were a spell hanging over the words. Brill claimed she didn't know what a lot of the words meant, and that frightened her. But Lev reminded her that he had been the first to read of Kumju and his origin.

Brill said, "No. I knew him before that." She began. And the story touched them as it always did with wonder and awe.

It happened in the village at the foot of the lava flow. Misu, in a self-induced trance, began to pat and shape the red clay of the region.

And the Ka of the god Kumju entered the figure. It had been intended as an elephant god to assist in the hunt for ivory. However, the Ka of Kumju guided the potter. There was the thickness of an elephant, with massive back and flattened forehead. But the Ka of Kumju did not care for tusks. The clay that was meant to curl forward, by his command was smoothed into a faceless mask. He allowed no features to be engraved, preferring a timeless appearance which he himself could mold through the ages. His extremities ended in a crouch, providing him with a solid base resembling the paws of the lesser Sphinx.

When Misu the potter completed the last thought-command, Kumju tossed the man's soul back into his mouth. The potter swallowed, stared at Kumju, and went into a fit. His arms and legs jerked, foam and slaver covered his mouth. Kumju was pleased. The man had expected to see a red clay elephant.

When the potter recovered, he crawled away and brought a saucer of milk. On entering the room he descended to his knees. Kumju continued to stare at him with his no eyes. Misu lowered himself to his belly and wriggled forward, pushing the bowl in front of him. When it was under Kumju's absent nose, Misu ate dust and backed off.

Kumju inhaled the fragrance of fresh warm milk.

Prince Sundiata, Hungering Lion, donned his mantle of ox tails to look on Kumju and win favor. He came with flowers of many hues woven into a chain. He too, when he saw the no face of Kumju, averted his eyes, prostrated himself and ate dirt. Kumju watched the powerful haunches of this princely warrior tremble and investigated his gift, sucking up the sweet, damp odor of jungle groundcover, catching a whiff of intensely rich and fecund humus that lay sprinkled on the spreading leaves.

So began his existence among men and men-gods. Ostrich plumes and the pelts of leopards, aromatic scents and fragrant resins quickened his senses. His duties were made known to him. He must drive away locusts, and assist the fields to produce a sufficiency of millet, sorghum, and tubers by summoning rain. He was responsible for bringing game into the area and fish into the waters. Red ochre, carnelian, baboons on leads of gold, and a naked palm slapping and quickening the beat of the deba until generations fell and the great ones were wrapped tightly in cotton bands and buried with caparisoned royal horses, standing. Such was the fate of Kashta, king god of Kush, who sent forces against Egypt. So ended Ali Ber, unifier of Gao.

This was the god the children stood before, and to whom Lev repeated, "We are the family."

After this their lives changed. There was nothing perceptible to the grownups they lived with. It was something felt by the three of them, a solid core, a common center. Brill would no longer think of pushing off without Lev.

She sat with him telling endless stories. Bea lay full

length on the grass while Lev was propped in the hammock, a pillow under his bandaged knee. Now Brill was older, she pretended Kumju related these odd tales to her. But it wasn't like that. Visions started in her mind like wellings from deep springs. She saw rain forests with leaf pushing up under green leaf, and a particular albino plant from which the chlorophyll was leached. Bea rolled on her stomach to listen.

"In the time of famine the people sat all day smoking."

"What's famine?" Bea asked.

"It's being hungry."

"Were they hungry?"

"Yes. Now be quiet and listen. The drum called deba never stopped. And the king's bathwater was powerful medicine and cured people."

"I wish I had some for my knee," Lev said.

"Well, if you don't want to hear. . . ."

"No. Go on."

"The medicine was powerful and the king was powerful. But not powerful enough to protect his favorite son. The great king feared for the life of his son, that one of his wives would kill him by poison. So he approached Kumju with dust and ashes on his head.

" 'How shall I guard the life of this son, whom I love best?'

"Kumju directed him to humiliate the boy in public while teaching him in secret the rain charms and the medicine charms, and to understand what the dogs with no bark said. It was done as he directed, but Kumju was not satisfied.

" 'It is not enough. Banish the boy, that he may be saved from the slow poison brewed by your wives with other sons. Banish him that he may return and rule.' "

Lev enjoyed these stories and her peculiar way of telling them. Bea clapped her hands and begged for more.

But Brill was troubled that they weren't stories in the sense of being made up. They were histories known to her. Memories that were no part of her experience.

She went with her fear to Lev. His solution—smash the god, throw him off the cliff.

Brill was horrified. "No, Lev. It's important for Kumju

to be here. But I don't want to be the one. I don't want to hear the stories anymore."

"Then don't listen."

"I don't listen. I hear them in my head."

"It's the same thing. I think you should make the decision to stop listening."

"What if he calls me?"

"Don't go to him, come to me."

"But you won't break him?"

"Not except he forces me."

So she no longer visited Kumju. He called her in sleep sometimes. "Earth mother, we must plant the baobab tree, and make sweet the wells of running water that the tribe of men have fouled. You are as a spear balanced for throwing. And I will arm you with the spur of a white cock."

Brill turned her sleeping head and would not listen.

They grew up, Lev more slowly, as boys do. He imagined many times asking Grandpa, "Who was my father?"

Then, as he was preparing to leave for prep school, he asked.

Angstrom turned his eyes on his grandson. He saw a fourteen-year-old, straight and determined. "You don't have to be ashamed of Lev Rosenfeld," the old man said.

"Lev? My name."

"Yes."

"And Rosenfeld? He sounds like a Jew."

"He is. He fought for the state of Israel. He was a soldier, first with the British, when he was only four years older than you. At Tobruk he saw some of the heaviest action of the war. Later he fought the British in the Resistance. When your mother knew him she was not quite seventeen. We, that is, your grandmother felt she was too young to marry."

"But she must have been married that same year to Dr. Knolls?"

"When it was found she was to have a child, the family thought it best to give you the protection of his name."

"Why couldn't I have the protection of my own father's name?"

411

"There was never any question of that. Rosenfeld was committed to a life of violence."

"And he was a Jew."

"That's true. Your grandmother, even if circumstances had been different, would not have agreed."

"My father never tried to find out about me?"

"He didn't know. He doesn't know. The family thought it best."

"You mean, I have a father somewhere who doesn't know I exist?"

". . . Yes."

Worlds spun in and out of existence and his stomach knotted. "I'd like to write him. Do you know where he is?"

"I met him once, many years ago when he was your age. At that time he lived in a settlement in the Valley of Jezreel called Ein Harod. They might know there."

"Thank you, Grandpa." He went to his room and wrote a letter telling about himself since he was born. Everything. The books he had read, the thoughts he'd thought. About being the grandson of Theodore Angstrom and oil and the sun. Especially the sun, because that was the source of all power, Angstrom power and world power.

He asked Lev Rosenfeld if he should come live with him. He asked him if he had a son. He hoped the answer to the second question would be no, that he would have a place across the world reserved for him, where he would fit as he had never fit here. He'd miss Grandpa, of course, but a grandfather wasn't the same as a father. He would take Brill with him, and little Bea.

When he reread the letter, he was ashamed of the way his longing tumbled out. Using that first letter as a guide, he composed a more restrained missive, including only the external facts of his life. "I have been told by my grandfather that I am your son. Have you other sons? And would you like to have one? I would prefer coming to visit you than going to Groton.

"You will be sad to learn that my mother died in a plane crash three years ago. Since then my two sisters and I live with our grandparents. I hope I will meet you soon. I am enclosing a recent picture of myself and would like to have one of you. Your obedient son, Lev."

Would the letter find him? How many days would it take? He waited for an envelope with foreign stamps. The reply from Ein Harod came within two weeks. It read:

"My dear son,

"It is a fine thing for a man to learn he has a son. You are my eldest. You are old enough to understand that I loved your mother and mourn her death. In the fifteen years which have passed, I am married to a good woman who would welcome you. We have four children, three boys and a girl. But your place. . . ." Lev let the letter drop.

The man was rich in sons. The last thing in the world he needed was a fourth son. He picked the letter up and finished reading. Lev Rosenfeld spoke of the death of his Aunt Sara. "A rare and beautiful person. In the 1956 crisis, she scoured the Gaza all night for wounded, and with a torch, led the medics to them. Her torch attracted enemy fire. *Sara Rosenfeld*, remember her name." He went on to advise him to finish his schooling, then if he wished, visit Israel.

His other suggestion was that he come for a summer and work alongside his family in the fields. A bunch of little brothers and a sister, and a strange woman, all speaking a language he didn't know. That had not been the way he imagined his reunion with his father. Besides his *real* sisters, Brill and Bea, had not been included in the invitation.

He made the decision to go to Groton. He reached a second decision. He no longer wanted to be Lev Knolls. He had been thinking of taking his father's name. But with three young Rosenfelds as heirs, that seemed superfluous.

He sought out his grandfather who ran the world these days from the end of a telephone. He looked up as Lev entered. "You had a letter, did you?"

Lev nodded. Nothing escaped the old man. "My father agrees with you, that I should get an education."

"Sensible," was his grandfather's comment.

"I was thinking. Before I go off to school. . . ."

"Yes?"

413

"I'd like to register as Lev Angstrom, if you've no objection."

The old man opened his arms and clasped the boy clumsily. "You and me Lev, it's going to be like me and my dad all over again. An Angstrom in the business. I can't tell you what this means. It's a wish at least twenty years older than you are. Well, as they used to say during the war, 'Praise the Lord, and pass the ammunition.'"

"Then you think it's the right thing?"

"We'll have your name changed legally. You'll enter Groton as an Angstrom."

"That's great," Lev said, not knowing how else to express the fact that he had made his position in the clan official.

"Okay, young Angstrom, tell me about the rest of your father's letter? He's well, I hope?"

"Yes, married. Hey, what do you know, I've got four Israeli siblings."

His grandpa laughed heartily. "He's quite a guy, your father."

"I told him about Mother. I thought he should know. And he mentioned someone who had died too. His Aunt Sara."

Angstrom's great gnarled fists closed and he struck himself a blow on the chest knocking the air from his body.

The boy was alarmed. "Shall I get you something? Shall I call for help?"

The old man got up and turned to the window looking out to sea until his breathing became regular. "Help? No, there's no help. The tide pool is still down there. It was a day much like this. . . . I'd like to see the letter, Lev. Or at least that part of it that mentions Sara."

Lev had it with him and placed it in his grandfather's hand.

"Leave me now. I'll return it to you later." Sara had been dead five years. He hadn't known. No wave washing up on shore told him, no storm cloud indicated it. 1956, the year France and Britain allied with Israel and tried for control of the Suez Canal with access to Middle East oil. He remembered how involved he had been.

The U.S., under strong pressure from key men, collaborated with Russia, and the triumvirate crumpled. Yes, America was run by key men without faces and without names. But Angstrom knew them. He had created them. One could say his damned oil had killed Sara.

—But really, he said sternly to her, it was your own inability to stay out of other people's troubles, taking on the burden of the whole frigging world, that didn't appreciate it anyway, that killed you, that wound up killing you. Cold, tired, walking over the Gaza, shining a frigging light, a beacon, a target. That was the kind of dumb stunt you would pull. I could count on you every time. It wasn't oil, Sara. It was your own goddamned stubbornness.

In the fall of 1965, Lev entered Princeton. Brill accelerated and was admitted to a small liberal arts college in the foothills of the San Gabriels.

She clutched the map showing the layout of the school. Repeatedly referring to it, she eventually located Wiley Hall, where she was assigned. Her roommate, Terri, had just taken a hot tub in her jeans in the hope of shrinking them to her own contour. She spoke casually of having been strung out the night before, and within five minutes was asking about Brill's love life.

"Well, actually, you see, I went to a girl's school."

"Oh wow? So what turns you on?"

Brill laughed to cover her embarrassment. "Just about everything, I guess. Being here."

"You'll get over that. That's frosh euphoria. It doesn't last."

Brill had trouble finding buildings and was always hurrying. Some of the books for her classes had not arrived. She worried about this. She was anxious to start out right, rack up a good record.

"Relax," Terri told her. "Enjoy. Look the boys over. Did you notice, I've got the kind of bod that can turn a guy on from the other side of the room."

Brill didn't know how to respond to these confidences. She began spending more time in the library. Her major was biology. In Reind's textbook she read, "Life may

415

have evolved from nonlife as gradually as multicellular from unicellular organisms, or birds from reptiles."

Where the road of life branched. . . . She stared into space thinking about it. Somewhere there was bifurcation, first life, simple unicellular organisms absorbing chlorophyll directly. They became plants. Others were feeders, capable of devouring and utilizing the stored energy of the plants.

Why?

Going up the scale, the carnivores ate the herbivores. *Nature, red in tooth and claw.* Was that God's plan for the world? A constant mindless feeding?

What if all these millennia nature had been working toward the product given uniquely to man, a mind? A mind so that the order of things could be changed.

Brill stopped eating meat. Protein could be gotten from other sources—soybeans, nuts, dairy products. She started patronizing the health food store off campus, munching sunflower seeds, not showing up at her eating club.

"She was Ray to her friends." The day Brill picked up *Silent Spring* her life changed. First she read the jacket material. The Nun of Nature they called her. She repeated that. Then dipped into Carson herself. "I believe evolution is the method by which God created, and is still creating life on earth." And again: "I felt bound by a solemn obligation to do what I could." Brill thought what it must mean to devote one's life to something significant. 99.9 percent of lives are lived and there's nothing left, no residue.

In the first paragraph she was reminded of Thoreau, who said of a fish he was watching in a brook, "Methinks I have need even of his sympathy, and to be his fellow in a degree."

The crux of the book came early. "Birds were moribund. They trembled violently and could not fly. It was a spring without their voices. No chicks hatched, the thin shells of eggs cracked and leaked into a sterile world. The trees did not pollinate. Roadsides were withered and sere. No fish jumped in the streams, a brown sludge carried what had been water to a slow trickling death."

Speaking from the pages, Rachel Carson said: "It was

not witchcraft. No enemy had taken this action. The people had done it themselves."

Brill forgot to go to class. She did not close the book but read to the end. Was it too late? That was the real question.

They turned out the lights in the library, not until then did she leave. She couldn't seem to catch her breath or be as she was before. This was a book sitting on the shelf with thousands of others. Yet it contained a call to arms.

Much more important than attending classes was to counterattack, fight-back, do something while there was still time.

If there was time. This chemical barrage was what they called spin-off. A result of World War II, of government agencies and corporations not anxious to go out of business. Lethal gases developed for war were modified to defoliants and pesticides. Chemists moved into agriculture.

"Spray," the farmers were told. The problem, as Carson pointed out, is that poisons increase and multiply in the earth. "If not another drop of DDT is used, it will proliferate in rivers for the next thirty years, the action of sun and water potentiating the lethal chemicals." They were sprayed from planes, covering thousands of acres. Even moderate spraying builds up fantastic quantities in the soil. Ponds and marshes are laboratories in which men unwittingly mix toxic substances which combine in new and deadly ways.

"All life," Carson lamented, "is caught in the violent crossfire."

Brill walked until she was sure Terri was asleep, then she slipped into bed without undressing. She dreamed of Clear Lake. It was here in California. They sprayed against gnats, using a dilute solution, one part DDD per 70 million parts of water. No harm in that. But it killed the swan grebe, a bird that fed on fish. An autopsy showed its body to have concentrated the DDD to 1,600 parts per million.

"It doesn't go away," she cried out in her sleep. "It doesn't go away."

Terri said in the morning, "You had a nightmare last night. You're cracking the books too hard. Better let up."

"I'm sorry I woke you," Brill murmured. Again she skipped class and found a quiet place, not to read, but to recheck certain passages and think it through. She found a tree to lean against. She was grateful. In her dreaming she thought there weren't trees anymore. "A few false moves on the part of man," Carson said, "may result in destruction of soil productivity, and the anthropoids may well take over."

Brill quivered for the millions of years it had taken nature in her blind turnings to at last, through man, provide herself with a brain, a thinking, logical brain. Was it an organ capable of consulting self-interest alone? Where was loyalty toward life? Was compassion no part of the cellular structure of the mind of man?

Streams were dumping grounds, the oceans overfished. There was no government agency for checking the pesticide in water. Cancer hazard from drinking water contaminated by chloroform and asbestos fibers was growing. Brill worried about life in the Carmel tide pool, the starfish, periwinkle, crabs, the brilliant rose and bronze sea slugs she had taken for granted. And the bottom-dwelling creatures: mollusks, glass worms, barnacles, clams, oysters, shrimp, anemones, or the small fish captured and released on the tide? Year by year they were dwindling with no one to note or care, let alone make a report of it.

It was obvious she couldn't sit under a tree all day. She glanced at her watch. She stood up. I've got to do what Terri said, she thought. I've got to get my head together.

She started walking. People knew. The kids kicked things around. But they were just bullshitting. And the professors, knowledgeable, full of statistics, not really caring. It was their job to talk, not to care.

Rachel Carson was dead. She was dying when she wrote her book. That proved people could care. It was a beginning. It meant hope, a nucleus.

Nucleus of what? She approached the idea cautiously. *People who cared.* There'd been such people in the past. The early Christians cared. Their sign, the cross, a pagan symbol of the sun's rays. Instinctively they had chosen the source of life. What was needed was a band like that. The

418

new humanity, who would not kill or harm living things, who would devote themselves to the protection of the earth.

Earth mother, Kumju told her long ago. She did not listen. She had not known what he meant. Perhaps she should not have turned away her hearing. The old god had been a watcher over cattle and sheep, over fish and people. He was of the earth. He could feel the poison seeping. He called to her, tried to rouse her. "You are a spear balanced for throwing."

Was that true? Could it be she? What had Kumju whispered in the garden so long ago? *In the third generation is born one of the priestly caste.*

What did that mean? A prophetess? Was that the way to rally people, make them understand? Her own family were the Pharisees, the money-changers in the temple. They were the defoliators, the manufacturers of the sprays. It was their pride, their tradition, beginning with Great-grandfather Angstrom.

Could it be these were her enemies?

And not hers alone? The enemies of mankind? And what about Lev? He was studying engineering at Princeton so he could take his place, accept the crown. It was a crown, as much as for the Saudi princes, to be an Angstrom.

What should she do? She wanted to take a stand. The New Humanity must resist the power of the state, be perpetually and forever on the side of life, fight the death that poured over them.

She began to see the scale of the effort to be made. It was necessary to be part Angstrom. Diamond cut diamond.

They would use the old sign. The sun would be the symbol under which they gathered.

"You don't come to the eating club anymore?" Terri said.

"No." She was startled, not realizing she had wandered back to the room.

"If you've found something better, let me in on it."

"You must be very careful, you know. I mean, of what you take into your body."

"I don't get you."

419

"Have you read *Silent Spring?*"

"Heard of it."

"You should read it. They are using sodium arsenite as a weedkiller and calcium arsenate as an insecticide. Mercury is compounding at a deadly rate in the bodies of fish. We're swallowing poisons with every mouthful of food we eat."

Terri came to a full stop, something she rarely did. "You mean you're not eating?"

"I can't. It isn't safe."

"Have you," Terri began tentatively, "talked to the doctor or the school nurse about this?"

"It wouldn't do any good." Brill's voice was gentle, but what she said was frightening. "They chose aldrin, one of the deadliest chemicals. Did you know it's an oil by-product? Shell Chemical is the principal manufacturer. My grandfather owns a piece of it. Aldrin turns into dieldrin in the soil. They were trying to wipe out the Japanese beetle. They sprayed from planes. They sprayed everything, children out playing, housewives on shopping errands. And of course, the animals. Birds trembled and fell from the trees. One woman watched her cat go into convulsions. They groom themselves, you know, by licking their fur. The veterinarian said to wash it off. But chlorinated hydrocarbons cannot be washed off, not from fruits or vegetables or children or cats."

"I know, I know," Terri temporized. She wondered if she was on something. She didn't think so. It happened this way sometimes. The pressures of college, trying to make friends, work piling up. And Brill seemed to have trouble just finding her classes. She was really hung up on this pollution thing. Maybe she was right. Perhaps you should lobby or take action. People just went ahead kind of half-assed, not knowing what the results would be. She herself was concerned. But it was one thing to be concerned and another to stop eating. She stared at her roommate. "Would you like to rap, you know, talk about it? I could get some kids from the dorm."

Brill hesitated. "They'd have to be sincere."

"Of course. What do you think? Just one thing," she stopped at the door, "you're not on pills, are you? You're not popping?"

420

Brill shook her head. "Why should you think that?"

"If we're going to help, we got to get it straight, you know?"

"It's you who don't have it quite right, Terri. I'm only interested in meeting people so we can form a nucleus. Can you keep a secret, Terri?" A fierce whisper passed her lips. "In this room the New Humanity may come into being."

Terri shook her head, but negatively. "Let me get some of the kids, okay?"

"Okay." Brill spent the time making additional notes. Of course Terri didn't understand in the slightest. She was an instrument, unknowingly working for the plan.

In twenty minutes Terri filed back with a premed student, a second year psychology major, a member of her biology class, and a severe looking girl interested in all aspects of theater, especially psychodrama and street happenings. Terri introduced everyone, although Brill had seen most of them around.

"Is there something on your mind, sister?" Ali Pasha, who was registered in her biology class as George Hall, asked.

Brill nodded.

"Why don't we hold hands?" the psychology major suggested.

Inez, the drama person, held out her hand to Brill, and rather self-consciously they formed a circle. Inez said, "Terri thinks you've got a problem."

Brill replied, "In the same sense that we all have."

"We're here to help," Terri reiterated.

Jim, the premed student broke in, "Have you been cutting classes, I mean, on a regular basis?"

Brill looked surprised.

"Just a guess. When a kid's in trouble, they tend to drop out."

"I know what you mean, man," Ali said. "You get so far behind that up looks down to you."

"It isn't that." Brill attempted to extricate herself from this misunderstanding. They had the wrong impression. "You see, I don't need help. But help is needed." She saw a rainbow trout trailing its rotten liver eaten by

421

fiercely multiplying cells enlarged with carcinogenic nodes.

"I don't hear what you're saying," Ali said.

"If you'll give me a chance," Brill replied. "We're all living in an atmosphere that is not quite fatal. I didn't say that. Paul Shepard, the ecologist, did. I want to organize a group. I want to start with the people in this room. We'll call ourselves *The New Humanity*. We'll spread the doctrine of Rachel Carson, save the earth and living things, even man, if he will let us."

There was a considerable pause. Inez finally spoke. "That's a cool idea. The New Humanity." She stared the others down. Most looked serious and even worried. "But you know," Inez continued, "to undertake something like that you need strength. Terri says you're not eating."

"I'm afraid to eat. Plants treated with benzene hexachloride, BHC, or lindane are monstrously deformed, they develop tumors and swellings. Their chromosomes are terribly swollen."

"Look," Ali said, "I don't like this. I don't think we should mess around."

"Let's hang loose. Okay?" It was the second year psychology student. He and Inez huddled, then called Terri, Ali, and Jim into their discussion.

Brill hardly noticed. She didn't notice people much anymore. She wondered about the nitrogen-fixing bacteria, that indefatigable band, the all but invisible threadlike creatures toiling in their dark realm to bind soil organisms together, working for life. When man introduces his herbicides the root nodules on leguminous plants are unable to form. The relationship is disturbed. It could mean starvation for the bacteria, surrounded by a sea of air-held nitrogen.

The psychology student was saying, "I feel she needs to be jolted out of this, not coddled."

"What do you suggest?" Ali asked abrasively. "Electric shock?"

Inez spoke positively. She was an upperclassman, used to deciding. "We'll stage a happening. It's a very effective technique. They use it in psychodrama with good results. We'll need to get more kids and divide up. People versus vegetables. We'll use aerosol cans and attack the plants, who will sink down defeated. Then the aggressors throw away the spray cans, go to them, lift them up. . . ."

"And eat them," Ali concluded.

Inez ignored him. "And shake hands. It's symbolic. Man has made a bargain with nature. Then we bring Brill up some dinner and sit with her while she eats it."

"Do you think it will work?" Terri asked.

"It will if you're here telling her what's coming off. Sort of a running commentary."

"Where do we do it?" Jim, the premed student, asked doubtfully.

"Right below on the quad. You bring her to the window, Terri."

"It can't hurt," Terri agreed.

"If it doesn't work," Jim concluded, "we have to take her to the shrink."

That decided it. The shrink was a fink, who telephoned parents. Terri guided Brill to the open window with an unobstructed view of the quad. The rest departed.

Terri didn't know what to expect from the drama about to be enacted. They had allowed themselves to be persuaded by Inez. Maybe it helped some people, maybe it didn't. Inez was not exactly an authority. However once the shrink got hold of you it turned into a real hassle. If they could avoid that. . . .

Minutes slipped by while the group improvised costumes, recruited actors, and wrote out placards. There was the beat of a drum.

Brill thought, the *deba*. The beat grew louder. Approaching each other from opposite directions of the quad were two groups. One consisted of students with signs pinned on them: *Government Protection Agencies, Wild Life and Fisheries*. These were farmers in straw hats and coveralls.

The other group was considerably more awkward. Hampered in their movements, they hobbled rather than walked. One person, completely encased in a burlap bag with the word POTATO stenciled on the back, tried to keep up with Carrot, wrapped in a long brilliant orange velvet cape, ripped off, for the occasion, from the wardrobe department of the drama school. Cucumber was similarly

423

attired in green with safety pins holding everything together.

Brill hardly noticed the figures. She was caught up in the music. Terri attracted her attention. "Look, Brill, down there. Just what you said, there are the farmers and government people armed with all those terrible things."

The aerosol cans of hair spray began their uncontested duel. Terri elaborated. She was the Greek chorus. "They are marching on the plants, spraying DDT, DDD, dieldrin, lindane, BHC, what was the other one, heptachlor, all the poisons."

Brill leaned out the window. The scene wasn't much different than that going on in her head. The cans were aimed and triggered. The plants reeled back, staggered, shrank in on themselves, withered, fell, sank down, stretched out dead before her eyes.

She pushed Terri aside and ran down the stairs, through the lobby and onto the quad. "Stop," she ordered the spray can holders. "In the name of the New Humanity."

They stood in disarray and allowed her to wrench the aluminum containers from their unresisting fingers. "The New Humanity owes a new fealty. No longer to man. Our loyalty is to *life*. If man can become part of the force of life, instead of backing death, manufacturing death, paying for death, if he can become part of life, then we accept him. Life is the rallying cry of the New Humanity."

There were calls of bravo! You tell 'em! Hear, hear! They thought she was playing, that she had joined in, thrown herself into their game. But Ali, who was the potato, got out of his sack. And Terri came bursting on the scene. They led Brill away between them. They took her to the student clinic. The resident psychologist was disturbed by what he saw, a staring, vacant-eyed girl.

"Was it a trick?" she kept asking in a bewildered way. "Were they playing a trick?"

"No," Terri told her, "they wanted to help you, that's all."

"I believed them because of the deba. I heard it." None of them knew what she was talking about.

An attempt was made to contact her father, but he was at Hanford, Washington, on AEC business. The grandparents were reached.

"I don't believe it," was Ted's flat reaction. "What does a school psychologist know? Bring her home, have David go over her, prescribe a tonic, and she'll be all right."

Brillianna sighed. These were complicated times, nothing was that simple anymore. But she wanted to be convinced.

Brill was duly sent for. Ted didn't like the look of her. She was pale, quiet, withdrawn and uncommunicative. Why was it that things always piled up like this? Two years ago there had been a political coup in Arabia. Saud, who succeeded Ibn Saud as king, mismanaged financial affairs to an unbelievable extent. It hadn't really surprised Ted when Faisal took over. He had met them both in '38. Saud hadn't a brain in his head; he was a puffed-up peacock with no guts, gumption or sense. Full executive power was quickly bestowed on Faisal by the council that "ties and unties." But it was obvious things couldn't go on like that. Why should Faisal do all the work, make the decisions, and Saud live like a besotted butterfly?

Still, a coup was outside Ted's experience. And now, when he was settling into a good working arrangement with Faisal, the British pulled out of Aden, leaving the Company and the American government isolated.

Brillianna knocked on the door of his study. She had come to discuss their granddaughter. Ted felt this was her province. In his opinion it came under household affairs. He had enough to look after.

"Ted," Brillianna broke in resolutely, "I want to talk about Brill."

"Yes, yes. Brill. Fanciful. Always was. But she'll be all right. She'll grow out of it."

"I don't know, Ted. I'm very worried. She absolutely refuses to eat. The doctor can't continue therapy in her weakened condition. He wants to hospitalize her and force feed her."

"No," Ted said vigorously. The problem had finally taken hold. He wrestled with it, leaving the British withdrawal from Aden in abeyance. He wasn't feeling up to this. He'd had a miserable session with his dentist yesterday. Suddenly he brightened. "Lev," he said.

"Lev? You're not thinking of pulling him out of Princeton?"

"That's no problem. He'll take a leave. Lev will know what to do about her. They're as close as peas in a pod. He'll talk sense into her, the way you or I or a half dozen psychiatrists could never do."

Brillianna hesitated. "But Lev's so . . ." she groped for the expression, ". . . far out, in his thinking."

Ted never failed to defend his grandson. "Just young, just young. Besides, let's face it, that's why he has a chance of reaching her."

Reluctantly, Brillianna agreed. She was not anxious for a hospitalization. At the moment Lev was the lesser evil.

Lev received the communication with concern. But he was not unduly alarmed. To have a breakdown was no big deal. If you were adjusted to this environment and this society, you had to be insane.

He agreed he was needed at home. His grandparents were too far removed from their generation to understand the special pressures kids now had to deal with. The heritage laid on them by their elders—the bomb and missile builders, the nuclear plant erectors, the food adulterators—was rejected. Kids everywhere turned off, dropped out. The government was escalating Vietnam, laying down a wall-to-wall carpet of defoliants. No wonder his sister flipped out. It was 1965 and there were peace signs in dorms all over the country. Fingers spread in a V was a greeting of the young.

American combat and support troops were in Vietnam. Lev's knee would keep him out of the draft, but if one were disposed to worry about things, well, there was quite a range. Lev himself had a letter folded into his billfold along with his driver's license and credit cards.

It had arrived four years ago. He never told anyone about it. He was at Groton when it was forwarded. Israeli stamps meant it was the reply he looked for. Lev had felt it necessary to inform his father he had taken the Angstrom name.

Addressed to Mr. L. Angstrom was an enclosure in

Hebrew and a translation. It was the prayer for the dead. It took Lev a few minutes to understand—he was dead to his father.

People lived with such things tucked away in odd corners of themselves. Brill worried about the strange stories of the earth which she claimed Kumju told her. It did not surprise him that all the evils lumped under the heading *pollution* overwhelmed her. He hoped his coming might enable her to talk it through. He would try to explain that most kids felt as she did.

Ten minutes at home reversed this thinking. He found Brill in the upstairs dressing room, the one done in gold and white with an excess of appliquéd butterflies. She was sitting on the floor, scratching them off. She didn't turn her head when he came in. She continued ripping at the butterflies. It was difficult to get them off without scarring the paper underneath. Once in a while her nails gouged too deep and she was down to raw board. Shreds of flaking gold paper sifted to the floor. *Especially Brill*, Mother had said. Lev picked her up. "I'm home, Brill." There was no response.

She regarded him with composure. He might have been a piece of furniture or another butterfly.

Grandbee was bad tempered about the butterflies. She thought the cat had got in and done the damage.

Lev sought out his grandfather. They shook hands warmly, and Ted clapped the boy on the shoulder. "You're looking in great shape, Lev."

"You too, Granddad."

"Oh, I don't know. I've decided people don't change as they get older. They just become more so. I'm more cantankerous than ever. My dentist made a goddamned bridge that won't stay in. I tell you, at my age, things are always falling down or falling out. Some great man said that. I forget who, but he was right."

Lev had not been listening. "I want to take Brill on a camping trip," he said. "Ten days, maybe two weeks. Show her birds flying, wild flowers by the side of the road. I want to show her what a psychiatrist can't, at least not from his office. I want to persuade her it is not that desperate yet. That there is time."

Ted pumped his hands. "That's the ticket. I knew I

427

could count on you," and he began to complain about the British pullout in Aden.

"What about Grandbee?" Lev asked. "Can we bring her around?"

"No problem there. She's desperate. Brill's just skin and bones. You saw her. Even Dr. Levinson can't get her to eat."

Grandbee gave in because she was at her wits' end. Lev wanted Bea Anna to join them. On this point she would not agree. "Absolutely not. I won't hear of Bea leaving school in the middle of the semester." Lev tried again, but she remained adamant.

It was already November, so they decided on Kauai. Brill showed no interest in the plans. Lev guessed she was bound up in a different existence. It was up to him to find a way to make the world real to her again.

At the air terminal, he took her hand so she wouldn't be frightened by the hubbub. She slept most of the flight, and he could see how worn out she was. She did not speak of the struggle that preoccupied her, but it showed. Her heavy lashes resided on lavender circles, which had no right on that young face. He could see the throb of the pulse in her neck, she was so thin and wasted.

The captain announced they were at 34,000 feet. They rode through valleys and craters of clouds, rimmed to brilliance by the sun. An ephemeral world that blew away. Lev loved flying just as he did sailing and climbing, anything that allowed you a different look at things. When Brill opened her eyes they were over tropical waters. They had descended to a lower altitude, and Lev was able to point out how clear and untouched the ocean was. The deep shades of color were reefs, around which currents rode, shelving into lighter hues.

"It looks clean," she said.

They made their approach toward the chain of islands rising from the ocean like humpbacked sea monsters. Breaking the trip in Honolulu so Brill could rest, they went straight to the Halekulani on Waikiki. The Angstroms were always given the same apartment facing the sea. The partitions between their sleeping quarters were Japanese sliding doors. The management had stocked the rooms with anthericum, wax-like in their red beauty.

There was an orchid lei on each bed. Lev crossed to her side and put the lei over her head.

"I don't like dying things," she said, and took it off.

He made her rest an hour and then escorted her into the dining room. A buffet was laid out and arranged like a still life painting. "Try the poi," he said. "That's too ancient to have any modern ingredient."

She nodded and picked up a taro chip to dip it with.

"And the fish," he said. "You saw that sparkling water."

She helped herself to a small portion. They ate outdoors, watching late bathers, looking at Diamond Head. Lev sipped a Scorpion, the orchid he cast aside, but there was a miniature paper parasol which Brill accepted.

Afterwards, they took a short walk along the beach, removing their shoes, letting the warm water lave their feet and ankles. The murmur of the sea was soothing and they turned in. He stole into her room twenty minutes later and was pleased to see she was asleep.

The next day they met their camping equipment, which had gone ahead to Kauai. They also met Bea, who was sitting on her suitcase waiting for them. Brill showed her first surprise and animation as her sister hurtled herself into her arms. "Bea! I can't believe it. Lev?" She turned to him for an explanation.

But Bea was full of the escapade. "It was incredible, it really was. I was called into Miss Heath's office, wondering which of my crimes had caught up with me. Then I saw she was holding one of those smelly lavender stationery sets with Grandbee's name in the upper right hand corner. I mean, it's unmistakable.

"Miss Heath said in that special voice people use when someone's dead, 'I'm afraid I've bad news for you Bea Anna, your Aunt Matilda has passed away.' You should have seen me, I was marvelous. I reached out for a chair unsteadily and sat down. I mean, the reason it was so marvelous, you don't sit in Miss Heath's presence. And she got me a glass of water with her own hands. It was like God waiting on you, you know? Then I recovered a little because I wanted to hear what it was all about. As soon as she said that interment was to be on the island of Kauai, I got the picture. Dear Aunt

Matilda. And dear Miss Heath, being unlike herself, all helpful and sympathetic. 'Your grandmother has included a ticket and asked that a school official put you on the plane. I will, of course, grant the leave for the purpose of attending the services. However, you will take your school books. I have asked your teachers to copy out the sections to be covered.' That's what makes my suitcase so heavy," she said to Lev, who had just picked it up.

He was the one to be hugged next. Caught off balance, he dropped the case. "Lev, it was beautiful! I don't know how you did it. There was Grandbee's spidery writing, and it even sounded like her, so proper."

Lev looked pleased. "I know," he said, "I've been considering a life of crime. Come on, we've places to go." He rented a car, dumping the paraphernalia in the back, and drove to Waimea Valley. Its immensity on a small island seemed unreasonable until he reminded them the island was the top of a volcano which extended to a broadening base on the sea floor three or four miles below. In that perspective, the vastness of the chasm was understandable. Comparable to the Grand Canyon, this was a verdant moss-covered declivity with shades of green mixed with brilliant blooms. A waterfall sent smoking spears into the jungle, the dripping could be heard from leaf to leaf, each a separate tonality.

"It's drenched in green," Brill said.

"In life," he reminded her.

"Yes."

Round one. Lev had fought for this.

He set up their tent on a remote beach beside a hau tree. Nearby a banyan put down stalks which in turn became trees, until there were a dozen. "The leaves are the size," Bea said, "not of dinner plates, but of platters. You know, Grandbee's huge Haviland platters from Armagh."

Vines twisted in strands through lush creepers with spiral leaves, elephant ears, mangos, bamboo, and stalk palm. Brill examined all this. "I didn't know there was so much beauty." Deliberately echoing Lev's phrase, she added, "So much life." Brother and sister exchanged glances.

Lev drove in the last stake and their tent stood an

outrageous man-made orange, a nylon sporting-goods orange. "Get into your suits," he urged the girls, "and we'll go after our dinner."

They changed, emerging to find him in the same torn shorts, to which costume he added a knife, swim fins, face mask, and handheld harpoon. They donned masks to watch and fins to keep up with him. The deeper tone of his skin was already a golden brown. They had to protect themselves with sun blocks and lotions.

In the water he seemed another, larger fish, gliding without effort. Before Brill's eyes adapted to the new element, she saw nothing. Then she realized she was swimming in an aquarium with striped sunfish and blue and white fish with banded tails of yellow trim. Maroon minnows came in a school, an almost transparent, oblong creature floated by her face mask. Some were gray with what seemed to be saddles across their backs.

But the gold silent fish that was their brother, whose dark hair streamed behind him, was hunting. He was intent, spear gun in position, stalking the surgeon fish, darting as it darted, closing, drawing back his arm. The spear flashed through the water entering the flat elusive side. A clean strike.

They surfaced, Lev shaking the hair from his eyes, laughing into their faces. Brill was invigorated by the swim, the salt water, the underwater gardens, even the chase for their dinner.

They foraged for wood, made a fire. Bea picked a mango and Brill washed it in the sea. Lev shook down some bananas and climbed for a coconut. The thirty foot tree bent under his weight, but gave up its fruit.

Lev degutted the fish, cooking it himself. For the first time in months Brill set to, she ate everything in sight. It was uncontaminated, taken from a clean sea and from unsprayed, uncultivated trees.

In two weeks it was a different girl who did her own hunting alongside the other two, who matched them joke for joke, who sang into the wind as Bea with her mellow voice led songs and rounds. Brill began to laugh back at the world.

One day as they lay on their bellies, full and replete, Lev said, "Do you want to talk about it?"

431

"I don't mind. I don't think I was crazy or anything. I just woke up to what they were doing, how they were treating our world. And I didn't behave in a sensible way, I flipped out. I think the kids meant to help, but they made it worse. You know, more vivid. If not for what happened on the quad I might have been able to keep it to myself. But I decided to save everybody. We were to be the New Humanity, under a cross that symbolized the sun."

Lev said, "Maybe it will still happen. . . . But you know, when you go back, and we've got to go back soon to that other world, the one that for some reason or other they call *the real world*, you're going to have to eat. Are you ready to do that, Brill?"

She nodded. "I've got it figured out. The problem was living in the dorm, going, or mostly not going, to an eating club. I need to buy my own food and prepare it myself."

"Won't that mean taking an apartment?"

"Yes, I'll do things right this time. There is a health food store in the area, but before, I only munched sunflower seeds. With a place of my own, I'll do all my cooking, buy organically grown food. No poisons, I'll boil the water, bake my bread. I'll stick to what is pure, and of course I'll eat."

Bea had been quiet, taking no part in this interchange. "Tell me about the New Humanity," she said, "what it means."

Brill thought about it carefully before putting it into words. "I think now it was a rebellion. Not exactly against the Angstroms, but against all the power they control and the pernicious use they make of it."

"*Pernicious*," Bea said. "How do you spell that? I'm going to use it in my composition."

"Shut up, Bea," Lev said. "Brill has hold of something. Angstrom power comes out black from underneath the world. Actually, there is much more power flooding down on us right now." They were stretched on the sand, the salt water not yet dried on their bodies, their eyelids warm.

"The sun?" Bea asked.

"Of course the sun. There's more power there than even Angstroms ever dreamed of."

"More than atomic energy?" Bea wanted to know.

"The sun *is* atomic energy, and every other kind. Oil and nuclear power are both stopgap methods. We'll run out of oil first, in about twenty-five years. And next we'll run out of uranium, and that's an end to nuclear power. But the sun is forever. Besides which, it's nonpolluting."

Brill followed out his thought. "There was a lot of talk at school about dropping out. Some kids did it with drugs. Some went off to farm and live on communes. The trouble with that, it was going back in time. But there's a new way. If we could figure out how to make all this glorious power spilling onto us *work*, then we could bypass the Angstrom power that kills the land and the water, that poisons fish and animals and man."

A distant look came into her eyes. "The New Humanity. The New Everybodies."

"And it starts with us," Lev said. He got up, and his sisters followed him to the edge of the sea where the ocean stretched to the sky.

"*We* are the family," he said.

They repeated, "We are the family."

"We are Angstroms, but a new generation. We reject the way power is used and squandered. We'll live a different life, a simple life, like we're living right now. Only instead of retreating into the nineteenth century, we'll move toward the twenty-first. Through the use of new technology we will be independent of the old power." He explained how they would go about it. "Brill, you have the vision, the true vision. You've got to think this through, work out the basic research. I'll use the resources of the company, try to channel them into alternative fuel exploration. And I'll do something I've always wanted to do, build a solar house."

Bea caught both their hands, her voice rising with excitement. "What will I do?"

"You're the pied piper. You'll bring us a following, extend the family, which should be an open community, into the New Humanity. You'll do it through your music."

As Lev continued to unfold their life to them, the great round globe sank in the sky. It remained full, giving the impression of nearness, seeming to reach the three on the beach, joining in the promise. This was the family Lev

433

founded when he was eleven and adopted when he was fourteen. Brill had almost paid with her sanity to move it forward. And Lev Rosenfeld still read the prayers for the dead over him. Any birth is hard, and this was a rebirth. He drew in the sand the source of their freedom and power:

The day before their intended departure, men in the khaki of island police broke up their camp, hustled them aboard an inter-island plane, and on to a 707 with the assurance their gear would follow. Bea's great eyes teared at intervals. "Do you suppose my roommate peached on me?"

Lev laughed. "You don't generally take a face mask, fins, a harpoon, and bikinis to a funeral." But it was not Bea's predicament that concerned him, or his own. It was the decision Brill had come to.

She sat beside him with set face. The world was about to fall in on them, and he could do nothing to prop it up. There was no way to have foreseen the length to which Brill would carry things. But he knew his sister. Brill's conclusion seemed to her a logical extension, a simple following out of their plan. She was no longer mentally ill or mentally stressed. Still, she possessed the Angstrom will, and was unshakable in her determination. Any reprisals the family might use against her would have less effect than his own attempts to reason with her.

Tomas met them; he was much sobered, like a jailer transporting his charges to a new facility. Very little was said in the car. Lev glanced surreptitiously at Brill. She was tasting her decision and finding it bitter. But that never weighed with Brill.

"Well," Tomas said finally, "you kids better have your answers down pat. They're all in there. Even your father, Miss Brill. And their mood cannot be described as one of joy."

"Grim?" Bea suggested.

Tomas considered. "I'd have to say heat that word up."

"Anger?" the youngest Knolls whispered.

"It doesn't matter," Brill cut in. Tomas looked at her in the mirror and shook his head. The gates opened as he employed the latest gadgetry and swung the car into the circular drive. "You'll find them in the living room."

Lev nodded. "I'll go in first," he said to the girls.

"We'll go in together."

The trio marched silently into the enormous room. There was a blaze in the hearth around which their grandparents and Dr. Knolls were sitting. Grandbee was doing needlepoint. The men looked up when they entered. Grandbee did not, she finished her row.

"Well, well." Ted spoke wtih a falsely hearty air as though police had not torn up their camp and put them forcibly on the plane. "You've done a good job, Lev. Brill, you look like a different person. Doesn't she, Brillianna?"

Grandbee looked up for the first time. "Did you really think you could get away with it, Lev? Did you think for a minute I wouldn't find out about Bea Anna?"

"Grandbee," Lev responded in a subdued tone, "can we hold the fire? It's the wrong battle."

His grandmother regarded him sharply.

"What he means," Brill said, "is me. First, I want to thank you for sending me to Kauai. I am completely recovered. Mostly because I had a chance to think things through. It goes very deep. My illness was a result of who I am. I find I can't be the Brill Grenville Angstrom Knolls any longer."

"Would you mind translating?" her grandmother snapped. "What exactly do you mean? That happens to be who you are."

"That was the trouble," Brill continued. "I was trying to be that person who lives here in this house and has all that I have. That was tearing me up. You see, I wasn't crazy in any crazy way. I know Angstrom money is funneled into chemical research and that we are responsible for the spraying and the poisons. Your arsenicals turn up

435

in feed to fatten livestock. Your mercury is dumped into the rivers and concentrates in the bodies of fish."

"Are you going to start all that again?" her father asked, speaking for the first time.

"Not really. I'm just laying a base, or trying to, so you'll understand. . . ."

"Understand?" Ted spoke in a constrained voice. "Understand what?"

Brill turned fully to her grandfather. "I am breaking off my relationship with you. My life is dedicated to fighting you. All of you are committed to a philosophy of killing our world. I can't be part of that. I can't live with you and be your granddaughter; I can't accept casually as I've done all my life the special status and wealth that comes from all this horror."

"Horror?" Ted repeated. "That's what your grandmother and I have given you?"

"And now that we're in Vietnam, the horror is increased. We are deliberately poisoning the rice fields there. My illness was my guilt. Knowing I am part of all this knots my stomach and makes me vomit."

Brillianna glanced apprehensively at her husband, whose eyes had become fixedly staring, and who seemed not to have words to answer her. "We were prepared," Grandbee said, "to be stern with you, Brill. But I see you are still quite ill. The best thing we can do is to get you back into therapy as soon as possible."

"I refuse."

"You can't refuse. You are not yet eighteen."

Brill outfaced them. "None of you have jurisdiction over me. Probably for the first time in my life I am completely well."

Grandbee laid her needlepoint aside. "You will do as we judge best. If you do not cooperate, you will be sent to Oakridge for your own good and until you've come to your senses."

Lev fastened compelling eyes on them in turn. "Then you'll have to commit me too, Grandbee, Grandpa, Dr. Knolls. If you don't allow Brill to leave, then I will leave. Of course," he addressed Grandbee directly, "you have the option of declaring us both mentally ill."

"Me too," Bea Anna said, taking her stand by her brother and sister.

Grandbee rose and, advancing on the young people, stopped before Bea and slapped her across the face. "As for you," she turned to Lev, "I shall not be dictated to by a criminal. Forgery, for your information, is a crime. Did you or did you not sign my name to obtain Bea's release from school?"

"I did." No excuse, no explanation.

"Brillianna," Ted interposed, "I think this has gone far enough." He proceeded, speaking this time to Brill, "I always imagined one of my blood would take pride. It was a great adventure, Brill. I'm sorry you don't see that. I never understood why the first act of rebellion has to be to tear down and disparage what other people have built up. My life has been oil. With it I put civilization into high gear."

Brill answered without hesitation. "I wish I could make you understand. There's no way I can continue here without despising myself." She added more softly, "I hope to be a worthy antagonist, Grandfather."

Ted acknowledged what she said with a nod. He did not speak to her again. "Drive your sister back to campus," he said to Lev. "I've had enough for one day."

"What about me?" Bea Anna spoke up.

"You deserve a hiding," Grandbee said, "practicing such duplicity. But I consider your brother chiefly responsible for that. You will go to your room, have dinner alone and reflect on your part in this. Tomorrow, Tomas will take you back to school."

"Yes, ma'am."

With the three gone from the room, Brillianna turned to Ted. Since Brilli's death he had been her principal concern. When there was a conflict she placed his interest even above those of the children. He settled down after the war, the episode with 'that girl' was never repeated in any serious way. His sexual life was kept under wraps. But she was content, especially as she grew older. She became his confidante in most other matters. He depended on her good sense and judgment. She had his respect, and in a way, his love. She knew how bewildered

437

he was by his granddaughter's attack on the company. "Brill doesn't realize," she said.

Howard Knolls walked to the window and stood looking out. He was pleased Ted had taken this kind of punishment. It gave him added satisfaction that it was Brill, his daughter, who told the old goat off. That was something *he* had never done. From the time Ted named his wife's son after that terrorist, Howard harbored resentment. He often thought he should have taken the million dollars she wanted to throw in his face. Ted Angstrom was capable of going on forever. And in the meantime he was tied to his job. There'd be a fortune someday, but he wasn't getting any younger either. He was not in sympathy with Brill's attitudes, but he was gratified at the outburst that demolished all Angstrom had ever accomplished.

Ted remained without movement, like one who has had a seizure of some kind and is afraid to test his parts. He did not reply to his wife, he replied to himself. "It is true, what the Saudis say, 'A man's enemies are his children and his posssessions.' "

A great many practical considerations followed Brill's break with her father and the Angstroms. Tuition was paid to the end of the quarter. This gave her time to look around and apply for jobs on campus. She took two: becoming a grader for Dr. Fredrick's Calculus 12 and a lab assistant. She stopped buying books, photocopying sections she needed or relying on the library. Those books she had, were sold. This was a wrench, as they had shared her dorm room, giving it the warmth of much handled surfaces.

Terri moved in with a boyfriend, which made it easier for Brill to find a new place. She spent a good deal of time looking for something she could afford with cooking facilities. She finally found a reconverted basement garage in the home of a professor. A mattress from the Salvation Army and her old lamp were supplemented by a wooden crate for her typewriter, and a chair borrowed from the professor's wife. This arrangement cost forty dollars a month. Her only other expenses were groceries conscientiously bought at the health food store, and prepared for maximum nutrition at minimal cost.

Bea popped in most weekends. She was the unofficial envoy conveying the well-being of the various relatives. And, in the course of this, carrying news of Brill to them. Bea was at first horrified at her sister's circumstances. She had never encountered such a makeshift existence as this bare room.

Brill, unperturbed by her reaction, was inspired to quote Marcus Aurelius, "A man can live well, even in a palace."

Bea began to see it in a more romantic light. "Every great scientist had a struggle," she consoled herself aloud. "Look at the Curies. This proves to me that you are probably a genius."

Brill laughed, "I don't think that's the right criterion, Bea."

"Well, even Grandbee says it shows a lot of character."

"And that isn't all Grandbee says," Brill guessed.

"I can tell you this, no one expected you to stick to it the way you have. Now they're beginning to think you'll do just as you said. Of course Lev and I could have told them that."

Brill made an attempt to interest Bea in the turn her own thoughts were taking. "We're studying crystals. Think of snowflakes, Bea, each one symmetric. That's because the atoms are symmetrically arranged in space. In a solar cell, radiant energy interacts with atoms and electrons in crystal lattices to produce electric current. The trouble is that an individual cell produces only about half a watt."

"Look, Brill, it's fascinating. I especially like the snowflake part, it's poetic. But I've got to dash. I'm meeting Grandbee for lunch. Love ya." This was accompanied by a big hug and the next moment the room was vacant.

Brill lay down on the mattress and closed her eyes. The picture became clear. A perfect crystal of silicon grown under high heat and sliced into wafers. These were doped with atoms of boron or arsenic in carefully controlled concentrations. Boron with a valence of $+3$ yielded a p-type wafer, arsenic with $+5$ an n-type wafer. When light struck a juncture of the two types, a small electric current was produced. She squeezed her eyes tighter—

now let's see if I have the valence figured out. Electrons in an atom can only exist in certain definite energy bands. Those closest to the nucleus possess least energy. Those in the outermost orbit, the valence band, are the most energetic. A small amount of light will release a valence electron so that it becomes free roaming. If it absorbs energy from a photon of light, it may jump into the conduction band, grabbing onto one of the implanted arsenic atoms.

Think of it, she told herself, as a knight's move in chess. It jumps over squares it is forbidden by the rules of the game to enter. When it jumps, it leaves a hole with one positive charge in the valence band. The electron and the hole form a pair that can be regarded as two particles, or particle and antiparticle. She remembered what her sister said. She too saw it as poetry of a kind, poetry in its high aspiration, but more like the movement of a ballet in its constant change of pattern.

Letting her mind wander she remembered two definitions of time, absolute changelessness and endless change. Her microscope made her believe in the second. In class she laughed out loud because she read that in 1577 a comet cut a swath across the sky. It did not know it had upset the Ptolemaic theory of constancy and changelessness. But it was very embarrassing because everyone saw it.

Brill moved all day as other students did, she crossed the campus half a dozen times, entered buildings, opened doors, climbed steps, rang for elevators. But the world to her was an extension of her thoughts. And thought seemed an autistic form of speech. Her isolated, subjective brain communicated not with the people she rubbed shoulders with, but the alchemists of old who told her, *Man must finish the work which nature has begun.* Or Paul Valéry saying of a poem, "One line is given to the poet by God, the rest he must discover for himself." She related this to science. If God would give her the dominant line for solar energy, she would devote her life to unlocking the rest.

If Brill's way of living and thinking was distorted by lack of human contact, she was not aware of it. Her thoughts interacted with her reading and with her experiences in the laboratory in which she watched a fraction of sunlight, equivalent to black body radiation at 6000° K, produce electric current in crystal lattices. The idea must be in both the person and the work, she thought. And ideas trembled in her mind. She didn't know enough yet to evaluate them. Were they foolish, completely speculative, wild? Or so eminently practical that they had already been worked out? She attacked knowledge fiercely trying to encompass it. Then she could begin to fan the intellectual fire that burned in her.

Sometimes she slowed down long enough to be lonely. She saw a boy and girl holding hands, and hurrying back to her renovated garage, stared at herself in the cracked mirror. A vibrant young face looked back: the coloring light, but the nature dark, intense.

She knew why no boy asked her out. Her preoccupied manner and rumored brilliance were only part of the reason. The episode freshman year was remembered. People whispered about her. She knew they did. They thought her strange, perhaps not quite right in the head. She didn't mind. The soul has no sex. She didn't need boys. Bea dropped by. Lev wrote. She talked with her professor about discrete energy levels spreading into energy bands. These human contacts were sufficient. Paul Tillich said, "The asking subject already has something of the object about which he asks." If that were true, she was part of silver and part of copper, freely conducting to produce a photovoltaic effect. She felt the sun shining on her for that purpose.

Her teachers spoke of her ability among themselves. It sometimes seemed she finished their sentences for them and raced ahead to the resolution of a problem before they had fully articulated it. She graduated with top honors at the head of her class.

Seated in the audience with other parents were her father, grandfather, grandmother, and Bea. Lev still had a week of exams at Princeton.

When the name Brill Angstrom Knolls was read off with the distinction *summa cum laude*, Bea stood to clap and cheer. The Angstroms and Dr. Knolls stood with her. Professors and then classmates joined the demonstration. Brill, in her long robe, looked like a young Erasmus, her bright hair flowing down her back. She faced the applause in stillness. It was the stillness of a deep wonder. These people she had passed every day, spoken to occasionally, worked with—had known and liked her, when she thought herself unknown and disliked. They felt she had earned the honors bestowed. The Grenville eyes opened very wide, as Grandbee's sometimes did. She turned to her classmates, her teachers, and her lips moved. Someone standing close might have heard her thank-you.

They did hear. They understood. The applause doubled. Brill paused a moment more, accepting the congratulations of the president of the college, and returned to her place. She had no idea her family was there. She hoped to see Bea, but Bea was a will-o'-the-wisp, maybe, maybe not. After the ceremony was concluded, her sister found her, planted a kiss on her mouth, and led her to where her father, grandfather, and Grandbee waited to congratulate her.

Her father shook her hand. "You did it, Brill. And we're all proud of you." She swallowed hard trying to keep her composure.

Then it was Grandbee whose narrow hand sought hers. "You may not acknowledge us, my dear. But we are very proud of you." An unwanted tear slid down Brill's cheek. She did not wish to call attention to it by brushing it away.

Her grandfather enfolded her in one of his well-remembered bear hugs. "You said you'd do it. And by God, you've carried it off in style. You've proved your point. You don't need us. But we need you. Why don't you come home?"

She looked from one to the other. "Thank you all for being here. It's very generous of you. Thank you for being proud of me. I'm proud of you, too. But nothing has changed. You are still tearing up my world in hundreds of ways. I can't be reconciled to that."

No one knew quite how to gloss over this. Why was it, Ted wondered, that he was able to deal effectively with kings, countries, and the Department of the Interior, but not with this reed of a girl. Her mother too, he had never known how to handle. The Angstrom strain made them willful and unheeding, but it was the untouchable quality, the aristocrat's stare that defeated him.

Brillianna, however, was able to finesse the situation. Taking Brill in with eyes matching her own, she managed to get the conversation into an acceptable mold. "Thank goodness you're looking well, Brill."

Such a simple comment and so impossible for him to come by. The plain truth of it was, he was not up to these women.

"I am well," Brill replied. "You look well too, Grandbee."

Her father asked if it was true she was to receive a National Science Foundation fellowship.

"Yes."

"Will you do your graduate work at Berkeley?"

"No. At Stanford. I was contacted by the chairman of the physics department, Professor Barrington. I'll have a free hand, and at the same time, high-powered advice if I need it, which I certainly will."

"Did you hear me yelling?" Bea interrupted. "When you walked out on the platform, I yelled my head off."

"Well," Ted cleared his throat for another try, "there's no point standing around. Can we take you out to dinner, just tonight, by way of celebration?"

Brill stood her ground. "No, Grandpa. But I do appreciate that you all came. I know you don't understand, and that makes it all the nicer. Thank you." The tall slender girl with the delicately chiseled features walked away from them.

Bea started to cry. Grandbee put her arms around her. "Come, come, my dear. You and I have lived with Angstroms too long to expect anything else. If there's a hard way, they'll take it."

"Now why should you say that?" Ted asked in an aggrieved voice.

"Because it's true," his wife replied.

Augmentation occurs both in a crystal and in a plant. Yet, are they growing in the same way? The crystal is regular and periodic, the living organism irregular and highly differentiated. But order is still there, proceeding from subtler axioms. With a pencil Brill traced drawings of stubby forms that reminded her of an aborted fetus. No wonder those Fermi surfaces were referred to as 'monsters.' But they must have been called that by someone working too late at night. They were just mathematical diagrams representing the energy structure of a crystal in momentum space. She should force her mind back to the experiment and stop musing about matter, life and order.

The experiment on which she had spent three years had yet to produce clear-cut results. The procedure was to start with the known forces between the particles and the known laws governing their motion. The whole mess of equations was then poured into the computer, whose predictions were tested by further experiment. These were found to be right in some respects, wrong in most.

There followed dread, immobile stretches where her brain, like a prisoner, sought and pried at crevices and crannies looking for escape. Sometimes a new hypothesis blew into her mind. Sometimes it was erected painstakingly piece by piece. So far there was nothing conclusive. Many times she thought she had hold of it, only working on to prove herself wrong.

But hadn't Bertrand Russell said, "A piece of matter is a series of events obeying certain laws"? On these sheets of paper she was plotting the future. This was immensely exciting, even if it was the future of an electron within a Fermi surface. She focused the extraordinary seeing of her mind's eye to follow the trajectories of quasiparticles in a magnetic field.

Brill pushed back her hair, a childhood gesture when it flowed about her face and got into her eyes. These days, it was caught severely back and held by a rubber band.

She had worked unremittingly for weeks, enthusiasm propelling her forward. But tonight she was tired. Professor Shonin, who shared the lab many evenings with her, appointing himself mentor and friend, looked at her with concerned, nearsighted eyes and said, "Do not forget, Brill, there is a world outside of academics."

Usually she nodded without looking up. But tonight she folded the Fermi surfaces into a manila envelope and listened.

"Remember Goethe: 'Gray, dear friend, is all theory, and green life's golden bough.' I sometimes wonder at our craving to make order and sense out of nature."

"Perhaps," Brill said, "we crave it because it is there. Newton thought that. He once wrote that everything may depend on certain forces by which bodies are either mutually impelled toward each other and adhere in regular figures, or are repelled and secede from each other. We know it's true for the large heavenly bodies. We know it's true for the smallest, those we can't see except by their movement."

"Give it a rest tonight, Brill. You look done in."

"I think you're right. Goodnight, Dr. Shonin."

"I'm about to call it a day too. I'll walk you across campus."

The offer surprised Brill. In the two years they had worked side by side she had never seen him look up from his calculations, other than to meticulously wipe his glasses or to quote good advice. He never dared supply any of his own. However, she accepted gratefully. It would be pleasant to have someone to talk over her hopes and frustrations with.

Dr. Shonin, it seemed, was determined the conversation proceed on a more personal plane. She evaded questions as to her family and interests outside her work, so he spoke of himself. He was preoccupied with the fact that his hairline was receding. Brill was surprised at this vanity in Dr. Shonin. She would never have guessed he gave a thought to his appearance.

"How old would you guess me to be?" he demanded.

"I don't know. I'm not awfully good at judging ages."

"Thirty-seven. I'm thirty-seven. And when I look at you, so dedicated, so full of enthusiasm, willing to work your life away, *give* your life away, I am reminded of myself. And what do I have for the long grind? Some interesting results, some publications. And I am on the tenure track."

"What should you have?" Brill asked him.

"What other people do. Friends, a little human warmth. Perhaps a family. I let it all go by."

Brill didn't comment. They had left the building and were standing hesitant in the grounds.

"Which way?" he asked her.

"It isn't necessary to see me home."

"I know that. I'd like to."

Brill took the usual turn, Dr. Shonin at her side. "I don't even suppose you know my Christian name," he said.

"No, as a matter of fact, I don't."

"It's Ivan. Although most people call me John."

"Ivan is more interesting."

"You have a strange name. Brill."

"It's derived from Brillianna. It's been in the family for years."

"Very interesting," he said.

She turned away in embarrassment, unsure whether he meant the name or herself.

Ivan Shonin made conversation at her doorstep, but she did not invite him in. Alone in her studio apartment she prepared herself a cup of tea and thought about him. Not actually about him, about herself. For the first time since she had moved in three years before, she looked at her surroundings, amazed the place was so pedestrian. Why had she done nothing to fix it up? Not an interesting texture, color, or even print had been added. It was as drab as the day she took it. She kept it clean. And it was tidy. But there was no hint, no evidence that Brill Angstrom Knolls lived here.

She realized that Brill Angstrom Knolls had slipped away from her. She hadn't thought about her recently. She had been too absorbed, too preoccupied with the trajectory of a conduction electron in a constant magnetic field. But wasn't there another kind of trajectory too? A personal one that had to do with herself as a woman? She was twenty-four. She had never slept with a man. She sublimated restlessness and physical urge in her work. Later, she always thought, there's plenty of time. But as she sipped her tea her thoughts returned to Dr. Shonin. Was he a projection of herself a dozen years from now? She freed her hair from the rubber band and got up to look at herself. She was pleased with what she saw.

Opening the bathroom mirror, she took out the pills that she had purchased several years ago. She read the instructions and saw that to prevent ovulation a course of two weeks was necessary. She had made up her mind— to be a virgin at her age was ludicrous and the remedy couldn't wait two weeks.

The next day, on the way to the lab, she stopped at the drugstore and bought a package of condoms, certain that it was not a commodity Ivan Shonin customarily carried. She ran up the steps of the physics building with her hair falling free down her back. Ivan Shonin seemed to have difficulty concentrating his attention on the resonance spectra he was subjecting to a statistical analysis.

Brill wasn't interested in courtship, romance, or marriage. Perhaps the only part of the plan she neglected to think about was Ivan Shonin. She had confidence in his physical health; he was certainly not promiscuous, so she ran no danger of venereal disease. Like a good scientist, she had controlled all factors. When they reached her door that evening, she suggested he come in. She could tell he was nonplussed. He had been prepared for a siege. Perhaps he was disappointed.

There were only two chairs. He sat in one of them. She noticed for the first time that the bed was a rather prominent feature of the room. "Can I fix you something? Some bread and cheese, maybe? And I have wine."

"No, thank you. It's very kind of you. Did you want to talk about your work, perhaps further elucidation . . . ?"

"No, I'm not thinking of my work. I'm thinking of the line from Goethe you quoted the other day. Remember? 'Gray, my friend, is all theory, and green life's golden bough.'"

"Yes," he said a trifle uncomfortably. "Well, there may be some truth to it."

"Ivan," she smiled to encourage him. "I'm going on the assumption that there is." And before his astonished eyes, she pulled her sweater over her head and stepped out of her skirt. The skirt, being well made, had its own lining, therefore she wore no slip. She seemed quite at ease in plain white brief nylon pants and a white bra across her wide, but far from full breasts.

"Brill." He stood up, knocking over the chair in his agitation. He picked it up and set it back where it belonged. "Brill," he said again, "I never imagined. . . . Are you sure you want to do this?"

She continued to stand there for his inspection. Surely the next move was up to him.

Ivan came up to her and put his arms around her. She had never been kissed by a man before. Tense and expectant, the embrace fell short of her expectations. "Aren't you going to take your clothes off too?" she asked him.

"Well, it isn't necessary."

"I'd rather you would."

He stripped down to blue shorts. He hadn't an athletic build, but was a slender man about Brill's own height. His legs were somewhat knobby and exceedingly hairy. "All the way," she said, and reaching around unfastened her bra.

Simultaneously they stepped out of the material that covered their sex organs. He was not in a state of erection, but looked full and quite lengthened. He approached her, and to her surprise she found herself placed on the bed. His hand stayed on her buttocks and she drew her knees up so that her labia presented themselves fully. He busied himself massaging and manipulating. A groan escaped from between her teeth. She had lost Brill and become demented. Her swollen genitalia demanded, coaxed for his. She felt him rubbery, semihard, bumping against her, unable to thrust sufficiently for penetration.

Her own frenzy subsided. "It doesn't matter, Ivan. Let's eat the bread and cheese now."

"We'll get crumbs in the bed," Ivan said.

"It doesn't matter." She got up and moved around the

room naked, placing the bread and cheese on a cutting board and pouring two half glasses of wine. She returned to sit beside him on the bed. They each helped themselves, munched and swallowed. Suddenly Ivan was at her again. This time he was successful.

Brill got up and took a shower. When she came back, she was wrapped in an old terrycloth robe. Ivan was completely dressed. He was doing a great deal of talking, making a great many plans. "A friend of mine has a cabin at Half Moon Bay. I can get the use of it weekends."

"No." Brill spoke so decisively that he stopped mid-course and looked at her. "No, you're a nice person, Ivan. But. . . ."

"It can happen to anyone the first time. It was all right afterwards, wasn't it?"

"It was," she said. "That's why I can't see you again, or let it happen again."

"What are you talking about? We've entered into a relationship."

She opened the door. "I'll move to a new lab. Goodbye, Ivan."

"But why? Didn't it mean anything to you?"

"Yes, it did."

"It didn't," he said. "You're a frigid bitch."

"I suppose so," she said indifferently.

"No, wait, Brill. Forgive me. You were alive with warmth and passion. I felt it. I failed you," he said miserably.

"No, please don't think that. It's that . . . it's that I can't have my life disturbed."

"God in heaven," he said staring at her incredulously, "I believe you."

"Goodbye, Ivan."

There was no use trying to explain. She shut the door. The tumult he roused in her would dissipate her energy. She was meant to be the constantly varying interior space through which current traveled and charges flowed. The passion in her could not be channeled toward one man, not even a man she liked and respected such as Ivan Shonin. She cleared away the food, rinsed, dried, and put the two wine glasses in the cupboard.

Somewhere between night and morning, tossing on her

no longer virgin bed, an idea came to her. She sat up and without turning on the light, scrawled the word *noncrystalline*. Then she slept.

When she woke, a mental paralysis held her. She couldn't remember what word she had written. She knew it had been only one. What if it conveyed nothing, was the result of feverish night speculation, a dream even? She forced herself to her elbow and looked at the word long and hard. Her heart beat again, and a great joy burst the circumference of her being, spreading out to grapple the entire world.

Doping, or adding of controlled impurities to semiconductor crystals, was accomplished by gas diffusion, or recently by more accurate but extremely costly implantation with an ion accelerator. By either technique, making a silicon solar cell was a high precision process, time-consuming and expensive. The word jotted in the night was her answer: noncrystalline.

Noncrystalline semiconductors were known. Certain plastics such as pyroid were thermally and electrically anisotropic. If their physical and electromagnetic properties could be analyzed mathematically by some extension of the Fermi surface method, the way might be open to fabrication of solar cells on a mass basis. The vision in her head was of solar cells reproducing themselves by controlled polymerization.

She let herself into the lab early. By the time Shonin arrived, her things were cleared out. There was no difficulty getting space elsewhere. She went first to Dr. Baines, the mathematician on her committee, before tackling her director of studies. Baines had a fondness for far-out ideas and often discoursed to her on his conjectures about 4-manifolds. She outlined her project in carefully constrained language, describing objectively while the heavens opened and angel wings pulsed, and a clear and present picture of Kumju filled her mind. *You are as a spear balanced for throwing.* Yes, yes, and she continued to lay forth her ideas in detail. "The electronic characteristics of silicon and other metallic semiconductors are understood and largely predictable by the theory of Fermi surfaces. My research will be directed to developing an analogous theory for noncrystalline materials."

451

"That's quite a challenge," Baines said. "How are you on Lie algebras? You ought to sit in on Wybourne's seminar this term. Just the thing you need. But I feel I must warn you—your proposal, while tremendously exciting, is not a simple extension of an established field. You'll be off in the wilderness all by yourself."

"I plan to start with polycrystalline alloys. They should have some similarity to the pure crystal case. Then, if I'm lucky, I'll get into completely amorphous substances."

"Good, good. Of course, you'll have to get Professor Barrington's approval. But I see no difficulty there. I'll talk to him if you want. He'll give you the same warning I did. You're cutting out an awful lot of work, and it could come to nothing. You're a lot safer doing your thesis on some little piece of Barrington's work, but this—this could be great." He bubbled on, writing on a pad, the board, his desk blotter, pulling books and journal articles out of piles that leaned against the overcrowded bookcase. "And look into long-chain organic polymers, such as Saran, the various vinyls, all those synthetic petroleum products."

Brill looked up sharply. Of course, it would mean working with petroleum synthetics. Perhaps an Angstrom could not escape the crude, even in her generation. Or was it more likely that no one of her generation could escape the by-products of the Company? She thanked Baines, went to her room, and spread out her notes.

"Arm me with the spur of a white cock," she whispered and plunged into months of investigation. She worked at white heat, as though the sun, that great outflow of fusion energy, showering the world so completely, wanted to cooperate through the mind of this young woman and transmit its ultimate gift to mankind.

Her professors took to dropping by the office she shared with two other graduate students; and people she didn't know joined in the discussions of electron velocity conventions, needles on Fermi surfaces, Fermi-Dirac statistics, quasiparticle pairs, space groups, and lattice vibration spectra. Half the time she nodded dutifully and copied down the chalk marks, hoping to make sense of them later.

Most of the leads she was given petered out. She was forced to develop her own mathematical tools. Her trips

452

to the lab became less frequent and finally ceased. The battle now was between her and symbols, integral signs, arrows, strings of parentheses. Her idea, so simple in concept, became intolerably complicated. She forgot an analysis done six months earlier and spent a week resolving a problem the answer to which was in one of her old notebooks. At this point she suddenly saw that the superposition of all possible space lattices was an utter impossibility. Three years of graduate work, three years of visionary hope drained out of her. She felt as though she had slashed her wrists and looked on while her blood poured out.

After an hour or so she gathered up her papers, walked calmly out the door, along the mall and past the medical center, looking for a wire trash basket that was not already overflowing. She found one with a chain around it, deposited her work in it, and returned to her room where she sat staring at the blank wall, sipping Pepsi-Cola. What embittered her most was that she had never taken time to hang anything on the walls or learn to drink something stronger.

She woke the following morning with the stunning realization that by restricting consideration to those lattices that satisfied some regularity condition, the problem could be solved.

Statistical regularity. That was the way to go—my God, her equations were at this moment in a wire trash bin. She raced to her bike and pedaled desperately past the shopping mall and across the medical center. Was this the day for trash pickup? Had dogs got into it in their quest for hamburger wrappings? She saw herself at the city dump searching through mounds of junk for her notepads, begging the watchman to help her find the key to solar energy.

Her papers were where she had thrown them. And from the moment she recovered them everything went miraculously well. Kumju tested her, and she had nearly crumpled. But now tests and hurdles were behind her, and the paper wrote itself. From the new axioms Brill was able to prove that her generalized Fermi surfaces were closed; consequently, particle motion along them was periodic. A host of corollaries followed from this

453

theorem, yielding specific clues to the nature of the non-crystalline materials that could be utilized. Now workers in the laboratory could begin the hunt for actual substances that satisfied the required conditions, the 'Brill A. Knolls conditions' as they would be called. Her job was done.

Professor Barrington called her into his office. "I like it. I like it very much. There's a wealth of new ideas here. When do you expect to have it written up in final form?"

"I've given copies of the rough draft to Professor Bitterbaum and to Dr. Baines, for their comments."

"Well, get on their tails. Don't delay. We've got to get this ready for publication fast. I was talking about your results to some people back east. The upshot is, the Institute for Advanced Study may offer you an appointment. This is almost unprecedented. Of course, nothing is official as yet. You must concentrate on publication. And in the meantime, allow me congratulations and all. I am very proud indeed to have had even a small part in the work you've done at Stanford."

Brill left his office in a daze. She had expended the power she knew herself to possess. It was a glorious feeling to have used yourself up. She felt like Copernicus who gave the earth its initial push: that it rotate. She had taken aim, the spear left hand and mind, traveling into imagined space unseen but knowable. It was a marvel, a thing of infinite beauty. She recalled that in her first fumbling explanation to Bea in her undergraduate years, she used the example of a snowflake. Her intuition told her even then there was beauty. And not beauty only, but a path into the future. Radiant energy followed paths she herself had plotted. In describing and predicting it she became part of the process. She imagined herself flowing like the current she controlled, flowing, not walking home.

The Institute. She was a young woman and the Institute had harbored Einstein. She couldn't quite take it in. There wasn't time for it anyway, she shook off the glory and began to consider how to compact years of notepads into sentences and paragraphs. Writing was difficult. Thought came to her in concepts, in great clouds, never in the words it must ultimately be translated into.

Having lived in a world of her own invention, she must now descend and cope with a real one. Typing was the next chore facing her. She hadn't the money to have it done by the department secretaries. But when she finished the title page, it was beautiful.

GENERALIZED FERMI SURFACES ON
A POLYLATTICE

A dissertation submitted in partial satisfaction of the requirements for the degree
Doctor of Philosophy in Physics

by

BRILL ANGSTROM KNOLLS

Committee in charge:
  Prof. H.L. Barrington, Physics, chairman
  Prof. A.J. Bitterbaum, Mathematics
  Prof. Y.N. Aliprantis, Engineering
  Prof. J. Baines,   Physics

1972

It took ten laborious days and three packs of Korectype before Brill was able to distribute legible copies of the dissertation to the members of her committee. To put semiconductor photovoltaic cells out of her head, she went to the movies. The next day she picked up a novel. How long it had been since she read to be swept away. Toward the end of the week Dr. Baines came to see her.

His task, he explained, was an unpleasant one. At first she thought he was trying to draw her attention to some grammatical solecism or perhaps correct a reference. But he quickly disabused her on this score. "It seems a graduate student of mine, Jules Fine—you know Jules?—anyway, after a careful perusal of your paper he seems convinced there is a flaw in your proof."

"A flaw?"

"Fine went over the question in point with me, and I must say his argument was quite convincing. But it is equally probable that we misinterpreted your meaning. What is at issue is that you proceed on the basis that your generalized surfaces are compact. Is that correct?"

Brill looked down at the manuscript, it blurred before her eyes. "I prove it, using the uniform boundedness principle."

"I read that proof and it seemed okay to me. The trouble is, Fine has a counterexample. In other words, an unbounded Fermi surface."

"No, that's not possible," she said. "The trajectories would fly off to infinity."

"Exactly what Jules Fine said. And in that case the paper collapses."

"But. . . ."

"Check your mathematics, comb through it carefully. It is easy for a small error to creep in, then be compounded. It happens to all of us. When you live as close to your work as you have, well, perspective tends to get lost. Then again, you may be able to clear this up. Anyway, good luck."

She could see his mind was already made up. He believed the calculations leading to her principal theorem to be wrong. In a panic she dug out all her old notes. These were the bare bones. On this skeleton the whole edifice rested. If the compactness theorem failed, the whole thing crashed.

She reworked page after page, her mind analyzing as though the work were some other person's, as though she had nothing to do with it. There it was, glaring out at her. A hole in the mathematics. Not a small discrepancy. But a hole so big you could drive a truck through it. There was no way to repair it. And out the window went compactness, and with compactness went her whole thesis. At that moment objectivity fell away. Light added to light had produced darkness. Her mind went dark as though someone had thrown the main switch. "In the secret hour," Jung said, "the parabola is reversed, death is born."

The death of her work was a trauma she did not know how to endure. It hadn't been properly born, but was somehow wedged in the birth canal. There it rotted and festered, swelling with noxious gases that invade any carcass. The trouble was, she couldn't get away from it. Even dead and deformed it was part of her.

Everyone was very kind. On the advice of her director, Brill wrote a short preface to her stillborn thesis, taking account of the counterexample discovered by Mr. Jules Fine. The doctoral committee, recognizing the effort which had gone into the paper, declared her research qualified her for the Ph.D. degree. This was awarded in absentia. Brill moved away from campus to a small apartment in Carmel, where she could walk on the beach. No public honors, no Institute offer. Not even a job offer. And what was most difficult to accept, the knowledge of wasted years, college and graduate school, eight years total, with no conclusion, no idea worth considering, let alone following through or implementing.

She lay on the beach, on the white sand, and the sun poured down on her. She closed her eyes against it until it radiated a helix of colors that spun in a spectrum she had been unable to reach. There it was, a fusion furnace drowning her in its rays, and she unable by the subtlest reasoning or the most daring constructions to enhance its dilute quality and make it assume the central place in civilization. You've failed, Brill Angstrom Knolls, she told herself.

It would be harder to tell Lev.

It was called picking up the pieces. How convenient that everything was called something. Otherwise how would you know what in hell you were doing? Brill, instead of finding a husband, instead, even, of a career, elected to teach second grade.

Her grandfather, when he heard of it, was incensed.

Her father, when the news came to his ears, professed himself shocked. "All that education going to waste." He felt so strongly on the subject that he telephoned.

"I'm happy," Brill said. "Doesn't that count for something?"

It was true at first. The respite was needed, and she enjoyed the children. Through them she hoped to catch a glimpse of the young Brill. Her class of youngsters was a way to reenter an earlier time of seeing and sifting. She had slipped through life to her twenty-fifth year. Not many mammals lived so long. Elephants, tortoises, a few horses, and she, Brill Knolls.

She turned almost exclusively to her seven-year-olds. She was at ease with them. Together they watched white mice scamper in their cage, planted a surprise garden on the windowsill from assorted seeds. Created a terrarium whose inhabitants were a small turtle and a chameleon, worked on a topographical map of the United States made of paste and cocoa, pinned up pictures, and joined hands in a large circle to dance.

In their more serious moments they did phonics from reading charts, sounding in singsong. They drew numbers on the board, adding two apples and two apples. Then two pears and two pears. Bridging eons of human thinking, they arrived at the abstract *two plus two equal four*. Two of *anything*. It was glorious. The class did not seem aware of what they had done.

Was she wasting herself as her father and grandfather believed? Is it a crime to be content when you have power in you? All her life that inner strength frightened her. Was she repressing it, denying it by temporizing? Was she wrong to relax with her children? Should she continue to force her mind? Force a breakthrough? *I don't want happiness, or love, or success. I want to use myself up.*

Summer vacation.

That meant time. It meant no further excuses. There was no obstacle now to getting to work in earnest, except the fear. How could she face another failure? If only she could brush the cobwebs away. She had been so close.

Or had she? Had she gone down a wrong path? When she took it up again, should it be from an entirely new vantage point? To try again was torment.

Yet unleashed forces trampled, raged and stormed through her. Embedded in these charged emotions were unformed concepts waiting to be seized, examined, and set into the hard, clear mold of logic. There are certain mites necessary in breaking down the residue of plants and converting them to soil. These mites can begin life only under the fallen needles of a spruce pine. *If these small creatures have their special purpose, then, surely, I have mine. I want to release myself, become myself. I want to be more than I have been.*

She went one afternoon to clear out her desk. The school with no children seemed a severe, impersonal place. She didn't like the halls, tunnels through which she passed. Opening the door to her room, she stepped into a carnival of color: a light, happy area.

There was a large yarn and peg picture of an outrigger canoe over her desk. The walls held cut-outs, paintings, and a clock designed of construction paper. A roll-down chart with small flags indicated the natural resources of the world. The oil flags were black: Saudi, the Bahrein Islands, Abu Dhabi, Kuwait, Abu Hadriya, Aladen, the Iranian field. Angstrom outposts.

More pleasant were the seeds on the windowsill, which had sprouted into small tomato plants. Heavy with fruit— she tied them up. The turtle and its companion, the chameleon, were doing well. Her glance took in the collection of sea shells in the process of being labeled.

She hadn't seen it coming. There was no time to duck or take evasive action. The Jabberwocky existence, which for a while made sense, lay in fragments.

She got up, and, going to her desk, opened the center drawer: pencils, chalk, erasers, packs of heavy paper, her class records in neat piles. She shoved the drawer shut. Let them stay there until September, or forever.

I won't be back, she realized, and took the turtle and chameleon and the tomato plants with her. *Life,* those things were life.

Crazy fancies plagued her on the walk home. The distance between her and reality was something she

459

couldn't account for. There was an odd time lag between herself and the world. Even when she reached out her hand for the door there was an unaccountable moment before she pushed it open. The brisk measure by which she lived fell away.

Brill started to work in a preliminary way. She got out her thesis and read through it. This was painful, almost devastating. She wrestled with a desire to take the same route again. She began reading articles in the solar energy field which had appeared since she left school.

Through all this she waited for a letter from Bea.

Bea was the maverick Angstrom. She took no interest in physics or geology and avoided mathematics successfully from the ninth grade. Her world was of song. She sang Mahler and rock, Schubert and jazz, touching everything with her own variants. Her interpretation from the beginning was distinct. Brill felt the music bottled in herself poured from her sister.

Bea's heart was set on Aspen Music School. Brill helped her select audition material. Together they read through the songs of Brahms, deciding on the "Zigeunerlieder." For the Mozart selection, they chose, "Vesperae Solonnes de Confessore." But Brill's favorite was "Vittoria! Vittoria!" which Bea sang a capella, head thrown back.

The tape was made and sent with crossed fingers and prayers. Three weeks later Bea was accepted. Lev was passing through on his way to check into the development of a gas recovery scheme which employed high-pressure fluids rather than explosives to crack oil-bearing sandstone. So the three of them celebrated with midnight doughnuts.

Since the fiasco of the thesis, Brill avoided her brother, wondering if he still believed in her. And she found herself beginning to question him. Did he work for the New Humanity, or routinely for the Company? She reproached herself severely for this doubt. She knew him to be resolute. His commitments were forever. If only she could measure up.

Lev was off first. She drove him to the field and waved goodbye as he climbed into the Cessna, envying him this freedom. There followed a few hectic days running

460

around picking up sheet music and scores, going shopping with Bea for a regulation long black skirt for choir. Then it was over.

Bea too was gone. And for Brill the three-month hiatus began.

A week went by. Finally, a phone call.

Bea laughing, because she shared a room with an oboist, "and a baboonist. I mean bassoonist. Can you stand musical jokes? I have all sorts. Listen to this. A bassoon is an ill wind that nobody blows good." Much laughter in the background. "That's Erin. That cracks her up. Do you know she spends all her time cutting reeds? Really. She carries this little knife. And she takes lessons in reed cutting."

'What's it like, Bea-Bea? What does your teacher say about your voice?"

"She says I have potential. And good cheek bones. It's important to have areas to resonate from. I wrote you a letter telling you about everything."

It was a typical Bea letter. It arrived late because she forgot to mail it. It was addressed to Brill to read to Lev when he showed up next "Although it's conceivable he'll come to Aspen. That tract of land Grandfather gave him is somewhere around here."

What tract of land? She didn't know Grandfather had given him a tract of land. She felt cut off from her family. Yet it was she who had insisted, who still insisted that her life run its separate course. She returned to the letter avid for news. Was that a symptom of her loneliness? Bea was bubbling. Bea was never lonely.

"But let me tell you how being at Aspen has changed my life. I used to envy the instrumentalists lugging around their cases that labeled them musicians. But now I am convinced I possess the best instrument of all. e e cummings says, 'a world of made is not a world of born.'

"All other instruments are artificial, mine is part of me. I know you were right, Brill, I am going to sing. That is my life. And I love it. You won't believe I'm up every morning at seven, I bike from the Continental Inn where we music people stay, to the school about two miles away. There I shut myself up in a carrel replete with soundproofing and piano, and sing my heart out. I don't eat breakfast at all. I have brunch about eleven.

"But I haven't told you what the country is like, *red*. Uptilted. Tableland covered with wild flowers. Columbine is the state flower, but perhaps it should be daisies. Remember, Brill, you looked it up in Father's unabridged dictionary and it was originally *day's-eye*. I thought of that. There are different kinds, yellow, white, and a fringed lavender. Oh, and by the road there grows a marvelous high thing called *fireweed* because it flames out at you. And red paintbrush and lupin and tiny bluebells hiding under leaves, also puffs resembling huge dandelions. Erin sprays them with hair lacquer and they make great arrangements.

"The music school is built by a clear, clean stream. And to prove it isn't polluted, fishermen still take trout from it. I, who swam in Southern California beaches in tan foaming sludge, swear to you, it is clear as around the reefs that winter in Kauai, a perfect mirror for Maroon Bells. Maroon Bells is the name of the highest peak rising 11,800 feet. But didn't Lev say they are going to press oil from the surface shale? It frightens me to think what that might do to this remaining bastion. Do you think Lev will have anything to do with this? I would hate it to be any Angstrom, but especially I would hate it to be Lev.

"There are trout ponds right on the school grounds. You can see the fish jump and watch the circled ripple spread and fade. The aspen are silver-gray with lollipop leaves in the dark green of the pines. The effect is a mottled two-tone forest with cleared slopes for winter skiing. Clouds spread shadows like eagles, like claws, like giant hands on the sideways-lying red strata.

"The town is a transplanted Zermatt, the hotels, like music boxes with geraniums at the windows. And mild dogs with heavy jowls and china blue eyes lie in the streets. They have demolished many of the old Victorian houses of American origin to make room for coy, overly cute Swiss music-box chalets.

"Must go and feed my instrument. There is this marvelous little omelette shop. A sidewalk cafe, actually, where you sit with homebaked muffins and coffee until the omelette arrives. You have your choice, they can

462

be had with avocado, crabmeat, mushrooms, or God help you, a combination. I intend to have a stuffup and watch the tourists, and the music students and the people from Paepcke Institute go by. LUV, Bea."

Brill had never seen Aspen, but she could picture it, even to the smell of the coffee and the taste of omelette.

There was a great in-gathering in 1973. This to mark the golden wedding anniversary of Brillianna and Theodore Angstrom. Ted himself took charge of the arrangements. It was to be catered from the Alta Mira, the best cellar wines dusted off and served. He submitted himself to measurements for a new tuxedo and cummerbund, expostulating to all who would listen that the size hadn't changed in fifty years. This was not accurate within twenty pounds.

His enthusiasm led to a shopping expedition with Brillianna which exhausted him. "I don't see how women do it." She selected a gray lace gown with folds of pink satin revealed by motion. He chose as his gift a diamond tiara, taking pleasure in anything that came from the earth. The colors had been captured and hardened in alluvial fires. They lived and flashed on the black velvet against which they were displayed. A necklace, he felt, was not for a seventy-year-old throat, even one as well preserved as Brillianna's. The tiara, however, set off her aristocratic bearing.

He ordered colored lights strung in the trees and pavilions set up on the lawn. He engaged three bands of musicians to play around the clock, orchids to be floated on the pool. A battalion of waiters was hired for the occasion, while the guest list included international dignitaries, heads of governments, heads of state, members of industrial empires, partners, royalty, and here and there someone Ted liked.

But nothing in life runs smoothly. A full scale Arab attack in November, immediately dubbed the Yom Kippur War, found the Israelis unprepared. Egyptian armies crossed the Canal. The Israelis quickly regrouped and in their turn bridged the Canal under General Sharon to march on Cairo. In the Sinai they surrounded and cut the enemy off from food and water supplies. The stranded Egyptian forces survived solely due to U.N. intervention.

Angstrom shook his head. "The weakness of the Arab is that he talks a better battle than he fights. Or to quote the Bedouin, 'The words of the night are coated with butter. When the sun shines they melt away.' That's what happened in '67. Nasser literally talked the country into mass hysteria. I don't believe he had any intention of going to war with Israel. But the louder he talked, the more he believed. He succeeded in convincing himself and his nation that the shrines of Jerusalem were theirs for the taking. This time it's different. Russia is supplying heat-seeking SAM VI missiles. They hone in on aircraft. Unless we come up with a counter-ploy, the airplane may be obsolete as an instrument of war."

The Arab oil boycott was a delayed time bomb. Ted knew it was coming and spoke with Faisal's minister of oil. Ted saw eye to eye with him, stopping the flow of oil would certainly drive prices up and independents out. On the political side, the minister explained, the shortage was designed to soften American support for Israel. Ted had no quarrel with this objective either. However he made it plain that it came at an embarrassing moment for him personally. He reminded the shaikh that an invitation had been sent to King Faisal. While the names had changed from his day, the high-sounding phrases were the same, completely beclouding the issue. When he hung up Ted didn't know whether the flow of oil would temporarily be eased or not. Probably not.

There were other Arab guests on the list, Prince Muhammad ben Sulaiman, one of the King's nephews and a Princeton alumnus; as well as 'Abd al 'Aziz al Sagr of the computer department of the College of Petroleum and Minerals at Dhahran. He had learned computer science at the University of Texas and spoke English with a drawl which endeared him to Ted. Who else? Oh yes, the minister of state planning, Hisham Nazer.

Ted counted on their good sense to refuse the invitations, as Saudi was the chief framer of the present crisis. Without Saudi, the Arab world made no moves.

"What terrible timing," Brillianna wailed. "Our fiftieth

wedding anniversary, and the czar of oil has to send his chauffeur at six in the morning to get gas for his Continental."

"I've always told you it is a game," Ted reminded her. "This is a show of strength on the Arab side. It won't last long."

"Tell your guests that," Brillianna said curtly. They had a small tiff about the trees. Brillianna felt it would be poor taste to light them in the middle of an energy crisis. Ted had already gone to the trouble of wiring and a flick of the switch would illumine his grounds in soft translucent colors. He was determined on achieving this effect, austerity or no austerity.

King Faisal sent his regrets and a marvelous set of diamond earrings. Brillianna breathed easier. She even began to look at the gas shortage through Ted's eyes, as good business.

Acceptances were pouring in. "It's going to be quite a bash," Bea said. She was a junior at Stanford this year and had an extremely good-looking young man in tow, Roger Cramer, who seemed a bit intimidated by so many Angstroms.

"Well, we're for it," Brillianna handed Ted a gold embossed envelope with a good many Saudi stamps and matching stationery.

"Which one?"

"The Emir Muhammad ben Sulaiman. What is he thinking of? Cars lined up for blocks at those stations still open. Motels, hotels, resorts, the tourist trade, all hurting. The price of food up again, due mainly to the jump in synthetic fertilizers. And shortages across the United States for the first time since the depression. Maybe he wants to see how we're taking it."

"I'll show him how we're taking it. I want to know when he arrives. Just before he enters the garden, I want every one of those floodlights on."

"But Ted. . . ."

"Every last one. I'll be damned if I give anyone the satisfaction of seeing an Angstrom cut back. Not where power is concerned."

"And why should we have to? Why are they so greedy?

Surely they are getting more billions than they know what to do with."

Ted smiled. " 'They' is us. And 'greedy' is what it's all about. Except you usually spell it *profit*. Of course, Faisal doesn't need to sell oil at inflated prices. He doesn't need to sell it at all. Oil in the ground is better than money in the bank. Especially with money meaning less and less."

Brillianna said severely, "You talk as if you weren't affected by this at all. Aren't you afraid that one of these days Faisal will nationalize you?"

Ted replied with an old Saudi proverb. "If you hear that a mountain has moved, believe it. If you hear that a man has changed his character, believe it not." He took his wife's hand. "It doesn't matter if he does. Saudi has already gobbled sixty percent, with concessionaire oil only forty and a small part of that under direct Company control. But the Saudis aren't able to handle the other aspects. We have the refineries, pipeline, transport, outlets, new products to play with. Of course they're learning. They no longer buy apartments in Beirut or gambling houses on the Riviera. The modern Saudi executive is well-informed in fiscal matters, but inclined to be chauvinistic and insular. The practice is for fathers to give their sons a substantial amount of money to invest at age fourteen or fifteen. Often the kid is a millionaire in his own right by the time the family sends him to Stanford or Princeton, or as in the case of 'Abd al 'Aziz al Sagr, the University of Texas."

In the days following, regrets and costly gifts poured in from Arabia. Abdul Hadi Taker, governor of Petromin, and the Shaikh Rashid declined with congratulations. "That Rashid is an interesting man," Ted said. "He is manager of Intercontinental Oil of New York, in which the Compagnie Française des Petroles has a half interest. He has a palatial home, sunken bar with a view of the pool. . . ." He broke off, recalling he was speaking to Brillianna.

But she kept up with the times. "I suppose the young ladies swim naked—except for their veils, of course."

Ted nodded his approval of her. "Well, Brillianna, what do you think?"

"What do I think about what?"

"The fifty years, of course."

"I wouldn't have missed them for all the oil in Dhahran."

"I wasn't always the best of husbands."

"Of course not. I had some miserable empty years. But you put me right on top. I like being there. It's bred into me."

"Yes, it suits you."

"The best years, the most fun, I wonder if you know which they were?"

"The first?" he said, hazarding the answer he knew she would reject.

She shook her head. "Too fairy-tale, not really enough. I don't think I quite believed in them. No, unlike most women, I found the second half of my life the best. You came back to me then, Ted. And we built together. I found it exciting, being part of things. Of course I always was, in a way. You could never have carried off the social end without me."

"Social end, my foot. It's you who stiffened my backbone to fight the U.S. government." He bent and kissed her hand. There was none to see. There was only the two of them.

They continued strolling. "Vincent Van Gogh did a marvelous canvas, a pair of old shoes."

"That was it? The whole picture?"

"But it said everything. Don't you see, that's us now, Ted. There was a time when I hated you. Don't look so shocked, you know it's so. I tore my insides out so you wouldn't have the son you wanted. All that was so long ago. I begin to think that maybe an accretion of fifty years, the good and the bad, is love, an overworked word I dislike using. The Greeks, who were much more civilized, knew one word wouldn't do. They had the necessary shadings, *eros* for the passionate, *philia* the brotherly. But the one that comes to mind when I think of our years together is *caritas*, caring. Through it all, I cared for you, Ted."

Ted forbore to mention that 'caritas' was Latin. Brillianna never liked to be corrected. Besides it was a pretty idea. It made him pensive. "Remember sitting on the porch swing at your aunt's house when I asked you to marry me?"

She laughed. "I thought you'd never get to it. All you could talk about was oil."

"I told you then you'd be taking a chance on me."

"Yes, I was forewarned. Tell me, Ted, do you think Brill will relent and come?"

"Of course I do."

"I wonder. Well, it is getting chilly. We must be going in." She wrapped her fluffy hand-knit shawl about her. "I hope you're the one to go first, Ted. I wouldn't want you to be alone."

"Our time hasn't come by a long shot, old girl. But when it does, we'll go together. There's a certain volcano, Mount Asama, I think, where thwarted Japanese lovers throw themselves in."

Brillianna squeezed his hand. "Let's hope we're still able to climb to the top."

It was their last minute alone before the party.

Ted had his way, chandeliers glittered, and the garden was a rainbow of light. Not until the last arrival did Theodore and Brillianna Angstrom enter arm in arm at the top of the staircase.

The diamond tiara caused a sensation. Brillianna's smile matched its radiance. Bea Anna tossed roses, strewing their path. An orchestra struck up "Let Me Call You Sweetheart." And Ted hummed audibly, "I'm in love with you." This brought a burst of applause. Champagne filled every glass, all lifted to the host and hostess. "Happy anniversary! And many more years!"

The Angstroms led the first dance of the evening, a waltz. They danced alone on the terrace, a handsome, white-haired, unbent couple. After this formality, a more swinging party got under way.

Ted passed among his guests. He was in great form, arguing against the stratigraphic trap theory and defending his tried and true anticline approach to oil discovery. As a raconteur he was at his best with the meeting almost thirty years ago on board the U.S.S. *Quincy*. "Ibn Saud admired Mr. Roosevelt's wheelchair, and damned if he didn't give it to him. But the President supplemented this, what you might call personal gift, with a Douglas C-3. Well, Churchill, who was interested in getting a foot in the door of my concession, gave the King a present too, a custom Rolls. But of course, being British, it was a right-hand drive, which put the chauffeur in the place of honor and the King of Arabia in an inferior position." Ted chuckled, then he laughed and finally roared at the idea. "I'm telling you, it was a disaster. And the funny part was, they had imprisoned the one man who could have prevented the blunder, John Eustace Nichols. But it's an ill wind you know. Churchill's gift undid the efforts of the butterfly collectors and the locust fighters."

"Who were they?" the chairman of Gulf inquired.

But Ted simply poked him in the ribs, "Oh no, I've got to keep something up my sleeve," and went on to repeat the joke about growing old: "You know what they say, everything either falls out or falls down." It made no difference that he had been telling it for years, that it had all been heard before. When Theodore Angstrom related an anecdote everyone laughed. For his part, he relished the audience, and enjoyed the assurances. He liked being told how well and vigorous he looked.

Lev returned for the gala by way of Colorado. He took refuge in the kitchen and had supper with Maria and Tomas. Tonight was none of their doing, but outside catering, food of which Maria was extremely suspicious.

Tomas jumped up from their meal to direct a dilatory waiter. He conceived it his duty to keep an eye out for pilfering. Maria was more philosophical. "It is a big outfit, the Angstroms employ the biggest. The food is not the freshest food I have seen, but the employees are bonded."

"You think the Angstroms need insurance money?" Tomas reproved. "It is their possessions they wish. While I am here, no one is going to walk out the door with a single spoon."

"Me," Maria said, "I am more skeptical of the guests."

Lev laughed and reached too quickly for one of Maria's rolls, burning his fingers.

"Nothing changes," she chastised him. "Not this one

at any rate. You should be out there attending the party."

"I'd rather be here."

"Underfoot." Unconsciously she used his mother's expression.

"As always," Tomas agreed. In their sixties, the pair possessed the timeless quality of those who have seen much and made their peace with all. It was healing to sit with them. Lev needed the good smells of their kitchen, the banter, the old associations. There was a new letter in his billfold which he had considered tearing up. But what would be the use of that?

"Lev Angstrom, this is Adam writing. Our father will not write since you are dead to him. But someone should tell you that our brother, whom you have never known, is dead. Avri crossed the Suez with General Sharon. Everything he fought for is already forfeit because the Saudi-California Company listened to the Arabs in the hope of a better price for oil. You traded what our brother gave his life for, the security of Israel. Live with it, Angstrom, if you can."

He thought of what Maria said, that nothing changes. He wondered if it were true for her. Had he only grown a taller boy who still burnt his hands on her muffins? Or was that her defense? What was his?

Did he need one? Why? He had named himself Angstrom. Was that a crime? He believed he could accomplish more working within the framework of the Company, using its vast facilities to develop alternative fuels.

Lev had made a judgment and he stuck to it. He counseled his grandfather, "Hold back on nuclear and breeder reactors." His hope was in a triad: solar, fusion, and shale. He himself was experimenting with *in situ* extraction from shale in the Colorado tract.

Lev was not a person to explain himself. If his father, Lev Rosenfeld, and his brother, Adam, condemned him, it was because he was an Angstrom. To them that spelled enemy.

Maria leaned confidentially toward Lev. "You can tell me," she said in a whisper that carried through the whole kitchen. "Is your sister Brill going to come?"

"I don't know." He didn't. Brill had not confided in

him recently. He understood her pride. But he too hoped that tonight she might be able to put it behind her. Perhaps talk to him about her thesis and confide her plans for another try.

"I mailed her the invitation," Tomas said. "I mailed it myself."

Brill couldn't park within blocks of the estate. She might have driven up to the front door and allowed her Saab to be parked by attendants. But that would have meant being officially announced. She did not want to come home that way. Especially as she did not consider this a relaxing of the principles which kept her away, but a human recognition of the passage of time, an acknowledgment to her grandparents. It was something she wanted to do. She had already made the decision when Bea dashed over to her apartment. Brill had no advance warning. Bea neither wrote nor phoned. She walked in the door and threw herself in her sister's arms. In many ways she did not seem like Bea at all. She had cut her hair, and was dressing with new chic and smartness. The first exchange was largely incoherent. Then Bea arrived at the purpose of her visit. "I've come back for Grandpa and Grandbee's fiftieth. You got an invitation, didn't you?"

"Yes."

"And you'll come. I know you'll come. They're getting old, you know."

"They *are* old," Brill said, "and yes, I'll come."

Bea hugged her. "I knew you'd listen to reason. I have to drive back that same night. I'm preparing for a big test. College is just a detour for me. I can't wait to get back to Aspen this summer."

"I know."

"Oh, I do hope this get-together will be the beginning of some sort of rapprochement. I never understood why you had to isolate yourself so completely."

"You understood once."

"Well, in the beginning, perhaps. Your moving out was a statement, an indictment. And I think you wanted to

471

prove you could make it on your own. But you have. I think it's marvelous to have such a brilliant sister. But don't you agree that the anniversary could be the opportunity for a new closeness?"

"Have you been reading about the oil spills from the new giant tankers? Oil cuts off oxygen and nothing can live."

"All right, Brill. But remember, they're your family. And none of them are really immortal persons as Grandfather likes to pretend."

"Tell me about yourself, Bea?"

Bea complied readily enough. But through all the chatter Brill couldn't find her sister.

Next to phone was her father's secretary, Peg Trotter. She also urged her presence at the upcoming affair. Miss Trotter took it as a personal triumph that Brill listened to her arguments and agreed to come.

Brill knew a way through the sunbaked brick wall, a crack partly covered by ivy, through which, at one time, it had been possible to squeeze. The ivy grew thicker now and she had some trouble locating the exact place. But once having detected it, she was immediately in the farthest part of her grandparents' garden.

It was Kumju's realm. She was dismayed to discover the patch of hillside he presided over neglected and weed-infested. She recalled that even in her time the gardeners were not anxious to go near the spot. Apparently her grandparents no longer walked to this distant perimeter of the estate. It had reverted to a tangle of underbrush.

"Kumju," she said. Unexpected tears flooded her face. She climbed up to him, taking no care for stockings or shoes. "Kumju," she repeated, touching his no eyes, no face, removing a creeper. "Arm me with the spear of a white cock, and I will take you away from here. You will come to me. It is a small patio, but the sun will shine on you and I will hang baskets of ferns and set out pots of bright flowers. No weeds, Kumju. I have need of your strongest magic. Do I need courage? Give it. Do I need insight? Show me the path. Kumju, I can be more than I am."

The moon had followed her to this spot. Its light bore down on Kumju, and her mind filled with his answer.

472

"The untried cannot lead the way. Therefore were you hardened in fire." She sat a long time in the garden, meditating on his words before joining the party.

It was a matter of pushing through animated groups. The symbolism of Bergman films was being analyzed at her elbow. A trustee of Stanford stopped her, holding out a refilled martini. "I was quoting Herman Kahn to the effect that any two consenting adults may play their consoles together." He fumbled for her hand.

She eluded him, working her way deeper into the crowd. An ambassador said, "*Elephantiasis Arabum* is a hypertrophy of the cellular tissues. Would you believe my balls got so big I could sit on them?"

"Blow, blow," someone declaimed scornfully. "Winds do not blow. Never did blow. They are *sucked* across the oceans."

Brill felt battered. Her original idea was to put in as brief an appearance as possible, but she spotted Lev engaged in a discusson with a young man she did not recognize.

"Salt domes," the young man was saying, "being geologically stable, are the perfect repository for storing ingredients to get civilization started again."

"What would those ingredients be?" Lev asked. He saw her and held out his hand.

"Those things you'd need to reestablish industry. Priority would be given to mining operations. We'd have to have petroleum, coal, and gas. Salt for human consumption. Limestone is necessary to produce iron and steel. You'd have to have sulphuric acid for fertilizer, and ammonia of course."

"Ammonia." There was an element of attack in the way Lev hit his consonants. "The only reason to include ammonia is as a source of explosives. But what if the race, starting out again, doesn't want to go that route? Suppose they've had it with aggression, wars, and guerrilla action? Presumably, the reason they're looking in the salt domes is because we let loose with the ultimate megatonnage and destroyed what it took two thousand years to build. So why should those remnants, those struggling inheritors want to emulate that? And wouldn't we be even more criminal to put temptation in their way? What

473

do you say, Brill? Brill, this is Roger Cramer, a friend of Bea's from Stanford."

After a polite interchange, Lev felt free to pull her away. "I'm glad you came. Really glad." He noticed she had fastened on glass beads. Her dress was quite plain. Anyone else would have looked odd and out of place. Brill carried it off.

"It's a gesture," she said. "It doesn't change anything."

"Have you seen Grandpa and Grandbee yet?"

"Only from a distance. I haven't been able to get near them."

Lev brought her punch. She thanked him absently, looking around. "Where's Bea?"

"I'm afraid you've missed her. She just split with Cramer."

At that moment she saw her father. He looked considerably older than she remembered. There was gray at his temples and scattered through his blond hair. He seemed haggard, nervous and tired. Brill didn't know she could still feel the kind of pain she experienced on seeing him. His manner with her was casual, as though it had been yesterday they last met. "I understand from Bea that you have given up your teaching position."

"Yes. How are you, Father?"

He dismissed the question. "Working hard, that's all. Tell me about yourself. Will you be going back to research where you belong?"

"I'm thinking of it."

"Excellent. I don't like to see training and brains go to waste. Do you need computer time? I could arrange that."

"Yes," the god in two pieces answered before she did, "I think I might be ready to try again."

"I'm off to Washington, but I'll have Miss Trotter call you."

The Emir Muhammad ben Sulaiman, the one who had not had the sense to stay away, touched her arm. "Excuse me. You were pointed out to me as Miss Knolls." He led her toward the dance floor. "Did you know, Miss Knolls, that when people die their amino acids turn to the right? It's a fact. One of those lovely facts that nobody knows what to do with."

474

The Saudi prince presented an opportunity she could not let pass. As she followed his somewhat flamboyant steps, she asked how women's rights were proceeding in his country.

The question puzzled him. "The Arab has always honored learning," he assured her. "Among the people there is a saying, a book is like a garden carried in the pocket."

"How lovely. But my question was, are your young ladies allowed to walk in this garden?"

"The new university at Jidda, the King Abd al-Aziz, is coeducational. Of course, the boys attend mornings, while the young women go late afternoons and evenings."

"My grandfather told my brother that male professors lecture through closed circuit TV. Is that correct?"

"Oh yes. The girls ask questions and receive answers through electronic gadgets."

"Amazing. I find you an amazing people."

He beamed, taking this as a compliment.

"For instance, you proclaim yourself part of the Third World. Yet, synthetically produced fertilizers have a largely petroleum base. Putting the price so high as to make them unattainable is causing starvation in much of Africa, particularly Ethiopia. I find this odd Third World policy, especially at a time when Saudi spending is astronomical."

"You think we are without compassion?"

"I think you might take the garden out of your pocket. Gardens like sunshine, you know." The dance concluded. There was a pause in the music. The drums began a slow roll announcing an enormous statue, perceived only gradually to be the anniversary cake. It was cast in the mold of a four foot high oil derrick. There was wild applause, cameras went off in everyone's face. How had the news media gotten in? No one knew. Ted delighted in going from group to group telling his guests what an ideal marriage theirs had been. Brillianna, at his side, watched him with wide Grenville eyes. She caught sight of Brill and tightened her hold on Ted's arm.

Following her glance, the old man beamed. Tears came to his eyes. He was easily moved these days. Brillianna waited for Brill to approach.

Brill spoke first. "Thank you for the invitation. You both look marvelous."

Brillianna pressed her granddaughter to her suddenly and fiercely. "Brilli's little girl," she said. Then, as though ashamed of the outburst, added, "You've behaved very badly, of course. But we won't speak of that this evening. The only thing I will say on the subject is that you are to come visit occasionally."

"That you are, Brill, that you are." Her grandfather clasped her in a tight hug.

Then it was over—a terrace and house littered with the debris of festivity, corks and crushed napkins, paper favors, dirty plates and glasses, empty punch bowls, and leftover canapés.

The anticipation, the excitement, the drinks, the hour, were too much for Ted. He felt alone and uneasy in his king-sized bed, even turning the electric blanket higher did not warm or relax him. He got up and knocked on his wife's adjoining door. "Brillianna?"

There was no response. *She must be asleep. After all that excitement; nerves of steel, that's what she had. Or perhaps she'd taken something.* He himself refused any type of medication. "The body renews itself," he always declared. *Yes, she was sleeping. Unbelievable after such an occasion, such an exhilarating occasion.*

"Brillianna, are you asleep?" he said in a voice calculated to wake her up.

"What's that?" she asked, partially rousing.

He approached the bed. "You weren't sleeping, were you?"

"That's generally what I do at night."

"Well, move over. I'm coming into your bed, woman."

She opened her arms to him, her withered arms, and he crawled into them. She clasped his bulk, holding him. For all that it was silent, their understanding was complete. She knew he was afraid. At their age each night is a small death. He felt the threat keenly because his existence was one of gusto, each moment full of doing and being, an embrace of life. When a living thing dies nothing familiar remains. All that is left is the word *why*.

A tear splashed onto her upper arm. It was not hers. "You're overtired, my dear."

"Yes. Promise me that you'll be with me, Brillianna, at the end, when my time comes." There was no talk now of romantic lovers and Japanese volcanoes. The hour was stark, cold, reality inescapable.

"Of course," she said serenely. "The tragedy of human life is that we cannot save each other. We can look on, we can suffer, but we can't avert. That is why, ultimately, you must place your faith in the Lord. Saint John said, 'Beloved, let us love one another, for love is of God.' "

"You know, Brillianna, you remind me of the cheramoya, that desert fruit. Outside it's kind of bumpy and green with warts, inside the fruit is pale and sweet like a pear." She smiled in the dark. For tonight at least she had banished his fear.

Downstairs in the patio, they were still cleaning up. "Fifty years," Brill commented to her brother. "And we are just beginning to see what it meant." It was unsettling to have been thrust suddenly into the midst of Angstroms. So many emotions surfaced and had to be repressed. On balance she felt her decision, taken eight years ago, was the only tenable one. And yet the ties went deep. Even unacknowledged, they were her people. But the evening had not ended. "Lev," she said, "I have something to show you." Lev was hopeful as he followed her past the cleaning crew, along the flagged path to the far garden.

She stopped abruptly. "Where is Kumju?" she challenged.

Lev looked around. The question was unexpected. This was not the talk he wanted to have with his sister. "He must be here somewhere."

"He is. There in that mass of weeds."

Lev peered at the old god. "I'll tell Grandbee to get after the gardeners."

"No. I want him. You'll help me, won't you, Lev? I want to kidnap him, take him to my place."

"Take Kumju?"

"He's not happy here. He wants to come with me."

Lev was alarmed when she spoke like this. He knew it was a conscious reversion to the way they referred to him when they were children, but he didn't like her adopting that mock-serious attitude.

"I'm going to take him, Lev. If you don't help me, I'll manage myself."

He saw Brill was determined and decided it would be unwise to oppose her. He nodded his assent.

"I think they still keep the dolly in the tool shed." She spoke calmly enough, but he sensed a hidden excitement. "It won't be hard to roll him onto it. We'll make two trips. I'll go for my car. I'll have to move it about a block."

Lev investigated the lock on the shed. It was all but rusted away, a sharp blow with a rock shattered it. Inside, against the wall, was the dolly. He wheeled it out and up to the god. The head was heavier than Lev imagined. Suppose he dropped it and the thing smashed on the flagging? Brill returned, so there was nothing for it but to wrestle it through the wall, first the head, then the thicker base. It took several heaves to get Kumju into the trunk of the Saab.

Lev swung the car in a U-turn. "What if the old stories come back, Brill?"

"That was a long time ago, Lev. I only want him for sentimental reasons. Because he was so important in my childhood."

"Perhaps Kumju knows certain things after all," Lev conceded. "But I doubt it." The need to confide in someone prompted him to add, "I doubt that even the God of the Old Testament knows why my brother Avri died."

Brill reached her hand out over his. "We are the family, Lev."

Lev nodded. She had not forgotten. "What about you, Brill? Will you try again?"

The question came easily and she seemed to feel no constraint in answering. "I've told myself that I will. But I have to wait."

"For what?"

"The way, Lev, the way."

The fact of Brill's presence at the anniversary party eased things considerably. Occasionally her father phoned her. One evening they had dinner and he was able to tell

478

her that office space and computer time had both been arranged.

"Well," she said somewhat too brightly, "I suppose I can't procrastinate any longer."

Dr. Knolls was again on his way to Washington. Brill was surprised the following day, returning from a long walk, to find his secretary waiting on the porch. "I hope it isn't an intrusion, Miss Knolls. But I am worried."

"Come in, Miss Trotter. I was about to make myself some tea."

"Thank you."

"Now, you were saying? Is it about my father?"

"I don't know if he has confided in you, but the whole AEC is coming under congressional fire."

"Why is that?" Brill asked.

"Well, it has to do with these." She opened a briefcase at her feet, crammed with documents. "Dr. Knolls asked me to do a summary on them, and in the course of typing, I . . . well, frankly, I became upset. Quite needlessly I'm sure. You see, I have no technical background. I'm in no position to judge. But I'm frightened. For Dr. Knolls too. He's been very nervous lately. Unlike himself, poor man. And I thought you could tell me if he is in danger of coming under personal attack for his part in this." She indicated the sheaves of papers.

Brill looked at them, and then at Miss Trotter. "These are marked CONFIDENTIAL," she said.

"I know. Technically, I suppose I am remiss in confiding in you. But I know you to be a person of immense personal integrity."

"What are these documents," Brill asked, "and why should I see them?"

"It isn't just to ease my fears regarding Dr. Knolls, although that is part of it. Actually, I felt I was typing a nightmare. That's when I decided to come to you. You could make sense of this and tell me if I should be so afraid."

Brill studied her a moment. "All right, Peg. Leave the file with me."

"Dr. Knolls will be home at the first of the week."

"I'll have it to you by then."

"I don't like acting behind his back. But it's for his sake, for all our sakes."

"I think you did the right thing," Brill told her.

Out of the pages of typed notes that accumulated as she placed them face down on the table, a singularly drear landscape presented itself. During World War II her father worked under Professor Eugene P. Wigner, who left the Technische Hochschule, Berlin, to accept a teaching post at Princeton. Wigner was in charge of the group concerned with the theory of chain reactors at Hanford, Washington. A well-known chemist, Wigner later moved to theoretical physics. Howard Knolls felt privileged to work with such a man.

The first disquieting thing that Brill picked up was expressed, oddly enough, by a Soviet scientist, V. I. Spitsyn. He spoke at the Second Geneva Conference back in 1958, stating that in his view radioactive wastes disposed of in metal containers must corrode. As she read on, she discovered that the tanks referred to by Spitsyn were actually the storage vaults at Hanford, Washington, underground concrete containers lined with carbon steel. The wastes were described as self-boiling material which would melt the containers in minutes if not for the cooling system. This circulated air and stirred the liquid to prevent formation of solids that otherwise would settle on the bottom and burn through both concrete and steel.

Brill took a break and washed her face before returning to the patio with Kumju looking over her shoulder. "Corrosive failure of the tank wall would release large amounts of radioactive materials. In the case of plutonium 239, alpha radiation is the major hazard. It is selectively absorbed by the bone marrow and highly carcinogenic." She thought of it as a force wrapped in a death heat.

She could understand Peg Trotter's anxiety. She was devoutly glad it was her father, a responsible man, a well-balanced man, who weighed these reports and added his careful summation.

The following year, at the Monaco Conference on Disposal of Radioactive Wastes, it was reported that radionuclides had actually leaked from the containers and seeped into the ground. She recalled years ago hearing her father say that the site at Hanford was chosen for its clay soil, which tended to hold spillage. She was eleven when they visited Hanford. She was told to wait in the car while her father conducted some sort of inspection. Was she making that bleak, barren, scarcely remembered terrain the repository for new fears?

The International Symposium, meeting in Vienna, 1967, insisted that it would take a thousand years for seepage to travel through the water table to the Columbia River. By that time most of the radioactive materials would have decayed. A report dated 1970 concurred.

Spitsyn again; three time winner of the Order of Lenin, director of the Institute of Physical Chemistry at the Academy of Science, and a specialist in radioactive elements in the soil, Spitsyn did not agree.

He agreed that radionuclides were at present a good way from the river. "But they are there. And they are moving. Surface water is subject to change which can be caused by any number of things, flooding, irrigation, the construction of dams. Radionuclides are moving and this movement is not under control. I find this disturbing."

Peg Trotter rang up. "Do you think I was neurotic to allow those reports to affect me?"

"Come have dinner with me," Brill replied, "and we'll talk."

The dinner was yogurt, nuts and honey in ceramic bowls. Candles added a festive touch.

"What did you make of Dr. Spitsyn's remarks?" Brill asked.

"The Russian? It made me feel strange that he was more concerned than we were. Of course I gather most of the material he was talking about was short-lived. Is that correct? So even if there is contamination in the ground water, that's still a long way from the Columbia River."

"And therefore would not constitute pollution, since there is no injury to human, plant, or animal life? A lawyer's description of pollution. They're talking about plutonium 239, the most dangerous carcinogen known to man. It is *not* short-lived. It has a half-life of 24,360 years and, in significant amounts, must be isolated for a half million years before it reaches innocuous levels."

"Maybe I didn't understand."

"The federal government has set the maximum amount of plutonium 239 that can be tolerated by an adult human, at 0.6 micrograms. That, Peg, is one fifty-millionth of an ounce. So, if just a few ounces reach the river. . . ."

Peg bit her lip. "They were trying to save money, I suppose, by reusing those tanks. You know how hard it is to squeeze money out of the government."

"There is no excuse for not replacing them."

"I remember once typing that they plugged a leak with salt."

"That seems a bit primitive," was Brill's grim comment.

"It worries you too, doesn't it?" Peg asked.

"Let me read more, Peg."

"You're worried," Peg insisted. "I can see that."

Brill dreamed that in the night she got out of bed. The texture under her bare feet changed from carpet to vinyl, from floor to stone steps, and finally to the grassy turf of the patio. Leached by night of color it was alien, almost unrecognizable. She felt the dew, saw it beaded on a branch. She passed the pear tree with its blossoms of black flowers. The earth under her feet seemed palpable and alive. She stopped when she looked into the no face, no eyes of Kumju. His hollows, she knew, had been the repository of red jewels set there to filter the world.

Kumju made a picture and placed it in her mind. She swallowed endless fields, leaned into a wind that blew off the sea. Once more she was over land, aware of wafted clover and the smell of cut grass. She wrinkled her nose at the strong burn of fertilizers. She had never possessed a highly developed sense of belonging to any one spot. She was born into the world, part of it. Wherever she was momentarily, was part of her. Sea, land, sky, she had temporary ownership of all. As she took it in, absorbed it, it was hers. In the same way she belonged to it.

She experienced a sense of being trapped in an invisible zone, confined by temperature, pressure, and the interaction of plants. It is a delicate, multibranched set of circumstances that supports life. "You have been tampering with it." Kumju spoke directly in words. "There is an abyss opening at your feet. Nothing in your knowledge has prepared man for what is to come."

And Kumju made a final picture: It was scrub country, desolate and bare. The only things that grew were some sheds, barbed wire fencing, and rusted machinery. She had seen the place before.

She left the small garden feeling cold. Her feet especially were cold. She got into bed and pulled the covers up. With the covers high she could tell herself that she had been dreaming, except there were traces of grass cuttings in the sheets.

The next day Brill decided not to go to the lab. The reading began routinely enough, she was into a dull batch—a letter, No. 1059, from a civilian contractor employed by the AEC.

It was a formal request that new storage tanks be built, citing the fact that 35,000 gallons of radioactive wastes had escaped into the ground. "The clay of the soil should not be counted on to prevent the contaminants reaching the Columbia River."

This evaluation was reaffirmed in a report stamped SECRET, which was addressed to the Joint Committee on Atomic Energy from the U.S. comptroller general. Her head ached, but she couldn't stop.

During the next seven years nine more tanks sprang leaks. Losses now ranged to 55,000 gallons. The same contractor renewed his request for additional tanks, estimating that the reserve storage would be used up by 1964.

Actually it was 1963 when they started to fill the last tank. And for the period 1963 to 1965 there were no reserve tanks available. If a major leak had developed, it would not have been possible to pump the liquid into a spare. Even under those conditions the reactors were not shut down.

Reports from the Illinois Institute of Technology were appended estimating the life of the tanks to be twenty years, and confirming that a twenty-nine-year-old tank had leaked a third of its capacity, or 115,000 gallons of radioactive wastes.

Ten additional tanks sprang leaks and fourteen others were weakened through structural stress and corrosion. But it was the official attitude of the AEC that the existing tanks could be made to handle greater amounts if temperatures were controlled through new cooling devices. When half a million gallons of radionuclides were accidentally discharged, they announced themselves to be in error.

There were documents separated by a rubber band stamped OFFICE OF THE COMPTROLLER GENERAL, NATIONAL ACADEMY OF SCIENCE, NATIONAL RESEARCH COUNCIL, OAK RIDGE NATIONAL LABORATORY, NATIONAL REACTOR TESTING SERVICE. This last was, in later papers, shortened to NRTS. Full texts of the Rand Report and the Stanford Institute Report, as well as recommendations for further grants, were contained in the file. The Stanford account was pessimistic regarding alternative energy forms, particularly solar and geothermal sources: "With fossil fuel in short supply, and in view of the intransigence of the Arab coalition, nuclear power is the only route."

The Rand report recommended a go-slow approach due to the safety factors involved. "A loss of coolant accident could threaten the lives of thousands by causing the reactor core to melt, releasing lethal levels of radiation."

Brill sat there and thought—what has man done with his blasting, mining, smelting, fissioning? He has unlocked from earth and rock and subterranean vaults substances such as cesium 137, known to concentrate in food chains; strontium 90, accumulating in bones and mother's milk; plutonium 239, the most toxic to man, attacking the genes and lungs; cobalt 60, iodine 125, carbon 14, ruthenium 106, tritium, and technetium 99. All radionuclides, all poisons. They were collected at Hanford and sealed into giant vats where they boiled with self-generating fumes.

It seemed a madness. But it wasn't madness, it was business. A billion-dollar business. And advising this business was also business. A new and immensely lucrative area of expertise. Corporations were given over to it, foundations, and top universities.

In their doomsday scenarios they concern themselves

with the most amazing minutiae. They postulate that the world is incinerated, and conclude regretfully that paper money cannot be adequately decontaminated. It must be discarded. Jewelry too must be thrown away, along with coins and watchbands. *A coolant core has exploded showering me with invisible death and I am worried about whether I can decontaminate my watchband.*

Don't knock it, she told herself, they got a grant of seventy-five thousand dollars for the study.

A subsection caught her eye. It was marked simply Z-9. The fact that there was no definition or description of what the cryptogram stood for, bothered her. Further along in a separate paragraph it was suggested that something be done to clean up the Z-9 mess. "If the media got hold of it, those opposing nuclear power would have a field day."

No other clue to what Z-9 could be. Her father came back from Washington and she had to return the documents to Peg.

Another summer was gone and with it her entire life. The letter did not come to her, but to Dr. Howard Knolls. Peg brought it over.

Brill had been washing up the breakfast dishes. She did not touch or pick up the envelope.

"It's from your sister," Peg said.

She knew. She had seen the handwriting. She stared at the fluttering window curtains. For a moment they changed to the old chintz that framed the sycamore in the backyard of the San Francisco house.

"It's marvelous news. She's getting married. That awfully nice Roger Cramer. I'm not really surprised. They'd been seeing each other a lot at Stanford, and when I heard he was at the Paepcke Institute, well. . . ."

Yes, the old sycamore. She saw the gray cement against gray bark. The tree doctor patched the hollow. In their childhood, she and Lev and Bea left notes for each other there, messages from the god in Carmel, money tied in a handkerchief, jacks, books lists, poems. But the tree doctor slapped in cement, his wrist flicking expertly back and forth as the trowel smoothed and blended until it was almost indiscernible from the texture of the tree.

Peg was smiling. She looked pleased. Her forty-year-old face young, more innocent than Bea's, and more naïve.

A few short months ago all Bea's thoughts had flown straight to her. Not this summer. Her sister wrote infrequently and with no detail. The omissions made lies of everything. She mentioned the Paepcke Institute for the Humanities, but not that Roger Cramer was there. She described the chair lift up the mountain, people passing on the way down calling greetings, the slanted meadows of mountain flowers, the granite peaks commanding the valley. She went on about a particular cloud. "The sky is often white here. And the weather is changeable. It usually rains for a while in the afternoons. As I write, storm clouds darken the sky except for a small patch of blue that is as light as morning."

She filled a letter without saying anything at all about Roger Cramer. Why had she kept silent? She talked of the music tent flapping under Mozart, the success of her own recital. She spoke of the rapt faces of students. She told of an early morning canter along Roaring Fork River. I thought she practiced then, the stray thought flashed through Brill's mind. Bea mentioned walks beside Hallam Lake before a performance. But she did not say she walked hand-in-hand with Roger Cramer.

They had often discussed the possibility of a great love, an unstoppable passion. But they agreed, the three of them, that the vow came first. No outsider could separate or change what they meant to each other. The newcomer would enter the family, which by this natural process, would grow, become a living thing. But the letter had not come to her or to Lev. While Lev was checking new processes, and was in and out of shale mines trying promising methods, while she had worked her brain to molten liquid on the damn Fermi surfaces, Bea blithely turned her back. The new humanity would not include her or Roger.

The New Humanity. How pretentious. There was nothing to back it up, no accomplishment, nothing solid beneath it. Only failure. Would it have been different if the bounded surfaces had proved out? Would the letter have come to her?

Bea had chosen. Rejection is choice too. But Bea was not the only one to reject her. She had rejected herself.

—I will start to be Brill, she thought fiercely. It was as though some huge boulder was blocking the entrance to her being.

—I'm going to find a way to roll it aside. I've been exiled. Worse, I've exiled myself. I am suffocating. I am strangulating. What I pushed down, what I subjugated, was myself.

—I feel strength. I feel it and I want to use it. I want to use myself. I abhor this sense of waste. Everything in nature does what it is meant to do, from a green sponge to flood gulls feeding on a rising tide.

—But people can choose. Even when they do nothing, or write letters. I rejected Brill too. Now I claim her.

She had gone to college to prepare. Gone to graduate school to prepare. Now she was prepared. But for what? To discipline herself to approach the solar cell from another angle? Could she rev herself up for another such struggle? She had been running data on the computer. Her father arranged it and Lev wanted her to try. So far, nothing. Pasteur claimed chance favors the prepared mind. But she hadn't been lucky, she hadn't found the current that propels thought forward. Her mind was stuck on the old shoals and sandbars of Fermi surfaces. She must free herself from those monsters and go on. She remembered a line from e e cummings. Bea admired cummings. "Move away still further into now." Yes, she must do that. Move from the past into the present. The trouble was, *now* was a prospect devoid of detail.

Except for the one she would have to deal with, her sister's marriage. It lay like a dud: no explosion, no shower of maiming, life-extinguishing fragments. Everything was carefully balanced, her response to Peg, her smile, her actions. All tightly controlled. For she was aware it might not be a dud, but simply slow to detonate. It might yet splatter her against the off-white wall and yellow curtains. Her ten billion nerve cells wove on the loom of her brain. Organic disturbances shook her, upheavals occurred.

Cemented over. It was odd that parts of yourself could be lost and people taken from you. One, two, three, O'Leary. Four, five, six, O'Leary. Seven, eight, nine, O'Leary. Ten O'Leary, the postman, sir.

"Where are you off to, Brill?" Peg was not annoyed that there was no answer. She went to the window, letter in hand, and watched Brill, tall as many boys and as slender, walk through the patio into the field behind the apartment. The light chestnut hair pulled from her face emphasized the severity and regularity of her features. She didn't look twenty-five. There was something perennially young about her, as though she were trapped in adolescence.

Brill stopped, she had almost stepped on a spider's web built in the tall grass. She focused on the swaying fragile filigree. Its tensile strength must be considerable. Like herself, it had power to be gathered. But only once more, for a single effort.

The phone at the Colorado tract was ringing when Lev jumped out of the jeep and bounded up the stairs. The door of the cabin was never locked. He lunged for the receiver and made it.

"Lev?"

He recognized Peg Trotter.

"This is Peg Trotter."

"How are you, Peg?"

He knew there was trouble. Peg was one of those women who somehow reach middle age without kith or kin, and, apart from their job, are totally isolated. As a result she identified with her employer and the somewhat attenuated far-flung family. Miss Trotter came into her own during crises. It was she who did the telephoning, the notifying, the sympathizing. She had even managed to get Brill to their grandparents' anniversary party. Bea claimed she was in love with Howard Knolls. But Lev, failing to see how anybody could be in love with Knolls, felt it was a more generalized sense of concern for and pride in being on the periphery of the Angstrom clan.

Her voice held a quality of restraint, meant to indicate

that a person without her powers of self-control would, by this time, be hysterical. "I've been debating whether to call."

The phone had rung a dozen times.

"—But I thought perhaps you should speak to Bea."

"Bea? You mean because she's getting married? I think that's cool."

"Oh, I do too," Peg hastened to say. "No one could be more thrilled. Mr. Cramer is such a handsome young man. And since he was at the Institute and Bea Anna returned to Aspen, the romance had an opportunity to flower."

"Yes," Lev said rather shortly. He did not imagine it was accident that Cramer arranged a guest lecture for himself. He was laying siege to an Angstrom heiress, and according to the note, a short epistle impressionistic with happiness received from his sister yesterday, Roger Cramer had been successful.

"Actually it isn't Bea I called about. It's Brill."

Lev waited.

"I was so excited when Dr. Knolls received the letter from Bea Anna announcing the news. Of course, your father," she insisted on referring to Knolls as his father, although she knew perfectly well he was not, "your father was terribly pleased. However, in the course of the letter Bea asked if he would break the news to Brill, as she didn't know how she would take it. As she put it, you three have always been so close. Well, Dr. Knolls was leaving for a conference, so he asked me to drop by Brill's place and use my discretion to soften the blow."

"Why should it be a blow? Why shouldn't Brill be pleased? I mean, why did everyone assume it would be a blow?"

"Well, it's generally the older sister who marries first. It's difficult when it's the other way around. Especially when there's such an age difference."

"Nonsense. Brill hasn't a petty bone in her body."

"I didn't mean it that way. It certainly isn't that. But you know yourself Brill reacts to things from her own point of view. Your father gave me the letter to show her. When I did, I knew instantly it was the wrong way to go about it. She became very withdrawn. I think she was terribly shocked."

"What did she say?"

"It was more the way she acted, as though she could only handle it by detaching herself. That's why I said she withdrew. I had a definite feeling of dislocation. She wandered away. I called after her. I didn't like her going out, wandering around in that condition."

"You say, *that condition*. Just what are you getting at?"

"It was my impression she wasn't dealing with the situation, but escaping, if you know what I mean."

"I'm afraid I don't." Lev spoke coldly, because he knew precisely what she meant.

"She just walked out of the apartment. I called to her but she kept going. It's hard to explain over the phone; I felt shaken. I do think Bea Anna should have written her. Of course it's too late for that now. My purpose in calling, well, I don't know how close you are to Aspen. . . ."

"Not close," Lev said.

"At least it's the same state. I realize it is a family matter, but Dr. Knolls *did* leave it in my hands. And I thought, if it's at all possible, you should see Bea Anna and urge her to phone her sister."

Lev had already made the decision to do just that. "I'll see what I can manage. Thanks for calling." Peg Trotter wanted to go over it all again, but he cut her off. He blamed Bea. Not to tell Brill first had been a deliberate and in his opinion, callous decision.

His concern for Brill was usually well sublimated. It returned now along with the old worry which began with that first episode in college and reappeared at intervals since. The work-load she carried at graduate school had bothered him, the extra units, the way she drove herself, her inability to let up. When her research crashed, he thought she'd never survive it. But she was tougher, hardier than he supposed. Still, Brill had no one to open up to. Only Bea and him, which made her vulnerable where Bea was concerned. This could send her out of control, groping for a reality he sensed was not as definite for her as for other people. The genius, which he never doubted she possessed, was at times too much for her to cope with. It was a different way of looking at things.

490

Her perception was not confined. Her mind slashed through questions, turning problems to new angles, approaching them in unorthodox fashion, using tools from one discipline, applying them to another, recognizing no artificial boundaries to knowledge.

For Lev, she had always been a strangely wonderful person who sometimes lost herself. He could see her walking past Peg Trotter, just walking.

When she took up a position as a second-grade teacher he was totally baffled. She explained it as a rest from the pressures of academic life. It was, she said, a time in which to recoup her ideas and strength. He didn't fully accept her reasons, and was glad when she gave it up, suspecting it was a way of hiding out from responsibility to herself.

And what about his responsibility to her? If he were honest with himself, Bea was not the only one to have slipped away. It was true he saw Brill when he was home. They talked at length about the experimental aspect of his job. She read his brief on geothermal energy, and he had just mailed her his analysis of the *in situ* process being investigated here. She listened to his complaints that lack of funding stood in the way of a major breakthrough. But in many ways they had lost touch.

He had to change this, rouse Brill to work again. Lev hardly saw the countryside. He was unaware of climbing into fantastic vistas, or breathing mountain air. His lungs might have been made of acrylic or some other synthetic. His senses were suspended. He didn't see the skin of the world wrinkled into canyons, stretched for a high jump, leaving an ice cap at the top. A strange kind of capillary action seemed to push him on. He was propelled, not along mountain curves, but toward a moment in time—the moment he pronounced himself and his sisters a family.

"I don't understand you, Bea. I mean Knolls isn't even your own father. Sorry," he said to Cramer who sat on the sidelines, "but if you're going to be part of things, there are certain facts you'll have to know."

"Don't mind me," Roger said cheerfully. "Besides, I was the one who advised her to write both Dr. Knolls and her grandfather."

"Didn't it occur to you," Lev asked—politeness no longer covered his anger—"that this might be a matter concerning the three of us?"

"Don't say another word, either of you." Bea inserted herself on a footstool between them. She took her brother's hand. "Lev, we all have to grow up. It's uncomfortable that I have to say this, but the truth is, Brill isn't very mature."

Lev looked at her incredulously.

"I mean, I think she has some sort of picture of Roger standing in front of Kumju and swearing an oath of allegiance to the New Humanity or the New Anybodies, or whatever we were. I was twelve. It seemed a great idea then. The trouble is, Brill still believes in it."

Lev stared at a large worsted yarn stitch, a kind of crewel in the form of an old sampler which proclaimed, *God bless our pad.*—Believes in it! It was what kept Brill going. And it had done the same for him when the socialites he dated, the plastic manikins broke, when an arm or leg or neck twisted at an odd angle and he could see the crack. Then he would jump in his car, climb a mountain, take up the Cessna, or head for home. At home there were people who didn't come apart on you. People who could be depended upon.

As an eleven-year-old he forged it. Their mother's death welded the bond. Lev Rosenfeld's unalterable decision, the Hebrew prayer and Avri's death were the matrix. It was this deep loyalty from which Bea Anna defected.

Bea wrote to the blond cardboard man at the instigation of Roger Cramer. The moment Lev entered the room, he remembered Cramer's face, a handsome face without flaw, first seen at his grandparents' anniversary party.

Had it been going on then? Had she confided the pact to him then? It must have sounded childishly stupid to an outsider. How had she put it? 'We vowed, we swore a solemn oath.' One didn't vow or make pacts anymore. You hung loose, man, ready to make the scene, any scene. Cramer had figured a lucky combination for himself, a rapid ascendancy. Marriage to an Angstrom heiress. He laid it on her, and laid her into the bargain.

More came back, the conversation about salt domes. He was a journalist. That fit, on the affable side, easy with people. Lev had never been easy with people. The security he built was being pulled down by this clown. And Bea, sensible little body, cheerful iconoclast, collaborated in the destruction. Her instinct was so normal. Should it be trusted now?

"I wouldn't have messed in," Roger was saying, "except Bea was psyched out at the idea of writing Brill."

"It wasn't that," Bea interjected hastily. "I wasn't *afraid* to tell her. I didn't know how. It seems silly. Roger couldn't understand it. But you know, Lev. It wasn't until I got away from home that I was able to sort it out. There's such a thing as being too ingrown, too dependent on each other. It isn't healthy or natural. I mean, have you ever asked yourself why Brill hasn't married?"

Lev replied quietly with his usual appearance of detachment. "Are you saying that loyalty to us cut her off from all that?"

Roger interrupted once more. At least, Lev looked on it as an interruption. "If that's the case, then this is a first step toward letting fresh air in, putting things to rights."

Lev didn't respond to him. He spoke to Bea. "I can't accept what you're saying. There is nothing unnatural, as you seem to imply, about standing together, backing each other, being. . . ."

"A family? But three children aren't a family, Lev. And you should recognize that when it's a question of three adult siblings, it becomes grotesque. We should all be pursuing our own lives. Doing our own thing. That's exactly what I intend to do. And I certainly have no guilt about it. I don't feel I owe Brill an explanation. All the same, I'm afraid she'll be peculiar and sticky about it. I *did* try to write her. But no matter how I put

493

it, it sounded as though I was breaking away. At least I thought that's what Brill would think, you know how she is, so intense and all."

"She counts on us," Lev said.

"And she *can* count on us. Getting married isn't deserting the Knolls or the Angstroms."

"Forsaking all others," Lev quoted.

"Lev, get with it. That's so old-fashioned. Roger and I are going to write our own ceremony and be married here in Aspen, barefoot under the Maroon Bells."

Lev chuckled. "Brill may not be the only one you have to reckon with. What about Grandbee?"

"She'll come around. She'll have to or miss the wedding. And you know how Grandbee loves weddings."

The door flew open. A girl with a disordered mane of red hair stopped in mid stride. "Oh dear, a family conference." She looked at and spoke directly to Lev. "Excuse it, please."

"It's all right, Erin," Bea said. "We're through with the heavy stuff. We've sent out for pizzas."

"Super." Erin sat down by Lev. "You're her brother?"

"And you're the bassoonist," Lev guessed.

"Right. I was Bea's roommate last summer."

"I should explain," Bea said, "that this is Erin's pad. She sort of lent it to us."

"Tell me," Lev asked her, "how does a girl decide on a bassoon as an instrument?"

"Please don't turn out to be a male chauvinist. You have incredible eyes. I generally don't trust a sister's description, but she was absolutely right about your eyes."

"You do believe in role reversals, don't you?"

"No. I don't believe in roles. If a girl likes the sound of a bassoon, why shouldn't she play it? If she thinks a guy has great eyes, why shouldn't she tell him?"

"But what does that leave the guy to tell the girl?"

"He doesn't have to tell her anything. No compliments, no pattern, just honesty." She gave him a sideways glance. "If you think I'm foxy looking, that's different. You could tell me that."

"I do think you're foxy looking." The description was apt. From the bottom-hugging jeans rose a slender,

494

provocative figure. Her face held a pleasant, elfin quality. "Are you a student?"

Erin answered obliquely. "You might say that since I arrived at Aspen, they are uncomfortably aware there are students on campus."

Bea laughed. "Erin teaches woodwinds in exchange for a class in music theory. The other night she received one of those delightful memos they send around if you are heard tootling on your instrument after eleven."

"Three bars of absolutely indescribable music descended on me. How else was I supposed to fix it in my mind?"

Erin's presence relieved the atmosphere. Lev wrung a promise from Bea to telephone Brill. That, at least, saved something. Perhaps Brill would be reconciled. The pizzas arrived and Erin sat on the back of the couch talking with her mouth full. He found himself enjoying her freewheeling exuberance. "I'm the only one that's ever had any talent in my family. We're a big family too. Five kids, all as undisciplined as me. Anyway, my mother once said that when it came to talent, the only parlor trick she could do was get up on the dining room table and have a baby. So when the Sisters sent a note home to my parents saying I had a special gift for the bassoon, that was it. I've had lessons ever since. I think they probably sent that note because they couldn't get anyone to volunteer for the bassoon, or else they had one left over."

"Don't listen to her," Bea exclaimed, "the Irish are not noted for their accuracy. Erin is absolutely mad about her instrument, and good. And now she's into writing, part of an orchestration workshop."

None of this did Erin deny. When Lev got up to leave, she accompanied him into the hall. Lev was conscious of the look his sister shot Roger.

The door closed on their goodnights and he found Erin still beside him. "You can drop me," she said. "It isn't out of your way."

"I thought you lived here," Lev said.

"I do. Or did. They've been using my place for reasons too complicated to go into. I thought I'd go home with you."

Lev tried to assume a level-headed stance. "You don't know anything about me."

"Wrong. I've known about you forever. How you fell, getting a metal post through your knee when you were eleven. . . ."

"All right, all right," he conceded.

"Bea says you were always wrecking yourself as a kid, falling on or out of things."

"Not true. The girls skirted the big moguls, you know, went whipping around them. I jumped them and never cracked up once.

"She told me you were going to climb Orizaba your sophomore year, but fell down the stairs at Princeton and broke your foot."

Lev laughed. "But I did climb Orizaba."

"You did?"

"Didn't she tell you? I climbed it the next year with three friends over summer vacation." They reached his parked Porsche and Erin jumped in, not allowing him to touch the handle. "Go on," she said, "about Orizaba."

Lev found himself speaking readily and with humor about himself. He wasn't always able to do this. "I've climbed since I was fifteen and I've had a long-standing agreement with Grandfather to phone the moment I was off the face. Well, this time I tried to place the call. But have you ever attempted to get through from Mexico City to Carmel, California? It was a comedy of errors. The operator couldn't make out my Spanish and switched me to someone she assured me was English-speaking. Then I was the one who couldn't understand. By this time there was interference on the line. I was told the circuits were busy and the connection went dead. I decided to try later.

"You know how it is. I was with these guys, a few hours went by. And there was a time change I hadn't taken into consideration. The result was, Grandfather flipped out. He went down to the local police station and asked for a Spanish-speaking officer. He told him his grandson, Lev Angstrom, was lost with companions on Orizaba. Grandfather insisted he contact his counterpart in Mexico City at once and arrange a rescue. The officer explained he couldn't comply with this request on his own, so his superior was sent for. After a combination of dire threats on Grandfather's part, plus the assurance that he would pay for the call, the sergeant finally agreed to take the responsibility.

"Now comes the funky part, my grandfather's Spanish-speaking officer, although of Mexican descent, couldn't make the Mexico City police understand him. In exasperation Grandfather takes the phone and gets across to them in a combination of English curses and kitchen Spanish that his grand-hijo and friends are lost on Orizaba.

"The next episode, an item in the San Francisco *Examiner-Chronicle*: 'Four Americans fail to return from expedition. Rescue being organized.' This is picked up and syndicated in the Mexico City press. The four Americans were listed as Sherri Adel, that was Jerry Adams; Wendy Matel, that was Wendell Maxwell; Bob Pine, that was Bob Ryan, and Web Angby, me. I see the article. . . ."

"Oh no," Erin burst out.

"Four fellow Americans stuck on Orizaba, which we have just climbed, and two of them girls, Sherri and Wendy. I call the Mexico City police and volunteer the four of us for the rescue team."

Erin enjoyed the story and his attempt to amuse her. But she was determined the conversation would not proceed on this level. "Why do you climb, Lev? I thought men climbed to prove something. But you're an Angstrom. You don't have to prove anything."

"When you climb," Lev said, "you are on your own. You've left your civilization and all its supports. You learn something about yourself. Tell me when you want to turn around."

They were winding along a high pass with enormous slabs of exfoliating granite braiding with extruded surfaces. An occasional pine broke through the granite.

"I want to see where you live," Erin said.

"It's a four-hour drive. We won't get there till daylight."

"Do you always figure things out hours ahead of time? Or maybe you figure in days or even years?

Maybe you have your whole life planned? I'm not like that. With me A rarely follows in a straight line to B. All sorts of possibilities intervene and sometimes I never leave A at all because there is so much to explore."

The great peaks over them were black shadows. They flowed from form to form as the car passed. "I don't think you'll find A in me, Erin. I don't even find A in myself. As a matter of fact, things just came apart for me."

"I know. Bea said you wouldn't like the idea of her getting married."

"You're close friends, right?"

Erin nodded.

"Did she ever tell you . . . say anything about the family?"

"Sure. The one you formed."

"I suppose it sounded pretty stupid. It did in there."

"Idealistic, maybe. Not stupid."

"We were the nucleus, we three. It was supposed to grow. This was to happen by bringing in friends and. . . ."

"And Roger doesn't take the whole thing seriously."

"Neither of them does. You see, it's more than a family, it's conservation, a simple life, that's at the center. But it was to be with the framework of technology. Brill, she's the genius, a unique person, clinical almost, detached. Except when it comes to Bea and me. Anyway, she's doing work on a solar cell."

"And you? What's your part?"

Only to a musician's ear was there a missed beat.

"I was to have built a solar house."

"But you haven't."

He didn't answer. Recently he had been toying with the old idea. He had even chosen the site, a bluff facing due south, with a lake fronting it for added reflection. Squirreled away in his desk somewhere was an abandoned set of plans. "I've been doing a few things," he said defensively. "Right now I'm taking a long look at alternative energy."

"Alternative energy means solar too, doesn't it?"

"Of course." Even with his eyes on the road he knew she was looking at him.

"I think you feel lousy about having put off the solar house. As though you let Brill down as much as Bea has. Because that's Brill's special interest, right?"

"To tell the truth, I don't know how practical my design is."

"Then you *do* have a design!" she said triumphantly. "But I don't think you're asking the right question. 'Is it practical? Is it possible?' If I asked those questions, I'd never write a note of music. Because, can you build a world with dimension, that you can actually enter, just out of sound? And one that has the added magical property of being called into being only at certain moments in time? Your faith is what makes it happen."

Lev muttered something under his breath.

"What did you say?"

"I was calling down a blessing on your untidy red head."

"Why?"

"Because I'm going to show you the solar house."

"But you said it isn't built."

"It isn't. I'm going to show it to you anyway."

She slept in the car and wakened when he turned off the main road onto a dirt track with a wall of coniferous forest on either side.

The mingling of night and morning culminated in streaks of light. Sunrise beat the sky to a froth of color. It filtered along the trees, outlining a meadow. He stopped and got out. "Are you ready?"

"What is this place?"

"You'll see." They were at seven thousand feet. The morning sun had not had time to moderate the frost of night. He followed the edge of a stream. The water struck at half-submerged rocks and ran backwards, creating slapping waves and white spume that threw itself against the down-rushing current. Lev picked up a stone and tossed it into the water. "Did you see that first tight circle? Children are a separate family inside a family. The larger circle, those are the grownups. From there on the circle widens, grows more diffuse, a few friends, schoolmates, the world outside. It's that first circle which needs to be protected. It's hard to define, hard to put into words. All sorts of things go on that only you three know. Like Brill's stories and the way she'd pretend they were real. She used to tell us Kumju told them to her, and we believed her. That is, Bea did. And I pretended to."

"Who's Kumju?"

"A god we used to have in our garden. Brill has him now."

"A real god?"

"Nobody knows. Grandfather picked him up in Egypt. But he never made it in one piece. They said he was freight-damaged. The truth is, he was broken in two. He's been a part of things as long as I can remember. He watched our mother grow up and then us." His eyes had been riveted on the stream. He wrenched them away. "Come on," he took her hand and they began to climb. She saw a waterfall far up the mountain. Snow fed, it poured out in torrents to swell the stream. At their feet he pointed out stripped aspen branches lying naked. "Beavers."

They approached the dammed shallows quietly, standing some minutes to watch. The pond remained still, without a ripple of activity. A nondescript bird, scorning the penned waters, dared the rapids further along, ducking its head in the swift current to drink.

They continued the climb, leaving stream and pond behind. At the top of the rise Erin stopped involuntarily. They looked down on a lake, like a tiny pocket mirror reflecting sky and clouds. Winds ruffled it breaking the image of massed pines.

"We've left the aspen behind," Lev said. He turned to watch the animation in her face. "What do you think of my solar house?" He pointed to a bare promontory several hundred feet below, that overhung the lake.

"It's marvelous. There are aspen growing down there!"

"Yes, it is sheltered by low hills to the north and is at a lower altitude. Do you want to go through the house?"

"Nothing but the full tour will do."

"Okay." He smiled into her face. "It's something of a scramble." They ran downhill to the bluff, brushing past clumps of wildflowers like hand-held bouquets. Even

500

the rocks were colorful, part of the red-orange earth. They arrived breathless at the bluff. "It only has one door," Lev said, erecting the house for her. "It's at the back. So when you enter you see the lake. It was going to be a hydraulic revolving door, in other words, an air trap. But I decided against it."

"Why?"

"Well, it would be expensive."

Erin looked puzzled.

"Brill wouldn't like it if I used my family money for the house. So all I can put into it is my salary, the money I earn."

"I like this sister of yours. She's really independent, isn't she?"

"She's been on her own since she was a kid."

"Well now, tell me, is the foundation poured? Is the framing up?"

"Of course, can't you see how peaked the roof is? And it's covered with black glass plates."

"I see, it's mostly roof area. That lets you get all the sun you can. I sort of feel in my bones the way it works. But you'd better tell me, only not too technically, so I'll understand."

It was as though he had found the plans at the back of his desk drawer. The details were clear to him. "Actually my first attempt was based on MIT's prototype Solar House IV. Then I started fooling around. That expanse of dark glass on the roof draws the sun which heats the copper pipes in the ceiling, which, in turn, heats the water flowing through them. This provides energy to both heat and cool the house, and to cook with."

"What happens on days the sun doesn't come out?"

"There's a storage reservoir that holds up to five days' supply. Then we go visit friends."

She was concentrating too hard to laugh. "Help me picture it. I've walked in the door. The roof comes almost to the ground, does that mean an A-frame look?"

"Right. A pyramidal metal frame. The sun not only supplies heat but also light. The idea is to convert this into electricity. Over there," he gestured in the direction of a squirrel that scurried off, "is a biconvex lens focusing sunlight on a battery of solar cells, surrounded by black concave mirrors which further condense and absorb. A transducer changes the condensed radiant energy to electricity, which is used both to power the house and for storage. Of course, Brill is working on a concept that would revolutionize the whole field. Solar cells have been used from the beginning to power spacecraft, but the process is much too costly for mass production. Brill's thought is—well, she'll have to tell you, it's a field of mathematics I never studied. . . . Now if you'll step this way, we are in the living room." He stood aside and gestured for her to enter.

She swept by him. "I love your furnishings," she said. "Very tasteful. Divine color scheme."

"Are you comfortable? Because the heat can be controlled by interior adjustable aluminum blinds. Also, if you'll notice, there is extra insulation and thermal pane glass."

"What percent of the total power will the sun really provide?"

"Good question. I hope about forty to fifty percent."

"It sounds a little cold and a little hot."

"It is. In this house you have to put on sweaters and take them off. It's not what they call a shirt-sleeve atmosphere. But I don't think it will be too bad. The air-conditioning works by using antifreeze in the pipes instead of water, creating an absorption-refrigeration process, much the same theory as the old gas refrigerators worked on."

They smiled shyly at each other, aware they were two complex individuals attempting to share something.

"I love your view of the lake," Erin said. "The clouds seem to touch it."

"That's its name. Cloud Lake."

"Is it really?"

"Of course. You just named it."

Her laugh was a joyous sound. "I wish your kitchen were better stocked. I could go for a good cup of coffee and breakfast."

"As it happens, that is entirely possible."

Erin looked skeptical. "The town is quite a ways back."

"I have a cabin, a prefab, set up not too far away. We'll walk over. You see, this is part of a large tract of land my grandfather deeded to me to avoid paying taxes on. We are experimenting with an *in situ* process, a technique for squeezing oil from shale without disfiguring the land. We work inside the mountain."

"You mean there's a mining operation here?"

"It seems to go with being an Angstrom, this interest in energy. When Brill broke away I decided to go the other route. I'm bucking the tide, of course. The reason I'm even permitted to investigate dark horses like shale, coal, geothermal, and solar, is the Arab stranglehold. The country is just beginning to scramble for self-sufficiency."

"It's good that at least other possibilities are being checked out."

Lev nodded. "Everyone knows there's been an influx of billions in OPEC funds into U. S. Treasury bills, and more billions flooding the U.S. economy. When a business borrows large sums, its creditors have a say in how things are run. The same is true of governments."

"You're implying Saudi Arabia has bought a voice in U.S. policy? That's pretty frightening."

"It's committee decision all down the line. And you don't know who is getting to whom. That's big business. I work for the Company, even own a small portion of it. But the Company is a process, an ongoing process. No one can control it any more. It interacts with government, national policy, international policy. And it is important which way it goes. No one controls it, but certain of us can give a shove now and again. That's what I'm trying to do. I think it's vital the Company wind up California, not Saudi. I mean the Saudis aren't exactly civilized. You should hear some of Grandfather's stories. Hands and feet of thieves hanging in the marketplace at Jidda. That was 1933. And slavery wasn't outlawed until 1964. So to me it seems important to break free and we can only do this by developing competitive forms of energy. The shah of Iran, who is pretty astute, made a good point. He said, 'Oil is too valuable to use as a power source. It is the base of all petrochemicals, fertilizers and drugs.' India, Africa,

503

Latin America are in for a rough time. But the U. S. has agriculture. The Saudis can't grow a damn thing. They can corner the money market, but they can't feed themselves."

"Then why don't we use that leverage?"

"Because we need to export. We've been pretty largely priced out of manufactured goods, so agriculture is it. We sell our wheat to Russia under most favored nation status, and it winds up in Saudi."

"And now they're not even going to let the Jews out."

"That's surprising," Lev said. "You'd think they'd want them all in one place so they could finish them off. That's a biased opinion. I'm half Jewish."

She seemed surprised. "How does that square with being an Angstrom?"

"It doesn't. That's one of my problems." He laughed abruptly. "But why get into that?"

"Why not? Moon, spoon, June went out with bobby socks."

Lev considered this a moment. "You sound spoiled."

She nodded agreement. "I'm the youngest child."

They pursued a zigzag course down the hill, sliding the last dozen feet in scree. Eventually they rejoined the stream, following it to the cabin. Itself unexceptional, it was set among trees in such a way that it seemed to grow like everything around it.

From the railed porch one could cast a line into the water. The living room was furnished hastily with a few bean bag chairs crumpled from a last occupancy, a coffee table and some candles. There was a single bedroom with a sleeping bag on the floor. Erin took in the monastic look of the place and became sweeter to Lev. She sat on the counter and gave advice as he prepared scrambled eggs in a buttered skillet. "You should use polyunsaturates, didn't you know that?"

"You want to cook?" he returned.

"No."

"Okay then."

She swung her legs back and forth. "Lev. . . ."

"What?"

"I'm the one asking questions all the time. Don't you want to know about me?"

504

"Why?"

"I want you to understand me, then maybe you'll like me more."

"It might work the other way. Here, it's done. Slide over the plates."

At that moment the toast popped up.

"I can see you've been a bachelor a long while. Your timing is perfect." But she seemed preoccupied. "Well, if you won't ask, I'm going to tell you anyway. Music is the most important thing in my life. I think because I know I'll always have it. You don't know that about people. You don't even dare hope it." She looked out at him over the rim of a glass of milk. "The bassoon is only part of it. I compose. I'm working on something new. It's monumental."

Lev smiled slightly. "Tell me about it."

"Well, one should really say, Opus 39 or whatever. But secretly I think of it as a tower, a great campanile. It's stories high, and each story is a work in itself, yet it is all interconnected. Have you ever seen Giotto's Tower, part of the Maria della Fiore church in Florence?"

He nodded.

"I picture it like that, proportioned so perfectly and strongly that it breaks your heart. Anyway, the idea is that everything men value, they shut up there."

"Salt domes," Lev said absently.

"What?"

"Nothing. Go on."

"I have this great idea, showing it through the bassoon, a simple repairman called in to fix the plumbing. One story is devoted to knowledge and philosophy, mausoleums of books containing the collected wisdom of mankind. Another is filled with works of art. Then at the top, where the bells are . . . well, no one knows for sure. Some believe God lives there. Some say God died there. Some say a giant computer sits looking out over everything and toting it all up with flashing lights and a myriad buttons. Did you know they don't press buttons any more to activate ballistic missiles and warheads? They turn keys. A physics student told me that. At the end of the piece there will either be a great

505

hallelujah or we will hear the key turn. I don't know which yet."

She communicated a vibrancy as she talked, in some manner sharing crashing waves of sound.

"Your eyes are green," he observed.

To escape his scrutiny, a great many suggestions poured out. "I'll do the washing up, you look in the fridge and get together a picnic. I want to go back to the solar house and spend the whole day."

"There's plenty of beer," he said, "and not much else."

"What about the eggs? I'll hard-boil them."

He put their lunch into a backpack along with the rolled-up sleeping bag and a couple of sweaters.

Erin gave him an odd look.

"It gets cold when the sun goes down," Lev said.

"We're not going to stay that long."

They left the cabin and hiked briskly back the way they had come. "I might as well tell you," she was slightly out of breath, "that I've had a thing about you since last summer. It's partly Bea's fault. I generally don't listen to sisters. But then she showed me a picture." She touched his arm to indicate a stop, and slipping her fingers into her jeans came up with a scuffed wallet, from which she abstracted a snapshot.

Lev looked, not at the picture, but at her.

"I ripped it off," she acknowledged. "But before you start thinking what you're thinking, let me go on. I'm a musician. I'm serious about music. And I'm good. But a bassoon can drive better men than you to jump off the bluff. And I practice every day. Not only that, I write for and perform with a group in Aspen. There are rehearsals almost nightly and performances weekends. This makes me unreliable, someone not to be counted on. My head's so full of music, I don't get other things together very well, like my life. I'm scatterbrained, sometimes I'm one place when I should be another. I forget about appointments. And when I get scared about a man, like maybe he's beginning to mean more than I want him to, I run." She looked into his face to read his conclusion.

Lev took possession of her hand, and they climbed

the summit. They stood a moment, taking it in, the life in them responding to the life of earth, sky and water.

They made their way through the dusty smell of chaparral to the imagined house. He unrolled the down bag, and she stretched out while he propped the backpack against a rock. Removing the cans of beer, he took them to the lakeside to chill in the shallows between rocks.

He came back and sat down beside her. Erin leaned against him letting her tousled red hair fall against his chest. "Bea told me, I guess she meant it as a warning, that she's never seen you with the same girl twice."

Lev gave that low rolling laugh of his. "Sheer protective coloring," he said, "mostly to keep Grandbee off my back. She's a great one for marrying people off. Although, until now, she's been singularly unsuccessful with us."

She could hear his breathing. It was perfectly even. Hers was a hissing in her ears, a ringing in her head. Signal flares were up.

Lev looked at her intently. She seemed fragile, young. There was no trace of makeup on her face. He pushed back the strands of unruly hair and kissed her ear. "Erin, you are the more of everything than I had thought, more artist, more person, and I suspect, more woman."

"You thought I was a spoiled, wayward brat."

"Perhaps I did. Perhaps you are." They undid the package of salt and hard-cooked eggs and went down together for the cold beer.

"Could I help you build this house?" Erin asked.

"I don't know. What about your music?"

"I could do both."

"What about all those dire predictions?"

She shrugged. "That's only in case I should get involved. Actually, you're not as good looking as your picture."

He laughed. "Well, let's see then, do you have your union card?"

"No, but I can climb ladders, roof, paint, get splinters in my fingers."

"You're on," Lev said.

507

The intercom on Ted's desk in his San Francisco office buzzed. "Mr. Roger Cramer to see you, sir."

"Who the hell is Roger Cramer?"

Consternation at a quiet, well-bred level. "You sent for him, Mr. Angstrom. All the way from Colorado."

"Well, if he's come that far, he can wait a little longer." Ted read his mail and a *Playboy* article. After what he considered a suitable interval, he rang his secretary. "Anyone waiting for me?" he asked.

"Mr. Cramer is still here, sir."

"Cramer? Well, if he's still there, you'd better send him in."

A well set up young man, scrupulously buffed and brushed, was ushered through the carved double doors. His feet sank into the carpet, making no sound. Ted had observed before that this seemed to disconcert people. "Well," he said, "who the hell are you?"

"Roger Cramer, sir." The young man came forward, smiling and extending his hand. Ted ignored it. The smile on the young man's face stiffened there.

"I know you're Roger Cramer. People have been telling me that for an hour. What I am asking you is, who are you? Who are you that makes you think you can marry my granddaughter?"

The smile disappeared. "I'm in love with your granddaughter, Mr. Angstrom."

"I don't think that answers my question."

There was a pause. "Well, I don't think there is a satisfactory way to answer it, sir. I met Bea Anna at Stanford."

"What did you major in at Stanford?"

"Business administration."

"Ah," Ted said with something like satisfaction.

"But I switched to journalism."

Ted's brows drew together, laying a carpet like an entry rug. "Journalism! What did you want to do that for?"

"They had a better department, sir."

508

He never forgets to say *sir*, Ted thought. "Have you ever held a job, an honest-to-god job?"

"Well, I got a lectureship at the institute in Aspen. I knew Bea was there, so I applied. And I was lucky."

Ted looked at him with more interest. "Lucky, huh? That's a plus, young man. The first plus I've given you. Luck is important, very important. A man can work his heart out and, if he's not lucky, end up as a middle management person." He uttered the last words with such scorn that it seemed there was no worse fate. "Now," Ted leaned back in his swivel chair and peered up at Roger Cramer, who had not been asked to sit down. "Now we come to the crunch. Although Bea's name is Knolls, I'm sure you are not unaware of the Angstrom fortune, and that she is an heir."

"I know that." Roger spoke up, he didn't mumble or seem embarrassed.

"Then you are also aware that if you marry, and notice I say *if*, it would mean marrying into an empire. Bea Anna is the modern equivalent of a Plantagenet princess. Except today's power and money and influence are something new, a phenomenon of our times. What I want to know is, how do you fit into this?"

"I don't know, sir. I haven't the slightest idea. I think it would be a tremendous challenge to be part of Saudi-California."

"Hmmm," Ted said. Then looked at him shrewdly. "Would you be willing to start at the bottom and work your way up?"

"No, sir," Roger said distinctly.

Ted broke into a big smile. "Sit down, boy, sit down. We're going to get along."

Ted took a fountain pen out of a block of marble and began to draw mysterious hieroglyphics on a sheet of paper. "I need a man in Washington."

"Just like that?" Roger asked.

"Just like that. The president of the United States, despite his statements to the contrary, is on the way out. And he is going to nominate the dodo bird in his place."

"The what, sir?" Roger leaned forward, intrigued.

It amused Ted that he had piqued his interest. "I look at it this way. Washington is the focal point, the center. We have a job to do there. I see it as launching a three-stage rocket. The first stage is about to fall back to earth, thrusting the second stage forward."

"The second stage is the dodo bird?"

"You're quick, you're very quick. But it's the third stage we've got to concentrate on, there's a whole constellation of appointments to be made, and kept in orbit. That's where you come in. The dodo bird has to be maneuvered, the Congress approached and the Senate softened up. Now, you're an affable young man, a fresh face. You think big, and you're lucky. So you're going to Washington."

"What about Bea?"

"What about Bea? The Kennedy Center of Performing Arts is about to make her an offer."

Roger Cramer's aplomb deserted him. "Good God, I can't believe this."

Ted also was surprised, as he had only that moment thought of the happy solution.

"You'll be fed various names at the proper time. They won't be unfamiliar to you. For the present, all you have to do is make friends with the right people."

Roger digested this a moment. "Then I have your permission, sir, to marry Bea Anna?"

"My permission, yes. And if all three stages come off without a hitch, you'll have my blessing."

"What's the différence?" Roger was beginning to feel at home with the old man.

"Considerable," Ted said.

Bea phoned Brill later in the week. Her sister's voice, sounding as though from the next room, asked, "Want to come to a wedding Saturday?"

Brill matched the lightness. "So you've set the date? Where is it to be?"

"Here at Aspen. Outdoors by the stream, under the Maroon Bells. I'll have to break that part to Grandbee gently."

"Suppose it rains? You said it rains some every day."

"Then we'll just move inside. Are you glad for me, Brill?"

"Of course, if you're sure. If it's what you want."

"I'm sure most of the time, and scared part of the time. But it is what I want." Superlatives spilled out of the phone describing Roger Cramer.

Brill listened a decent length of time and then cut in. "Have you contacted Lev?"

"Yes, he'll be here. Did you know Grandpa sent for Roger, gave him a regular grilling, but he passed with flying colors."

"That's nice."

"We're having a wedding supper Friday night so the whole family can get to know Roger. Why don't you come then?"

"Okay."

"Phone," Bea said, "and we'll meet the plane."

"No, I'll come directly to the hotel."

"All right. Brill? Wish me luck."

"I do."

There was a pause as Bea waited for something more spontaneous.

"See you Friday," Brill said and rang off. She remained by the phone, which was in a small alcove. She had never noticed the wallpaper design before. Ferns and flowers, living things, pressed into an ugly pattern. She began to tear at them with her nails. It was a slow job but she was patient, pieces and shreds of torn paper settled at her feet.

When Grandbee was notified, she was equally upset. "Outdoors! It sounds pagan. I, for one, will not feel they are married. If they don't want a church wedding, if they want to keep it intimate, just the family, I have seen some charming home ceremonies. Our own daughter was married here."

Ted didn't argue, but he knew if Brilli had not been pregnant at the time, nothing but a church wedding would have done.

Brillianna continued her complaint. "To expect two elderly people to travel half across the country to see

511

them married in a park like hoboes or gypsies, I do think is unconscionable."

Her real animus against the marriage she did not mention. To her way of looking at things, it was extremely inconsiderate of Bea, who was five years younger, to marry while Brill was still single. Bea had plenty of time, and it was unseemly to point up her sister's spinsterhood. Also, the marriage made more immediate the disposition of the Haviland china reposing regally in the Louis XV cabinet. In the early days she imagined the china would pass to Brill. And she had, through the years, kept that possibility open against the time Brill came to her senses. She had never understood why the girl found it necessary to deny her own family. She feared the Grenville inbreeding was at work there. That, combined with the Angstrom character, drove her. Like all Angstroms, she quested. But for what, her grandmother didn't know.

She was aware of the contrast in her granddaughters. A flighty streak marred Bea's nature, as it had her mother's. Poor, lonely Brilli, who sought love in unlikely places. On further consideration, Brillianna decided that in this swinging generation it was as well to get Bea Anna married. Although whether a young female *could* ruin her reputation, she was unsure. Still, recalling Bea's breathless in-a-hurry manner, it seemed wise while she was in the mood to marry, to encourage her in that direction. It could be looked at this way: one down, and one to go.

Ted seemed singularly pleased by the whole thing. He was, Brillianna thought, an incurable romantic. Any excitement pleased him. Besides, the wedding presented another opportunity to polish and trot out the old stories. "Have my cummerbund cleaned," he instructed Maria.

"You won't need your cummerbund," his wife told him acidly. "The whole affair is going to be barefoot in the grass."

"What?"

"It's the vogue today." Brillianna took pleasure in being current and dumbfounding her husband. "They even write their own marriage ceremony."

"Is it legal?" Ted asked.

512

They met in the gaudy, impersonal setting of a hotel lobby. An exclamation of dismay escaped the bride-to-be when she saw her sister. Brill seemed a wraith, her eyes ringed and dark. Bea fastened a look of inquiry on her as though trying to understand if she had done this. And in that instant became as pale as her sister. But Roger stood beside her, and Lev came in looking marvelously tan and kissed her. Grandfather gave her one of his bear hugs, and Grandbee was sniffing into a lace handkerchief, while her father, or the man she had always known as father, escorted her into dinner.

A lavish display of flowers entwined in frosted wedding bells ran the length of the table. The banquet area was private, waiters moved like shadows, this was the Angstrom family. The preordered dinner started with a toast to the young couple. Lev was seated across from Brill. He noticed she seemed incapable of finishing a sentence, letting them float vaguely away.

Dr. Knolls and the Angstroms met the Cramers with restrained enthusiasm. Roger's parents attempted to appear at ease. They still couldn't believe their son, whom they had more or less given up on, was marrying into this fabulous, monied clan.

Roger's face was guarded. But there was a quality of alertness about him. Ted, at this closer proximity, was well satisfied. Bea had made a good choice. Still, it appalled him, these young girls, ready at a moment's notice to leave their family and their homes. Biology was a devastating thing. However, Cramer would fit in. He might even bring off the Washington coup.

Glasses were once more raised, and by consensus Bea was declared beautiful, even for a bride; and Roger's father, who had indulged too much before dinner, swore his son was a lucky bastard.

Ted didn't take to the father. He sized him up as middle management. But the son was a different proposition. With Angstrom backing he'd move right along.

A nagging memory spoiled the rosy picture. . . . His own girl. He and Brillianna had expected marriage to solve the problems. It had solved everything all right. Eleven years later she was dead.

Without the memory of Brilli that haunted this evening, he would have felt the oil pastures ensured happiness, providing with abundance a guarantee against the vicissitudes of life. But the great black gusher had not been powerful enough to carry Brilli's fragile life.

The music of a Renaissance flute broke across the hushed voices of the guests assembled on the lawn before the music tent. Bea stood in a small group that included only her family. She wore her mother's wedding dress, which had been secretly sent for.

Grandbee had a moment of giddiness when she saw it. Ted thought it an ill omen. However Bea looked so lovely that he could not believe the fates would be unkind a second time.

The moment arrived. Bea smiled on them all, hugged Howard briefly, clung to Lev, kissed her grandparents and approached Brill. Brill turned to watch the flutist.

Bea walked to Roger and joined him. Together they proceeded across the grassy slope toward the minister. Grouped on both sides of the wedding pair were students from the music school. Friends, her father's secretary, and relatives watched, as hand in hand the young couple came to the mound where the minister stood waiting. He was a giant of a man, dwarfing Roger, who looked slight and boyish standing before him.

Were all brides beautiful, Erin wondered, her eyes on Bea. Her thoughts turned to Lev. He insisted they attend separately. He had flown down last evening leaving her to drive out this morning. She had hardly been able to catch his eye. When she did, he had only a reserved smile for her. An appropriate smile, one wedding guest to another. The music was stilled, the ceremony began. Erin's eyes wandered to the other sister, Brill, who elected to wear a dark suit. It was the only spot of gloom in the whole festive company. She looked the part of the uninvited fairy godmother about to make a dour wish.

Brill, feeling herself scrutinized, allowed her glance to roam casually. Who was that rather fey-looking girl with red hair? Possibly the bassoonist who had been

Bea's roommate the first year. Erin, meeting her eyes, smiled. Brill drew herself together. It was a trial to be stared at, pitied. Especially as she honestly wished Bea well. Since it wasn't Bea, why not?

Bea, her Bea, had gone away and never come back. So why not wish this stranger, with the strange young man, well? She heard the wedding vows without emotion.

Erin worked her way through the assembled group, appearing unexpectedly at Brill's side. She caught hold of her arm. "Brill, I'm Erin. I want to know you."

"Bea Anna's friend?" Brill asked, trying to sort things out.

Erin brought her cheek against hers. "Lev's girl." She kissed Brill and looked deeply into her face.

"And I am the executioner," Brill said, "who walks by his side."

"What did you say?" Erin's voice was flat with shock.

"It's time Lev had a girl. I hope you'll be part of the family, Erin."

Erin tried to respond, but she was held in a kind of paralysis.

Brill returned home. "Bea got married," she told Kumju. "And I met Lev's girl. It's Erin, the bassoonist."

The brief interlude occasioned by the marriage seemed unreal. But Peg Trotter called to talk about it. "Wasn't it lovely? I thought the setting, those snowy mountain peaks, indescribable."

"Did you meet Bea's roommate?"

"The red-haired girl? Yes. Lovely, isn't she?"

Brill was impatient at Peg's lack of differentiation. She enthused about everything equally in identical vocabulary.

"I liked her too," Brill said, and changed the subject.

Fresh ideas were gathering in her head, ways of grappling with unbounded Fermi surfaces in her model. The resistance would depend not only on the orientation of the magnetic field and the current but also on the direction with respect to the crystallographic axes. But before she could turn her mind to that, she must find out about Z-9. The secret was there somewhere in the files Peg had in her possession. Her need to know was partly to satisfy herself as to the extent of her father's involvement. She also meant to discover what the cryptogram Z-9 represented. "Peg, I need another session with the files."

"But how can I? Suppose Dr. Knolls asks for them?"

"Just the last section. If he asks, bring him what I've already gone through."

"Suppose there's something in the last part he wants to refer to?"

Brill said nothing.

". . . All right."

"Drop them off tonight. I'll have them back to you by noon tomorrow."

Brill read most of the night. Toward morning a subsection caught her eye. *Trench Z-9*. She gathered her energy for a final effort. "The accumulation of plutonium in this crib has reached a level that suggests it is possible a nuclear chain reaction could be touched off through earthquake or sabotage. It is recommended that this crib be mined in the hope of recovering the plutonium." There was a note attached directing attention to the 1967 Vienna Conference Report, which said in part: "A substantial amount of radioactive fluid was dumped into a sump at Hanford during an emergency. The action caused the ground water to fluctuate, exposing contaminated mud, which dried and became airborne. Since then, lower or intermediate level waste has been disposed of by dumping into this sump. Most of the material is relatively short-lived radioisotopes that decay rapidly. However, there has been criticism within the AEC of this deliberate dumping."

The card index also referred to an article dated 1970. ". . . In summation, papers presented identify long-lived radionuclides in the ground water beneath the installation. These materials are trapped by relatively impenetrable layers of rock at different levels. This perching phenomenon delays the movement of the substances, allowing time for radioactive decay. It has been suggested, however, that springs form in much the same way, trapped between layers of rock. Eventually, they re-surface elsewhere or feed into a stream. This hot material concentrated beneath the cribs could conceivably be carried into subterranean aquifers which supply drinking water, or be leached directly into the Columbia River seven miles distant. On reaching the river, radionuclides would be extremely dilute, but cesium 137 could concentrate a thousand times through the levels of the food chain."

Brill leaned back. She couldn't take it in. The accidental spills she had been concerned about were one thing, but to deliberately pour radioactive debris into open pits was a crime. Perhaps against a humanity that hadn't yet been born. But did that make it better, the fact that the consequences were deferred?

What was her father's part in this? The thought kept invading her mind. She couldn't get rid of it. She shook her head. He was a responsible person. Still, he brought the papers home to study. What did that indicate—concern, a very real worry? Did the molten poisons eat into his sleep? And in his waking life, between appointments, phone calls, seminars and consulations, what dreadful possibilities crept into his mind?

She recognized her schizoid approach, terror at the thought of Z-9 and an equal fear for her father. As an officer of the AEC, had his opinion lain with the majority? Had he voted for expediency, sacrificing caution, risking disaster?

It was important for her to know. She had to know. Surely the decision regarding Z-9 could not be laid at his door. But there was no way to question his part in it without exposing Peg.

Brill turned in early, not to sleep, but to quiet herself. She was having another attack of nerves. Kumju was part of it. His role shifted constantly, crystallizing her fears. He spoke of domestic animals, sheep, cattle, swine. "Birds are more resistant than animals. The adult species can survive *one thousand*. Cereal plants such as wheat, barley, oats can take up to *four thousand*. An oak tree begins dying in its upper structures at *ten thousand*. Natural grasses and grazing land can withstand

517

twice that amount. Insects are more impervious, their larvae, eggs and nymphs are sensitive, but an adult insect will survive a *hundred thousand roentgens.*"

A wave seemed to pass over Kumju's featureless face causing it to undulate. "Bacteria. Viruses. It takes a *million roentgens* to destroy them." Daylight touched the room. Brill lifted her head from the pillow. Still sleeping, she sought another spot. The next moment she brought herself upright. There was a terrible fear in her. She thought that all the oak trees had died.

Why had that frightened her so deeply? After having read the catalogued results of radiation in human beings, beginning with a murky softening of the skin and ending with retinal impairment, it seemed that the extermination of oak trees was nothing to get exercised about.

Brill got up and went into the bathroom for a glass of water. She peered at her face in the mirror. Her skin had taken on a new pallor. Was it separating from the bones? She felt cold. It would get colder in all rooms everywhere. You couldn't drive your car at seventy. The bowl in the tree was cemented over. You couldn't assume that because something was, it would continue to be; because gas was unrationed, it would remain unrationed; because lettuce was thirty-nine cents, it would stay there. Nothing could be taken for granted. There were no guarantees in this world that was passing. The whole fabric was shot through with breakdown and corruption. Manipulated shortages, dumping of milk, smothering millions of baby chicks, the massacre of calves. There was no fuel for schoolrooms. But the military commandeered millions of gallons of gasoline, and millions more were shipped to Saudi after being refined here. Americans despaired. High government officials were dismissed, the president resigned. And in Alice in Wonderland fashion was pardoned while denying there was a crime. The safeguards built into the Constitution were violated; enfeebled, they no longer protected. Taxes like a swollen river swept away homes, blotted out lives. The rich barricaded themselves behind guarded condominium gates. The poor preyed on each other. Senseless crime, mischief turned crime, soared.

The blacks were frustrated; middle-class working people, furloughed.

With the ground shifting under your feet was it enough to keep your balance? She knew it was not. She knew what was required.

They laid out and staked the house themselves. It took sophisticated calculations to make sure the roof collectors would be properly oriented to the winter sun and that the overhang was right for the latitude. At the same time, as he pointed out to Erin, they were squaring the corners by the oldest method known to man, the 3-4-5 triangle the Mesopotamians used to build the ziggurats.

Crews were brought up to pour the foundation and erect the steel space frame. Then they retreated down the mountain, leaving quantities of nails and cigar butts. Lev and Erin stared at the skeleton in the shape of a truncated prism, steep to the south, which they were to fashion into a dwelling. Footings had been sunk for a dual opening fireplace, which puzzled Erin.

"It's not exactly solar energy."

"No," Lev said. "It's in case we have a week of bad weather and use up our reserve. Or in case something goes wrong with the circulation system. Or in case nothing goes wrong and we just want to lie on a bear rug in front of a roaring blaze. Synthetic bear," he said, catching her eye. Erin didn't stand for things made out of animal skins.

They worked till about one each afternoon. Then Erin would wander off, take out her knife, and whittle at her double reed until it felt right to her fingers and tongue. As she inserted it into the crook and attached the wing joint to the butt, long joint, and bell, she explained, "All these twists and turns are so a five foot five inch woman can play an eight foot woodwind."

She teased him with a Beethoven scherzo, of such compellingly fast rhythm it was impossible to keep to his more plodding pace. He finally dropped down beside her to rest and look over the elevation plans. Copper pipe for the radiant heating system had to come down through the partitions. Lev chalked the places he'd have to drill plates and joists, and nail on reinforcing scabs. "You know, it's taking on the appearance of a house. So far, a house that birds fly through. But in a few weeks. . . ."

Erin took the bassoon from her mouth and blew out hard a couple of times. "That was a tough passage."

"It sounded good."

"It isn't only a question of your wind. The bassoon is completely irrational in its fingering. But listen to this. I'm going to take it up three octaves from low B-flat." She proceeded to do so and it sounded rather pleasing. "That's its melodic range, roughly the same as the tenor voice. Now I'll take it to treble E. See how you like that."

He listened, but did not know what he was listening for.

"Well?" she demanded.

"Yeah, sounds good."

"It's an authentic Johan Adam Heckel, made of mature European maple. You know in Mozart's time there were only four keys. Anything outside the scale of C had to be cross-fingered. You're not interested, are you?"

"Yes."

"No you're not, you were sneaking looks at your blueprints all the time."

"Is that some sort of crime? We are trying to put up a solar house."

"That's not the point. The point is I'm making a gigantic effort to be part of your life. And you're not putting out an effort of any kind. You're not even interested."

"What do you want me to say, Erin? That the bassoon is my favorite instrument? It isn't. But that doesn't really have anything to do with you and me, does it?"

She shook her head. "No. It's just that rehearsals start tonight on the concerto. I won't have time for supper, I'll have to dash."

"Okay."

520

"And I won't be back till morning. But don't worry. I'll catch a few hours sleep at the prefab and be on the job by noon."

"I'll get some of the crew back, then."

"Is that what I've been?" Her voice attacked him. "Another back, hands?"

"Erin, you told me at the beginning this would happen, that you'd have to go down the mountain."

"You could at least tell me you didn't want me to go."

"I would if I thought I could stop you."

"Oh damn, I'm as irrational as my instrument."

"It will be hard on you, that long ride into Aspen and back."

"I know."

"Perhaps you should stay over every other day."

"Perhaps I shouldn't come back at all."

He pulled her to her feet and into his arms. "End of break." They worked another two hours. Erin was unusually subdued. She dredged up an old grievance that weighed on her. "Why did we have to go to the wedding separately?"

His reason was one he had explained before. "So as not to load Brill with more than she could handle."

"She handled it just fine. I told her I was your girl."

Lev was astounded. "You told her?"

"Of course."

"You were taking a chance." He seemed pleased however.

"She's a strange person." And she mentioned Brill's sinister pronouncement, which she hadn't been able to get out of her head. Lev only laughed, "That's part of a Kumju story," he said.

Still she worried. That was the trouble. She worried too much about him. "There's a couple of cans of tuna," she burst out, "and a part of a head of lettuce."

"Fine. I'll manage."

"I know you will. You managed before me. You'll manage after me."

He grabbed her with grimy hands. "There's not going to be an 'after you.' It's just you, understand?"

"It isn't the long drive or the schedule of rehearsals.

521

I get into it. I start thinking music, hearing it, living it."

"You'll juggle things, just as I do at the mine. Look," he took her by the shoulders, "if it were another man, that would be one thing. But I promise not to lay a hand on your bassoon. Now, you'd better get going."

She kissed him quickly and passionately, seized her instrument, and hurried off. Lev turned to study the corner bracing.

In the past he enjoyed the prefab retreat with the quiet bearing in on him, crickets and the murmur of the stream the only sound. This night he found himself expecting Erin's fluting laugh, or the movement of her through the rooms. Mouthfuls of food were not palatable without her conversation. The tuna was flat. He'd forgotten the mayonnaise and relish. That was Erin's department. She added the condiments. He squeezed lemon over everything and ate. Later in the evening he placed a phone call to the mine and took notes on the report. "I'll be by in the morning," he told the foreman. Next he arranged for a full crew to spend the day at the solar house. The rest of the night he studied the specs.

Things at the mine were not going well. The men grumbled at the introduction of new methods and when the machinery he ordered arrived, it was too large for the working space, which only confirmed the men in their skepticism. However the house proceeded at a good clip. The crew had put in four hours by the time he arrived. The outline began to fill in between the ribbed steel girders. He didn't know until then how important it was to him, a tangible expression of confidence.

He began looking for Erin around eleven-thirty. By twelve-thirty he was irritable with his crew. When they stopped to open their lunch buckets, he kept working. He heard her whistling before she came into view. She swung along with inner rhythm and waved. He waved back.

"Hi, Sandy, Don, Al," she said to the men, and— "Hi, Lev," her voice changing to a different note. She surveyed the morning's work. At least that's what he thought she was doing. "The woodwinds were terrific, really effective. We wove a chain, holding back, hold-

522

ing back, then breaking through with tremendous power. The fingering is fantastic."

"It went well then?" he asked.

She laughed. "Let's say it's in framing. We have to solidify yet, you know, put up interior partitions, pack in the insulation, and see if we can collect the sun in glorious amounts on our roof."

So she had noticed. With her usual enthusiasm she climbed to the as yet unfloored attic space; and stepping from joist to joist, scrutinized the insulated panels and inspected the apical ventilator. This was one of Lev's latest ideas, to put a thermostatically controlled vent at the peak of the building, coupled with inlets around the perimeter for a controlled air flow.

At four o'clock Erin went back down the mountain. By the end of the week she was worn out. "Come in with me for the weekend," she suggested. "You can come to some of the rehearsals, and just fool around."

Lev shook his head. "We're having problems at the mine with the new machinery. And too much needs doing here."

She accepted this. There were obviously countless details left before the glass plate collectors could be positioned.

Erin didn't come back. She telephoned. "I'm staying in town, Lev."

"Okay."

"Are you mad at me?"

"Don't be childish."

"You are."

"Is this the kind of conversation you want to have?"

"No."

"All right then, we've been making good progress here. I'm trying a heavy metal soap to reduce convective loss. I've been doing some reading. And I see the importance of having the black coating wavelength selective. That is, black in the visible spectrum, but effectively 'white' in the infrared."

"Oh Lev, my darling. I don't know what the hell you're talking about. I could tell you about the canon I wrote in the Lydian mode for the third floor of the

523

Tower, and how I see it coming together. Lev, I've decided. I'm not coming back. Goodbye, Lev."

"Erin!" The phone at the other end was dead. He jumped into his car and started down the mountain. He drove with the wind stinging his face. What had she said that first day? When someone becomes too important, I run. Why is it that people don't listen? Why had he not listened? Perhaps it was her commitment to music which made her special from the beginning. Something was important to her. What it was didn't matter, it could be music or shoe repair or botany. Her dedication fulfilled her, making her a whole person. Why go down to Aspen and argue her into dividing herself again? She told him at the beginning it wouldn't work. He turned the car around.

Angstroms gathered for marriages, births, anniversaries, and deaths.

Brillianna had known for some time that the malignancy was metastasizing within her skeletal frame. She delayed telling Ted. He looked florid to her, a heart attack or stroke could carry him off first, and then what would have been the use of upsetting him?

When the indomitable old lady took to her bed, the household became alarmed. Ted was informed his wife had a cold. For the moment he accepted that, regaling Brillianna with the Company's plan to outfox opponents of oil. "There is a movement afoot to repeal the oil depletion allowance," Ted chuckled. "It gives the dogs a bone to worry on. The real golden gimmick is not the twenty-two percent that allows a write-off on gross income. The brilliant move was hit on twenty years ago, namely calling foreign royalties *taxes*. At first I was mad as hell. We'd kept our end of the bargain, built the King his railroad. And he taxed us anyway. Then my accountants pointed out that was the best thing that ever happened to us. We can't be taxed twice, and that is the real shelter. It cut over one billion from our federal tax last year. While the depletion allowance saves only about twenty million. You can see where it's important to entrench, dig in, so to speak."

Her wasted hand reached out from under the covers for his. "You know the best way to double your money, Ted? And that's to fold it once and put it back in your pocket."

He patted her clumsily. "You haven't changed, Brillianna."

She smiled at his not noticing. He never had noticed.

"Say, did you know the kids are all landing in on us?"

"Yes, I'd heard. Seems like a month of Sundays since we had them all here."

"Our anniversary, I think." He started to withdraw his hand, but she wouldn't have it.

"It seems unfair," she said in a mildly reminiscent way, so that he didn't know at first she was talking about herself, "that when you're old, with aches and pains to contend with, when it's hard sometimes just to get through the day, that you are asked to take on more. The truth is, Ted, I can't stop with you much longer. But we've had fifty years. Who's had that?"

"What are you talking about?" he asked bewildered. Then more belligerently, "What are you saying?"

She told him apologetically about the medical diagnosis.

"But we always agreed I'd be the first to go," he said in an accusatory voice.

"I know, dear. I know."

"Why wasn't I told? Even the children were told."

"I thought it best," Brillianna said firmly.

"Oh, you thought it best. Well, you take too damn much on yourself, always have."

"It's the Grenville strain. We like to manage things right up to the end."

"Don't talk about the end. I won't hear of it. I won't let you go. You can't just die on me."

"I know it will be difficult for a while. But you have the Company."

"The Company?" He didn't seem to know what she meant.

"Straighten my pillow so I'm sitting up more. That's

525

better. Now I want you to make an effort, Ted. I want to talk to you about a *living will*."

"What the hell's that?"

"It means that I have written out instructions witnessed by my lawyer, to the effect that I am in sound mind. And being so, I relieve my physicians of any responsibility for taking extraordinary or heroic measures to keep me alive. Any medication is to be for the relief of pain only. I do not wish to be indefinitely maintained with intravenous feedings, heart-lung machines, or any of the gruesome possibilities modern science has made available. When my time comes I want to be let go."

"You mean you're not going to make a fight of it?"

"It's a carcinoma, Ted."

"Where's your spirit, woman? Where's your fighting spirit?"

"Don't argue with me, Ted. My mind's made up. And I'd rest a lot easier if you'd make the same kind of will. With your money, Ted, they could keep you on supportive life systems for weeks, even months."

"Well, I should hope so. You think an Angstrom gives up without a struggle just because some doctor puts a fatal name to something? I'm going to demand everything, including extrathoracic heart massage."

She shook her head. "My poor Ted, what it means to be an Angstrom."

When he left her he went into the study and phoned the doctor. "MacMenimen, this is Angstrom. You're off the case. And not only that, I'm going to test this living will nonsense before a board appointed by the AMA. Where's your Hippocratic oath? You're willing to let your patients die without benefit of modern technical help, and you call yourself a doctor!" The man tried to defend himself, but Ted hung up.

He placed another call to a member of his club, also a doctor. "Look Paul, I want you to take over Brillianna's case. It has been seriously mismanaged. Not only that, I want consultants. I want the biggest men in this country, and in Europe. I want them flown in. Any fee. Whatever they want. But I want them here immediately."

"Ted, I don't think this is wise. You've got a good man in MacMenimen, one of the best. Brillianna has confidence in him."

"Well, I don't. Do I have a right to choose a physician or don't I?"

"If that's the way you want it. I've certainly no objections to calling in consultants, the more high-powered the better. But from what George tells me, it's useless. It's a classic case. . . ."

"I don't give a shit what George says. I'm having him up before the AMA. He doesn't practice medicine, he practices euthanasia. What I want is a panel of experts, top men in the field. See to it for me. What's the point of living in an age of medical miracles if there's no miracle for you?"

Having set the wheels in motion he stood in the doorway and bellowed for Lev. A servant discreetly fetched his grandson.

Lev came up to him, running, "Is it Grandbee?"

"They're trying to tell me your grandmother is dying. I won't have it, you know."

"But Grandpa. . . ."

"They've got her brainwashed. She's too weak to stand up to them. They've got her believing it. They've interfered with the natural will to live that's in all of us. She's got a will to die, which they've instilled in her. They've had conferences behind my back, Lev. She signed some document called a living will."

"If it's what she wants—" Lev said.

"She wants out just because the going gets a little rough. Hell, it's rough for me too. You got to tough it out. I'm lining up some heavy fire. I've hired the best, the biggest men in their field. We're going to make a stand."

"Don't do this, Grandpa. Let her go her way. I understand how you feel, but—"

"What the hell do you mean, you understand how I feel? When you've lived with a woman fifty years, come talk to me again."

"Okay, Grandpa. You're right there. But you've got to respect her wishes. And face up to the fact that it's the end. For God's sake, let it be easy."

"Since when are you qualified as an M.D.? You've let that incompetent pill pusher get to you. Anyway, MacMenimen is off the case."

"You can't do that. Grandbee trusts him. She has confidence in him. Let me phone him back."

"All right, all right. But he's got to go along with the consensus. After all, cancer is just a word. It kills by scaring you to death. But countless people have recovered."

Lev said quietly, spacing his words for emphasis, "Grandbee is not going to recover." He thought his grandfather would strike him.

"Get out of here," the old man roared. "I counted on you to help me. I counted on your Angstrom spirit. But you're about as much help as a gatepost."

Brill had moved into her old room without a word to anyone. She took her brother's arm, walked with him out of the house and along the steps to the beach. "Leave it alone, Lev. They'll be fighting right to the end, the way they always have. That doesn't mean there isn't love behind it."

Lev nodded. There was a wind off the sea. The sun dispersed its light. But consciousness flowed only one way.

By the weekend Brillianna had failed visibly but refused hospitalization. "I'm going to die in my own bed. Hospitals are dehumanizing. I'm going to die right here with my family around me. That used to be the custom because then one could look into the eyes of one's immortality."

She became less lucid. The young people each came, took her hand, and kissed her. Ted was impatient of all this. He motioned them away.

"Remember Ted," he bent to hear her, "the time we fought the U.S. government? The whole Angstrom fortune was in the balance."

"That's right, Brillianna."

"Remember, Ted. . . ."

"What?" His cheek was against hers catching each faint breath.

"Right at the beginning, at Aunt Lillian's."

"When I asked you to marry me?"

"Yes, then. I asked what it was we had to put back. You know what it was, Ted? Our lives, our whole lives."

The medicos descended—a dapper Italian, someone from the Kettering Institute, a Harley Street physician, and a specialist from Stanford. MacMenimen was there but refused to speak to Ted. He repeated loudly several times that he was a personal friend of Brillianna's. Dr. Potter acted as the welcoming committee. Each was aware of the reputation of his colleagues and a great many greetings and salutations went on in the entry.

"What is this, a convention?" Ted asked. "There is a sick woman upstairs. My wife. These local men tell me they can't save her. That's why you're here. That was no free plane ride, you're going to work for those fees you'll send in. And you're starting now. Follow me." He led the way upstairs. The small battalion of doctors stood in the doorway of Brillianna's room, each with a black bag.

She regarded them, her eyes widening in shock and disbelief. MacMenimen was unable to return her glance. She turned to her husband. "Ted, what have you done?"

He took her wasted hand. "These men disagree with the diagnosis. They've even convinced George he's wrong." He turned and winked at the doctors. "They're going to get you back on your feet."

She closed her eyes as though this was her last refuge. The doctors stepped up, deposing Maria, who stood resolutely by the bed, and examined Brillianna.

The hospital was contacted. Within twenty minutes, two attendants were lifting her onto a stretcher. Covered quickly by several blankets, her pathetic dimensions were camouflaged. Ted followed alongside the stretcher. He reached under the blanket to free one of her hands which disappeared in his. He did not let go of her, but climbed into the back of the ambulance. It was only a matter of ten minutes, but she was monitored by Dr. Goodwin, the Englishman, every moment.

They were met at the emergency entrance and the wheels of the gurney lowered. Brillianna was conveyed through the corridors to a large airy suite. Ordinary admittance procedures were waived, Lev was talking to them at the front desk.

The room filled with flowers as the news spread. "Say, this is nice, honey. Why don't you open your eyes and look. Some pretty yellow flowers, mums, I think. They're from Bea and Roger. And wouldn't you know, the biggest display of all from Maria and Tomas. They're good souls, you know. Friends. At a time like this you really get to know who your friends are. And these roses, they're from Bill Brenner. You remember Bill, he's the chairman of Mobil. In '53 Kim Roosevelt masterminded a coup overthrowing Premier Mohammed Mossadegh who nationalized the Iran fields. It was a little deal we'd worked out with the shah. We kept him in power and he let American oil in. Well Bill Brenner was operating there as quick as I was. That man can really move. He's a real oilman. You must remember him, he was at the anniversary."

When he turned to look, she had been hooked up to an IV machine, an EKG above the bed was monitoring her heart, and there were half a dozen leads taped to her chest. A catheter was inserted and urine flowed through plastic tubing to a basin on the floor. A peripheral pump was attached to her leg. Dr. Potter explained that this boosted her circulation and relieved the heart of its full task. A breathing cup had been placed over her mouth and nose. Her eyes, those Grenville eyes of softest gray, were on him.

"Well," he said heartily, "that's better. That's more like it. Now we've begun to fight. All this allows your body to rest, recover its strength. Then with your vital forces high, you'll fight the cancer. That little Italian doctor explained it to me. So you just get those ideas out of your head, about slipping away. There's that little item you've got to supply, the will to live. You hear me, my girl, the will to live.

"We'll go on a cruise when you're better. I've been giving a lot of thought to it, the Caribbean. Sitting out under a steamer rug, soaking up sun. That's what you need. But in the meantime, I'm right here with you. I'm not going to leave your side. See, they brought in a bed for me too. We can watch television later if you feel like it."

Her eyes hadn't moved from his face. Their expression was difficult for him to fathom. He turned in when they put out her light. It was a fitful night's sleep in a strange room with its medicinal smell. Nurses came at intervals to check the IV, empty the basin, respond to an incipient fibrillation on the EKG screen, and administer digitalis. Ted thought of himself as standing vigil.

By morning he was exhausted. But breakfast set him up. The team of specialists arrived at eight. The examination took about ten minutes. Brillianna didn't speak during the course of it although several questions were addressed to her.

Ted followed the medical men into the hall. "Well?" he demanded.

"She's responding nicely," he was told.

"We've restored the circulation. She's resting comfortably."

"How long do you think it will be?" Ted asked.

The doctors looked at each other.

". . . until we get her out of here," Ted hastily amended.

"There's no telling. She hadn't been taking proper nourishment at home."

"I knew it," Ted said, "I knew it." He turned to confront Dr. MacMenimen, but was told the doctor had excused himself. He would no longer be in attendance. "Who needs him," Ted said. "He's a defeatist."

He was reassured by Dr. Goodwin, who told him the IV should soon overcome the nutritional imbalance.

Holding on to those words he went back to his vigil. The nurse was trying to find a new vein, the one used during the night collapsed. Ted approached the bed. He smiled, a big, bright smile, a winning Angstrom smile. "Well, how goes it? Feeling better this morning? Nothing like a good night's sleep." Those great pale eyes watched him without a flicker.

By the end of the week Ted could no longer convince himself she was looking better. She looked, in fact, as though she had been in the ground all week and exhumed. Her skin was ashen. They had moved from the veins in her arms to those in her legs and the back of her hands. They kept changing the needles. The glucose

531

dripped more slowly, her body could no longer accommodate it.

She made no complaint. She made no sound at all. Her eyes never left Ted.

"What's wrong with her?" Ted asked the doctors. "Why doesn't she speak?"

"It's possible she is comatose."

"With her eyes open?" Ted yelled.

"It is possible."

"It may be paralysis," Goodwin said. "She may not be capable of speech."

"Oh she's capable of speech all right. She's a Grenville."

"It could be that her mind is gone," said the Stanford man.

"What the hell are you saying?"

"We fought for the body," the Italian put in soothingly, "but perhaps the mind cannot endure."

"Are you trying to tell me my wife has become a vegetable? I place her in your hands and you dare stand here and tell me such a thing? You're fired. Get this man a plane ticket."

"That will not be necessary, sir."

"You're a goddamned charlatan," Ted yelled after the retreating doctor. The others demurred, he had attacked the integrity of an eminent man, a man whose articles had appeared. . . .

"Shove his articles up your behind," Ted told them and went back to his wife. Her eyes met his. He knew she had all her faculties. He spoke to the intelligence he saw in her. "You know me, Brillianna. You know I have to fight. It's the way I am. I know you're angry. I know you wanted to be left in peace. But I've discovered, you can buy anything. This room, do you know what it costs, the doctors, specialists, the treatment . . . none of this would be possible without the oil. The oil has given us a chance. The oil enabled us to fight, and we're going to win. You know why? The oil made us immortal." There was a staring quality to her eyes, they no longer focused. Ted spoke louder so she would hear. "Immortal persons. That's what we are, immortal." He glanced at the monitoring device over her bed, the trace was flat. He doubled his fist and punched the instrument. Glass tinkled, striking all about him. His knuckles were cut and bleeding. He picked Brillianna up from her pillows and shook her. "Immortal! Immortal!" But Brillianna Grenville Angstrom was dead.

Ted howled his grief. He struck out at the doctors. He wouldn't let them near him with their opiates or hypodermics. He initiated suits against every one of them. The family let him be. The suits were withdrawn, the doctors mollified with cases of scotch, tickets home, and prompt payment of their considerable fees.

Not until her death did Brill realize the force that Grandbee had exerted. Her thin, ramrod body stood between them and change. Her inflexible will saw the amenities observed, the Armagh china trotted out. Her anniversary, even her death, called the family together. Now everything was in danger of falling apart.

"I've got to get away," Bea said to her. "You'll be all right, won't you, Brill?"

"Of course."

When she had arrived ten days earlier, her sister hugged her and said, "Oh darling, I've so many things to tell you. We'll have a long talk. The first real one since I got married." And from that moment took care to avoid her.

Brill was not surprised when the couple returned to Washington. Roger was doing PR work with the oil lobby. Bea had been offered a contract with a prestigious opera company. Shortly before, the trustees received an endowment of two million dollars. She was beginning to understand her position as an Angstrom heiress.

Bea took the Haviland china when she left and set her table with it. The jewels Ted showered on Brillianna were retrieved from the vault. "Take them," her grandfather waved them aside, "they're yours."

"Even the diamond tiara?"

"Enjoy it, Bea," the old man said wearily. "It's yours."

533

"Ours," she said to Roger, and bought him a car.

"Ours," she declaimed and purchased a condominium.

The facts were—Brill ticked them off—Bea was gone, Grandbee, and long ago, Mother. Depression, like an oil slick, rolled over her, thick, black, viscous.

She tried.

She moved back to her own place but that didn't help. She found herself crossing off the days on the calendar before she started to live them. It was time to take herself in hand. Forget death, look to the future. Toward this end she perused the offprints and journal articles ordered from the Stanford library. The idea was there. Kumju was whispering to her. Atoms in a crystal might be regarded as oscillators tuned to identical frequencies. They were capable of resonating with one another and conceivably might be shaken into increased activity by an external magnetic field. At times she could almost formulate it. If only her head would clear and misfortune leave her alone, she would be able to pin it down.

Lev stuck close to his grandfather. Concerned over the old man's periods of depression, his own spirits rose when Ted showed signs of bombast and the familiar meandering tirades. Lev listened to his raging grief, listened to him pour it all out, how in love with Brillianna he had been. The next moment confiding what a prig she was. His voice dropping to a whisper, he said, "She deprived me of a son. But you know," making a final assessment, "what matters is the years. Just as she said, going through it all together. We came to have tolerance for each other. Respect. I do honestly believe I came to love her. I sure as hell miss her nagging."

That was one tack. Lev nodding, aware it was his physical presence that was required, not his understanding. On the other hand the old man was quite capable of focusing on present situations. He defended double dipping. "What the devil are we supposed to do? Angstrom corporations are floating bonds at eleven percent. Those damned Saudis are draining all the money

534

out of the country. They move in here with their billions on short-term investments, garner their interest and out. Where would those camel herders be without me? Ibn Saud, that urine-drinking fool, was looking for water. I tell you Lev, we've got to recycle Arabian investments, get them to commit themselves long-term in Western economies, so that it will be equally unprofitable for them to keep prices high. Recycle, it's the only way. Give me that phone. Operator, patch me through to Jidda. I want to speak to King Faisal. That's right, Faisal. That's right, he's the King."

Lev knew it wasn't the world situation, but the eleven percent that was bugging him.

"Without American funding, without us setting up equipment, that oil would be untapped. Camels would be cropping the ground above it and none of them the wiser. I won't stand for this kind of squeeze. Those goat herders are threatening the democratic process." Then into the mouthpiece. "What do you mean, he's not there? Where is he? Maybe you don't understand, this is Theodore Angstrom."

Ted hung up, looking vacant-eyed. "They said he's not there." One minute shrewd and nimble-witted, the next he embarked on a rampaging indictment of men and events long past. He frequently vented his spleen on Mayor Wagner. Twenty years ago he had been mayor of New York City, and twenty years ago he refused to receive the King. He disallowed a ticker tape parade as well. Ted approached the mayor through congressmen, senators, even the president. But Wagner remained adamant, claiming the King was an anti-Semite: "And from another Semite, that's too much."

"Well," Angstrom wound up, "as it turned out, he was right. I've been sore at him all these years, but he was right. All of Fort Knox is a drop in the bucket to what I've given Faisal. A three hundred percent jump in oil prices, twenty-eight billion petrodollars this year, a projected two hundred billion by 1977. And a mind-boggling half a *trillion* by 1985, and he has the nerve not to be in."

Lev was thinking he should get back to the mining operation. He decided to fly down and check on the solar house as well. He had turned it over to a regular contractor who was in touch almost daily by phone. But he wanted to see it. It had become a symbol, rising above his grandfather's incoherent sense of loss and concern with finance, Bea's absence, Brill's withdrawal —rising above death itself. He recognized the incompleteness of the list—he had left out Erin. He must throw himself into his work and the building.

He must get back if only for a weekend. The phone call to Jidda was evidence that his grandfather was beginning to interest himself in the Company again. He was ready to give them hell in Beirut, Riyadh, Caracas. But what freed Lev was the Rockefeller appointment to the vice-presidency.

Ted received the news from Roger on his private line before it was made public. The straws had been in the wind, but confirmation was something else again. "We're in the driver's seat," he told Lev jubilantly. "Now we can move. The Saudi government is ready to sign a 335 million dollar contract for military hardware. Out of this, 77 million pays for on-the-spot military training to the Saudis. It's a new concept. It started in a small way with TWA mounting a program to train Arab pilots. But this will be the first time the U. S. Defense Department has awarded a foreign military training contract to a private concern. Roger has been in on it from the beginning. He's going places, that boy." This was a dig at Lev, who he felt was too easily sidetracked from main-line Company interests.

This spawning oligarchy of oil left Lev with a bad taste in his mouth, his decision to leave was taken on the spot.

Within the hour he filed an instrument plan and turned his radio to 124.0 San Jose Tower. "Centurion 87 Romeo ready for takeoff. IFR—Denver."

From ground control: "Centurion 87 Romeo taxi into position and hold." He performed the pre-takeoff check, warmed the engine, set his transponder to 3470 and taxied onto runway 30L, lowering his flaps ten degrees for good lift.

"Centurion 87 Romeo cleared for takeoff."

536

He eased the throttle forward, enjoying the rapid acceleration along the centerline.

He thought of himself, a small bright dot on the screens of the controllers as they sat in darkened rooms watching over him with radar advisories. He had the feeling he'd known as a child that someone cared what happened. God was scanning his radar screen, all was well with the world. Death was left behind. Both the death Grandbee wanted and the one she had died. He put it out of his mind, along with the glimpse he had into the machinations of the Company. He understood his grandfather. He was an oilman. His side was winning and his hat was in the air.

Things are in the saddle and ride mankind.

Not things—they had a name: Multinationals.

It helped his grandfather to be maneuvering behind the scenes. What helped Lev was reaching 18,000 feet. Victor 244 led over the Sierra Nevada. He looked down on the peaks he had so often scaled. The disk of the world rimmed below him. Problems dropped away, bottomed out somewhere below.

He was Lev Angstrom who raced the sun. This was his moment, pacing that great orb. No haze, no smog, particulates, or even clouds obscured it. He felt himself absorbed into its power.

Altitude was a good gauge. If something was important up here, then it was important in a real sense. The solar house held up against this measurement. It was what one man, *he*, could do about things. According to reports from his foreman, insulation was in and the solar absorber positioned. The piping had been installed two weeks ago. It waited only occupancy for the heated water to flow and the storage vessels to fill. It waited for him.

He began whistling, but cut it off mid-phrase. It was something Erin whistled, he didn't even know the name of it. Lev's mind veered. He locked it in another direction. Suppose they could switch from the tyranny of oil. Because of the relatively low wattage of the photocell, conservation would be part of any changeover to solar energy. Heating, lighting, and communications such as telephone, television, and computer banks, could be powered by the sun. But heavy industry, big machines, tanks, planes . . . forget it.

It would be an interesting civilization, sophisticated in communication systems, but bodies staying put, or using bicycles or the old horse and buggy. That would effectively put an end to foreign interventions and devastating wars. Perhaps eventually the missiles would rust away in their silos.

In this reverie he crossed the Rockies. Denver descended him to 11,000. He cancelled IFR, the small field he would put down on had no instrument approach facilities. It was, in fact, not much more than a cow pasture. He arrived over it with an ample supply of reserve fuel, but acutely aware that individual flights such as this were hardly in line with conservation. He had consumed in the course of this trip what would heat and serve five families for a year. He was addicted to flying. It would be a lot harder to give up than cigarettes. He greased the wheels on the concrete in a full stall landing, a perfect flare-out.

Lev jumped down conscious of bracing air. It was still early, plenty of time to rent a car and arrive at the site by five. The workmen would be gone. This was important. He didn't want conversation. He wanted— in fact needed—to be alone, inspect the work himself, commune with the structure and the place.

For him this was home, much of it built by his hands and hers—he turned off that course for the second time. Here, in plateau country, mountains rising salt-sprinkled, it was hard not to think of Erin. Erin hammering her finger, her nail turning black. Erin rushing about being busy and excited, humming under her breath or whistling. Music was always spilling out of her. In this she reminded him of Bea. He saw her climbing ladders, whittling on her double reeds of mature . . . what was it, maple? No, that was the instrument. He didn't allow himself to go on. He sealed Erin in a compartment of his brain. Another dungeon. Mother's death, a father for whom he was nonexistent, his brother dead in Egypt, Grandbee. Locks to turn, doors to avoid.

Lev drove fast, impatient that he was on the ground. He zeroed in on the property, kicking up dust and the

538

sun-warmed smell of chaparral. The feeling was strong in him, he was going home. For the first time that was a physical place. Now at last he belonged somewhere. The idea that took hold of him almost ten years before was realized.

He saw the heavy tread marks of earth-moving machinery, slowed, and parked. He walked along the stream and mounted the crest for his first look at the peaked roof with its nonreflecting light-absorbent panels. There was a rush of pleasure, a physical reaction, expanding corpuscles, freer breathing, a heady quality. It was up.

Standing.

He strode over the orange rock, then arrested himself mid-motion. Someone sitting on the porch looking out over the lake, got up. Not someone. *Erin.*

He continued to stand pinioned to the spot.

Erin ran down the stairs, across intervening space. She stopped just short of him. It was Lev who took the final step between them. Her fingers flew across his face, into his hair, over his shoulders.

"Erin. What are you doing here?"

She tossed back her russet mop. "I've been here right along."

"Al never said. . . ."

"I know. I swore him to secrecy. I knew it was just a question of time. But why did you stay away so long?"

"My grandmother died. I couldn't leave the old man." She put her hand in his and they walked toward the house. She didn't say she was sorry, she didn't waste time with things like that, the quick pressure of her hand told him. "Nothing must spoil this moment for you, Lev. You are going to enter your own creation. It's happened to me a few times. It is a holy thing. Like they want churches and mass and communion to be. Usually it isn't. Because there has to be creation, that is part of holiness, the main part." She fell silent and watched him as he approached the steps, climbed them, and reached out his hand, touching the black panels. She knew that gesture. It was gentle, one he used sometimes with her, exploratory, yet holding back in awe, wonder and disbelief.

"It's working, Lev. Your house is a working success-ful solar house, and has been for about ten days now."

"You've been here ten days?"

She shook her head. "I told you, I came back right away. Right after you left to tell you I was utterly wrong, utterly miserable. I've been here almost a month. I did the concert, commuting back and forth. Killing myself, but proving I was tough enough to do it, if I had to. And I do have to. Either way it's only half a life."

They went inside. He saw the stitchery taken from the old place: *God Bless Our Pad*. He smiled and re-moving a couple of ceiling tiles, examined the copper piping, gingerly laying his hand on it. He pulled away immediately.

Erin laughed. "Is that hot enough for you?"

"Seems to be." He went down to the basement to investigate the stored water in the tank. "And you say it's been working without a hitch?"

"It gets a bit cool evenings. So I spread the sleeping bag in front of the fireplace. Unecological, but so com-fortable. And in the middle of a forest with wood just lying about, it doesn't really waste."

Lev turned his attention on her fully. "You've been here all this time?"

She nodded.

"And drove back and forth every day?"

"Yes. I worked on the house from one to four with the rest of the crew."

"You've logged more hours than I have."

"It was the only way I knew to prove to you that I wouldn't tear us both up again. I won't Lev. I'm here for good, if you'll say it's all right."

He remembered the day he had gone down the moun-tain after her. He remembered turning the car around. "What about the Tower? Your music?"

"I'll handle it. The Tower sort of quit on me. I don't think I'm ready to tackle it yet. I'm working on some-thing else. It's based on the legend of Daedalus. He was the architect who contrived the labyrinth for the Mino-taur in Crete."

540

"Yes, I remember the story. Weren't he and his son imprisoned in it?"

She smiled. "The labyrinth was so complicated that even Daedalus forgot its secret. He got through only by following a lowly ant. Once outside, he built two pairs of wonderful wings so that he and Icarus could make their escape. He cautioned Icarus not to fly too close to the sun or the wax would melt and his wings drop off. So the two flew lightly, without effort, from Crete. But the boy, Icarus, was drawn to the sun. He soared closer to its glory and power." She looked at him with her multicolored eyes which at this moment were green. "I've dedicated it to you, Lev. I would never have thought of a sun theme if not for the solar house. I've spent hours on the porch staring until that great orb turns black, wondering if it is our future. Daedalus was a builder and a dreamer, and in my mind you've become one."

"You've really come back to me?" Lev asked. "You won't fly off on a sunbeam, Greeneyes, or run around a church widdershins and disappear?"

"I'm glad you're afraid to trust me, Lev. That means it went deep with you too. But I won't disappear in the clap of a chord, or allow anything to separate us. I will continue to be a musician, but I'll be here to open the door and kiss you hello. If you want it that way?"

In answer he scooped her up against his body. "The Saudis say to be as a king, a man must have a well of pure water, a woman, and a singing bird. You are an endless well, you are woman, you are my singing bird." They built a nest of jackets and parkas and sank into it, rediscovering by touch, by feel, by lips and fingertips what they had lost. Her breasts seemed to swell, her body undulated under his hands and separated. He invaded, but the conquest belonged to them both.

It was with shock on reading the morning paper that Brill encountered a lead story on Z-9 and the deliberate dumping of plutonium 239 at Hanford, Washington.

541

The article contained precisely the information Peg Trotter had been slipping her. Here it was, public property, spread all over page two of the *Chronicle*.

She had always felt keenly her good fortune, that she, and she alone of the children, had a father. But he allowed himself to be used, a pawn of the Angstroms. He lent himself to this horror.

She drove to San Francisco, the newspaper beside her on the seat, folded open to his name. He had been forced to appear before an investigating committee. Cleared of any wrongdoing, still how dreadful and sordid the ordeal must have been. An hour later she knocked at his study. Dr. Knolls disliked being disturbed. Brill was aware of that.

"Yes?" She detected a tinge of annoyance in his voice.

"I want to talk to you, Father."

"Is that you, Brill?"

She entered. Walking up to his desk, she placed the article on it. She had no pity for her father's embarrassment. "I certainly didn't expect this kind of publicity," Dr. Knolls said. His initial shock on perusal of the article wore off, and he attempted to come to grips with it. "The entire AEC is under fire and will be defunct in another couple of months. It's to be reconstituted as ERDA, the U.S. Energy Research Development Agency. Heads are going to roll. They are retaining only eighty percent of the old AEC personnel."

"*Only* eighty percent? It's the same crew then. And the same old policies of secrecy, inefficiency, and playing games with plutonium."

"No, we're setting up a policing board, NRC, the Nuclear Regulatory Commission."

Brill's laugh was harsh. "Headed by a former AEC member. Isn't that putting the fox in charge of the henhouse?"

Knolls shrugged. "All I know is, I'm fighting to protect my reputation. My entire career is at stake."

"Were you aware of the dumping?" Brill asked bluntly.

"I was opposed to it. You must believe that. In my private correspondence there are letters, one in particular to the acting director, in which I state my opposition. But this is terrible." His hand on the paper trembled. "I was hoping the lid could be kept on. I had no idea the press would get hold of it, blow it up out of all proportion."

Reaction took place in a series of washboard knots as assessment of what he said traveled from mind to stomach: "Out of all proportion? Is that what you think? The Columbia River is seven miles away. It's true ground water can move as slowly as fifty feet a year. But it has been known to travel as fast as a twentieth of a mile a day. And don't tell me about the clay soil."

Dr. Knolls possessed a mobile face, anxiety showed on it. "I don't want this to upset you."

"It seems to me you are upset only for yourself."

A noticeable coldness appeared in Dr. Knoll's manner. "The media is playing up sensational aspects." He struck the paper contemptuously. "In my opinion there is no real threat."

"In my opinion the plutonium lost in the ground constitutes an extreme and present danger."

Dr. Knolls was livid. "I refuse to argue with you, Brill, in your state of mind."

"You mean you refuse to debate me because you know I'm right."

Knolls' light blue eyes were milky with emotion. "I take it then that I am cleared by an investigatory committee to be condemned by my daughter?"

"I came here to beg you to free yourself of this mess. You don't need it. You don't need the Angstroms, or the AEC, or ERDA. You're a scientist. Why should you lend yourself to this? They're using your brains, your prestige. Dad, make the break that I made years ago. You say you were exonerated by the committee. Now, I'm begging you, exonerate yourself."

"What are you talking about? The risk from nuclear power is equivalent to being a hundredth of an ounce overweight or smoking one cigarette every eight years."

Brill stared at him with an incredulity that changed to hostility. "When you can show me where the plutonium has got to, we can talk again."

The roll call was lengthened since last she ran

through it: no Mother, no Grandbee, no Bea, and no Father. Two through death. Two through defection.

And Grandfather approaching eighty. That left her and Lev, with Lev gone much of the time. At the moment he was here, returned from Colorado. She thought, although she hadn't asked, that Grandfather sent for him. Lev insisted she spend the week at the Carmel place with them. Since Grandbee's death she had relaxed her prohibitions. There was only a lonely old man left, what was the good of keeping up the protest against him? A year ago they had filled two houses. Now each estate was a near-silent place.

The article on Z-9 was one of a series. Brill, always an early riser, was the first to bring in the paper and pore over it. Incomprehensible to her was the apathy into which the catalogue of horrors fell. Was it too technical for people to read? Did it simply add other hazards in a world becoming daily more hazardous? Was the apathy symptomatic of a general feeling of helplessness? The free enterprise system was built on the right of every man to make a profit. This was the American way. When the Colonies rebelled one of the first things to be revoked was the Queen's Charter, dating from Elizabeth I, which granted companies the right to incorporate only after they had demonstrated in what manner their business contributed to the welfare of the people. That very sensible proviso had been abandoned. How could you safeguard nature, for instance, when people felt it was their inalienable prerogative to despoil, exploit, ravage, take, pollute, make barren, render sterile, as long as it paid them to do so?

Her perusal of the paper uncovered the fact that other countries—presently Japan, Canada, and Italy—were shipping their radioactive wastes to the United States. Deadly isotopes were being imported under contract by American firms, who found more profit in obtaining reusable uranium and other radioisotopes extracted from fuel rods than they did in financing and building the original plants.

Brill read on: "The Allied General Nuclear Services has petitioned the newly formed NRC to receive spent fuel rods at its reprocessing plant in Barnwell, South Carolina. These wastes remain in this country under what GE, the pioneer in this field, calls *perpetual care*."

Her father had failed to mention this newest wrinkle. "So," she said aloud, "we have become the radioactive dump for the entire world." She was so incensed she could not contain her indignation. "If the world goes, you go too!" she wanted to shout at the profiteers.

It wasn't only Barnwell, South Carolina, and General Electric. The next paragraph stated that Saudi-California was producing fuel rods in Seattle for nuclear power plants. "We're in it, are we? *The Company?* You're only an immortal person as long as there are persons, don't you understand that? Your face too can dissolve and turn soft. Your eyes become blind. You can vomit for three weeks before you're dead. Doesn't anyone understand that?"

It was all a kind of round-robin. Tentacles reached from the central body. Oil firms spread on the waters of the world, the snow at the Arctic contained radioactive traces, a half billion pounds of lead were released into the atmosphere each year, plutonium was lost in the ground, and runaway technetium 99 with a half-life of 200 thousand years was on the move. Cesium 137 spilled from an atomic plant in, not surprisingly, South Carolina, and contaminated a five-square-mile area of the Savannah River. Vinyl chloride fumes were killing factory workers. *Kiracoo, Kiracoo,* said an old nursery rhyme. *Guard thy kingdom on the west.* But who knew where, or from what direction it would overtake them?

And what was 'perpetual care'? It used to mean flowers on graves forever. Now it meant the graves themselves. Stuff the lethal wastes down a hole somewhere. Or cram them into the leaking, corroded, already overfilled storage tanks at Hanford. Or put it down a salt dome. Isn't that where they were going to preserve the artifacts of the present for insect eyes on long stalks to gaze at? She tried to recall what had been said at the anniversary party. Salt domes were stable and usually surrounded by gas fields, which further protected them.

The trouble was, if you stuck it all down a salt dome, you couldn't take it up every few years to see if it was still there. It would mean permanent disposal with no way to monitor it. No reports to make out? Unthinkable! No, they would bury it in the ocean and the day would come when fish and surfers floated belly up.

By then everything would be hot, contaminated. She was systematically searching the house for Lev. He wasn't in his room. She checked the pool. A wet towel proclaimed an earlier dip. Where was he? She looked into the garage, his Porsche was there.

He must be with Grandfather. He had been very good to him since Grandbee's death. The old man made unreasonable demands on his time. Sending for him from Colorado on the pretext of business, Brill guessed was pure loneliness. Lev indulged him. But it seemed to her the two were on a collision course. The day would come when Lev would not respond. The basic conflict in their ways of thinking would prevent him.

Brill heard voices coming from the study. She slipped quietly into one of the settees in the adjoining anteroom to wait until her brother was free. Perhaps she was wrong, perhaps he would find middle ground on which to meet his grandfather. She knew the strength in Lev that he mined from some deep well. It was always there. Her strength was of a different kind. It would be summoned. And it had to do with Kumju. She was afraid of her strength.

They were talking about the Colorado shale mine. Grandfather was saying, "We need an alternative fuel if we are to ride out the next twenty-five years. And I want to know if we can look to this *in situ* method. Or should we start moving on surface mining?"

She wondered if Grandfather knew when he gave him that land in Colorado that Lev would oppose surface mining. He sent the right man, but not for his purpose. She smiled to herself.

Lev allowed his grandfather's question to lie for the moment. Then he said, "If we can't work out the *in situ* approach, we've got to forget shale. I tried to imagine those canyons, those stretches of mountains and forests, filled with the sludge machines leave when they bite a thousand acres of raw land and chew it up. They spit out walls of spoil a hundred feet high. When it dries, it supports no life of any kind."

"You've been listening to the damned conservationists."

"It's the future, Grandpa. You said you want to be part of the future. Surface mining is out of the question. There'll be erosion and flooding and you'll wreck the water tables. You know the enormous quantities of water needed for processing, the estimate runs as high as six barrels for each barrel of oil. This is water normally used for agriculture. Even if it could be spared, it means spillage into the Colorado, increasing the salinity until the water is no longer potable."

His grandfather nodded briefly, taking account of his points.

"Then there are other things that bother me." Lev said.

"Such as?"

"Politics. I don't like the close tie between the oil industry and the top echelon in the Interior Department."

Ted flinched. It had taken a lifetime to set up this chain of command.

"It seems a bit blatant," Lev went on, "when the assistant secretary of the interior leaves his position in government to head the oil shale operation at Atlantic Richfield Company, in Colorado. It's like dominoes changing places. The executive director of the Colorado Mining Association then takes his place, going to work for the Interior. Interchangeable pieces."

Ted wondered if he had been wrong to put the lease in Lev's name. He decided to be blunt. "The reason you got a lease on a 515 million-dollar tract for 210.3 million is that I promised you'd get into production."

Lev brought his hand down on the desk. "There is no way I will work on the kerogen on top."

"All right, Lev. But the small print says, *produce*. And if you aren't ready with your *in situ* process, I don't see that you have a choice."

"It'll take time. There are lots of problems," Lev

said. "The machinery needed to heat the shale in place underground is too big to bring in. And retort temperatures run too high. They just don't make refractories that will stand up to it. The only way the *in situ* will work is to dispense with retorts altogether."

"How can you do that?"

"I think we can generate enough heat to gasify the whole works by an atomic explosion."

—No. That isn't Lev. He hasn't joined them. He hasn't.

The old man thought it over. "The trouble there is radionuclides can escape through rock fissures and endanger your ground water. Much the same sort of thing they are running into at Hanford, and more recently in the Savannah River. There have been some hysterical articles in the papers."

"Whether they are hysterical or not is too early to tell. I understand in Hanford, plutonium 239 got away from them. That's about as serious as you can get. And the cesium in South Carolina isn't pleasant to think about either. However, a carefully monitored blast is certainly preferable to strip mining. Besides, our site is several miles from the Colorado. I can't see any danger of it getting into the river."

—There was no warning. Just the explosion. And local fallout compounded of radioactive debris, gases and volatile fission products. The iodine istotope was the one she felt first. She clutched her throat. It was on fire. Iodine absorbed selectively, massing in the thyroid. It burned.

"Brill, you're so quiet. I didn't see you sitting here."

"How's Grandfather?"

"He seems in pretty good spirits. But you know, Grandbee told him when to come in out of the rain."

"Lev, can we talk? I know you'll be going back to Colorado. And we haven't really talked."

"Sure. Is it anything special?" He was tempted to tell her then and there about the solar house. But they were still working on it, putting on finishing touches. He wanted it perfect. Also he should prepare her for Erin. At the moment she seemed nervous and upset, this was not the time for confidences.

"Special? Yes." She glanced at him. "Remember when Mother died? You stole the car out of the garage and we drove around half the night."

He sensed agitation behind her words. "I've been thinking of Mother too," he said. "I suppose one death makes you think of the others."

"Lev, will you let me drive your Porsche?"

"Sure. If you want."

"We'll drive and talk."

"Okay." He found the keys in his pocket and handed them to her.

"I'll tell you a Kumju story like I used to. Would you like that?"

He nodded. She had something to say, let her get into it any way she could.

The engine turned over and she took off with a jackrabbit start. "Tame lions are prowling the temple. We're at Musawarat es-Sofra where Mujaj commands the clouds. The people dance and sway and bring gifts, beads of ostrich egg shell, pottery incised with red and white pigment. Mujaki's heart is softened.

"But an ancestor holds her arms. The rain does not come. The people suffer. Hunting shrines are set up in the jungle. An animal is brought down, its stomach becomes the bag for carrying away tongue, brain, and those portions not eaten on the spot. The bag is closed with twisted gut."

Twisted gut. Her gut twisted and was drawn tight. She suffered with the people who propitiated the earth.

"They prayed for rain. *Why is there no water?* Kumju heard. 'It is unsafe to drink. Substances that will outlive you many times have seeped into the ground. The people suffer and will die.' "

Lev waited for more. There was nothing further. "That wasn't a very pleasant story," he remarked.

"No."

"What was the point of it?"

"The point is Colorado."

"I see." She was driving too fast, taking the curves at too high a speed. "Look, Brill, at the moment the work there is purely experimental."

"To cut into the earth, Lev, is like cutting open your

549

own body. Because we are part of the earth. And this cut would be not only deep but poisonous. Remember Grand Junction, where radioactive fill was found under homes and schools, and the lead poisoning among the children exposed to the smelting going on in Idaho?"

"That's why the *in situ* method is worth pursuing."

"One pound of plutonium 239 will produce nine billion. Do you know how many zeros there are in a billion—000,000,000. 9,000,000,000 cases of lung cancer for a thousand generations."

Lev was disturbed by her manner. "The nuclear-type blasting I was discussing with Grandfather is very low yield."

"All you need is a milk bottle, just a milk bottle full of plutonium."

"We were considering the various possibilities. You have to do that, Brill."

"A great tremor like an earthquake follows the blast. It's bright under the earth, unseen brightness that reaches the temperature of the sun. It can create fissures, passageways to the surface, to soil, water, grasses, the bones of men. Did Grandfather ever tell you about the oil fire he witnessed in East Texas when he was young? What you are planning is the inverse of that, not a tower of flame, but a burrowing. . . . Did you know that the fire bounces and keeps exploding? New flames constantly unfold and burst, turning the ground into a volcano, a boiling mass of liquid."

Lev noticed on the straightaway she repassed the Hamm's truck that had passed them on the down grade. "Did you ever think of it the other way?" he said. "A two-week absence of people, if for example they were in hiding against radiation, just two weeks without them, might be more disastrous to the earth than all we have inflicted on it. I mean, think of it a moment. All the ecosystems, food plant cultivation, irrigation, the feeding of livestock, domestic animals, transportation, distribution."

She interrupted him. "Lev, the mullet are declining in Hawaii. Remember the schools we swam through, the clear water? The new string of hotels and condominiums are dumping raw sewage directly into that sea. That wonderful bright water. I can hardly bear it.

"Do you know when I can't stand things that I bury myself inside. I control my heart beat and respiration. I travel with Kumju over the world, across the web of living substance, where all is coeval, tied in a single umbilical cord. I see the poisons we have injected swirl in the troposphere and watch them float down. Radio waves travel with us at infinite speed in straight lines. Heat and light and gamma radiation are traveling too, on their own energy and wavelengths. The ultraviolet radiation raises the temperature of absorbing objects— that's you and me, Lev, and Grandfather, and Bea—by several hundred degrees.

"It only lasts a few thousandths of a second. But the high energy X-rays penetrate. It melts granite. That's matricide, Lev. I can't let you kill our mother. The earth is our mother, Lev. And I am a spear balanced for throwing, armed with the spur of a white cock. I will not let you call down fire. Only the Son of Perdition may do that. Are you the King of Fierce Countenance? No, Lev. I won't allow it. Revelations—Antichrist is to be assassinated!"

Lev threw himself on the steering wheel. His hands fought hers. The Porsche left the road. She pressed the accelerator to the floor, the car careened crazily over rutted ground. He tried with his foot to pry hers off. Too late.

They were in a spin. The car rolled over. There wasn't time for fear, or to fix a definite thought in his mind. But his body knew. It held rigid against final impact.

Final. . . . Final. . . .

He opened his eyes and lay looking up. He couldn't see the sky. He saw a rain of bright filaments passing before his vision. He was watching his own internal hemorrhaging, watching the blood sift past his inner eye. It occurred to him that he should test various parts of his body. Did his arms and legs work? Was his spine injured? Total lethargy overwhelmed him.

Later.

Later thought returned. His fingers clawed against sand, that meant he had been thrown clear. Clawing, that was the only movement he made. Then implosion: memory.

Brill.

Her name triggered a motor center. "Brill!" He could hear his voice sounding miles distant. He began to scrabble more vigorously with his hands in the sand. He pushed himself forward, he crawled. "Brill, where are you?"

There was no sound. He was alone on a windy scrub highland, blind, with bright curtains, gay particles sifting from some bleeding internal chamber. Did the brain have blood? He couldn't remember.

"Brill?" He asked it tentatively. "Please Brill, answer me." He swept with his hands in front of him, they struck rock, manzanita, space, more space. He dragged himself after his hands. _Especially Brill._ Was this what Mother feared? Did she have some inkling even then?

"Brill," he pleaded. "There won't be an atomic device. I swear to you. You can see for yourself. You'll come with me. Brill, do you hear? Are you listening?"

He bumped into the car. It was on its side, heating up in the sun. She lay not far away, he stumbled over her. She was prone, her arms flung out.

He blinked hard and rubbed his eyes. A grayish kind of light showed her to him. He put his hand on her chest and felt life. He laid his head beside hers. "Brill. What have I done? Brill, you're all right, aren't you?"

"Okay, buddy, let's see what we have here. Let's have a look." It was the man who drove the Hamm's rig. "You all right? Can you stand? Here, let me give you a hand."

Lev found himself hauled to an unsteady vertical. His vision was clearing. He looked into the thick, florid face. "I seem to be all right," he said, surprised.

"Your Porsche is totaled. I saw it turn over five times. By rights, you should both be goners."

"How is she?"

"Breathing pretty good. I radioed for help. We'll just let her lay, that will be best."

"But you think she's all right?"

"You were thrown clear. The doors on both sides are sprung. Didn't you have your seat belts on?"

"If we'd had our seat belts fastened. . . ." Lev pointed to the bright red wreck which had been smashed, compacted to a few feet in height.

"I believe in seat belts," the Hamm's man said.

"But the evidence clearly indicates. . . ." His head was pounding. Why argue, if his seat belt had been fastened his head wouldn't be hurting.

"Lev?"

He bent over her. "It's all right, Brill. The car went out of control."

"Are you all right?"

"Fine."

"Am I?"

"Yeah. Right as rain." It was one of Grandbee's expressions, and she smiled up at him. She didn't remember. Thank God she didn't remember.

Superficial injuries were the excuse for keeping her in the hospital. She didn't know it was the psychiatric section. After two weeks of intensive examination they were able to rule out physiological impairment. The somatic tests began with X-raying her teeth. It was a complete workup. They attached electrodes for a continuously monitored EEG.

Could they detect that every sentient organ in her body was crying *enough?* Brill began to understand when she was administered written examinations described as projective techniques, starting with the Multiphasic Personality Inventory. "The purpose here," her doctor explained, "is to come by the CQ, or conceptual quotient score."

"It isn't the accident. All this has nothing to do with the accident. You think I'm crazy." She began to fight hysterically. Restraints were used.

Lev explained the situation to his grandfather, putting it in as mild a way as possible.

"She's insane then?" The old man cried. "That's what you're trying to tell me. A homicidal maniac."

"No, Grandfather, no. It's acute depression. She can respond to treatment. There is every chance for a cure, just like before."

"Before, she didn't try to kill you."

"It wasn't just me. It was herself too."

Ted didn't hear him.

"We've received nothing but hurts, wounds from that girl. When I think what those years did to Brillianna, when she wouldn't even see us. Well, I thank God she's not here to know about this."

"It isn't a disgrace, Grandfather, to be ill."

"Ill? So it's ill, is it? All right, have it your way. As long as you're standing here in front of me, Lev. When I think how it might have been . . ." his voice became unsteady.

It took him a week to work himself to the point where he could see his granddaughter. It was the same hospital, which made it more difficult. He never imagined himself entering it in a conscious state and of his own will. Maria had remembered flowers, two dozen yellow roses. He should have thought of it himself, he wasn't functioning clearly. It had jolted him more than he admitted. His own demise was something he was geared for. But the thought of Lev lying on the sand, haunted his sleep. It could happen. The young were not immune. He remembered Brilli.

He had a bad moment going up the steps, facing those glass doors. It was bad again when the odor hit, a typical hospital odor, carbolic soap and disinfectants. It was all associated in his mind with Brillianna's death.

The elevator took them to a different floor. Lev was with him, but Ted indicated he would see her alone. He entered the room. Brill lay staring at the ceiling. Her slender body followed the contour of an electric bed, raised slightly at knees and head.

She didn't turn when he came in, or give any indication she knew he was there. "Hello, Brill." He crossed to her and laid the flowers beside the pillow.

Brill's eyes shifted, first to the roses, then slowly lifted to his face. He smiled reassuringly. She continued to look at him, it was as though she peeled back the epidermis. He thought of medical books he had seen,

554

layer after layer of glassine stripped away, gradually paring deeper into the anatomical structure of the body. He made an effort. "How are you, Brill?"

She started at his words, then snatched at the flowers and threw them on the floor. She turned away from him to the wall.

Ted bent stiffly, retrieved the flowers and went out. He was holding the bouquet upside down. A nurse took them. Lev led him out of there. He couldn't have made it on his own.

Lev decided they should stop by the club for a drink. He watched his grandfather cradle the Courvoisier. He couldn't seem to bring himself to taste it.

"It didn't do any good," the old man said finally.

"It may have done her good."

"No. She turned away from me."

"We have to try," Lev said, "and keep on trying." There was another silence. Lev spoke into it suddenly and decisively. "Granddad, I'm giving over the mine."

Ted swirled the contents of his glass, looking into it deeply. "You've turned from me too, turned to the wall."

"No," Lev protested.

"What do you know," his grandfather said. "There's Chuck, from Occidental Petroleum."

"Grandfather, can't we talk about it?"

"Hi there, Chuck. Come join us. . . ."

Lev had an interview with the doctor. "When can I take Brill home?"

"I don't think you understand, Mr. Angstrom. Your sister is in a depressive phase. She needs institutional care."

"No."

"How can I put it to you, Mr. Angstrom? Your sister, at present, is a danger to herself and to others."

"I'll make arrangements," Lev said.

"Arrangements?" The doctor seemed puzzled.

"Yes. I have a home in Colorado. It's isolated, completely away from people. She can be looked after there. I'll look after her myself."

555

"You'd need a professional with her. Even on tranquilizers, in these cases violence can be a recurring pattern. Or she could slip into a catatonic state."

"I'll employ a nurse. You see, I know Brill. She had an episode like this, well not as extreme, nine years ago. I was able to bring her out of it. She depends on me."

"It is true that there is every hope for eventual cure, but no guarantees and no time estimates. You take each day as it comes."

Lev won out with the doctor. Brill would be released into his custody. There were things to do.

He phoned Hank, his mechanic, to have the Cessna ready. He was acting on instinct, convinced he knew what was needed to bring Brill back to mental health and stability. The countryside would calm her, allaying the fears that broke out in impulses toward death and violence. Also, he was counting heavily on the solar house to bring her around. There it stood, a monument to his faith and dedication.

Besides he didn't dare leave her with the doctors. Doctors like to probe until raw fact is exposed. He had no intention of allowing that to happen. Facts were something Brill could not survive.

He phoned Erin to meet him, and she told him enthusiastically that she was staining the wood trim and reupholstering a beat-up leather chair. She thought of the solar house as home. She had crawled over the roof placing panels of glass, caulked, painted, planed surfaces, tested pipes. She was part of the project and the place from the first. And he was ready to admit it now, part of him. Not many people had been let into his life. The power and fortune of the Angstroms set him apart. It was better to cleave to the family you had than trust yourself to strangers. For some reason Erin had never been a stranger. Her belief in the house had been the initial spark. When he left, she had returned. That seemed natural to him now.

He dreaded asking her to leave. However the doctor had been blunt, "A danger to herself and others." He couldn't take that chance. It was a remote one, but he couldn't take it. Besides he was confident it wouldn't be for long. It had taken two weeks in Hawaii that winter.

Only two weeks. Of course this was more serious. It might be months before Brill was able to pick up her own life. She probably never heard the things he muttered at the time of the wreck. Nevertheless, his first commitment was to Brill. He resigned his position. It meant abandoning the experiment. The *in situ* was his baby. It was hard to let go. They would certainly go ahead with surface mining. His last gesture was to file a plan for fill and recontouring. He also negotiated to keep the few acres surrounding the house.

For the first time since he could remember, his grandfather was angry with him. He felt Lev had betrayed the Company by walking out.

"You saw Brill," was Lev's reply.

"But to allow the vagaries of a sick girl to influence your work. . . ."

"I don't think I've made a good Angstrom," Lev said. "Perhaps I should have tried to be a Rosenfeld."

"You'll be back at it, Lev. The Company is in your blood." This was said more to convince himself than his grandson. And so it was left.

Unwanted thoughts were part of the headwinds he bucked. He was the Son of Perdition, of Fierce Countenance, who called down fire. Yet even in her most frantic moment, he had been Lev.

She tried to kill him.

But she was willing to die with him to save him from committing the ultimate in horror her frenzied brain could invent. The capacity for fear, he thought, is in all of us, but like a child, she didn't know what to invest her fear in. He remembered, as a small boy, being frightened of the bulky dresser after the light was turned off. It must be like that when madness seized her. She feared her brother. The thought jarred him as much as the accident had done. He brought the plane in, but his landing was far from perfect.

Erin ran onto the field, hugging, kissing, claiming him. "Was it really true you weren't hurt, Lev?"

"Not a scratch." The problem now was how much to tell her.

"But you don't look well. You're so pale."

"It was a close thing. I suppose there's always shock."

"How's your sister doing?"

"Brill's still in the hospital."

"Anything broken?"

". . . No."

"No internal injuries?"

"No. They aren't satisfied though. They want to keep her a little longer, a day or so for observation."

"How come they didn't keep you for observation?"

"Me? Oh, I'm tough."

She laughed. "Wait till you see the changes in the place. I'm putting in a cactus garden, in hanging pots of course. So I can bring them in when it snows. Do you know one of them, the prickly kind, burst into the most extraordinary blooms."

Although he smiled, she sensed his reserve. As they approached the car, he said, "I'd like to drive."

"Sure." The doors slammed on either side. Neither said anything as he looked for the summit road.

"Wow," she said, "I'm getting bad vibes."

"There are a couple of things I'll have to explain."

"Like, you can't stay. You're going back."

"That's part of it."

"All the harmonies suddenly dissolve, discords build and you can't do anything about it. You play a fifth and it comes out a tritone. You modulate and it blasts your ear drums. What's it all about, Lev? Why are you here if you can't stay?"

"I thought we'd get home first, have a drink, lie out under the stars, find the Big Dipper and the Dog Star, the only ones I can identify. . . ."

"I want to know now."

"It's heavy, Erin. Brill was more seriously hurt than they realized at first. There's going to be a long period of convalescence."

"How long?"

"They don't know yet."

"And you want her to recover here?"

"I think she'd do best here. She's not getting on well with her father. And Grandfather isn't up to any additional strain. This is the only place I could think of."

"Couldn't you send her on a cruise or something? I mean, you're all so damned rich."

"She needs me. I'm the only family she has left."

"So you want me out of the picture. Pack up, my girl, your services are no longer required."

"Erin, it's not like that. I want you to marry me." He hadn't meant to propose in the course of a quarrel, but it was out.

There was silence between them. She felt for his hand on the wheel covering it with her own. "I've been a pig," she said.

"It won't be long, Erin."

"I, Erin, take you Lev," she said musingly. "You did say you wanted to marry me?" She moved close against him, her fingers ran caressingly into his hair. "Bring her, Lev. We'll have her well in no time."

"Not we, Erin. You have to go back in the morning. This is something I need to do alone."

"But why? I could help. Help nurse her, cook, make myself useful in dozens of ways."

"It wouldn't work."

"Why not?"

"Brill's strange about outsiders."

She withdrew, plastered herself against the door. "I see."

"No, you don't see."

"Then explain it to me."

"Erin, the sickness isn't a result of the accident. It's the other way around."

"What are you saying?"

"It's a mental breakdown. She ran us off the road."

"You mean she tried to kill you?"

"She was hallucinating. Having some sort of attack."

"Oh God." She slumped back in the seat.

"She's depressive. But those are the very ones, the most unpredictable, violent even, who have the best chance of a cure."

"I am the executioner who walks by his side. . . . And you propose to stay out here in the wilderness and take care of her yourself?"

"No. She'll be traveling with a specially trained nurse."

"But isn't this a condition that can go on for years and years?"

"I don't think so." He told her about Hawaii.

Erin said slowly, "It may be like that again. But suppose it isn't?"

"The other thing I didn't tell you, is that I precipitated this acute episode. Grandfather and I were discussing *in situ* mining, the possibility of an atomic charge of some kind. Brill overheard. That's what triggered it. So no matter what it takes. . . ."

"Yes, I understand." She sounded grim. "No matter what it takes, your life or my life or anything else in the process, you are prepared to see it through."

"I don't know what else I can do."

"Of course." She gave his hand a squeeze. "You're right. You're always so goddamned right and logical. I'll go back to the conservatory and work on Daedalus or maybe try to finish the Tower. I've got a new floor to look in on, one where human hope and despair are hung on coatracks."

When he finally turned off on the private road and brought the car to a stop, they continued to sit there.

"If I weren't such a healthy cow," she said bitterly, "you'd love me more."

For the first time Lev laughed. It wasn't a happy sound.

"You would," Erin insisted. "You'd feel I needed you. With you, needing and loving is all mixed up. Is it because you had no parents? Oh Lev," she put her arms around him, "let me give you all that. I can. Being without you has taught me. I can."

He took her into the house with its peaked shiny black roof, through the double-insulated door. Once inside, it was much like any house. Erin had made it comfortable with many touches, from a heavy handloomed Irish rug, to copper pans hanging in the kitchen and plants dangling from strands of hemp and leather.

Firewood and pinecones were heaped in the hearth, ready for lighting. He touched a match to it and they stretched in front of the blaze. He stared mesmerized into the fire, watching its center change as it fueled itself.

"What if she harms you?" Erin asked.

"She won't."

"That's the reason you're sending me away. You're afraid for me. Well, I'm afraid for you."

"There's no reason to be, Erin. Brill is a gentle person."

"A gentle person who tried to kill you."

"Since then she's had treatment."

"Great."

He went to the bar, but not finding the mix he wanted, continued into the kitchen.

"I'm working on the Daedalus theme. It's like weaving, picking out threads, modulations. I've come to the part where Icarus flies into the sun. What if it is prophetic? What if it is you who are flying too close, whose wings will melt and drop off?"

"Did you say something?" he asked coming back in.

"Must I really go in the morning?"

"Yes."

"It's so hard to go. It's the hardest thing I've ever done in my life. Lev. I'm going to write out the phone number at the conservatory, in case you need me, or just feel like talking."

"There's plenty of time tomorrow."

But she was on her feet, racing around after pencil and paper. "No. Now, while I think of it. Remember I can be here in four hours."

They didn't turn in but stayed by the fire, waking fitfully to whisper, kiss, and complete each other's bodies. Erin said, "I can hardly think of poor Brill. Just of what it means to you and me."

"You don't know her."

"Is she anything like you?"

"She has a brilliant mind, delicately balanced. Her second-graders loved her. But at the same time, she won't let people close to her. Only us."

"How will she take our marriage? I mean, once she's well?"

"It will have special significance for her. She needs a sister."

Erin nodded. "She is one person working alone. She is afraid to fail again. I understand her. It's an obligation, like with music."

He made breakfast as he had the first day. She sat on the counter swinging her legs, watching. "The frying pan should be hotter."

"You want to do it?" he asked.

She laughed shakily. Later she choked on her eggs and had to be slapped on the back. "I could pretend to be another nurse."

"She knows who you are. She saw you at the wedding."

"I kissed her at the wedding. I went up to her and kissed her. She looked so highly tuned, as though her strings might snap. And they did. You're right, Lev. She has enough to cope with. I'll be patient. I'll wait."

He dropped her at the conservatory on his way to the airport and watched her trudge away, bassoon case under one arm, her suitcase under the other. He put his car in gear, wishing he could do the same with his mind, suppress the churning, stop the ceaseless going over of the situation.

He struggled to get a grip on things. He had to be calm himself to impart calm to Brill. He thought of what Grandbee once said: "The weak eat up the strong." He put away such notions.

He drove into the mountains. Their very abiding induced a sense of peace. That's what he must try for. Mountains were sheer being at its most awesome. Stillness was strength, the kind of strength he was going to need.

Brill looked very pretty in a rose-colored suit, not sick at all or . . . he repressed the word. He refused to think of her in those terms. He always forgot how attractive she was, perhaps because she didn't like being thought of in that way. Her manner was purposeful, indicating urgency. He remembered that quality from the small, determined little girl she had been. Relax, he wanted to tell her. Don't march out to meet life in full battle array, let it roll over you, enjoy it. The woman traveling with her was introduced as Mabel Travis. She was a large person, comfortable looking and retiring. She would do her job efficiently and keep her distance, as people do who have always lived in someone else's house.

Brill gave her brother a searching glance. "You're all right, aren't you, Lev?"

"Perfectly."

"I don't know why they wouldn't let me see you in the hospital."

He had seen her in the hospital, repeatedly. She turned her attention to the country. "How marvelous," she breathed deep. "There's a seventh sense, isn't there, the pleasure of drawing pure air into your lungs." She got in beside him; Mrs. Travis and the bags were piled in back.

"Why didn't I come to Colorado before?"

"You should have."

"It's the scale of things that puts us human beings in our place. Is this another Porsche, or the same?"

"Another."

"I don't know how I came to pile us up, Lev. I'm usually such a good driver."

He murmured something about the mechanical failure.

"You know, I don't remember anything about the accident at all. It's completely blocked out. Is that because of the concussion?"

"That's right."

"But you're all right, Lev? I could never forgive myself if anything happened to you."

"I'm fine."

"And I feel fine." Her voice took on a sprightly tone. "You know, I think the rest was good for me."

"Well, next time how about checking into the Acapulco Princess?"

She laughed. "Look Lev, those great cresting waves frozen into solid rock." She rolled down her window. Her hair, even when it blew, had a groomed look about it. He thought of Erin's tossing, undisciplined red mane. He thought of her eyes crinkled in laughter behind granny glasses. He thought of last night. The road was winding sharply and he slowed.

"You said on the phone you had a surprise. When will I see it?"

"When we arrive."

"When we arrive where? I never asked where we are staying?"

He laughed. "You're getting warm, as we used to say when we were kids."

She leaned back and watched the texture of silver aspen leaves interspersed with the darker pine.

"How is Grandfather?" Lev asked. "Did he see you off?"

"Oh yes. Physically, I'd say he's great. But he rambles a good deal. Gets on those talking jags."

"Well, that's nothing new. He's used to holding down the floor at board meetings. I think there's something gallant about him. Bulling through Grandbee's death. Storming around, making as much noise and commotion as ever." He remembered Mrs. Travis in the back seat and asked if she was comfortable. As a matter of fact, she was not used to these speeds, but declared herself entranced with the scenery.

Lev turned onto a private road.

"It's posted," his sister pointed out.

"By me," Lev said.

"This is the surprise? It's the land Grandfather gave you."

"Wait!" He was glad he had not torn down the A-frame. It was the ideal place in which to lodge Mrs. Travis. She would be on hand during the day with medicines and regimens, but during the evening she would retire here, a quarter mile from the house.

"What a lovely setting," Brill said. "Will we all fit in?"

"This is just the first stop. These are your digs, Mrs. Travis. And the car parked out front is for your use."

"But where—?" both women asked at once.

"A bit further on. That's the surprise." He carried in Mrs. Travis' grip. She couldn't get over having a place of her own and a car at her disposal. "And this little stream rushing by. I'll sleep like a baby. Of course, there is a telephone in case I'm needed?"

Lev showed it to her. "Why don't you unpack, Mrs. Travis? Settle in a bit. Then just jump in the car and follow the tracks, you are two minutes from the main house."

"You built a house here?" Brill asked.

"Even a road leading up to it."

"I can't believe it." They came in sight of the lake. She caught her breath. "It's a perfect thing." Her voice was hushed. "Lying there it reflects a perfect day." Then she saw the house.

"Lev!" She jumped out of the car and approached, incredulous. "Does it work? How efficient is it?"

"About forty-percent efficient. The problem is the initial cost. It's pretty much a custom job."

"But it works! It works!" She hugged him and would have hugged it, if she could have gotten her arms around it.

"A Harvard professor came out to look it over when I first put it up. He was impressed."

"I should think so. Nonpolluting energy. And that it should originate with us, Angstroms, who have polluted from the Persian Gulf to the Catalina Channel. It's fabulous, Lev. More than that, a dream, an impossible wish. Is the design yours?"

"It started out as a version of MIT's Solar IV. But the finished product doesn't bear much resemblance. It changed, I changed. Yes, I'd say it's mine."

She scrambled to the roof, nimble as a goat, exultant, taking in the solar collectors under protective plastic shields and the bank of silicon photocells.

She slid down again to stand beside him. "Oh Lev, and to think an Angstrom did it! I'm so proud, Lev, so proud." She kissed him on the cheek, a rare display of affection for her, and immediately added, "You could have used triple glazing instead of shielding the glass with plastic. You're losing energy by reflection."

Lev replied that the outer surface was sprayed with a Dow nonreflective coating, and they argued the point. He won her complete approval, however, for his use of "selective black" on the collectors themselves.

"Beautiful," she said. "Do you have performance curves for this particular goop?"

Lev assured her they were in the book of specifications, and she could study them at leisure. He demonstrated the louvered aluminum windowscreens, thermostatically regulated for indoor temperature control. Brill thought the arrangement too elaborate. Since the problem was seasonal, a hand-cranked system was simpler, cheaper, and more efficient: "Just raise them like flaps in summer to provide shade and circulation."

"You'll be my consultant on the next try," he said, and

opened an access panel to show the copper tubing connecting with the storage tank in the basement. No one understood as she did.

The view, other than its unobstructable exposure to the sun, was no longer of consequence. The furnishings, the color scheme Erin had worked over, Brill didn't see. It was his vision she applauded.

There were tears on her face. "Angstroms grabbed it off when power sources were young, four decades ago. But this, this shows the way, Lev." She removed her coat. "They've calculated that the energy released from a single solar flare could power the world for a million years. The supply is infinite, clean and free. If only I—if someone could find a simple way of converting it into electricity. Those silicon cells you have up there probably cost you more than you'll get back from them in a hundred years."

"Sure," Lev assented cheerfully. "It's experimental."

"We've got to look in a different direction. The silicon cell will never be suitable for anything but high-cost applications, like space probes. There's got to be a better semiconductor that's not dependent on a precise crystal structure, that's inexpensive, easy to fabricate, that can stand a few impurities. There are thousands of compounds to try."

Lev was caught in her excitement. "The problem is as much political as scientific. Under the present administration, research into solar energy receives less than two percent of the total energy budget. It's a stepchild, with no lobby, no support from the private sector."

"But I understand from Grandfather that oil corporations are buying into fledgling solar companies."

"The old fox only told half the story. They're buying in to control any promising new patents. They're betting on nuclear fission."

She faced him, eyes blazing. "I'll tell you something, Lev. The octopus is going to turn on itself. One tentacle is going to fight the others." She stood a moment longer, then made an abrupt transition. "Well, now, show me the house part of it."

He gave her the tour she asked for, but the actuality of living in a solar-powered home was the true wonder and delight. "We're not *taking*. For the first time in three generations, we're *giving*, pointing the way. What you have done gives direction to my entire life."

Lev was pleased, at the same time a bit perturbed by her enthusiasm. He had promised the doctors quiet; a serene atmosphere to hasten recovery. However, she was obviously happy, that must be racked up on the plus side. He showed her to the room Erin had prepared for her with wild flowers in a vase by the window. "You've had a hard trip, Brill. Turn in, get some rest. I'll call you for dinner."

Her suitcase was on the bed. She sat down beside it.

"Do you want me to help you with anything?" Lev asked. "Hang up some of your things?"

She smiled. "Don't treat me like an invalid, Lev. I'm fine."

"Okay." He closed the door with a feeling of relief. She seemed her old self. Apparently the accident and the period following in the hospital were still blocked out. For this he was grateful. There were certain facts Brill was not equipped to deal with.

An hour later, Mrs. Travis drove up. She did not consider it professional to comment on her employer's home, but her expression was a curious mixture of surprise and disapproval. Nothing, however, was allowed to interfere with her schedule. She looked at her watch. "Miss Knolls should have her medication."

"Is it necessary to wake her?" Lev asked. "It was a long trip and then she was all over exploring the house."

"I do think it's important, yes. If she is feeling tired, I'll serve supper in her room." She opened the door and an exclamation of dismay passed her lips.

Instantly Lev was at her side. Brill was sitting on the bed beside her unopened case exactly as he had left her. There was a rigidity in her position as though by inaction she balanced, kept back some terrible flash flood ready to engulf her. He brushed by Mrs. Travis who spoke urgently to him. "Mr. Angstrom, sir. It's better if you leave this to me." She went into the living room where she had left a commodious bag and extracted a vial and a syringe.

Lev knelt before Brill. He took her hands in his. They were icy. He began to rub them. Brill stared unknowing in front of her. Her psyche in retreat, her face a mask. What went on behind it was impossible to know. It could be that all was serene and calm in that recess she had found, or perhaps the impenetrable barrier was against the King of Fierce Countenance, the Son of Perdition, himself. Or was it a wild gyrating swirl awash with poisons and encroaching pollutants?

Mrs. Travis slipped off Brill's jacket and rolling up her sleeve rubbed her upper arm with cotton. The smell of isopropyl alcohol reached him. She plunged the needle into the firm flesh. "Two cc's," she said, "that should do it."

It took a few minutes. A convulsion passed over his sister. Her lips moved. "Oh please," she said. "I can't be this."

"You won't be. You aren't," Lev told her.

"I get cold, the numbness starts in all the extremities at once, I can't do anything to fight it. I can't lift my hands, or scratch or kick or bite. The outer skin is pulled over me, and you know what I am? A thumb. A gigantic, perfectly smooth thumb. A thumb is the most helpless form there is. And I am encapsulated in it, I can't defend myself."

"You don't need to defend yourself, Brill. I'm here. I'll help you."

"Oh Lev, what can you do? The cuticle grows over me, the skin of the thumb holds me. A thumb can't even think, Lev."

He put his arms around her. Her speech had become thick. He helped Mrs. Travis lay her down. He took off her shoes.

"I'll make her comfortable." Mrs. Travis assured him, and he was banished to the living room. He had looked into his sister's madness, it was not frenzied activity, but imprisonment in a womb shape, an innocuous shape. There was no way to resist when it slipped its cocoon over her. Her power of thought was in abeyance, and the possibility of defense removed. She would have fought with her teeth, bitten the balloon surface. But a thumb has no teeth, no throat to scream its despair, no hands to batter a way back to the world.

A thumb. He looked at his own. The most flaccid

things he could imagine and the most helpless . . . except they pressed, as hers pressed the steering wheel that day. He relied on Mrs. Travis' hypodermic, and the mountains, and the solar house and the healing rays of the sun itself.

Mrs. Travis came into the room. "She's alseep," she announced.

"But what was it? A relapse? Does it mean she's regressing?"

"It's a setback, yes. She hasn't had an episode such as this in quite a while. But I'm sure it's the strain of the trip, the excitement."

"Do you think I was wrong to bring her here? To insist?"

Mrs. Travis was detached, professional. "A good sleep will put her right."

A drugged sleep, Lev thought.

"I'm confident she won't remember this."

"Then you don't think I was wrong?" The weight of his decision oppressed him. He had taken her away from doctors, assuming he knew best what Brill needed. And at the first close look at the unreason he was dealing with, panic and cold sweat overcame him.

"I'll stay here tonight, Mr. Angstrom."

Lev shot her a grateful look. "Take my room. I'll turn in on the couch."

Morning dawned clear and bright, topped with white clouds. The coffee pot, inscribed in Swedish, whistled at nine o'clock. Mrs. Travis set out a substantial breakfast, consumed mainly by herself. Brill appeared looking somewhat pale, but cheerful. Mabel Travis was right, she seemed to have no recollection of the hallucination. And there was no recurrence, although Lev remained alert for any lapse.

After the first week he began to relax. She seemed perfectly normal, herself again. Their days quickly assumed a routine. Brother and sister took long walks around the lake and along the stream, or explored the forest.

"I don't know why I need a nurse," Brill complained. "I feel marvelous. I'm sure my concussion and memory loss after the accident were largely iatrogenic. That's the word, isn't it, when it is caused by the doctors themselves?"

"We'd need somebody," Lev replied, "even if it weren't Mrs. Travis. And she seems a good soul. Think of her as a housekeeper."

"I would, except she keeps pushing pills at me. I don't take half of them, just hold them in my mouth and get rid of them at the first opportunity."

Lev looked concerned. "I think you should take them, at least for now. That was a heavy scene, the hospital and all."

She didn't answer. Some cloudy intimation may have kept her from pursuing the point. "Look! Wild raspberries." Immediately she was in the fields. Together they sought them on the prickly stems and under furry leaves, plopping them into their mouths.

"How delicious. And how tiny."

The peace of the high plateau entered their lives. And the glow of health returned to Brill's cheeks. Sometimes they took the car and drove into the cantilevered desert regions where great peaks stood above them. She delighted in the softness of the colors there. The pale lavender sage with gray leaves, the mauve granules under their feet, cactus that flowered only for a day, but then in brilliant velvets, vivid orange, red and yellow. The sky tinted like the inside of a shell, seemed a footloose wanderer blowing past them. Occasionally she thought about the girl who rushed up and kissed her at the wedding. Erin said, "I'm Lev's girl." It surprised her that Lev had not spoken of her. She felt he would, in time.

One of Brill's favorite spots was the confluence where the stream spilled into the lake. She allowed her eyes to follow the swift-moving water as it gleamed and frothed. "In the East, the mystics have a word, satori. That's when one realizes there is no path to choose, that one is already there. One is already at the center."

"That makes sense," he said. "We're each of us at the center of our lives."

They watched a hard-shelled insect scuttle to safety under a pebble. "Exoskeleton," she said, "as opposed to us. We wear our bones inside."

"The advantage seems to be of size. There's a limit to

what you can carry around, and the weight of our bones is half floated in our body."

"Yes. It allows a brain, a mind. I've often thought, Lev, that man's mind is the way evolution has devised for being conscious of itself. Through our minds nature can see itself, be aware of itself. Yet it is our brains that syphon up the black pastures, that split the atom, that build nuclear reactors. . . . You know, that's what I was going to tell you the day of the accident. That's why I went to find you. The latest scheme of the—what does the AEC call itself now, ERDA?—working with the Interior Department and the Company, is that we build reactors all over the world, including the Middle East. And the agreement is, that the nuclear rods are returned to us so we reprocess the radioactive wastes. It's terribly profitable, and makes us the dumping ground for the entire world. More deadly isotopes will be collected in America than any place on the globe. Isn't it odd, that's just come back to me now. And there are other things as well, still hiding out of reach."

"Leave it alone, Brill. You're not here to go poking into the past." His words persuaded her and she smiled.

"The sun is the answer, Lev. And your house is a beginning."

"It's been comfortable so far. It stayed cool on the hot days, and when we needed heat on those crisp mornings, we got it. The test will be winter."

"How much reliance do you expect to place on the fire-place?"

"I think there will be days when we go around indoors in parkas. The NSF estimates solar engineering can supply thirty-five percent of the nation's total heating and cooking requirements. I think this design is closer to forty. There are other solar houses, of course. In Florida, Israel, Australia, Japan. I thought we'd compare notes with them."

"Cloud Lake, Colorado, to Japan." She turned her eyes on him. They were uncomfortably like Grandbee's. "What's happened with the shale mine?"

Lev shifted his glance from her. The operation was proceeding, as he knew it would, with surface mining. He was aware, although they took pains to hide it, that they were glad to see him go. His watchdog attitude and insistence on *in situ* methods had not been popular. Now they had a free hand. . . . But one battle at a time. Right now there was Brill, asking and expecting a reply. Brill, much too close to remembering. "I don't know that shale is the answer."

"The answer," Brill said, "is a cheap, efficient solar cell. It's the only way to stop nuclear fission, breeder reactors, and oil from poisoning our planet."

Lev had never felt as strongly as his sister on this matter. It seemed to him that power had to go through phases. Certainly, burning fossil fuels was an improvement over human muscle. The twentieth century lived on oil. If by some magic oil disappeared from the world, you wouldn't have a clean, beautiful, natural utopia. You'd have starvation, disease and death, unless there were replacements ready. Nevertheless, he shared Brill's profound concern about what the next step was to be.

He replied, "I'd say the most reasonable course is to develop alternate forms simultaneously. Geothermal has potential. But in the Imperial Valley they're bringing up brine along with steam. It gets into the turbines and clogs them."

"And geothermal is only effective in the western states, while the sun floods all of us and everything." She herself seemed to glow with a secret source of power.

"Our main problem," Lev conceded, "is to hang in there until we can bring either fusion or solar along. Fusion, like solar, is clean. By using multiple laser beams to trigger it, they have succeeded in containing a reaction at 130 million degrees centigrade."

Brill shrugged this off. "For five one-thousandths of a second. Solar is further along than that."

Lev agreed. "When the time comes, Brill, I'm willing to scrap with the big boys. I'd like to see legislation right now underwriting a private solar industry, in which participation by oil, nuclear and coal companies would be prohibited."

"What about an independent government organization devoted to solar research?"

"No. I guess I'm too strongly Angstrom to want government horning in."

"You sound just like Grandfather."

They both laughed.

One evening Mrs. Travis suggested a hand or two of gin rummy. Brill looked up from a notebook she had taken to scribbling in and said she had work to do. When Mrs. Travis departed for her A-frame, Lev asked, "What are you writing, a diary?"

"You might call it that. Evenings are so quiet. And what you've done here has inspired me to get back to work myself on something I thought about a long time ago."

"Tell me about it."

"I'm not ready to talk about it yet. But it does seem interesting possibilities may jell. I'll need to look through current journals though."

"You're back at work on a solar cell," Lev hazarded.

She inclined her head. "But I don't want either of us to get our hopes up. I have a great deal of checking to do before I can even get started."

"I don't know if you should get started just yet," he was anxious about her. "It may be too early. I think you should hold off a bit."

"But Lev, the thoughts are there. I can't prevent that."

"It may be pushing things, Brill."

"It's simply an aggravation if I can't get it down. Besides, all it amounts to is keeping a journal of the things that occur to me during the day. Please don't restrict me there, Lev. I don't want to live as a vegetable."

"Okay. If that's the way you feel."

"The point is, I'll need help. I'll have to check the literature."

Lev was relieved to see a way out. "We'll have to wait a while on that. The library at Boulder University would be the closest source of material."

Brill nodded agreement. "I know it's a terrible job to load on you, Lev. But I would be so grateful. It won't take more than a day or two to run everything down."

Lev hesitated. "You want me to go to the university? But that would mean leaving you alone here. I don't like it."

"With Mrs. Travis? You know I'd be perfectly all

right. Besides I'm not ill anymore. All you have to do is look at me to know that. You and your house and your mountain have wrought a miracle."

Lev smiled. It was what he wanted to believe. That night after Brill turned in, he phoned Erin. "Can you meet me tomorrow at Crystal Lodge in Boulder?"

"Oh, Lev. I don't know what to say but *oh, Lev.*"

"It's going to make scintillating dinner conversation."

"Your sister must be much better."

"Only a month and she's well on the road back."

"Oh, Lev."

"There you go again."

"I know. No words that I can think of are adequate. Perhaps I could sing something?"

"How's the music coming?"

"I'm working on Daedalus. There's a group here that wants to do a recording of it."

"Fantastic."

"I know. The reason it's come along so well is that we're sharing the sun. You built with it your way, and I'm trying to catch some of it in the music."

They rang off without saying they loved each other. Do you say to your arm or your leg, I love you She had become that, himself.

They met in the room he reserved. She arrived first and he found her struggling to light the pot-bellied stove.

"This is part of what every woman should know," he said, marching in, dropping his bag and going to her assistance. He rearranged the kindling and it went up with a roar.

He rose from a crouching position to face her. "Being able to light pot-bellied stoves is something I demand from the woman I marry."

"Maybe we'd better continue to live in sin," she whispered.

"Didn't Whitman write a poem, *Song of Myself?*"

"I think so."

"For me that poem would be called Erin." They didn't bother to turn down the bed. He caught her to him and entered slowly. She rose toward him, lifting as he thrust, arching in a dozen pliant movements. When it happened, she cried out and they were returned to themselves. "For me," she said, burrowing into the crook of his arm, "Lev and music and mountains are going-on-forever things. You're gentle and then it's a firestorm. We seem to change bodies."

They lay sleepless on the bed. She wandered from topic to topic, wanting to share at once and forever those things which made her Erin. "I walked into the old Sanborn's in Mexico City. They call it the House of Tiles, and in the ladies' room, on the wall there is a Siqueiros mural. Unbelievable!"

"What's it doing in the ladies' room?"

"Well, the place used to be the Jockey Club. They redid it to make a restaurant. I guess that's the only place they had for the john."

She told him about a fire in the dorm freshman year. "The girls came dashing out in their pajamas and robes, and every one of them was clutching a stuffed animal."

Lev laughed. "A security blanket."

"I guess. My security blanket is you, Lev. In never being farther from you than I am right now."

They fell asleep for a while, although they swore not to. Erin woke with a start. "Oh dear, time has gone by, our precious time. And I didn't even ask why we're in Boulder."

"The university library. I'm picking up some books for Brill."

"What kind of books?"

"She's back to her research."

"But should she be doing that kind of thing now? So soon? It must be very taxing."

"I think it's good therapy for her. There's very little to do out at the house. We spend all day walking and hiking. At night she studies. I don't know that there'll be any momentous breakthrough. But I can't see that taking an interest can hurt her."

"She's very intense, isn't she? She could overwork or build fantasies."

"Brill is pretty realistic. If she gets enthusiastic it will be because she has hold of something. Remember, she was very close at Stanford. The Institute for Advanced Study was interested. All her professors were excited."

"I tried to tell you once before, but you didn't hear me.

575

When I get to the part in the music where Icarus disregards common sense and flies directly into the heat of the sun, all sorts of diminished chords gather."

"What are you saying, Erin?"

"I don't know. I really don't know."

"You're afraid to let yourself believe that everything is going to be all right. But it is. I'm with her every day. I see the change. She's no longer withdrawn. We talk quite freely, naturally, on every subject."

Erin seemed to bring herself to a decision. "Does she know she tried to kill you?"

"No," Lev admitted. "That's still blanked out. And I hope it stays that way."

"Doesn't she have to remember? I never took psychology, but doesn't everything have to surface and be accepted before . . . before she's well?"

"That's the Freudian school. It isn't adhered to much anymore. It's where you are *now* that counts."

"I'm sorry, Lev. I didn't mean to make you go through this over and over. I just want us to be together."

"Soon, Erin. Soon, believe me."

Lev was lucky with his haul from the library. The books he found were outdated, but there were a number of articles in the journals. NSF-sponsored scientists from Martin Marietta Corporation and the Georgia Institute of Technology were working with a French team in the solar laboratory at Odeillo. At the University of Missouri they had designed an aluminum-silicon diode with a thin insulating layer of silicon dioxide between the metal and the semiconductor, which yielded light conversion efficiencies as high as thirty-eight percent. Dow Corning offered an exceedingly thin silicon web crystal. Several researchers were investigating organic materials that exhibited semiconduction effects, such as polyvinylidene chloride and dyes of the indole and phthalocyanin families.

Before driving back he placed a call. Mrs. Travis answered. "I'm so glad you phoned. Your sister has been looking for you."

"Looking for me?" His heart muscle contracted like a squeezed sponge. "But she knows where I am."

"I know, Mr. Angstrom. I think she forgot. Just a minute, I'll put her on."

"Lev?" She sounded breathless. "Lev, is that you?"

"Is everything all right, Brill?"

"Of course. I thought you'd be here by now."

"You know how far it is. It will be another five hours."

"That's all right. Don't drive fast. As long as I know."

"Know what, Brill?"

She evaded this and asked how he'd done at the library. He enumerated the titles and she sounded pleased.

Lev hung up.

Had she forgotten he had gone into Boulder? If so, she did a good job of dissembling. It may be that she had gotten lonely, or been confused as to exactly where Boulder was and how long it would take. Because it was ambiguous and various explanations were possible, Lev became even more perplexed and worried. Was he over-reacting? He didn't know. Perhaps he was underreacting.

Brill was delighted with the material, especially the work on organic dye films. She stayed up after he turned in, saying, "I'll just be a minute more." When he heard the door to her room close, it was almost morning.

The next day she was reluctant to go on their walk. "There's a section I'd like to finish transcribing. And some calculations to go over."

"Oh no you don't. Fresh air and sunshine were prescribed. And I'm here to see you get them."

She gave in cheerfully. "You're right. I shouldn't be poring over papers on such a glorious day."

"Perhaps we could talk about it," he suggested.

"Why not? That stuff you brought back yesterday gave me a big lift. It shows I'm on the right track."

"Really?" It was power she was talking about, and he was an Angstrom.

"Even in my graduate work I was trying to get away from the silicon crystal into amorphous substances— chalcogenide glasses, plastics. But recently I've been thinking, carbon is in the same group as silicon and germanium, why not look at carbon compounds? And the best bet among the carbon compounds are dyes and pigments,

577

which already have electron transport properties. So when I read the article on phthalocyanin dyes, I kept saying 'of course!' You see, what it amounts to is a different kind of order."

"No, I don't see," Lev said.

"The trouble with the silicon cell is it has to be a flawless crystal lattice, donor and acceptor atoms stuck in with subatomic precision. It's keeping this under control, putting it together like a puzzle, that makes the solar cell prohibitively expensive. It's the need for absolute order."

"And you see a way to get around that?"

"Now I do, yes." There was a teasing expression on her face, as though somehow if he could see with her eyes it would all fall into place. "I'm going at it a totally different way. There are many kinds of order. Crystalline, geometric, that's one kind. Then there's the order you find in recursive systems, in DNA, in proteins, in the neuron-linkages of the human brain. Like yours, Lev. I couldn't describe what you're thinking by group theory. Yet I know what's going on in your mind. 'She's overtired, overstimulated. She should lie down.' You want to turn the conversation into a more neutral channel." She caught his hand. "But I'm not tired. I've got some great ideas down on paper . . . and I'd like to start testing dyes. Can you get me some Monastral blue, a few glass flats—"

"Hold it, hold it. Are you talking about a laboratory?"

"Who needs a laboratory? We've got a solar house. What better place to test solar cell materials? We can stick them in your V-ridge panels right next to the silicon cells and compare performance. All we need is a good volt-ammeter and a bench in the basement where I can paint the samples."

"We'll need a hell of a lot of other things," Lev said. "But Ed Simon at the mine can get them for me. And if you want special shapes, he can have them precision cut."

Brill's eyes were shining. "We've turned this into a collaboration, Lev."

He laughed. "Hardly. My contribution is the legwork. But I'm glad you're into experimentation. I never did see how you could do solar research entirely on paper. It stands to reason you need the sun."

"The paper comes first. That tells you what to try."

"You make up your list, and I'll go see Ed."

She had become thoughtful. "Of course, the problem eventually is going to be financing. Anything that looks good here will have to be developed on a professional scale."

"Why should that be a problem? Grandfather always claimed you can't do better than back yourself. What I said about other companies wouldn't hold true here: Grandfather would play it straight with us. When you've got something concrete, something you can show him, we'll get the old boy down here. He'll throw the weight of the Company's R and D behind you."

She hesitated. "I walked out on all that, remember?"

"It won't have anything to do with you personally. Inflation is hitting the multinationals hard. They're paying eleven percent for money. That hurts. If your results impress him, that will be the clincher."

Several weeks later she stood before him with a resolute expression. "Lev, I must have another work period."

"I don't know about letting you work harder."

"What about a couple of hours after lunch? Just until I push this through."

"Don't force it, Brill. It'll come."

"What you mean is that so far none of the dyes has worked. But we've got the data I need to stake out the energy gap characteristics of the whole class of compounds. And instead of substituting the central metallic atom, I'm going to change the indole group. I think if we replace it with the much simpler pyrrole, we have it."

"Sounds reasonable," Lev said, "but it also sounds like a big project, and you'll need the help of an organic chemist."

"All I want to do is design the molecule. Then Grandfather's R and D people can take it from there. What do you say?"

"You're here for a rest, you know." It had become an old refrain.

"And I have rested, I feel great. Don't you see, Lev, it's all coming together. I've got the data I need, and you don't have to scare Mrs. Travis out of her wits anymore, climbing on the roof. Now it's just a question of equations."

He came to a decision. "All right. We'll try it. Two hours after lunch, if you take a nap."

"It's odd," she mused. "Once before, I thought I had everything solved, and a grad student punched a hole in it. The math got away from me. They call them Fermi monsters, mine were so horrible they ate each other up. But now it's different. Totally new. And simple. That's the mark of a discovery. It's there all the time, only you never looked in that direction."

"If there's anything more I can get you. . . ."

"No. All I need now is lots of pencils. This time it's going to prove out."

Lev decided to go fishing. He bought an inflatable boat and sat in it with his hat over his eyes and a line over the side. He speculated on the possibility that Brill might actually make the discovery she felt was so close. The workings of her mind were often too rapid and complex for him, but one thing he could appreciate and admire was the way she extracted information from everything that happened, favorable or not. He must have gone up that ladder a hundred times and placed a hundred different mixtures in the battery. Each time there was some fractional difference in the reading that would impel her to change the formula. Rest? She never rested. Even when he forced her to lie down and put on records, he could see her fingers tapping the blanket as if it were a calculator. If determination could do it, Brill had it made.

He found that he wanted it to happen very badly. He cautioned himself that he must not allow this to cloud his judgment. He must be alert and critical. Brill must not be hurt a second time.

Yet, there was every chance of a breakthrough, right here at Cloud Lake. It wasn't only determination. Brill had genius. In a few weeks she had duplicated and confirmed the current work on phthalcyanins, and struck out on her own. And he had to admit that although progress was painfully slow, there was a day by day rise in the wattage per square centimeter. It could happen. It could work, it could. . . . In between dreaming there was an occasional fish for dinner.

One evening they had a guest. Peg Trotter drove up, announcing she wanted to see Brill with her own eyes. Brill somewhat reluctantly appeared from the basement she had turned into lab and office. "Peg, what are you doing here?"

"I had to come, Brill. I had to see how you are."

Brill's smile was tender. "As you see, I'm fine."

"And I wanted to tell you, I made the decision to leave your father's employ. I couldn't in good conscience play even the small role I played. I want no part of it."

"But what will you do?"

"That doesn't worry me. Dr. Knolls gave me excellent references. I won't have difficulty getting another job."

"In the meantime you must stay here. Mustn't she, Lev?"

Lev's eyes met hers. He had somehow never thought of Miss Trotter as part of the extended family. But he took it as a further sign of health that Brill was willing to accommodate to people, that she was reaching out to the world again. Also, he saw immediately this first addition would pave the way for Erin. "You're welcome to stay, Peg."

"I can pay my share."

Lev smiled. "We'll talk about it later."

Peg had brought along several boxes of Brill's personal effects. "I stopped by the apartment. I didn't know if you wanted any of this. . . ."

Among dishes and bottles of shampoo was Kumju.

Brill didn't seem surprised that the god had found her. But Lev was not happy at the reappearance. It had started with a Kumju story, and the next thing he knew Brill was racing a Hamm's truck. Logically he couldn't blame a terra cotta figure in two pieces or imagine as he had a moment ago that it had taken incantations and thought commands to impel Peg Trotter to put him into the back seat of her second-hand car. In penance he helped Brill drag Kumju to the red clay of the bluff and position him facing sun and lake.

Peg's presence gave Mabel Travis someone to talk to. They initiated an exchange of recipes and exotic desserts. Peg was a fanatic about the house. She went through it daily from stem to stern, and planted a window box of herbs and dwarf tomatoes. She filled a shed with roots and promised to dig them in after the thaw.

Brill left the basement when the sun was at its zenith and worked beside Kumju, covering her notepad with equations. Lev's attempts at a limited schedule, a sensible regimen, were abandoned. She worked incessantly, hardly exchanged a word with anyone, left the table abruptly in the middle of dinner "to jot down a thought," and never came back. Mrs. Travis was disapproving. She retreated to the late afternoon nap, and there she held firm.

Lev, seeing Brill totally absorbed, decided to let things take their course. Her color was good, that was on the physical side; her attitude positive, affirmative, that was proof of her mental stability. He thought perhaps his job was done.

When he phoned he discovered the group Erin performed with was out of town until Monday. He rocked in the boat between sky and water and phoned Monday. Erin listened in silence while he explained it was now possible for her to be there."

"Is it some sort of emergency?" she asked.

"No. No emergency. I just thought. . . ."

"Because we're booked into Denver the next four weekends. It's really exciting. We're performing *Daedalus*. And it sounds, well, the brightness of the sun seems to pervade the auditorium. Everyone felt it."

"Then you can't come?"

"Well, not right away. Except you need me."

"No, no, that's all right." He talked some more, he couldn't remember about what. He did need her. It was an emergency, every cell in his body longed for her. But if she didn't feel the same way, the hell with it. He went fishing. . . .

Brill hailed him from the bank. "Phone Grandfather," she called. "Phone him!"

"You've got it?" A few strokes of the oar brought him to shallow water. He jumped out ankle deep and pulled the boat up on dry land. Then swung her off her feet. "Really, Brill?" He realized he had been both skeptic and believer, afraid to believe even when he inserted the panels and recorded results. But at the same time, certain she would eventually hit on it.

"Put me down!" She waved a sheaf of papers over his head. "Do you want to dump my results in the water?"

He complied, still grinning. "Just now? Just this minute? Have you had a chance to go over it?"

"That's what I've been doing. I wouldn't want to send for Grandfather until I'd checked and rechecked every detail. How soon do you suppose we can get him out here?"

"I'd say if we can reach him in Carmel, Hank will fly him up right away."

"That's what I was hoping."

They walked toward the house. "And you've solved it?"

She nodded. "The engineers could start costing it out tomorrow. We can make solar cells a hundred at a time, a thousand at a time. You see, you either handcraft something, build it piece by piece, or you take advantage of a natural process that does it for you."

"I hear what you're saying. But you haven't told me how."

"*How* is in here." She held up the papers she was clutching. "Remember, I started with phthalocyanin dyes, which showed some hopeful semiconduction effects in thin films. We tinkered with them for weeks and got enough data to calculate they would never work. At first glance that was disappointing, but it was really the turning point, because I saw it was the indole structure of the dyes that was at fault, and I turned to pyrroles instead. Well, if you follow the same pattern, that is, link four pyrroles around a central metal atom, you get a well-known ring, porphyrin, which occurs in all kinds of common organic substances. So, cost will be nothing. The real question is efficiency. But I knew in advance that the low energy gap measurements on the dye pigments were due to the benzene half of the indole groups. Eliminate the benzene ring and you've got pyrrole, so there's no doubt but we'll get high conversion efficiencies from sun to electricity—circa twenty percent across the whole spectrum. That beats the silicon cell hollow. Cost of materials is negligible, and fabrication—we can practically grow the films. I'm going too fast. Look, here's the [Monastral blue molecule. These are the indole groups. . . ." She began to sketch on the back of her pages.

"I'll tell you what," she interrupted herself, "there's a schematic drawing, a completely detailed blueprint on my desk. I'll go over it with you when we get home. It will clarify everything. But the important thing, the wonderful thing is, I've done it. I've done my job. And I owe it to you. No, don't wave it away, Lev. Let me tell you. It was coming here, being so impressed by the example you set . . . and it was other things as well. I know I was sick when I came. I wouldn't admit it. But there were times when I was so full of lethargy and, what is that beautiful old-fashioned word, miasma? But the walks with you, the long hikes in this mountain air straightened me out. I know you've taken time from your own life to do this for me. And I want you to know what it meant. First of all, my health. And then a tranquillity such as I haven't known in a long time. And suddenly I found my reason for being. It's more than a theorem in solid state physics, it's a matter of redemption, personal redemption and redemption for Angstroms, who took and took and took."

All this from Brill somewhat embarrassed him. "Tell me more about the schematic drawing, is it an actual working drawing?"

"Of course. That's what I've been telling you. We'll go over it in detail. It's very simple to follow. You'll see immediately, it's so much more graphic than formulas."

However, Mrs. Travis had other ideas. She met them at the door, informing Brill she had missed both her medication and her nap.

Brill submitted to the scolding, smiling apologetically at Lev. "I admit it, I'm suddenly exhausted. But I had to push it through. You understand, don't you?"

"Of course," Lev replied. "Go have your nap. You have a right to be tired."

She smiled back at him, "It's a good feeling to give in to it," and allowed Mrs. Travis to lead her off.

It was not a sudden suspicion which unfolded. He simply was not convinced the drawing existed. He knew better than anyone how ill she had been. Was it possible, in spite of seeming so normal. . . ? This invention, didn't it conveniently answer her guilt regarding Angstroms? She had just said so herself.

Yet they had discussed so many aspects, he had secured the pigments, helped paint the chips, double-checked the measurements, even corresponded with other researchers when she was pressed for time. When it came to making a statistical analysis of the data, of course he was lost. He knew allowance had to be made for latitude, altitude, time of year, angle of orientation, cloud cover, and dozens of other factors. How these were all shaken together to produce a single percentage efficiency figure with a confidence interval, Brill tried many times to explain to him.

He often peered curiously over her shoulder at the chemical diagrams. His own organic chemistry was dim but he recognized various heterocyclic compounds and complicated electron transfer equations. Brill knew what she was doing. She was trained, she was brilliant, but— the truth of the matter was he was afraid the model might be wholly in her own head.

Without hesitation Lev invaded the basement laboratory and with his penknife pried at the locked drawer of the desk. It gave under his persistent efforts, and he removed a large black notebook marked simply B.K. He opened it, thinking oddly enough not of Brill, but of Erin. He took it to the window.

He began turning pages, scanning line after line of her small neat hand: a review of the literature on semiconduction in organic pigments; a summary of the chemical properties of pyrroles, indoles, phthalocyanins, and related substances; a log of experimental findings; a table of intramolecular potentials; sections on group-theoretic order, statistical order, recursively generated order. And there it was, a meticulously delineated illustration, the working drawing of the solar cell—an extraordinary design, comprising intricate junctions of mediating structures and cross-sections.

It was, in fact, a powerful, coherent unity.

He closed the notebook.

From the highbacked rocker in a corner of the room, Peg Trotter spoke to him. "You have no faith, Lev. You must have faith."

"There was something I wanted to check out," he said by way of excusing the broken drawer and rifled notebook.

The chair began to rock. He went upstairs, phoned person-to-person, and reached his grandfather in Carmel.

"Lev, boy. It's good to hear you. How's Brill? The two of you still in Colorado?"

"That's where I'm calling from. We were wondering if you could join us for a few days."

"Well, that's mighty nice. But my traveling days are pretty well over. The way these new air terminals are set out, they just about got you walking to your destination."

"Take my plane. Hank can fly it. He'll have it juiced and ready to go. There's a nice little landing strip near here."

"I don't like that word *little*."

"Well, I wouldn't care to land a jumbo jet on it, but for the Cessna it's perfect. We'll meet you this evening."

"Hold on. What's the rush?"

"We've got something to show you, Grandfather. Plans for a solar cell that will bring the whole area competitive with fossil fuels."

"The devil you say. Well, if it's business, that's different. What time will Hank be ready?"

"I'll talk to him and have him ring you. Start packing."

The old man sounded like himself, Lev thought with satisfaction. Ever since Grandbee's death, he'd dreaded having him go too. The old man was Angstrom tradition. More power resided in his gnarled hands than in those of any king, now that Faisal had been assassinated.

The Company was expanded in so many directions it would take a compendium to look it all up. The Angstroms were a dynasty. A dynasty moving toward the sun.

He phoned Erin. "Look, you asked me if it is an emergency. It is. I want you. Is that emergency enough?"

There was no response. He called into the phone, "Erin?"

"I nodded," she said apologetically.

"You're crazy, you know that?"

586

"Everything's going well?"

"Super. Call me here this time tomorrow. We'll make plans. Okay?"

"Okay. Lev, this time I want to say it. I love you."

"That's great." He hung up and found himself whistling. He dialed her back. "Me too," he said, then contacted Hank and made the arrangements.

Brill emerged from her rest refreshed and in a gay mood. It matched Lev's own. "Grandfather's flying in tonight. How'd you like to go out to dinner, splurge on a good wine, and meet him?"

"I'd love it."

They dined by an enormous stone fireplace. "Very inefficient method of heating," Brill observed, as he knew she would.

For lovemaking only, he wanted to say, but modified that to, "You'll be glad of ours this winter, I promise you." They were served mountain trout and chilled Chablis.

"You know, it's interesting," Brill said. "The Saudis are going nuclear for the prestige and clout it gives them. But their real hope is solar."

"Well, that's what they've got, oil and sun. You know what the Jews say, if Moses had wandered thirty-nine instead of forty years in the desert, stopped just a bit short, *they* would be sitting on top of all that oil."

"Oil again. The moment Grandfather tapped into a subcontinent of the stuff, our lives were determined. My father was advanced in the AEC, and this scandal has destroyed him. He takes a great deal of blame on himself even though he won't admit it. He was vindicated, but how can someone else vindicate you? And Mother, neglected by everyone. She was the kind of woman who couldn't make children her life. She flitted like a bee with her too much oil money, looking, looking. . . . Then Bea Anna, the first time she left the family she wound up married. It's very nice for Roger Cramer, who never held a job before, to be part of the Washington inner circle. We can add your father to the list, Lev Rosenfeld, saying the prayers for the dead over you. And Avri, killed for the disposition of borders which was decided in locked committee rooms. It's possible Bea may escape through

587

her music. I hope so. As for me, I've always had an uneasy conscience, as you know."

"The price of oil keeps going up," Lev said.

"Not any more," she declared.

"Will you tell me what you were doing teaching second grade?" her brother asked.

She smiled because it was a question he asked frequently. He was never satisfied with her answer. "Don't you remember what fun second grade was?"

"I guess I don't."

"Colored chalk, growing plants, visiting rabbits and things. I loved it. Anyway, it was necessary. I kept my balance, enjoyed the children and waited." She paused. "Do you understand?"

"No. But I've found that isn't always necessary."

It was an hour later the Cessna set down and Ted stepped into the whirling air unsettled by propellers. His grandson grasped his hand firmly. His granddaughter planted a kiss on his cheek. He checked her over under cover of thick overhanging white brows. The girl looked fine. Animated. Good color. A different person than he had put on the plane. He tried to banish from memory the hospital room and the wan creature who turned to the wall. He had never been close to Brill, or Bea for that matter. He never wanted to be close to a little girl again. It was too dangerous, an exposed relationship with the leverage all on the other side.

Lev did most of the talking on the drive back, telling him about Brill's new technique. "It will enable the Angstroms to corner the energy field. Think of it . . . a solar cell that could cut costs to three hundred and fifty dollars for a unit capable of continuously producing one kilowatt."

"That would put solar power in line with electricity generated by conventional means," Ted said, his skepticism implicit in the remark.

"That's right."

The fact that Lev gave him no argument, just a simple reply, engendered confidence.

"And that," the old man said, "would be a new ball game."

It was after ten by the time they arrived. Ted, who had not seen Lev's solar house, insisted on being taken over every inch of it. He was surprised to see Peg Trotter there. She gave him a tepid hand and retired.

Mrs. Travis broke in on them at eleven to say it was Miss Knolls' bedtime. Brill looked anxiously at Lev.

"It can wait until tomorrow," Lev told her.

"Of course. Goodnight, Grandfather. I really thank you for making the trip. Goodnight, Lev."

Lev turned to the old man once they were alone. "How about a nightcap?"

"Just the thing. Those planes take it out of you. Not like the old days where you went at a reasonable clip by train. Things were more civilized then. You had dinner, played a round of poker, turned in, and in the morning you were wherever it was you were going."

"Scotch?"

"Right on, son." He surveyed the ice in his glass. "Well, here's to your solar house. The goddamnedest thing I ever saw. Seems snug as a bug in a rug, and it is nippy outside."

"This is primitive, already outmoded. You probably noticed we're using the fireplace tonight and the heatolators. But with Brill's invention the sun will provide all heating, cooling, air-conditioning, and cooking needs electrically. We'll tell the gas and power companies to go fly a kite."

"Not so fast," Ted said, freshening his drink. "You'd be putting me out of business."

"One business," Lev agreed. "That's the whole idea, Grandpa. But it'll take a while to get into production, and by that time oil will be pretty much used up anyway. What you want to do is to be there first with Brill's photocell."

"Maybe. My people tell me breeder reactors by the late eighties or nineties, and fusion by the middle of the twenty-first century. Solar is way way down the pike. But I'll listen. I'm really amazed at the change in that girl. I can hardly take it in. She's an Angstrom, you can see that. Now tell me, this idea of hers, it's commercial? You've

589

seen the results? You know what I'm talking about. Theoretical breakthroughs, they're a dime a dozen, we've got thirty-five Ph.D.s on consultancies making theoretical breakthroughs all the time. What I mean, can we patent it?"

"Commercial development is going to take work," Lev answered honestly. "Brill isn't an engineer, the cost projections are rough. That's where you come in. Bring in your consultants, your production people. With Brill's approach you'll be able to stamp out whole batteries of photocells like integrated circuits. Remember, you've got the sun working for you full time, a nonpolluting, nonhazardous, inexhaustible power source."

"And free," Ted chuckled. "Well, that's all I wanted to know, that you had checked things out. Any more ice? And a spot more liquor while you're at it."

"Sorry," Lev said. "I thought your stomach was still at 17,000 feet."

"Forget my stomach. I have. Ever since Brillianna went, I've stopped worrying about myself. I'm trying for the long view, looking beyond my time. I see the plan clearly, the self-perpetuating plan. Yours may be the newer vision. But for me it began with oil." He tapped the scar indelibly etched into his cheek.

"Postwar, that was when everything changed, the catalytic cracking of crude, the quick freezing of food, radar, nuclear power, space technology. That's when the corporate umbrella spread out. We ourselves bought into a hundred companies. Oh, it started in a small way in 1927 with Standard of New Jersey building a refinery in the Soviet Union. Then Vacuum Oil, a subsidiary, made a deal to market Russian oil in Europe."

—Amazing, Lev thought, he never forgets, not when it concerns oil.

"But it didn't really catch on then. It took four decades. The free enterprise system, the communist system— they're just slogans. Business around the world supports them both. Let everyone believe what they want as long as they buy what we have to sell. You know, I brought in management consultant firms who produced two hundred and four volumes of analysis, and that's what it boiled down to: support both the Democrats and the

Republicans, the communist bloc and the Free World, so your friends are never out of power.

"1966, that's when oil got top representation at the White House. 'Most favored nation' tariff agreements were signed with Eastern satellite states, and two weeks later the *New York Times* reported that the U.S. had removed restrictions on the export of more than four hundred commodities to the USSR and Eastern Europe: vegetables, cereals, fodder, crude and manufactured rubber, pulp, waste paper, textiles, textile fibers, crude fertilizers, metal ores, metal scrap, petroleum gas, chemicals, dyes, detergents, plastics, medicines, and scientific instruments are a few that come to mind, because they were all owned in part by Angstrom.

"Amtorg Trading Corporation is the official Soviet agency exporting to us. They have a real oligarchical clique running things there. Three percent of the hierarchy controls the total wealth. All governments today are puppet governments. And that's the way it should be. Thomas Jefferson said, 'Government governs best that governs least.' It's the consortiums that make basic policies. Do you think Kissinger's jetting around the world at that crazy pace changed anything in the Middle East? Of course not. It was a red herring. Things cooled down when we promised Egypt and Saudi what they wanted, nuclear power."

"But it was the Compagnie Française des Petroles," Lev interposed, "who wrecked that bit of diplomacy by agreeing to supply the Arabs with nuclear know-how whether or not they clobber Israel."

"Quit worrying about Israel. She has a strong ally."

"Us?"

Ted shook his head. "Russia. Without an Israel, Russia has no excuse for being in the area, and her oil companies need the Mediterranean and the Suez Canal."

"That may have been true five years ago. But now a radicalized PLO is aiming for an eventual takeover of Israel. That would put Russia in an even better position. And with atom bombs all over the place, how will your consortiums handle it?"

"Look, everyone is worried about proliferation. But we've already got it. Those Middle East countries are

591

packed in there like sardines. If Israel goes, they all go. The Arabs know that. They still dress like Valentino and face Mecca five times a day, but they're no crazier than anyone else. At least not much crazier. They assassinate their best men, but so do we. No, they're businessmen. The proof is they just lent the Common Market three billion dollars. Sure they're buying armaments like mad. But with overkill twenty-five times the population of the earth, and since you can only kill a person once, it's rather a low yield investment. None of this hard stuff will surface except in guerrilla actions, which you'll still see in the Middle East."

"I wouldn't consider the loss of Israel a guerrilla action. Do you know about my brother?" Lev asked.

"I heard."

"And do you know that for fifteen years my father has read the prayers for the dead over me?"

"I'm telling you, Lev, we're off the blood standard, just as we're off the gold standard. It's an *economic* world today. Natural resources, commerce, transportation, that's where to focus. For the first time you're seeing world economic conferences. Rockefeller and Eaton, super-capitalists, led the current push. In 1969 they set up two synthetic rubber plants at a cost of two hundred million— where? In Russia. They also have a fifty-million-dollar aluminum plant there. GM is sending enormous amounts of earthmoving equipment. Boeing is selling them whole fleets of 747s. We divide our wheat with them. And the new opium of the masses in Moscow is Coca Cola. You think this is a bad thing? Pernicious? Right?

"Wrong! You can become wealthy selling armaments, just as you can printing money or minting coins. But it no longer pays to finance governments to fight each other. Too many of your own markets would be destroyed. Can you see the Japs bombing Los Angeles with all those Datsuns and Toyotas on the street? They wouldn't do a Pearl Harbor on Honolulu today. Why should they? They own most of it.

"At the moment Saudi is stage center buying up California, New York and London. Kuwait recently spent seventeen million dollars for an island off Charleston, South Carolina. Japan lent its old enemy Russia a billion to prospect for natural gas. In return the USSR agreed to purchase Japanese mining machinery. The U.S. Department of Agriculture owns Middle Eastern air lines. Australia exports thirty-one percent of its goods to Japan. The National Bank of Hungary has borrowed a hundred million dollars from American banks this year. A Western bank just opened a branch in Bucharest. The Saudis are into banking in Detroit, and they're working on other deals. Iran is recycling its oil money, lending Britain 1.2 billion dollars. It is also purchasing ten percent of our rice exports, while my old drinking buddy the shah—actually, what we drink together is coffee—just came up with the best proposal of all: to negotiate an international treaty tying the price of oil to twenty other basic commodities. He's the first Muhammadan to wear a business suit, to understand *that* is the royal purple of the twentieth century. He also bought twenty-five percent of Krupp, which in turn donated two million dollars to Harvard University. You notice Hitler comes and Hitler goes, but Krupp goes on forever. Sony plans a plant in France. Ford Motor Company is preparing to move back into Egypt. Kaiser Resources Limited of Canada is selling coal in Japan. Chrysler's Argentine company signed a twenty-four million dollar sales pact with Cuba, and Alcan is pitching for an aluminum remelt factory in Havana. Dart exports Tupperware kitchen products to thirty countries in Africa, Asia, Europe and Australia, with $17 million in earnings last quarter. Gimbel's department store, across the street from Macy's, is British. It wouldn't surprise me to learn that Colonel Sanders is a Hong Kong conglomerate. Even our company—nationalization can't hurt us. With a profit jump of three hundred percent, someone has to bring it to the marketplace.

"You get the picture? It's like macrame. The world is being woven together. The strands are bonds of interest, not friendship, brotherhood, or any of that crap. Do you read me, boy? The world tried putting itself under the protection of the Church. That led to a blood bath that lasted centuries. Then we placed our hopes in philosophers, Locke, Jefferson, Engels, Marx. More war, hot and cold. You know why? It was all so damned idealistic.

"But now we've got a chance. Yes, I believe we have.

And do you know why? The guys who are out for *number one* like me, are running the show. And you can believe it's a global show. We can't let India or Ethiopia or Bangladesh go under. We can't let them starve.

"Why? Because we're noble and high-minded and humanitarian? Rubbish. Because, damn it, those are markets. And you've got to keep your markets alive and kicking. Nobody needs to write me out two hundred and four volumes of reports to make me understand that.

"It's business. And business is healthy. Don't slap wage and price controls on business, put them on government. Of course, in a way, the multinationals are governments, we use a systems approach to transfer resources within our own empires. There are so many businesses proliferating from the Seven Sisters alone that the skeins could never be separated out. Self-interest is what keeps us in line, keeps us civilized. Self-interest is going to keep us from blowing up our investments and our markets. What I say is—watch out for the fanatics who want to make the world safe for democracy, or protect us with the domino theory, or save our souls with their particular brand of truth. Altruism has caused more havoc in the world than any other ism. Give me the man who says honestly he's out to make a buck.

"I know you're worried about the Arabs. But I'm telling you, they're worldwide investors. Sure, a generation ago they chopped off their neighbor's head to grab the booty, now they just shear him. None too gently, it's true, but they leave him enough so he'll be able to stagger back next year to the marketplace for another trimming.

"You see, at my age I can't be sure about tomorrow, but I can span a century in my thinking. Oil will peter out. I know that. And fission and breeder reactors are damned poisonous. You may not believe this," he cast a somewhat embarrassed glance at Lev, "but I've been turning over a few things. After all, my Old Man changed with the times. You've got to do that, or get left behind. You've convinced me that in the long run, the long run mind you, it's solar, or possibly fusion."

Lev felt a surge of affection for the old fellow. All the time he'd thought he had turned a deaf ear.

"Which will be practical first?" Ted shrugged. "We

594

may have the answer tomorrow. In any case, let my experts battle it out. I'll bet on both. The idealists fouled up. Now Angstrom and subsidiaries are going to truss up the world. Even if we have to borrow at a goddamned eleven and a half percent to do it."

There was a long silence before Lev spoke. "So it's to be *one world* after all. But hardly according to traditional forecasts. And you, Grandfather, you are sort of the new J. Christ, Muhammad, Locke, Jefferson and the 'Godfather' rolled into one. The world leader whose face is *not* on the cover of *Time*. Brill wouldn't recognize you, but you may even head up her New Humanity. That self-interest you speak of may eventually force the blinders off, you may start to take care of the world to protect your investments."

"The New Humanity?" Ted laughed. "Could be. There has to be a humanity of some kind to tend the immortal persons and their proliferating activities. They trade, as I have shown, in everything under the sun. But you can't fold up an oil barge and put it in your pocket. The legal tender is still money. And essentially money's got no religion, no race, and its color is green. It's the most unprejudiced thing there is. It's the flag of the multinationals."

"Grandfather, how about some sleep before you finish your coup? I know if I don't turn in, I'm going to start believing you."

"Well, if everything goes according to Hoyle tomorrow, I'd like you to head up this solar energy thing. Now mind you, all I can do is put your name before the proper committee. But at least I know which one that is, because I set it up myself."

"We're sitting in a solar house, so you know I'm interested. But what I really want is to check into shale again. I guess I'm sort of a bulldog. It seems to me, though, that we're going to need either that or a low sulfur coal while we convert to solar."

"Sounds reasonable. Me now, I look ahead, way ahead. Past you, Lev. The Company is immortal, self-perpetuating. I told you once, like a dividing cell. Now if it was a matter of oil, no. You're part Rosenfeld, there's divided loyalty there. But never forget oil gave you a chance to sit in on the game. Within the framework there are a lot of options. Outside it, you are part of the great herd, a consumer. They used to be the rabble, the peasant, peon, serf, slave, but we've elevated them. Now they're consumers."

"I think you're getting a bit carried away,"—but Lev enjoyed his boardroom tirades.

"At least I'm a good replacement for the White House economists on the one hand and the doomsayers on the other."

"You're right, there. In that respect I begin to think you've got it all together." He helped his grandfather up, it was hard for him to get out of low chairs.

"And I can promise you, boy, when I send in the name Angstrom to any department, they won't say no."

"Thanks, Granddad. See you at breakfast."

Lev dreamed his grandfather was dying. And as he died, oil rushed, spurted and gushed from his eyes, his mouth, his ears, his anus. "Nothing of him that doth fade, but doth suffer a sea change into something rich and strange." An oil sludge of blackness was replaced by morning.

He could hear Mrs. Travis in the kitchen. He smelled bacon, coffee, and pancakes. She was aware that today was an occasion. Sensing the excitement, Peg kept to her room.

Brill was already at the table and their grandfather came in shortly afterwards. "That brother of yours kept me up till all hours," he said to Brill. "So you'll forgive me if I'm not too bright. Also remember, my background was geology, and that was a long time ago. So try not to get too technical on me."

"I won't." She gave them a serene smile. There was no hint of nervousness in her manner.

When Ted had consumed more than he should, and a second cup of coffee to wash it down, Brill suggested they repair to the porch with its view of the lake and distant low humped mountains.

She went to fetch her notebook. Returning, she said, "It must have snowed last night. Look, high in the crevices."

They glanced up and it was true, there were traces of white running like thin ribbons in the rock.

The men seated themselves and Brill stood with the table between them, on which she laid her notes. "The sun is the ultimate source of all energy on earth, including stored energy in fossil fuels, wind and water power, and nuclear energy. Direct solar radiation is an inexhaustible supply of light, heat and electricity." She reached out and plucked an aspen leaf, by way of illustration Lev supposed. He settled back to listen.

"We are led to consider the photovoltaic cell, which is any device that converts photons or light energy into electrical energy. The silicon solar cell depends for its effect on extraordinarily precise control of the regular geometric arrangement of silicon atoms, replaced at regular periodic intervals by donor and acceptor atoms of other elements. This is mathematical order of an unusually high degree. Let us call it crystalline order. It is typified by the perfect symmetry of the Platonic solids, of crystals, of snowflakes.

"But there is also another kind of order, to be found in DNA, in enzymes and proteins, and in living structures generally. This order has nothing to do with symmetry. It escapes the net. It's a growing, living, developing order, self-generating, dynamic. But it is just as structured, precise, controlled as the static geometric order of the crystal. And in this structure is the clue to continuous, efficient photoelectric conversion. Take this leaf I'm holding. It exposes its largest surface area to the sun. Between the veins of the leaf is a spongy mass of cells, the chloroplasts, filled with a green pigment, chlorophyll. What is chlorophyll? Simply a porphyrin ring with a central magnesium atom and an aliphatic chain. Solar energy is stored as glucose by the action of chlorophyll on carbon dioxide and water. Actually, photosynthesis takes place in two main stages, the photochemical or light-dependent stage and the enzymatic or dark stage."

The sun was climbing higher. It had been a big breakfast and Ted was beginning to feel logy. "Yes, yes. Can't we skip the preliminaries and get on with it?"

"You do understand," Brill said conscientiously, "about the sunlight? And that my concern is with the mechanism of energy transfer. The excitation of the chlorophyll molecule is due to its structure, which is

597

ordered in a totally different way from the geometric form of the silicon crystal—"

"What is the girl talking about?"

Brill stepped around the table. "I filled the notebook with material Lev brought me from the library. I made pages of observations of phthalocyanin pigments. I went from indoles to pyrroles to porphyrins. Then I saw it was all meaningless. The perfect porphyrin was chlorophyll. God gave us the perfect solar cell in this leaf." She laid it reverently in the old man's hand. "In every leaf in the world." She smiled beatifically on both men, who stared back at her.

"Brill," Lev said, "the invention."

"You heard her," Ted snapped. He flipped the pages of the notebook. "Copied. Copied from the journals you supplied her with. She's mad as a hatter."

Lev took the notebook from him and began hunting frantically for the diagram of the solar cell. He came to the maze. Of course. His stomach turned over. All that was needed was to trace the outline of an aspen leaf around it. What he had read as an engineering drawing was a highly schematic rendition of the structure of— insanity.

"You're not pleased?" Brill asked. "You won't back my invention?"

Ted patted her hand. "We'll see, we'll see. It's not up to me, you know. All I can do is set it before the proper committee. Lev, drive me back, will you? I'm not up to this. I'm too old. Brillianna would know what to do. That was her department. If one of you children was sick or ailing, it was up to her. I'm an oilman. That's all. Only thing I know well. I don't know what to do about this. Brillianna now, she'd have some hotshot psychiatrist out here."

"It's all right," Lev said. "I'll handle it."

"Handle it how?"

"We've been getting on very well. There are long walks during the day. We have books, we're building quite a library."

"And at night we can play gin rummy," Brill said.

—*Especially Brill.* "It was my fault, thinking it could

598

move so fast. I let her overwork. This time we'll take it slower, much, much slower."

The old man stood in front of him. "I laid it out for you last night, Lev. There are plenty of top managerial slots for an Angstrom."

"I can't," Lev said. "I don't want both sides of the family reading the prayers for the dead over me."

"If you stay here, I'd read them myself, if I knew what they were. Buried here you're as good as dead."

"I see it differently," Lev said.

Mrs. Travis came out. "Phone for Mr. Lev."

He didn't remember until he heard her voice that he had asked her to call. "I'm sorry, Erin."

It took a moment for her to answer. "That's it? You're sorry?"

"That's it."

"I see. . . . You flew too close to the sun."

He hung up slowly. There would be a great deal of time from now on. It was the crop he would harvest.

His grandfather was impatient to be off. Impatience is a young man's trait. Lev felt they had, in a way, changed places. He was old. His life behind him. Theodore Angstrom was chafing at the bit. He would be on the phone to Washington later in the day, to Jidda and New York. He was the immortal person.

One did not look at the knotted varicosed veins of his hands or the dentures that didn't fit. One must not look too closely at an immortal.

The withdrawal was complete, as though the powers of speech, of thought even, had been eradicated. Brill no longer uttered a sound. She moved only when she was moved. Peg fed her, Mrs. Travis carried her to the porch for sun and air.

Lev was almost as silent as his sister. He walked miles every day, staying away from the house. It was all he could do to force himself to look at this nonexistent Brill. It was harder knowing what had happened, that the cuticle had crept up and enclosed her. Somewhere past his seeing, his sister was held in a cocoon the shape of a thumb.

No thought entered there, no scream forced its way out, there was no passage, no throat. "Oh, please," she had said to him sitting on the bed by her unopened suitcase, "I can't be this." Then he was able to reassure her. Then she would hear him.

For some reason he identified her with Kumju, without differentiation, no eyes, no nose, no mouth, a non-Brill sitting placidly where she was left. Sometimes he forced himself to say a few broken sentences to her.

Peg Trotter, passing him, a shadow herself, murmured, "Have faith."

"Faith? In what?" In the no eyes, no nose, no mouth of what had been his sister? Suddenly he was out of control, beating Kumju with an oar which broke in half. He continued smashing the clay god with the heavier end. He concentrated on the head, so it couldn't look at him pounding it into terra cotta pieces, and then pounding the pieces until they became chips and powder. He turned his fury on the broad haunches, swinging maniacally, covered by sweat which ran into his eyes. He could barely see, but the target disintegrated.

Mrs. Travis moved to stop him, but Peg put out a hand, restraining her. They both looked at Brill who sat under blankets in the sun. It was not possible to say if she watched the incident. She was turned toward it.

Venting his anger with such violence was a release for Lev. And the queer notion came to him that he had released the god too. He was ashamed of his unreasoned action, but his load was lightened.

Gradually he began to live his life. Day piled against day until somehow they had gotten through the winter. The sun shining on their black peaked roof warmed the occupants within. Early wild flowers burst open. Roots were taken from the shed and planted, seeds scattered. The people in the solar house watched over them. There was a feeling of hope, of activity throughout the circles broadening in their still pond. But the stone at dead center was inert. They wheeled her outdoors and placed her in the sun where she could watch them work the garden. But Brill's eyes were turned inward. She didn't see.

There was quite a bit of traffic to Cloud Lake now the pass was open. People were interested in the solar house. They asked for permission to inspect it, they asked for advice in building others. Lev listened. It excited him that here and there someone wanted to make the attempt to break free. But as long as Brill was what she was, this too would have to wait.

One afternoon when he had gone into town for supplies and the others were at work around the place, the phone rang. It was picked up on the fourth ring. "Long distance calling. Mr. Angstrom, please."

"Mr. Angstrom isn't here. Can I help you, this is Mrs. Angstrom."

A male voice broke in on the California operator. "The devil you say! The only Mrs. Angstrom I know about was my wife, Brillianna Grenville Angstrom."

"Well, this Erin McKenna Angstrom."

"You mean, Lev got married?"

"Yes, he did."

"Without letting me know?"

"The way you left here, Mr. Angstrom, he didn't think it would make any difference to you one way or another."

"Nonsense. Of course it makes a difference. He's my only grandson. He bears my name. Now who are you, young lady?"

"I don't know if you remember me. I was Bea's roommate at Aspen. I came to her wedding."

"The girl with all that untidy red hair?"

Erin laughed. "I'd only let a grandfather talk to me that way."

"Well, bless your heart and congratulations to Lev. Tell me, did you survive in that solar house?"

"Yes, we did. Quite comfortably."

"That's great. I hope Lev has a patent on it. I called because there's an item in today's *Chronicle*. It concerns Brill. How is she doing, by the way?"

"The same."

"Too bad, too bad. It seems some Japanese professor got hold of a microfilm of her thesis. His name is Yamata, with the University of Osaka. Brill's name is here too. Let

601

me read it to you. 'Yamata's new theory of semiconduction is based on unpublished work by Dr. B. Knolls, contained in her 1972 Ph.D. dissertation.' Then comes a lot of technical stuff. 'But by imposing certain conditions, her theory of boundedness,' that's what it says here, *boundedness*, 'holds up.' Apparently it's a big breakthrough in solar energy. I thought it would please Brill to know her original line of investigation is responsible for it. Put her on a minute and I'll read her this."

"I wish it were possible, Mr. Angstrom."

"That bad, huh?"

"Yes, that bad."

"But you can explain it to her? Explain that it wasn't all wasted."

"Mr. Angstrom, Brill hasn't spoken in six months."

"My good God." There was an interval of silence. "And Lev's sticking like glue, isn't he?"

"Yes. Yes, he is."

"Well, you tell him to have Hank fly me up now the weather's decent again."

"I'll do that."

". . . Not in six months, you say?"

"No."

"Well. . . ." She could feel the force of Theodore Angstrom as he rallied. "Say hello to Lev for me. He'll be pleased about the development. It was nice talking to you, Erin. Another Mrs. Angstrom. It proves that one way or another things go on."

Erin went back to the garden. "What was it?" Peg asked.

"Damn," Erin said, trying to keep from crying.

A dust storm swirled along the road. Lev's Porsche screeched to a stop in a choking cloud. Erin went out to meet him, her face so white every freckle showed. She told him about his grandfather's call.

Lev dropped the boxes back in the car. "Have you tried to communicate with Brill?"

Erin shook her head. "You know it's hopeless, Lev."

He approached his sister. Her face was lifted to the sun. Lev knelt in front of her. "Brill, it happened. Just as we said. We're a family, and we're living in a solar-powered house. Your work proved out, you know. In

602

certain cases the Fermi surfaces are bounded, just as you thought. You've won through, Brill. If Grandfather's multinationals don't succeed in winding the Arabs into their macrame, then the only hope we've got is your bounded Fermi surfaces. Think of it, they'll yank the countries of the world back from monetary ruin, revolution, and mass starvation. What do you say, Brill? Those old Fermi monsters that kept you up so late at night."

There was no response.

In desperation Lev grabbed up a stick and fastened her fingers around it. Holding her hand in place, he guided it to draw in the dirt their compact, the symbol of the sun's rays:

Brill's eyes focused. They stared at the sign.

The sun: an orgastic litany of heat, momentary mountains thrust from turbulent oceans of gas flows. Radioactive cataclysms hurl spirals, vortices and funnels, to create and cannibalize energy. Great flares of scarlet vapor swell, sheerest bubbles, to burst a hundred thousand miles in space. An ionized zone thinner than gas wraps an electrical field on which a dazzling corona shimmers, crowning the boiling mass. This cauldron is the energy that fuels all life. It began with the sun.

THE BEST OF BESTSELLERS
FROM WARNER BOOKS!

MORE LIVES THAN ONE? by Jeffrey Iverson   (89-372, $1.95)
More Lives Than One? reads like a detective story and is the most thorough attempt to authenticate experiences of "previous incarnation." **8 pages of photographs.**

DARE TO LOVE by Jennifer Wilde   (82-258, $2.25)
Who dared to love Elena Lopez? Who was willing to risk reputation and wealth to win the Spanish dancer who was the scandal of Europe? Kings, princes, great composers and writers . . . the famous and wealthy men of the 19th century vied for her affection, fought duels for her.

THIS LOVING TORMENT by Valerie Sherwood (89-415, $1.95)
Perhaps she was too beautiful! Perhaps the brawling colonies would have been safer for a plainer girl, one more demure and less accomplished in language and manner. But Charity Woodstock was gloriously beautiful with pale gold hair and topaz eyes—and she was headed for trouble.

A STRANGER IN THE MIRROR by Sidney Sheldon (89-204, $1.95)
This is the story of Toby Temple, superstar and super bastard, adored by his vast TV and movie public, but isolated from real human contact by his own suspicion and distrust. It is also the story of Jill Castle, who came to Hollywood to be a star and discovered she had to buy her way with her body. When these two married, their love was so strong it was—**terrifying!**

 A Warner Communications Company

THE BEST OF BESTSELLERS
FROM WARNER BOOKS!